14,444

Salt and Steel

SALT AND STEEL

Peter Padfield

C

CENTURY PUBLISHING
LONDON

First published in Great Britain in 1986 by
Century Hutchinson Ltd, Brookmount House,
62–65 Chandos Place, London WC2N 4NW

ISBN 0 7126 9489 7

Photoset by Rowland Phototypesetting Ltd
Bury St Edmunds, Suffolk
Printed in Great Britain by
Anchor Brendon Ltd, Tiptree, Essex

For Jane and our family

ACKNOWLEDGEMENTS

I should like to thank all those who helped so much by talking to me of their days before yesterday, and I am grateful to Constable & Co. for permission to use excerpts from *The Anatomy of Courage* by Lord Moran. The poem on page 559 is from *Marlborough and other Poems* (C.U.P. 1916), by Charles Hamilton Sorley, whose small number of war poems surely rank with the very best, higher than many to be found more frequently in anthologies. I should also like to acknowledge my debt to Kathleen E. Burne's *The Life and Letters of Father Andrew*, published by A. R. Mowbray.

PROLOGUE

She didn't think she could bear it. How people chattered!
She had forgotten what it was like. She had become unprac-
tised; it was the first family gathering, practically speaking
the first social gathering, she had been to since – she couldn't
think.

They were all trying to pretend everything was back to
normal and nothing had changed. Some, perhaps, were not
pretending. Probably they believed nothing *had* changed.
She had forgotten how stupid some people were, her relations
especially. And their hats!

Of course one had to pretend; it was all a pretence. One
couldn't go around saying what was really in one's mind –
even if one knew. That would stop the game. She imagined
the stunned silence if someone actually said what they felt.
Was there no half-way house? Was it not possible to be
agreeable without assuming an interest in the servant problem or the prospect of unrationed food again – after carrying
one's *sugar* with one out to tea, I mean to say, feeling positive
guilt at accepting *butter* from one's hostess's restricted allowance! Most were not pretending. How else could they discuss
these things with such unending zest? They were the things
which exercised their minds. Dear Lord – four years of
slaughter, a lifetime to think about those who would never
come back, in order to get on with this again! It was incomprehensible. There was no relationship between this and the
agony endured to achieve it, the brute frightfulness. Images
from the casualty clearing stations still rose unbidden at odd
times of day or night, mostly night. This was what it had
been for, and the reason for all the gaps that could never be

1

filled again; the young men with firm young bodies who had borne their dreadful wounds so philosophically – screams in the night. She remembered Andy screaming in the night.

In church she had been moved and had glimpsed the design. There had been moments like that in France – not belief as an act of conscious faith, but insights which caught her suddenly off guard. It usually happened when she was dropping from exhaustion. It had happened at the christening today as the Rector, stepping down from the font, handed the little, screaming bundle back to her. What a splendid little fellow he was! How he had bellowed!

Uncle Richard was coming up. She smiled. He was one who *would* understand. He had always been there as long as she could remember.

'Well –!' He stood in the straight way he had, gazing at her for a moment, the laughter crinkles fanning out from his blue eyes. 'Nothin' wrong with his lungs!'

She laughed. 'How did you guess? What I was thinking,' she added.

'Elementary, my dear Watson!' He leaned towards her ear. 'I caught you smilin' to yourself!' His expression had changed. 'A rare pleasure these days.'

'Uncle Richard!' She felt horrified. 'Am I – surely I don't –?'

He placed a hand on her arm to stop her. 'No, no – you are *yourself*, Henry. You always will be.' He looked round briefly at the others. 'Don't think I don't feel the same meself at times.' His fingers pressed her arm.

Was she so transparent? She wondered if everyone could see into her so accurately. Surely not. Uncle Richard had always been like that; obviously he still cared for her or he would not have noticed.

'I shall have to try harder,' she said, smiling.

An image rose of that perfect July evening and Uncle Richard and Robin, the westering sun brightening their flannels and the sides of their heads, one fair, one dark, as they held the newspaper in front of them, reading it together.

'Looks rather like war, old thing,' Robin had said as he came towards her afterwards with that loose, swinging walk.

2

It had been difficult to take it in. Babs had come bounding out from the house. 'D'you think there's going to be an absolutely *tremendous* battle in the North Sea? Willy does.' Robin had laughed.

Had that girl sitting out in the sun by the tennis lawn, feeling prickles of apprehension – had it been her? What had she actually felt? She could only remember the shock and incomprehension that this could happen – in the twentieth century –

Uncle Richard was gazing at her. 'You can't take it all on your own shoulders. There has to be a limit, otherwise –' He shrugged.

She knew what he meant.

'The more one sees of it,' he went on, 'the more one realizes how powerless one is. Even as His Majesty's servant. It can come as something of a shock after – well, perhaps there is the odd occasion – if one is very fortunate and the ball comes your way – one might be able to give it a nudge in a certain direction –'

It was odd to hear him talk like this. As children, listening to his stories of adventure, they had thought him capable of toppling empires.

'But the big things,' he went on, shaking his head slowly, 'I fancy the world will look pretty much the same when we go out as when we came in – don't you?'

She thought of little Jack in her arms in his muslin robe trimmed with satin and his trusting eyes staring up. 'That's *too* cynical!'

He put a hand up to stroke the end of his moustache. 'To tell the truth, Henry, I fear it may look a good deal worse.'

'*Worse!*' He *looked* as if he were serious.

'I'm off to Russia in a few days – the Soviet Republic!'

He turned as her great aunt May came up to them in the red velvet hat which had been so noticeable in church, not unlike a gendarme's in shape with a little peak and a cockade of two curled feathers nodding as she walked. It was splendidly jaunty, perfectly setting off her grey dress and pearls and loose jacket.

'Richard!' She turned her lorgnette. 'Henrietta! You *are*

3

looking fetching today,' and turning back to him briefly, 'Isn't she, Richard!'

He raised his brows, examining her. 'Now you mention it –'

'You *tease*! You know she is, yes of course you are, my dear. Being a godmother agrees with you – and little Jack, isn't he too *scrumpy*, why, I could have *eaten* him, positively *eaten* him!'

She smiled. Aunt May always had been slightly inaccurate in her use of what she thought was the up-to-the-minute word.

'He has a useful pair of lungs, I'll grant you!' Uncle Richard laughed.

'Oh *hasn't* he! What a *frightful* noise!'

'I daresay he'll go to sea!'

'I should *think* he will!'

They laughed.

'There is his mother!' Aunt May was looking over Henrietta's shoulder. 'I've bin meanin' to –' she lowered her voice. 'I didn't manage the wedding – of course you probably know that. It was up in –' She frowned.

'Hull.'

'Hull. An odd place for a weddin', I thought. She looks rather – nice –'

'She is nice,' Uncle Richard said firmly.

Aunt May looked at him. 'I'm quite sure she is. I must go over.' Turning a gracious smile on each of them, she left, feathers bobbing.

'*And* her father's in the stud book!' he said in a low voice.

She laughed.

'*Not* that he has any tin. Perhaps that won't matter so much in our new world fit for heroes!' He obviously didn't believe it.

'It won't matter to *them*,' she said sharply.

'Ah!' He raised his brows at her tone, smiling as if to say 'that's more like the old Henry!' and nodded. 'No – I believe you're right. He's one in a million, your brother. It won't matter a scrap to him.'

'I'm so pleased for them.'

He rested his hand lightly on her arm again. 'You're *all*

4

one-in-a-millions!' and smiling as if perhaps embarrassed at allowing such a deep expression into his eyes, 'Hanged if I know how Robbie managed it!'

'Why are you going to Russia?'

'Ah!' He stroked the end of his moustache again. 'I'm afraid they've started somethin' there.'

'The Bolsheviks?'

He nodded. 'I fear it'll not be stopped.'

'The Whites, won't they be able to stop them? If we support them properly.' *More* fighting. Why on earch had she said it?

'We *are*, Henry. But it's not geographical you see. Look at Germany. Look at our own Reds. The new Utopians! It's in men's imaginations – the most precious and the most dangerous thing God gave us. I sometimes think His trust was misplaced, don't you?'

'Bolshevism will spread, you mean?'

'Sure to. It'll be the French revolution all over again. Moscow instead of Paris preachin' to the oppressed – before gobblin' 'em up! But look here! What are we doin' talkin' politics! Let me fetch you somethin', I haven't bin lookin' after you –' He reached down for her empty plate.

She handed it to him, shaking her head. 'I won't. Why shouldn't we talk politics?' He would not have said it if she had been a man.

He made a pretence of nearly dropping the plate in surprise at her tone.

She smiled. He was a dear. She needed to talk about substantial things. There were so many doubts and questions in her mind: she needed really to *talk* to him because he understood and she knew she could trust him, and he could see things in odd, different lights; he would give himself, not take or repeat the expected things. But he was right; it was not the time.

'Tea?' he asked. 'An ice?'

She smiled, shaking her head, feeling suddenly weary. 'D'you think I've done my duty?'

He put his hand on her shoulder. 'Splendidly! By Jove! You were marvellous –'

5

'I mean in here. I mean –' She looked around at the groups of relatives.

He understood at once. '*Beyond* the call of duty, I'd say! Look here, you slip away. I'll square your mama. She'll understand. If she don't – I'll make her!'

She bobbed up on her toes and pecked him on the cheek, feeling his moustache tickling. Funny, she remembered as a young girl thinking how exciting *really* to kiss him. He had so much glamour; he still had.

She made her way to the door, smiling and exchanging a few words with people eager to accost her. She couldn't remember who all of them were; most she only ever saw on this sort of occasion. They might have been to her own christening. She felt ashamed of her earlier thoughts. She belonged. In that way things *were* the same.

There were so few young men.

It was mercifully quiet in the hall when she escaped, although she could hear the high pitch of the conversation inside the drawing-room. Her grandfather studied her with heroic eyes from the canvas beside the stairs, one hand resting on the barrel of a cannon, a line of sailing battleships in the background. She had known him as a sweet old man, not like that at all. He would have loved today. She could still remember the pang she had felt when she learned one day by accident that he had passed on and they would never be going to stay with him again.

Arriving at the first floor landing, she looked along to the end of the corridor at the white-panelled door of Scopey's room. Mrs Harding had been in that room for goodness knows how long now, but it was still Scopey's room to her. She thought of the odd feeling she had had at Whitestone Pond that morning as she realized it had changed. It still had the same name and was in the same place, with the same shape, yet it was entirely different. She had had to shut her eyes or turn her head away to see the real Whitestone Pond they had walked to and played around as children.

She turned for the flight up to the night nurseries; she was in her old room again as the house was so full for the christening. If Whitestone Pond and Scopey's door changed or remained unchanged entirely in her mind, that surely applied to other things, probably to everything. Everything was subjective, nothing real. She herself was a product of her own imagination. She felt herself looking on, watching this young woman climb the stairs; how preoccupied she was with herself. It had not been like that in the war when she came up here. She had been so anxious for them all, George and Andy and Willy, and Harry later, although he had been so much younger he had never been so close. She had looked at their photographs and possessions, wondering. The picture of them all at their prep school, that would be up there. Now she knew which of them would not be coming back, and all she could think of was *herself* –

The treads creaked near the top exactly as they had when they were children. She was a ghost returning from the future.

BOOK ONE

1895–1910

1

When she remembered it in later life, as she often did, Henrietta had the impression it happened in Piccadilly outside the Egyptian Hall. She was holding her little brother, Willy's hand as she recalled it, trying to give him a sense of the awful marvels she had witnessed inside – the witch who had been locked, protesting, into a cabinet and transformed in an instant into a monkey was one she remembered most vividly for she had seen the spirit of the witch afterwards, flying away in the darkness above and had never been able to get a satisfactory explanation of where she had gone. But the little fellow had been more interested in the two giant stone figures over the pillars on either side of the entrance and she had pulled him away in disgust. It was then she saw her father.

It was a trick of memory, for Willy was little more than two at the time and asleep on a rug in the garden of Felpham House while Nurse, who would have liked to doze off herself for it was a broiling June afternoon, kept half an eye on him and the rest of her attention on his brother, Andrew; who had learned to run surprisingly fast and was teasing her with sudden forays. It was actually George who was with Henrietta that day. He was four and a half – a year younger than her – and perhaps because he was younger the incident made no impression on him; it may be though that even then he was less sensitive to intuitions and auras than she.

Mrs Scopes, the housekeeper, had the afternoon off. The 'Mrs' was a courtesy title she enjoyed by virtue of her position; she had no husband or family of her own, only an ample capacity for love, and she lavished this on the Steel

11

children, Henrietta especially since she had been the first and was so bright and responsive and, as the only girl amongst so many boys, needed extra mothering – so Mrs Scopes had convinced herself. To have Henrietta to herself was her greatest pleasure in life and that day, as the weather was glorious, she had suggested she might take her to St James's Park.

'Why not take George as well?' Mrs Steel had said. Her brisk manner left no doubt that this was an instruction, but there was a hint too, as Mrs Scopes perceived it, that she should not take such an exclusive interest in the girl.

Equipping the two of them with bags filled with chunks of stale bread for the ducks, and herself with a hat sporting blue-green kingfisher feathers which might almost have served as a decoy, she led them out after luncheon while Mrs Steel was in her dressing-gown, preparing herself to do duty by the afternoon callers. They caught the omnibus to Trafalgar Square and sat on the open top deck, an experience in itself, but one that resulted in Henrietta throwing bread excitedly to any pigeons she saw, and soon emptying her bag. George, showing the determination to achieve set goals which was to distinguish his later career, clutched his bag to himself and refused to let her 'borrow' from it. When she tried artifice, promising she would buy him some more as soon as they got off the 'bus', he told her she could not buy stale bread.

'No more you can't,' Mrs Scopes said, relapsing into the vernacular in wonder at this precociousness, although it was nothing new so far as George was concerned.

It was after they had left the omnibus and were walking in the shade of the trees by the side of the Mall, Henrietta still thinking about how she was going to make the stingy George part with his bread, that she saw her father. He was strolling the same way some distance ahead of them and it was difficult to say what first made her aware of him because from the back with only his hair and strong brown beard visible beneath his top hat he looked much as any of the other dignified figures strolling there; perhaps his height or something about the swinging way he walked, not quite the rolling gait associated with sailors in books, but a distinctive sort of swagger, alerted her. He was with a lady with a very thin waist and a marvellous hat piled with rolls and bunches of gauze and colourful silk ribbon. Perhaps it was this that first caught her attention. He turned smiling as he spoke to the lady with the hat and Henrietta saw she was not mistaken: it *was* him.

'Look!' She tugged at Mrs Scopes's hand. 'It's papa! There – over there!'

Mrs Scopes stared in the direction she was indicating, then abruptly came to a stop.

'Why have you stopped?'

Henrietta tried to release her hand so that she could run forward to her father. 'It's papa – I know it is – I've seen his face –' but the more she pulled the tighter Mrs Scopes's grip became until she had to cry out in pain. Looking up, she was startled by the expression she saw; there was something horribly wrong and for a moment she forgot her impulse to run after her father.

'It's the heat,' Mrs Scopes said, and letting go of George's hand, fiddled with her high collar, trying to pull it away from her neck. 'I'll have to rest a moment.' She half-closed her eyes and sank to the grass, pulling Henrietta down into a bending position. 'Henry, darling, do you look after George and see he doesn't run away. There are so many people. What would your mama say if we were to lose him. It would be the end of me –'

Henrietta was more struck by Scopey – the magisterial – appealing to *her* than by the sense of the words themselves. She cast a glance at George, watching them, then quickly back to Mrs Scopes whose eyes were now completely shut. But there was something about those trembling lids and the upright way she was sitting on the grass and the firm grip still around her hand which told Henrietta it was play-acting.

There was no doubt about her distress, but it was not caused by the heat. She knew instinctively that it was the glimpse of her father and the lady with the hat and the waist that was the real cause of the trouble; it flashed into her mind that he should not have been walking with her and turning to smile in the way he had smiled, although she could not have put the feeling into words. Far more alarming was the

13

effect it had had on Scopey. She did not want it to be the end of her. Felpham House without Scopey was unthinkable. She found herself entering into the spirit of the act, taking off her straw boater and fanning Mrs Scopes's face as she had seen her mother do after a strenuous game of tennis on the lawn at home. Gradually the grip around her other wrist eased and dropped away and the lids fluttered open, and soon after that a smile began to play around the corners of the lips almost as if Mrs Scopes guessed that she had guessed.

'Thank you Henry, I do feel much more like myself again now. You may stop. But I think we should wait a little longer, then I shall be quite recovered.'

Without thinking, only aware that somehow the incident gave her power, Henrietta said, 'Make George give me some of his bread!'

The smile faded. 'But I can't do that –'

'Yes, you can –'

'No! It's mine!' George squealed, backing from her.

'Of course it's not, it's ours –' and turning, 'isn't it, Mrs Scopes!' She knew from the look she received that she was behaving abominably, but she didn't care. It *had* been papa, and whatever he had been doing with the hat lady it excluded her. 'If you don't tell him to give it to me I shall take the *whole* bag –'

'*Henry!*' There was astonishment as well as reproof in Mrs Scopes's tone, and extraordinarily a hint of moisture gathering in her eyes. She turned her face away so that Henrietta would not see it, and as she did so caught sight of George running as fast as he could from them. 'George –!' She started up. 'Come back – *at once!*'

Henrietta, appalled at the tear she had seen, also called out and started running after George who, looking round anxiously, cannoned into a man's legs, overbalanced and fell. The man helped him to his feet while Henrietta raced up.

By the time they had calmed him and resumed their walk towards the lake neither their father nor the hat lady were to be seen.

*

14

The notion of duty ingrained in his midshipman days still burned bright in Robert Thackeray Steel: duty well done left him with a warm feeling of integrity and gave shape and purpose to his life which might otherwise have lacked a moral centre, have been no more than a round of self-indulgence and idle talk – itself an indulgence since he was, or had been a raconteur of international class. He had challenged the celebrated Yankee, Commander Josiah Steevens, on his own ground, the wardroom of USS *Naragansett*, and bested him in an all-night sitting that had been the talk of the station for the rest of the commission. He had earned a tie with the 'Dockyard Liar', the notorious P.W.W.Rimington, in one famous clash at the Senior in St James's that had been immortalized in the diary column of the *Morning Post*.

It was this singular gift of invention combined with the honesty of his eyes, which were blue, widely spaced and set rather deep below a noble forehead, and his voice, honed to thespian standards by the need to project it from the quarterdeck to the foretop in a gale of wind, that had earned him his present station of ease: without these qualities he would probably not have captivated the heiress, Alice Brookes, nor won her father, a shrewd East Anglian who had taught himself a version of accepted English pronunciation while creating single-handed the Imperial Sewing Machine Accessory and Components Company, a multi-million pound empire of shining spindles and bobbins, needles, thimbles and fastenings, which he had started from a second-hand lathe in the front parlour of his terraced house near the Ipswich docks.

Had Robert Steel been a thoughtful man he might have reflected on lives betrayed by their own genius: to convince an Ipswich tradesman that what he needed to expand his already astounding empire – and carry it on after him – was a lieutenant, Royal Navy, on half pay and with an actual distaste for trade in any form had been a consummate piece of work; to persuade his daughter, the refined product of Cheltenham Ladies' College and Madame Dupuis in Paris that his principal pleasures were in reading the Latin poets and singing duets – in his admittedly splendid baritone – at the pianoforte had been a virtuoso performance and a sterner

15

test of staying power than his all-night epic with the Yankee moonshiner. Had he been a thinking man he might have considered these tremendous efforts not wasted, for he led a very agreeable life, but unproductive: it had not taken old man Brookes long to find that his son-in-law was incapable of sustained effort in an office nor that his talent for improving on facts was a liability, while Alice, who had a sharper eye even than her father, soon became aware that the Latin poets and that lovely voice could be put to use in other delicate ears. Meanwhile the art of creating baroque fantasies from the most trifling everyday incidents began to wither from lack of first-rate competition into something only a little more spicey than garrulousness.

But there was duty. This neither Alice nor her father – who had tied up Alice's money in trusts which he told everyone would take more than the labours of Hercules to unravel – could fault him. Had his mind been analytical he might have reflected that there was no duty – with the single exception of dismissing maids caught out in peccadilloes – which did not agree with him, indeed which he did not actively enjoy. His duty to his station in life, to Felpham House, which he loved, to the servants Alice employed – who loved him – to the exigencies of entertaining and sending his guests home with a chuckle in their bellies and a heightened sense of wonder at the crises which could befall a fellow on his way to the club, to his twelve tonner yacht, named *Peacock* on account of her glittering brasswork and brightwork, above all his duty to the children with whom God had blessed him. One of his pleasantest duties when he was at home in the early evening was to make his 'rounds' of the 'nursery flat' and hear the eldest's prayers, afterwards sending them to sleep with extravagantly textured bedtime stories.

It was during this duty on the Sunday following Henrietta's afternoon in St James's Park that he was surprised into the first glimpse into the possibility of self-doubt that had struck him since he had become a man of leisure.

Henrietta had not given a thought to the episode on the Mall until that Sunday. Then, following her father and mother walking side by side into church, she had remembered her glimpse of him with the lady with the hat, and had felt again the stab of possessiveness she had felt then – for she loved him even more than she loved Scopey, or believed she did; but she saw him so little her emotion was more akin to hero-worship. Kneeling inside the church she had found herself asking God to protect Papa from the 'hat lady', for it had suddenly occurred to her she was a witch in disguise, in fact she was sure of it or why should Scopey have looked so horrified when she saw her, and then put on such a silly act to stop them getting near?

That evening, when her father came up on his rounds, she was reminded of it again as she knelt by her bed.

'Please God, look after Mama and Papa and George and Andrew and Willy and Mrs Scopes and Bliss –' she ran fluently through the names of the domestic staff.

'And Grandpapa and Grandmama –' he prompted her.

She repeated them, '– and keep them safe till morning – and please God, don't let the witch harm dear Papa – Amen!'

She jumped into bed while Robert Steel, a little puzzled, moved over to hear George's prayers.

When George was in bed he came back and sat beside Henrietta, looking down at her quizzically with his honest blue eyes.

'Who has been telling you stories, Henry?'

'Stories –?'

He opened his eyes in mock alarm. 'The *witch* I have to look out for!'

'But I saw her.'

'*Saw* her?'

'Mrs Scopes saw her too. She was in the park.' Henrietta gazed up, surprised he was being so dim. 'She was with you, Papa –'

'With me!' Robert Steel's brows had drawn down and he gazed at her with an expression she had not seen on his face before. 'What park?'

'On the Mall.'

He continued to stare at her for a moment, then his face broke into a smile; she was glad to see it; she had felt a touch of alarm.

'She was no witch,' and looking at her earnestly, 'Can you keep a secret, Henry?'

17

She nodded energetically.

'Then I'll tell you who that was – but you must never tell anyone – not even Mama – especially not your Mama.'

'I promise.'

'Very well then.' He paused. 'It was your cousin.' He nodded at her look of surprise. 'Yes – and you have not even heard of her.'

She shook her head.

'Of course you haven't. She is your cousin on your mother's side, and she has brothers and sisters.' He leaned closer and lowered his voice. 'But we never visit them, we never even speak of them – and that is why your Mama must never know you have seen one of them –'

'Why do we not speak of them?'

'Because, Henry, they are not our *sort*. And it would hurt your Mama, it would hurt her very much to know that you knew that she had cousins from that sort of people –'

'What sort of people, Papa?'

'I do not say they are not good people, they are – very good people – indeed I would rather pass an hour or two in the company of your cousins than with many of our sort of people – but it would not be right –'

'Why did you do it then, Papa?'

'I feel sorry for them. Consider, Henry – here is your Mama in this great big house with her dresses and servants and you know all the beautiful things she has – and there –' he waved an arm '– are your poor cousins far away in Suffolk where the winds are always in the east from the ice and snows of Norway cuttin' their poor hands and faces till they are raw red like a Norfolk ham. And they live in a poor little, straw-covered cottage with two pigs that come in at night when they can't *stand* the cold wind any longer – and rats in the rafters chasin' each other and havin' rough and tumbles so your poor cousins can hardly sleep for the squealin' – and spiders hangin' down as big as your fist – who gobble each other up – so the flies have free reign and they have a grand Derby round the single wick in the lamp that burns all night so your cousins can have a little heat – round and round –' he made a humming noise '– and every so often one of the little devils burns his wings and drops to the table so in the

18

mornin' when your cousins rise at first cock to milk the cows and feed the poor hens –'

'What's first cock, Papa?'

'The first call of the cockerel of a mornin'.' He made a good imitation. 'So you see what a very different sort of life they live compared with you and me and our sort – and I confess it Henry – I feel sorry for 'em –' he had a distant look in his eyes '– so – I do what I can, little enough though it is, and every now and again I ask one of 'em up to London and I take 'em for a stroll in the park and I give 'em a good, square meal in Jimmy's. That, Henry, sets 'em up no end. It sets 'em up for a twelvemonth –'

Henrietta was puzzled; the description of the cousins hardly fitted the brief glimpse she had had in the park. 'But where do they get their fine clothes?'

'Number one Sunday best,' he replied smartly. 'Everyone has number ones – you've seen 'em in church – even the poorest in the land. They hang 'em in their wardrobes all week –'

'Do the cousins have room in their little cottage?' she asked, thinking of the huge wardrobes she had seen in her mother's dressing room.

'Just for one – one lovely dress for the girl cousins and one number one Sunday suit for the boys, and they take turn and turn about – one takes communion, one attends matins and one goes to evensong. That, Henry, is why I invite them to London – one at a time.'

Henrietta, looking up at him through tears forming at the thought of her poor relations, realized she had never known quite what a good man her Papa was, and impulsively reached up to hug him.

It was the tears and the spontaneous embrace which planted the first seed of doubt in Robert Steel's mind. He could reassure himself afterwards that his story had its basis in fact: there were relations of old man Brookes who farmed precariously somewhere in Suffolk – he had never corresponded with them, much less visited their 'poor little, straw-covered cottage', but that was mere embroidery without which no story was worth telling. Alice never spoke of the Brookes either; probably she had never met them, their ways

19

had diverged so. Yet while he tried to shut out the thought that he had told her deliberate falsehoods by convincing himself that he could hardly have told her the whole truth, the sight of the tears in her trusting blue eyes, so like his own, would not leave him. He was a sentimental man and they changed soon into the tears of innocence deceived. That he could have deceived her became a reproach he found it increasingly difficult to live with. Perhaps the deception on which his whole life was based would have caught up with him in any case at some time, yet this was the scene that came to epitomize it in his mind. The vision of it was a cancer that gnawed at his self-esteem.

It was a significant awakening for Henrietta too; while the initial effect was to make her adore him more than ever, as she grew older and, emerging from childhood, appraised him with searching eyes, the thought of it undermined all confidence in him. It was then the memory of the lady in the hat became mixed up somehow with a Christmas outing in Piccadilly which took place some two years later.

Alice Steel noticed the change in her husband as she noticed most things and, without being fully conscious of what she was doing, used most things. She had been the strength in the partnership from the beginning. She had known from the beginning that was how it would be and perhaps even recognized that for her it was how any marriage needed to be. It had nothing to do with her large income from the trusts; it was the ascendancy of her sharp, practical mind and clear, essentially political vision – although never in a party sense – that saw people and things as they were and what might or might not be done to change them to her advantage, and her determined will over his mind of infinite suggestibility and capricious fancy.

Robert believed he had wooed and won her. He had, for she had recognized in him the very attributes she lacked; his family was beyond reproach: on his father's side the Steels of Worcestershire and the Collingwoods, both of whom had provided generations of officers for the Royal Navy, on his mother's side the Earls of Saxmundham, whose noble origins were lost in the mists of antiquity. His easy manner added to the aura of lineage, and his looks – his eyes then had been able to summon her blood in a way her mind was unable to comprehend, let alone deal with rationally. In these conditions she had recognized his imagination as something splendid which she entirely lacked and needed – just as she recognized that she could provide the steadiness he needed. In that sense he won her; but it was she who had to make him aware of victory and guide and hold him to the path to the altar, in that sense he was won and in that spirit their marriage was a success, each supplying what the other conspicuously lacked, opposite poles of a strong attraction.

After the deception he practised on Henrietta, however, the self-doubt, confirming perhaps something he had sensed for some time but never acknowledged, began to reveal itself. Most obviously it inhibited his social gifts. The imagination that had glowed at Alice's dinner table and made her 'recitation evenings' memorable, lost some of its inspired fantasy; his stories became repetitious and he was content for long periods simply to listen to others talking. As if in compensation, his taste for port grew.

As a result the balance of the marriage altered; not only was one of his most important contributions depreciating, but Alice, noticing his weakness where before she had admired his gifts, worked on the flaw – not because she wished to hurt him particularly but because it was her nature to work on whatever was to hand. This increased his lack of belief in himself. He began to see that, far from having won Alice and a way of life dreamed of by sailors, he had been snared and diverted from his true profession. Seeing Alice as the cause, he rebelled in little ways, staying on at the club to alarm her that he would be late for one of her musical soirées, loudly praising Ipswich at dinner as a much under-rated spa town which he had a mind to visit next year, a drollery that amused his guests but brought twin spots of colour to Alice's cheeks and a darker look to her brown eyes. Rather late he realized these tactics only played into her hands; had she looked for excuses to correct him she could have found none better.

By the end of the year following the revelation at Henrietta's bedside – by which time another boy, John, known as Jack, had been born – the Steel's marriage had changed irreversibly: from the dominant, Alice had become the dominating partner, ever more insensitive in her treatment of her defeated husband while he grew more careless in his spasmodic attempts to break free. She would have been horrified if told that she bullied him; she believed he was hopelessly irresponsible, she was simply keeping him up to the mark; strangely she never considered his most sacred and intimate obligations 'to love her, comfort her, honour and keep her, forsaking all other', nor his promise to honour her with his body, which he kept rather as a duty although less frequently since the spirit had departed; it never occurred to her that the spirit might have been breathed successively into the young women she knew he entertained at Jimmy's. That she allowed because it was 'done' and, although she was not conscious of it, because it provided another flaw to exploit.

It would have shocked and revolted her to be told that her need for more than his routine and mechanical performance – which left her with a feeling of distaste that she should have to allow herself to be used – gave deep emotional edge to her domination.

Just as she was unaware of her own deepest needs, she was unaware of his; she thought she knew him through and through; without the divine spark of imagination what she really knew was what she had made him, not what he could have been or might be still in his fantasies – while he only knew or thought he knew what he might have been without her.

The chief sufferers from this imbalance were the older children. He could take himself off to his club, to his yacht for August, to Jimmy's with his fancies; the servants could retaliate in the many subtle ways in which as a class they were skilled. The children were easy targets and although Mrs Scopes did her best they were defenceless. It was on them that the weight of Alice's unconscious unhappiness fell; as a result they became a tight, secret sister- and brotherhood, like all such setting great store on rituals and signs, presenting a united front to the outside world.

2

'Now, Henrietta,' Mrs Scopes said with satisfaction after inspecting them in their clothes, smelling of laundry, 'I'm off to see to Master Jack. Do you take the boys down to the hall for me and when the carriages are come, remember, ours is *third*,' she could not keep the excitement from her voice, 'not second mind, that's for godparents.'

Henrietta thought of the odious people she had been forced to shake hands with in the drawing-room the day before. Everything about her latest brother was horrible; the fact that he was another boy had struck her as unfair from the start; Scopey had promised to speak to Mama about having a girl this time; then his face was so ugly and everyone crowed over him, lying about what a pretty fellow he was and how his blue, staring eyes were just like Papa's and yet he had a look of his mother too. Actually he looked like a crumpled up little monkey. And they were calling him *Henry*.

Mrs Scopes's eyes were moving over the boys again from their shining, brushed hair to their polished shoes. 'Now, don't get in the way, there's more than enough for everyone to do without looking out for you boys. Stick close to Henrietta and follow into the carriage.' She gave Henrietta a final glance and hurried out.

Henrietta turned to the three, watching her for a lead, bright eyes above white and blue sailor suits, Willy who was just four and wearing his for the first time standing unnaturally still as he stared up, frowning with concentration, George with an eager look as if he couldn't wait to get downstairs, and next to him Andrew – inspiration seized her.

23

'Andy!' she said sharply. 'Why are you not wearing a dress?'

Andrew's brows rose.

'I *told* you you were a girl.'

He shook his head. 'No, Scopey says –'

'Scopey doesn't know,' she interrupted scornfully, moving across to the toy cupboard where the dressing-up box was kept. 'I shall find you something –'

'I'm a boy,' Andrew said, looking down at his sailor suit.

William looked at it too, and compared it with his own while George, impatient to be downstairs, turned to her, 'Oh, come on, Henry! That was yesterday Andy was a girl.'

She rounded on him. 'People don't *change*. You're either a boy or a girl. You can't change.' Pulling the box out, she rummaged for the white dress they had used the day before.

Andrew ran to the door. 'I like my suit.'

'You can't go,' Henrietta called. 'Scopey told you to wait for me.' She pulled the dress out and tried to shake it free of creases and crumples.

George's expression changed as he realized she was serious.

'You can't, Henry –' He thought of the visitors waiting downstairs in their fine clothes, and the carriages about to draw up and was seized with fright.

Henrietta had the same kind of sickly ball of fear in her stomach as she approached Andrew with the dress, but knowledge of the dreadful consequences actually strengthened her: she would show Mama what she thought of Henry. It was as if she was determined to seek punishment as the only way to express the magnitude of her feelings.

Andrew backed hard against the door as she came towards him, pleading, 'I like my suit, Henry –'

She began to feel sorry for him. 'We're going to church,' she said gently. 'Girls aren't allowed to wear boy's clothes in church – surely you know *that*!' She heard through the open windows the sound of hooves on gravel.

'They're here!' George dashed to a window and craned out although he knew the view of the drive was shut out by the side of the house.

'You'll have to be quick,' Henrietta said urgently. She

24

dropped the dress to the floor and seized Andrew's tunic with both hands. He struggled, shrieking.

'George!' she called. 'Come and hold him!'

George turned from the window. 'There isn't *time*, Henry –'

She straightened. 'You don't want to, that's all. Just because you're a *boy* –' she spat the word out. 'You have no imagination,' an accusation she always hurled at him when he would not comply with her wishes, and then suddenly feeling the injustice of it all welling up, burst into tears. 'It isn't – it isn't – fair –'

William, who had been watching her with tense interest found this too much; his face crumpled up in sympathy.

Henrietta sobbed. 'All you – all you – boys – and I have no one –'

George had moved across from the window. Put like that, perhaps she was right; it was unfair. He looked at Andrew, his mind working fast and practically as always.

'Andy, if you do as Henry says, I'll let you be Wellington next time –'

Henrietta stopped crying and wiped her eyes as she looked to see the effect on Andrew.

He was staring up at his elder brother through somewhat narrowed lids. 'Every time? I want to be Wellington every time.'

George's brown eyes, so like his mother's, grew harder. 'You can have two turns – and that's all –'

Andrew, recognizing the look, realized he had squeezed as much as he could from the situation. 'Promise?'

George moved across to the large, leather-bound Bible on the corner table which was used on such occasions and gave the ritual formula; Andrew, unable to prevent a beaming look of anticipation transforming his face, held his arms up for Henrietta to remove his sailor's tunic.

The change was soon effected. Henrietta in another sudden moment of inspiration, dashed to the mantelpiece and took the jay's feather Willy had found a few days ago, thinking she could brighten up her new sister's dress in the coach; then she opened the door.

It was none too soon. The new maid, flushed with the

25

excitement downstairs, was coming towards the nursery.

'Oh, Miss Henrietta! Thank the Lord! Mrs Scopes is all a-flutter –' She caught sight of Andrew in his creased and grubby dress, staring as she flattened herself against the wall for them to pass.

Coming to the head of the stairs, Henrietta turned and hissed, 'Andy, keep behind me and George – *hold your dress up* or you'll trip.' Her heart was pounding furiously as realization of the enormity of what she had done hit her. George was looking unusually solemn too, she noticed, biting his under lip. She took his hand and feeling him squeeze her fingers, realized how much she relied on his no-nonsense solidity.

The hall was empty when they reached it; from the sound of voices it was apparent everyone had gone outside. They passed through, a silent group, Henrietta and George hand in hand in front, behind them Andrew clutching William's hand while still dutifully holding his dress up with the other.

Greetings and smiles from the few guests who had not yet boarded conveyances greeted them as they emerged down the steps from the front door. The warmth of the June sun and the brightness everywhere made a sharp contrast to the dark furnishings and cool air inside the house. Henrietta smiled and nodded to the aunts and uncles and the few she didn't recognize. Why couldn't it be just an ordinary day? It was so beautiful. Just in time she saw Marsala bounding up from behind a knot of people to the left; the Dalmatian had caught the air of occasion; her pink tongue lolloped out from the side of her open jaws; she was coming straight for them, and her mate in mischief, Port, was not far behind, yelping. As she shouted and tried to prevent them from jumping up she saw from the corner of her eye Mrs Scopes standing in front of a carriage further up the drive, waving frantically with one arm, while little Jack held on to the other. Then the Dalmatians pounced. All was confusion.

In the midst of it she heard her mother's voice, 'AN-DREW!' It was from behind, freezing her blood.

George had let go of her hand and was struggling to pull Port away from William, who had fallen on his back on the

26

gravel. Marsala's paws were on her shoulders; she could feel hot breath on her face.

'HENRIETTA! MARSALA! DOWN!' from her mother.

Then she heard Papa's voice and struggling round saw the two of them on the steps before the front door with Nurse just behind, holding the baby, Henry, who had started to cry at all the noise. Her mother turned. Papa, a great smile splitting his beard, ran lightly down the steps towards them calling to the Dalmatians, who bounded away.

'And then the band played!' He looked down quizzically at Andrew, who retreated, backing into Henrietta.

'I'm a girl,' he said defensively.

His father let out a bellow of laughter. 'I see – I thought perhaps – I thought you was the Holy Ghost –!' He was still smiling when he heard the determined crunch of footsteps on the gravel behind and his expression changed.

Her mother's eyes were like flints as she looked into Henrietta's. 'How dare you play your stupid games –' she hissed in a low voice. 'At a time like this!' She seemed scarcely able to contain her anger. 'I'll attend to you presently. Now – take – Andrew – inside – and see he *changes*!' She turned to her husband, now looking suitably serious. 'Find Mrs Scopes this instant, Robbie, and send her in to see me – what is the woman thinking about?'

Henrietta heard no more; her parents, the visitors, the warm sunshine, the house itself fell out of her consciousness; she could only feel Andrew's hand as she pulled him, only think of Scopey, hearing again her mother's voice, 'what is the woman thinking about –' Her legs scarcely carried her; they felt weak and strange as she realized what she had done – Scopey, the one she loved more than anyone, who stuck up for her and all of them against her mother, who had endangered her own position several times by so doing, but this time –? She wished she could sink into the black, bottomless void she felt inside.

It was a silent journey to the church. Mrs Scopes sat very upright with a strained, unnaturally white face, avoiding Henrietta's eye; George had a serious expression and the other children infected by the mood, looked equally solemn – except for the eighteen-month-old Jack who was constantly pointing to people they passed and trying to stand on the seat to show himself off while practising the repetitious sounds he used for words.

Inside the church Mrs Scopes passed Jack silently to Henrietta. She took his hand and led the boys into the second pew immediately behind their parents and the godparents and Nurse, cradling the infant in his swathes of muslin, lace and satin. She moved a cassock into place for Jack, one for herself and knelt, encouraging him to do the same. Then closing her eyes she prayed fervently for Scopey, more fervently than for anything she had ever wanted for herself – although it was for herself that she prayed that Scopey would not be dismissed, that her mother's anger might be vented on her instead because it was her fault, not Scopey's and in fairness Scopey should not be punished. She vowed that if Scopey was allowed to continue at Felpham House, she would never again do anything wicked, never rush through her prayers without thinking at night, never think horrible thoughts of her mother –

Jack had started jumping up and down on the seat beside her and as she moved to restrain him she saw her mother's eyes on her, penetrating it seemed into her mind and discerning the guilt there. She rose and put her arms around Jack and pulled him down to the seat again, then started showing him how to form his chubby hands into the shape of a church. 'Here's the steeple. Look inside –' she turned the hands back to back and wiggled his fingers about '– and see the people!' He chortled. Concentrating on keeping him quiet she forgot her own troubles for a time, only to feel sudden throbs of apprehension as she remembered again.

The service started, and she concentrated hard when Jack allowed her to, determined to prove she could keep the vows she had made on first kneeling. And when the priest said, 'Ask and ye shall have' it came as a personal message, '– so give now unto us that ask –' he went on. Squeezing her lids more tightly shut, she endorsed the plea with all her powers and by the time they came to the interesting part of the service she remembered from Willy's christening when, all standing round the font, Nurse untied the satin ribbons to remove baby's hood, and passed the bundle to a godfather

28

– on this occasion Uncle Joseph – who passed him on to the Rector, she was sure that her prayer would be answered. As a check however she had arranged for a sign: if Henry cried when he was dipped in the water all would be well, if not – the worst would happen. She could not believe God would allow this, nevertheless found herself scarcely able to breathe as the Rector carefully inclining the bundle over the font, recited 'Henry Collingwood Thackeray –' not a sound from the infant – and made the sign on the pink forehead with his finger, 'I baptize thee in the name of the Father – and of the Son – and of the Holy Ghost – Amen.'

She stared in disbelief. Henry was mute. He was returned to a more upright position gazing into the Rector's face, and then as if suddenly realizing that the tangled eyebrows and highly-coloured nose before him were strange, unnatural features, he opened his mouth and yelled. Henrietta smiled happily with the others as the bawling continued. Nurse stepped forward to take him back. Henrietta looked up into the high darkness of the roof where God moved invisibly and uttered silent thanks.

Afterwards the formal tea at home was exciting enough for her to forget she was due for a scolding. Delicious, wafer thin sandwiches with savoury fillings only to be tasted on such occasions – she couldn't even guess what they were – tarts lumpy with glistening strawberries, petit fours of every colour, éclairs, meringues, it was impossible to make a choice without looking at the same time at the other plates ranged tastefully among flowers down the length of the damask-covered dining table – wondering. The men, choosing for their wives, didn't make it any easier; they asked her questions, complimented her on her dress, teased her about having so many brothers; she could tell by their eyes they liked her, and at one point she overheard Uncle Joseph telling her father it wouldn't be many years now before she was the belle of the ball; conscious of being watched and liking it, she made her way up the room to the far end where the maids in starched white aprons and caps were pouring tea from behind tables spread with delicate blue and gold cups, and further along ices in dessert glasses. She saw George eyeing these while stuffing half a meringue into his

29

mouth, and went quietly up behind him. 'Bread before cakes.'

He started, then turned to reply but couldn't because his mouth was full.

'You are a *disgusting* little boy,' she said, and moving back to the long centre table selected a single sandwich and put it on her plate.

In the evening, after the visitors had gone and the half of the white christening cake remaining had been removed from the drawing-room, and the gleaming silver presents had been put on the mantelpiece, and the mossy bank which had served as a backdrop to display them had been dismantled and taken away, and the Canterbury bells and convolvuli and lilies of the valley growing out of the mossy bank had been replaced in the conservatory, and the carpet swept and the piano and chairs and settees moved back to their usual positions, she and George were called down to answer for their trangressions. It was very quiet after the hubbub of the afternoon, and cool after the warmth that had been generated then by so many people. Only her mother was there; Papa was absent; he usually was on these occasions – something Henrietta wondered at when she was older, but at the time accepted as a law of nature. Her mother had changed for dinner and was looking very striking in a black chiffon gown with lacy shoulders, over which she had thrown a scarlet embroidered fichu apparently carelessly, although it seemed to Henrietta that there was something studied about her pose among cushions at the end of the settee, holding an open book up as if she was consciously demonstrating self-control.

She began quietly, asking whether they realized how stupid their prank had been, and what dreadful shame they had brought on the whole family, especially little Henry, who was too young to speak for himself, whose special day this was, and what an affront to the Lord if Andrew had actually found his way into the church in that shocking dress; how everyone had worked hard for days to make it a pleasant and memorable occasion yet all *they* could think of was of drawing attention to themselves with a thoroughly thought-less and inconsiderate charade –

30

Hearing it coldly like this, Henrietta marvelled that she could have been so selfish; at the same time she took comfort from the stream of reproof, thinking that the more they took the less would fall of Scopey, for the sign He had given her at the font had not been entirely convincing; she had said *when* Henry was dipped, not *after* – or she thought she had, it was difficult to remember now –

'And what have you to say for yourselves?'

They remained silent, convinced by the exposition that there was nothing they could possibly say, knowing in any case from experience that excuses usually provoked more.

'Which one of you was it thought of it –? Henrietta, you are the eldest, have you no sense of responsibility!'

Henrietta saw more than disapproval in her mother's eyes, there was dark anger unconcealed. She felt her own will harden and said nothing.

Her mother's control cracked. 'I will not have insolence!' She stood as if poised to come across to bend her over and administer a smacking. Henrietta flinched involuntarily, then braced herself. Instead, her mother stepped to the bell-pull beside the mantelpiece and gave it a sharp tug. They waited in silence, her mother, not looking at them, moved across to the window with set face, staring out; the sun brightened her cheek and tight hair; the song of a thrush, then another further away could be heard distinctly from the trees outside in the garden. Henrietta wondered why her mother was still so cross; it was all over; in any case Papa had laughed and during tea everyone had been friendly and cheerful; no one had noticed the incident really. Why, she wondered, was Mama always angry. She felt George's fingers gripping hers, then the door opened.

Her mother turned. 'Ask Mrs Scopes to come down, Hilda.'

The maid bobbed out again. Henrietta felt hollow with despair and heard herself saying, 'It wasn't Mrs Scopes, it was me.'

'And me,' George seconded her stolidly.

'Ah – you have found your tongues at last.'

'It was Andrew,' she lied desperately. 'He wanted to put the dress on and we let him.'

31

'I thought a moment ago you said it was *you*.'

'We let him. We knew we shouldn't –' she floundered desperately.

'And you expect me to believe that!' Her mother looked at George.

George hesitated.

'I see.' The angry eyes moved back to Henrietta as George said in a stumbling way that he couldn't remember how it started. 'Well, I imagine I know. You are determined, Henrietta, always to be at the centre of attention and never to allow anyone else to share it. You could not bear it when you saw poor little Henry taking the attention from you and you thought up that little game to spite him – and me. Well,' her voice rose, 'I am simply not going to put up with it. I have spoken to your father and we have decided to curb your wilfulness. You will stay in your room for two days to reflect on the necessity for reserve and modesty – and a further day for telling untruths to me here, blaming Andrew for your own misbehaviour – you understand?'

Henrietta felt tears of rage and impotence welling up; that had not been the reason. She tried to hold them back, but failed and had to sniff and wipe her eyes as her mother turned to George and said she would come up presently to slipper him for abetting her. Then they were dismissed.

Lying in bed in the awed silence after her mother had given George three whacks on his bottom – heard distinctly from across the corridor separating her room from the boys' – she seethed with the injustice of it. Forgotten were her vows in church; she hated her mother with all her heart; all she could think of was seeing Scopey, feeling her comforting hug and hearing her soft, reassuring voice.

She waited, hearing from downstairs the muffled tones of the grandfather clock in the hall, and soon afterwards the dinner gong. The birds were still singing in the trees outside, the westering sun made patterns on her wall. She waited several more minutes, then threw back the sheets and put her feet to the floor; she could feel her heart beat as she wiggled them into her slippers and tiptoed across to the door – and out. There was no need to tiptoe; she knew her mother would be well out of the way in the dining-room, yet it was possible she had read her mind and decided to lay a trap, and was waiting quietly at the foot of the stairs. So she trod very carefully, stopping for a long time to listen whenever a board creaked beneath her, hearing only a subdued murmur of talk from the night nursery – and then down the stairs to the first floor. At the bottom she peered cautiously around the corner along the passageway to Scopey's door at the end. It was empty. Picking up her nightdress, she ran and giving only the faintest tap on the door, quickly turned the handle and pushed.

She stopped aghast. Scopey was slumped in her easy chair, her eyes moist and red-rimmed, a long, racking, almost silent sob tearing up from her chest; the dinner tray on the table before her was untouched. She turned at the sudden intrusion, as shocked as Henrietta, who knew somehow in that moment of stunned silence that the die had been cast: she was going to lose her. She rushed forward; arms opened to receive her and burying her head in that ample bosom she burst into uncontrollable tears.

She remembered little more of that night, only that she woke up in the morning in her own bed with one of Scopey's handkerchiefs clutched in her hand.

When she came down after three days of confinement – during which no one was allowed to come in and speak to her except the maid bringing her tea, although she kept up a correspondence with George through notes pushed under the door – Scopey had gone. The little room was empty. There were the same curtains and the colourful framed picture of a multitude of birds and butterflies and animals bordered all round with the words 'All Things Bright and Beautiful, All Creatures Great and Small, All Things Wise and Wonderful, the Lord God Made Them All', but the few photographs and the work basket and all the ornaments and the feathered hats over the wardrobe and the cushion covers had gone. It was clean and bare and odourless and as utterly lifeless as she felt as she looked in.

The same morning her mother, eyeing her curiously she thought, handed her an envelope addressed in a large, rounded hand. She knew at once it was from Scopey although she couldn't remember having seen her writing before, but

33

in any case no one ever wrote to her except at Christmas and birthdays. She ran up to her room and tore it open.

My dearest Henry,

I was very sorry to leave after all the years and specially leaving My Own Henry and not even time to say goodbye but I trust Master George did convey my Farewell.

Do not fret Henry I will come on my day off and we will have fun as ever we used to and do not worry over me I have a good job with a family in Dover Street and very considerate. Also *you must not blame your mama* twas I had to go because we did not hit it off which happens between people you will learn that when you are older and I have my pride same as anyone else and it would not have been right to go on as we have been. So it is all for the Best you can be sure so do not fret My Henry and God Bless you and the dear boys.

Hoping to see you soon   Your Old Scopey

She read it through a second time. She felt numb, emptied of feeling. After a while she went to the drawer in which she kept her special box, a painted black enamel tin with a tightly fitting lid, opened it and emptied the contents on to her bed – a fir cone from which you could tell what the weather was going to do, a ring from a Christmas cracker set with a brilliant red paste stone, some small, folded pieces of paper with the code she used to send secret messages to George, a stone with strange markings she had picked up on the beach at Thorpeness, two marbles she had won from George and a shark's tooth given to her by her father. Then she fetched Scopey's handkerchief, folded and smoothed it and put it in the tin, and the letter on top of it. She studied the collection on the bed, after a moment picking out the shark's tooth and putting it on top of the letter, then she closed the lid and replaced the box in the drawer.

Mrs Scopes's departure and the arrival some days later of Mrs Harding in her place was an emotional milestone for Henrietta, but for the rest of the family it was eclipsed by

34

the Queen's diamond jubilee celebrations at the end of that month. For George, the culmination at the Spithead review of the fleet remained all his life his most vivid childhood memory. While Henrietta and the younger boys and their mother saw the review as guests of their grandfather, Admiral Sir George Steel, from the deck of the Admiralty yacht, *Enchantress*, George joined his father for the day in the *Peacock*.

He had been aboard the yacht before, but never out to sea. The unfriendly cold green of the water and its perilous closeness to the gunwale of the dinghy as they were rowed up river from Gosport through an early morning mist, the sting of salt on his cheek when occasional spray from the tip of the oar spattered his face, the wild eyes of their oarsman, introduced by his father as 'my man John', left an abiding impression, as did John's bare feet and white, mis-shapen toes. He grunted as he rowed, occasionally winking at George and parting one side of his mouth in a twisted grin. He chewed continuously; once when George thought he was about to grin again a stream of dirty-coloured liquid spewed out instead in an arc over the gunwale. He winked as George stared at him. Truly this was a new world.

There was another sailor aboard the yacht, who caught hold of the painter as they came alongside. John introduced him to his father as Jessup, adding in a stage whisper the man was intended to hear, 'A galley-stoker, your Grace, as ever I seen!' He steadied the dinghy for them to climb out. 'There's no reel sailormen to be 'ad in all Pompey, not this week.' He winked up at George, 'I reckon they 'ad the press gang out to man the fleet!'

His father laughed hugely, then telling John to pass up his traps and the picnic hamper, motioned George towards the open cabin hatchway, 'Down y' go!' He followed afterwards with the bags and hamper, which he placed with a grunt of satisfaction on the centre table of the cabin.

'By Jove, we're goin' to enjoy ourselves today, George! Mark my words, this will be a glorious day! And *you* are the *most* important fellow.' He pointed to the hamper. 'You are appointed steward – in charge of the victuals – open up now!'

If this was a new world, his father in his blue reefer jacket, yachting cap and pressed white flannels, was a changed man; he seemed to have left all his cares and a large part of his dignified character on land when he stepped into the dinghy. As together they identified the delicacies in the hamper and stowed them so that they would not shift when the yacht rolled, he was like a fellow conspirator, his blue eyes popping with assumed surprise and real delight at each new item. Three bottles of champagne in straw envelopes were lovingly examined, then wedged in a locker beneath the starboard settee full of bottles similarly encased.

'You must be very careful of those three, George. If we was to drink the Queen's health today in anythin' less I should be sorry.'

By this time the yacht had begun to move and judder in a lively manner beneath them, and a tattoo of slapping canvas could be heard from above. His father pulled a gold hunter from his pocket and studied it briefly. 'Still an hour of the ebb – not that the confounded tides here know the meanin' of punctuality.' He leaned towards the barometer on the forward bulkhead and tapped the glass with his finger. 'By Jove, it is! It's rising! I give you a glorious day – caloo, calay –' motioning him towards the steps, he chortled in his joy. 'But one more thing –' He leaned forward again towards a nest of shallow drawers fixed on the bulkhead above the centre table and pulling one out tipped it so that the contents could be seen – a row of cigars packed in what looked like tea leaves. 'Now you know where all the important materials are.' He motioned him out again, raising his beautiful voice to declaim, 'When the breeze of a joyful dawn blew free – in the silken sail of infancee –'

John was waiting as they emerged, nonchalantly holding the boom steady with one hand; he made a bow as he saw George and brought his other hand up to his squashed blue cap. George grinned, uncertain how to take the exaggerated salute. The great area of tan sail was banging frighteningly close overhead, the hanging reef lines dancing a jig out from the canvas, rope tackles tautening and slacking, slapping the scrubbed white deck planking. He felt his father's hands on his shoulders pressing him down into a sitting position in the angle of the cabin hatchway.

36

'That's your station, Steward – sit y' tight!'

He did as he was told while his father settled himself further aft at the tiller, hauled in the main sheet and nodded at John, who ducked under the boom to make his way forward, yelling at Jessup as he went. His father pulled the tiller, the bow sheered to starboard, a black iron mooring buoy came into view to port, rolling as the line slipped through the ring and splashed into the water. The sails went suddenly quiet, filling in flat curves and heeling the yacht. George gripped the coaming behind him and held on, seeing his father nod and smile approvingly through his beard. Then John was back, tending the jib and staysail sheets as he sat on deck, his legs over the cockpit coaming; right aft the main sheet blocks rumbled as the boom swung out, the tan sail above casting shadows beneath the translucent skin of rippled water slipping by.

His father was leaning towards the high side of the deck, one hand lightly on the tiller, glancing up at the curve of the topsail way above, leaning to peer under the foot of the main in the direction they were turning, up again at the topsail.

George looked ahead. Across on the far side of the channel the blunt, slab-sides of an old ironclad, the lower links of her stern cables hung with green weed, emerged from behind the jib, and as they continued falling off the wind, pointing ever further down river, he saw her aftermast, then a long upper deck and, tucked beneath like two trains in a tunnel, huge drum-like turrets from which the stubbiest of gun muzzles poked.

'The old *Monarch*,' his father called. 'Beastly steam kettle! I turned down a commission in her not a hundred years ago. Can't say I'm sorry – though it cost me my advancement in the service. Can't stand an independent-minded fellow, the rulers of the Queen's navee –'

He continued his commentary as they brought the wind right aft and the yacht came upright; the sense of motion gave way to calm; they seemed to glide almost silently under the huge spread of the main and the topsail on its swaying pole above. There were more warships anchored below the *Monarch* along a line of pale-coloured water stretching far away and merging with the mist to port.

37

The reserve fleet, his father said. 'It gives one food for reflection. How many millions of public money went into that little lot do you suppose! And to what purpose! I'll wager you can't find any two of 'em alike. Progress it's termed, George, progress and the advancement of science. Heaven knows where it'll end – I'll lay odds the Lords of the Admiraltee have no more notion than you or I on that score –'

'D'you see there, the old *Black Prince*,' John called out. 'There's a *ship*! D'you see the lines of her!'

'Ah – supposin' you was hopin' to arm her with a couple of eighteen inch Armstrong breechloaders weighin' a hundred tons apiece!'

John shifted the quid in his cheek and propelled a stream of juice over the side. 'I'd stow 'em down in the orlop – fer ballist.'

His father chuckled. 'Best place for 'em if you want my opinion! Stand by to wear!'

George's attention had shifted from John's mouth to his bare feet and those twisted toes; they were curved around the edge of the bench like thick white talons and they twitched at his father's order as if taking a firmer grip.

'Look out for the boom, George!' He pulled the tiller towards him. ' Watch y' nob!'

John ducked quickly over to his side to release the runner, then back, juggling with his sheets and shouting at Jessup to boom out the staysail. The main boom creaked overhead, the canvas swelling to port. The bows were now pointing down a straight stretch of water bounded by docks and jetties and crowded with craft of every size and description from passenger steamers to yachts and rowing boats, moored or under way; beyond them the narrow harbour entrance was just visible against the mist over the open sea behind. George, wondering how his father could possibly steer between all those moving and stationary craft, thought one must be the *Enchantress*. Henrietta had said it was a hundred times bigger than Papa's yacht; she had poured scorn on his adventure. He wished she could see him now with Papa and John and the mysterious Jessup huddled in the bows – although if she were here she would want to be steward so it was as well she wasn't. He wondered if she was steward in the *Enchantress* and became aware of an empty feeling in his stomach; it had been a long time since they had eaten that early breakfast.

'– you may not like Armstrong – and I confess I could wish his mother had thought of somethin' better to do with herself than bringin' such a clever fellow into the world – at all events he's English and that's a thing we should never forget to be thankful for. What a queer chance it is – it's a thing I never cease to wonder at – take any prodigy of intellect you care to mention and ten to one his mother's an Englishwoman – ain't that so, John?'

John's brow screwed up in concentration.

'Take Nelson,' his father went on without pausing, 'he's a fellow you're not unacquainted with if I'm any judge – we'll soon be payin' our respects to his flagship, George – the *Victory* of glorious memory – consider – had the noble Horatio's mama been of a somewhat lively disposition with dark eyes, you know how they are – and a way of conversin' with her hands and shoulders – and a fancy for certain tasty portions of the after legs of frogs, and his father, instead of an honest Norfolk parson one of your jesuitical Hail-Mary's from across the water – what then d'you suppose our history would've bin! I believe I can tell you – I fancy we'd not be here now settin' out on this glorious mornin' to pay our respects to the grandest fleet that's ever bin – no –'

He was interrupted in full tongue by a yell from close to starboard, swelling into a furious medley of shouts and banging. George, startled, half-raised himself from the bench to see what was happening, but all he could make out over the cabin top were a number of deeply sun-reddened faces and raised arms with clenched fists, and one standing figure holding an oar, all glaring at his father, shouting ferociously as they passed down the side very close from forward aft. He could hardly distinguish individual oaths from the din, but whatever strange words they were they sounded dangerously hostile. The thought of pirates flashed into his mind. Thoroughly alarmed, he turned to his father and was astonished to see him smiling, raising his cap politely to the strangers. John had turned and was answering them roughly, but his father cut him short, telling him not to use language abaft the mast – a mystifying instruction, but with effect. Balked, John turned to Jessup in the bows asking if he was asleep or plumb fagin blind –

'Language!' his father shouted, 'I'll four-water your grog!'

They left the strangers astern; George saw they were in a clinker rowing boat which had once been white; the standing figure was sculling with his oar over the stern, the others still staring angrily at the yacht, shouting and waving still; they wore coarse sweaters like fishermen.

'I hope you was watchin' that, George,' his father said. 'There are few events in life we cannot draw a useful lesson from. You noticed how I paid 'em every civility – despite their nauseatin' language?'

George, still shaken by the fierceness of the encounter, nodded.

'That's the way you must deal with that sort of person. Never lower yourself to their level – try and raise 'em to yours – ain't that so, John?'

John chewed resolutely. 'It's Jessup needs raisin' – I reckon 'e needs raisin' up from the dead.' He turned, shouting forward, ''Ere! Jessup! Keep y'r daylights open! I swear I'll not be answerable for my temper if we loses so much as a chip a paint by your dozy ways –'

'Do 'e sing?' his father asked.

'Sing!' John looked briefly puzzled. 'I 'opes not – oh, I 'ope 'e don't try. 'E can't do nothin', Jessup can't. If 'e was to sing –' He tossed his head, rolling his wild eyes.

'I hope he can,' his father persisted. 'At all events we must keep our eyes liftin' – and the steward here will keep a weather eye open to port – ain't that so, George! But first – you must bring me a cigar. I confess I need somethin' to relax my nerves after that little rencounter –'

George, jumping down into the cabin to fulfil the request, found it difficult to believe his father's nerves had been affected; he had behaved as if greeting acquaintances in the street. It was his first glimpse into the possibility that adults should not always be taken at face value, but it was no more than a flash of insight, he had no time to ponder as he went to the nest of drawers on the bulkhead; the wood was of a lighter colour than the rest of the cabin panelling; it was the colour of his father's cigar boxes, and it smelled the same as he pulled the top drawer open, a spicy smell. The cigars were thick and firm; he wished he could smoke. He also wished his father had thought of eating something to relax his nerves.

When he returned to the cockpit and handed the cigar to his father, he saw the one he had taken earlier still sticking up from the pocket of his reefer, and pointed it out.

His father looked down. 'Hang it! That's for the next time then! But you must see it don't happen again, George. Sing out whenever you see anythin' ahead or lookin' as if he might be crossin' – especially one of those confounded fishermen.'

George wedged himself into the angle of the coaming, hunching his shoulders and lowering his head so that he could see under the boom; the space between it and the shining mahogany rail around the side was limited though, and feeling anxious that he might miss something, he turned and asked if he might go forward to see better.

'A splendid idea! Yes, do you go for'd Steward – but keep low – hang on the rail – I don't like to think of it if we was to come on the *Enchantress* and your poor mama lookin' down over the rail – and you gone!' and turning to John, 'I dare say I shouldn't hear the end of it!'

Jessup scarcely seemed to notice him as he clambered by where he was sitting, back to the mast, gazing vacantly ahead. He took a half-lying position, one arm over the rail, gripping it tightly with his hand lest the yacht heel again – although it had been a most gentle ride since they had been steering down river. There were various craft ahead, two yachts rather like themselves and going the same way, a paddle-wheel steamer which seemed to be going astern with a great threshing of foam from the paddle boxes and a cloud of black smoke hanging in the breeze above her tall, yellow funnel; there was also a launch with a polished brass funnel manned by statuesque sailors and flying a white flag with a red cross, speeding across their course. He called back, itemizing each of these possible threats.

'Bravo!' his father replied, 'A model report! Now – keep y'r eyes on the two sailin' boats – let me know if we make on 'em,' and George heard his aside, 'A future sea king, I'll be bound!'

41

He felt a thrill of pride. He had not considered a career before – apart from momentary enthusiasms soon forgotten – now with the bustle of activity in the harbour ahead and the water tinkling and sighing around the stem close below, and his keen sense of responsibility for the safety of the *Peacock* he felt there could be nothing finer than this life at sea. Even his empty inside was forgotten as he reported the proximity of craft, especially powered launches, that appeared suddenly from behind other vessels ahead.

The strains of a military band were coming from some-where in the city to port; cheering swelled, died away and broke out again in long peals. The paddle steamer which had been going astern drew in alongside another steamer tied up to a pier whose decks were crowded with people; bright colours of dresses and hats stood out against the white paintwork of the ships; excited cries and shrieks of laughter carried across the water. He heard the whistle of a train and saw its smoke rising in puffs from somewhere behind the steamers. Then his father called him aft again. He was aware of Jessup's eyes on him as he turned and crouched his way back under the boom, gripping the hand rail along the cabin top.

'You make a first-rate lookout,' his father greeted him. 'Now see what you can do as steward for I've a mind to break out the first of the "boy". You remember where we stowed the bottles?'

'The champagne?' he asked.

'That's it! And two glasses. And while you're down there see if you can find the rum for my man, John. Bring the chammy up first – I intend givin' the *Victory* a decent salute –'

He was down the steps before his father had finished speaking, and soon found the champagne; wedging a bottle carefully between his calves, he investigated the nearby bottles, pulling off their straw covers until he found one labelled 'rum', then leaving it temporarily uncovered, ran up with the champagne bottle and handed it to his father. Afterwards he fetched two wine glasses from the rack, then the bottle of rum and lastly filled a flask from the water cask and brought that up, interrupting a discussion about whether Jessup should be allowed grog after his miserable performance; his father decided to allow him a four-water tot to encourage his singing voice and John yelled forward to the man to bring two mugs aft and look slippy about it.

His father pointed ahead to starboard. 'There she is, George! D'y' see her?'

He moved across the cockpit and John, sitting on deck there, shifted his legs to enable him to see.

'The *Victory*!' his father called.

She looked broader and more stubby and solid than he had imagined from pictures of sailing ships in books. He was struck by the width of the yards over the bulging black and white checkered sides, and the dark tresses of rigging spun around and below the thick masts.

'It was just such a mornin',' his father said, 'a light breeze – the sun tryin' to get through – she bore Nelson towards the enemy line at Trafalgar. Picture it, George – can you see her – sails all set – movin' to the long, slow swell of the Atlantic – then suddenly from the signal halyards – flags – telescopes snatched up on every quarterdeck astern – "England expects –" ' there was a catch in his voice, ' "England expects that every man will do his duty." And they did. By God, they did! And there she is, George –'

He stared, trying to imagine the scene, but found it difficult. The great ship seemed so solid and firmly anchored against the buildings and green land behind and the bustle of moving craft all around, and to clothe those lifeless masts with canvas was beyond him. He found himself more interested in the moving figures of two sailors jumping like monkeys down the ladder-like rigging of the centre mast; they seemed to be racing one another.

He heard the pop of a champagne cork behind and looking round saw his father catching white froth from the bottle in one of the wine glasses; seeing his glance, he nodded at him to come across and take the other. Just as he was holding it to be filled, he heard a bugle from the direction of the *Victory*, shouted orders and the sound of a band; turning he saw the old ship alive suddenly with flags, lines of fluttering colours stretching from the bowsprit up over the masts and down to the gilded stern, where a huge white ensign flapped lazily up the staff. It was a magical transformation.

43

'We could not have timed it better,' his father said delightedly.

Wherever he looked around the harbour now there were flags and ensigns waving in the breeze; peal after peal of cheering rang out from the passengers on the paddle steamer, and from somewhere just beyond it the beat of the military band throbbed more loudly than before; he caught a glimpse of troops with dark faces, brilliant red turbans and blue uniforms marching to the beat down the pier, then the view was shut out by the bulk of a black passenger steamer slewing under a pall of smoke as dark as her hull; she too was dressed overall with flags.

'I give you a glorious day!' His father's eyes reflected the animation of the scene. 'A most glorious day for old England! Now, George, when I say "The Queen!" you are to repeat it and drink up.' He gazed into his eyes. 'The Queen! God bless her!'

'The Queen!' George repeated dutifully, and lifting his glass, drank. The bubbles stung his palate.

His father was gazing at him still. '*Confound* her enemies!'

'*Confound* her enemies!' George repeated, drinking again.

'Bravo, George! Well said! Now, let us toast the *Victory* and remember Nelson!' He stood, turning to face the old warship which they had brought almost abeam. '*Victory*!'

'*Victory*!' George gulped another mouthful; it was pleasant. He enjoyed toasting; he wondered who they would toast next.

But apparently it was over for the moment, for his father now had John and Jessup stand and face the *Victory* as they glided by her, and led them all in cheering, 'Hip-hip-hip –'

'Hurrah!' George joined in, snatching off his cap as he saw the others doing and waving it wildly.

This they did three times, after which his father said the excitement had made him peckish, and sent him down to break out the victuals – caviar and Bath Olivers for himself, 'And whatever takes your fancy, Steward. John here will have a fresh plug of baccy – ain't that so!'

He was busy for some time with the snacks, choosing a pot of bloater for himself and spreading it thick on lumps of fresh bread which he tore from the loaf; by the time he came

44

up again he was satisfied – even rather full. He saw his glass on the side bench had been filled and as his father nodded at him encouragingly, he took it, gulping down a mouthful as he gazed out at a shingly beach on their port hand; sightseers were already congregating; some were waving at them. He waved back.

'Shall I be lookout again?' he asked.

His father roared with laughter. 'No, George. We're clear of the harbour now. Do you sit and enjoy yourself –' and he swept an arm towards the side opposite the beach. 'When the sun comes through – and I can promise you it will – you'll see an incomparable sight – a sight such as no other nation on earth could match. You can see the start of it there already,' he pointed, 'D'y' see the torpedo boats – and beyond them the torpedo boat destroyers they're called now – and beyond them again can y' just make out the fellows that look after the destroyers – the cruisers? And we'll see the big ships presently – the battle line – the backbone of the Navy, whereon,' he declaimed, 'under the good Providence of God, the wealth, safety and strength of the Kingdom chiefly depend –'

George, seeing only two lines of disappointingly small vessels well over a mile away and disappearing into the haze, asked what torpedo boats did, whereupon his father launched into a story, difficult to follow at times, about an engineer called Whitehead – another prodigy of English intellect – who had invented an explosive machine that swam under water and caught ships by surprise below the armoured belt. Englishmen could not agree with such unsporting methods, so Whitehead had thought up an amazingly clever scheme.

'He sold his invention to the foreigners. You have to hand it to the fellow, George. Then – back he comes to the Lords of the Admiraltee. "Look here," he says, "the Froggies have these infernal devices I invented, don't you think it wouldn't be half bad if you had some of 'em too?" – just like Armstrong and his hundred-ton guns you see – well, what could they do but scratch their nobs a bit and look at one another and say, "Well, it ain't fightin' as you and I understand it, but if our lively neighbours have these infernal machines I dare say we ought to have some too. Can you make us a better one?"

"Naturally!" Whitehead replies, cool as brass, "I'll make you one with two screws – those Frogs will never know what's hit 'em!" "Splendid!" say their Lordships, grinnin' at one another as they picture the look on those Froggy faces, "We'll have a couple of hundred – just as a start." And that's how it was, George –' he waved his arm towards the torpedo boats. 'The truth of it is, with such an unscrupulous enemy an Englishman has to bend his principles at times – if once our fleet was beat – you could say goodbye to old England and the empire –'

George, who had finished his glass of champagne and was twirling it absently in his fingers, had stopped listening. It had flashed on him that the way to prevent the torpedoes sinking British ships was to tow nets like the fishermen did either side. If each ship had spars like bowsprits but sticking out *sideways* towing these nets the torpedoes would be trapped in the mesh. It was such a breathtaking idea he turned to tell his father.

But he was looking back over his left shoulder at a ferry crammed with passengers overtaking them fast; it was heeling at what looked a dangerous angle since all the passengers were crowded on the starboard side, staring towards the fleet.

'By Jove!' His father turned back to glance briefly at the set of the sails and the course. 'There's some pulchritude! D'y' see the one all over in lilac, John? I swear she has the blackest eyes!' He lifted the champagne bottle, wedged at his feet, about to fill his glass when he realized the bottle was empty. 'Steward!' he called.

George, divining instantly what was required, darted down into the cabin, opened the locker beneath the settee, and pulled out a second champagne bottle. Starting up again he heard his father's voice raised in 'John Peel'; John had joined in with a rasping bass.

> 'D'ye ken John Peel, with his coat so grey?
> D'ye ken John Peel at the break of day?
> D'ye ken John P-e-e-l . . .'

He sang on as he took the bottle with a nod of approval and, wedging the tiller against his thigh, tore off the gold wrapping and untwisted the wire fastening from the cork. Then, still singing at the top of his voice, he waited as the ferry came up close on the port side. The passengers had started to join in and by the time the bow of the beflagged and smoking, listing vessel was abeam her decks rang with the chorus. His father stood, then pointing the champagne bottle towards the girl in lilac eased off the cork. It flew high but was blown back and fell in the yacht's wake. Filling his glass, he called to George for his. It was nowhere to be seen.

'Did y' leave it below?'

He jumped down and found it rolling around the cabin floor; the yacht was twisting and pitching in the ferry's bow wave now, and he had to snatch hold of the table to steady himself as he chased and caught it, mercifully unbroken. He hurried up again.

His father filled the glass, then raised his own and his splendid voice at the same time; it carried across the ferry's decks, subduing most of those still singing. 'I give you – THE QUEEN!'

'The Queen!' George piped after him, and put his glass to his lips. The yacht rolled and he had to lean, spilling some of the champagne down his chin and front as cheers and shouts of 'The Queen!' came back from the ferry. Everyone seemed to be waving and the girls were blowing kisses. Caught up in the excitement George put the glass to his mouth for a second attempt, successfully finishing the contents this time, then waving the empty glass to the people on the ferry, he waved the other hand as well and to emphasize his feelings, jumped up. The bows lifted in the ferry's wash; the cockpit floor rolled away and he came down banging his knee on the bench and his glass on the coaming; it smashed into tiny fragments, and as he crouched, numbed with the pain in his knee, he saw blood welling out between his fingers.

He felt hands around his waist lifting and turning him gently to a sitting position and heard John's voice in his ear, 'Lay casy lad – easy!' The sailor prised open his hand with his strong fingers, making reassuring noises as he looked at the lacerations and picked out pieces of glass still sticking in his palm. George felt his breath coming in gasps as, clamping his teeth, he fought back tears of sheer mortification.

'Brave lad,' John said, and to his father, 'He's a good 'un, this one,' then soothingly, 'Lay easy now – I'll be back in a trice –' and he left to go below. He returned shortly with a medicine box and a mug of water and started very gently to wash the blood away from George's hand, examining the cleaned wounds minutely for slivers of glass that still remained and pulling them out. George, conscious of an odour of spirits and tobacco and other indefinable smells was surprised at the tenderness he showed; he was like a nurse.

'I trust we won't need to amputate,' his father called.

'He'll be right as a new guinea,' John replied, sharply George thought.

'You've earned a mention in dispatches, George – wounded in the line o' duty.' His father paused. 'I fancy your mama may not be pleased. I think it best we don't mention you was toastin' her Majesty's health, George, at the time you suffered your injuries – I fancy we can cook up somethin' –'

The breeze snatched at Henrietta's dress as she stepped out on deck after lunch. The water shone in the sun; she had caught glimpses of it through the saloon ports when the day first brightened; now as she walked to the rail she caught her breath. Over moving bright and shadowed bands of green and blue sea, pointed up with little flashing crests of waves, line after straight line of warships spread out – black hulls ruled red at the water, shining white upperworks above, yellow masts and funnels reflecting points of sharp light framed in curving lines of multi-coloured flags, diminishing in the distance, seeming to merge into haze way beyond the land as if they stretched on for ever. And around and between the moored ships, pleasure craft packed with sightseers and the sails of scores of yachts moved slowly – one of those was probably the *Peacock*.

Her attention was caught by a hail from close to; an officer with a megaphone to his mouth was standing in the stern of a launch with a bright brass funnel surging by in patterns of laced foam – 'Clear the line! Bear up! Clear the line!' She tried to see who he was shouting at, but the craft was evidently around the other side. It might even be the *Peacock*; she felt again a twinge of jealousy that George was out on his own with Papa.

Not that she would have exchanged places with him: she was having the most exciting time ever. From the moment she had seen Grandpapa that morning transformed from the benevolent, straw-hatted and stooped old gentleman she knew into something out of a fairy-tale with a three-cornered hat, gold epaulettes and braid and stars, and medals tinkling at his breast, and a hanging sword gilt-handled at his side, she had realized this would be no ordinary day. The young officer of the *Enchantress*'s boat who saluted Grandpapa had had a look in his eyes as he handed her aboard, and she had been aware of the sailor, motionless with a boathook at the stern, gazing sideways at her intently.

She was, of course, a princess; the information had been withheld by her mother because she was not her real mother and was jealous of her. It explained much about her behaviour that had not been clear before. The idea was confirmed when they arrived aboard the *Enchantress*. Splendidly uniformed, starred and bemedalled admirals greeting Grandpapa had smiled at her with expressive looks, and their wives could not have been more gracious. Then there had been the boy at the next table at luncheon; she had liked the look of him; he was older than her and had a straight nose and very direct eyes with which he had kept her under observation when he thought she wasn't aware; evidently he, too, knew her real status.

She felt a tap on her shoulder, and Grandpapa pointed to two vessels steaming out towards them from Portsmouth; she recognized the second as the royal yacht, *Victoria and Albert*, which they had passed earlier. Large flags blew from each of her raking masts, two very grand ones from the mainmast, which Grandpapa explained signified that the Prince of Wales representing the Queen, and his sister, the Empress of Germany, were both aboard. Watching, she felt the rail begin to pulsate beneath her arm and saw the water sliding past the side below. Their bows turned towards the royal yacht, and Grandpapa motioned her to walk forward with him; as they walked she saw men running along the decks of the moored battleships nearby; soon the sides were lined with sailors and on the quarterdeck of the nearest sun glanced from bandsmen's instruments.

She became aware that Grandpapa had stopped and was talking to someone; it was a younger officer although just as splendidly uniformed, and beside him as she turned she was startled to see the boy she had noticed at lunch; he was gazing at her with that direct look and this time his eyes did not move away. She smiled, he smiled gravely back, and seemed about to say something when the officer introduced him to Grandpapa as 'my young nephew, Alastair'. Grandpapa then introduced her, and Alastair held out his hand in a formal, very self-possessed way. As the men resumed their talk he asked her if she was enjoying herself.

She nodded vigorously.

'Yes,' he agreed, 'it's awfully jolly, we've had the whole week off school – have you?'

'I don't go to school.' Wondering suddenly if, as a princess, she ought to, she added quickly, 'not that kind of school.'

He looked a little puzzled. 'I'm going to Eton next half –' then as they heard a dull, thumping sort of explosion from a distance, he turned quickly; she followed the direction of his gaze and after a moment saw puffs of whitish smoke rising from the nearest battleships; almost immediately afterwards a ripple of reports reached them.

'They're firing the royal salute,' he said, turning back, 'twenty-one guns.'

She was impressed by his knowledge. 'Are you going to be a sailor?'

'No,' he replied in a matter-of-fact way. 'I'm the eldest,' and realizing she didn't understand, 'In my family the eldest always goes in the army. Isn't it the same in your family?'

She shook her head. 'I'm the eldest in our family.'

He smiled. 'They won't send you in the army!'

'I have five brothers,' she said quickly, feeling herself colouring, and to cover her embarrassment, 'well, they *think* they're my brothers, but really they're not because my mother isn't really my mother.' She looked quickly round in case Grandpapa was listening, but he and Alastair's Uncle, still talking, had moved a little distance away. 'You mustn't tell them. Two of them are here. They don't know.'

He smiled again, a pleasant, open smile like his greyish eyes. 'Honour bright!' Then he told her about his own brothers and sisters, and she learned that he lived in a castle in Scotland, which disappointed her as it sounded so far away and she had never met a boy so assured and knowledgeable and at the same time so good-looking in a strong, serious way. But when he learned that she lived in Hampstead, he said they had a place in London, off Piccadilly.

'We often go there!' she exclaimed. He seemed pleased so she told him that her real mother lived in Piccadilly, and whenever she went there she hoped she was going to see her, but never did. He thought he must have met her because they knew no end of people there.

'She's very beautiful,' Henrietta said. 'She's tallish and she has lovely hair – about the same colour as mine but much much smoother and silkier and she wears diamonds in it and she rides in the Park every morning and you should see the men who come out just to see her – and her photo's in the *Graphic* – nearly every week –'

Alastair had been eyeing her speculatively. 'Does she look like you?'

She thought for a moment, then nodded, 'Yes – she does really.'

'I thought so. I must have seen her.'

She was alarmed. 'You mustn't tell her. You mustn't tell anyone.'

He promised and she believed him utterly; it was a secret between the two of them. No one else would ever know.

Cheering in unison and the beat of a ship's band some way ahead diverted their attention; a passenger liner with black hull, buff-coloured upperworks and black funnels had interposed between them and the royal yacht, which they could just see steaming into the lines of battleships; their own ship was evidently turning to follow the passenger liner. Grandpapa and Alastair's uncle beckoned to them, and they followed to the forward rail. It was there she was separated from Alastair for the deck was crowded, and one full-bearded admiral, seeing her craning her head for a view, stepped back and shepherded her into his former place at the rail. She smiled, thanking him, but afterwards the afternoon seemed strangely empty.

George, lying on the settee in the cabin, wished they could just sail back. His knee was painfully stiff and ached if he moved it, his hand was sore still beneath the bandage John had put on, worst of all he felt horribly sick with the motion of the yacht since the wind had got up. He was tired and he didn't wish to see another ship; the hundreds he had gazed at that afternoon and his father's descriptive comments were blurred together in images of light off water and white topsides and yellow funnels, and bands playing and cheering sailors waving their caps, and flags and this nausea in his stomach. He wanted to be at home in his motionless bed and just go to sleep. His father had said Nelson was always seasick; he didn't suffer himself so he couldn't know what it was like. His singing had become a hateful sound; it meant he was content to stay out here. John was joining in the chorus.

'Oh, my bonny sailor laddie, Oh, my bonny sailor he,
Well I love my sailor laddie, blythe and merry he be –'

He thought he heard rain on the deck above, heavy drops, and hoped it might induce his father to steer for home.

'Sailor lads has gold and silver,
army lads has nought but brass –'

The song stopped abruptly, turning into an exclamation as the drops became a thunderous tattoo. There was a different motion to the boat now, and he heard John down in the cabin; he was cursing, pulling oilskins from a narrow cupboard. Then there was a crashing thump from above, the yacht seemed to jerk and his father shouted, 'Where the devil are you? The bloody runner's gone!'

George's heart sank. If there had been an accident they might never get in.

There was no more singing then, only the sound of the rain falling in solid waves and lightning flickering through the dim portholes and the crash of thunder afterwards, and John's voice cursing and shouting at Jessup to fetch things, and every now and again thumps on deck. Gradually he drifted into a fitful sleep, waking from time to time with terrifyingly vivid dreams of trying to escape from the cabin or, once, of his father beckoning to him from the dinghy which was rolling wildly but he couldn't move to jump in; on another occasion he was being shaken out of his sleep by Mrs Scopes who was saying he must move away from the fire; he was practically on the flames although strangely they were not hot and nor was he asleep but she kept on saying 'Wake up, lad –' and he realized it was John shaking him by the shoulder. He sat up, wincing at the pain in his knee.

John's eyes were close; he thought from their intent expression the *Peacock* must be sinking.

'Fancy you can git up on deck?'

Feeling it was important to leave the cabin quickly, he swung his legs down and followed John up the steps, stifling a cry of pain as he bent his injured knee. It was late; the rain had stopped, but clouds darkened the evening sky. He saw a row of lights astern, then emerging fully gazed round in surprise. There were lights everywhere. All the ships he had seen that day, the further ones scarcely more than shadows above the sea, were outlined in electric light, the shape of their hulls, superstructure, funnels and masts picked out by a myriad bulbs which formed clusters and aisles of illumination for as far away as he could see. Here and there a flag at a masthead was formed by white lights crossed with red; at another distant point he could just make out a red V R in the middle of 1837 in white bulbs; as he watched it changed to 1897.

'Worth waitin' for, George!'

He looked round at the other side. One ship quite close to them had a giant eagle picked out in coloured lights above her bridge, another, graceful sweeps of red and white festoons, another was shooting up fireworks, and next to her was a ship with an arrangement of rapidly changing shapes and colours like the advertisements he had seen at Christmas in Piccadilly Circus; this one had two flags illuminated by beams of bright light at her mast; one he recognized as the white ensign, the other had horizontal red and white stripes with a blue corner covered with rows of white dots.

'The *Brooklyn*,' his father called. 'What you'd expect from a Yankee – they have no navy to speak of so they have to make that vulgar brag. Don't it make you sick!'

Henrietta couldn't remember having been up so late before; she didn't feel the least tired, only excited by the pools of light on deck and the lights dancing in the dark water below and the bustle and talk all round as people made their farewells to one another and agreed it had been a memorable day – the most marvellous day they could remember.

'Who was that boy, Henrietta?' her mother asked, 'the one who came up to say goodbye?'

'Alastair,' she replied as if it were the most obvious thing in the world.

'Lord Vauncey's boy,' Grandpapa put in.

'Indeed!' A new note entered her mother's voice. 'I saw you talked with him at tea. Did you like him?'

Henrietta looked up as she gauged her answer, and was surprised to see a smile of warm approval. She took her cue from it, 'Yes, I did.'

'There's nothin' wrong with Vauncey,' Grandpapa said, 'I knew his brother.'

'His eldest son?' her mother asked.

'Yes,' Henrietta replied. 'That's why he has to go in the army. Will George have to go in the army?'

'Army!' Grandpapa shouted. 'Henry, the boy's goin' to sea. Ain't that so, Alice! God bless my soul!'

'I wonder where their London house is,' her mother was saying. 'It would be rather nice if he could come over – after the holiday perhaps – you would like that Henrietta? You seemed to get on well with him.'

'Army!' Grandpapa chuckled. 'Talkin' about the army today! Ain't the sea service good enough, Henry!' He tilted her chin up with his hand. 'Well – don't you see George cuttin' a brave figure in one of those battleships?'

She hadn't thought of George doing anything in particular when he grew up; it was a novel idea. 'Will he be an admiral?'

Grandpapa roared with laughter. 'That's up to George! But from what I've seen of the lad – yes, Henry – I believe he will. He has the right stuff in him.' His expression changed and he seemed to gaze right past her. 'A pity I shan't be here to see it.'

She felt very sorry for him; his eyes looked old and tired but his expression was like a boy denied a treat he had been looking forward to. She thought it must mean a lot to him. She pulled his arm in to her body and snuggled up. Soon afterwards they started moving towards the gangway down to the boat.

3

The idea of the castle in Scotland took hold of Henrietta's imagination over the following weeks. At Thorpeness on the Suffolk coast, where every August they rented a timber holiday house, she detailed her plans to George as they wandered the beach looking for useful wreckage washed from the sea, or cornelians in the shingle, or stones with holes right through them; George was not a good listener; he interrupted her thoughts with questions and difficulties – how did she know that Alastair would *want* to marry her? Keeping crocodiles in the moat would frighten people and no one would call on her. Grandpapa would not *want* to live in one of the towers; he liked his own house. You didn't get boys or girls just because you wanted them; it was chance which type you got –

'Why does Mama have boys every time then? If it was chance she'd have girls too.' She found herself growing fierce. 'You don't know a thing about it.'

'Yes, I do – Scopey told me –'

'Oh – and *what* did Scopey tell you?'

'She said you couldn't have babies until you were married.'

'Well, I *am* going to be married – *to Alastair* –'

And the cycle started again.

Finding George so difficult, she started confiding in Andrew or William and she made the discovery that Willy, although not quite four and a half years old, had imagination. Before that she had thought only girls had imagination while boys liked making real things work or hitting things. But Willy, she found, could enter her world and become a part of it. He suggested that if she got her crocodiles as babies

56

they would grow up liking her and they would all be able to swim in the moat and go for rides on their backs like the Greek boy who rode on the back of a dolphin – he had been much impressed by a picture he had seen of this episode. And they could come into the drawing-room in the evening and lie around in front of the fire.

'Would they bark,' she wondered, 'if anyone came?'

He thought. 'They'd probably make a noise. They have very big mouths.'

'I could have two dogs as well –'

'They'd lie in front of the fire,' he objected, 'and the crocodiles would eat them,' and after pondering a moment, 'The dogs can lie in front of the fire in the day and in the evening they have to change places with the crocodiles – then they can see if someone is coming because everyone who wants to come into the castle has to go across the moat and the dogs are swimming in the moat so they can easily see them –'

Previously Henrietta had looked on Willy rather as one of her charges, a little boy who had to be told what to do and what part to play in her games. During the holiday she came to see him as a character in his own right with a mind capable of soaring fancies complementing her own. Often, while George and Andrew built fortifications of sand and stones together, afterwards defending and attacking or demolishing them with bombardments, she and Willy went off together, walking for ages planning the future course of their lives or telling each other questions that had come into their minds – if you dug a really deep hole in the sand and got in and covered yourself right over your head could God still know everything you were thinking? Or, after Henrietta had confided to him the existence of their Suffolk cousins – which she had never told anyone else, not even George – wasn't it lucky that he had been born her brother or he wouldn't know her.

'You might have been born anywhere,' she said, feeling very strange, for once you thought about being born as someone else it was difficult to follow it up and think how *you* would feel if you were not you because then you wouldn't know what it was like to be *this* you.

'I know,' he replied, kicking up sand with his toe as he walked, 'I might have been a spider. Then I would have eight legs. I'd like eight legs, Henry –'

That was another great difference between him and George; he had a fascination with all living, moving creatures, even spiders. George liked throwing stones at seagulls in flight or chasing mice in the stables with a stick, but things like that almost threw Willy into a fit; he would even step over or around ants rather than tread on them. Once on one of their rambles they saw a herring gull lying near the line of seaweed and small debris left by the receding tide. It looked dead, but as they approached they were startled to see it move and flap and hop down towards the sea, rising sometimes a few feet in the air, each time falling back.

'It's hurt its wing,' Willy called, seeing immediately what was wrong, and running after it.

The bird increased its frantic efforts to get away; it scrabbled into the sea and was carried out in the tow of a receding wave. Willy ran in after it.

'Careful!' she shrieked, and dashed after him, for he couldn't swim.

He was standing with the water half way up his calves when she reached him. The gull was thrashing some ten yards further out. It had managed somehow to lift itself over an incoming breaker, which surged in and struck them, crashing up her legs inside her skirt and soaking her knickers, and it would have knocked Willy flat if she hadn't held him.

The soaking didn't seem to affect him; he stared out towards the bird as the wave passed, then wriggling free of her hold, shouted at her desperately, 'Get it, Henry! Go and get it!'

'Don't be silly!' she said crossly, trying to catch hold of him again.

He was too quick for her. He had seen the gull caught in the breaking crest of the next incoming wave, and was pushing sideways through the water to intercept it. She went after him, catching him just as he plunged to catch the bird. As she pulled him to his feet, she saw he had it in his arms, his right hand bending around its neck to hold the head still. It seemed paralysed with fright; she saw its eye fixed on him.

As she helped him back out of the water, he was examining

its wing and when they were beyond reach of the waves, he said, 'It's just a piece of line – you hold him, Henry –'

He seemed to know instinctively how to handle the creature with its wing closed so that it wouldn't hurt itself trying to escape, and reluctantly she took it from him in the same way. The thin line, evidently discarded by a fisherman, was wrapped around one of its legs, from which a loop had caught around the wing, preventing it from extending fully. He worked away carefully, muttering, 'It'll be all right – don't worry – oh dear – that feather's broken –'

When he had freed the line, he straightened, looking at the bird and touched its head softly as if to stroke it.

'Let him go now Henry.'

She bent and released her hold. Immediately there was a thrash of wings and she felt air on her face as it seemed to hop up from the sand and rise noisily past her ear. She watched it climb up slowly over the sea. Willy was waving at it. It rose higher and higher as if thankful to prove that it could, then floated on the wind, then flew again. They watched until it was no more than a speck among other distant specks in the sky.

She realized suddenly she was cold; the breeze through her wet dress was chilling despite the sun. 'Come on!' She started running back towards the others and Willy ran and jumped beside her, evidently very pleased with himself.

'I wish we could've kept him, Henry.'

'You can't keep seagulls,' she said rather crossly; she admired him tremendously for what he had done and, knowing she would not have done it herself, felt vaguely annoyed.

'No,' he agreed, 'but he would have died – wouldn't he?'

'He might have.'

'He would – I know he would –'

'*Someone* would have found him.'

He hadn't thought of that, and the eagerness faded from his face as he considered the implications. 'He might have died before they found him.'

'That's why God sent *us* to find him.' When she thought about it, it occurred to her that they usually walked in the other direction. 'Don't you remember – I said we'd go this way today. That was God. He was talking through me – like he talked to Abraham in the burning bush.'

'D'you think God will show us another one tomorrow?'

'You have to be very good or God doesn't talk to you at all.'

'I'll be very, *very* good,' he said rather breathlessly for they had been running for some time.

By the end of the holiday a pattern had been established; there were quarrels and shifts of intimacy and from time to time a closing of the ranks when their mother worked herself into a mood or Nurse scolded one of them or the show-off children from another holiday family were invited to tea, but in general she and Willy had become very close, and Andrew, who looked up to George because he was older and stronger and resourceful and looked commanding with dark eyebrows and bold eyes, did whatever George wanted to do.

Jack, who was not yet two years old was something of a nuisance to everyone, although Willy, perhaps looking on him as a young creature needing attention, spent a great deal of time keeping him amused – to her extreme annoyance – and as a consequence Willy had become Jack's favourite. As a girl she was expected to help Nurse look after the infant, Henry, a disgusting chore which she thought unfair: if her mother wanted another boy she should look after him instead of farming him out on her and Nurse, who had enough to do keeping up with the wretched Jack. It was especially horrible when the sun was shining outside and the boys were on the beach. Sometimes she wondered whether she should accidentally drop the little crybaby when Nurse gave him to her to hold for a moment, but she couldn't do it deliberately, and there were times when he gurgled up at her with a bright look in his eyes and a sort of smile on his chubby face when she thought that it really wasn't his fault that she had to stay in and it would be quite wrong to drop him.

Alastair never did come to see her after they returned to Felpham House. Whether her mother sent him an invitation or not, she never knew, and she didn't ask, partly because she knew her mother disliked her and she wasn't going to play into her hands by asking favours, mainly because Alastair had become more of an idea than a real person, an idea she could

60

talk with in her head and plan for just as well, probably better when he was not physically present. She was happy with *her* Alastair, content to know that if she ever needed the real one he was there in Scotland or sometimes in Piccadilly or at Eton and she could see him simply by looking up his address in Burke's, which often lay on a table in the drawing-room. Probably she would see him when she was older; no one ever got married until they were at least eighteen; she would ask him to her coming-out party. Since she thought only in terms of herself it did not occur to her that Alastair was several years older and would be of marriageable age before her.

'How do people leave their cards if you live in a castle in the middle of Scotland?' she asked her father one evening when he came up on his 'rounds'.

He stroked his beard. 'An interestin' speculation, Henry. It would be a long way to dispatch one of the servants, would it not! The *middle* of Scotland, you said?' His eyes were glinting, then he looked serious. 'Well, I dare say they'd post 'em – as a matter of fact some of these professional fellows are doin' just that now – in London – especially their PPC cards –'

'What's a PPC card, Papa?'

'It's dreadful Frenchified jargon – *pour prendre congé*, Henry – in a manner o' speakin' goin' away – so people know you're going away –'

'The opposite of at home cards?'

'Exactly so, Henry!' he laughed. 'Which brings me to a matter I've bin talkin' over with your Mama. We've decided it wouldn't half be a bad idea if you – and the boys of course – was to have a governess.'

She sat straight up.

'Your Mama feels that gels of your age all have a governess and she's bin remiss in not seein' to it earlier but she thought – with Aunt Emiline teachin' you writin' and a little French and with your dancin' and piano lessons and all – but now I fancy she finds you a little – wild at times –'

'Mama doesn't know – she never sees me – hardly ever –'

His brows rose with a sad look, she thought. 'She knows everythin', Henry – every last thing that happens between these walls. And beyond.' He rose, leaning to kiss her on the forehead and stroking her hair gently. 'You'll like her, I know you will. It's better than goin' to school now – ain't it!'

Miss Carstairs lasted scarcely more than six months. She was a pedantic woman, prematurely matronly with no sense of humour or feeling for the real interests of her charges. In awe of Mrs Steel, who had engaged her, she said, as much to bring order and discipline to the elder children as to educate them, she tried to instil obedience and punctuality by punishments graded according to the offence, a system that worked well enough with the pragmatic George, who could see no point in asking to be kept in in the afternoon to write out lines just for the satisfaction of being late for the start of lessons after breakfast in the schoolroom – a former boxroom with bare cream and brown paintwork fitted up with a blackboard and two desks. Also he was attracted by the different coloured stars with which Miss Carstairs bribed them to work. Top was gold. George could scarcely open his exercise book fast enough to see if he had a gold star pasted on the top of the page; it was the lustre of the colour as much as the fact that it was top award that attracted him; he ran his fingers sensuously over the sheen as if physical contact added to the visual pleasure.

Henrietta regarded this as disgusting toadyism; having taken an immediate dislike to Miss Carstairs's unsmiling strictness, her obsession with time and rules of grammar and her seeming remoteness from all real feelings or affections, she made it her business never to give her the satisfaction of awarding *her* a gold – although she found making deliberate mistakes in spelling and punctuation – the only areas that seemed to interest Miss Carstairs – meant knowing the correct modes; otherwise it was possible to get it right by mistake. Consequently she found herself working rather harder than when Aunt Emiline had taken them through *Alice in Wonderland* or *The Jungle Book* in the comfort of the drawing-room. She also found it a challenge to her ingenuity to think of plausible stories for why she was late – which again meant knowing the correct time, or she might be early.

One of her better inventions was the ghost she met in the passageway. The tale was dismissed out of hand, which made her more determined.

'It was a ghost – and I know *who* it was.'

Miss Carstairs rose beautifully to the bait; one of the games Henrietta played with herself was to see how long she could keep her talking before she started the lesson.

'*Who* was it Henrietta?' she sighed.

'Lady Ottolene Murray,' she replied pugnaciously; the name had come into her head that instant, although it was a good choice since she had been the previous owner of Felpham House.

'Lady Ottolene is alive and well,' Miss Carstairs replied briskly, 'as you well know, Henrietta. That was a very stupid story – and,' she added as if realizing the enormity of it suddenly, 'a very wicked story. Imagine if Lady Ottolene could hear herself described as a ghost. You will have to stay in again this afternoon and –' pulling out her watch, 'you are twelve minutes late so that is –?' She turned to George.

'A hundred and twenty lines,' he said smugly. If Henrietta's intransigence had taught them one thing it was that you simply added nought to the number of minutes late to calculate the number of lines you had to write.

'But why should I get lines just because I saw a ghost? It's not fair –'

'It is not because you saw a ghost, Henrietta, it is because you were late and told me an untruth to try and escape your just punishment.'

'It wasn't an untruth because I did see a ghost and you can't say I didn't because it's disappeared now – through the wall –'

'That is enough, Henrietta!'

Henrietta shrugged. 'I know it was her. She seemed to want to say something to me – she had an *awful* look –'

'*That is enough!* George – go down to the study and ask your father if he can affirm that Lady Ottolene is in good health.'

Henrietta could scarcely believe her success.

George returned after a while with a copy of the morning's *Times*. Papa had told him, he said, that Lady Ottolene was quite well on the Wednesday before last because he had been invited to a soirée at her home, and he hadn't heard of anything happening to her since although there was no telling with the traffic in the streets these days and Miss Carstairs was welcome to look in the obituary columns just in case. As for the awful look which Henrietta had described, he thought that was quite possible because as he understood it Lady Ottolene had sold the house in order to pay off her debts – but of course they must never breathe a word to anyone.

There was no mention of her in the obituaries and Henrietta had to spend the early part of the afternoon writing out, 'I must not speak ill of the living' one hundred and twenty times. Having done this she wrote on the following page, 'I hate Miss Carstairs, oh, how I hate Miss Carstairs, she is a –' She was wondering what word or selection of words to use when George burst in and said hadn't she finished yet because Bliss wanted help taking the horses out. She had intended tearing the page from the book when she had finished her essay on Miss Carstairs, but forgot when she heard about the horses, slapped the pages shut and jumped up to follow George outside.

The next day she was down in front of her mother to answer for what she had written, receiving a lecture on the sinfulness of hate, the need to love all men as the Lord had taught, and finally three stinging cuts on her outstretched palm with the cane and a sentence of confinement in her room for the whole day.

There was an extraordinary sequel to this episode; the following week George was called in to the study after breakfast to be shown Lady Ottolene's obituary in *The Times*. Apparently she had caught German flu the previous week – about the time therefore that Henrietta had claimed to see her ghost. Miss Carstairs appeared stunned by the news, and was rather pale as she looked at Henrietta.

'Perhaps I owe you an apology, Henrietta.'

Henrietta returned her look with silent superiority.

'Perhaps the *awful* look was because she knew she was going to die,' George said. 'Perhaps she did die for a short time when she first caught the flu and came back here to haunt us, then the doctor made her better and she went back to her house through the wall –'

'That is hardly likely, George. Doctors cannot bring people back from the dead.'

Henrietta's eyes narrowed. 'Sometimes they think they're dead and they bury them and then they hear tapping inside the coffin.'

George cut in to point out that she would not become a ghost just because the doctor *thought* she was dead; she would have to be really dead –

'Come, come, now children! This is a most disagreeable topic –'

'No, it's not,' Henrietta contradicted. 'D'you think there are ghosts now, Miss Carstairs?'

Twin spots of red had appeared on the governess's white cheeks. 'I will excuse you this one time, Henrietta – you evidently think I was wrong last week, but you must *never* contradict your elders. Now – open your books –'

'But do you think there are ghosts?' Henrietta persisted.

A doubtful expression came into Miss Carstairs's eyes. 'Some people say they have seen ghosts but I do not believe it has ever been proved –'

'But why don't you believe me – if other people have seen them?'

She managed to keep the controversy going for several minutes longer, counting it a great victory, especially as she had sensed that Miss Carstairs was badly rattled. But thinking about it in her room that night she became very frightened, convincing herself that even if she hadn't seen anything, there must have been *something* there or why should she suddenly have made up the story and correctly given the name of a person who was that very moment falling ill? Then she thought that perhaps she had seen into the future – and if she had really seen into the future that meant that Lady Ottolene was going to come back to haunt them – which meant that she was back already because she had died yesterday. Then the door creaked. She froze, not daring to move even her head to look around and see if anything had come in. She stayed rigid with terror for what seemed like half an hour, then the door creaked again. She screamed.

George was in the room first and tried to calm her, then the other boys and finally Nurse.

'I saw her!' she choked out between sobs. 'It was her –'

'Who –?'

'Lady – Lady Ottolene – she-she – opened – the door –'

'Now – now –' Nurse said soothingly stroking her hair, and sending the boys back to their beds, she stayed with her until she fell asleep.

In Papa's hands the affair became a great joke. If anything was mislaid in the house it was Lady Ottolene who had taken it, and the trick was to devise an amusing explanation of why she needed it. If a picture fell, or a vase was broken or a window that was thought to have been shut was found open, it was Lady Ottolene who disapproved of the subject of the picture because it was too lively, or did not like the flowers because they reminded her of cemeteries, or needed a breeze to rustle her dress while she was haunting. In this way she became somewhat less frightening, but more real; none of the children doubted her presence in the house.

Another result of the episode was a sharpening of Miss Carstairs's relationship with Henrietta; feeling that somehow she had been made to look a fool, she became even stricter, and Henrietta, sensing that despite this increase in severity, the governess had lost some of her former assurance, found more ways of probing beneath her guard until even George, his enthusiasm for gold stars staled by repetition, joined in. Miss Carstairs changed her tactics, trying to curry favour, but it was too late; the new attitude only invited fresh liberties and so, eventually, more desperate punishments. Henrietta would have been surprised to know how insecure and unhappy Miss Carstairs was, caught between Mrs Steel's displeasure at her failure to curb them, and their own schemes to undermine the lessons in the hated schoolroom. But miserable as she was, the governess was determined to preserve her dignity, and Henrietta, never guessing, only feeling that they had her on the run, hounded her unmercifully.

The final episode had more to do with Willy than with her or George. It happened the following June. Uncle Richard had been invited to a tennis party to which their close neighbour, the West End actor, Gerald Gilbertson –

'Geegee' to their father – had also been invited. 'Geegee' fancied himself as a tennis player, but Uncle Richard was one of those fortunate men who played all ball games practically to international standard; his tennis was wonderful to watch. He had adopted the new American service and could make the ball whizz over the net at phenomenal speed shaped like an egg so that when it bounced on the grass it cut away sharply. There was great speculation about whether 'Geegee' would be able to cope with this service, but on the morning of the party it was overtaken by the greater sensation of a series of heaps of freshly disturbed earth which had appeared overnight in an almost straight line from end to end of the tennis lawn. The heaps were removed by the gardener and the bare patches cunningly replaced with turf so that it was difficult to see where the mole hills had been, and the party turned out a great success for the Steels with 'Geegee' so totally outclassed he was forced to claim a bad fall in rehearsals the previous night at which he had strained his right shoulder. However, the earlier distress afflicting both Mr and Mrs Steel and transmitted to the rest of the household as a sense of impending social humiliation, resulted in their determination to hire a mole catcher to ensure that it could never happen again.

The catcher appeared two days later. He was an oldish man with a wide, deeply-weathered face with grey stubble on his jaw and a deerstalker pulled well down over his ears; his name, he said, was Abe, and the children, who followed his every move as he surveyed the mole's work, soon learned that he earned a penny for each 'little crittur' he caught.

''Tis a bad year usm dowent catch two thou'nd,' he told them.

'Two thousand pennies!' Henrietta breathed in awe.

'A toidy sum, miss – but this ol' patch –' he looked around, 'i'nt worth more'n a thruppenny piece – if usm lucky!'

He opened the drawstring of his sack and showed them one of his traps, a short wooden tube with a wide V notch cut out from the underside and five holes in the topside through which string nooses were arranged. He had George poke his finger in the tube, then suddenly pulled the nooses tight, roaring with laughter at George's cry of surprise.

67

'But Master Mole's a rare clever little crittur,' he said, releasing the finger, 'you 'as to snare 'im in 'is main road,' pronouncing it 'rowéd'. ''Tis of no use a-settin' your traps in 'is side la-ens – you 'as to ketch 'im when 'e's a-drivin' along 'is great north rowéd –' he chuckled at the joke.

William asked what moles ate; worms mostly, Abe told him, and beetles and other little grubs and 'hants and most anythin' 'e come on with 'is little ol' snout – but when 'e come on one o' my snares – 'e dowent eat no more worms then 'e dowent!'

William asked him how the traps worked; Abe told them to follow and he would show them. He had already worked out the approximate run of the main road, and he probed at the edge of a rose bed beyond the tennis lawn until he found it about four inches down; he made an opening just large enough to admit one of his wooden tubes, and after smearing the nooses inside with earth, placed the trap in the hole so that it formed a continuation of the mole's tunnel; he then adjusted the nooses with a trigger which the mole would dislodge with his snout and piled earth all over so that not a chink of light could penetrate below. Finally he stuck a three foot length of whippy ash stick in the ground nearby and pulled its top down to insert in a loop coming up through the earth from the nooses.

Henrietta should have been warned by William's fascination with all the details for she knew his sensitivity to hurting any living creature, but she was so interested herself she didn't realize until Abe had gone and they were back in the house changing to go downstairs for tea that there had been purpose behind all his searching questions.

'We've got to set those traps off,' he said, 'before Moley.'

She looked at him in surprise.

'It's easy,' he went on. 'I know where they are – all of them!'

The more she thought about it, the more appealing the idea became; it would drive her mother mad; it was she who had been more upset by the damage to the lawn. But how could they make it look like an accident?

'I don't care,' William said, 'I'll do it and she can give *me* a whacking.'

'What about Abe?' George asked. 'He'll lose his thrupp-ence.'

'*We'll* give him thruppence,' Henrietta replied promptly, realizing immediately afterwards that she had more or less committed herself. Three pennies proved impossible to find between them, however, they could only scrape together a penny ha'penny. She said she would wheedle the rest out of Papa that evening, which meant they would have to spring the traps that night after they had gone to bed. She shivered as she thought of Lady Ottolene, then had a flash of inspiration. 'Lady Ottolene can do it!'

Andrew jumped up in excitement. 'Then they'll never know it was us!'

George looked at him doubtfully, but Henrietta convinced him that if he and Andrew and Willy did the work, she would wait in her room and when they had finished and were safely back she would start screaming and wake the whole house, and when they came up she would tell them she had seen Lady Ottolene walking in the grounds, and would point out just where.

Even George seemed to think that sounded like a water-tight plan, and they went down to tea in a state of high, nervous excitement.

In the event almost everything miscarried. The sheets which George tied together in best story-book fashion to climb down from the first floor WC window slipped from the pipe around which they had been tied. Andrew and William tried desperately to hold the end as it went, but were forced by his weight to let go, and he fell, fortunately landing in a bush below and not sustaining serious damage. The dogs started barking. Robert Steel, roused, decided to pay a visit to the WC just as Andrew and William were coming out to go upstairs and ask Henrietta what she thought they should do next. They darted back inside and locked the door. Robert Steel, slightly puzzled, continued downstairs to see why the dogs were making a noise, and then Andrew found that he couldn't unlock the door. Eventually he started banging on it from the inside and shouting in panic. The banging must have eased the catch for when Robert Steel arrived back and, talking to him through the door to calm him told him to try again, the heavy key turned and the lock opened. Emerging very shaken, they said they had come downstairs together because they had been frightened by the ghost. He scratched his head, for normally they would simply have gone in the chamber pots beneath their beds, but finding them incoherent, sent them upstairs again.

Worst of all, George, without the sheets from the WC window, could not climb inside again and this meant that Henrietta could not do the screaming act – which she had been looking forward to – because that would mean George's absence from his bed probably being discovered. She and Andrew and Willy discussed it for a long time in urgent whispers when they thought Papa must have returned to his room, but they could see no solution. Whatever they did must lead to discovery; eventually they decided the only thing to do was to leave George to sneak in when the doors were unlocked by the servants, who would not split on him. Henrietta threw two blankets out of the window to land near the knotted sheets and hoped he would have the sense to come back and find them when he had finished springing the traps.

'But he won't know where all the traps are,' Willy said for about the tenth time, far more worried about the mole than about George's fate.

'Yes, he will,' Henrietta replied, annoyed. 'He was there too. We must all go to bed now and pretend nothing's happened.'

The next morning passed normally, although George was hollow-eyed and slower than usual at his desk in the school-room; after lunch they were discussing why it was the sprung traps had not been discovered when the blow fell. They were summoned down to the drawing-room, all except Jack and Harry who were evidently considered too young to have taken part. Henrietta, looking at the boys' tense faces, braced herself and without thinking about it, took Willy's hand; whatever happened, they were all in it together.

Their mother was standing at one of the side windows, gazing out into the garden as they entered; they lined up silently some distance away from her and behind one of the armchairs as if it would offer protection from the wrath to

70

come. But when, after a moment, she turned to face them she looked more weary than angry; there were dark shadows beneath her eyes and uncharacteristic wisps straying from her tightly-caught hair. She stepped towards them with an almost puzzled look until she had nearly reached the chair, then moved across in front of the fireplace – where Papa liked to stand, Henrietta thought, wishing he were here. It would be a joke to him; he would laugh it away.

'I am not going to ask which one of you it was,' she started, then spreading her hands, 'but *why?*' and she looked at Henrietta.

There was a knock on the door which opened to reveal the housemaid.

'Beg pardon, m'um, but Bliss jes' come back with a message from Mr Steel.'

Her mother's face hardened. 'Yes?'

'He says how he can't manage to get back tonight – for the musical soirée, m'um. He says he's awful sorry, he hopes as how you understands –'

Henrietta, gazing into her mother's face, saw her eyes darken with sudden anger, which as quickly faded into something like hopelessness, and her voice was very controlled as she said, 'Thank you, Millie.'

The door closed. Mrs Steel turned, preoccupied as if she had forgotten their presence, and moved slowly back to the window again. Henrietta, studying her expression, saw her, perhaps for the first time not as a parent to dress up for and pretend good manners or manipulate or defy, but as a person with feelings of her own which were unconnected with them; at the same time she saw in her face how deeply unhappy she was, and wondered in a flash of intuition if it was Papa's erratic way of coming and going and treating things as a joke that made her so unhappy.

When her mother turned to them again she had regained her composure. She held up three pennies.

'Mr Frost found these pennies at the three traps that someone sprang last night.' She looked hard at George, whose cheeks showed livid scratches from his encounter with the bush. 'I imagine they belong to one of you – and since you have wasted Mr Frost's time I shall return them to him.'

71

She closed her hand decisively. 'I had hoped, Henrietta – and George – that by bringing in Miss Carstairs and setting regular hours of schooling, I might have expected some improvement in your behaviour. On the contrary –' she paused '– I am forced to send you both away to school. Henrietta – you will be going to St Mary's – and George – I shall be making enquiries whether they have a place at Birchfield House. In Kent,' she added, looking at him deeply and, Henrietta thought, sorrowfully.

There was silence for a while, and she gazed at each of them in turn. Henrietta thought she looked lost, rather as if she recognized them as adversaries but wanted to be friends, and did not know how. Then she dismissed them.

'Boarding school!' George said wonderingly as they climbed the stairs.

Later, Henrietta remembered this as the moment her childhood ended. She didn't feel this at the time, nor was it. If there was any such moment it was, perhaps, when she emptied the contents of her special box on to her bed after Scopey's dismissal. But she continued to move in and out of childhood and the fantasies of childhood for many years, indeed its hopes and terrors remained with her always, often more real in retrospect although never again so vivid.

The next week Miss Carstairs left.

4

For Willy, Lady Ottolene's ghost was real, as real as any member of the family or staff or the dogs or horses; he knew exactly where Henrietta had first seen her because he had questioned her, and she, happy to oblige, had shown him. He never passed that part of the passage between the linen cupboard and the head of the stairs without being aware of Lady Ottolene's presence, always increasing his pace and steering himself away from the place on the wall through which she had gone – half-hoping, but more in fear that she would show herself to him.

He knew what she looked like; Henrietta had described her minutely from her ash-white hair 'sort of blowing even though there was no draught' and her burning eyes down to her pointed button boots which made no sound on the floor as she walked.

'Why did she come back, Henry?'

'Perhaps she never wanted to leave – when she sold us the house. Perhaps she doesn't like us here.'

'She can't *do* anything?'

'She can frighten us.'

'Papa isn't frightened. Is he?'

Henrietta looked at him shrewdly for a moment. 'He *pretends* he isn't,'

At night, Willy would rather have thrown himself from his bedroom window than have walked past the linen cupboard on his own. That, he was convinced, was *her* room. It puzzled him that Mrs Harding could go into the cupboard and take things out and move things with impunity. He warned her the first time he saw her do it; she told him not to be silly;

73

there weren't such things as ghosts. After a while he had realized Mrs Harding could get away with it because she wasn't a member of the family, not in the strict sense of being related to them, although he couldn't imagine the house without her.

Over the following year, Lady Ottolene gradually faded from his consciousness to be replaced, shockingly, by a more personal ghost.

He never forgot the numbing sensation that came over him after Mama told him Jack was dead, nor the look in her eyes as she said it. He didn't see his ghost and never told a soul he was aware of it, but it haunted the empty bed near the door for a long time, and the sensation it caused returned at odd moments in later life. It came most vividly aboard the depot ship in 1918. He was late back from a patrol, tense and strained. He saw the envelope with Isobel's writing, and knew she had had a boy and he would call him Jack. He could rationalize it afterwards; he had wanted a boy perhaps. But at the time it happened he knew, and in the instant of knowing he was aware of Jack's empty bed by the door of the night nursery.

Henrietta knew something was wrong as soon as she entered the house. Perhaps it was the unnatural quiet, or perhaps she sensed emanations as dogs do when someone dies. She ran up the stairs to the nursery with a feeling of unease; no one was there. Dropping her satchel, she went out quickly, through the door to the backstairs and up to the night nurseries. Willy was half-sitting, half-lying on his bed, his shoulders against the wall, his eyes large and misty. Harry was on the floor, absorbed with a toy horse, which he was jumping over a slipper; he didn't turn his head as she came in.

Willy gazed at her, his face working as if he was trying to say something; then it came out suddenly. 'Jack's dead.'

She thought of Jack lying in bed, barely able to speak because of his sore throat, turning and continually shifting position and trying to throw the blankets off as she read to him, his eyes, whenever she looked away from the page,

74

staring up desperately at the ceiling, his forehead damp; the next day her mother and the doctor had left the room with grave faces, not speaking; on the day after that a nurse had come.

'Dead?' she heard herself saying, an empty, sick feeling in her middle as she tried to imagine it.

Willy nodded silently; Harry was looking up, studying her reaction.

Mama had looked so tired when she told them they must all be very quiet in the house. Papa had said they must pray very hard. She had an image of Jack and Willy in the nursery, each talking at top speed, not really listening to what the other was saying, yet very much together; they had played together ever since she had been going to the convent – over two years now; it had been annoying to come back and see them so happily immersed in their game when *she* wanted to be Willy's closest friend. She felt a sting of guilt as she thought of the times she had been so jealous of poor Jack, and had tried to turn Willy against him – impossible to imagine him not there any more –

She found herself sitting on Willy's bed, holding his hand; it was quivering as if he was crying inside, but no sound was coming out. She felt very protective, and at the same time numb, as she had been when Scopey left.

Although she couldn't imagine it then – or allow herself to believe it – Jack's death became real when she went downstairs and saw the expression on her mother's face; it was her look rather than her black dress trimmed with crape that told her, and the look on the maids' faces and the subdued way they talked; then she knew she would not see him again; the numbness turned into a desperate sense of loss.

Later in her bedroom, waiting anxiously for her father to come up on his rounds – although he was not so punctilious now as he had been – with half her mind aware of Nurse across the corridor trying to soothe Willy to sleep, she wondered if Jack could see them all down here from where he was now – whether he was looking at her in bed, whether he could tell how much she hated herself for being beastly to him and how badly she wanted him back with them all.

75

Then she had an odd feeling that perhaps it was all a game God was playing with her; perhaps she was the *only* real person in the world; everyone else, her family, the servants, the girls she met at school, the nuns, everyone was pretending they were people to make things happen to her; perhaps Jack was in the game too; perhaps he had not died because he had never been real just a kind of puppet God had been using to make her believe she had a family. Even Willy – how could she know whether even Willy and Nurse were real; perhaps when he told her about the strange thoughts that came into his head, he was pretending to be her close friend. Perhaps she was quite alone.

She would ask Papa when he came up – but that would be no good because if he was pretending, he would simply go on pretending and there was no way of testing if he was real because she couldn't see inside his head to find out.

He did not come, nor did her mother. Nurse came in later and stayed with her. Jack was in a better world, she said, she should not grieve for him. Nurse appeared real enough, and her hand on her head was cool and comforting, yet the worrying thought would not leave her: was everything happening only to herself? Was everything she looked at like a scene in a theatre designed so that she would think she lived in a real world? But if God invented the game, who invented God? He couldn't suddenly have appeared from nothing; something must have existed before God; something must have created Him, and there must have been something there to create Him from – what put that something there in the first place if not God, but He could not have created Himself from nothing. What was there in the first place –?

She found herself falling into a void and there was nothing she could catch hold of to stop her descent, and nothing below except darkness, and God was down there somewhere, and she would soon see Him if only she could stop this terrifying fall; then she saw Jack; he was in his christening robes, but he looked just as he did when playing with Willy in the nursery except that he was gazing at her with a strange, sad expression. She tried to reach him to comfort him but she was on her stomach in thick, gluey mud which prevented her from moving; she could only call to him and tell him to come to her because she was stuck, but he didn't seem to hear. She called and called; she could near Nurse telling her not to worry –

'It's all right, Henry – *Henry* –'

She felt her hand on her hair.

'My child,' Father Geoffrey said when she had told him, and laying his hand on her arm, 'my dear child.'

She had never confided in him before, although she had often felt she would like to. He came to the convent every Thursday to teach Latin to those girls whose parents had requested it, and who were thought capable of coping with the subject; they were unusual lessons, very different from those taken by the nuns; he made the ancient Romans come alive, their thoughts and feelings as real as if they were actual, living people, and she wanted to learn so that she could read the stories for herself – as well as please him. He had a wide, gentle smile and deep-set brown eyes, but perhaps the most attractive thing about him was his beauti-fully modulated voice; she thought of him as the absolute personification of goodness and wisdom; she also found herself interested in him as a man for he was quite young. It was rumoured that all the money he received from teaching went to the mission he worked with in the East End.

'You remember the story of Isaac. Abraham was prepared to sacrifice his son, Isaac because he was certain it was God's will. We have to submit ourselves to God's will, my child. There are many, many Isaacs sacrificed –' He had a deep look as he gazed at her, 'believe me, I see them every week. I see the suffering of those who ask "Why?" as you ask now. No one on earth can answer these questions, we can only have trust in God – perfect trust in Him that all will be well.' He paused and she felt he was looking right into her heart. 'You will not forget your little brother but – in time – his passing will appear in a different light – I promise you. Even if we cannot explain them, all things appear differently when we see them in the light of God's love – for *us*.' He squeezed her arm with his hand.

She wondered, on her way home, why he had chosen the

story of Isaac because Isaac had been saved. But she was convinced – almost despite his words – that she could have perfect trust in him. She wished she could have the same trust in her father; with him it was the other way round; she had begun to suspect that he made up things to tell her, his flippant manner a device for getting around difficult questions. And when she needed him, he was never there; she hadn't seen him since Jack's death; he had not been home. Mama had spoken to her about Jack the next morning. She had never felt so close to her as then; it had been plain from her eyes and the puffy skin beneath that she had been crying all night, but she had not cried when she told her about Jack passing away in his sleep in the hospital. She had admired her self-control; she had strength; she was *real* in a way Papa was ceasing to be somehow. And compared with Father Geoffrey's deep concern Papa's refusal to take her or anything at all seriously was annoying and silly. He had always made up stories, she realized; she had an image of the lady she had seen him with outside the Egyptian Hall in Piccadilly and the way he had turned to smile at her. She couldn't imagine Father Geoffrey smiling at anyone in quite that way.

'Master George? And Master Andrew?' The new man looked at them in turn. It was strange not to be met by Bliss. George remembered now, his mother had written to tell them he had gone to South Africa to fight the Boers; he had forgotten. It was going to be strange at home without him; he wondered if this new man would let them help in the stables; he appeared a grimmer character altogether with a fierce moustache and a very upright bearing as if he had been a soldier; he wondered why he had not gone out to South Africa.

'You've come in Bliss's place.'

'Coachman,' the man replied as if mention of his predecessor was unwelcome. He had a funny accent. He indicated the way out to the street and started off; George exchanged a glance with Andrew and followed, and behind them came the porter with their trolley, its axles squealing.

George addressed the new man's back. 'Do you live above the stables too?'

He stalked on. 'Aye.'

It was going to be very different. He wondered how long Bliss would be away; old Phipps had told them the war would be over by tea time; he hadn't understood what he had meant by that; there had been a great many tea times and several battles since then.

He turned to Andrew and said in a loud voice, 'You can bet Bliss is teaching the Boers a lesson!'

Andrew caught the spirit of it. 'I wish I was old enough to go out.'

'I wouldn't be here if I was older you can bet. Old Bliss'll have some yarns when he gets back –'

It seemed to make no impression on the new man. Perhaps he couldn't hear with all the noise. Several newsboys were bawling excitedly, their calls merging so that it was difficult to tell what they were saying; people were jostling about them, some trying to get near to buy a paper, others who had just bought one impeding them by standing where they were, reading with rapt faces.

'Terrible reverse –' he made out one of the calls before the rest of the sentence was drowned by a rival, and then between the crowding figures he caught a brief glimpse of a newsboard.

BULLER RETREATS FROM COLENSO
LOSS OF 2000

'Terrible reverse of British troops!' the nearest boy shouted again.

He thought of Bliss. Two thousand was a frightful number. Even as they followed this new man on the way home for poor Jack's funeral Bliss might be lying dead on the veldt. It was an awful thought – as difficult to think of the stables without Bliss as the old nursery without Jack jumping up and down talking fast at the top of his voice, Henrietta scolding him and telling him not to show off –

After the lights of the station the street seemed very dark. A light drizzle had begun to fall and damp cold penetrated inside his shirt. He thought for a moment they had lost the coachman, then saw him standing by Bacchante – he recognized her immediately by the pale blaze on her forehead. Good old Bacchante! He ran up to stroke her nose and talk into her nostrils the way Bliss had shown him. She smelled just the same as she stamped her hoof and twisted her neck in recognition. Good old Bacchante! The dreadfulness of Jack's death hit him suddenly. It had been a shock in old Phipps's study when the news had first been broken to them, but here with Bacchante – thinking of Jack with him by the brazier listening to Bliss, it struck him more deeply.

Henry would have cried, and Willy. He and Jack had been very close. But it would have hurt Henry most; she pretended to be as tough as a boy but she wasn't really; he had had to comfort her often enough after she had stood up fearlessly to their mother, then afterwards just broken down in tears. Henry looked on all of them as her charges; she ordered them around, but she loved them all and he remembered her discussing only last summer at Thorpeness how naughty Jack was turning out and planning what they should do to curb him, or otherwise he would grow up into a very disagreeable young man. She must have taken it very hard. His mind had been filled with Jack up to now, and how strange that he would not be there when they got home, and he would never see him again; now he wondered why he hadn't thought more about Henry; she would need him.

The new man helped the porter with their trunks, then took his place on the driving seat without a word. Bliss would have let them sit up there with him; he would have talked throughout the journey, commenting on the carriages they passed, the way they were driven and kept, proud of his ability instantly to recognize the coaches of the grand families by the retainers' liveries. This time the journey seemed to go on for ever. The drizzle shone in the flare of the street lights as they passed them; people walked fast, looking down under glistening umbrellas; ladies clutched their dresses. A commissionaire in blue with a row of medals on his full chest stood beneath a striped yellow and white canopy over the front doors of a hotel, his arm raised to summon a cab; inside lighted windows two waiters set tables for dinner – white cloths and wine glasses, napkins arranged like bishops' mitres and plush red backs to the chairs; a flower girl beneath a parasol was showing her wares to a tall man in a burberry coat with a pipe sticking from his mouth, bowl downwards, waggling as he talked; he was smiling, so was the flower girl. At the corner a man in a top hat was buying a paper from a newsboy.

BULLER'S TERRIBLE REVERSE
THOUSANDS LOST

Old Phipps would be eating his words when they came back next term.

He thought of that moment in the study, 'Some bad news, I'm afraid – this is a letter from your mother. Yes – your brother – Jack – has been ill – very ill – rheumatic fever. It proved too much for him. You will, of course, be leaving before the end of term – matron has all arrangements in hand. I am sorry. Think of your mother. It helps to think how others must be feeling. I know you will not let her down – good man –'

It had taken some time after they had left the study for the meaning of the interview really to sink in.

'– good man –'

His mother must have heard the horses; she was waiting at the garden door as they came through the colonnaded way from the stable yard. She was dressed all in black but her smile was as wide as it always was when she welcomed them home and her brown eyes were alight with warmth. He felt bewildered.

'You must be cold – brr! What a beastly evening!' After hugging them both – for fractionally longer than usual, he thought – she turned and led them to the drawing-room – the holy of holies where they were allowed only on special occasions. His father was standing warming his back at the flames in the fireplace.

He smiled in his great beard. 'George! Andy!'

Henrietta had jumped up from her seat and was coming towards him – she too was in a black dress trimmed with

81

crepe – and he saw Willy and Harry craning their heads from around the settee, then Henry's arms were about him; he tensed, standing his ground as she kissed him. It was so different from what he had expected. The family – it was almost too much. He felt himself quivering all over and his lip trembling, and bit into it fiercely.

'Mackinnon found you then –' his father boomed.

'Go near the fire,' from his mother, 'you look utterly perished –'

They were asked about the journey.

'There was a queer fellow in the carriage –'

'He asked us if we were imperialists. He said England needed young fellows like us –'

'He said that by the time we grew up, the empire would be on trial – the time of trial is coming sooner than *they* think.'

'For the Anglo-Saxon race –'

'Yes, the Anglo-Saxons. What d'you suppose he meant? He said he wished he was young again –'

'So do I!' his father roared, slapping his full waistcoat. 'He's right, I'm hanged if he ain't right –'

Millie wheeled in a trolley of muffins and cakes, and he and Andrew were put to toasting the muffins; it was a show of normality and talk for their benefit, he realized, and played his part, experiencing a sense of kinship such as he had never guessed at before. Jack, who was not there, had brought them all together.

Afterwards in bed he wanted his father to say something about Jack, he didn't know what, but he felt after he had said his prayers that he needed to talk about him. His father reiterated Phipps's advice that they must all think of Mama tomorrow. Jack would want that, then quickly changed the subject.

'There are too many mothers grievin' their sons tonight, George – it's a bad business.'

'Why have so many been killed?' he asked. 'Old Phipps told us it would take no time to teach Kruger a lesson.'

'Ah!' His father pulled at his beard. 'It's come as a sad surprise to more than Mr Phipps, George. I have to confess – I don't know the answer. But it's on the tapis Bobs is goin'

82

out to take charge. He'll settle the business, I can promise you –'

'I wish I was older. I'd go out – so would Andy – so would all the fellows at school –'

'I dare say,' his father's blue eyes seemed to look beyond him, and he repeated abstractedly, 'I dare say they would, George.' He moved as if to leave the room but then leaned closer, 'Keep this to yourself, old man – I don't wish your poor Mama to know until after – y' know what I'm drivin' at –' with a significant look, 'until *afterwards*. I'm goin' out myself –' He held his hand up. 'Not a whisper now – strictly *entre nous*!'

George raised himself on one elbow, staring. 'Have they sent you a commission?'

'No, no – not the naval service, George. But they need fellows who can shoot a bit and ride a bit – by Jove, that's what Bobs'll need – play Johnny Boer at his own game –' He held a finger to his lips and whispered, 'Night, George – old man!'

The next morning they learned that Bliss was missing. Mrs Harding had been to the War Office notice board – she had, she said a favourite nephew who had gone out to South Africa – and had come back with the news about Bliss.

'I wonder what it will be next,' she said dramatically to Henrietta. 'Bad luck always comes in threes.'

When Henrietta told George, he thought of his father, and hoped the war would be over before he got out there. The Boers always aimed at the officers.

As if to compensate for Jack's death, another child was added to the family the next spring. Henrietta couldn't believe it when Mrs Harding told her it was a girl; she had never felt so happy. She was christened Caroline, but came to be known, after young Harry's name for her – 'Baba' – as 'Babs'. Returning from school every day, Henrietta went straight into Nurse's room to help with the infant, and at the weekends enjoyed nothing better than to push her pram up to the Heath, proud of the smiles and greetings elicited by her young sister, thinking of the day she would be able to walk and hold her hand, and they would go on picnics together, and she would design dresses for her and show her how to feed the ducks on Whitestone Pond.

She was often accompanied on these walks by her great friend from St Mary's, Mary Edgehill. Mary was the daughter of a judge who lived in Admiral's Walk, close to Felpham House. She and Henrietta had met and played sometimes as children, but it was not until they found each other in the same form at the convent that they came to know each other well. Mary was no beauty; she had a plump face with nondescript, brownish hair that hung straight without being smooth or shiny, and a short, dumpy figure; her only striking features were her eyes, which were greyish, seeming to change shade with the day or colour of clothes she wore, and fringed with lashes so thick and close as to appear dark. They were steady eyes which gave an impression of absolute sincerity, but they could set with granite determination. She admired Henrietta for her quicksilver originality and vivid looks; she would sit for ages combing and brushing Henrietta's hair until it gleamed like burnished gold.

Henrietta admired her for her independent mind, loyalty and strength of will, regarded by the sisters as mulish obstinacy, and an apparent disdain of what others might think of her – although this was an act adopted since she was convinced she was irredeemably plain.

That autumn, when Willy joined George and Andrew at Birchfield House School, leaving only the three-year-old Harry and her infant sister at home, she and Mary became inseparable in school and afterwards at one or other of their homes.

In Mary's home, Henrietta was regarded as an expert on the war; this was after it became known that her father had gone out to South Africa as a volunteer. Sometimes a maid would come up to the nursery with a question starting, 'The Judge wishes to know, Miss Henrietta –' More often she was summoned downstairs and cross examined by the Judge in person, a large man with grey eyes and round cheeks like Mary's – except that his cheeks were veined and red – and an extraordinarily high forehead suggesting enormous intellect.

Henrietta was at a disadvantage in these interviews because her father had been invalided out of the Imperial Yeomanry before seeing a Boer, and had been convalescing at the Cape ever since. His infrequent letters home were filled with social gossip – for the war had become the thing for everyone to do – and to preserve her status as an authority and his as a hero, Henrietta was forced to invent.

'What about Buller – I hear he's been sacked? What's your father think?'

'He's quite pleased, sir.'

'Pleased is he –!'

'Yes, he said in his last letter, Buller wasn't up to it.'

'The deuce he did!'

'He told us we must never tell anyone – however much we trusted them,' she added hastily, 'in case de Wet's spies managed to find out.'

'Not up to it! I had heard it was political. The Bull's not up to it then! I'll be hanged! It explains some aspects of his campaign I found puzzling. But he's pleased with Bobs?'

'Oh, yes! He thinks Lord Roberts the greatest general since Hannibal –'

'Hannibal!'

'Give Bobs a few elephants,' she extemporized recklessly, 'and he'd beat de Wet in two weeks, that's what he wrote –'

'African or Indian, I wonder?'

'Indian, I think –'

'Of course! They'd have to be Indian! That's all most interesting, thank you, Henrietta, thank you very much.' He seemed in much better humour when she left; he usually was.

She did not tell Mary about her father's real status; it was about the only thing she didn't tell her. But she worried afterwards about what she had said and whether the Judge would find out the truth when the war was over and her father came home, and one Thursday after school confessed to Father Geoffrey, asking him if she ought to own up.

He smiled. 'I don't think that is necessary, my child. As long as you confess to God – and try to become more truthful in the future – I see no reason why the Judge should know as well!'

'But he might find out –'

'That may be the time to confess then! I think it unlikely. After all, your father will not wish to speak too much about his part if he is spending his time as you say he is.'

A perceptive remark, she realized, thinking of her father; she was more than ever convinced of Father Geoffrey's wisdom, but at the same time a little disappointed he had taken her confession so lightly.

'Why do there have to be wars?' she asked. 'Papa said he met Rudyard Kipling at Cecil Rhodes's house –' she tried to think of the name.

'*Groote Schuur*,' he prompted.

'That's it! Kipling told everyone how the war was a good thing because it showed how unprepared we were, and it gave us a chance to put it right for the big war that's coming. Why do we have to have a big war?'

The half smile on his mouth had gone, and he looked very serious. 'I hope he is wrong, my child.'

'He thinks we are too proud and –' she hunted for the word he had used, but could only remember the sense '– too fond of a soft life, and if we really care for our civilization we must learn to work and to fight for it.'

'I think, perhaps, he is right about our pride and our love of luxury. But our civilization –' he gazed up past her head, pressing his fingers together '– there is much that needs to be done here in England – before we can be truly proud.'

'We are better than other people, though.'

'There is One who is better and greater than all of us, my child. We are in danger of forgetting that when we set ourselves up as judges of civilization. We must trust in Him – not in ourselves. He came to bring light into our darkness. We must allow Him to light the way for us.'

She felt he wanted to say more, but he didn't and she remained puzzled. Once again he had not really answered her question.

5

Willy had realized from the first day that he would be standing in George's shadow.

'We expect great things from you,' Phipps had said. 'If you do half as well as your brothers, I shall be very satisfied. Do you play cricket?'

Without giving him time to answer, he had gone on to detail George's exploits in the cricket and football XIs, both of which he now captained. He said nothing of Andrew's scholastic prowess although he picked up several prizes each year.

'What are your hobbies?'

Willy tried to think.

'Butterflies?'

'Yes, sir, I like –'

'Mr Hapgood takes butterflies and moths. You will need to think of something for the winter though. Many of the boys collect stamps. Do you collect stamps? I understand your father is in South Africa with the volunteers – you must be proud of him – you should ask him to send you letters from different states. You'll have to be quick about it or you'll miss the military franking. You could build up a British empire collection. Several boys are doing that. Your collection will grow with the empire –'

George had told him it was best to keep in with old Phipps since he ruled the place like a tyrant; also he was very generous at handing out sporting gear for good performance on the field; George had collected two cricket bats, besides several balls and pads and gloves. Willy knew he wouldn't match up to George's excellence; he had tried to earn his

87

approval in family games for as long as he could remember, but George was out on his own when it came to games; he was going to be another Uncle Richard. His compact figure seemed to be made of indiarubber; he could leap and catch balls at extraordinary heights and distances and had a marvellous eye which served him as well at archery as for shooting or cricket. Willy knew he could never match up to George, nor for that matter was he anything like as clever as Andy. He had left Mr Phipps's presence that first day with the awful certainty that he was going to be a disappointment.

The feeling turned to desperation on the second evening after lights out. Lying in bed listening to the older boys in the next dormitory who had just come back and were unpacking, and the interjections of Matron and a master whose voice he didn't recognize, he was overwhelmed with despair and longing for his bed in the attic at Felpham House, and Nurse tucking the sheets in and staying to read a story. And he thought of Henrietta; Henry would understand. He could tell her things he could never tell his brothers. As he thought of walking with her along the beach at Thorpeness in the sun only a week before he felt tears choking him and turned his face hard into the pillow to smother the sobs he could not control.

He had recovered from homesickness after about a week, but the feeling that he couldn't live up to the reputation of his brothers, particularly George, grew stronger as he found out what a school hero George was; even the senior boys talked decently to him after they found out his name, and the masters who took the new boys for football in those first weeks always made him captain of one of the sides, and made him play at centre forward. He tried his hardest, knowing all the time that impossible expectations were being placed in him. After a few weeks they realized he was not like George, but he never lost the feeling he should be.

It was worse when George left after his first year to go to a crammer's for naval exams for his legend actually increased with absence. Old Phipps, who was the last to realize that Willy lacked his older brother's brilliant talents, said encouraging things whenever he saw him as if taking it for granted he would step right into George's shoes. When at last, half way through his second summer term, Phipps watched a game of cricket in which he was playing and saw him miss three balls in a row, then fall to the fourth, clean bowled – and afterwards in the outfield shouted at to change position at the end of the over – the change in attitude was immediate; there were no more encouraging talks, no questions about his family, indeed their eyes seldom met. It was as he had known from the beginning; he had let him down.

They had to shout at him in the outfield because he was studying a clouded yellow; it had alighted on a buttercup some yards away and he was closing in cautiously, making sure his shadow didn't fall across it because he had never seen one before and wanted to identify it. He was only about three feet away with bent knees, leaning towards it breathlessly when the shouting started; he jerked involuntarily and the butterfly rose and fluttered away – not before he had made out the greenish yellow underwing and the central white spot, which he described to 'Happy' Hapgood that evening. Happy invited him into his room and pulled out his tray of specimens to show him two clouded yellows, a male and a female; they had agreed that his had been male.

He had never been to Happy's room before, and he thought afterwards he would avoid it if he possibly could in future; for one thing he hated seeing butterflies and moths pinned in cases; they looked duller than the ones he saw flying, and unnatural; when butterflies settled they usually closed their wings or fluttered them half open, half shut. They did not look real stretched out in motionless rows. For another thing Happy would come so close; he had made him sit in a chair while he fetched the tray, which he placed on his lap, then half-kneeling by him, he pointed out the different species while resting one hand on his knee. His jacket smelled strongly of the tobacco he smoked; there were hairs on the back of his hand, and his manner was odd. Without knowing why, Willy had felt alarmed. He had even thought at one time he wouldn't be allowed to leave, but directly Happy lifted the tray from his lap, he stood and moved quickly to the door, and saying 'Thank you sir!' made a hasty exit.

After that, he decided to do stamp-collecting on hobby

89

afternoons in the summer as well, but was not allowed to change.

'Is that all you've caught, Steel?' Happy asked him one wet day towards the end of term when they were inside in 1A formroom setting their specimens.

'Yes, sir, I'm afraid so, sir.' He didn't tell him that he hadn't actually caught any, and the few miserable specimens on his board with torn wings or other imperfections were all discards from other boys; he couldn't bear the thought of popping the beautiful creatures in the killing jar or, the recommended method, squeezing the thorax.

'Not much for the best part of a term's work?'

'No, sir, not really, sir.'

Happy studied him for a moment. 'Come along to my room after *Cena*, I could show you some I've just pinned out. You might like one or two –'

'No, sir, thank you, sir – I have some,' he said desperately.

'I understood you to say these were all you had caught.'

'Yes, sir – but you see – I don't like –' He stopped.

'Yes, boy?'

'I can't, sir – I can't – I don't *like* – killing them, sir.' Now it was out, his humiliating secret, the thing that separated him from his brothers and the world of boys and men, made him fit only for the company of girls. And of all people, he had had to tell Happy.

Extraordinarily, Happy didn't seem annoyed. 'You don't like killing them?' He was gazing at him with a funny sort of expression.

He wished he wouldn't talk so loud; the others were listening.

'No, sir,' he said in a low tone. 'I like seeing them when they're alive, sir.'

Happy laid a hand on his shoulder. 'If that's how you feel –' He smiled sympathetically, nodding his head, then turned to go to the next boy.

After that, he detected a change in Happy's attitude towards him; he was treated as a person rather than one of a number of small boys, and on the last outing of term Happy walked with him and told him about his own life, particularly his time as an undergraduate at Oxford, which he had

90

enjoyed more than anything else. He said that he ought to aim at going to Oxford himself; he was just cut out for it. And afterwards he kept him back when the others were going and told him to come to his room for a moment.

There seemed no way out of it this time; he went with great trepidation although Happy had been talking so decently to him, and waited just inside the doorway as Happy stepped briskly to his desk, opened a drawer and took out a large book with a rich, greeny-blue cover and red edges to the pages. Turning, he held it out towards him.

The title, *British and European Butterflies and Moths*, gleamed in gold in a fashionably skewwhiff sort of script, the letters lined with black on one edge so that they seemed to stand out away from the cover. Below the title was a butterfly embossed all in glinting gold perched on a spray of golden oats, small flowers with blueish petals and brilliant golden eyes behind. Stepping forward and taking it as Happy seemed to want him to, he thought it the most splendid-looking book he had ever held. It smelled good too; it was obviously spanking new. He wondered what he was supposed to do with it.

Happy was watching with an amused expression. 'It's for you, Steel! Have a good hol! Now – cut along!'

He raced up to his bed in the dorm and opened the book on it, kneeling down on the floor to run his hands over the shiny paper. It was by two people called A.W.Kappel, FLS, FES – assistant librarian of the Linnean Society – and W.Egmont Kirby, LSA. He wondered what the letters meant. There were thirty coloured plates, he saw, by two unpromising sounding people, H. Deuchert and S. Slocombe. Leafing idly through the introductory pages until he came to the first plate, he stopped, staring in wonder: he had never seen such illustrations. The brilliant sheen of the scales, the soft texture of the underside of the rear wings, and in later ones as he turned the plates the furry feel of the bodies of the moths and larvae were more lifelike even than the real thing. He expected to feel them as he ran his finger over them, and as he did so it occurred to him that there was nothing he would like to do more when he grew up than paint butterflies and birds and animals of all sorts. He would never do anything half as good as these, but it would be a decent sort of way to spend one's time. He must tell Andy, and show him the book.

Closing it, he lifted it from the bed and sped out and down the stairs, jumping the treads two or three at a time, then scooted towards the seniors' day room, slowing to a walk as he approached in case there were any masters about.

Andy was coming towards him down the corridor.

'I say, Andy!' He held the book up. '*Look!* Look what Happy gave me!'

Andy stopped, an extraordinary expression coming over his face, and he stared at him a full five seconds before repeating, '*Happy!*'

He nodded silently. Something was wrong.

'Have you been along to his room?'

He nodded again. That was fairly obvious.

Andy looked quickly back down the corridor before hissing, 'You've *been* to his room!'

'Only once –' He shifted the book under his arm; it was rather heavy. 'One and a half times.'

'Did he try anything?'

Willy stared at him, puzzled. 'He showed me his clouded yellows. Why? *Why,* Andy?' He had been right about that uneasy feeling he had had. 'What happens? Have you been along?'

'*No.* I jolly well haven't! Nor would you if you had any savvy.'

'Why? *Why?*'

'He's a wrong 'un.' Andy sounded exasperated. 'He likes touching fellows,' and as he still looked uncomprehending, 'Doesn't he read you stories at night in the dorm? He sits on our beds. Hasn't he read in your dorm?'

Willy shook his head, still baffled. 'Matron reads to us.'

'Well – when he does – if he sits on *your* bed – keep your blankets tight round you.'

Willy began to half understand.

'Of course, some of the fellows let him.' Andy gestured towards the book. 'I'd watch out if I were you, old man.'

Shaken, Willy turned back towards the stairs and went

slowly up again, wondering where he could hide the thing until the trunks were brought out.

There was no one in the dormitory when he arrived, and he decided to have one more look at the magical colour plates before he put the book under the mattress. Opening it on the bed, the flyleaf fell back, and he saw there was a neat ink inscription.

'To my most original butterfly catcher,
Ernest Hapgood – July '02'

Looking at it, he felt terribly sad for Happy; it seemed so sad he had no one else to give such a splendid present to.

His mother was standing in front of the fireplace with a letter in her hand when he entered. He wondered what it could be about. It didn't look like one from the Pater – as old Phipps insisted they call their fathers. And why should anyone write a letter that concerned him? He approached cautiously.

His mother smiled. 'It's all right, Willy. You haven't done anything wrong – at least not that I've heard of!' She paused. 'Do you like your school?'

The question caught him by surprise. It was not something he had ever thought about. He hated going back at the beginning of term, but once he was there – it was the place where people went; he had no particular opinions about it. Some of it he liked very much; he loved singing lessons, and the drawing lesson once a week, and it was great fun in the summer to roam the beautiful grounds by himself and lie in the long grass in the sun and wait to see what insects or sometimes little animals came unsuspectingly by; once a mouse with large ears had peered out at him for what must have been several seconds before it suddenly darted back into the undergrowth.

'Yes,' he said.

His mother gave him a searching look. 'I've had a letter from your headmaster,' she waved the letter. 'He is –' she seemed to search for a word '– a little worried – about you.'

He frowned, trying to think why old Phipps should worry about him; it must be his cricket.

'It was just bad luck he was watching that time. I had some decent innings afterwards – nothing as good as George's –'

'This is not about cricket, Willy. It's about *you*.'

'Me?'

'He says,' she looked at the letter, scanning quickly down the lines, 'it would not be fair to compare you with your brothers because of course all boys are different, but – here we are – "I find William too dreamy for his own good. We have tried all we can here to instil in him the spirit of manly endeavour and ambition, but I regret to have to tell you he has resisted our most determined efforts. Not to mince words, he is indolent in the formroom and on the playing field. It would be wrong of me not to draw this to your attention since it can only be to his advantage –"' she turned the page '"– if he is brought up sharply while still at a young enough age to benefit. He is obviously capable and it is evident from the example of his brothers that he comes of first class stock. Do not think me presuming if I earnestly recommend that he follows his brother, George, into the Royal Navy. The *Britannia* training, I feel sure, would administer just the electric shock that is called for in his case."' She looked up. 'Well –?'

He wondered if George knew he was going to be given electric shocks.

'I must say,' she went on, 'I am inclined to agree with Mr Phipps. And there will, of course, be no difficulty in obtaining a nomination for you.'

'I'd rather go to Oxford,' he said, then wondered suddenly whether that might not be almost as dangerous; he might end up wanting to touch fellows.

'*Oxford!*'

'Cambridge,' he corrected quickly.

'Whatever gives you that idea?'

'I'd rather go to Cambridge than the *Britannia*,' he struggled. 'There's no end of boating at Varsity,' he added, thinking of what Happy had told him.

'Boating!' She gazed at him steadily. 'It seems to me that Mr Phipps is right.' There was a hard look in her eyes now.

He told Henrietta about it as soon as he left the drawing-room. 'They're going to send me into the Navy – like George.'

Henrietta looked at him, remembering what Papa had written about Kipling saying there was a big war coming, and she had an image of Willy and George in one of the battleships they had seen at the Spithead review sailing out in a great concourse to fight the French. 'You'll be able to wear a uniform like Grandpapa's.'

'I'd much sooner go to varsity.'

'Like Andy?'

'Is Andy going?'

'Mama says he's going into the church. You have to go to varsity to go into the church.'

'I wouldn't like to go into the church,' he said, thinking of the old Rector talking to even older ladies after Sunday services. What he really wanted was to look after animals and study them and paint them, and perhaps write books about them like the book Happy had given him.

'Come on,' he said, 'let's see how Limey's getting on,' and started out.

'Limey?'

'You know,' he called back. 'I showed him to you – my lime hawk moth caterpillar.' He pushed through the door to the attic stairs and ran up. Limey probably needed fresh leaves.

George was woken by the banging of steam in the heating pipes for the salt water bath. The clewlines of the nearby hammocks stretched across his vision, taut in the early light. The air smelled stale. Unconsciously he braced himself for the day ahead.

'. . . Never forget – you wear the uniform of the finest service in the world. You have set your feet to the path. If at first you find the going steep – and hard – I know you would not wish it otherwise –'

He would never forget his first sight of the *Britannia* and the *Hindustan* moored just ahead and connected to her by a covered bridge. The September sun played on their chequered hulls; black and white reflections danced among the white gigs and moored cutters and blue sailing dinghies between them and the shore, yet despite the brightness of the scene and the setting of river and gentle green and wooded banks beyond, he had been seized by apprehension. What alarming customs, what trials of fortitude and hard, bare decks were concealed behind those great painted walls? Both hulks had been stripped of masts, except for one forward in the *Britannia*, rather shorter than seemed necessary for the bulk of her; instead each had her upper deck covered with a long, sloping roof like the roof of a bungalow.

Approaching in the pinnace, the sides towered above, apparently lifeless save for a floating white ensign at the stern and an officer watching from the top of the gangway. The smell wafted to him even before they came alongside; it was perhaps his strongest impression as he reached the top of the gangway and stepped in through the entry port cut in the sloping side timbers, a smell of wooden decks and paintwork and close, lived-in odours which seemed to stretch back through generations of cadets. He did not belong with them; would he ever? The deck spread wide and low from white-panelled bulkheads aft up to the timbers of the bow. All was immaculate, all strange.

They were mustered in silent, nervous lines by a petty officer with the girth of a bull and a voice to match, and presently the Captain appeared, the sound of his heels sharp on the deck planking as he stepped towards them, a row of medal ribbons at the chest of his uniform jacket, the four rings of gold on his sleeve very bright, his face clean-shaven and sunbrowned with fine wrinkles fanning from his eyes.

'Welcome aboard!' He had a pleasant, friendly voice. 'I need hardly remind you, I think, your school days are over!' He allowed the idea to sink in for a moment. '*Britannia* is a naval establishment. You are all now members of the Royal Navy – its future officers. As such you are bound by naval discipline. If there are times you feel it unnecessarily strict – or your officers unduly harsh – remember, the time will come when you in your turn will be responsible for the well-being and discipline of men under you. To command it is first necessary to learn to obey. You are expected to obey every order you receive here promptly – intelligently – rapidly –

without hesitation – or argument.' He smiled suddenly. 'That, after all, is what you will expect when it is your turn! Never forget – you wear the uniform of the finest service in the world. You have set your feet to the path. If at first you find the going steep – and hard – I know you would not wish it otherwise –'

His neck was aching from the unnatural position into which he had been forced by the sag of the hammock; he turned, gazing up at the deckhead beam, layer upon layer of paint smoothing and rounding its pitted surface. Snores were coming from his next-door neighbour, Selby.

'Watch out for the second term!' Selby had warned him on the day after their arrival. Selby had just been beaten by one of them for answering the seemingly innocuous question, 'Eight minus five?' Too late he had learned that second termers were known as 'Threes' – they had served three months aboard – and such was their superiority over the recently arrived 'News' that mere mention of the word Three constituted disrespect. They found out afterwards that Threes in their turn were not allowed to breathe the soubriquets of the two terms above them, 'Sixers' and 'Niners'; nor of course were the lowly News.

The rules of the cadets' unwritten code were far more bewildering than the law administered by authority, for they had to be picked up by experience – if one were fortunate the experience of others – and many and devious were the traps laid for the innocent and unwary.

He had weathered the first week; he had not expected to enjoy it, but often had: the daily race up the rigging of the single mast, hanging out upside down like a fly from the futtocks as he went over the tops, dodging the clumsy attempts of the Sixers or Niners within to bang his knuckles with rope ends as he came over had seemed daunting in prospect, but in practice enormous fun – better than tree climbing. And there was landing for games; he had chosen to play association football for his first term, reasoning that it would be better to do something in which he knew he could shine than to start Rugby or hockey or one of the many other options. He was on trial for the firsts that afternoon; his nerves tingled with anticipation. Archer-Smith, who seemed to arrange all the games, had been good to him; a Sixer, he never tried to make him feel small as some of the others did, but seemed genuinely to like him and respect his ability on the field. He had invited him to a table with other senior terms in the 'stodge shop' and talked very decently to him.

Other News had not approved of this fraternization; in particular a large Irish boy named Fitzdunnon with a broad face, thick belligerent mouth and a voice that had evidently broken long before had accused him of toadying. He was a wild brute who in the first few days had thought he could do just as he pleased. He had been brought up sharply for showing disrespect to a Niner while fagging for him; summoned to a 'Sanc' in the woods ashore – one of the secret dens where the Niners gathered to dispense fearful justice, so it was rumoured, or make sport at some unfortunate junior's expense – Fitzdunnon had been made to dance an Irish jig which, according to his description, had his tormentors rolling on their backs with laughter. The incident had made him something of a hero among the News.

If Fitzdunnon thought he could stop him talking with whomever he pleased, he was mistaken. The hulking fellow had little brain, or made little use of what he had; moreover he was too clumsy to be good at games; even climbing into his hammock without falling out the other side had proved more difficult for him than for most. He would prove easy enough to deal with. Selby did not care for him, nor did Leadwith or the smaller boys Fitzdunnon tended to push around.

He heard movements on the ladder and tensed, waiting for the call; footsteps sounded on the deck, then the bugle from above, and the boatswains' mates were striding between the hammocks.

'Tumble aht! Tumble aht!'

'Where ARE you – the sun's scorchin' your eyes aht!'

'Rahz aht! Rahz aht! Show a leg!'

Wriggling free of his blankets, he gripped the hammock stretcher by his head and described a neat circle to the deck by his sea chest while most of the others were still struggling from sleep. He darted for the 'heads', then to the long salt-water bath; he loved the early plunge, at least the tingle and freshness generated when he was out, and discarding his pyjamas quickly, plunged in. The water, barely warmed, enclosed him; he flailed and yelled. The day had begun.

Henrietta watched her mother reading George's letter; there was not a lot of it, just one side and the reverse, but she took a long time, going over it twice slowly as if trying to read between the lines before she passed it on.

Papa took it and read it through quickly, chuckling as he handed it back to her. 'Brings it all back, by Jove! Stoke Fleming – brings it all back –'

Her mother looked at him coolly as she slid the letter across the table to Henrietta.

Dearest Mama,

This is a ripping place. Our term lieutenant is called Hepplewaite-Adams, we call him H-A and he's an awfully good sport. He plays soccer and rugger and was picked for the United Services last year. I've been picked for the soccer XI and he was awfully decent and said he was all for fellows who put their backs into it and he was sure he and I would get along swimmingly what he could not bear was dodgers. There are one or two in our term and he says if they go on as they are they won't be here next term. I like him very much. We also have a chiefy for our term. He shouts at us fearfully but I haven't been punished yet. So long as you do things quickly he is all right. Everything here is done at the double, you should hear us going up the ladders they shake as if it's an earthquake. In class we do no end of maths and we also do seamanship which is easy for me after the old *Peacock*. We also have knots and splices which is the same and semaphore and engineering and naval history and French. We rib the French master no end.

We are now going to walk to a place called Stoke Fleming where the fellows say you get A 1 cream teas with real Devonshire cream and buns. We get buns every afternoon at the stodge shop by the playing field and you can buy cream and jam for them for 1d.

Your loving,

George

Henrietta handed the letter back. She could picture it so well, George chumming up with this Hepplewaite-someone and taking care not to be caught by the one who shouted. She thought of Willy; he would not take to it in the same way when he went; he would probably be one of the dodgers – not really a dodger but he was so absent-minded when he was interested in something he was sure to be caught by the man who shouted.

'Well –?' Her mother was evidently expecting a comment.

'He's still a greedy pig,' she said.

Her father guffawed. He had been less restrained in Mama's presence since his return from South Africa – a war hero – although he never talked about what he had done out there.

'I'm very glad he is enjoying his food,' her mother said rather primly, and looking at Papa, 'From what you led us to believe, he'd be eating nothing but ship's biscuit and weevils.'

Henrietta squealed.

'So it was in my day,' he said, looking at her, then turned to her mother. 'They treat 'em soft now – I don't say it's a bad thing. If there's one thing I remember from my time as a snotty – it's hunger.' He placed a forkful of liver in his mouth and chewed. 'Oh – that hunger –!'

Her mother looked across at Henrietta with raised brows; she half-smiled back, surprised at what she took to be a sense of humour. But she had been acting strangely lately, not exactly making friends, but *including* her more; she now took luncheon in the dining-room with her parents and any guests they might have, saying nothing of course unless she was addressed, and assisted on 'at home' days, handing round tea and cakes and obeying other whispered instructions aimed at making the visitors more comfortable. After the first excitement of taking part in the hitherto barred world of grown-up society, she had become very bored; the things

100

they talked about were horribly predictable; she had come to the conclusion they were all just out to make a show to each other, the events they had been to and the names they had met. They never really talked as if they were much interested – unless someone had done something really bad; they pretended interest, then came out with something completely different designed to show off who *they* knew or what they had just heard at so-and-so's. Another very tedious topic was where you could buy things most cheaply; it was amazing how people dressed extravagantly in the most expensive costumes and hats with jewellery hanging all over them could spend so long under-bidding one another.

'I don't think I really want to come out,' she said to Mary Edgehill while they were walking the four-year-old Babs up to Whitestone Pond one grey afternoon after a luncheon party.

'*Henry!*' Mary glanced sideways with her appraising expression.

'I don't think I could bear it. Mama spends all morning dressing up and all lunch just being polite, and then she says "Thank *goodness*! That went off all right!" ' She took off her mother's voice so well, Mary started laughing. ' "I was *so* afraid Colonel Beauchamp would retreat into his shell at being *surrounded* by ALL THOSE LADIES!"'

Mary shrieked with laughter.

Henrietta fell silent, depressed by the memory of the Colonel's everlasting stories about horses.

'You'll have to come out,' Mary said. 'Or else what are you going to do?'

'I could go to India. Geraldine says her parents can't afford to bring her out – and all her sisters – so she's being sent out to India. There are any number of officers in India – in the hill stations –' she wondered why they had stations up hills.

'India's an awfully long way, isn't it?' Mary was looking solemn. 'Just so that you don't have to come out.'

'I could go to the East End. I could help Father Geoffrey.'

Babs, neglected, decided to make her presence felt by running across to the other side of the road. A dray pulled up sharply for her as Henrietta ran out and picked her up, scolding. She had become a wilful creature, always needing to be the centre of attention. She carried her back to their side and putting her down, gave her a slap on the hand. It wasn't hard, but she started crying, then turned and ran away back down the hill. Mary went after her this time, and led her back, talking soothingly.

This was how the boys treated her when they were at home, giving in to her every whim; as for young Harry, Babs could make him do anything she wanted; she was becoming thoroughly spoiled.

'We don't *have* to go to the pond,' she said to her crossly as they came up. 'We're doing it for you. *We* don't want to walk up there – do we Mary?'

Mary shook her head.

Babs looked from one to the other, her dark eyes seeming to gauge how much credence to put in the statement. Then she reached up, put her hand in Henrietta's and started skipping along the way they had been going. 'This way, Henry – come on!'

She would speak to Nurse about her; if she was not curbed soon, she would grow up into a really horrid girl.

'I'd like us both to come out together,' Mary said.

She looked round; she had never thought of coming out *with* anyone. It would be fun with Mary.

'All the men would be sure to come just to meet you,' Mary went on. 'I'd dance with the ones you didn't want!'

'Don't be silly!' She felt pleased by the compliment, nevertheless, and it was true, men were already smiling and paying her compliments. It would be a pity to miss all the parties. 'I could come out with you, then go to the East End afterwards.'

'Where is the East End?'

'I'm not sure. It can't be very far if Father Geoffrey works there.'

'We could both go. When we're really out!' She giggled and Henrietta joined in.

It was not until some three weeks after this conversation that Henrietta found a chance to catch Father Geoffrey's eye after the Latin class. She asked him if he needed any help with his work in the East End.

He seemed surprised, then he smiled. 'The Lord needs all the hands he can muster, my child. But first you must finish your education. Then – if you still want to –' he left the sentence unfinished, but the look in his eyes suggested she probably wouldn't.

'Oh, yes – I know I will. So will Mary. After we've come out.'

He laughed, the first time she had seen him really laughing, then laid his hand on her hair. 'Bless you, child!'

Helping in the East End entered her private world rather as Alastair had years before, a pleasing image to hold and shape as she would and to plan for alone with Mary, and escape to while present at grown-up conversations, able to think to herself that she would not be doing this when she was grown up.

6

George could not shake the thought of the fight from his mind; it had been with him for two days, catching him unexpectedly with foreboding at odd times; now there was less than a day to go.

Scampering back down the line in the Roger de Coverley, he felt a breathlessness that was not due to his exertions, and a heightened sense of awareness of the other cadets; he knew what they were thinking when they looked at him, and he tried not to catch their eyes. Most were for him, he thought. Fitzdunnon and the few would-be-bruisers who followed him were generally feared, or at least treated with reserve as unpredictable and dangerous to cross. He felt the familiar flush of apprehension. 'Fitz' was at least two inches taller than he was and built like an ox. Everyone had watched him put Watkins down inside twenty seconds with just three flailing blows, the last of which had knocked the smaller fellow sideways practically off his feet and left him with a dislocated jaw –

Shouts of laughter and barracking came from the head of the line: 'Johnny' Walker and 'Hedgepig' Smith had circled the wrong way; in trying to move quickly back in the other direction to right the mistake, Hedgepig overbalanced, practically bringing Johnny down on top of him before they recovered and, without completing the movement, loped off down the line shamefaced. George joined in the renewed shrill hoots and calls, almost forgetting for a moment – yet it was still there at the back of his mind.

The servants' band came to the end of the dance; in the silence that followed he heard Hedgepig panting at the end of his line. Then the drum rolled and he stiffened for 'The King'. Immediately after the last notes faded came the blare of the bugle; he rushed at the head of the scramble for the gangway, pounding up the shaking treads to the poop to assemble red faced and breathing heavily for prayers. He looked down and closed his eyes at the call to pray, but the chaplain's words passed over him as he willed his fervent request to a God he had called on often in his first weeks in *Britannia* but somewhat neglected since. He asked chiefly that he might not disgrace himself; imagining as he had so often those flailing, bent-arm blows that had felled Watkins, he asked for the strength to withstand them that he might get in a few blows of his own to mark Fitz and draw blood; lifted by that image, he dared to ask for a miracle – if he closed both Fitz's eyes –

'Please God, grant that I may find his eyes – grant that I blind him quickly, God –'

It was his only chance, to get inside those round swipes with a straight arm to the brute's eyes; he had started boxing lessons in the gym ashore, and knew he could throw a useful straight left. The trouble was that scientific boxing went to the winds in these bare-fist contests; the five he had seen had been desperate, headlong mauls from the first second with no attempts at parrying or defence. If he tried science and failed would he be branded a coward? But if he did not, he would undoubtedly fall to the sheer weight and aggression of the Irish ox –

The words of the Lord's prayer sounded from the cadets around him, cutting into his thoughts, and he joined in, strangely calmed after his brief communion; God had seemed quite close for a while, almost telling him he must use his head. Had not David slain Goliath?

'Lighten our darkness, we beseech thee, O Lord,' the Chaplain intoned, 'and by Thy great mercy defend us from all perils and dangers of this night – for the love of Thy only Son, our Saviour, Jesus Christ –'

George responded with an ardent, 'Amen!'

They sang 'Eternal Father', then broke up in the customary stampede, jostling shoulder to shoulder down the quivering gangways along the deck into the timbered bows, out along the covered way, swaying beneath their feet to the *Hindostan* and down to the lines of hammocks stretched between the low beams of the orlop.

Kneeling to brush his teeth over the basin in his sea chest, George heard Fitzdunnon calling from the other side of the deck to one of his hangers-on; he was looking forward to a nice walk in the country tomorrow afternoon! It was greeted by a burst of laughter. A cadet captain shouted to them to stow the noise. George felt himself colouring, thankful for the dim lighting.

'He's got nerves,' Selby said in a low voice from the next chest.

It had not sounded like nerves to him.

'We've spread the buzz you won the boxing cup at your prep school.'

He looked up briefly, smiling his thanks. Selby was a splendid fellow; whatever happened Selby would stick by him. It could easily have been Selby fighting Fitz tomorrow; they had been together when the dispute began, arguing about a mooring exercise they had been shown in the seamanship room, when Fitz and two of his followers had come up, jackets wide open, caps flat aback, swinging their key lanyards vigorously as the junior terms were supposed to for the hated 'general cheek' ordered by the cadet captains.

Although he and Selby had their jackets open and their caps pushed to the backs of their heads, they were using their hands to emphasize their arguments rather than swing their lanyards. Fitz, pushing belligerently close had 'supposed' they thought they were excused 'cheek' since he (George) played in the XI and licked the Niners' arses. George, stung but keeping his hands deliberately away from his lanyard, challenged him to repeat that. Selby, quick as always, asked why one of Fitz's jacket buttons was done up. Fitz fell for the bait and looked down, and Selby, taking a step towards him swung his key lanyard either by accident or design flicking his cap off his head.

He apologized with mock unction. 'I do beg your pardon, old man!'

Fitz's eyes had been narrow with anger. 'I'll thank ye to pick it up – *old man*!'

Selby only smiled and Fitz, losing control, let go of his own lanyard and grabbing Selby's with both hands, twisted it close around his neck, pulling his head down.

Instinctively George brought his extended fingers up under Fitz's armpit, surprising him into releasing his grip, and Selby shook himself free. Fitz's attention now concentrated on George, an expression in his green eyes as if this was the moment he had been waiting for; his wide lips had parted slightly, but he hadn't smiled.

'No one strikes Fitz – not you, *Steel*! I'll see you. On Sunday.'

'Sunday it is!' George replied with an assurance he had not felt.

Selby was staring at him, the blood which had suffused his face while he was half strangled draining away to leave a mottled impression.

He had turned to Fitz. 'I knocked your cap off – if you want to meet anyone on Sunday –'

He had been interrupted by a group of Niners approaching, demanding to know why none of them was 'cheeking' and why Fitz's cap was on the deck. Selby sought to take the blame by saying he had knocked the cap off and it was his fault they were arguing over it; this had been to no avail; they had all been caught out; the only question was what form retribution would take. After discussing whether they should be required to report to their sanc ashore, the Niners' spokesman, a small, sharp-faced cadet whom George could not remember having seen before, called for instant punishment; the others agreed and – Fitz first because he was capless – they had bent and taken two hefty cuts each with a broom handle. Straightening, tense-faced but silent, they walked off rather stiffly, swinging their lanyards feverishly. George made a point of catching up with Fitz and calling out, 'I'll see you on Sunday, Fitzdunnon!'

It had caused an immediate sensation among those of his term who heard; by lunch it had become the chief topic of speculation and by the afternoon had even spread to the senior terms. On the soccer field that afternoon Archer-Smith, 'Archie' as he now knew him, reminded him of the local Derby they were playing against the town school on the following Wednesday; he hoped he would take care not to get himself injured.

'You can handle him – keep moving – play him like the clumsy great bull he is. *Don't forget*, we need you on Wednesday!'

Back aboard afterwards in the steaming salt-water bath, he and Selby had asked Leadwith to judge who had the better welts across their bum; impossible to tell, Leadwith had replied: Selby's stripes were crossed with the yellowing bruises from a previous beating – he attracted beatings, he was so careless; he reminded George in some ways of his brother, Willy. On this occasion Selby's bum had been so colourful he had been christened the Blue Baboon.

The lights went out. He was in his hammock although he couldn't remember actually getting in. He gazed up into the darkness thinking that the next time the lights went out he would have won or lost, and for an instant he wondered if perhaps the result was ordained – but it was for a moment only as he occupied himself again with the practicalities of tactics. 'Keep moving . . .' Archie had said, 'get in underneath –'

As if reading his thoughts, Selby called across softly, 'Use your head. Fitz is an ass –'

'WHO'S TALKING!' The cadet captain's voice seemed to reverberate around the deck – King, not one to be lenient.

King's footsteps sounded on the planking as he came down the line of hammocks. George held his breath for Selby.

The footsteps neared, then King's cane clanged on the metal hammock rail.

'It was here somewhere. If someone doesn't own up I'll turn the section out.'

'Me,' Selby said in a small voice.

'OUT!'

George felt his stomach turn over; on top of Selby's existing bruises and with only his thin pyjamas as protection it was going to hurt; he prayed Selby wouldn't utter.

He heard his bare feet land on the deck; the silence seemed to take on added intensity.

'Over!'

108

George heard the swoosh as the cane cut the air; the crack as it landed was sharp and awful. He felt as tense in every nerve as if he were taking it himself – then the swoosh again and the sharp crack. Selby made no sound.

King's footsteps moved away, and he heard Selby climbing slowly back into his hammock; his breathing was uneven with little catches in it. George wanted to say something encouraging, but that would be asking for it. He found himself thinking of Fitzdunnon's wide face and officious green eyes instead, and his fists clenched tight; he would pay out Fitz for this. He could feel his heart pounding and hear his own heavier breathing.

Hardly anyone spoke as they headed for the far bank in the pinnace – at least that was George's impression. Perhaps, lost in his own thoughts, he didn't hear. Purely by chance Fitz was in the same boat. Looking at him out of the corner of his eye, George was surprised by his expression; he seemed almost subdued. Could Selby have been right? Was the brute affected by nerves? Had the story about his prep school boxing cup actually put the wind up him? It was hard to believe – yet there was no doubt, he was not his usual ebullient self.

Some years afterwards on their sublieutenant's course at Greenwich Fitz confessed to him that it wasn't Selby's tale that had alarmed him, but a snatch of talk overheard between the instructors in the gym, evidently after a boxing lesson. One had predicted he would make a champion out of Steel, and had listed George's attributes in such glowing terms, he had given up all hope there and then! Like George, he had gone into the fight anxious only to preserve his reputation by going down with colours flying.

On the same occasion he confided that he had disliked George during those first terms in the *Britannia* because of his swelled head about his prowess at games and indecent friendliness with the senior terms and 'authority'. To Fitz authority was and remained always the enemy. Added to this, he had contrasted George living grandly, he supposed, in London with his own country background and had credited him not only with more sophistication but with greater brains.

'You were a wild fellow,' George said, smiling over his tankard.

'Indeed I was – aren't I the same wild fellow now! But that was a fight, beGod! That was a *fight* –'

'I don't think I remember too much about it –'

'You don't remember –!' Fitz roared. 'He doesn't remember! Come to think of it – neither do I!'

They neared the jetty – only a few minutes now and they would be at it. George could see in his imagination the ring of cadets, feel the expectant hush before the start and see the eyes darting between the contestants – he'd been a part of it all before – then the shouting, and Fitz coming at him with those derisively parted lips. That was not exactly how he looked now as he stared towards the shore.

He wished desperately that it was just an ordinary Sunday. The day was so perfect, crisp and clear, the thin sun warming his face, the river bright with moving reflections, the bare branches of the trees ashore still and sharp against the blue of the sky. He thought of Stoke Fleming and the young waitress who had served them the last time they had walked to the tea house. She had smiled, enjoying their ribbing – Mary her name – it had seemed to him she had smiled at him particularly. He wanted to see her again –

There was a shouted order and the tinkle of the telegraph; the deck quivered as the screw went astern, and they were slewing in against the tide – out fenders – a gentle bump on the timbers; it was nicely judged.

They split up in groups after jumping ashore and strolled off with assumed nonchalance in different directions, keeping up a pretence that it was just an ordinary Sunday; everyone knew it wasn't, from the Old Man down. 'H-A' certainly knew; he had not said so because the officers were not supposed to be aware that these contests took place, but from odd phrases of encouragement he was in no doubt that H-A would be pleased if he managed to take Fitz down a peg. A good thing if our Hibernian friend could be brought up with a round turn, he had suggested, it might be the making of him; he had the right stuff in him. Probably Fitz had never been brought properly under restraint. Even here

110

he got away with far too much; the usual punishments made little impression, and he was bigger and stronger than anyone in the senior terms, possibly older too.

'Strictly between you and me and the sternpost, you understand, Steel.'

'Yes, sir.'

It had been an embarrassing interview; normally H-A would never talk critically of another cadet, not to him.

They turned off the path into the woods; he wondered if the keeper would be alert just this once and chase them out. He never was; some boys said he was sleeping off his Sunday dinner at this time of day, others that he was perfectly aware of the ancient custom and would never disturb them unless they did damage. It was too much to hope he would put in an appearance on this Sunday –

He was content to follow Selby and the others, picking their way through the saplings, twigs cracking beneath their feet, the brown leaves of last autumn still thick in places, rustling as they kicked them up. No one spoke much. They had been full of encouragement earlier in the day; they didn't really expect him to win though; they wanted to see him hurt Fitz; if he could do that he would have fulfilled their hopes. He felt the recurrent sick feeling he had been getting in his stomach, and a weak spasm passed down his legs, but then as they came to a fallen tree across their way, and climbed over and jumped down the other side he found himself very aware of fitness and sure balance, and the feeling passed as quickly as it had come on; whatever happened Fitz would not have an easy time; he was so clumsy he would catch him with good blows early on – if he aimed and timed them right – it was all a matter of timing – he had to keep his head – not allow himself to be rushed –

They emerged into the clearing sooner than he expected. It seemed that everyone had arrived before them, but scanning round he saw Fitz's party had not come yet. They were all gathered in little groups and they turned to look as he appeared. Sensing the atmosphere of excitement he adopted a deliberately casual attitude, thrusting his hands into his jacket pockets.

He turned to Selby. 'I'll wait until they come.' He hoped

the unevenness he detected in his voice was not apparent to the others.

Selby looked at him curiously.

'Before I strip down,' he explained.

Selby laughed, rather more loudly than the misunderstanding warranted. George laughed too, and the others.

'I expect he's lost his way,' Leadwith said.

'He's probably knocked up the keeper to ask him!'

There was another round of laughter.

George realized he was flexing his knees and moving his legs about rather as he did before going in to bat and stopped.

There was a momentary hush in the talk around the clearing, then a renewed burst of voices; he knew Fitz had arrived before Selby told him.

'Here he is!'

He turned casually, hands still in his pockets. Fitz and his party had seen them and were making their way to the opposite side of the clearing. The other cadets were already moving, the groups dissolving into what was beginning to look like a ring. He felt his heart pounding and had to swallow hard as he turned back towards Selby and unwound his scarf from his neck. Selby took it, then helped him off with his jacket, Leadwith taking the other arm and pulling. He undid his tie and tossed it casually to Selby, shivering slightly in the cold air. But the activity had calmed him; he was glad the moment had come at last, the waiting was over; he was even looking forward to it. He removed his shirt and pulled his vest up over his head. Selby was looking like an animated clothes horse. He clutched his arms across his chest as the cold hit him, and jumped up and down.

It was as he had imagined it in the pinnace – the eager ring, the quiet, the air of tension as he turned to look for Fitz. He too was stripped to the waist; his skin was very white over his barrel-like rib cage and great shoulders, his arms were thick with muscle. He had the physique of a young man, not a boy.

'Ready?' he heard Selby call.

Fitz nodded, and started towards them with his awkward gait, jaw thrust forward, a look of ferocious determination in his wide, green eyes. George's world narrowed to those

112

eyes. He saw them flick down and up again and knew an instant before it happened that Fitz was going to charge. Instinctively he balanced on his toes and bent knees, left leg leading, as he had done countless times in imagination, waited fractionally for the moment, then punched out straight with his left. Fitz's face came on to his fist like a football, jarring right up to his shoulder. He saw the eyes widen with surprise, and Fitz was actually shaking his head as if in wonderment when he caught him again, this time over the right eye with the full weight of his body up on his tows behind the blow. Fitz's head jerked back, his face changing into an expression of wild rage, lips drawn up at the corners, brows lowering. George saw a spot of blood on the right brow and felt a sense of exaltation.

A tumult of shouting had risen all around; he heard his own name repeated. Fitz was charging again, head down this time. George could not see his eyes, only the curly brown hair at the top of his head. He swayed back on his toes and leaned to the right, and as the hunched figure hurtled in, arms flailing, brought his right fist jabbing up from underneath; he felt it connect with something hard and heard an animal grunt as Fitz, overbalanced by his own momentum, fell to his knees, only his hands saving him from going flat on his face. The shouting reached a new crescendo; for an instant George, carried away with the excitement, wanted to jump in and punch him as he struggled up, but he held back.

The blood welling from above Fitz's eye had spattered down his cheek, and the skin around the eye was puffing, giving a slightly lopsided look to his contorted expression as he rose; he was breathing heavily, and seemed to sway.

'Is it a fight?' he rasped, 'or a bloody dancin' lesson?' His arms were held, bent about the level of his lower ribs.

The yelling about them rose another pitch. George felt himself master of the situation and reading another desperate charge in Fitz's eyes, he stepped in himself with his left to the face again. Fitz seemed to duck at about the same moment and he caught him somewhere on the forehead, feeling a jarring pain in his hand. The blow failed to stop Fitz, who came on, head butting, throwing ferocious, bent arm punches, one of which caught him painfully on the right

113

shoulder as he leaned and swayed. He jabbed at the lowered head to try and stem the onslaught, but was forced backwards by the sheer weight of the assault and found himself amongst the spectators before Fitz stopped, raising his head at last and blowing hard. He looked frightful, the right side of his face streaked with blood, spatters of which had fallen on the white skin of his chest and shoulder; his right eye was a gleaming trench between red swellings and he was twisting his head as if to fix George properly in the sights of his good eye. His mouth was open, drawing deep breaths, and even his teeth seemed stained with blood from a cut on his upper lip. Suddenly his knees sagged and he staggered leftwards as if his balance had gone.

The shouting boiled up around George's ears; he heard Selby scream, 'GO IN! FINISH HIM -', and the chorus was taken up by others, 'FINISH - FINISH -!'

He stepped in, twisting savagely to throw all his weight behind his right as Fitz half-turned his head again to bring his good eye into play. Too late he realized that the apparent lack of balance had been a ruse; Fitz had recovered and was waiting for him with bent knees, moving his head sideways to avoid the punch; whether or not it landed, he never knew, for in the same instant the breath was knocked from his lungs by a blow beneath the 'V' of his ribs that doubled him, choking and fighting for air, scarcely feeling the punches now landing thick on his head; then he saw the ground coming up fast to meet him and felt it hit him on the ear, but rather softly as if it was rubber. From a long distance away he heard his name called. Still fighting for breath, he scrabbled to his knees, but fell away again to the side. He tasted blood in his mouth and spat it out.

At last, fighting down nausea, he reached an all-fours position, then managed to stand. Selby, an anxious look in his wide eyes, clutched his arm to steady him. He shook it free, turning to see where Fitz had gone. He was standing ten feet away, his chest heaving, head twisted so that he could watch him from his good eye. What a low trick! He would not get away with it –

He started towards him. The whole left side of his face and his ribs ached as if he had been kicked. He would get the brute's other eye. The watching cadets had gone silent, quite silent. Fitz was waiting, a wary look in the good eye. George feinted as if to move towards the blind side, then launched his right, feeling it land flush on the unmarked half of that wide face; the big head jerked back. He closed, throwing caution to the winds in his determination to keep his right hand hitting the target – if only he had more strength –

Fitz seemed to swing the whole upper part of his body to avoid the blows, then butted in head down and caught him another shuddering blow in the ribs. Instinctively, he moved away. Fitz came on, grunting as he swung his arms like flails. George, weaving, taking punches on his arms, feeling the breeze of others past his nose or ears, saw on the odd occasion Fitz lifted his face a tell-tale reddening around his good eye and knew that if he could only last out he would win. Fitz, perhaps sensing this too, seemed to make a final effort, hurling himself bodily behind a slugging right to the side of the chest that knocked George temporarily off balance, then caught him with his other fist on the side of the left eye, and as George jabbed to keep him away another grazing blow to the side of the jaw.

He was unclear how long the fight lasted after this or what happened to him. The strength finally ebbed from his legs and arms as he tried to trade punches, then his balance went again. He had an impression of looking up at trees against the blue sky and Selby and the others crowding round, bending and staring, but he couldn't see too well as he felt his left eye closing up. When they reached down to help him to his feet he had to cry out to them to go easy; his middle felt as if it had been crushed, his jaw and the whole left side of his face throbbed with pain; his right hand was agony; he thought he must have broken all the bones in it.

He had a desperate sense of failure. 'I chucked it!' It hurt to open his mouth.

'Rot!' someone said, and others, crowding round curiously as he stood supported by Selby and Leadwith, added encouragement. After a while he gathered that Fitz had also ended the fight on the ground. Practically unable to see, he had

115

stumbled with the effort of his final burst of punches and lain, coughing up sick until lifted by his supporters.

The fight passed into term legend; stories of how both he and Fitz, their eyes completely bunged up, had to be led aboard, guided up the gangway steps and turned at the right point to salute the quarterdeck while the officer of the watch discreetly left the deck so that he would not be a witness to the scene gathered embellishment by the hour.

Both George and Fitz spent the next few days in the sick bay, as their sight returned, able to admire their handiwork on the other's face. They were in adjacent cots and they talked the fight over blow by blow, Fitz generous in praise of George's skill, George equally generous about Fitz's guile!

'And what else could I do! With me one eye! I'd not touched ye then, had I – had I –?'

'I thought I had you beat,' George said, still tormented by his stupid mistake.

'So ye had – and so ye cannot hold it against me now. It was a legitimate ruse of war. Didn't Nelson himself hoist French colours when he felt the need!'

George agreed. It wasn't the trick which irritated him, but the fact that he had fallen for it. The more he mulled it over, the more annoyed he felt about his own naïvety. Fitz had grown up half wild among the farm lads on his people's estate; he should have known he would not stick by Queensberry rules. He determined that it would be a lesson he would never forget; he would never again judge other's conduct by his own. Within the Service, this stood him in good stead, but since he never realized the extent to which his conduct and habits of thought came to be moulded by the *Britannia* and all that followed, he lacked the self-knowledge – or indeed the imagination – to appreciate how, outside the enclosing circle of service life, attitudes might be very different; in these wider fields the lesson was lost.

The more immediate result of the contest and his spell in the 'sanny' was that he and Fitz became fast friends. He was impressed by Fitz's subversive or careless attitude to almost everything except, he learned, horses. Fitz conceived an admiration for the way George thought things out before acting or even opening his mouth, and made an effort to emulate him; this produced a remarkable change in his behaviour, exceeding even Hepplewaite-Adams's hopes before the fight. On George's end of term report, the lieutenant commented:

. . . his conduct and bearing have been such as to have exerted a beneficial influence on others.

The Captain summarized:

Another highly successful term in all fields. He continues to show great promise.

7

Willy had been unable to contain his excitement for days. Now, perched in the bows of the dinghy approaching the *Peacock*, he was silent at last, his feelings overwhelmed by the scene. Barges, loaded down to the tops of the gunwales, slid upstream, their great patched tan sails stiff with wind, white or grey topsails above and little houseflags with different devices fluttering out against the summer sky, sail after sail they came in endless procession. Nearer, a steam tug with red and white bands around its funnel, pouring smoke, was towing a string of empty lighters diagonally out across the tide. Willy was fascinated by the way the water slipped down into a long hollow behind the roll of foam at her bow, swelling up again into a boiling froth under the stern. A man was walking along the side of the nearest lighter, calling down to someone sculling a dirty old boat bobbing in the wake. Beyond, a paddle ferry with more black smoke blown from the funnel was slewing into the jetty, her rails lined with passengers, and further out in the middle of the river a cargo steamer blew two blasts on her siren.

But, for Willy, the focus was the *Peacock*; he turned to look at her again. She lay straining at her mooring some twenty yards off now, a thoroughbred among the moving commercial craft, her gunwales and varnished coach-roof skylights glinting in the sun, reflections from the waves rippling up her shiny black side; a rope leading to the mast-head was slap-slap-slapping with a curious, interrupted rhythm against the wood as if calling them away, away-ay, away-ay-ay –

He had never been away in her for a cruise. George went

118

every summer; Andy had been last year for the first time; this year he was included – instead of going to Thorpeness – and Henry too. George would keep Henry under control.

George rowed, grunting with the effort against the tide. He was acting as 'John'. The real John had absconded with the harbourmaster's wife, so his father had said, but he didn't believe everything he said; at any rate they would have no crew until they reached Plymouth. There, he was going to be shown the Hoe where Drake had played bowls before sailing out to defeat the Spaniards. And there they were going to find a 'real west-country sailorman' as crew for the next stage of the cruise to Ireland.

In the meantime George was 'John', and had been since early morning. He must remember; it would obviously be more important aboard than it had been in the train, where he'd slipped up once or twice on the journey to Gravesend.

'John,' he mouthed under his breath. 'It's not far now, John –'

'What's that?' George – 'John' – said.

'Nothing – John.'

He saw Henry staring at him from next to his father in the stern. 'John!' she mimicked. 'Toad!'

He was about to reply in kind but his father cut in boisterously, 'Quite right, Willy! You are promoted – Bill,' and turning to Henrietta, 'D'you hear that, Steward – Bill!'

Henrietta raised her brows coolly as if he were being extraordinarily childish, then turned to look over the side.

'Now, Henry,' he said more gently. She continued staring out with fixed gaze. '*Henry!*' he repeated, and when she did not respond, roared with laughter, 'Bravo, Steward! Bravo!'

She turned to look at him with a gleam in her eyes and he twisted with another roar and squeezed her leg. George had said he was a different man in the boat; so it was proving. With his small-topped yachting cap rammed down over his hair, bunching all round below it, faded blue reefer with two rows of brass buttons bulging over his ample middle, his white flannels and plimsolls, he looked as Willy imagined he must have done in his prime at sea. There were heavy folds of skin beneath his eyes and the whites were veined with pink, but they looked clearer nonetheless than in the mornings at

119

home, as if the tangy breeze off the river and the sunlight on the water had brightened them already.

Aware of the scrutiny, he called out, 'This'll be a voyage you shan't forget, Bill, I promise you!' and raising and twisting his head as if to sniff the breeze, 'If the wind goes round – as it might – and the steward stows the victuals in time for us to catch the first of the ebb – as she will –' he gave Henrietta an amused glance, 'we'll fetch up snug in Dover harbour by nightfall! How's that appeal to you, Bill! A capital day's sailin'?'

He nodded happily, wondering where Dover was, but not caring; he just wanted to board the *Peacock* and feel her move.

'Now then, Bill,' his father went on, 'You'll jump aboard with the painter, take a turn for'd and pass the end back to John in the dinghy – then come aft and put the boardin' steps over. You'll find 'em in the starboard locker – in the cockpit.'

'Aye-aye, Papa!'

'Aye-aye!' his father repeated approvingly, and looked at Henrietta. 'That's how we answer orders aboard ship, Steward – Aye-aye.'

'I know,' she replied tartly. She was evidently going to be difficult.

'And we jump to it!' John put in with a rough voice.

'Why do I have to be steward?' she asked without looking at him, and turning to her father, 'I don't see why I should.'

'*I've* been steward,' John said coldly. 'You have to start as steward.'

'No arguments in the boat!' his father said, 'And Steward, elbows off the gunwale! We don't want a one-armed steward!' He added, 'They only do half the work. One-legged stewards now, we don't mind them, but we can't abide a steward with only one arm – ain't that so, John?'

'We only get half the grub,' John said.

The steward tossed her hair disdainfully; how striking she looked in a mood, Willy thought; her determined chin and the strong line of her brows gave her a dauntless look; he could imagine her riding a chariot like Boadicea at the head of the Iceni, hair streaming; she wouldn't care a bit for the Romans.

120

His father was looking at John, chuckling; John would be smiling back in a knowing way.

John had been decent to him lately, since it had been fixed that he was following him into the Navy – so long as he passed the exams of course. He'd spent the last few days instructing him in seamanship and especially knots in preparation for the cruise; he could do a clove hitch, reef knot, round turn and two half hitches, fisherman's bend and a rolling hitch in the dark without having to think, and he knew the international code flags.

They were almost up to the yacht now; the lines of the seams and ends of the hull strakes were plainly visible beneath the glistening black paint; the waves lapped along the red boot-topping with the thin white band separating it from the black above. Willy wondered how they got the sweet curve of it so perfectly; he was sure if he tried it would be a wiggly line. Everything about the *Peacock* was perfect. The tide sucked eddies in the dark-shadowed water under the counter; it must be deep out here.

He felt the thrust of the bow as John put extra strength into the final strokes; they were abreast of the yacht now, pointing in the same direction as her with about five feet of clear water between, then John turned the bow and the tide caught it, sweeping them in towards her. He tensed, seizing the end of the painter. The end of the starboard oar bumped and slid towards him as John shipped it, and he felt a splash of water cold on his hand. He was about to reach out to fend off imminent collision when John dug the port oar in the water, checking the swing and they fetched up gently alongside, perfectly positioned near the stern. He reached up and caught hold of the gunwale and scrambled aboard, hearing his father's 'Bravo!' whether at the excellent way they had been brought alongside or his own quick pounce he was not sure, but he felt a glow of pleasure. The deck was comfortingly steady beneath his feet as he hurried forward with the painter, passed it through a fair-lead and down again to John in the boat. There was a smell of new varnish and paint and warm timber and tarry rope.

'A creditable effort, Bill!' his father said as he put the steps over for him.

When he and Henrietta were aboard, John cast off and pulled away for the shore to fetch Andy and their gear and provisions which he was guarding. His father took him by the arm.

'Now, Bill, we must make sure you know the ropes.'

Willy gazed down into the water curling past the *Peacock*'s stem but did not see or hear it; his mind was in Africa. He had been chosen to go out by the Royal Geographic Society. A swallowtail butterfly with a span of over a foot had been reported; he had been asked to see if it was true. He knew more about butterflies than anyone in England; this one would be named after him if he found it – Steel's swallowtail. The Germans had sent an expert too, a professor who had started out a week earlier. Willy had the advantage of owning his own yacht though; he had convinced the committee he could overtake the professor by sailing up river into the heart of the country while his rival went overland.

'You're not afraid of crocodiles, Steel?'

'No, sir.'

It was not true. He had seen them floating like great logs on the yellow water as the river narrowed –

'Bill!'

He looked back, wondering who Bill was. His father was beckoning him from the cockpit, and he remembered. Casting a quick glance ahead, thankful to see nothing at all close, for he was lookout, he scrambled to his feet and balanced his way to the shrouds, then aft, holding on to the rail on the coach-roof with his left hand; the low shoreline seemed further away now; they must be almost out to sea.

'A spell at the helm, Bill? Think y' can manage?'

He nodded, seeing John looking up at him from the side of the cockpit. Astern the dinghy rose and swung briefly to starboard on a quartering wave, then jerked back as the tow-rope tautened.

'Nothin' to worry about. Wind's steady.' His father pointed with his arm and flat hand over the port quarter.

'You see where it is? See how the waves are comin'? If it holds there you've nothin' to worry about.'

He made way for him on the bench, but kept one hand on the tiller after Willy had taken it to steady her for him. With his other hand he indicated the tilting compass bowl. 'There's your lubber's line, d'y' see, Bill? She's on – *now*! Sou-east a half east. See if you can keep her there –' He pulled the tiller up as the card started to swing again, pushing it back when the yacht responded. After a moment he said, 'Now – have a try!' He took his hand away and leaned back, gazing up at the set of the topsail, then round again into the wind over the quarter and down at the compass card.

Willy had held the tiller for short turns on day trips, but had never steered a compass course before; in his anxiety to prevent the point from straying from the lubber's line, he put on too much helm, then corrected too far, steering a zig-zag which caused Henrietta and Andy to pop their heads up from the cabin.

'Ah! Steward!' his father said. 'Cocoa and biscuits for the watch on deck, and you can fetch me up a Havana.'

She seemed surprised at these peremptory orders, and turned scornful eyes on Willy when John barked at her, '*Aye-aye – sir!*'

She rounded on him. 'Don't you tell me what to say!'

'Steward –' his father interrupted.

She turned. 'No! I'm not going to be shouted at.'

Willy felt sorry for her as she stood up to both of them; John should not have used that tone, although she had been picking at him. She was so prickly these days; she seemed to like quarrelling, especially with John when he tried to put her right.

'You shall have your trick at the helm,' his father said, obviously attempting to soothe her. 'But it's important orders are obeyed on board and no argument.'

'I don't mind him *pretending* to be John, but it doesn't mean he can shout at me –'

'I didn't shout –'

'Quiet!' His father's voice was sharper. 'I'll not have argument on deck. Do you go below, Steward, and do your duty!'

Her head went down. Andy's had already disappeared.

His father leaned back, sighing.

123

John said, as if to himself, 'I'd like to see her in the *Britannia*!'

'What's that y' say, John?'

'I wonder what would happen to her in the *Britannia*!'

His father roared. 'It don't bear thinkin' about, John!' He looked at Willy. 'It's as well both of you find out about it now, it'll stand you in good stead later I can promise you. Let 'em once get the upper hand – and they try, oh, they all try – the more like angels they look, the more certain it is they'll try –' He seemed not to finish whatever it was he was saying.

Willy had the feel of the boat now; he found himself able to anticipate the movement of the card and check it before it swung too far. He was enjoying it. The sense of restraining and focusing all the power he felt through the hull as they leaned and surged, and the pressure of the tiller like a living thing in his hands exhilarated him. But at the back of his mind was a disturbing image of Henrietta angry and unhappy down in the cabin.

He had seen his mother in her for a moment just then. He had not noticed it before; it wasn't in her looks, it was something about the set of her mouth and chin and the way a dark shutter dropped down behind her eyes when she was angry. He couldn't imagine anyone getting the better of her – not for long. John would feel her tongue before the day was out – so probably would he himself?

It occurred to him suddenly that she might be unhappy when she grew up. She was so sharp and critical. He had these odd feelings at times. When he thought about them, they vanished. It was difficult even to imagine her grown up. He had thought at one time when he was eleven it would be a prime age; now he was eleven and he felt no different. He thought he would be content at fourteen, Henrietta's age, but he couldn't imagine being grown up.

The bow fell off the wind and from behind the jib as he pushed the tiller down, he saw a large passenger liner some distance away astern of two cargo steamers he had been watching before. She was heading obliquely towards them. He pointed her out to his father.

'A P&O if I'm any judge, Bill.' He leaned forward to pull

the binoculars from the rack on the bulkhead and held them up to his eyes, leaning out over the coaming as he studied the ship. 'P&O she is – one of the new ones I dare say.' He lowered the glasses and replaced them. 'Know where she's from, Bill?'

By this time Willy had become more concerned about a barge which he had caught sight of astern, catching them up. Rolls of foam jumped around the black stem; the brick-red sail stretching way above was full of wind, straining in dark creases at the corners.

'Never mind about him,' his father said, catching the direction of his gaze. 'His duty to keep clear.'

He wondered if 'he' would know his duty – or if 'he' could even see them; he couldn't see anyone aboard, only that great sail obscuring everything behind the mast.

'India,' John said.

'D'y' hear that, Bill? I should like to hear the yarns aboard her – there'll be some yarns I can promise you. You know what they used to say –'

They heard barking from astern, and looking round, saw the white face of a dog bobbing up and down above the barge's side near the stem with its blue and red and gilt scrolls.

'There's y'r lookout, Bill!' his father chuckled. 'Ah, you scamp, now let's see what happens!' And as the dog continued to bark excitedly, 'All right you scallywag! You've roused 'em out by now!'

Willy, trying to concentrate on the course, looked round again. The barge seemed closer already – ominously close, he thought, and still he could see no sign of life except for the little dog jumping about first on the far side of the stemhead, then poking his eager snout under the foresail on the near side.

After some minutes, as she still came on, his father said, 'Perhaps we'd better come up a shade. Down with the helm, Bill!'

Thankfully, Willy pushed the tiller away from him. The *Peacock* responded like the thoroughbred she was, starting to turn at once.

'That'll do, Bill –'

His father leaned suddenly with surprising agility, seized the tiller and pulled it back, but by then they had come round far enough to spill the wind from the sails, and she swung upright, then lurched as a wave, broadside on, lifted them.

Henrietta, balancing up from the cabin at that moment with two mugs, fell against the entrance, crying out as cocoa spilled over her wrists.

'You did that on purpose, William Steel!'

His father held the tiller and with his other hand hauled in on the sheet so that the main filled again.

'There you are, Bill, keep her up there for a bit. Come back to the old course when he's clear.'

'Sorry,' he said, feeling he'd blundered terribly.

'You're doin' well Bill – ain't he, John?'

'Yes, he is.' John sounded as if he meant it.

Henrietta held out a mug towards him. 'The rest of it's on the floor.'

'Deck!' John said.

She looked at him coolly for a moment before placing the other mug on the bench some way from him. *'Andy* made it.'

'Good!' John said, stretching for it. 'It'll be all right then.'

'Avast you two!' his father called. 'By George, if we're to put up with this all voyage –' then with a suddenly gentler, almost cooing tone, holding out his arm towards her, 'Do you come by me, Steward! We'll keep an eye on how Bill keeps his course.'

She was extracting a long cigar from inside the sleeve of her jersey. She pointed to one end wet with cocoa. 'That's how he steers! I'll fetch you another –'

But her father took it from her, chuckling, reaching into his pocket with his other hand for his clipper. As Henrietta sat by him, Andy appeared at the entrance with a mug. He handed it to her, then held out a tin lid with biscuits on it.

'There's a little fellow over there wouldn't mind some of those!' His father nodded towards the barge, whose stem was now almost level with the dinghy, but some distance from them; she must have been keeping away even as they rounded up to avoid her approach. The dog was silent now, staring at them, panting, his red tongue lolling out from the side of his mouth. A small, round man with white hair and beard stood by the wheel astern, also looking at them.

'Salt of the sea!' his father said, and lifted his cap to him.

Willy, concentrating on bringing the *Peacock* back to her old course, did not see the response.

Andy stepped into the cockpit with a mug of cocoa for himself, and sitting down by John, stared at the barge as it overhauled them, black side high out of the water and heeling showing green growth below the waterline and heavy, raised leeboard. The sun glanced off his spectacles.

'Where are we?' he asked.

'Makin' up for the West Spaniard, Andy.' Willy smelled a delicious whiff of his cigar. 'And Bill's layin' such a dead course we shall have to look out we don't hit it – ain't that so, Bill?' He leaned out over the coaming, gazing ahead. 'There she is – right on the nose –' He pointed. 'D'y' see, Steward?'

Henrietta was already looking out with him. 'It's got black and white stripes –' her voice was normal again.

'That's it! And y' see the shoal – y' see the nasty sluice to the sea – there can't be much water there now –' He leaned aside as Andy came over to look too. 'D'y' see it, Andy? Watch y'r course Bill. Many a good ship's ended her last voyage up on the Spaniard!'

Henrietta looked round at Willy, her eyes rather blue and wide as if she wondered whether they could trust him to steer clear. He felt pleasantly important and stared ahead, trying to make out the extent of the shoal. He could see it now it had been pointed out; there was a lighter look to the blue and a mass of little running whitecaps lit by the sun. He felt a shiver, wondering how far it extended. The black and white buoy he could see appeared to be some distance from the whitecaps. He hoped his father would watch out when they got nearer.

'What's that big ship?' Henrietta asked. The liner was much closer now.

'That's a P&O,' his father replied. 'She's come from India. There'll be some happy faces aboard her this evenin' – and some tears.'

'Tears?' she asked surprised.

'It's hard to keep y'r eyes dry when you haven't seen your native land for twenty years, Henry.'

'Do they have to stay out that long?'

'Not many nowadays. Not now they can get home in just four weeks by steamer. Four weeks, Steward, and look at her! You'd fancy she'd just come from dry dock – not rolled across the Bay of Biscay-o!'

'Geraldine's going out to India,' Henrietta said. 'She won't have to stay out for twenty years will she?'

'Bless you, no!' her father roared. 'She'll make a good catch, you may be sure.' He looked at her fondly and for rather long, Willy thought, wondering what he meant by a 'good catch'.

He was glad the row was over; he hated it when they quarrelled. He thought suddenly it was a pity Mama wasn't here too, and Harry and Babs and Nurse and Mrs Harding, and wondered what they were doing at Thorpeness. He could imagine the timber house and the shingly path down to the beach beside the rough grass almost as if he were there. He wouldn't be anywhere else now than where he was; there could be nothing as exciting as steering the *Peacock* towards the Spaniard.

He looked at John and their eyes met. He thought he saw approval and a gleam of humour. He was glad he'd not made a fool of himself. He knew he'd done well. He was glad he was going into the Navy; there was no end of sailing, as much as one wanted, according to John. He looked at the compass and eased the tiller up; the card hesitated, started to swing. He pushed the tiller away. A stronger gust caught the sails, heeling her further and he pulled the tiller again to meet the swing.

Henrietta looked down anxiously at her father's face against the cushion. The light coming in the cabin ports was strangely yellow, seeming even to give a yellow tint to his eyes, narrowed now in pain. Poor Papa. His forehead was creased and there was a sort of pink furrow which had been pressed into the skin by his cap brim, dividing the red of his face exposed to the weather from the pale skin above. How grey and old he looked suddenly, so utterly different from the man he had seemed until a few minutes ago, but he wasn't old, not really old.

'Do you go up on deck, Steward,' he muttered, 'I shall be right again in a moment.' Even as he spoke, he couldn't help gasping and raising his hand to pass it across his forehead.

When he had withdrawn it and was looking at her again, she placed her own hand lightly there. 'I'll stay with you, Papa.' She had an image of herself as a sister of mercy, giving up all thought of personal happiness to nurse the suffering.

'No,' he muttered, 'no need. I'll be best alone.' He closed his eyes, then his hand came up again to touch her fingers. 'Bless you, Steward!'

She thought of him as he had been at Dover, so boyishly delighted to have made it all the way from Gravesend before the light faded completely.

'Didn't I promise you we should have our dinner in Dover harbour tonight!'

The lights of the town rising between the grey cliffs, and the lights of the esplanade and from the ships at the pier and landing stages reflected in the smooth water had made a magical setting she thought she would never forget. It had been so still after the motion of the yacht in the sea. He had sent her down for a bottle of 'the boy' and they had toasted 'the finest passage ever made in a twelve tonner in the twentieth century!' He had added, 'And the finest crew it's been my pleasure to command!' She had begun to feel lightheaded with tiredness, and so hungry, and burning from the sun and wind during the day. The smell of sausages cooking had wafted up the fore hatch. John had volunteered to cook because she was so tired – perhaps to make up for his beastliness during the day. She had felt guilty because she had been deliberately beastly to him. But he had been so protective then, serving her first when the meal was ready and making sure she had everything. It had been the most perfect night; the best of it all had been Papa's high spirits; he was seldom like that at home now, indeed they seldom saw him. It had been like the old days when she was small.

The next day had not gone so well. Making for Rye, where Papa intended to visit an 'old ship' who owned a public house there, the wind had forced them to steer in long zig-zags out to sea and back; there had been nasty, short waves splashing spray up over the bow on occasions and Papa and George had done all the steering. She had felt rather seasick at the jerky motion, but had not disgraced herself. Willy had gone quite green but bravely insisted he was all right until he had dashed suddenly up from the cabin and been sick in the cockpit.

When finally they arrived off Rye in the late afternoon, they had to anchor to wait for the tide to go in over the bar and up the river; Papa was determined to do this without a pilot; he had used those rogues on previous occasions, he said, and had taken good care to learn the marks so he would not have to submit to their beastly arrogance again. The wind had gone round – blowing on to the land by the time the water was high enough though, and with the tide under them and the wind behind they had raced in between the low timber breakwater and the equally low stone pier at terrifying speed, especially as they had to avoid fishing boats in the bay beyond; she could tell Papa was rather scared as his boisterous manner had gone completely and he had just issued curt instructions or queries about what they could see ahead. After passing the untidy houses of the port, they had steered up the river towards the town itself, only to drive aground long before they got there.

She had been terrified as they bumped and tilted; the sails, loosed, had thumped and cracked like thunder.

'She'll come off as the tide rises,' Papa had said after the boys lowered the canvas, and things were quieter.

But the tide had only driven them more firmly on to some obstruction which they found out afterwards was a sort of submerged breakwater made of wattles. When all hope of getting off on that tide had passed, Papa, strangely, recovered his spirits. He stopped cursing the blackguards who had designed a buoy which you couldn't tell if it was port or starboard so they could wreck honest strangers and pillage and murder their crews – a story he abandoned quickly at the sight of Willy's wide eyes – and announced he was going ashore. He had disappeared into the cabin, emerging half an hour later in a tweed suit with a check waistcoat, carrying a homburg hat, gloves and walking stick, and had given them a homily on accepting disappointments and difficulties with good grace.

'It's a lesson you'll learn in sail – fair winds are followed by foul – it's the law of life. You make a swift passage and feel no end of a dog, then some scoundrel shifts the marks and puts you aground. It's the law of life. You won't learn it in steamships. It's difficulties make good men – and women too I dare say. Remember that when you're in a scrape, Steward. Plain sailin's no good for anyone – savin' soldiers and engineers. I thank God I'll not have to serve with another beastly oil-rag – as you shall John – and you Bill. They'll try and make you into an engineer, Bill, when you go to Osborne. That's Fisher's idea. He won't succeed – by Jove, he'll not make a Steel an engineer. Now John, do you fetch the dinghy alongside and take me ashore.'

Henrietta smiled to herself. It had not been amusing at the time. They had wondered, after he had gone striding along the dyke, whether the buoy really had been shifted in order to wreck the yacht – they had all heard of wreckers on the Cornish coast. In the dark, when Papa had not returned she had become really alarmed, especially when George handed each of them a knife or a spike to defend themselves, and set watches so there would always be someone awake during the night. It had been a dreadful night. She had hardly slept even when it wasn't her watch.

Early the next morning George and Andy set out along the dyke to the town to find Papa. They had knocked up two publicans before coming to the right one, or rather his wife, who told them their father was still asleep; he usually slept late when he visited since he and her husband had been together in the same ship in the West Indies – anyway, she would see if she could raise him for them. While they waited she had treated them to an enormous breakfast, and when she learned there were two more still aboard the yacht had filled a basket with rolls stuffed with ham and potted meats, and added cream pastries for them to take back.

Papa had been surprised and not at all pleased to see them when he had come down eventually; he seemed to have a bad headache. It was probably the first symptom of whatever it was he was suffering now, she thought. That had been five days ago, though; he had soon recovered then and returned to his former boisterous spirits. She prayed he would do so now; it hurt her to see him looking like this.

He seemed to be falling asleep; his breathing had become louder, almost a snore, and his hand which had been holding hers, had fallen away. She lifted it and placed his arm in a more comfortable position along his side.

The yacht was rolling terribly, swinging in long arcs; she could hear the boom jaws banging against the mast and the sheets and rigging rattling and clanging each time they leaned to these huge swells. There was just no wind; the surface was oily calm. She could see it through the ports, smooth and dead-looking; there were hardly any reflections even, and as the yacht rolled and the ports lifted so that she was looking at the sky, there was no sky, only hazy yellowish light.

'What's he doing?'

She turned. George was peering in. 'He's asleep,' she replied.

'Wars!'

He hung there as they described another great arc and the shackles and blocks banged above. Wondering at his expression she said, 'Why?'

'I don't know.' There was an anxious edge to his voice. 'It's getting darker. I can't see the land any more.'

She looked down at her father, then turned and clinging to the table with one hand and the cabin top with the other, made her way to the steps. George moved away. As soon as she put her head outside she saw what he meant. In the direction in which she remembered the cliffs there was only a bank of darkness, and all round the haze shut them in a small area of that filtered yellow light and limpid water she had glimpsed through the ports. Beneath the surface skin of the sea great forces moved, raising ridges with smooth sides which drove towards them.

She saw Andy and Willy gazing at her with wide eyes; she could tell they were alarmed. So was George, although he hid it better. Their feelings communicated themselves to her, or was it simply the oppressive, sticky stillness of the day

132

which made her suddenly anxious. It was scarcely past noon; it might almost have been twilight.

'I think there's going to be a storm,' George said.

There was a low rumble which she felt as much as heard, as if it had welled up from the sea and was transmitted in the haze.

'I think we should wake Papa.'

'Yes,' George said. 'Tell him, Henry.'

She went down again into the cabin and took him by the shoulder, shaking gently. He groaned, moving his hand up to his head.

'Papa!' she said, 'Papa, there's a storm coming.'

'Storm?' he muttered, opening his eyes.

'Yes.'

'What's the glass doing?'

Why had she not thought of that! She moved to the barometer on the forward bulkhead and tapped it as she had seen him doing. The needle fell; it was already way below the brass pointer.

'It's going down,' she said.

He had levered himself up on to one elbow, and with the other hand gripping the central table, was trying to peer out of the ports on the other side.

'Where's the wind?'

'There isn't any, Papa.'

'No wind!' Slowly and painfully he put first one foot, then the other down to the deck, and stood, holding on as the yacht heeled, then moved carefully to the steps and up.

She was aware of a flicker of light outlining his figure in the entrance; it was strange, as if his appearance outside had triggered it off. Then she saw another, this time chiefly through the ports, a crooked flash of lightning. It was going to be a thunderstorm. She should have realized; she had felt this oppressive heaviness preceding summer storms before.

She heard her father telling the boys to take all the canvas off. His voice sounded better, thank goodness. She followed him up, but as soon as she appeared, he told her to go below again and don her oilers and sou'wester.

When she came up some minutes later, moving awkwardly in the stiff coat, he sent Andy and Willy down to get theirs on. He smiled at her; his eyes looked a better colour now, as if the prospect of the storm had allowed him to forget his head.

'Do you go forward, Steward, and lend John a hand. Take care now!'

She realized, as she moved forward, stopping and hanging on to the coach-roof rail with both hands as her side of the deck swooped low, that a wind was getting up. She felt a gust pulling at the brim of her sou'wester and saw the surface of the water swept into confused movement.

George, right up in the bow, was wrestling with the jib as she reached the mast and hung on to it; he had lowered the sail and trapped a section under his legs, but a large part must have blown out in the gust and was floating in the sea. He looked up and told her to grab the sheet, nodding to a rope leading from over the side near the canvas and passing across the deck in front of her. Stretching and grasping the shroud to her right, she bent and took hold of the sheet.

'Pull!' George said.

Wedging herself between the shrouds and clutching the forward one between her arm and body, she pulled. George, similarly hanging around the forestay, heaved at the canvas, and between them they soon had the sail on deck, then rolled and bundled and pushed it down through the open fore hatch.

'Well done!' George said.

His dark eyes were unusually expressive; he was enjoying it she realized. She was too. She liked the feeling that he trusted her. She didn't mind him acting as if he were older and telling her what to do. She admired his strength and competence; the fact that he was giving orders seemed natural and right.

He had already lowered the staysail before she arrived, and restrained it with temporary stops; now he told her to hold the bunched canvas while he took the stops off. Soon they had bundled and pushed the sail below on top of the jib. He told her to go back to the cockpit while he closed the hatch.

Andy and Willy, enveloped in oilskins and sou'westers, were kneeling, pulling a rope from the locker beneath the

134

side bench when she arrived back. Her father was sitting, swaying with the tiller, looking out to port, wisps of his hair plucked by the wind. The gusts were stronger now, the thunder closer and more frequent. Following the direction of his gaze she saw above a retreating ridge of water the darkness she had seen when she first came up; it was quite black and she thought she glimpsed white below it in an interrupted line, then she clung to the coaming as they heeled and all she could see was another wave-tossed ridge rolling away from them into the blackness.

'We're goin' to see some fun,' her father said.

As if in answer, the sky lit in a series of jagged bursts and streaks; moments afterwards they heard the crack of the thunder beginning again.

In the quiet after it died, she thought she picked up another noise low and far off; at first it sounded like a wave running up on a beach, and she wondered if they had drifted in to the land, but it continued at the same level and she realized it had a pulse; looking at her father she saw he had heard it too.

His eyes met hers. 'A ship!' His forehead was creased again, and his eyes anguished, whether in pain or because he didn't like the idea of the ship, she couldn't tell.

He leaned to take an end of the rope the boys had pulled from the locker, and twisting with it, started to make it fast on the metal rail on which the main sheet block was shackled.

'All secure for'd!' George said from behind her; he was leaning on the coach-roof.

'Very good, John. Do you go below now and find your oilers.'

'Shall we be setting the trysail?'

'No, John, we'll run on a bare pole.'

George looked surprised. 'I've got it up.'

'Pass it aft then. Andy can stow it till we need it.'

The day grew darker, the blackness to port more profound and the motion of the yacht increased as the swell they had been experiencing was crossed by short, steep seas which lumped into ugly shapes, seeming at times as if they would topple and fall aboard. Always the *Peacock* rode over them.

'Watch below, go below!' her father said abruptly. 'That

135

means all of you,' he added as they looked at one another. He turned to George, who had come up in oilskins. 'I'll sing out if I need you. But y'r to secure a lifeline around you if y' have to come up,' he nodded at the rope whose end he had made fast, and looking at them each in turn as they stared at him, 'That goes for all of you. Anyone goin' over the side is dead.'

His eyes were stern. Henrietta felt her insides turn over. Moving to follow his instructions, the white of a wave some way off under the darkness to port caught her eye; looking, she saw it was at the bow of a battleship with piled superstructure almost the colour of the background murk, but lighter; there was another similar ship behind it and she could just make out others behind that, a line of dark grey shapes emerging from the storm, waves tossed at their bows or passing along their sides. She called out and pointed.

'The fleet's at sea,' her father said, and with a hint of his old gaiety, 'We shall sleep soundly in our bunks tonight!'

She had a treacherous feeling she would rather sleep in one of the battleships even though they had engines. They looked impregnable. No waves could overwhelm them. She thought of the solidity of their decks underfoot as the *Peacock* rose, heeling sickeningly, and the boom with the rolled mainsail shifted just above her head. She clung on, swinging into Willy, close behind in the small space, and felt very afraid. They had no real crew; even George, sturdy and dependable, was only a boy. Papa was not even well. Soon that dark cloud would envelop them, and how could the yacht survive larger waves than this?

They swung upright on the crest and hung there for a moment, when the sky to port lit suddenly and the line of battleships was thrown into silhouette. It was a scene she never forgot. Whether it was the menacing aspect of the vessels with their long guns and smoke from the funnels blown in a line which cut off the tops of their masts, or her own precarious situation, or whether it was a portent glimpsed in her subconscious, the image remained with her always – a line of black ships against flickering lightning; whenever it returned to her she felt an echo of the anxiety she felt then.

It was oppressively hot below. She took off her sou'wester and opened her oilskin coat as she and Andy and Willy sat squeezed together on the settee where Papa had been lying. George, restless, stood, gripping a beam overhead, peering out of the ports on either side. She found herself wondering what her mother would do if the *Peacock* went down and they were all drowned. George was her favourite; she would never get over him – or Andy or Willy. She loved the boys. She would mourn them always – and never forgive Papa even though he were dead too. What would it be like to drown in those endless waves? Impossible to imagine Felpham House with only Harry and Babs. Her mother would not worry about her. Papa would if he were saved, but he wouldn't be saved in this weather. Anyone who got in the sea was dead – he had said so.

She began to pray very hard, but kept her eyes open, pretending to gaze out of the ports so that the others wouldn't know she was praying. She prayed for them all, but especially for Papa.

'Restore his strength, dear God, that he may bring us all safely through this storm. Please do not send too much wind for him. It's not all plain sailing that I ask You for – but Papa is *not well* –'

His eyes looked so dulled and sunken.

She found it difficult to concentrate with the motion and the wild, lopping green waves rising just outside the ports.

For years afterwards when Willy was reminded of the storm, he felt dreadful guilt. No one blamed him at the time, or subsequently. He never knew whether they really blamed him in their minds but didn't tell him, or if it was all in his own imagination. He told himself over and over it was not his fault; with the sudden violence of the squall, it would have happened in any case, and his father was not well before he went on deck. No amount of reasoning could prevent that sudden stab whenever the subject of the storm came up though. He never brought it up himself, and whenever one of the others did, he always tried to introduce some

137

reminiscence which led away from the subject of the mainsail blowing out lest even then he might be accused, or merely because it was too painful for him to contemplate.

That it was somewhat irresponsible to leave one half of the great mainsail to be secured by an eleven-year-old occurred to him later in life when the memory and the guilt had lost their sharpness. But he refused to blame his poor father, who had trusted him to do it, and it left a dull hurt. He never could remember how many stops he had put around the sail or how tightly he had pulled them or whether he had left pockets which the wind might catch in. He could only remember his excitement at the time. He had not felt in the least seasick since that awful passage round to Rye; the wildness of the scene and his sense of being part of a great adventure, and the achievement of hanging on and doing a sailor's task while the *Peacock* rose giddily and fell down the sides of those amazing seas were his only impressions. Reef knots – he must have made the stops fast with reef knots which he had been practising for days.

Lightning flared to port; in the intervals, after the brightness, it looked very dark on that side, thick purpling darkness beneath which he sometimes saw a white line of waves.

His father seemed tired when he and Andy returned to the cockpit after completing their task. There was a greyness about the skin around his eyes and the weathered surface of his face was like a mask from which all blood had drained. It was the peculiar light, he thought, startled, and probably he still had a bit of the headache which had caused him to lie down earlier.

'There's some line in the locker,' he told them, pointing. 'See what you can find.'

They found several lengths of hemp and pulled them out; it was impossible to coil them down neatly and his father told them not to bother, just do it quickly.

Suddenly he ordered them below in a strange, impersonal tone quite unlike his usual voice. For the first time it occurred to Willy that something might be seriously wrong. He looked into his father's face. He was telling John something, but he didn't hear what he was saying as he stared at his expression, seeing the same kind of look in his eyes as he had glimpsed

138

when they were shooting through the channel into Rye harbour.

His father saw him staring and spoke directly to him in that strange voice again. 'Anyone goin' over the side is dead.'

Alarm gripped him.

'Look!' Henrietta called. 'Battleships!'

Following the direction of her arm, he caught a brief glimpse of them, then the yacht rolled and she fell against him, pushing him down on to the coaming; he gripped it tightly with one hand, holding on to her oilskin with the other.

As he went down into the cabin, he looked at his father again; he was taking a turn with one of the lengths of rope around himself. It was another confirmation of their serious situation. He wanted to ask John, when he came down what it was going to be like, and how many storms he had been through in the *Peacock*, but it would suggest he was afraid, and he kept silent. John's presence was reassuring nonetheless; impossible to imagine anything happening to him; whatever he did, games or fighting or tree-climbing, he always came out on top.

Seeing Andy sitting on the settee next to Henry, he sat beside him. Andy would know what they were in for, but he didn't look in the least scared. Henry glanced at him for a moment after taking off her sou'wester as if she didn't see him, then stared out of the ports with a set face; her eyes looked unusually large and dark. He had never seen her like that before; she was afraid. He had not imagined she would be afraid of anything. It was even more alarming in a way than the look in his father's eyes.

He began to hate sitting with nothing to do but listen to the swirl of the seas buffeting the side, and the frames and timbers groaning, tensing himself now one way now the other.

'How much longer will it be?' he asked. There was a false edge to his voice; he wished he hadn't said it, and was thankful that John, standing gazing out of the ports on the other side, didn't seem to hear.

'What?' Andy asked. 'Will what be?'

He was going to say he wished he could go up on deck

139

again and see what was really happening – he might have said it – but all he was aware of was a blast and roar of wind which even inside the cabin came as a physical shock, sucking the air out. The yacht lurched and he found himself hurtling towards John, also dislodged by the suddenness of the movement; he landed on him, hearing Henry scream. The sea was surging along the deck outside which seemed to be below him somehow; he was staring through a port into dark submarine depths; they had been thrown on their side and they must have gone straight down. He felt no fear; it was so quick he couldn't grasp what was happening. Light flickered through the green on the other side of the glass and he felt the cabin moving back towards the upright. The glass cleared; he was slipping away from John. He twisted, and seeing the table leg close, grabbed it with both hands. Henry's hair was hanging down near his face; she seemed to be lying across the table. He tensed and clung as the yacht went over again the same way, but more steadily this time, and he heard urgent noises in the water alongside as though they were being driven forward at express speed.

He started to pull himself up, feeling his head throb with pain; he must have banged it on something.

Andy laughed as he saw his face coming up above the table and Henry who had pulled herself back into a sitting position joined in. He started laughing himself, he didn't know why.

'Stow it!' John called roughly. He had moved aft to the steps, and was leaning half way up, looking out. Willy was amazed to see past him through the hatchway the dinghy poised high above them on a wave streaked with lines of lacy foam; spindrift blew out in sheets horizontally from its crest. He could hear his father shouting, but the noise of wind in the rigging and a sea falling against the foredeck prevented him from catching what was said.

John turned, motioning him to come up beside him. 'I'm going on deck. Stay here and watch out in case you're needed. The mainsail's blown out. I'm going to try and pass a line.' He added, 'So you'll know where I am.'

Willy's heart seemed to stop for a moment. He could hear the canvas now, beating like a great drum somewhere

140

forward. It was his fault. He had not secured it. He ought to be going up there, not John. He pulled his way up the steps, trying to grasp John's oilskin, but the bows rose and he had to clutch at the sides of the hatch instead.

He watched John clamber into the cockpit, keeping low, holding on motionless for several seconds as spray whirled about him. His father was hunched, twisted in his seat to look aft at the next rearing ridge, struggling with the tiller. He was capless, wearing only his reefer jacket and flannels without an oilskin. His hair and beard streamed water, and he shook his head continually as if to clear his vision. Beyond him on the quarter the dinghy careered after them, adding another spray-blown path to the long patterns of white spindrift down the threatening slope of water. They were moving very fast; he felt the hollow sensation inside as he thought of the reason for it; he could hear the canvas drumming and cracking forward. He wondered how much had shaken free, and tried to indicate to John that he wanted to help him, receiving only a decided shake of the head and an indication to stay put.

John crawled by him on his way forward, a rope around his chest, leading back into the cockpit, carrying a tangle of line in his hand. The yacht heeled suddenly as they lifted on the crest. John flattened; he glimpsed his father thrown to the side against the coaming instants before he closed his eyes. Water hit him in the face and chest and sloshed down past him into the cabin. The howl of wind in the rigging reached a crescendo drowning all other noises for a moment, then as the yacht eased upright again he became aware that the sound made by the canvas had changed. The drumming and thumping was accompanied by fast whip-like reports.

He opened his eyes. John was still flattened on deck nearby but he could hardly make out his father for blown water. As it passed he saw him pushing desperately on the tiller. The dinghy was right out on the other quarter now, pointing half away from them, very low in the water. The painter tautened and it swung sluggishly after them. John had started moving again; his legs disappeared from sight. Willy followed his progress by watching his jerking lifeline, concentrating on it with such intensity, willing it to keep leading forward, fearing he would see it tauten suddenly and fly out to the side, he was scarcely aware of the water inside his oilskin, seeping down his neck.

Someone was squeezing up beside him. It was Andy.

'What's happening?' He had to shout.

He told him, wondering if he would have the same awful feeling; for all they knew it might be the part of the sail Andy had lashed that was blowing out. If he had any such feeling, he didn't show it. He had taken off his spectacles; his pupils looked large and misty blue.

'Where's the Pater's oilskin?' he shouted. 'We'd better fetch it.'

Willy wondered why he hadn't thought of that, but the impossibility of his father ever putting it on while wrestling with the tiller and with that rope around his middle occurred to both of them at the same time.

'Better wait till it eases,' Andy said.

Willy found the idea that it would ever ease extraordinarily comforting; it hadn't really occurred to him before. Andy was always level headed; he had an answer for everything and it usually turned out to be right.

Another crest lifted under them and again the yacht went over and the ghoulish shrieking in the shrouds rose discordantly. Andy's weight pressed him against the side of the hatchway. There was not so much spray blowing across this time and he could see his father fighting the tiller, trying to keep the stern from being thrown to one side. He began to sense a pattern in their motion. The dangerous time was while they climbed, exposed to the wind and those vicious, curling crests which might come at them from one side or the other, knocking the stern round. Afterwards, as they sank into the valley between the seas, the yacht seemed more manageable and his father was able to relax slightly – or so it seemed to him.

John's lifeline stopped moving; he had arrived. The cracking noise of the canvas continued though. Willy climbed another step and, twisting, raised his head out of the hatchway as the stern slipped towards another trough and their headlong speed seemed to lessen. The expanse of sail straining out was horrifying. He wondered if John would ever get it under control. Much of it had been torn into strips which were blowing out over the foredeck, but a section near the mast was still intact, ballooning like a small spinnaker. John, one arm around the boom where the sail was still secured, was lying on the open pocket as if on an inflated mattress, stabbing at it with his other hand. Willy saw the flash of metal. There was a crack like a cannon going off and the canvas opened into two halves with John, unbalanced, sliding through, swinging under the boom on his arm. At once the motion of the yacht eased.

John fought to regain his position, then started passing the line he had taken with him through the rent he had made and round under the boom. He paused, clasping the boom to him with both arms as the yacht went over again and spume flew overall. Willy ducked his head quickly inside.

'Does he need help?' Andy shouted.

He shook his head. John would manage; he always did. Someone else trying to cling on in that small space would only be in the way.

Looking aft, he saw something had happened to his father; he was rolling, slumped against the coaming, the tiller swinging from his loose arms. Andy became aware of it at the same time. Turning, Willy saw his startled eyes.

They tried to climb out together, but obstructed one another. Willy held back, deferring by habit to his older brother, then crawled after him, possessed by a sick feeling that when they reached their father they would find him dead. He had rolled on to the floor of the cockpit; the line around his middle stretched up over the coaming to the sheet horse. Willy looked for a sign in Andy's face as he reached him, but had to throw out both arms as the yacht was hurled bodily sideways and over on to its beam. The sea came in, pushing him against the bench, then lifting and tugging him back. He clutched wildly, feeling Andy's legs and holding on.

As the yacht swayed back and the water receded, he found himself half way over the cockpit coaming, gripping his father's legs. Andy was lying over the rest of his father's body, his arms clamped around him.

He slithered down into the cockpit as Andy lifted his head, looking around in a dazed way. Seeing Willy, he seemed to recover himself, looked down for a moment at the form he was lying on, then started working himself along to the point on the sheet horse where the lifeline was made fast. Willy looked at his father. His head was propped at a funny angle against the corner of the cockpit above swirling water, but his eyes were open, gazing at him with a lost expression. The muscles in one cheek moved as if he were trying to say something, but nothing came out; his mouth seemed to be frozen half open.

They had to get him into the cabin. He looked up to see what Andy was doing; evidently he had the same idea, for he had begun to loosen the hitches in the lifeline. He felt the yacht going again and, stretching to seize the rope where it went around his father, yelled a warning to Andy, thankful to see him duck and fling both arms around the main sheet tackle. The sea came in, immersing him; he felt it up his nose and down his neck. His legs were swept away; they brought up hard against the other side of the cockpit and his wrists twisted until they were almost breaking as his father's body also moved, but he held on.

When the yacht righted again, his father's face was half under water surging across the cockpit. He let go of the lifeline and crawled up to his father's shoulders, taking his head in both hands and lifting, trying to push with his legs beneath the great shoulders.

Andy shouted. Looking up, he saw he had unfastened the lifeline. He hurled it towards the cabin, but it fell across the bench.

'Quick!' Andy yelled, 'Take it into the cabin. Make it fast!'

He wanted to stay where he was supporting his father's head above the flood, but there was no time to argue. The yacht would go over again at any moment and the sea come rushing in. He stretched for the line and scrambled back towards the hatchway. Henrietta was there, watching him. Her eyes were wide and her face very white but she looked composed against the torn background of waves. He saw spray rising over the bow and blowing away to starboard.

Reaching her, he thrust the line into her hands and shouted at her to take it down quick, and tie it to the table leg, the only solid thing he could think of at that moment. She took

144

it and backed down the steps without a word. He turned to see if they were about to be rolled over again. To his astonishment he found they had swung broadside on to the sea; there was a ridge with an ominously smooth glistening hollow beneath the foam riding the crest high above them to port. He made a lunge for the hatchway and scrambled in as it hit them. The crash of water and the sensation of being hurled over and carried along by giant forces shut out every thought, but somewhere at the back of his mind he retained an image of Henrietta with the line in her hand and the table leg a long way away from her. She could not possibly have reached it in time even to take a single turn.

He had a sick feeling as the yacht started to right itself again and rushing sounds of water all about him began to abate, that the rope must have gone and with it his father and Andy, lost for ever in the meaningless scend and reach of these seas. Miraculously, he saw the rope was still there, taut across the steps leading out to starboard. He climbed out; it was leading forward, and he saw them both, Andy and his father, clasped together half way along the deck towards the bow. He couldn't think how they had got there. He saw John leaning down from the coach-roof, stretching his arm towards Andy, who had raised his head.

None of them, not George or Andy, Willy or Henrietta, could have described afterwards how they hauled their father aft along the narrow deck beside the cabin ports, eased him round and down the steps into the cabin and somehow lifted him on to the settee while the yacht rose and lurched like a cork broadside on to the seas, nor could they have said how long it took. But they did it. Their father said nothing; he gazed at one or other of them in intervals between the seas coming over, and when at last they got him on to the settee he tried to speak, but could not get his lips around the words; there was a strange lopsidedness to his mouth; a look of despair entered his eyes when he found he couldn't make them understand.

'Row –' he seemed to be saying, 'Row – row –'

Much later they learned he was probably trying to tell them to stream the drogue.

Even if they had understood, it is doubtful if they could

145

have managed it. They were utterly done up. They fell asleep as they were, wedged, crouching into corners while water slopped from side to side and outside the wind howled.

When they woke the yacht was still rolling, but not so wildly. Extraordinarily, there was a man crouching in the cabin hatchway, peering down at them. He had a grizzled head and a full beard and, marvellous to see, the grey hairs were edged with sunlight and blue sky beyond. Then Willy had a sudden thought he might be a pirate, and felt a rush of fear through his whole body.

His expression seemed more puzzled than fierce though as he gazed at the bunk over the side of which their father's arm swung loosely. 'You all right then?' He gazed round.

John was scrambling up from where he had wedged himself between the stove and the other bunk. 'My father's ill.'

The man started down the steps into the cabin and, crossing to the table to steady himself, leaned over to peer into their father's face.

'Row –' came up in that strange, strangled voice Willy remembered from yesterday.

The man scratched the side of his beard. 'You be halfway to France here, sir –' There was a comforting burr to his voice. Willy began to like him.

'He needs a doctor,' John said, and as the man turned towards him, 'The main's gone. In shreds. We need a tow.'

Henrietta bobbed up beside him. 'You must give us a tow back, *please*! Father will pay. We must get him to a doctor –'

'Father will pay,' George repeated earnestly.

The man straightened, holding the coach-roof beam by his head and Willy, also standing now, saw his father's eyes following the stranger's with helpless intensity. It was terrible to see him so helpless. His whole face seemed twisted, and only one side of his mouth seemed really to move as he tried to frame words that would not come out.

The man looked down at him again. 'That'll be salvage then, sir –'

'Can't you see he can't talk,' Henrietta interrupted, 'he needs a doctor.'

The man twisted to look at her, and suddenly his teeth showed in a grin. He put a hand up to grip her shoulder. 'You rest easy now, Miss. We'll have you in Plymouth afore sundown, that we will, aye, if the wind do hold.'

8

Willy seldom noticed what anyone wore, sometimes not even what they looked like; he had general impressions of people he met, their height or stoutness or the darkness or lightness of their clothes or the high pitch of a female voice, but often, if asked, he would have been unable to supply any more precise details. He was the reverse of Henrietta in this respect; after a visitor left the house she would nearly always comment, very often disparagingly, on their clothes or the way they were worn, or the colour of their hair, or their jewellery or the length of their fingernails. Her observations amazed him with their detail. Once she told him she was sure Mama's solicitor had something wrong with his behind; she had counted him scratch it four times while admiring the plants in the conservatory. On the other hand Henrietta could not understand Willy's absorption in things like the number of spots on a variant butterfly. She could not understand how it could possibly matter. Butterflies were pretty or not so pretty. She didn't really want to know their names even, although she pretended interest when they were sharing their deepest thoughts, and she knew all the common ones well enough from their walks together.

Willy's lack of general interest in the human species had few exceptions, but one was their father's younger brother, Uncle Richard. They seldom saw him. He was always travelling in Africa or Arabia or the Mediterranean, or on a cricket tour with the I Zingari, then suddenly without warning, he would be in the hall telling a cabbie to be 'awfully careful with that box, my man.' They would know that inside the box were presents, not the ordinary sorts of presents, but things like a Masai spearhead or a locket containing the hair of a real Persian princess, lumps of brain coral, shells of all shapes and convolutions, phials of sand from the Holy Land, illuminated Persian texts, a musical instrument made from rough, hollowed wood, crudely painted African fetish masks. Once he had brought their father a pair of carved ebony figures which their mother had whisked away before they had been able to see them properly. He had laughed hugely at their protests and especially at their mother's refusal either to bring them out or explain. She had points of colour in her cheeks when he teased her, she often did have when he came, and an unusual brightness in her eyes.

Discussing the figures afterwards when they were alone, Henrietta had said they were men without clothes; she had seen one of their tail things in front, 'like yours but bigger –'

'Bigger!' George snorted sceptically, and Andy laughed in an embarrassed way. 'You didn't see anything,' George went on. 'There wasn't time.'

'I did see, and it was bigger than yours, George Steel.'

George had become extraordinarily angry then, saying she was such a liar no one could believe anything she said; in any case she hadn't seen him in the bath for years now. Willy had hoped she wouldn't turn on him for a comparison; she had seen his quite recently. Fortunately the argument with George about her lying became so frenzied that the cause of the quarrel was forgotten.

On this occasion Uncle Richard had not brought the usual box of presents. He had not been expecting to come; it was only the news of their father's stroke and the near disaster in the *Peacock* that occasioned the visit. In any case he had just returned from Germany and had been rather fortunate, he told them, to bring his own skin back in one piece – indeed he hadn't quite. He had pulled the point of his moustache down to show them a livid scar on his cheek, only recently healed.

Willy gazed at what he could see of the scar; he had purposely placed himself on Uncle Richard's left at tea so that he would be able to look at it. They had not been told

149

how he had acquired it. 'Spot of bother with the natives!' he had said with a fractional lowering of one eyelid.

Willy knew there were no natives in Germany; Germans were much like the English people according to his father; the chief difference was that they were ruled by a Kaiser who was half mad. But while they had no savage tribes or cannibals, they did have a place called the Black Forest; the name exerted a sinister hold on Willy's imagination, and he was sure that whatever had happened to Uncle Richard must have happened there. But what –?

The girls were showing off as usual. Babs was sitting on his lap and now Henry had started tickling her; she could be very, very stupid. The grass was hard under him; he shifted his position, drawing his knees up and clasping his arms under them. When he grew up he would have lavender flannels to play tennis in like Uncle Richard, and a full, dark red tie and a floppy sunhat with I Zingari colours on the band; the trouble was his cricket probably wasn't good enough, and if he was at sea he probably wouldn't be able to play anyway. He would have some club colours on the band, and he would have a lavender coloured handkerchief matching his trousers just flowing out of the left cuff of his shirt. He would grow a straight moustache and wax the ends. The moustache gave a fierceness to Uncle Richard's face, the lower half anyway. If you took the upper half alone with those curving, bleached flaxen eyebrows and the smiling blue eyes you might think he was a good sport who liked bringing back curious presents. Then you looked at the long, clean-shaven jaw, lines sharply etched in it, and the firm mouth and the bleached moustache with pointed ends and you realized why he so often seemed to be 'in a spot of bother' on behalf of the government.

Mama rose from the tea table, gazing round at them all. She looked unusually nice; her eyes had a sparkle in them and she had a sort of playful air like the girls which she never usually had. Her long white tennis clothes set off her dark hair. He felt proud of her.

'Now, who's going on next?' she asked.

Henrietta started pulling Uncle Richard's arm, shouting she bags be his partner. Sometimes Willy hated her for her pure selfishness; she had already partnered him twice.

'No,' his mother said firmly, 'Uncle Richard wants some peace. You've been doing nothing but badger him all tea. You can be *my* partner, Henry. We shall take on the boys.' She looked round, 'George! Andy!'

George and Andy jumped up, scenting an easy win. They had suffered nothing but defeats at Uncle Richard's hands; he gave no quarter when playing them, although George had got the hang of his Yankee service now and caused him some problems with hard, low drives.

'And Babs,' his mother called, 'you can leave Uncle Richard alone and come and fetch the balls for us.'

Babs looked around, obviously thinking how to escape this chore. She was the limit; she wanted everything her own way and as the youngest usually got it. He saw her gazing at him speculatively with her dark eyes, and stared back hard. She turned away and went jumping and skipping to his father, sitting in a basket chair at the other side of the tea table, his poor father. He had a rug over his legs although it was warm. By comparison with Uncle Richard, he looked so unwell, blotched and greying. He had recovered his speech now, but couldn't use his right leg yet. The worst thing was having to sell the *Peacock*. Mama had forbidden him ever to sail again, or said the doctor had said so, even if he did recover the use of his leg.

Babs bounced up to him; he smiled and held out his arm to hug her. He always had given in to the girls.

'*Babs!*' his mother called sharply from the court. 'Leave your father alone!'

But he had his arm around her, and she pretended she couldn't get away.

'Now then, Willy!'

He looked up, startled. Uncle Richard was standing, gazing down with his humorous eyes. Unfolding his legs, Willy scrambled up, feeling blood rushing to his face. He had never been on his own to talk to Uncle Richard. George always had most to say to him, and Andy usually showed off his knowledge; more often Henry monopolized his attention. He liked teasing her, and she liked pretending to him she was gullible and asking him questions with wide eyes –

'You're followin' George to sea, I hear.'

151

'If I get through, Uncle Richard. The exams.' He feared the interview more, but didn't like to say so.

'*If!*' Uncle Richard exclaimed, putting a hand on his shoulder. 'Come on, let's go and see if we can find some butterflies. What can you show me?'

'There are no end of peacocks. We might see a painted lady.'

'Take me to her!' The blue eyes had laughter crinkles from the corners.

They started walking.

'You must never say "if", Willy.'

He looked up.

'If you wish to do a thing, you must do it. D'you wish to go to sea?'

'You can bet I do!'

'Then that settles it!'

Willy felt his hand on his shoulder, strong fingers squeezing. They entered the orchard and picked their way around the low branches, laden with apples.

'Uncle Richard –?'

'Yes.'

'When you were in Germany – did you have to go to the Black Forest?'

'The Black Forest! Lord, no! No I was a goodish way from the Black Forest, Willy. Why d'you ask?'

'I thought – well, I thought –'

Willy stopped as his uncle turned to pick an apple. They started walking again, Uncle Richard tossing the apple from hand to hand, imparting a terrific spin, Willy noticed, with his fingers. Then he said abruptly, 'Not every day a fellow has to thank someone for savin' his brother's life.'

Willy looked at him, wondering what he meant.

His eyes were serious for a change. 'Specially when it happens to be a nephew he's known – off and on – since he was the veriest little nipper.'

'It wasn't me, Uncle Richard. It was Henry.'

'Henry?'

'I told Henry to take the line to the table leg, but she knew there wouldn't be time so she put it round the step at the bottom and held on – right through the roll when we went right over she held on to it. Henry saved them, Uncle Richard. Otherwise they would have been swept into the sea – they *were* swept into the sea, but –' he stopped. Uncle Richard had heard all that.

'That shows remarkable presence of mind, if she did that, Willy. She's a remarkable gal, your sister, d'you know?'

'Oh, yes, I know,' he nodded.

The apple fizzed back and forth. 'Your father told me how you saved him from drownin', Willy. He'd about given himself up for lost, d'you know? In an agony because he couldn't do anything for you children. He was certain you'd all be followin' him to Davy Jones's locker, he said – he couldn't bear the thought of *that*. Then he saw you makin' for him with your eyes fixed on his like a mongoose goin' for a snake and no thought for your own safety.' He looked down at him.

Willy was surprised to hear what he'd done described like that; he knew about mongooses from books, but he'd never seen one.

'You did the right thing, Willy. I've known full-grown men I'd have trusted whatever happened lose their heads when it came to it. You don't know a man till you've been through a scrape with him. It's not how 'e shapes up beforehand – what 'e *tells* you he'll do – it's what 'e *does* that counts – whether he can stick it out. You don't find that out in a London drawin'-room, Willy. You don't find it out about yourself either. It's the first question a man asks of himself, d'you know that? Don't think I didn't ask myself when I was a youngish fellow. You're fortunate. You'll not need to ask yourself again. Although I dare say you will.'

Willy didn't fully understand what he was talking about; he wished he would stop. His sense of failure was sharp and vivid. Sooner or later, he was sure, Uncle Richard must hear about what had happened to the mainsail; then he'd wonder why he hadn't owned up at once instead of allowing him to carry on telling him what a good fellow he was. He thought of his poor father's slurred and indistinct speech since the stroke; that was his fault too; his father would not have had to fight the tiller like that if the sail hadn't blown out and set them on that scorching course downwind; he wouldn't have overstrained himself. It had been George who had really

153

saved them by cutting away the ballooning pocket of canvas with his knife and managing to secure the rest of it – and Andy who had the idea of passing his father's lifeline back to the cabin – and Henry who had taken a turn and held on.

He looked up. His uncle was examining him, curving brows raised as if wondering if he'd taken in what he'd been saying.

'Uncle Richard – did you have someone with you in your scrape in Germany?'

His uncle regarded him for a moment longer, then burst into laughter, clapping a hand on his shoulder as they walked. 'So that's what's on y'r mind! The Black Forest! I'll be bound!' He spun the apple up, catching it with a smack in his left hand. 'This is what we'll do, Willy, we'll make a compact. You shall find me a painted lady – and if you do I shall tell you about my scrape – is that fair?'

Willy nodded doubtfully. 'I think we *might* find one. They come out again about now.'

'After their tea and scones?'

He smiled, holding out his hand for a more cautious approach for they had come through the orchard and reached the gravel path between the side of the house and the lawns and flower beds, and he could see the buddleia he was making for stuck all over with peacocks and some red admirals he thought.

'There, Willy!' His uncle pointed to a bed of gloriosa daisies in a bar of sunlight to his right; two butterflies were spiralling up and down above as if chasing each other.

Willy shook his head. 'Tortoiseshells, Uncle Richard.' He led off the path across the lawn past the wooden seat towards the buddleia, every sense alert, wishing he'd said something more common than a painted lady; he had only *hoped* they might see one. It would be exciting for Uncle Richard if they did.

Approaching the bush, they stalked in a cautious circle as the peacocks fluttered and settled like dark leaves on the lilac-coloured panicles of flowers.

'This is capital sport, Willy!'

'It is when you see something rare, Uncle Richard.'

'Is a stonechat rare?'

154

Willy followed the direction of his gaze up to the top of the blackthorn, where the bird was perched, twisting its neck to watch their approach, raising its head and uttering its clicking warning call. 'No, she lives here.'

'She!' Uncle Richard looked at him with curving brows, then up again to the bird, but it had flown. 'Does she have a husband?'

'Yes, I can show you their nest.'

'I'm not sure she'd like that, Willy. I'll tell you what we'll do. I don't believe in chance, do you? I believe it's meant – all the queer things that happen to us.'

'I'm not sure,' Willy replied. He'd had odd thoughts like that, but never felt he had the knowledge to tell whether it was so or not.

'Nor am I, Willy, but I have a hunch, that's all. I'm going to play my hunch now. I believe that little bird was sent to us – our *painted lady*.'

Willy looked at him. That was cheating.

Seeing his doubts, his uncle took him by the elbow and guided him round until they were heading back towards the seat on the lawn. 'You have to allow I proposed the compact, Willy. I fancy that gives me the privilege of interpretin' the rules – that's fair now?'

Willy smiled, disappointed still that he had not succeeded in finding a real painted lady for him, but flattered by the way he was talking to him, man to man.

'You must agree, she couldn't 've bin a more prettily painted little lady, Willy!'

He laughed.

They sat on the bench, the late afternoon sun pleasantly warm on their faces, a hovering insect buzzing above their heads like a wasp, and from what seemed a long distance off the sound of voices on the tennis lawn, Henry shrieking as she missed a shot.

'We're very fortunate in England,' Uncle Richard said. His eyes were deep-shadowed from the brim of his floppy hat. Above, the gold in the I Z band gleamed like a ribbon of burnished metal. 'You must never forget that, Willy, for I fancy we shall have to fight for it – you and I and George and Andy and Harry.' He was gazing into the distant sky

155

over the elms, fine puckers fanning from the corners of his eyes. 'Sooner than most people imagine.'

Willy stared at him, images forming from line drawings in his history book of battles in the English Civil War – transposed now to Hampstead Heath, and Uncle Richard with helmet and raised sword turning in his saddle, beckoning them on.

Uncle Richard looked at him. 'Germany's a queer place, Willy – deuced queer. A bit like the desert. There are queer rules you need to learn. Once you've learned 'em, you can turn 'em to your advantage. It's run by soldiers and officials, y'see, stationmasters and postmasters and all manner of fellows in uniform. They're whales for uniform, Willy. You're no one over there if you can't dress up in a peaked cap or a helmet and long cape and polished boots. And they live by the book. If you play it by the book you can't go far wrong. Now, Willy, what I'm about to tell you – you won't repeat –?'

'No, Uncle Richard,' Willy came in quickly, 'I promise I won't repeat it.'

Uncle Richard smiled. 'Good man! I know you won't.'

9

Robert Steel had seen the inside of a good many clubs, but not Addison's. He made it a point to despise 'literary' people, and the few he had met in Alice's drawing-room had not caused him to alter his opinion. He wondered why the Judge chose to lend the authority of his presence to such a coterie, and even more to the point, what the devil he wished to discuss with him – probably something to do with Henrietta since she was so thick with his own girl. But what? He felt a pleasing tingle of importance, all the more pleasurable for being so rare these days.

'The Honourable Justice Edgehill, sir? The Judge is expecting you –' The porter came out of his cubicle to indicate the way to the smoking room. 'You will find him there, sir.'

The room was almost deserted and he spotted the Judge immediately. He was slumped in an armchair as if consciously throwing off the dignity he needed to summon in the court-room, his legs stretched towards a blazing fire, his eyes under the intellectual forehead apparently fixed on a bronze lion couchant atop a clock on the mantelpiece.

'Ah! Steel!' He stood in welcome. 'So glad you could make it.' He looked as if he meant it. He stepped a pace towards the wall and pressed the bell. 'What will you have?'

'Gin and bitters thank 'ee Judge.'

'Splendid!' The Judge indicated a chair close by his own and waved him into it. 'I've already ordered. You're not a vegetarian by any chance?'

'Good Lord!' Robert Steel laughed, easing himself down into the chair with the aid of his stick. 'I fancy I've gorn hungry sufficiently often at sea - no wish to risk it as a permanent condition!'

'Quite so!' A humorous light in the Judge's grey eyes showed he appreciated the remark, and lowering his voice, 'There are several vegetarians here you know – not to mention faddists of other sorts,' he gave a meaning look.

Robert Steel raised his brows, wondering what on earth he meant – surely not faddists of a compromising sort – not the Judge, surely. 'The literati!' he said.

'Exactly so. And there's a very good reason for it you know.' He looked up as the waiter appeared and, ordering the gin and bitters, told him to let the butler know they would be in in ten minutes. He turned back to Robert Steel, evidently casting around in his mind for the subject they had been discussing. Unable to summon it immediately, he turned to common ground.

'Remarkably fine looking girl, that one of yours.'

Robert Steel tried to hide the pleasure he felt. Henrietta had indeed blossomed recently, although he had detected on occasions a certain lack of the warmth she had always shown him before – even downright contrariness at times. Yet she had never been an easy girl, and it was only to be expected now she was undergoing a physical metamorphosis – or so Alice had said.

'You won't have any trouble getting her off your hands,' the Judge went on. 'Mary's a different kettle of fish, I fear –'

'No – no,' Robert Steel cut in gallantly.

'Oh yes.' The Judge's steady grey eyes cut through his protests. 'Oh yes – but fortunately she's not unprovided for. And if young men are the same as they used to be –! I dare say they are! What!'

Robert Steel took the glass from the tray the waiter was proffering, wondering for a moment if the Judge was about to propose an oriental marriage contract; he dismissed the thought: George was younger than Mary, and whatever else was going to the four winds these days, it was still accepted that the girl must be younger. The Judge would certainly hold to that.

The Judge went on, 'But how is your eldest boy doing?

What a very fine life he's chosen.' His brows drew down and he leaned closer. 'Tell me, what d'you make of Fisher?'

He thought about the answer. The Judge, from all he knew of him, was a Liberal; he might well be sympathetic to the First Sea Lord's beastly so-called reforms of the Service. 'I know a good many who fancy he's goin' too fast – a deuce too fast,' he added more warmly.

The Judge eyed him. 'That's the view at the Senior is it?'

'Some of the younger fellows may go along with it all for all I know – you know what they are – young Turks! If it's good enough for their fathers – let's change it all!'

The Judge nodded slowly. 'I gather you don't approve.'

Robert Steel took a deep draught of his gin and glowing pleasantly, for he had fortified himself at the Senior beforehand, decided to be frank – after all the Judge might well have some influence in the Liberal party – might even have political ambitions himself, he thought suddenly, and wondered if he had been invited here to provide ammunition for a foray into politics.

'It's madness,' he said. 'Take the common entry scheme. They've scrapped the old *Britannia*. What was wrong with the *Britannia* training! It served George well enough – made a sailor out of him – a damned scientific sailor, hang it! You'd never credit half of what they stuffed into that poor boy's brains. I'm glad to say it wasn't like that in my day. And he was never hungry –'

'Apropos of which –?' the Judge suggested, placing his hands on the arms of his chair and leaning forward.

Robert Steel drained the remainder of his drink, and they rose and started out.

'Where is the lad now?' the Judge asked.

'In the Medy.'

'You don't say so.'

'First rate sport. Capital!'

'Ah yes.'

'We gave him a Winchester for a leavin' present – from the old *Britannia* – he made senior cadet captain you know –' he tried to look modest.

'Did he, by George!'

'Not that that cuts any ice in the gunroom of a first rate!'

159

The butler greeted the Judge inside the doors of the dining-room and showed them to a window seat. Spatters of fine rain were being blown against the panes from the night outside. They sat and unfolded their napkins.

'I think you will enjoy our chef here – something of an artist in his way.' The Judge turned to inspect a bottle proffered by the wine waiter, and nodded. 'I'm pleased to hear about your boy. You must be proud of him. He'll go far I've no doubt.'

Robert Steel was certain George would go far – barring accidents that could happen to anyone. He had the qualities to make the top – so he had been informed by an 'old ship' who had it from the former captain of the *Britannia* himself. Certainly his reports made good reading, not that he would have dreamed of mentioning any of this. His expression said much of it. His pride in George and his high hopes for him were almost the only things that lent savour to his life these days – that and Henrietta when she was in one of her increasingly rare sweet moods.

'It's the girls I'd like to speak with you about,' the Judge went on.

So this was it! He smiled. 'A difficult age – Alice is always sayin' so at all events. I'm inclined to believe they're no sooner out of one difficult age than into the next!'

The Judge nodded vigorously. 'You know why I specialized in commercial law, Steel, I'll tell you. I made up my mind – from the beginning – steer clear of the better half. In professional matters you understand! *Ex natura rerum.* Do you read Pope?' His voice took on a different timbre as if delivering sentence. ' "Good as well as ill – woman's at best a contradiction still." Tell me,' he stared intently at him, 'd' you understand this suffragette nonsense?'

The waiter placed bowls of steaming consommé before them.

'Does anyone?' Robert Steel said, more interested in the savoury odours rising around his nostrils.

The Judge waited until the waiter had moved out of earshot, then leaned across the table. 'I'll tell you why I ask. My wife is one.'

Robert Steel gazed at him. '*Naomi!*'

160

The Judge nodded. 'It's a bad business. None of my colleagues know naturally –'

'You can rely on me.'

'Oh – absolutely – no question – no – the reason I tell you, you see, she's infected Mary. And Mary – perhaps you know already –?'

'Henrietta?'

'Have you had no indications?'

Several remarks Henrietta had made recently fitted suddenly into place. 'I'll be damned! I had no idea!' He thought of his wife. 'And Alice –?'

'Oh, no – no, no – Alice is much too – sensible. She has her feet on the ground, I don't need to tell *you* that. No, there's no danger in that quarter. But you see, I'm in a deuced awkward spot – with the two of them you see.' He swallowed a mouthful of soup. 'Looked at scientifically, there are two things we need to do.' He motioned with his spoon. 'First – isolate them – second – give 'em something to occupy themselves with.' His brows rose in interrogation.

Robert Steel thought how close and indeed inseparable Henrietta and Mary seemed, and how Henrietta's moods varied alarmingly, and wondered what the results might be if they were parted. Henrietta was capable of anything –

The Judge read the doubt in his eyes, and went on determinedly. 'What I have in mind is this. Mary was asking her mother – this must have been two years ago – whether she and Henry could come out together. Well now, if we can agree to it – you and I –' the Judge fixed him with his grey eyes so amazingly like Mary's, 'we could broach the idea – in the right quarters – it's not much more than two years now when you think about it. My guess is it would meet with thorough approbation.'

Robert Steel tried to gauge how Alice would take the suggestion. Her ambitions for Henry were high; how would she rate a joint launch with a judge who had neither the lineage, so far as he had ever heard, certainly no title, nor even a name known to the public, against for example one of his own noble relatives as Henry's sponsor. He tried to think of a Steel who might be suitable and willing, but could only conjure up depressingly plain faces and matronly figures from the Midlands. On the once illustrious Saxmundham side the position was no better; they had sunk into East Anglian obscurity. On the other hand the Judge was undoubtedly wealthy; his house in Admiral's Walk was more imposing than Felpham House, with splendid grounds; he was on familiar terms – so it appeared from his conversation – with the nabobs of the literary and artistic world – and while this was not the milieu Alice would want for Henry, there was no doubt society figures were drawn to it. Furthermore, in Naomi he had a lively, charming young hostess who was something of a draw in her own right – so long, of course, as her apparently feminist views were not by that time public property.

He saw the Judge gazing at him quizzically, and nodded. 'Yes, I fancy Alice would take to that –'

The more he thought about it, the more certain he became. Naomi Edgehill was seen at the right places. He remembered a photograph of her in *The Tatler* with the Earl of Selborne quite recently – where had it been? It reminded him of Fisher again and his beastly schemes – Willy would be going to Osborne instead of the old *Britannia*. It was well known the King had always hated Osborne as a house; why should they make it into a naval college for hundreds of other boys to hate, *and* try and make gentlemen into engineers. Poor Willy might come out of the place an engineer by all accounts –

'Something wrong?' The Judge was nodding at his soup.

'No, no – Naomi will be splendid. I know it.'

The Judge's brows rose and he gazed at him for a moment, then reached down for his napkin to wipe his lips. 'The essence of the scheme is, one –' he held up a finger over the top of the napkin, 'separation, and two –' suiting it with a second finger, 'influence. As to the separation, Mary will be leaving the convent at the end of this term – Naomi went to Paris you know – at all events I'll make certain she's placed sufficiently far away she has to board –'

The waiter took their empty bowls and substituted plates of pâté.

'You'll enjoy this. It's his own recipe you know.' The Judge indicated their glasses – Robert Steel's was empty – and the waiter filled them.

They broke the thin toast that appeared with the pâté and crunched in more or less silent satisfaction, interspersed with nods at one another and little grunts of approval.

'By Jove!' Robert Steel exclaimed at last, 'We've nothin' like this at the Senior.'

The Judge's eyes warmed. 'These literary fellows – they're not all vegetarians! Now – as to influence –'

'One thing that's occurred to me,' Robert Steel put in. 'Henry'll be goin' off at the same time –'

'Of course,' the Judge nodded.

'Is it your plan they should go different ways?'

'Heavens, no! No – just so long as Mary and her mother are separated. No, I've a high opinion of Henry – a very high opinion. That's why it's all so damnable –' he shook his head. 'Naomi's doing of course. Once she's fixed herself on something it's the devil's own job to shake her.' He spread a slice of pâté and gazed at it for a moment. 'Now – as to influence, I rely on Alice. She and Naomi are bound to come together much more once it's decided – you know what a meal they make of this sort of thing –'

Robert Steel agreed.

'Alice must convince Naomi,' the Judge went on, 'no young feller in his right mind would want to saddle himself with a feminist – as I understand they call themselves, why, when they're trying to ape *men* I cannot for the life of me understand, can you?'

'It's puzzlin'. But they are –' He felt the pangs of self pity as he thought that Alice scarcely needed the vote or feminism: she and her father had done for him without either. If only the Judge knew what Alice was like –

The Judge, reaching into his inside pocket, drew out his wallet and took a folded sheet of paper from it.

'Do you read Pope? You should. A constant solace – especially in my present troubles with Naomi. He hit women off perfectly you know. They talk of the new woman. Read his essay on the characters of women. You'll find her there – in all her strange variety! Her who laughs at hell – but – like her Grace – cries "Ah! How charming if there's no such place!" ' He smiled grimly. 'All she asks is liberty – the freedom to live her own life in her own way – but look closer,

163

Steel, look closer!' The grey eyes were like augers. 'What that woman really wants – if life does not give her *everything* she asks – is death. Death!'

Robert Steel felt suddenly out of his depth, and was thankful to see the Judge passing across the sheet he had taken from his wallet; it relieved him of the need to reply. He took it; there were four lines of verse, written in a small, disciplined hand.

> She who ne'er answers till a husband cools,
> Or if she rules him, never shows she rules;
> Charms by accepting, by submitting sways,
> Yet has her humour most when she obeys.

He looked up to find the Judge's eyes on him intently.

'Was it ever better put, Steel? Or if she rules him, never shows she rules. They are so much *better* at being women – they really do it very well, don't you agree? They rule us already. Why in heaven's name d'you suppose they want to become *men*!' His expression was anguished.

Handing back the sheet of paper, Robert Steel wondered if there was more than just feminism behind the Judge's difficulties with Naomi.

The Judge waved the paper away. 'No, no – that's for you.' His lips twitched in a stiff smile. 'Your brief, you might say! If Alice can only convince Naomi of the folly of her present course –' He fell silent, looking down and fondling the stem of his glass.

Robert Steel took up his, emptying it and glad to see as he put it down that the waiter was approaching with two silver-covered dishes.

The aroma was delicious as the covers were lifted. 'I think you'll enjoy this,' the Judge said. 'Bécasse. The chef has them expressed from the Mediterranean.'

'The Medy!' Robert Steel felt on safe ground again. 'I remember in Platea, we once bagged seventy couple in a day.' He picked up his knife and fork. Edgehill might be a deuce literary, but there were evidently other good reasons for his membership of Addison's.

10

Henrietta was not sorry to be leaving the convent. Only one of the sisters had ever meant anything to her, and she had left her behind in the second form. Her present form mistress she loathed as the embodiment of all the narrowing rules and observances that inhabited the bare corridors and large, plain rooms of the school. Since Mary was also going there would be nothing left for her in any case – except Father Geoffrey. She would miss him.

On the last Thursday she and Mary stayed behind after his class to say goodbye.

'So you're both going,' he said, smiling, but with a wistful look she thought. 'Surely St Mary's will never be the same!'

They laughed.

'I fear it's true. You two have brightened up my Thursdays.'

'You brightened up ours,' Henrietta said, and Mary nodded.

'You must not let it all go now that you are to be "improved" into young ladies –' he looked from one to the other with the hint of a smile on his lips, 'I hope they do not altogether succeed –' and as they giggled, 'Virgil is not inappropriate to some of these establishments I believe.' He raised a brow. '*Facilis descensus Averno*! But you don't need me to preach to you.' He put out his hand.

The gesture had a dreadful air of finality – or perhaps it was the look in his eyes.

'D'you remember,' Henrietta said quickly, 'you told us – if we wanted to help you in the East End – when we finished –'

165

He regarded her gravely. 'You are both going on to other schools –'

'But we'd like to come just once or twice so we can see – if we do want to – when we leave school –' She turned to Mary who was gazing steadily at her.

'Yes, we would,' she agreed.

Henrietta had the impression he was pleased although his expression scarcely changed. 'You can always ask for me at Plaistow – St Philip's Church or the community house there.'

'Plaistow,' Henrietta repeated.

He nodded, an amused light returning to his eyes.

She smiled back. 'We'll come and see ŷou.' She felt suddenly enormously happy.

Mary asked how they could get to Plaistow, and he told them two ways.

'*Deus vobiscum*!' He placed his hand on their heads in turn, Henrietta thinking she felt his touch rather longer than she might have expected, experienced a thrill right through her and hoped she was not colouring.

Looking back on it from much later, she marvelled at her forwardness then. Evidently much smitten by his ascetic masculinity and grave, gentle brown eyes, she could not have recognized her feelings for what they were, or how could she have thrust herself at him like that? As for him, how must he have felt at her importuning? He liked her, she had known that, but not entirely for her conscientious preparations of Ovid surely!

'I wonder what he thinks of votes for women?' Mary said on the way home.

'I'm sure he's never thought about it,' she replied, unaccountably irritated by the idea. 'You don't need a vote to enter the Kingdom of Heaven!'

Mary looked at her rather quickly. 'No – but where he works he must see so many – fallen women –' she paused at the thought.

'Fallen women' formed the subject of several of their intimate talks. They knew in a general, horrified way that these lost souls sold their favours to men, but exactly how and in what circumstances and why men should actually want them were topics of puzzled speculation. Mary was sure of

166

one thing – from her mother – the reason they 'fell' was financial; they could not earn enough in honest employment.

'Perhaps we could ask him to one of your mother's meetings,' Henrietta said, suddenly hopeful. Mrs Edgehill was always saying how necessary it was to educate working women to the cause; Father Geoffrey was in just the place to do so.

Mary was gazing at her with that steady, grey look. 'You said he was more interested in the Kingdom of Heaven.'

'Yes – he'll want to stop them falling into sin.' There was a contradiction somewhere, she thought, but didn't bother to analyse it.

'That's what I said.'

'You said he'd want votes for women.'

'So he should.'

Henrietta gave her a withering look. 'We shall have to convince him. He is a man –'

'Lots of men come to mother's meetings – sometimes –'

The argument continued stupidly, and they parted in bad humour.

Arriving home, Henrietta ran up the stairs, to be confronted at the top by Babs asking why she was late. She ignored her, but was pestered all the way to her room. Pushing her away roughly, she shut the door. She wanted to be alone. She threw her satchel down on the floor and sat on the bed.

She had not realized before how much she had looked forward to Thursdays and the preparation beforehand so that she would win Father Geoffrey's approval; it was only now they were over she realized how empty it was going to be without them. She would miss them terribly.

Henrietta had seen such streets from trains. Travelling south to Grandpapa's from Victoria, she had gazed out on the backs of narrow houses joined to one another without a break, row after row of them, and had wondered how people lived such cramped lives with only dirty bricks to look out on, and the smallest patches of grass at the back for gardens; no one was ever in the gardens; they seemed to be for hanging

167

washing. The rooms behind the windows were always dark. She had imagined white-faced people who never saw the sun or heard birds in the trees, and always felt enormously thankful for her own very different life.

These houses in Plaistow were much the same; seeing them from the front, they were not quite so uninviting though; the doors behind the narrow arch of their porches and window surrounds were painted brown mostly, and the stone steps scrubbed clean. It was impossible to see inside the windows because of the lace curtains, but sometimes when the woman of a house was talking to her next-door neighbour the front door was open and she caught a glimpse of a dark-painted passageway. Conversations usually stopped as she and Mary approached, eyes following them curiously; afterwards they heard the talk starting again, no doubt discussing the two of them and what they were doing there.

She felt an intruder in a community where all knew each other and recognized her immediately as a stranger from a different world. Men at street corners in shapeless dark suits and wide caps, often smelling disgustingly of drink, gave them bold, disrespectful stares and as they were going by passed comments and laughed. Sometimes they spat; she thought when she first saw this that it was a comment on their presence, and blushed scarlet, but she soon realized it was habitual. She felt trepidation as they approached another group and breathless anger that anyone should dare to look at her as these men did – but also a rather startling awareness of herself, the tightness of her dress across her breast, the swing of her hair beneath her straw hat. Turning to Mary to make a deliberately casual remark, she felt their eyes all over her.

They passed the public house from which the men must have come, a strong smell of drink from its darkened interior overpowering the otherwise ever-present biscuity sort of smell in the air, and she wondered how Father Geoffrey could possibly work in such a place; thinking of his beautiful voice and grave, brown eyes she could not imagine what possible use all his knowledge could be here. She had thought before she had never met such a saintly man; now she knew it.

168

By extraordinary coincidence they met him in the street. The community house had been pointed out by a girl they had asked in a baker's shop; it stood, slightly taller and wider than the adjoining houses, for it had three storeys and three square windows on each storey, at the opposite side of a square of rough-bordered grass, on which a piece of paper was blowing in the wind. They had just started towards it when they heard the sound of children in a road leading off to their right, and looking that way saw a figure approaching in the Franciscan's brown habit surrounded by small boys and girls who clung on his hands and clutched at his skirts, jostling for attention. Although they were coming to see Father Geoffrey, it took Henrietta a moment to realize it was him; he looked different in these unfamiliar surroundings, and she felt her insides sink as she wondered if he would welcome them. He looked so at home; she felt alien. She began to think that perhaps he hadn't really wanted them to come, but had only agreed because they had asked so persistently. They should have warned him in any case; Mary had said they ought to write first.

'How d'you know he'll *be* there if we don't?' she had asked.

'It doesn't matter if he isn't. We'll have shown him we are really interested – we can write afterwards and arrange to come another time –'

Why she had been so adamant they shouldn't warn him, she could not think. She had had the idea of surprising him; somehow it was more *inspirational* to appear suddenly. Perhaps, too, she had felt he might try to dissuade her.

He was certainly surprised when he saw them waiting for him at the corner, but he didn't appear too horrified. After the first start of recognition, he smiled and called a cheerful 'Hallo!' as if he had known they would come some time. The children were more put out. Some hesitated and held back until he encouraged them, others huddled in closer to him; all went suddenly silent, staring with wide eyes. How grubby many of them were, as if they had been having rough-and-tumbles in the street – as they probably had, Henrietta thought, remembering groups of running, shouting children without any supervision they had passed on the way. Eyes

169

stared at her from white faces, some pinched with hunger; one little girl had dark and yellowing bruises on her cheek. And how *old* some of them looked – experienced, adult heads on small frames in ill-fitting clothes, handed down, she thought, from elder brothers and sisters. She forgot the surroundings and her feelings of strangeness as her heart went out to them.

Father Geoffrey stopped as he reached them, and gravely introduced each child by name. They stared up, quite silent, eyes feasting on her crisp, white dress with its bands of blue satin, and her straw hat; one little girl he introduced as Anna couldn't keep her gaze from her hair, and thinking she was not noticed, shuffled round to the side to get a better view. A boy with a very wide, floppy cap much too large for him came up slowly, pulling one ear with his fingers and put out the other hand to her dress; thinking of the grubby marks he might leave, she wanted to draw away, but checked herself. She put her hand towards his and he took it gingerly.

'Now,' Father Geoffrey said, 'these are my good friends – Henrietta – and Mary – who have come to see you.' He smiled briefly.

Two boys were fighting to take her other hand.

He called to them sharply, and seeing Anna almost behind her now, told her she could take Henrietta's hand if she wished.

Two other girls attached themselves to Mary, and they started off towards the community house. Just before they reached it Father Geoffrey stopped and asked them if they thought they could keep the children occupied while he went inside for a few minutes. 'You might teach them some games,' he suggested, 'or singing?'

Henrietta looked at Mary in alarm as he strode off with a wave.

'I know a gime, Miss,' the little boy on her right said, and others took up the chorus. She felt Anna's fingers gripping hers as the noise increased. They were all jumping up and down trying to gain her attention, and for respite she started leading them across the road to the grass square.

Mary looked at her. 'Blind man's buff?'

The noise increased; she couldn't tell whether it was

170

because they liked the game, or were still championing their own preferences. She tried to raise her arms to still the babel, but Anna was holding on so tightly to her left hand she couldn't shake her grip. She called for quiet, and Mary did the same.

Eventually they had the children arranged in a rough circle on the grass. Realizing by this time that if she asked who wanted first turn the boys would start fighting, she looked for a suitable choice. Her eye fell on the girl with the bruised cheek; she was standing stiller than the others, a withdrawn look on her face; but as Henrietta approached, her eyes widened in alarm and she backed away. Henrietta bent and spoke softly; she turned and ran.

The others started laughing.

'Stop that at once!' she called angrily, and to her surprise they did, watching her in awed silence again.

Noticing that Anna had not laughed, but was looking at the other girl anxiously, she called to her and said she should be first. The next problem was to find a suitable blindfold. Discussing it with Mary she decided that Mary's small handkerchief folded and fastened with the blue ribbons from her own hat would do. There was an audible gasp as she took her hat off and tore the ribbons away. Bending to fix the makeshift blindfold around Anna's head, she explained what she had to do, turned her round once and started her off.

'Road's out of bounds,' she shouted as they scampered away, and realizing from puzzled looks they hadn't understood, 'Keep on the grass!'

From the way some of them doubled up with laughter as Anna blundered about after them she wondered if they had played the game before; whether they had or not, they went at it as if their lives depended on it, the boys seeing how close they could get to danger before hurling themselves away with shouts of derision, the girls jumping up and down with excitement.

A brewer's dray stopped nearby, the driver looking on, and several men appeared and stood, hands in pockets at the edge of the grass, watching silently and, she sensed, appreciatively. Others drifted up until quite a crowd had

171

formed and the children, aware they were being watched, played up to them.

Absorbed in her efforts to keep her more demented charges running too far from the 'blind man', she was not aware that Father Geoffrey had come out of the community house and was standing amongst the spectators; suddenly she caught sight of his habit among the shabby, dark suits, and saw his eyes on her; they moved away quickly as he realized she was looking, and a moment afterwards he was walking out of the group towards her, smiling.

'Splendid!' he called as he came up. 'Would you like to keep it going, I have one more visit I must make,' but seeing the disappointment in her face, 'or would you prefer to come with me? It's an elderly lady,' he added. 'She's dying.'

She didn't know what to say to that.

'Come on, then!' he said.

Intent glances from the men followed them as they walked away, she on his left, Mary on his right, the children crowding to take their hands and shouting for another 'gime'. She felt like a princess and the pied piper at the same time; so far as these children were concerned, she and Mary *were* princesses; as for the men, there was a less hungry look on their faces now and some looked as if they wanted to be friendly.

'Come to 'elp the Father?' one called.

She gave him a smile.

'There'll be a few signin' up if she 'as,' another shouted, and there was a burst of laughter.

'They've taken to you,' Father Geoffrey said quietly.

She asked him what 'signing up' meant.

'Signing the pledge I expect. Not to drink alcohol. It's the curse around here. When they're sober, they're as decent, honest fellows as you'd find anywhere. As soon as they get a little money though –'

One of the boys was tugging insistently at her dress.

'Where d'you live, Miss?'

'In Hampstead,' she replied.

'D'yer live in a big 'ahse?'

' 'Ow many gimes d'yer now, Miss?'

'C'n I 'av the ribbon, Miss – off of your 'at –?'

She couldn't keep pace with the questions, and it seemed

172

no time before Father Geoffrey arrived at one of the small front doors, all looking alike, and knocked. The children fell silent as they waited. After a while the door started opening jerkily and they saw a girl peering at them from the opening. Her eyes were large and dark with shadows beneath, her white skin drawn over fine features; she might be really pretty, Henrietta thought, but there was something missing; she seemed to lack animation even when she smiled briefly in recognition of Father Geoffrey, and pulled the door wider to allow him in. He beckoned to Henrietta and Mary, and they followed; Anna came too, refusing to let go of her hand; some of the other children remained watching on the pavement outside, while others began dispersing. She felt a twinge of disappointment that her fascination was not sufficient to hold them all.

It was dark inside, like the little hallways she had seen from the road, and the air was stale and heavy. A door on the right was half open and she could see an armchair with a chintz cover in which all the colours seemed to have greyed with age; the arms were shiny on the tops and threadbare. Behind it was the smallest fireplace she had ever seen with a black iron surround decorated with curling designs in relief; on the mantel above a twisted glass candleholder streaked with solidified wax held a bare half inch of candle. Next to it was a sepia photograph of a man with drooping moustaches and a rather plump woman against what looked like a painted woodland setting, and on either side of these cheap china ornaments were crowded between vases at each end. There were more ornaments and thick china jugs on a table covered with a stained white cloth next to the fireplace; above a diagonal crack in the wall led up to a fan of cracks in the angle of the ceiling, which was discoloured with large stains in rings of lighter colours at the outside, becoming darker in the centre. She was struck by the mixture of poverty and attempted homeliness. As she passed the door, she heard loud snoring from somewhere inside.

The stairs led straight up from the passage in which they were; they were even narrower than the attic stairs at home with a deep brown rail at one side and on the other only scored, chipped brown paint. The girl who had opened the door led the way, Father Geoffrey followed with Mary behind him, and she and Anna brought up the rear. By the time she reached the top Father Geoffrey had gone in through one of three half-open doors there; the girl was standing at another watching everything with her big eyes; behind her Henrietta glimpsed an unmade bed with crumpled sheets thrown back anyhow and two chamber pots showing beneath; one was badly cracked. She felt oppressed by the smell and dust everywhere, wishing she hadn't come; she wasn't tall, but the grey ceilings seemed to press down on her, shutting out fresh air; everything was in miniature. She followed after Mary, squeezing between her and the wall of the room Father Geoffrey had entered.

A woman with sunken hollows for cheeks and eyes glittering from dark sockets stared from her bed as Father Geoffrey introduced them. Her lips moved in a chewing motion, but she said nothing. Henrietta felt herself weighed up; the eyes had a remarkable intensity. They didn't look as if they belonged to someone who was dying – although from the rest of the woman's emaciated condition she could believe it. The eyes were curiously alive, though, more alive than those of the girl who had opened the door to them – presumably her granddaughter.

'It might make a change if one of the girls read to you today, Mrs Griggs,' Father Geoffrey suggested.

Mrs Griggs continued her chewing movements without speaking, staring at the girls in turn.

'Perhaps you would read –' He was looking at Henrietta with raised brows, 'while I have a word with Jenny next door and,' turning again to the woman in bed, 'your husband – I expect he's downstairs.'

He had drawn a Bible from somewhere in the folds of his habit, and he flicked through the pages, handing it to Henrietta opened. 'We've got to Luke, twenty-one. She enjoys the stories.'

Mrs Griggs had removed one bony grey arm from her blanket and was tapping the bed. The last thing Henrietta wanted was to touch any part of the bed or Mrs Griggs or even the room, but seeing Father Geoffrey's gaze on her, she sat, straight-backed on the edge, knowing as she saw the

174

woman's bird-like eyes fixed on hers that her feelings were divined.

As Father Geoffrey took Mary and Anna out with him, she started to read.

'And he looked up, and saw the rich men casting their gifts into the treasury –'

Wondering what it could possibly mean to this woman dying in this oppressive room, she felt Mrs Griggs's fingers feeling the material of her dress; her flesh crawled; she lost the sense of the words she was reading, only wanting to get through with it as quickly as she could and get out again into the air. But Father Geoffrey hadn't said how much she was to read. She could hear his voice from next door as he talked to the girl; from the sound of it Jenny was not talking much herself; no one in this family appeared to say much.

She felt Mrs Griggs's fingers prod the flesh of her leg, and tried to draw away. The prodding followed, more insistent.

'– when ye shall hear of wars and commotions,' she raced on, stumbling over the words, 'be not terrified, for these things must first come to pass –'

' 'Ere!' Mrs Griggs said in a husky voice, digging her fingers in again, ' *'Ere!*'

Henrietta looked up from the Bible, hoping desperately she didn't want – the image of the cracked chamber pot beneath the bed in the next room filled her mind – she couldn't do it, she wouldn't. Father Geoffrey had no right to leave her like this.

'Yer now wot,' Mrs Griggs was saying, 'My ol' man, yer now wot 'e is?'

Henrietta shook her head wildly.

' 'E's a pisspot!'

She stared, wondering if she had heard correctly.

'Pisss pot!' the old woman repeated with sibillant emphasis. 'Allers 'as bin.'

Henrietta felt transfixed by the glittering eyes.

'They give me a cent'ry for Jinny –' seeing the incomprehension on Henrietta's face, she repeated that as well, '*Cent'ry* – a 'undred thick 'uns – 'undred pahnd for Chr –' she stopped herself. ' "Ow much they give yer?" '*e* says. "A pony," I says. "Gorn! Gi' away! I seen the carriage she come

175

in," 'e says, "Come on, 'ow much they give yer?" "All right," I says, "they give me fifty – *fifty*," I says, "an'" I says, "I'm keepin' 'em – all on 'em. I mean to bring Jinny up proper," I says, " 'er dad's a guv'mint minister –" "Wot's that!" 'e says, "wot's that you jes' said?" " 'Er dad's a proper minister o' relijun," I says quick, "an' I means to bring 'er up mos' partikler –" "A guv'mint minister, you said," 'e says, "A guv'mint minister is 'e –!" an' 'e gives me a look. "I reckon thet'd mike interestin' noos – in the pipers," 'e says. "You –'" she checked herself again. " 'You *pisspot*!" I says, "You'd niver –" "Oh –!" 'e says, "jes' you watch me!" "Well," I says, "I'll give you 'alf." "All!" 'e says, "*All!*" an' 'e fetches me one – in me left eye. "You'll not git none o' them now," I says, "not likely!" so 'e fetches me one in me *right* eye, an' I'm lyin' acrosst the bed, see, an' 'e's under the piller quick as lightnin'. 'E don't find nothin' so 'e pushes me off of the bed an' gits under the mettress, an' still 'e don't find nothin' so 'e turns the 'ole bed over like a madman an' 'e come an' sits on me stomick –'

She stopped as Father Geoffrey appeared in the doorway.

'I was tellin' 'er abaht Jinny,' she said defensively. 'If *'e* 'adn't a drunk it Jinny could 'a had fine cloves an' all –' Henrietta felt her fingers feeling the material of her dress again, 'An' a posh school – 'e took it – 'e took it all –'

'Have no fear for Jenny,' Father Geoffrey said quietly, 'We shall look after her – if ever you can't – I promise you that.'

Mrs Griggs's lips started working as they had when they first came in.

'Shall we say the Lord's Prayer together?' he said.

Afterwards, as they were leaving, Mrs Griggs looked at Henrietta. 'Them white gloves – Jinny'd look all right in white gloves – I reckon –'

Henrietta returned her gaze for a moment, feeling dreadful she had not thought of giving something, but her gloves –! She started peeling them off, then laid them on the bed where she had been sitting. 'I'd like Jenny to have them. Goodbye, Mrs Griggs.'

Mrs Griggs watched her leave, chewing silently.

'She's devoted to that girl,' Father Geoffrey said when

176

they were outside. 'She talks of nothing else – she has several others, but Jenny's the one she cares for. It's strange.'

'But she's so old,' Henrietta replied, wondering how she could have any children, let alone several others.

'Not really. Besides, they're not her own – I expect she told you?' He looked at her as if wondering, and she nodded although she had not fully understood what she had been told. 'She takes them in as babies,' he went on, 'and looks after them. It's a business you might say. But if they do it with love – like Mrs Griggs –' He broke off to greet two women who were approaching.

'She's marvellous,' he went on when the women had passed. 'She's in the most terrible pain, but you'd never know. Most of the time –'

'What's wrong with her?' Mary asked.

He turned quickly as if realizing he had been paying most of his attention to Henrietta. 'Cancer. It's eating her away – she's light as a feather. But she won't give in, she simply refuses to die. She has her "Jinny" to look after you see. Goodness knows, I've told her often enough that Jenny will be well cared for by us – much better than poor Mrs Griggs can look after her – although of course I don't tell her that.' He smiled briefly. 'It is marvellous what the human spirit is capable of. I see it here every day – in the most depressing circumstances.'

Henrietta wanted to ask who Jenny's father was and why, if he was a government minister, he should want his daughter brought up in such a place, and scores of other questions, but children were beginning to come up and attach themselves, and the time for serious talk was past. She realized suddenly that Anna was not holding her hand and commented on it.

'She's one of Mrs Griggs's,' he replied.

She lay awake for hours that night, her mind a maelstrom of images, among which Father Geoffrey's serene face and the fierce glitter of Mrs Griggs's eyes jostled for predominance. She saw Jenny standing at the half-open door of that room with the untidy bed behind her in which four other children slept as well, Mary had told her on the way home – *boys* as well – and her expressionless, large, dark eyes taking

177

everything in; she tried to imagine her wearing the white gloves – surely they would be too large.

Downstairs in that poor front parlour Mr Griggs was snoring in the middle of the afternoon; she imagined him like the men loafing in their baggy suits outside the public houses and shivered for Jenny and for herself as she thought of their eyes as they looked at her. ' 'E's a pisspot –'

She kept on turning and shifting position to try and get to sleep, but the images and questions tormented her. Jenny's eyes reminded her of Babs's, and her face too in a way; she was not so attractive, but that might only be because Babs was so full of life and self-assertion; Jenny had neither; her eyes were like empty pools; she thought of the dark pools from which Mrs Griggs's eyes glistened. Her eyes and her skeleton fingers were the only parts of her still alive; the rest was already dead. Her voice was dead and she spoke of events that were past and gone – when she had taken the baby Jenny in for a hundred pounds –

'Of course!' Mary had said on the way home on top of the tram with the wind in their faces and the friendly street lamps and houselights beginning to glow all around in the dusk, 'Didn't you know!' Mary must have learned it from one of her mother's suffragette meetings. 'That's how they get rid of the babies they don't want –'

'Don't want!'

'The ones they have with – not with their wives.'

'Why do they want to get rid of them?'

Mary had not seemed so confident about her answer to this question. 'So that nobody knows.'

Henrietta had the image of her father with the lady with the feathered hat outside the Egyptian Hall in Piccadilly. It had *not* been one of her cousins – she had been aware of this in a vague way for some time – now other ideas raised themselves.

'We could have brothers and sister we don't know about,' she had said, wondering if it was really possible.

From her expression, it was evident Mary had not thought of this – the Judge was not that kind of man, Henrietta thought. But how could you tell?

Images of Babs and Jenny mixed with woolly sheep as she

lay, eyes tight shut, willing herself to sleep. The sheep disappeared; Jenny's dark-shadowed eyes remained. Why should she believe Mrs Griggs's story that her father was a government minister? It might as easily have been her own father. She turned violently and spread her arms wide so that her left hand dangled over the edge of the mattress. Jenny might be her sister.

They had told Father Geoffrey they would come and visit him again. He had seemed pleased. She would take something for Jenny. She would take something for her every time she went to Plaistow – she would invite her back home – how to explain it to Mama? Perhaps when she went to her new school she could pretend Jenny was a girl she had met in the street. She pushed the sheet back and turned on her other side. Father Geoffrey might help. He might write to Mama asking if Jenny could visit them.

He had been glad of their help, she could tell from his face when they left. What a fine life he led – when you thought about Papa's life, or the people who came to lunch and the stupid things they talked about. Father Geoffrey was doing something real. He had given up everything – like Christ himself. *She* would give up everything when she was old enough, and help him – all the time. She thought perhaps she loved him. She had discussed love with Mary, but they had not been able to get at what it really was. It was something you knew when you were 'in love'. But she didn't know; she just thought she probably was – she admired him tremendously, and she felt a thrill when he gazed at her with his deep, gentle brown eyes.

She felt her mother's eyes on her as she came in and walked round the table to the sideboard; she didn't want to eat at all, she just wished she could go back to bed. She had a slight ache over her eyes and the smell of the kidneys and bacon as she lifted the covers made her feel sick. She helped herself to a single poached egg.

Her mother was still eyeing her as she sat down. She returned the gaze challengingly, thinking of what she might say when it was discovered that her new gloves and the

179

ribbons from her hat had gone; after a moment her mother looked down to eat. Willy was also looking at her, but with an amused expression, and she smiled back, looking forward to recounting her escapade of yesterday in all its shocking detail – and her feelings for Father Geoffrey. That would stun him! Willy's eyebrows lifted slightly. It was good to have the boys back, Willy above all. Soon he would be going to Osborne and Dartmouth, then to a battleship like George and she would hardly see him except for odd days home on leave. Andy was going to Marlborough; he would be coming home for holidays but she had never been really intimate with him, not as she was with Willy. Harry was too young. She had a premonition as she had at times when she was happy, of the remorseless passage of time, changing everything –

Papa spluttered over *The Times*; the Kaiser! It was always 'Mad Billy' or 'the Huns'. Her mother looked towards him coolly over her napkin.

'War?' she asked.

He lowered the paper to tell her it was no joking matter, Henrietta suspected from his look, but seeing her face he just stared for a moment. There were pink spots in his eyes which had been clear; all trace of his former fine looks had gone – irretrievably lost in the pouched breadth of his cheeks above the grey-bordered beard – receded with his hair-line over the brow revealed now as none too noble. Henrietta felt a terrible pang like an ache for the time she had admired him as a god and a generous, loving father at the same time, and with it contempt that he had let himself come to this; she hated him for it.

'Well!' her mother prompted. 'What has he said this time?'

'He's landed in Morocco, the damn fool!' He started chuckling.

Henrietta wondered if he was going mad; he said such pointless things and laughed at them.

'On a white horse,' he went on, 'white charger I dare say. Where's the fleet now? Where's George? Where was his last letter from – Gib wasn't it –?'

'That's all right, then!' her mother said acidly.

He sat quite still, his mouth hanging half-open as if he had been about to say something, then he smoothed out the paper and lifted it to read again.

Henrietta hated her mother for what she had done to him. She thought of Father Geoffrey's calm eyes and clean jaw and the real life he lived, and wished she could join him.

Afterwards in her room she held Willy and Andy spell-bound with her description of Plaistow and its inhabitants. She made sure first that Harry and Babs were in the nursery; Babs could not be trusted with any secret; she made a habit of deliberately blurting out things in front of her mother which she could only have learned by eavesdropping.

The boys could not believe how Mrs Griggs had referred to her 'old man', and asked her to repeat it. She did. They collapsed with laughter and rolled about the floor chanting 'Pisspot – pisspot –' between spasms.

'Quiet!' she hissed. 'Nurse'll hear –' They were amazingly stupid. 'If you don't stop, I shan't tell you any more!'

They stopped and she continued the story, dwelling par-ticularly on Jenny, rather exaggerating how beautiful she would be if only she could be persuaded to show some feeling; carried away by the story, she said that Jenny looked so amazingly like Babs she believed her real father was Papa. They stared, silenced by shock. In fact she had discarded that idea while looking at Papa over breakfast that morning – along with several other of her jumbled fancies of the night.

'I'm going to help her,' she went on. 'I shall take her clothes from the dressing-up box –' and seeing a smile forming on Andy's face, 'they're far better than the ones she wears! And I shall take her some money each week so she can save to buy things for herself.' She looked at them, an idea forming. 'You could give up some of your pocket money too.'

'*Ours!*' Andy said as if stung.

'She is your sister.'

'How do you know she is ?'

'Why d'you think Father Geoffrey took me to *that* house! There are hundreds of other houses – thousands he could have taken me to.'

Willy was looking at her speculatively.

'Even if she's not our real sister,' she went on hotly, 'and she is – probably – isn't *everyone* our brother and sister!' and, working herself up, 'why should we live here like this with all we have –' she waved her arm, 'while she's starving. You should see how thin she is. Soon she won't even have a home. Mrs Griggs will die – probably she's already dead –'

She didn't tell them about Father Geoffrey saying he would take care of the girl when the old woman died.

They were silent for a moment.

'She can't be our sister,' Andy said.

'She's still starving, isn't she? Any money Mrs Griggs gets, *he* goes to the public house and gets drunk.' She looked at Willy. She knew he would crack first. He couldn't bear suffering in any creature.

'I could sell my stamp collection,' he said slowly.

She wanted to jump up and hug him, but she looked serious instead as if considering it carefully. 'How much would you get for it?'

'I don't know. Quite a lot I should think.' He thought of the set Papa had sent from Natal through the military post office during the war, and his pages of Indian stamps, some with Queen Victoria's head. It was going to be a loss; he had become attached to them. But he wouldn't need the collection next term – the summer term – and in the autumn he was going for his Nomination Board for the Navy; from George's tales of the *Britannia*, it was unlikely he'd need a stamp collection at Osborne.

He saw Henrietta had turned her attention to Andy; she was gazing at him with that aggressive light in her eyes. Without George here, she would be able to get him to do whatever she wanted; he was already moving about nervously, and he shifted his position again, left palm on the bed, feet twisted together. 'Whatever would Pater have gone to Plaistow for?'

'I thought you were supposed to be going into the church,' she replied quickly, and before he could think of an answer to that, 'What about your trains? You could sell them easily.'

'Henry!' Willy was shocked. Even for Henry, this was going too far. Andy's trains were his prize possession; added to every year at Christmas, they were something they all enjoyed, even Babs; impossible to imagine Andy without them. He saw him staring at Henry like a rabbit transfixed, his lips trembling.

'I can't sell my *trains* –'

'Christ gave up everything. If you can't give up your silly trains!'

'Where could I sell them!' His eyes behind his spectacles darted between her and Willy. 'No one would want them –'

'Mrs Harding is sure to know where we can sell them,' Henrietta said matter-of-factly as if it was agreed.

Willy, looking at Andy's expression, hoped that Mrs Harding would not know. He admired Henrietta, but feared her sometimes. When she wanted something she was without scruple. Andy, with all his brains was no match for her; George was the only one who could stand up to her when she was set on something, and now he was away there was no stopping her.

Here he was wrong, for in asking Mrs Harding where they could sell the trains and all the track and signals and paraphernalia that went with them Henrietta made a fatal mistake. Realizing immediately that something very serious must be up if Andy were prepared to part with the toys which engrossed him above everything, Mrs Harding called him into her room that evening and cleverly using his anxiety about the trains wheedled the important points of the story from him. They had a sister in the East End; she was starving, and Henry wanted the money for her.

Mrs Harding couldn't believe her ears – couldn't even speak for a minute as she tried to think out the implications. She knew, as they all did, that Mr Steel was one for the ladies – or had been she thought because with his drinking nowadays he could have little energy left for such activities. But for his past to catch up with him in this way, and for his own children to discover it – surely it was not possible.

'What makes Henrietta think this girl is – her sister?' She could hardly bring herself to say it.

'She saw her. Her name's Jenny. She looks just like Babs –'

'Like Babs!' Babs was Mrs Harding's favourite.

'Just like Babs,' he insisted, and went on to tell her how a priest had taken Henrietta to the exact house, repeating

183

Henrietta's rhetorical question about why should he have taken her to that particular house if Jenny was not her sister.

'A priest!' Mrs Harding exclaimed, impressed.

She turned it over in her mind for two days before finally deciding she had a duty to let Mrs Steel know, but even as she was telling her she couldn't quite believe it – nor did she know whether she was doing the right thing, for she was certain Mrs Steel had no idea Henrietta had been to the East End.

'Thank you, Mrs Harding,' Alice Steel replied, tight lipped. 'You are quite right to tell me. It's one of Henrietta's stories of course –'

'I thought – with Master Andrew going to sell his trains –'

'You were quite right. I'll speak to her.' There was a distant look in her eyes. 'She's convinced him, I've no doubt. She can be extremely persuasive. Were you here when she saw Lady Ottolene –?'

Mrs Harding nodded, smiling until she realized that was not the expected response.

'She seems to need to draw attention to herself,' Alice Steel went on. 'I thought she was growing out of it – but this time – it's gone beyond a joke –' She was containing herself with difficulty, but it was important not to let Mrs Harding think she attached any importance to the story.

Remembering the missing gloves and ribbons, she knew exactly when the visit must have taken place; Henrietta had been with Mary Edgehill that afternoon – for a long walk on the Heath, she had told her, where a gang of poor children had called them names and chased them. They had been lucky to escape without greater loss, and would not have done so if a gentleman with a dog had not come up just at the right moment. Even knowing Henrietta as she did, Alice Steel was shocked at her brazen imagination.

The story of finding her sister in the East End was more serious, though: it showed a knowledge of closed and guarded areas which it was improper for girls to be aware of. Undoubtedly this was Mary's doing. Thought of the Edgehills induced a wave of anger that Naomi should be so thoughtless as to spread her absurd views to the young who had no knowledge or experience against which to measure them. Naomi was the real culprit here. Alice Steel briefly congratulated herself on outwitting her – and the men – in the matter of finishing schools; she had allowed Naomi to finalize arrangements for sending Mary to Paris, agreeing she would probably send Henrietta too, then at the last moment had come out against it on the grounds of expense, choosing for Henrietta an establishment at Sunningdale run by a German, the Baroness von Witzhof. The Baroness was patronized by some of the best families; Henrietta would make friends from more suitable backgrounds.

It crossed her mind that she might begin the separation from the Edgehills at once by forbidding Henrietta further contact with Mary for what remained of the holidays; she dismissed the idea. Henrietta would be spurred on to clandestine meetings which might have far worse consequences; above all it would sour relations with the Edgehills and put paid to the prospect of the two girls coming out together which, for the present at any rate, she favoured.

No, she and Naomi would have to work together; she would call on her tomorrow and explain what she had discovered – hardly necessary to elaborate on the danger of the two girls making further secret excursions into the East End alone, surely even Naomi must appreciate that. If together they cut off the girls' pocket money, made sure they could not draw on their savings accounts and warned them of the terrible risks they ran – she was momentarily seized by a hollow feeling inside as she thought of the drunks and idlers, of the depression in trade, the violent assaults reported in the papers, the disease and dirt – the WC was probably unknown in Plaistow; the thought that Henrietta might already have used one of the privies there brought on another weak spasm. Pray God she had not become infected!

Still planning her campaign in bed that night, she heard Robert Steel blundering drunkenly against the door of his room as he tried to get in, and thought as she often did of the tares he had sown in *her* children. Undoubtedly Henrietta had inherited his incorrigibly romantic outlook and inability to adhere to the truth, probably to judge by her recent deceitful excursions his loose moral character as well, although of course she was a far tougher character. The

185

strength came from her side of the family, like her quick perceptions and ability to persuade others to her own way of thinking. In that respect she reminded Alice Steel of her own father. What a gigantic blunder poor Papa had connived at when he blessed her union with Robert – probably the only serious mistake he had made in his life. She was thankful he was spared the sight of what Robert had become.

It was left to her to rectify the mistake; all her children had their particular qualities; she had to build on them; with discipline and reason she could do it; with reason anything was possible – she began to think of the names she had been toying with for Henrietta's coming out; with her looks she could aspire to the highest levels if only her contrariness could be curbed. If she *wanted* to marry well nothing would stop her; what *she* had to do was implant the desire and nourish it –

She heard a more than usually heavy thump from Robert's room; he had missed the bed. She allowed herself a terrible moment of despair at her inability to stem the disintegration of his health and appearance – even his sanity – she looked into the abyss of the future, then with a tremendous summoning of the will she turned her mind back to her children. A *priest* had taken Henrietta to this house; she wondered who that could have been –

Confined to her room to think over her wickedness, the first thing Henrietta did was write to Father Geoffrey. It was long and impassioned, indeed a love letter. She told him how much she wanted to help poor Jenny but was unable to because her pocket money had been stopped and she had been forbidden to visit Plaistow ever again. Despite this, she would leave home secretly and *walk* there if he had a place for her in his mission. She would far rather that than the school she was being sent to in Sunningdale to be prepared for the stupid life she had no wish to lead. All her mother wanted for her was to have her pictures in the weeklies and to make a 'good' marriage, but why should that be the only thing a girl could look forward to! Here she was echoing the ideas Mary had imbibed from her mother, and conscious of

186

this after she had written it, she asked him what he thought of the women's movement.

'Please say I can come and work for you,' she wrote finally, then hesitated a long time over how she should end; 'sincerely' was too formal; 'love' she sent to her family, but flushed as she thought of using the word to him. At last she wrote 'your friend' and felt her cheeks tingling again as she added 'always', but having done it she left it. It was true. She signed it with a flourish she had been practising, then found herself making a drawing below as she often did at the end of letters to Grandpapa. It turned out to be a girl in a straw hat, ribbons blowing as if in a wind.

She smuggled the letter out to Willy via the maid who brought her tea, together with a note stressing the importance of posting it at once – if necessary going to the Edgehills house to get the money for a stamp from Mary.

The next days she spent in a fever of secret expectancy and apprehension. Longing for his answer to be positive, she felt shivers at the thought of leaving home, sure that even if she wanted to come back again, after such deliberate disobedience her mother would never allow it. Lying in bed at nights she tried to imagine not seeing her brothers or little Babs again and cried herself to sleep.

The reply came on the fourth morning. She recognized his precise, rounded hand immediately from all the comments he had made in her exercise books, although cleverly he had posted the letter in Hampstead. Her mother kept glancing at the envelope as it lay on the table beside her at breakfast, not saying anything since they were scarcely on speaking terms since the episode, and it was left to her father to make a joke about her not opening it.

'Expectin' a dun are you, Henry!'

She looked at him frostily, and felt sorry immediately as she saw his eyes fall away from hers.

Afterwards she ran up to her room and sitting on her bed almost afraid to see what was inside, started picking the envelope open.

My dear Henrietta,
I hope I may call you that now? I was sorry indeed to

187

hear that you are forbidden to visit us, although I think probably I guessed your last visit was 'unofficial'! If you still feel as you do when you have completed your education there is always room here for those who feel the call to help. It would be best if you took a course of study first to enable you to gain a better understanding of the problems and some of the ways in which we try to alleviate them and I will gladly send you details of such courses when the time comes. Until then I am afraid there are many reasons, including legal reasons connected with your age, why – much as we are in need of people of your vital spirit – I am afraid I cannot condone what would amount to your absconding from home. You will be sorry to read this. I have sensed for some time your impatience to taste life outside the walls of your home, but be patient. You have all the time you need in front of you. Do not be impetuous.

You asked about Jenny and poor Mrs Griggs. I visited her again yesterday and she talked of nothing but your visit, asking repeatedly when you would be coming again. I shall tell her how much you have been thinking of her and 'Jinny' when I see her next, it will please her enormously I know.

You mention the women's movement – it is something very close to my heart for I see here all around me the results of woman's subservient condition – her dependence on man, the temptations to which she is subject and her eventual punishment when she falls. If one considers that the whole fabric and welfare of society depends on women, especially perhaps working women, and the way in which they bring up and set an example to their families one is struck more than ever by the low position accorded them in society. Three halfpence an hour is, I believe, their average wage in employment, while on the other side – but you have tempted me to a sermon and that will never do! Sufficient to say that because I believe there is no finer career for a woman than to be a good wife and mother to her children – although you do not appear to share this view at present! – I believe wholeheartedly in the fight for women's rights. That may seem a contradiction to you now, but *tempora mutantor, nos et mutamur in illis* – if you remember!

I hope you are not too disappointed with this reply.

God bless you and keep you always – Geoffrey

Below there was a small line drawing of a monk.

She found she was not too disappointed; in a way she was relieved that the decision had been taken from her; now she couldn't run away. There was no reason and nowhere to go. It was reassuring that she would not have to leave Willy and Andy and everyone.

She read the letter through again, searching for signs that he *would* want her later and was not simply treating her as a silly child, and found them in his reference to 'legal reasons' for not taking up her offer immediately, and especially in the phrase 'much as we are in need of people of your vital spirit'. She wondered what he meant by 'vital' and ran to find the dictionary in the old schoolroom:

> Belonging or relating to life, contributory to life, necessary to life, being the seat of life, being that on which life depends.
> 'The dart flew on and pierced a *vital* part' *Pope*.
> Animate, living, full of life . . .

She read the letter through happily a third time, then folded it and returning it to the envelope, went back to her room and placed it under her clothes in the bottom drawer of her chest, where over the years it was joined by many others from him.

11

'What is the capital of Germany?'

In his mind Willy saw Uncle Richard's long, lavender-flannelled legs stretching out in the sun, and heard his voice, so like his father's but crisper.

'Berlin, sir,' he replied. He didn't like this member of the Nomination Board with his cold eyes and spectacles lowered on the bridge of his thin nose; he had already christened him 'the Beak'.

Some of his feeling must have communicated itself through his voice, for the Beak's lips seemed to have been hardening during the quiz and his stare sharpening, although so far he hadn't caught Willy out. Perhaps that was why he was annoyed.

Before he could frame the next question, Willy went on, 'It's really only the capital of Prussia, sir. There isn't such a country as Germany.'

He felt the sudden silence around the table, and almost heard his heart thump in his chest. He wondered what on earth had made him say it. The blood rushed to his face.

'No such country as Germany!'

It was the large man sitting opposite him at the top of the green baize covered table who had opened the interview with very decent remarks about his father and grandfather; he had a broad face and his eyes, beneath dark, tufted brows, had been cheerful and friendly; now they bore into his.

'Not really, sir.' The stare grew harder. He couldn't turn back now. 'It's really a lot of different kingdoms and duchies, sir, and the King of Prussia is their Emperor. His palace is in Berlin – sir –' he stumbled on.

'Doesn't that come to much the same thing, young feller?'

'Yes, sir, I suppose it does. But –'

The tufted brows rose fiercely. 'But –?'

'But it's not quite the same, sir, because the other king-doms are bullied by Prussia.'

The eyes moved away from his to meet those of another member of the Board to his left. Willy thought he saw a smile and felt the tension lift.

The big man turned to the Beak. 'That's fair enough. The youngster's hit the nail on the head, wouldn't you say?'

'A complex point,' the Beak replied, scribbling something on a pad before him.

Willy had an impression the answer was rather irritating to the large man, he didn't know why. He heard one of those on his left addressing him in a friendly voice.

'What else d'you know about Prussia, young man?' There was a humorous glint in his eyes; it was the one who had smiled, Willy saw; he liked him and felt grateful.

'They're all soldiers, sir.'

There was a ripple of laughter around the table. The man who had asked the question was looking at him encouragingly and smiling, so he went on, 'They have the greatest army in the world, and now they're building a fleet so they can take on our fleet –' He wanted to tell him what Uncle Richard had seen at the Krupp's gun works and all the steel and armour plate he had seen stocked up in the Wilhelmshaven and Kiel shipbuilding yards he had visited under the guise of a Chilean naval officer – that would certainly convince him – but he had sworn he wouldn't tell a soul. 'They think that when they have a fleet they will be able to sink ours, then take our colonies and have a great world empire – like ours, sir.'

'And what do you think of that idea?' the large man at the head of the table asked.

'Me, sir?'

The man leaned forward, his big chin jutting, eyebrows moving. 'You – sir!'

'I think it's a rotten idea, sir.'

Everyone laughed except for the Beak, who was staring down at his papers.

'I'll tell you something, youngster,' the large man said, 'so do I!'

There was another chorus of laughter. Willy smiled, beginning to enjoy it.

Unfortunately, the big man, after complimenting him on his grasp of world affairs, said they had better turn to the spiritual side.

'Padre!'

A clergyman sitting to his right smiled at him.

'Would you say there were peoples somewhat like the Prussians perhaps in the ancient world?'

'No, sir,' he replied smartly. George had told him to answer everything as if he knew, whether he did or not.

'No?'

It was evidently the wrong answer. 'Well, something like them, yes, sir.'

'Who were they?'

His mind went numb. He gazed towards the ceiling, trying to recollect scripture lessons with old Phipps; a name came to him.

'The Philistines, sir.'

The clergyman smiled. 'They will do very well! Can you remember any particular incidents in the wars between the children of Israel and the Philistines?'

'David and Goliath, sir.'

The clergyman nodded encouragingly, his lips open seeming to form silent words as if he wished him to continue.

'David went to the river, sir, and found five smooth stones. He put one of them in his sling and went out to meet Goliath and when he got near him, slung the stone and it hit Goliath dead in the middle of his forehead and sank in, and Goliath fell down dead.'

The clergyman nodded, smiling, and turned towards the head of the table. 'I am satisfied, Captain.'

The large man looked round at the others, then back to Willy. 'That will do, thank you, Steel. You may go. Remember to close the door as you leave,' and as Willy got up, 'I think we shall all remember what you have told us about Prussia.'

'Thank you, sir.'

192

The others were smiling, all except the Beak; he felt he had done rather well. And he'd been asked none of the questions he'd been mugging up for so long, the names and gunpower of all the first-line battleships, the endless marriages and births in the royal family back to Tudor times; he hadn't even been asked the number of his carriage in the train up from Kent, or the number of the taxicab he and old Phipps had taken from Charing Cross.

He followed the porter along the lifeless corridors, round corners, past closed doors from which no sounds came, their two pairs of heels clicking on the polished linoleum as if they were the only people in the great building – apart from the seven members of the Nomination Board, now deliberating on his fate.

They arrived back in the room where they had assembled originally for the written English papers. The boy who had been sitting in the next desk smiled at him. He had a pleasant round face with brown hair smoothed down and shining with some hair juice, and lively brown eyes. He went across, grateful for someone who looked friendly among all the unknown faces of the other boys who eyed him curiously.

'How did you get on?' the boy asked.

'Not bad,' he said, pulling a grimace, although he still had the feeling they had liked him. 'How did you get on?'

'Pretty mouldy.'

They exchanged questions about what they had been asked and then their schools and where they lived; the other lived near Guildford and went to a day school there. His father was a vicar. He had an eager way of talking, not in the least reserved, and Willy began to like him a lot. It wasn't until they were both called out together that they learned each other's names. His was Peters.

They followed the porter again along more corridors to be shown in to a room furnished with little but two desks and in the corner opposite them a green screen. Something about the smell of the room and the look of the elderly men in heavy suits and waistcoats behind the desks told Willy this was a medical examination.

The nearest man pointed to the screen and told them to

go and take their clothes off and come out again. He had a bored voice with a soft, Scots accent.

'Which one of you is Peters?' he asked when they emerged together, naked and acutely embarrassed.

'Me, sir,' Peters said.

The man pointed to the other desk, then beckoned Willy. 'Come over here, boy – come on, there's nothing to be afraid of. Right up to the desk!' He looked him over as if he were a prize pig at market.

Willy tried to think how Uncle Richard would deal with the situation. It had become habitual nowadays in awkward or difficult situations for him to suit his behaviour to what he thought Uncle Richard might do in the circumstances. He squared his shoulders, put his hands straight down by his side and looked over the top of the doctor's head as if he didn't care what he did to him.

'Cough!'

He coughed.

'I said cough, boy!'

He coughed again, hollowing his stomach in spasms and bowing his shoulders with the effort.

'All right! All right, boy. Now turn round – right round. And bend over.'

'. . . It's very curious,' Uncle Richard said, 'have you noticed Willy, it's seldom what we fear most proves the most unpleasant when it comes to it. You're wonderin' how I came by this scar. Nothin' whatever to do with what I'd been sent across to Germany to find out, d'y' see. I'd been all over the Krupps Works as I've told you, counted the big gun mountin's, I'd been shown their special armour and the stockpiles of nickel and tungsten they need for hardenin' the noses of their shells, I'd been over Blohm & Voss and Germania and seen the keels of the big ships and all the steel they'd laid by, I'd sailed from end to end of the Kiel Canal, taken the depths, made sketches of the locks at both ends – never a hint of trouble.

'Then I took my eye off the ball, Willy. I went into one of their *Weinkellers*. In Kiel. By chance it happened to be one that the naval officers had made their own – you know how it is – there are bars like that in Portsmouth our officers make their own more or less. Visitors are not made welcome. That's how it was here. The officers could tell I wasn't one of 'em and they pretty soon made out I was an Englishman. I'd dropped my dago manner by that time – heartily sick of it I can assure you! They started passin' comments in English – loud so I'd hear. I'm afraid to say I fell for it. I couldn't sit there and listen to 'em, nor could any Englishman.

'I went up to them and said "Perhaps one of you fellows would like to step outside and repeat what you have just said." Oh, yes, they were makin' the most damnable remarks about the King, Willy. I can't repeat them; they'd stick in my gullet. I expected to take one of 'em outside and lick him in a fist fight – they're not taught to use their fists as we are. One of 'em, as evil-lookin' a fellow as you're likely to see – tall with a longish face, rather fine features except he had a Mongolian slant to his eyes, and an arrogant way of starin' at you, short, straight blond hair – a regular Prussian – this feller stood up, clicked heels and bowed his head an inch or two to show me it was an insult not a compliment. "I should be very pleased to oblige," he said – first class English he spoke. "You would prefer swords, or pistols?"

'Then I noticed the scars on his face. He had two, one on his cheek, the other on the side of his jaw. My heart turned over I can tell you, Willy. I hadn't been sent across to get myself killed. But I couldn't back down. That would've proved 'em right in what they'd bin sayin' about Englishmen. "Swords," I said. I did a bit of fencin' at school. I didn't expect to best the fellow, he had the looks of an expert, I fancied. I thought I might suffer a cut or two for honour and retire – somethin' you can't do with a pistol ball in your chest.

'There were no more insultin' remarks after I'd said, "Swords!" My stock went up no end. We became the best of friends. They were all good fellows at heart – all except the fellow I was picked to fight! They provided me with two seconds for the business side of it – duellin's forbidden, you see – officially that is. My seconds arranged a venue and a time. I said I'd be there. And there I was, Willy – next mornin'. It was a grand spot, overlookin' the harbour, great trees growin' down to the water's edge almost, and the larks

195

singin', it was a capital mornin' like you might get on the west coast of Scotland in spring. There was somethin' about it told me I'd got nothin' to fear. One has feelin's like that. Your brain tells you it's all up, but all the time somethin' else is tellin' you it's not – not by a long chalk. That's how it was this mornin' in Kiel. That's how it turned out.

'He was a skilful swordsman, but I soon found he didn't like to move, not with his feet. He had a long reach and he'd been used to havin' things his own way without too much footwork, so I teased him a bit. I nicked him on the neck. He saw things were serious then, and steadied down, but I caught him again on the arm. He had some pretty patterns on it soon. To cut a long story short, Willy, he gave me one mark – by the mouth here as you've seen – and I gave him three. By that time we were both pretty well done up. My second patched my wound and invited me to their *Kasino*, that's what they call their wardroom mess ashore. We toasted each other in schnapps, and they asked me if Sir John Fisher was going to send the fleet across – when he became First Sea Lord – to round up their little navy and take it across to Portsmouth before it became big enough to make a nuisance of itself. "Not a sportsmanlike thing to do," I said. "But you did it to the Danish fleet in eighteen hundred and seven," they said. And it was true, Willy, we did – without even a declaration of war.

'I believe they know more about our naval history than we do ourselves. And that's how they plan to beat us. They say that Nelson proved the smaller fleet always beats the bigger so long as it's better – ship for ship – and well handled. And they mean to do it, Willy. And the way they're goin' now they have every chance. But I'm glad to say Fisher'll be takin' over the Board of Admiralty in October. You'll see things will be different after that – I promise you. He has ideas for surprisin' Tirpitz. They'll surprise our fellows too. It has to be done, Willy.

'And now, I fancy we ought to see how the others are gettin' along. We don't want to seem stand-offish do we? And not a word about all I've bin tellin' you. It's a secret between us – you and me and Admiral Fisher!'

196

After Uncle Richard had left, Willy asked his mother if he could take up fencing.

'*That*'s what you and Uncle Richard were talking about!' A funny look came into her eyes. 'He was a good swordsman at one time, Willy. He won the schoolboy foils. He could have made a name for himself they said, if he hadn't started travelling.'

'He didn't tell me he was as good as that.'

'He wouldn't. The best never *tell*, Willy. Only second-raters blow their own trumpet.'

The next time Willy saw Peters was again in London, and at adjacent desks. He was very pleased to see him; he had been wondering if he would ever since old Phipps had given him the good news that he had passed the interview, and the not so good news of the date he had to go up again to sit the main written examination.

Afterwards they compared impressions of the papers; both decided they had failed.

'It'll probably mean I shall have to become a parson,' Peters said gloomily.

Willy thought of Varsity; it seemed a pale substitute for the Navy now. Despite his recurrent feeling of guilt for what had happened to the *Peacock*'s mainsail and his poor father, the cruise had left him with a taste for sailing and the sight and scent of ships and deep waters which Happy's stories of boating at Oxford didn't quite match up to. His talk with Uncle Richard had clinched it; he would join the Navy, he had said, if he were their age. That was where the strain was going to come when the Prussian challenge began in earnest. He envied him and George.

He wondered what he would be able to say to Uncle Richard next time he saw him.

'Nonsense!' old Phipps exploded, when he confessed his failure to him. 'You must buck up, Steel. Modesty is becoming in a boy, but only if it is kept within proper bounds. Taken to extremes it is positively unmanly. You don't want to be thought unmanly do you?'

'No, sir.'

'Well, buck up, boy! Buck up! Think of your brothers. The idea of failure never even entered their heads.'

'No, sir.'

'I don't put boys in for examinations if they are going to fail. Only two boys have ever failed the naval entrance from Birchfield House. One had a history of insanity in the family. I had to get rid of him when he took to sitting up in a tree all night. The other was a fool. You're not a fool, Steel.'

'No, sir.'

'No, you've a good head on your shoulders. But you must – not – hold – *back*. Push yourself to the front. Otherwise, how is anyone to know you're not a fool?'

'I don't know sir.'

Far from reassuring him, old Phipps's pep talk made him more worried. To be only the third boy ever to have failed the naval entrance from Birchfield House, when one of the others had been mad and the other a fool, was an awful prospect. He couldn't come back after the holidays to face that; he would have to change schools.

'Let's wait and see, shall we!' his mother said, when he told her at the beginning of the holidays. 'I wasn't going to tell you this, Willy, but your father heard that you made a very good impression at your interview. Now you must never tell anyone because, of course, they're not supposed to say what happens.'

One morning after Christmas a man in a dark suit called at Felpham House and asked for him.

'Mr William Steel?'

He had only been called 'Mister' once before – at his naval interview. He wondered if they sent people around to your house to tell you when you hadn't passed. He nodded apprehensively. 'Yes.'

'I am from Gieve, Mathews and Seagrove, sir – the naval outfitters. Your brother, George, is a valued customer.' He paused. 'Would it be convenient, sir, for me to take your measurements now?'

Willy stared. 'How d'you know? That is – I may not have – I don't know whether I've passed or not –'

The man smiled. 'I shouldn't worry about that, sir, if I were you.'

198

Willy discussed this delphic utterance afterwards with Henrietta. 'It was his *look*, Henry. It was as if he knew but wasn't allowed to say.'

'Of course you've got in, stupid. If George can get in, you can!'

'I'm not as clever as George.'

'George is clever at some things, but you're much cleverer at others – things George doesn't even *know* about.' She was thinking of Willy's questioning mind and the soaring fancies it threw up, and the insights he had sometimes into what other people were thinking and feeling.

He could paint and draw better than George, Willy thought, and he knew far more about butterflies and birds and animals. 'But they don't ask you about those things.'

'Listen to me, William Steel, if George got in and you haven't, I'll – there's something wrong with them. We'll lose the next war.'

Willy laughed. Surely the Gieves man *had* known?

A week later his mother called excitedly from downstairs, 'Willy! Willy! You've passed!'

He rushed down, his tie undone, and she hugged him. 'I *knew* you would.'

'So did he,' Henrietta said, coming down after him ostensibly on the way to breakfast. 'He just wanted us to feel sorry for him.'

'That's not fair, Henry!'

'Oh?' She stopped and gave him her scornful look.

He stared back, warning her with his eyes not to say anything of what he had confided to her about not going back to Birchfield House if he failed, and running away from home if they tried to make him. He had been feeling desperate that night.

She continued on her way. 'He was trying to make himself important.' It was her 'silly little boy' tone of voice.

His mother turned back to him, a tender look on her face as she saw his expression. 'You *are* important, Willy. You're going to be a naval officer.' She hugged him again.

Later that morning his father called to him from the study as he was about to go out to the shop with Henry and Harry to buy some stodge in celebration of the occasion. He held *The Times* up as he came in.

'Somethin' that might be of interest, Willy.' His speech was much better, almost back to normal.

Willy took the paper and looked down the page at which it was opened; near the bottom was a list of the successful candidates for the Royal Naval College, Osborne. He scanned until he came to his own name – 'W.L.S.Steel' – the first time he had seen it in print, and in *The Times*! The intense feeling was heightened by the name just above his own, 'J.R.d'O.Peters'.

'You might like to cut it out,' his father said.

'May I?'

'You've earned it, Willy.' His eyes were bluer and clearer than he'd seen them for ages.

Outside, he whooped, 'Peters has got in too! Henry! Henry! Peters has got in!'

Of the confusion of impressions assailing him on his first day at Osborne, the one that stood out most clearly for Willy all his life, perhaps because it was so unequivocal at first sight, so puzzling on deeper reflection, so true in his later experience, was the legend engraved in great gold letters across one end of the assembly area or 'quarterdeck' known as 'Nelson'.

THERE IS NOTHING THE NAVY CANNOT DO

He stared up at it after making the salute to the quarterdeck they had been taught on the way across in the tug. The concept was overwhelming. He couldn't take it in; there was NOTHING the Navy could not do. It was so amazing because he had not thought there was anything much the Navy did do except steam about at sea and if it came to war, fight battles. What did they really do, he wondered, and thought of the secret missions Uncle Richard went on for Admiral Fisher – and what would they want *him* to do? There were any amount of things he couldn't and never would be able to do.

His other chief memory of that day came before this momentous awakening; it was of the passage over to the Isle of Wight, where Osborne was situated. Most of the new cadets, immaculate in uniforms retaining the fresh smell of the heavy cloth, had left their parents at home or on the platform at Waterloo Station, but a few families accompanied their sons in the special train to Portsmouth. Among these was Peters's. The first Willy saw of him was on the quay in the dockyard with his mother and two younger sisters. He recognized the look on his face immediately, remembering his own first day at boarding school: Peters had been to a day school. He wasn't blubbing; his lips were not even quivering, but it was obvious he was not listening to his sisters' chatter. He was casting odd glances at his mother's face – as she did at his. Willy made up his mind to go to him as soon as they were aboard and try and take his mind off things. His sisters looked good sorts. They had the same eager brown eyes and round faces; there was a distinct family resemblance.

He lost sight of them as he followed in his group up the gangway past the paddle sponson and on to the deck of the Admiralty tug that was to take them across to Cowes. The crew were getting their hand luggage aboard and stowed, and he saw the captain looking down at them from the bridge under the tall yellow funnel stained with smoke around the top. There was a hiss of escaping steam and a slight almost imperceptible movement of the deck underfoot. The senior cadets who had accompanied their party from Waterloo with a lieutenant called Packham, were shepherding them to the far side out of the way of those still coming aboard.

The water of the harbour was an opaque green, lopping gently, on which all sorts of craft, some grey and obviously naval, others in all sorts of different colours, lay at moorings or alongside quays or plied in different directions. There was a sense of activity, and in wafts between warm odours coming up from the tug's engine room, he smelled the distinctive tang of salt sea he remembered from the *Peacock*'s cruise. He felt a wave of nostalgia, and thought of his father with the stick he had to use for getting about now, and his mother's

201

farewell embrace before he left the house, and Henry shouting he must write to her *every* week –

'*You!*'

He wheeled quickly to see one of the senior cadets regarding him with an unpleasant expression. 'Name?'

'Steel.'

'Cook?'

'No.' Wondering if the cadet were deaf, he raised his voice, '*Steel.*'

'*Cook?*' the other cut him short. It was one of the tricks George had warned him about, but he hadn't told him of this particular one.

Another senior cadet next to the belligerent one said kindly, 'What's your cook's name?'

'Hoskins – Mrs Hoskins,' he replied gratefully.

'*Mrs* Hoskins!' the belligerent one repeated as they left him. He felt relieved; he had thought he was in for punishment; things didn't seem to have changed since George's time in the *Britannia*.

The steam whistle sounded and he heard a tinkle of bells from the direction of the bridge. Looking that way he saw a huge white ensign; it was blowing out from the stern of the battleship berthed ahead of them. He had seen it as they marched along the jetty and wondered if they were going aboard. From this angle it looked even more impressive. There was a verandah-like walk all around the stern windows in the hull which gave an oddly domestic look until you saw the rows and rows of rivets fastening the heavy grey plates, and above the side rails the turrets and muzzles of the guns, brass ends gleaming, and rising above them thick grey funnels and masts with circular fighting tops on two levels and wide yards with halyards. There was nothing homely about her; she looked cold and menacing.

He heard a senior cadet chivying late-comers up the gangway and, turning, saw Peters reaching the deck. He was looking sick, gazing straight ahead with a fixed expression as if he might break down if he actually noticed anything. His face was very pale. As he walked across the deck towards them, Willy went out to greet him.

'Hallo, Steel.' He smiled wanly in recognition.

'I was jolly glad to see your name in *The Times*,' Willy said enthusiastically.

'I was jolly glad to see yours.'

Willy was about to ask casually if those were his sisters he had seen on the jetty, but stopped himself just in time. What was there to say that didn't touch on home and family? He couldn't think of anything. Peters was very close to breaking down, he could see. It was no use repeating how ripping it was to see him here.

He searched his brain desperately. 'What do two and one make?'

Peters's eyes widened slightly in surprise.

'You mustn't answer that,' Willy went on. 'George told me. He's my brother. He went to the *Britannia*. It's the same here. They ask you trick questions to catch you out, then they beat you. They asked me the name of my cook.'

'What did you say?'

'I told them.'

'Did you get beaten?'

'No. Someone told me what they meant, you see. They just say "Name?" Then they say "Cook?" Like that.' It seemed to be working: Peters's eyes were showing interest. He went on quickly, 'Another thing they ask is "Are you pi, tart or blag?" At least they asked George.'

'What d'you have to say?'

'George said "Blag".'

'Did he get beaten?'

'No, they laughed at him. It means blackguard.'

'What do the others mean?'

'Pi means pious. I don't know what tart means.'

The tug was starting to turn; looking down Willy saw a circle of pale green and white-laced water spreading from the paddle wheel on their side. He glanced back at Peters's face, and was thankful to see the immediate danger was past; his eyes had regained the eager look he remembered from their earlier meetings; there was more colour in his normally ruddy cheeks and his lips were no longer pressed tight. He would feel dreadfully homesick tonight, just as he would himself. He always did on the first night. It would be dark then. No one would see.

'I've never been on a ship before,' he said, 'not a big one.'
'Nor have I,' Peters replied.

They saw masts, fully rigged, ahead on the other side and crossed the deck to look at them. 'The *Victory*,' they heard someone say. Willy stared at her. He had mugged up all Nelson's battles before the interview. It was strange to think this was the actual ship he had sailed and been killed in – a hundred years ago. If only he hadn't worn all his medals and ribbons the marksman probably wouldn't have shot him; it had always seemed such a terrible waste and tragedy. Grandpapa had told him that when young he had served with men who had fought at Trafalgar. They had wept when Nelson died. He had not been able to imagine that. Men never cried. Of all the things he had heard or read about Nelson, that had made the deepest impression. He would have told them at the interview, but they never asked about Trafalgar.

And there she was! He tried to imagine sailors aboard her weeping as they heard the news from the cockpit below. He didn't find it so impossible now, looking at the ship. She belonged to another time; everything must have been different, the men too. Nelson had asked Hardy to kiss him before he died. That, too, he could understand now. He imagined Nelson as he had seen him in pictures with his cocked hat and his eye patch and his loose sleeve and stars and decorations, pacing with Hardy before the marksman got him and felt a catch of pride as if in a very humble way he was joining their company.

He became aware of surging interest among the cadets around him, and saw them pointing and craning for a better view of something ahead, and heard the word 'submarine' repeated excitedly. He leaned out over the rail, surprised at what he saw. Three men in white sweaters were standing on a thin, raft-like thing scarcely rising above the surface of the water. A large white ensign fluttered just behind and above them. He wondered if the deck would get higher, but it didn't; the craft just came on towards them, a small wave playing up and sometimes over the bow and along the sloping side.

'I wouldn't like to go in one of them!' Peters said.

'No fear!' He had an image of the water darkening on the other side of the glass port when the *Peacock* went over and he had thought they were plunging straight down. Yet the men standing there in their white sweaters looked splendid, as if they were proud of their strange little craft, and he was disappointed when the submarine turned almost back on its course to enter a bay inside the fort at the harbour mouth; he would have liked to study it from close quarters.

It disappeared behind a small warship moored alongside a jetty leading into the bay. The tug was heading for the narrow entrance between the forts now. He and Peters crossed back to the other side, gazing at the little quays and ramps and squashed-up, painted houses and the round stone fort as they swept by. A few people walking on the esplanade outside stopped and watched them; a group of children waved; they waved back, Willy very conscious of his new uniform.

He heard Packham telling the senior cadets to form up, and turned to see three of them approaching their side of the deck; he was thankful the belligerent one who had quizzed him earlier was not among them. They separated the new cadets into small groups, each taking one, chivying them into lines properly spaced and 'dressed'. The one in charge of his group spent a long time going along the lines thumping them between the shoulder blades, ostensibly to get them standing straight; Willy knew he was quite straight when he received his. Then standing in front of them, their mentor demonstrated the naval salute, long way up, shortest way down. He showed them twice, after which he told them to do it and shouted at them for doing it slackly. Their sightseeing was over.

Yet he always remembered the sights – or his *impression* of the sights of that voyage better than any voyage he made afterwards. He remembered the water flecked with the smallest whitecaps stretching away to the fields and woods of the Isle of Wight, and the sky above clear, wintry blue with high tails of cloud. He remembered very sharply two lines of battleships anchored in Spithead, seemingly stubbier and smaller against the distances than the monster that had been tied up ahead of them at the jetty, but with the same grim presence, still, dark fortresses in a world of water and moving light. He remembered the three-funnelled Atlantic liner they saw turning gracefully away down the Solent, and four destroyers as black and low and vicious as the smoke roaring from their short funnels, sharp, turtle-backed bows throwing out screens of spray while the water piled up astern.

He remembered the verdant colours of the Isle of Wight, occasional clusters of farm buildings amongst dark trees, ruins of an ancient Abbey, his first sight of Osborne House, the twin towers and palatial façade flanked by wooded grounds sloping to the shore suggesting a grander version of Birchfield House. Above all, he remembered the crispness of the day and a sense of space and long distances beyond the land which keyed in with his feeling of setting out in a new direction from which there was no turning back; nor did he wish it. This was what he wanted.

He remembered talking to Peters after the instructional class was over; what they said faded with that day; echoes must have sounded though over their time at Osborne and afterwards at Dartmouth and in the training cruiser that had taken them to the West Indies as the closest companions.

Several lifetimes later he came across the photograph they had had taken together in Cowes during that first term at Osborne. What funny little fellows! What untouched faces! What would-be insouciant poses! What were they thinking in that far-off time, those half-children, half sailors? What did they know of anything? What did they apprehend of the future? If you looked closely perhaps it was there – in the angle of Jollion Peters's cap, in the broad smile which made his face appear rounder even than it was, in the frank, wide-apart eyes challenging the world keenly and good-humouredly – always surprised if the world did its worst – or was that hindsight, Jolly? *Jolly* –

His own eyes held that pensive look with which he was still cursed, but the camera had caught humour there – in his eyes rather than in the smile which just touched up the corners of his mouth; his lower lip looked rather obstinately full – not a bad looking young shaver though, not bad at all! He had always taken a good photograph. Self-conscious he had been; his stance, simulating brag, was so much stiffer than Jolly's easy chest-out, head-thrown-back style – brothers in arms! Nelsons to be! Better to travel hopefully – certainly than not to arrive. Were those two hopefuls as carefree and happy as he remembered? Bound with restrictions, harried by senior cadets, although not seriously bullied – that had only come later – their young minds moulded like plasticine to conform to the service ideal of what England expected – today it would simply provide mirth – or mutiny – yet that was not how he remembered it. They had expected nothing else. They had known why it had to be. Today's youngsters knew so much more about everything, yet it was doubtful if they made any more sense of it all than they had in their day. They had known the things that mattered, duty and love of country and love of friends – manly love untainted by thoughts of – Lord, they hadn't even known such things existed except as filthy vices indulged by brutes.

Perhaps it had been too easy. Cold baths and petty terrors and humiliations – and other things, but most of those seemed to have been filtered from his mind, and certainly he had only the pleasantest memories of both Osborne and Dartmouth Colleges – it had been a small price to pay for the absence of relativity in thought and morals they enjoyed.

He wished he could test his theories out on Jolly as he used to then. His matter-of-fact intelligence had been a good corrective for his own too speculative habits of thought. His memory would have been useful too, to amplify the flood of memories released by the photograph. Alas, that it could not be. There they were, the two of them in their new cadet's uniforms, their bright faces ready for anything that life could bring, and one would fall in the war just around the corner of the years, one would not. However hard you studied the picture you couldn't tell which or why it should be. Had it already been decided when the photographer removed his cap from the lens?

Or – supposing time did not run in the way experience suggested – if for instance it were simply another dimension – would Jolly die gloriously at Jutland because he was studying his face 'now' in the photograph, and feeling the emptiness he felt 'then'? Not causality as he understood it perhaps, yet if time did not behave in the generally accepted way, neither did causality. Who could tell? Even 'now', as he looked at the picture, he might be making the decision for those two boys to enter the photographer's establishment in Cowes! He couldn't for the life of him remember who had suggested it.

One thing was fairly certain; if it had been the other way around and it was Jolly looking at the picture 'now', he wouldn't waste time asking silly questions. The thoughts, if they came unbidden, which was highly improbable, would be dismissed into the classification of 'the great unknowable'. Jolly had always been certain that when finally he was called to account for his sins the 'great unknowable' would be made dazzlingly clear. He had few enough sins, poor Jolly, compared with those he himself had managed to accumulate since those long-dead, innocent, marvellous days together.

12

'Master George!'

Henrietta heard Millie's surprised greeting as she was coming down for tea, and leapt the rest of the stairs two at a time.

He turned as he heard her, his eyes lighting. After more than two years away, he hadn't changed so much as become a thicker, stronger-looking version of his earlier self. His dark brows were very sharp against his tan, his eyes clear with health. He was wearing a very new tweed suit with creases in the trousers.

She threw herself at him. 'You *beast*!'

'*George*!' Mama had come out of the drawing-room behind her. 'Why didn't you let us *know*?'

He disentangled himself. 'I didn't know myself till yesterday. I thought I'd surprise you. Actually – I didn't have enough for a wire –'

'Fie!' She held her arms out for him. 'Where did you get that suit!'

He looked down with a studied casualness that revealed he was not as mature as he seemed. 'Oh – Gieves knocked it up for me.'

Willy and Andy, alerted by his voice, were whooping down the stairs.

'*Quiet*!' Mama called, and to George in a smothered voice as he embraced her, 'Why didn't you come in uniform?'

He laughed. He was as tall as her now, and so broad the back of his jacket was stretched tight as he put his arms around her.

Henrietta thought she saw a tear glistening in her mother's

209

eye afterwards as she turned rather quickly, telling Willy to go up and fetch Harry and Babs. 'We'll all have tea in the drawing-room.'

That tea glowed for Henrietta afterwards as a golden moment: they were all together as they had been as young children; Papa, animated by George's appearance, was almost his former self, shooting questions and responding to George's tales with long stories of his own time in the Mediterranean. They heard of Platea and Lemnos and other strange ports which she had to look up in the atlas, and Lord Charles Beresford – 'Charlie B' to George. Although Commander in Chief of the Channel Fleet, Charlie B had treated George and all his boat's crew to a famous picnic at Gibraltar after they had beaten the flagship's boat in finding a man who had fallen overboard. They heard about the Kaiser's holiday villa on Corfu –

'Mad Bill!' Papa interrupted with a shout, looking triumphantly at Mama. 'Didn't I tell you George would not be far off! Get a close look at the feller, did you George?' He leaned forward eagerly.

'Not really. But some of our fellows were entertained in his escort cruiser. They said the German officers were very decent sorts. They got on famously with them – much better than the Frogs –'

'You don't say so! They're goin' to fight us – ain't they George?'

George grinned. 'I trust they are, Pater –'

'Course they are, George! This feller Tirpitz, he's not playin' bumblepuppy. D'you know, there's not one of the new Hun battleships can steam further than Land's End. You know what that means!'

'They mean to fight us in the North Sea.'

'How I wish I was your age again, George!'

Mama sat listening with a happy smile on her face even at the prospect of George in a battle in the North Sea, which, of course, she dismissed as fantasy – another indication of her husband's softening of the brain. The boys listened, wide-eyed. Babs made her presence felt as always, asking outrageous questions that brought shouts of laughter. Millie grinned again at George as she came in with fresh hot water for the pot and extra muffins. The spring sun slanted in through the windows, burnishing the pile on the velvet curtains.

Even as she basked in the outbreak of family warmth, brighter for the disagreeableness that had begun to seem normal now, Henrietta was struck with a sort of sadness. Whether it was a presentiment that this short period of George's leave would be the last time the family would all be together – apart from poor Jack; she wondered who else was noticing his absence after the dulling effect of the six years since his death – mama would, she was sure, although she gave no sign – or whether it was that acute sense of the remorselessness of time that afflicted her in her happiest moments, she could never tell. But when she recalled that teatime afterwards, as she often did, she had a distinct recollection of thinking that in less than a week the boys would be back at school and she would be back at the Baronesses's, and then George would go away in another battleship and they wouldn't see him for years.

After tea she and the boys walked up to Whitestone Pond just as they used to. Willy and George walked close together, talking about the Navy – for Willy had been one term at Osborne and George seemed very eager to compare it with the old *Britannia*. Willy struggled to insist it was no softer even if they did sleep in beds in dormitories. George began to shift his position, treating both *Britannia* and Osborne as nursery schools compared with real life in the gunroom of a battleship.

She felt sorry for Andy; he had been George's constant companion in the old days; now, as he hung on George's other side listening to the cadet jargon she could tell he felt left out. He looked very different from the other two; perhaps it was the spectacles he wore, but she thought it had more to do with his manner. Beside George in his guise as travelled man of the world he seemed suddenly very young and unsure, and although he was only a year younger than George his voice had not broken; he was evidently conscious of this for when he spoke it was in the gruffest pitch he could manage.

Lying in bed that night and thinking how George had changed, she was not sure it was all to the good. He had

211

always been very confident; today he had seemed almost cocky, telling them how he had been chosen as the Commander's 'doggie' – whatever that was – and how he had gone shooting with the great man, and he thought he would probably get a good 'flimsy' because of various successes he had contributed to in the regattas – and he was going to specialize in the gunnery branch because that was the way to get rapid promotion now. You had to be A 1 at maths, but he thought he could manage that as he had never found any difficulty with the subject. As she thought about all that he had said, she realized he hadn't *changed*, simply become more like himself, more determined to shine, more respectful to authority, more focused on success. And he had become less accessible to her. It was as if the Navy had taken him; he was still her brother, as dependable as ever – she knew she would always be able to rely on him utterly – but he no longer seemed to speak quite the same language. The Navy had given him its own language and its own goals and he couldn't see that there might be anything else. His certainties reminded her of the sisters at the convent. The Navy was like a church: it swallowed people whole. The echoing hulls of the battleships were like great grey steel cathedrals; they had become George's whole life and his faith. She realized with a little shiver that if ever he had to choose between her and the Navy, it might not be her –

She hoped the same thing would never happen to Willy. She couldn't imagine it would. He had always been different; beneath the briskness he had acquired at Osborne, he was still different – willing to conform to what was expected but not adopting it as his own. Not far below the surface of that argument he had been having with George about the *Britannia*, the real Willy had been looking on amused and detached, she felt sure from what he had told her before; he seemed to look on the strange customs and ordeals he was put through as an obstacle race which he had to negotiate, but which scarcely involved him. There was an essential Willy which the Navy would never touch. Because of this, he would not do as well as George; he might not do well at all –

The next day it was her turn to feel left out. After breakfast the boys took George to see the Lanchester which had been acquired since he had been home last. It was housed in what had been the stables; it just fitted because the engine, instead of extending out in front, was alongside the driver. She hated the machine. When it was used it was smelly and noisy, but most of the time it merely served as an object of devotion for Mackinnon; he was forever taking the engine or wheels apart, or polishing the paintwork or leather. But most of all she hated it because it had taken the place of dear Bacchante and Endymion – for that it could never and would never be forgiven, nor could she forgive Mackinnon for transferring his affections so spinelessly. She had wept for two nights over the horses, but when she asked him whether he had he had laughed at her.

Mackinnon was delighted to show off the machine, especially as George seemed to know about the parts of engines and how they worked, asking questions which necessitated poking around with spanners. Babs was with the boys, chattering nonsense, which also delighted Mackinnon; she had been a favourite of his since she had first tottered into the stables to help him feed the horses; he was stupidly devoted to her.

When George climbed into the driving seat and Mackinnon leaned in beside him explaining the gears and dials, Henrietta left. She walked back through the colonnaded way to the side door, her mind filled with things she would like to do to Babs – ought to do to curb her showing off. The boys only encouraged her, laughing at the personal remarks which she thought up deliberately to provoke them, while Nurse had given up long ago; anxious only to make sure the spoilt little devil behaved herself in front of Mama, she bribed her with unlimited licence elsewhere. Babs appreciated the situation, behaving like an angel in the short periods she saw her mother, at other times tormenting anyone not prepared to fall in with her every whim.

Arriving in her room, Henrietta sat in front of the mirror and glared at herself. She gathered up the hair falling down her back and piled it on top of her head, catching at the strands escaping, inclining her face to study the effect from different angles. Letting it fall again, she rose and lit the candle kept on her bedside table for emergencies and held a

213

hairpin in the flame until it was black, then seating herself at the mirror again, she started working at her eyebrows. After several visits to the candle she felt she had achieved the desired effect and put the pin down, opened the top drawer and took out a jar of cold cream and a cadmium red pastel she kept wrapped in tissue there. Scraping some of the pastel into the lid of the jar she began mixing in the cream with her fingers, then dabbing the composition on her cheek. She studied it, then added more cream and repeated the process. Afterwards she took her comb and more hairpins and started putting up her hair properly.

She was engaged in this when she heard running steps along the passage, followed by rapid knocking at her door. She had heard them all coming up the stairs some minutes before, but she knew from the sound of the feet this was Babs – the last person she wanted. If Babs saw her in this state it would be all over the house by tomorrow. She had not locked the door, though; before she could move, it was opening.

'Henry, Henry –' Babs started. Seeing Henrietta's reflection in the mirror, her eyes widened.

'Come in!' Henrietta hissed as she turned. 'Close the door!'

For once Babs did as she was told, gazing at her in silence.

'What is it?' Henrietta asked sharply. She could almost see the mind working behind those black eyes fixed on hers.

'They've pushed me out, Henry – I know they're doing something.'

'Of course, they're doing something.'

'They're doing something they shouldn't. They told me to get out because I was a girl.'

Henrietta's sooty brows rose. 'Because you're a girl!'

Babs nodded indignantly. 'You go, Henry – see what they're doing.'

She thought for a moment, listening to the sounds from the other end of the passage; they were evidently in the nursery. 'All right,' she said. 'Promise me you won't say anything –' she gave her a significant look, 'about – me.'

'I promise, Henry.'

'Cross your heart.'

214

'Cut my throat – ugchh –'

'Go and see if anyone's coming.'

Babs did as she was told, popping her head back around the door to say there was no one.

Henrietta rose and left the room, tiptoeing along the passage until she came to the door of the nursery, which was shut. She stood listening; she could hear George's voice; he seemed to be telling one of the others he had not kept his legs straight. She heard scuffling sounds and Willy saying, 'it won't hurt –' and realized suddenly it must be one of those tortures played in the gunroom which George had described at length; they were putting Andy or Harry through it. Angry, she seized the handle and flung the door wide open.

They turned at the sudden intrusion and remained for a moment still like a tableau. Andy was standing on the table, one hand on Willy's shoulder; George in shirtsleeves was at the other side and Harry was beside him; their expressions were incredulous.

George was the first to move; he shook his head, closing his eyes and passing a hand across them with an exaggerated gesture before opening them again.

'What are you doing to poor Andy?' she said fiercely, and to Andy, 'Come down at once!'

George recovered himself. 'No girls allowed.'

She advanced towards him, fire in her eyes. 'Who do you think you are, George Steel! You've been at home one day and you start ordering people around as if you were on a battleship – where you're only a little *doggie* anyway. I've as much right to be in here as you and I'm not going. And Andy –' looking up at him, 'I told you to come down this instant –'

George was leaning on the table by this time, shaking with laughter, and she saw Andy glancing down at him, also starting to laugh. She felt herself colouring and looked at Willy. He was gazing at her with a half-amused, half-puzzled expression.

'What are you doing to Andy?' she said sharply.

'Nothing. We're trying to help him, that's all, Henry.'

Andy was down on his haunches on the table now, appar-

215

ently helpless with laughter; Harry too had joined in and Willy was evidently having difficulty restraining himself as she continued to stare at him.

She tried to keep her voice very calm. 'You're all behaving very stupidly. I shall stay here until you tell me what you are doing.'

'I've told you, Henry, we're trying to help Andy – with his voice.'

'His voice!'

'Capstan drill,' George said from the other side.

She turned to face him.

He shrugged. She was amazed, seeing him without his jacket, at how thick his neck was; he was like a young bull. 'It's to get a fellow's voice to break,' he explained. 'You have to jump off the table keeping your legs straight when you land – only Andy always bends his knees.'

'And how does *that* make his voice break! I should think it would break his legs.'

George looked past her to Willy and collapsed again with laughter.

On the last morning before he went back to school Andy rose at five. He had scarcely had any sleep for thinking of the unhappiness ahead, but was not aware of tiredness; the hollow ache behind his eyes was simply a part of the misery overlying him like a cloud that he had observed a week or so back as a puff over the horizon, but which now obscured the sky; there was no chink of blue.

Always on his last morning he rose early to stretch the precious final hours at home. Time ran slowly when everyone was asleep; even when the servants got up and the maids clattered in the passage it could still be contained – even when he heard Millie coming with the hot water, and the family moving there was still time to think these normal activities part of a normal day. Breakfast was the turning point; after breakfast, he knew from experience, there was no holding anything; the day took over, accelerating to a crescendo of last-minute events and their inevitable conclusion – Mackinnon in his chauffeur's cap and livery

216

wheeling his trunk out through the vines towards the stables. Then there was no time left.

He padded in his socks to the window, careful not to wake George, who would despise him if he knew. Probably he half-despised him anyway. George had never worried about anything in his life; he wished he were like George –

The air through the window as he pulled the curtain aside was keen, spiced with a thousand garden and tree scents; there had evidently been a shower during the night, unlocking them. The sky was washed clean, the birds chorusing the fresh day and spring tangible in every breath he took. He felt a desire to be part of it, to be outside, walking, and thought suddenly he would like Henrietta to be with him. He let the curtain drop and walked quietly to the door and across to her room.

She thought at first it was a joke George had put him up to, then she realized he was serious.

'It's the middle of the night –'

'No, it's not. It's a lovely morning – honestly, Henry. There won't be time after breakfast.' In any case, he thought, it would have changed by then.

She could hardly see his face, only a faint gleam from his spectacles, but she could tell he badly wanted her to go with him, and it struck her for the first time that he was unhappy at Marlborough. She knew he always suffered from home-sickness before going back, but so did all the boys – except perhaps George. She sensed this was more than ordinary homesickness. There was a hint of desperation in his voice. She felt sorry for him and touched that he had come to her for reassurance; she had never been so close to him as she was to Willy.

Her bed was warm and comfortable. 'Half an hour,' she said.

'It'll be too late then – please – Henry –'

'Quarter of an hour.'

He hesitated. 'All right, quarter of an hour. I'll wait for you in the orchard. Please don't be long, Henry.' He knew that as soon as the servants woke time would start moving again.

It was cold waiting in the orchard; the chill air and the

dawn light took him straight back to Marlborough – the early morning walk from the house to school wrapped against the bitter wind, fingers stiff around the books in his kishe. Cold and Marlborough were inseparable – cold water in the basin in the morning, freezing 'sweats' over the Downs, snow blowing in the open entrance to the bogs behind the house, Downton jamming the window in the tiny study they shared to stop the icy draught. This time tomorrow he would be there, still asleep he thought. He had an image of his dormitory. It was only after lights out and in the few minutes he lay awake in the morning before the bell that he was able to be himself and think his own thoughts.

He started moving to try and shut out the images, but they persisted – Hutton and Squires and the asses who followed them around, aping their attitudes. He could remember the moment he had rebelled against being one of them himself – no particular incident – they had been hurrying back to the house after first lesson, warming their hands on the penny rolls they had each bought outside the gates as they did every morning, empty insides craving breakfast. Hutton was saying he had been given a note by 'Hairyjohn' about not learning his verbs properly; he was speculating on how many 'cuts' Sandy would give him. The others joined in, eager with examples of beatings they had received, when suddenly it had struck him they were talking just to impress Hutton. It had been like the conversion on the road to Damascus – except in reverse. One moment he had been a member of the group, happy to sink his personality with theirs, toadying to the stronger personalities, the next he had been an individual, observing them all from the outside – himself included – despising himself for being the same as them.

He was alone in the house. The few others like him also on the outside were mostly wet – except for Reeves. He had thought he might chum up with Reeves, but he was a queer fish who seemed to go his own way from a naturally perverse spirit –

He heard a twig snap behind and turned. Henrietta was coming towards him, flapping her arms to get warm. Her eyes were very dark against her pale skin just tinged with colour on her cheeks. He had been amazed recently at how

218

pretty she could look – pretty was not the word perhaps – *striking*. He felt himself instinctively brace; he had always been a little afraid of her. She had her aggressive expression now.

'Where d'you want to go?'

'Nowhere in particular,' he replied, and started to move away through the trees towards the tennis lawn and the side gate. He wondered why he had asked her; she looked as if she was not going to enjoy it. It would have been better to walk alone as he liked to on Sundays from school through Savernake Forest –

He looked so dejected as he turned towards the lawn, Henrietta was attacked by guilt. She had been thoroughly selfish to show she was doing him a favour. In reality she was glad now to be out so early; there was a crispness and promise in the air that excited her; she felt almost light-headed.

She ran up and slipped her hand into his; he looked round, surprised.

'We ought to get up early more often,' she said. 'Come on!' and started running across the lawn, swinging his hand. Two thrushes rose in alarm.

Outside the gate they turned instinctively left, the usual way up the hill towards Whitestone Pond and the Heath.

'I wish I could go in the Navy,' he said after a while when they had stopped running. 'I'd like to go to the Mediterranean. I'd like to go to Greece – Athens. I'd get up early and climb the Acropolis – when there was no one there.'

She looked at him in surprise; she had never guessed he wanted to go to sea. 'Couldn't you still?'

He shook his head. 'It's my eyes.'

She thought for a minute. 'Do they have parsons aboard ship?'

He turned his head to look at her earnestly. 'Do you think there is a God, Henry?'

The question took her by surprise. 'Of course there is!' She thought of Father Geoffrey, and began to feel annoyed that he should question something to which wise, good men like Father Geoffrey gave their lives. 'What d'you mean?'

'How do we know what parsons really think? Even if they do think there is a God, how do we know it's not just because

219

that's what they were taught – and the people who taught them were taught it and you go back and back – until Christ –'

'That's how you know!'

'But how do you *know* that Christ knew? Only from what his disciples wrote about him. They were *men*.'

He had obviously been thinking about it a great deal. 'Because He rose from the dead,' she replied. 'He couldn't have done *that* if He was an ordinary man!'

'No.' He didn't sound convinced.

Later in the morning, after he had been driven off to the station with his trunk and cases in the Lanchester, bravely concealing the dread she had glimpsed beneath his words, she ran upstairs to her room and wrote to Father Geoffrey, telling him about how, until then, she had not known, not really known her own brother.

His reply came a week later, after she had returned to the Baroness's at Sunningdale.

My dear Henrietta,

Poor Andrew – but you must not blame yourself. It is a very common experience to miss the very things that are under our noses. I worked in Bishopsgate several years ago and walked past the Church of St Michael in Cornhill almost every day. I hardly realized it was there until I chanced on a picture of it in a book I was reading and found it was built by Christopher Wren, the tower supposed to be one of his masterpieces. My eyes were opened!

On the other hand Andrew has probably changed. Boys do change a great deal when they go to their public school, and for some I am afraid it is rather a wretched experience, school. There are many reasons for this. The boy is a herd animal and his herd instincts are positively encouraged at all our great schools so that if for one reason or another a boy finds himself out of favour with his fellows his life can be very disagreeable. I am sure you have observed this at your own school among the girls. From my observations of boys I believe one of the great causes to be the different rates of development; thus one boy may have at the age of fourteen the physical characteristics almost of a man while another two years his senior (in age) still shows the characteristics of a boy, even his voice may not have broken. The stage of development reached has an obvious bearing on a boy's prowess on the games field – as you know games are the only god of our schools! – so a boy whose physical development is slower than the average may find he is regarded as a duffer at the only thing that really *matters*! So he loses confidence and is eventually rejected by the herd, which can be far crueller than individuals. It is not always easy for masters to spot these cases, although I am certain that once spotted at a school like Marlborough, where the masters are generally first rate, every effort would be made to prevent bullying and encourage the boy in other directions. I have a slight acquaintance with the housemaster of Cotton and could write to him if you would like me to do so. You did not say what house Andrew is in. If it is an in-college house, a move to one of the out-college houses like Cotton which are I understand regarded as more 'civilized', might be the answer. Of course, I do not know if this is possible once a boy has started at a house.

At best that can only be a *partial* remedy. The real answer lies within Andrew himself. One day he will realize, like Wordsworth, that misery and hardship are bricks without which no strong character can be built, and that all his 'terrors, pains and early miseries' have a part

> And that a needful part in making up
> The calm existence that is mine when I
> *Am worthy of myself!*

As for the big question, it is much the same, for it is only through doubt, I am convinced, one finds the Lord. I will tell you how I found Him. I was seventeen. I came home at the end of the Christmas term and found my mother very ill with pneumonia, and my father with a letter from my headmaster suggesting I had not been working – which was true. I had discovered painting and was spending most of my time in the art room. My father gave me the most fearful talking to. He was overwrought because of my mother and threatened to withdraw me from school if I was going to waste his money. The next day the doctor came and was with mother a long time, and afterwards my brother and I were called in to see her; she was very low; she didn't recognize us. It was the most terrible moment of my life. Afterwards I went to our church and knelt in front of the altar and prayed as I had never prayed. I told Him that I did not know if He existed, but I had come because there was nowhere else I could go. I told Him I had made a terrible mess of my life, and now I feared I was about to lose my dear mother without whom I could not imagine life at all. Finally I told Him that if He would return her to me I would give Him my life. I was there for hours, I may have fallen asleep, but when I left I had an extraordinary feeling of calm and knew my mother would be safe. The next day she rallied. But even before that I had determined to dedicate my life to Him because I knew *He had been there with me* at the altar.

So you see, dear Henrietta, faith is not a matter of believing in this or that doctrine, it is knowing Him, knowing that wherever you are you can be sure of His presence – indeed knowing Him as a *friend*.

I do hope this letter may be of some use to you, let me know if I can do anything, and may God bless and keep you always – Geoffrey.

She read it through again, wondering whether she ought to ask him to write to Andy's housemaster; yet what could he write? Andy had said nothing about bullying, not even about being unhappy; it was not from anything he had said she had divined the ordeal he was going through, and if she were to ask him he wouldn't tell her, she was certain. All boys went through these trials – judging by George's and Willy's descriptions of the Navy. Andy would not wish to be thought soft; he would keep it, whatever it was, to himself. Perhaps, in any case, she had imagined it; perhaps it had been just homesickness; perhaps by now he was quite happy.

She knew she had been right though.

There was the usual row in the changing room, Hutton's voice a very audible part of it; he was calling for everyone to witness the fact that all his clothes and his socks were

222

hanging on hooks. Andrew, glancing at him as he entered, and seeing the yellowing welts across his bare buttocks, felt again the inadequacy of his own unmarked bottom. Instinctively he made for the further side of the room, thankful to see a space by Reeves.

He started undoing his tie, slowly so that by the time he came to take his trousers off, Hutton and the others would be in the bathroom. He hated bath nights; conscious that his muscles did not match up to those of the larger boys and his body was shamefully hairless, he disliked taking off his clothes. Reeves had dark hairs growing above his cock, even darker than Hutton's, and a mass of hairs on his chest as well.

Reeves had removed his underpants; he was turning his bottom for Andrew to examine. Dark, purple bruising spread over a wide area, contused on the right cheek into one swollen mass, in the middle of which was the raw line of an open cut.

'How many?' he asked, shocked.

'Ten. He started with seven. He asked me if that would do or if I wanted a man's share. I wasn't going to let him get away with that.'

The noise around them had stilled; everyone was crowding in to see Reeves's bruises, Hutton foremost.

'He's drawn blood!' Hutton's voice was awed.

Reeves nodded casually, making his way through the press of bodies into the bathroom; the others turned and followed. Most of them had fading yellow stripes, but none could boast anything to equal those livid furrows. It was typical of Reeves to have asked for more. He imagined him straightening afterwards and staring at Sandy with that disdainful expression.

The most Andrew had ever received from Sandy was three; that had left him biting his lip to keep his face straight. He was certain Reeves wouldn't even have given Sandy that satisfaction. He remembered in their first term a group of seniors holding Reeves's hand under the hot tap in an attempt to get him to take back a remark he had made about not caring whether Preshut won the house rugger cup. He hadn't made so much as a sound.

He hung his shirt over the hook on which he had slung his

tie then his vest after it and taking off his trousers placed them carefully over the next hook, an idea forming as he did so that he should perhaps leave something on the floor deliberately; compared to what Reeves had suffered, two from a fug was a small price to pay for stripes. He bent to tug at his socks, still debating it with himself as he hung them over his trousers. Then, quickly stepping out of his underpants he left them where they lay and ran through to the bathroom.

The noise had risen again. He saw Reeves standing up, throwing water over himself, evidently unable to dip his bottom in. The sight made him ashamed of what he had done. Reeves had earned his stripes honestly; he was cheating – and worse, cheating to impress the others, doing exactly what he despised in those around Hutton and Squires.

Paddling through the water on the floor, he fetched one of the few remaining tin tubs from the corner and weaved through the din and splashing to a vacant tap on the side wall; turning it on, he was thankful for the steam which began to rise about him, but couldn't free his mind of the image of his underpants lying on the floor outside and what they signified. Some lines Henrietta had put in her letter which had given him a strange feeling of comfort when he read them surfaced again to accuse him – 'the calm existence that is mine, when I am worthy of myself.' Henrietta would never have done what he had. She was like Reeves in that sense; she just did not care what anyone thought.

He wished he could see her.

13

The thing that puzzled Henrietta most when she looked
back on the Baroness's establishment from the long perspec-
tive of the years was that she had realized from the start –
although perhaps the *very* first day was a trick of memory
– how out of date it was. What knowledge or experience
had led her to this? Practically speaking, none. Cocooned
at home in her parents' world of the nineteenth century,
at the. convent in the nuns' world of everpresent sin,
she had yet known instinctively in the way young birds
know when they are ready to fly, that another, different
world was ready for the taking. It was not from the weeklies
she saw with pictures of the great and the beautiful, nor
from the talk she heard around her from the daughters
of society. She had picked up vibrations through other
senses, the keen sense of the young about the world they
were growing in. It was a mystery; she had rebelled from
the first.

Not everything was rotten: the music periods she loved,
and the poetry. They were made to learn whole poems by
heart, Keats especially. She had scarcely touched Keats at
the convent and her response was immediate; he transported
her to regions she had long been aware of, but only dimly,
illumining them with vivid colours and images that became
a part of her. She was amazed and delighted to find in him
all her own obsession with the fleeting moment and the
inexorable passage of time; he unlocked so many ideas she
thought her own she came to feel she knew him almost
personally. Perhaps it was partly through him she sensed the
graven artificiality of the Baroness's world; strange if that

225

were so, that the Baroness, apparently much taken with Keats herself, did not also see it.

> Let then wingéd Fancy find
> Thee a mistress to thy mind . . .

Lavinia's laugh cut across the room.

'*Female hooligans!*' she called. 'Isn't that just too absolutely! *Etty!*'

The clouds were radiant white against the sky. Reluctantly Henrietta turned her gaze from the window. Lavinia – 'Popsy' – was lounging in the most consciously inelegant position between two chairs, her arms spread across an opened newspaper on the long table beside her. She would hold this attitude, however uncomfortable, until Miss Snape-Hervey came in, then watch the mistress fawn. Henrietta disliked her intensely – not in a personal way, she disliked her for what she was, self-absorbed, spoilt and so pleased with herself. She was also malicious, but so openly, predictably malicious it was funny. No one could leave the room in her presence without knowing they would be the butt of some outrageous story the moment the door closed. She told them with charm, and very amusingly.

Henrietta she regarded as incorrigibly bourgeois, a hopeless case of 'moral values', her sympathy with the women's movement an amusing naïvety. Had she known that she corresponded with a Franciscan missionary in the East End – and even thought she was in love with him – her inventions would have known no bounds. She herself received letters from 'Bobo', a captain in the Blues; she went round after lights-out to the rooms of her hangers-on and others she considered amusing and read Bobo's letters aloud, adding her own flourishes, Henrietta was certain; no man could be so stupid as this one appeared. Letters from men were, of course, strictly forbidden. Popsy got away with it as she got away with everything; daughter of one of the premier earldoms, she was the brightest feather in the Baroness's cap and none of the tame mistresses was going to risk her position by complaining of the Lady Lavinia's letters, or her rudeness or appalling language.

226

'Etty –' she went on. 'They've dog-whipped a poor bobby! Don't you feel that is a teeny bit rather?'

'I expect he deserved it.'

'*Au contraire* – frightfully chiv the poor lamb – they all *are*,' she drawled, opening her eyes in exaggerated innocence.

Henrietta smiled. It struck her that Popsy's idea of bobbies might change if she were involved personally in a scuffle. She wondered why she hadn't thought of it before. She would be the ideal demonstrator – not from conviction one way or the other, conviction was 'much too rather' – but for notoriety, self-advertisement, the fun of it, and because Popsy, the Lady Lavinia, could do 'but absolutely anything' and get away with it.

'Do you think so?' she asked, equally innocently.

'*Everyone* knows they are.' Popsy looked around for agreement.

Miss Snape-Hervey came in then. Those who had been sitting rose. Popsy leaned sideways over her newspaper as if immersed in it.

'*Bonjour, demoiselles!*'

'*Bonjour, Mam'selle!*'

'I say –' Popsy called without moving as the others seated themselves or drew chairs around to face the front of the room, 'don't you think it disgraceful, Mam'selle, the way the suffragettes give us all a bad name?'

'I do indeed – yes indeed!'

'What d'you think they should do, Mam'selle?' Henrietta asked, 'if Mr Asquith refuses to see them even?'

'*Pourquoi veulent-elles rendre visite à Monsieur Asquith, Henriette?* Tchhh –!' Miss Snape-Hervey pulled her mouth into a grimace.

'*Peutêtre,*' Henrietta replied, '*parcequ'il est le grand ennemi des femmes. Monsieur Lloyd George l'a dit!*'

'*Il y en a qui pensent que ce sont bien les sufragettes, les grandes ennemies des femmes, Henriette!*'

'*J'approuve!*' Popsy cried, taking her legs off the chair at last. '*Et au diable le Monsieur Lloyd George!*'

The others laughed.

Miss Snape-Hervey's brows rose. She turned again to Henrietta. '*Il faut comprendre, Henriette, que le mouvement*

227

féministe produit toujours des grandes passions. Non! La femme, elle a sa place – ce n'est pas à Westminster, c'est chez elle! Là, elle est la maîtresse! Alors!' She looked around the class. *'Il faut commencer –'*

It was three days after this episode, as Henrietta was walking back from the tennis courts that Popsy, who played to about the same standard and had been partnered with her for much of the afternoon, surprised her with an invitation to the Eton-Harrow cricket match at Lords the following week – not so much an invitation as a royal command in the way Popsy handled these things. Henrietta looked at her, wondering about her motives. Why should she want to add her to her retinue of hangers-on? Perhaps she was trying to make the others jealous? Or was she trying to impress her? It was hard to think of a reason.

'Thank you,' she replied. 'And you must come to a suffragette meeting with me.' She had never been to a public meeting, and until that moment had no plans to go to one.

Popsy's initial surprise turned to amusement. 'Would you risk it! I'd probably say dreadful things.'

'You won't mind if they say dreadful things to you, then!'

'You really believe all that ricky stuff, don't you!'

'Why don't you come and find out about it?'

'Is it a condition?'

'Yes.'

'In that case, Etty, how can I – *possibly*?'

'If it were not a condition?'

'I'd adore to!'

Henrietta smiled. 'I'd adore to go to Lords. I've never been.'

'You haven't!' Popsy exaggerated surprise. 'You *must*. It's *too* simply! You don't need to *know* a thing about cricket –'

'I love cricket.'

Popsy eyed her suspiciously. 'Bobo will be there, and – *heaps* of other chums.'

It was Henrietta's turn to look round quickly. The wide eyes met hers innocently, but she felt a twinge of apprehension as thoughts of the 'fast' circles Popsy moved in induced more speculation about the motive for the invitation. It would amuse Popsy to cast her to the wolves.

'I shall see the famous Bobo!' she said.

'I wrote to tell him I'd be going.' Popsy wobbled her head, raising her eyes and her free hand at the same time. '*Et par conséquence –!*'

Henrietta laughed.

It was amusing over the next days to see the changed attitudes occasioned by her elevation to Popsy's circle. Those already in and hurt that the invitation should have gone to a complete outsider took pains to cut her or close ranks against her by adopting an exaggerated version of their idiotic drawl in her presence – unless Popsy were also there, when they pretended silken friendliness. Those who wanted to be in tended to court her. Her own circle, however, made it clear they disliked Popsy and could not understand why she had been such a dupe as to fall for the invitation, particularly as she knew no one who went to Eton or Harrow – jealous, she thought, just like Popsy's lot.

The friend she liked most, Cynthia fflyte-Davison – 'Flighty' to most although Popsy called her 'The Balloon', which was particularly wounding as she had an ample figure – told her that Popsy's mother had been a favourite of the King when Prince of Wales.

Far from turning her against Popsy, this added to her glamour in Henrietta's eyes.

'Do you think Popsy might be –?'

'I will say this, she doesn't look in the *least* like her papa – not that many people see him these days.' Flighty prided herself on her knowledge of society. 'And you must have noticed her eyes, Henry, surely!'

Any resemblance between the King's somewhat protruberant blue eyes as they appeared in his portraits and Popsy's wide hazel-green ones had not struck Henrietta before, nevertheless she couldn't look at her after this without a thrill of speculation.

With the rational side of her mind and instincts born of her mother's 'at homes', and now the more stifling atmosphere of the Baroness's, where the goal and end of life appeared to be the deep curtsey on presentation at Court, she rejected Popsy's world; at the same time she was excited by the thought of it and, despite herself, increasingly apprehensive as the day approached. Her knowledge of the opposite sex was confined practically to her brothers and Father Geoffrey. The thought of Bobo and his soldier chums was alarming.

She was trying out different angles of her hat before the mirror and a half circle of 'helpers' on the morning, when they heard the motor car in the drive. Her insides went hollow. The others crowded to the window, chattering; the chauffeur was young and dark with a gorgeous uniform, she gathered, then they were turning, giggling, urging her to go down as they wanted a closer look.

She adjusted the white chiffon over her hat with nervous fingers and tied it under her chin; was it a shade angled?

'It's perfect, Henry – come on!'

Popsy, looking chic in a blue dust cloak, blue flowers showing through the film of white silk around her hat, was in the hall with several others. The obsequious Bursar, Mrs Maune-Blackaway, was also there, no doubt to ensure they were both properly turned out. The chauffeur was apart from them by the open front door. His uniform was dark green with a gold and red stripe down the breeches and the same gold and red around the cuffs of his jacket and on his lapels and peaked cap. He was tall with dark eyes and cheeks glowing with the freshness of young manhood. Standing there, he seemed to cast an aura of strained silence, extending even to Mrs Blackaway. Henrietta imagined it bursting immediately they drove away; they saw few young men, let alone *such* young men. She smiled as he turned his dark eyes towards her, but there was no response. Then Popsy, beckoning impatiently, swept by him through the door and into the early sunshine. She followed, conscious of his maleness and the studied impassivity of his eyes.

The car, dark green with shining black guards over the wheels and thin lines of red and gold around the tops of the doors like the lines on his uniform, had its hood folded back. There was still a nip in the air, but as she stepped up on to the running board a warm infusion of leather and wood and polish and petrol assailed her, taking her straight back to the Lanchester, tugging her with the security of home as she turned and sank back into the seat. He pushed the door to and strode to the front, bending over the starting handle. As he turned it the whole car swayed, disturbing her with a sense of his strength; the engine rattled into life.

Popsy was gazing at her with an amused expression as if divining her thoughts, and broke into a gurgling laugh. Then they were away, bumping over the ruts in the drive. She turned and waved to the faces crowding the windows in the old house.

'Blissful!' Popsy sighed, smiling round at her again. 'You do look *quite* simply, Etty,' and leaning closer, 'I'm sure Johnson thinks so, he's a hopeless baby. I think he has gypsy blood, have you seen his eyes?'

Henrietta looked at the flat back of his cap, wondering if he could hear; perhaps she meant him to –

'Alex said she could feel his eyes *peeling* her bodice away,' she went on, 'she felt as naked as a cuckoo, her legs went to jelly.' She laughed. 'Did he do that to you? Mama can't resist dagoes, all the footmen are dago – we'll be going in the drag by the way, you'll see some of them – they're known as the banditti –'

Whether it was release from school and the character Popsy adopted there, or whether she was really being friendly, Henrietta found herself unexpectedly drawn to her. Flippant and vain as she was, she seemed less consciously so now; in place of tricks of speech, there was a natural irony, instead of utter cynicism a detached amusement at the foibles of those she dissected. Chief among them were her own family, and as she talked Henrietta thought she glimpsed perhaps the reason she behaved as she did. She seldom saw her father apparently – rather confirming Flighty's remarks – and scarcely knew him; her parents had been moving in separate orbits for as long as she could remember.

'Tell me, Etty, truthfully, do I look quite – English – Anglo-Saxon? I do want the truth –'

She was a small girl, imploring help.

Looking at her face framed in the triangle formed by her hat and the silk scarf around it and drawn down either side of the wide brim in to her neck, Henrietta was struck with a resemblance she had not seen before; the wide, hazel-green eyes, the pugnacious tilt of the chin reminded her suddenly of Sister Anne at the convent.

231

'Is there some Irish in you?'

'Irish!' Popsy's eyes hardened and she turned, staring ahead, the corners of her mouth which had been lifting a moment ago set petulantly. Then she leaned forward and, clutching the seat in front with her left hand as she jolted, tapped Johnson on the shoulder with her right, shouting at him to go faster.

He half-turned his head. 'Can't go no faster, my Lady. I'm over the speed limit now.'

She stared at him. '*Damn* you Johnson!'

Sitting back, she looked to see Henrietta's reaction, flashing her a quick smile.

Whether it was her request or her language, it was soon evident they were moving much faster. The breeze pulled at their hats and scarves; clouds of dust blew up either side from the wheels and were sucked in around them, and Henrietta had to grasp the struts of the hood beside her to steady herself as she was bounced about in the seat.

'Come on, Johnson!' Popsy shouted.

Approaching a bend they slowed again; it was as well for as they came around they saw a farm cart piled with empty milk churns holding the very centre of the road. The single horse drawing it shied away as it heard them; Johnson put the brakes on and Henrietta, feeling herself sliding forward, gripped her strut as they stopped ten yards from the terrified beast.

After a good deal of shouting on the part of the other driver and careful manoeuvring by Johnson, they were past and on their way again.

'Johnson!' Popsy called. 'You were *absolutely*!'

'Thank you, my Lady,' he replied drily.

They seemed not to be going so fast though, and presently, entering Egham, they slowed even more.

'Twelve mile limit, my Lady,' he called back, 'in towns.'

Popsy looked at Henrietta. 'Rot!'

They both laughed.

The day was pleasantly warm now, but later, after they had crossed the river and were slowing again through the houses of Hounslow, the sun and the taste of dust from the roads had taken the first careless edge from the day. Popsy fell silent; Henrietta's thoughts returned to Bobo and his friends; how would they take to her? What could she possibly find to say that might amuse them? The life they appeared to live was so different from any she had known –

It seemed a long time before more imposing terraces on either side told her they were approaching central London. The traffic had become heavier, familiar red or brown motor buses with familiar advertisements along their sides moved majestically past the carts and drays and horse buses; cabbies wove insolently through them all, cracking whips, yelling at those they narrowly approached.

The terrace on the left hand gave way to a park which she thought she recognized, and she saw the white stone fretwork of the Albert Memorial glinting in the sun – Kensington Gardens. Distant images of walking with Scopey and George and Andy when they were very small flashed into her mind; she wondered how Andy was now. His last letter had been much more cheerful; he had been playing piano duets with the music master; from the way he had written he evidently got on very well with him and spent a great deal of time in the music rooms. From his enthusiasm she guessed he had discovered Schumann and Mozart rather as she had discovered Keats.

A horse snorted close on her right; turning she saw the beast's flanks as he went by at a fast trot, drawing a dog cart. A flashily dressed young man was driving – a K-Nut! In her interest she forgot herself so much she gave him a second look. He raised the brim of his straw hat to her with his whip hand; he had nice eyes and nice, even teeth below his blond moustache as he smiled. She turned away quickly. They had been slowed by a stopping bus; Johnson was turning the wheel and they edged out, following the dog cart, but then a cab pulled out from ahead and they lost it. She felt strangely disappointed; what would the Baroness think!

They had to slow again approaching the pillared arches at Hyde Park Corner where a dense knot of traffic had formed. She could see fashionable groups strolling in the Park, morning coats, white shirts and shining toppers setting off the summery colours and delicate materials of the ladies, who held bright parasols to the sun – an exquisite scene. How far it was from Sunningdale! She felt her earlier spirits returning and with them a happy sense of companionship with Popsy who had staged her release; catching her eye, she smiled.

Then she saw the dog cart again; it was inside them now, jammed between a bus and a motor car carrying two Indians dressed like Rajahs at least, which was turning up into Park Lane. Johnson, also making for Park Lane, steered behind the car and for a few moments they were driving along beside the dog cart. The blond K-Nut, catching sight of them, turned to her and again raised his hat, bowing his head and giving her an even broader smile than before.

Popsy looked round quickly. 'Who is *that*, Etty?'

'I haven't the least idea.'

Her eyes widened. 'Are you sure?'

'Perfectly.'

She gazed at her a moment longer. 'You see what you have done with your votes for women. We are nothing to them now.'

Henrietta laughed, wondering what Popsy's reaction would have been if he had saluted *her*.

The traffic was moving steadily up Park Lane, and Johnson was soon turning into Upper Grosvenor Street. A few minutes later the trees of Grosvenor Square opened before them. He pulled up outside a house hung with pink and yellow roses at every window, with a green awning striped with the familiar red and gold leading from the front door to the pavement railings. Jumping out, he strode round to open their door.

'Thank you, Johnson. Shall you be coming with us to the cricket?'

'No, my Lady.' His face remained impassive.

She gave Henrietta a look before turning for the awning.

Inside the house the first impression was of flowers everywhere and their scent, the next of the great height of the hall, and the delicate curve of the banisters of the grand staircase opposite them across the black and white chequered floor. They untied their hats and handed them and their dust cloaks to the footman – dark eyes and brows accentuated by his white wig. Henrietta suppressed a smile as she followed Popsy up the stairs.

234

After washing away the dust of the journey, they went down again to the supper room, whose tall windows looked out on the garden at the back. A cold sideboard was awaiting them, and a maid who bobbed a curtsey as she told Popsy that Lady Lynne had lunched and was in her room dressing for the afternoon.

She appeared as they were finishing delicious glasses of strawberries and cream, a striking figure, slim and straight with auburn lights in her hair cleverly matched by a russet sash around her cream silk dress, and she stood in the doorway for an almost theatrical split second as if it were a habit before she swept in.

Henrietta felt an immediate change in Popsy; it was nothing said, rather a coolness in her voice as she introduced her, matched on her mother's part by something watchful behind her smile. She had the impression of two strong characters, neither prepared to concede.

'It is as well you did not arrive earlier,' Lady Lynne said, and looking at Henrietta, 'I am not sure that a whole day at Lords is such an unqualified pleasure!'

Popsy took this as an implied rebuke – as it was probably intended. 'Etty likes nothing better than to watch cricket.'

Lady Lynne gazed at her with interest. 'A dear friend of ours had a gal who *loved* cricket – could think of nothin' else I believe. She followed Lord Hawke to Orstralia. One shudders! A sea voyage at her age!' Her eyes were expressive. 'My dear, that was the last *anyone* saw of her.'

Popsy came in quickly, 'You know she has a perfectly huge estate –'

'Property.'

'As large as France –'

'*Darling!*'

'And she is quite ecstatically!'

Lady Lynne's brows rose a fraction. She looked at Henrietta. 'Such a pretty gal too.'

Henrietta smiled, embarrassed in the cross-fire. Lady Lynne swept out, telling them to be ready as soon as they could, she had to attend the other members of the party. Henrietta's heart sank.

They were introduced in the drawing-room, Admiral Sir

235

Henry and Lady Claude-Coburg, he small and thin in a dapper suit, looking quite unlike her idea of an admiral apart from a parchment coloured skin and a thousand crinkles around his eyes, she as large and full as he was spare; Patricia, Marchioness of Oban, another matronly figure but with a more open smile, and finally Popsy's elder brother, James, and Bobo Fitzmaurice. Henrietta was surprised by both. James – 'Eggy' from his title Lord Eggledon – was not in the least like his sister. He was exceptionally tall with a long, almost gaunt face, startlingly blue eyes and sandy-coloured hair and moustache. Like Bobo he was an officer in the Blues, and he looked every inch the soldier. Bobo obviously tried to, but did not quite manage it; it was hard to tell why; he had the posture, but there was something soft about him; his eyes were softly protruberant and his lips beneath his moustache were full, pink and looked rather loose; to be kissed by them, as Popsy claimed she had been more than once, was a nauseating thought. He greeted Popsy with almost obsequious friendliness and the most drawling drawl she had ever heard. Popsy sounded normal by comparison.

Lady Lynne led them to the hall, arranging the seating for the drag as she went.

'Popsy, you and Henrietta must sit inside.' She turned to the Marchioness, 'Would you like to go inside, Patricia –?' and looking round for the Admiral's wife, 'and perhaps you would like to make up the four –'

'I shall be perfectly happy inside or outside. It is such a lovely day.'

'That is settled then.' The Countess moved past the statuesque footmen at the open front doors, calling back, 'James and Bobo can guard the hampers on top –'

'You can depend on us!' Bobo turned to Popsy, snorting with laughter.

He was a perfect idiot. Henrietta, following the ladies under the canopy, found the Countess's eye on her. She was evidently expected to enter the carriage first. She had to think for a moment which foot to start with; there was only one step she saw. Holding her dress up – they had decided it was too warm for their cloaks – she placed her right foot on the step, then her left inside and turning easily sat in the far front seat, feeling very satisfied with her performance. The Marchioness followed, smiling as she sat heavily opposite, rocking the carriage –

Dearest Mary,

I had a real taste of the *haute monde* on Saturday, I can't tell you what it was like. I wished all the time you had been there, it was so funny and so *dreadful*!!! And they have to keep it up all the time in the season, meeting all the same people again and again. Popsy, the girl I went with has asked me to go with her to Henley, I'm half tempted as her brother is rather a sweet. He says nothing, but underneath you can feel there's *heaps* going on. His chum, Bobo is the reverse – saying most ridiculous things all the time and you know that underneath there's *nothing*! But you'll never guess who I saw – do you remember me telling you about Alastair, the boy I met on the *Enchantress* at the Jubilee review of the fleet with the castle! I was pots on him for ages. He was there! Not only there, he was *captain* of the Eton side and scored the most perfect half century – well I was trying to watch but I was supposed to talk or at least listen at the same time. They 'walk round' you see 'chatting' it's called to everyone they know. I knew no one, but I had to go round. I was asked a thousand times if I was a Worcestershire Steel. One old boy asked me if I liked chopping wood, I thought from the *wicked* look in his eye it must be a catch-question or their way of suggesting you know what and Popsy told me afterwards I coloured charmingly, but apparently he asks everyone that. All the time Alastair was hitting beautiful fours all over the ground. I hardly recognized him he is so tall and good-looking now, but the worst of it was I never had a chance to talk to him because while we walked round he was batting and by the time he was out it was time for us to go back and have tea by the drag. All the carriages are drawn up in rows, I've never seen so many and the hostesses dispense tea and cold drinks and sandwiches and rolls and brioches, even lobster salad! Our tea was very 'pop' as Popsy puts it, not I think because of the excellence of our hamper but because Popsy's mama, the Countess of Lynne, is an absolute magnet for men! It was more like a court. I enjoyed tea in a way because although I was *aching* to walk round again to see if I might bump into Alastair, there were boys simply everywhere, I felt really quite important meeting all the names that normally one only reads about – nearly all tories, it was like a gathering of the opposition, one could imagine every sort of intrigue.

I amused the Admiral afterwards, he was a sweet old man in our party, I discovered he was actually in the Mediterranean when George was out there, and a great admirer of Charlie B, from what I gathered he thought Lord Charles Beresford would make a very much better First Sea Lord than Fisher, whom he *detested*! It was rather like that – *intriguing*! Anyway, I said to him 'the Baroness expects us to be able to hold an intelligent conversation with a cabinet minister for ten minutes. Do you think one minute each with ten ex-cabinet ministers qualifies?' He thought it tremendously funny, said he would dine out on it for weeks and Bobo, the ass, kept on saying 'ten ex-cabinet ministers, don't y'know, haw, haw –' every time he looked at me until Popsy told him to chuck it. The more beastly she is to him, the more he likes her. Popsy is going to marry him, she says. When I asked her if she loved him she looked at me as if I were simple. This was while we were having a *deep* discussion on the way back to Sunningdale. She doesn't believe in God or anything, all she believes in is *herself* she says! I said surely Popsy you can't only consider yourself, even if you say there's no God, there are other *people* you're going to hurt – as she does at school although I didn't tell her so. She called me an idealist. I should grow up, then I'd see that in the real world one only had oneself, and if you didn't get the better of other people they jolly soon got the better of you, and in a way I could see what she meant because if you don't believe in God or our Lord's teachings, what is there to stop you doing just what you want in this world because there probably isn't another afterwards? One could have so much more *fun*. From what Andy said to me before he went back this time I don't think he believes there is a God either. I'm in a terrible muddle now, I can't write to

Father Geoffrey because I know he believes utterly, he's already told me how he came to know Him – actually *know* Him. I feel so mixed up inside and there's no one here I can really talk to, do please write soon, you *owe me* a letter anyway.

Must close now as the Baroness is most strict about lights-out, do write soon. Thine always – Henry

P.S. I went with Popsy on condition she came to a suffragette meeting with me, perhaps your mama will be able to arrange one!

When she looked back on it, the suffragette meeting appeared to Henrietta the one clear and certain turning point in her life – her act of attendance a conscious choice of a new road leading away from the easy high road along which she would otherwise have continued, the meeting a sort of barrier which opened one way only; once through she could never have got back to the old road.

Had she disclosed this picture to her mother or the eldest of her brothers or anyone who knew her as a girl she would have been surprised to find they did not share it, and hurt by their laughter; wilful, ever dissatisfied with the path prepared for her, she had been seeking to make her own way off it almost from the moment of her birth, and had it not been that meeting it would have been another, or something else – 'Honestly, Henry –!'

She never did discuss it because she did not reflect on it until later in life, and then as a reproof that things would have been very different if – but that was unproductive for everything had been utterly disrupted by the war, and the easy high road she imagined would have been blown up with it, as it was for so many others. But without discussion, it became a fixed idea, reinforced when she retailed it as a fact to younger generations who had no reason to doubt her.

Her memory played her false: it was not conscious choice that took her to the meeting. During the long summer holidays after the visit to Lords, the idea of the return outing had lapsed and by the time they returned to school both she

239

and Popsy had almost forgotten the pledge. It was not until the beginning of their last term at the Baroness's when the suffragettes again came prominently into the news, chaining themselves to the railings outside the Prime Minister's door, trying to storm the Houses of Parliament after concealing themselves inside two furniture removal vans, that the idea surfaced again, then chiefly in Popsy's mind. It was the exploit with the furniture vans that appealed to Popsy, as it appealed to the newspaper columnists.

'Isn't this too screamingly, Etty! Do listen – "Until yesterday, when the suffragettes outwitted the policemen by the use of a pantechnicon van, we never believed in the Trojan horse. We are inclined now to place more credence in the story than heretofore." I do so wish – but you *promised* you would take me!'

It had been an up and down relationship between them since the summer, Popsy at times seeking her company and her sympathy with stories of the beastliness of her family or chums, at other times cutting herself off with ferocious verbal assaults and rudenesses which Henrietta found it difficult to credit. However, she had come to know her well enough to realize that beneath the brittle surface Popsy valued her counsel, even liked her and respected her quaint 'values', so she attempted to take the explosions philosophically. It was difficult at times.

It had not been long since the last one; perhaps Popsy was attempting to make up, but she seemed genuinely eager to see one of these stormy women's meetings. It was, after all, their last term; soon they would not be able to go together.

Henrietta doubted if the Baroness would allow it: Eton and Harrow was one thing – the third Women's Parliament quite another. 'She'll never give us per.'

Popsy's brows curved up. '*Un peu difficile?* We shall see *Henriette. Laissez-moi faire!*'

How she managed it, Henrietta was not sure; she said she had pointed out how important it was for them to have personal experience of such a vital political topic; the cabinet ministers they were supposed to hold in conversation were more likely to be interested in first hand accounts than

240

third-hand gossip from the papers! Probably she used more compelling social arguments.

However it was done, early on Thursday morning, 13 February Johnson arrived – it would have been unthinkable for the Baroness to allow two of her young charges to take the train to London by themselves – and drove them away, this time with the hood and windows up and wrapped around with thick travelling rugs. As it was nominally Henrietta's outing, he took a different route, north of the Park and then up Baker Street and the Finchley Road to Swiss Cottage, and so up Fitzjohn's Avenue and Holly Hill, where she guided him to the old stables behind Felpham House. However, the chief reason they went to her home for lunch was that George's ship had returned from the Mediterranean and he had a few days leave. Popsy was anxious to see him, Henrietta quite as anxious to show him off; she had talked about him and her other brothers often enough. Popsy would see she had not exaggerated.

To her surprise, as they came in through the colonnaded way and the side door, she found George had a friend with him, a freckle-faced young man with reddish hair and keen eyes.

'Leadwith,' George said, introducing him, 'generally known as Stinger.'

Leadwith smiled, extending his hand.

'Stinger!' Popsy exclaimed with her wide-eyed look. 'Do you?'

He seemed surprised by her directness. 'No. No fear of that!' He laughed uncertainly.

They learned in stilted exchanges that he and George were due to join the same ship next week at Sheerness, 'Sheernasty' they called it. Both seemed too abashed by the presence of the two girls to think of asking why *they* were here.

This was left to her mother, waiting for them in the drawing-room; she left no doubt of her pleasure at being introduced to the Lady Lavinia. Henrietta could imagine her scouring Debrett the moment they left, adding more names to her mental lists for the 'coming out'. She felt a little thrill of apprehension to think of how close it was now.

'We're going to the Caxton Hall,' she said.

Her mother looked puzzled for a moment, then her eyes widened. 'That's where the women have been meeting –'

She nodded, finding she enjoyed it as she turned the screw. 'We're going to the final session.'

Popsy said, 'The Baroness wants us to give a talk about it to the school.'

Henrietta looked at her sharply.

'Of course,' her mother smiled. 'How good she should have chosen you two! She must think well of you.'

'I don't know,' George put in. 'Perhaps she hopes Henry'll land up in the rattle!'

Stinger laughed loudly, then checked himself.

Her mother was looking at George as if the remark had been in poor taste. 'At least it will be more educational than your excursions to the West End.'

'Do tell,' Popsy said eagerly.

George looked at Stinger.

'The Gaiety?' her mother put in, 'Or was it the Empire this time, George?'

'You *must* see the Merry Widow,' Popsy said. 'Lily Elsie is too simply *absolutely*. You'd adore her.'

Henrietta was amused to see the effect of her wide eyes on George.

'You two won't be here tonight, I suppose?' He gave a token glance in Henrietta's direction, then quickly back to Popsy.

Chump! Henrietta thought; if he knew what she was actually like!

'I thought they were paying a visit to Bow Street!' Stinger said.

'*Worse!*' Popsy gave him one of her grimaces. 'We have to be back at school.'

He laughed rather more loudly than the remark warranted. George gave a snort, but he was obviously disappointed; he never had been able to hide his feelings; his eyes kept returning to Popsy's face like a retriever's, Henrietta thought.

'There's a new play reviewed in this morning's paper,' her mother said. 'Lena Ashwell is in it, I forget what it's called.

It is not one I shall be *rushing* to see! Another "moral" tale I fear, dressed up as a comedy.'

'Bernard Shaw again?' Popsy asked.

'No. Cicely Hamilton – very much in his *genre* though by the sound of it. The idle rich – the unemployment problem – "dossers" I think they're called on the Embankment – overworked shop girls, there is *nothing* right with society. Where you are going this afternoon reminded me. I do think the women's movement has a lot to answer for.' She turned to Popsy. 'I do hope that in your talk you will remind the girls there are a great many women who do *not* share Mrs Pankhurst's views and who are deeply ashamed of the rowdyism –' she was interrupted by the bell for lunch. 'It is the few who make the noise,' she concluded, rising, 'the majority who have to suffer the shame, do you not think so?'

Henrietta wondered where her father was, but did not want to ask. She had the impression her mother was very keyed up; she was talking such a lot.

At lunch the conversation passed as it seemed to when George was at home to naval incidents and characters, and both he and Stinger told amusing stories – she wondered how true.

'– there was a good yarn about Luigi when he was on the China Station. He was on a court martial – some stoker had done something rather serious. He was asked – the stoker was asked, "Do you object to any members of the Court?" "Yus," the man replied smartly, "I hobjects to Commander Bayly." "On what grounds?" "Well," he said, "jes *look* at the blighter!" Actually that was not the word he used!'

Popsy hooted with laughter; George, basking in it, tried to smile modestly.

'Will they court martial Percy Scott?' her mother asked.

Stinger and George started speaking at the same time, both shaking their heads; each gave way.

'But what is the feeling in the service?' she pressed. 'We are told so many different things, it is difficult to know what to think about it. Is it Fisher's doing, this – I suppose we have to call it a feud?'

Before she had finished George had come in, 'Anyone

243

with sense is steering well clear of taking sides, mater.' He looked at Stinger for support.

'Speaking for myself,' Stinger said, 'Charlie B is the most charming old fellow you could hope to meet. Even if he was my Commander-in-Chief!'

'But it is a *most* serious situation, is it not,' she persisted, 'when the *First Sea Lord* and the *Commander-in-Chief* of our main fleet are at loggerheads,' she raised her brows, 'to put it no higher –?'

George nodded. 'You're absolutely right. It's no joke. I feel sorry for Percy Scott,' and looking at Stinger, 'Charming or not, Charlie B had absolutely no call to dress him down in public –'

'But wasn't it fearfully rude of Scott,' her mother interrupted, 'that signal he sent –'

'That was a private semaphore to one of his own cruisers. The fleet was nowhere in sight then. Charlie B didn't hear about it for *five days* –'

' "Paintwork appears more important than gunnery!" Wasn't that a little –?'

George shrugged. 'The fact is Percy Scott's in the Fish-pond –' he turned to Popsy, 'a Fisher man –'

'Popsy knows all about that,' Henrietta interrupted, realizing suddenly that she ought to warn him, and fixing him with a hard gaze. 'Her mama is a *great* friend of Admiral Claude-Coburg.'

George's eyes widened; he looked at Popsy again, then down at his plate to start eating.

Her mother gazed at him, then at Stinger, now also busy with his plate.

Popsy said brightly, 'C-C says Fisher is a half caste.'

The tension broke in laughter.

'He told me Fisher's ma was a Cingalese princess.'

'That's one of Charlie B's,' Stinger laughed.

'Whatever will happen!' her mother said. 'I mean, it's terrible. Of course your father has always disliked Fisher and all his works.'

'Where is the Pater?' George asked.

'At his club,' her mother replied, and went on a shade quickly, 'And what about the new battleship, the *Dread-*

nought? Everyone seems to think it quite mad to throw away our entire naval superiority by building a completely new type of ship. One might just as well say to the Germans, "Let us all start afresh!" And surely they will be able to catch us up now if they wish. If the new battleship is as much of a revolution as is claimed –'

'Hang it all!' George laughed, 'You seem to know more about it than we do –'

'But we read about nothing else these days. If it isn't Fisher quarrelling with Beresford, or Beresford quarrelling with Percy Scott or someone or other writing to *The Times* "a plague on both your houses", or the latest German Navy Bill – there has been so much about that recently – and what the Kaiser has to say – nothing else seems to matter nowadays, we are all naval experts!'

There was a silence after she finished, then Stinger said, 'We seldom see the papers –'

'And when we do we have no time to read them,' George finished for him.

'Oh, come!' she laughed, and turning to Stinger, 'How long have you to go now – before you "ship a stripe" isn't it called?'

He smiled. 'About a year if all goes well.'

'You and George joined about the same time then?'

'The same term,' he nodded. 'He'll steam ahead of me after the exams though. I'm not very good at exams!'

'But I'm sure – if you work hard?'

'Not in my case, I'm afraid,' and looking at George. 'Of course some people don't have to work!' He addressed her mother again. 'He'll play cricket all summer, then walk off with six ones –'

'Six ones?'

'A first in each of the exams. There's a scale of promotion – depending on how many firsts you get. We ordinary mortals won't see him after that –'

'Rot!' George interrupted.

Her mother looked at him, trying unsuccessfully to keep the pride from her eyes.

Afterwards, as they were tidying themselves up before leaving Popsy said, 'You didn't tell me he was clever, too!'

'He isn't!' Henrietta replied. 'Well, he is in a way – but it's only because he *has* to do well. That's always been his fault –'

'Etty!' Popsy laughed. 'But aren't they just too! They're like big puppies.'

Thinking of Bobo and other sophisticates she had met at the Eton-Harrow match, Henrietta had to agree, but she was not sure she liked Popsy putting it into words; she made no reply; there was plenty she could say about Bobo if she wanted to.

The 'big puppies' suggested they dress up as ladies' maids to accompany them in case things became rough. Popsy clapped her hands and squealed with delight, but Henrietta and her mother squashed the idea, so they ordered a taxi-cab and went with them 'to see the fun'.

'Why should we pay to go to "The Girls of Gottenberg",' George said, 'when we can see the Suffragette Follies free!'

Henrietta turned on him. 'How *dare* you condescend to us – you don't know a thing about it. You're only a snotty – you never even read the newspapers, you said so. You're like the rest of them, you see no further than the end of your nose. You can tell the driver to stop now, and get out –'

He made a stupid pretence of falling back, fending off her attack.

'Don't be silly,' she said coldly, but Popsy encouraged him and he and Stinger continued to play up for her benefit. She was glad when at last they arrived.

There were policemen everywhere around the hall, and knots of spectators, among them girls handing out leaflets and selling badges and white 'Votes for Women' buttons.

'Thank you,' she said coolly as George handed her out of the cab. She wished the others weren't here; she wanted really to talk to him, she would not see him again for ages. And she wanted to hug him, but after his idiotic performance in the cab she couldn't. She was surprised when he bent his head and brushed her cheek with his lips.

He stood back and raised his hand. 'Good luck Henry! Don't get into a scrap!' He sounded more like an elder brother; perhaps, after all, he had grown up.

She made her farewell to Stinger. He lifted her gloved

hand in a charmingly hesitant way to kiss it, so that she wondered for a moment what they were doing here. There *was* a difference. It *was* nice to be treated courteously; things were ordered very well as they were, so why should women of all people wish to change them. It wasn't until a moment or two after she had waved her final goodbyes that she thought suddenly of Father Geoffrey, and then of Jenny and Mrs Griggs, and realized again how important it was to change things.

A policeman nearby smiled and gave a friendly salute as they passed; *condescending*, she thought, like George and all men – with a few exceptions. It was all a huge joke to them; there was almost a carnival atmosphere here despite the greyness and dampness of the day. The spectators were expecting to see girls screaming and kicking as they were carried away, the police were probably looking forward to some amusement too; probably they liked rough and tumbles with girls – she felt a very strange sensation as she thought of their hands around her legs and arms and body –

Inside, the hall was packed. She sensed the excitement immediately in the talk and could see it in the eyes and smiling greetings as they looked for seats. A few men's heads turning looked out of place amongst the rows of flowered hats and bonnets and scarves.

She squashed in beside a young woman who looked as if she might work in a shop, or was perhaps a lady's maid on her afternoon off.

The woman turned to her eagerly. 'They say Mrs P come dahn from the north this mornin'.'

'Has she?' Henrietta was a little surprised at being addressed so familiarly, but found she did not resent it. 'I didn't know that.'

'She'll be 'ere all right, depend on it!'

'Oh – splendid!'

The woman looked her over for a moment. 'Know 'er gels do yer?'

'No, I'm afraid I don't.'

'That Christabel, I seen 'er lars' year. A real goer – wiv 'er bell an 'er pipers an' all, men shahtin' an' peltin' 'er. But she give as good as she got!' She rose suddenly as the noise about them swelled into shouts and clapping, and looking down called, ' 'Ere she is! 'Ere she is!'

Henrietta stood, but could barely see above thickets of hats and waving arms and pamphlets. She shifted from side to side and stood on tiptoe, managing to catch a glimpse of several women moving along the raised platform at the front of the hall led by one she recognized immediately from all the pictures she had seen as Mrs Pankhurst; she was wearing a light grey cloak and seemed to be walking with a slight limp, the result of the cowardly attack on her at Newton Abbot, Henrietta thought, but her head was high as she turned to acknowledge the cheers and calls with a wide smile. Then Henrietta lost sight of her as she sat on a seat at the centre of the platform.

When all had taken their places and those in the body of the Hall had quietened, Mrs Pankhurst rose; there was an immediate expectant hush. She began quietly, welcoming them to the final session of this Women's Parliament, then describing the by-election she had just returned from in South Leeds. She had led a torchlight procession to Hunslett Moor, joined along the route by enthusiastic crowds finally numbering a hundred thousand, who chanted all the way, 'Shall us have the vote?' followed by the response, 'We shall!'

She had come to London, she went on, feeling as never before the seriousness of the struggle. Her experience in the country had taught her things that cabinet ministers without this experience did not know, and she felt the time coming when they might not be able to control their forces, which were increasing daily; she had to make one final attempt to see the Prime Minister and urge him to reconsider his position before some terrible disaster occurred.

She moved the resolution, 'This meeting of women is of the opinion that the most urgent of all constitutional reforms is to make the House of Commons representative of the people by enfranchising the women of the country. This meeting, therefore, calls upon the government before dealing with the House of Lords to secure that the will of the people shall prevail in the House of Commons by granting the vote to duly qualified women.'

The motion was seconded by a girl with lovely fair hair

248

who spoke with a northern accent – Annie Kenney, Henrietta thought, and it was confirmed the same moment by the woman next to her in a low voice filled with admiration.

There followed some minutes of shouting and disorder as women from all over the Hall tried to dissuade Mrs Pankhurst from going in person with the deputation that was to take the resolution to the Commons; she might be arrested and they would lose their leader. An amendment to this effect was moved, but was ruled out of order, and Mrs Pankhurst herself cut through the arguments by saying that the deputation had already been chosen and she was determined to go. A young women rose beside her on the platform – 'That's 'er!' Henrietta's friend whispered excitedly, 'Christabel!'

Christabel confirmed that the deputation had been selected and all on it had signified their willingness to be arrested under an Act of Charles II, which the authorities would use to prevent their approach to the Houses of Parliament; very matter of factly, she explained the terms of the Act.

Her voice rose. 'Every woman who has been selected for our deputation is prepared to be tried under this Act. There is an idea on the part of some of our oppressors that women are as cowardly as they are. It will be shown this afternoon that they are mistaken!'

As she finished speaking to enthusiastic shouts and clapping, she and Mrs Pankhurst and others members of the deputation started moving from their places. The audience rose with them and crowded towards the doors to cheer them on their way. Henrietta found herself swept along in the wave. She turned back to Popsy, reaching out her hand, but they were already being forced apart, and she could not grasp it. By the time she had been swept through the inner doors into the passage she couldn't even see her, and the pressure towards the main entrance was so great she went along with it.

She wondered if, perhaps, George and Stinger would be waiting outside, but realized as she emerged that she would not see them if they were; the road was lined with police, and the women coming out of the Hall were being forced by their pressure into a tight bunch behind the deputation, which had not yet started. Something was happening near the front; she saw Mrs Pankhurst's head rising above the others; she was being helped into some kind of trap. Then the trap started to move, and she was looking back, smiling and waving her hand to her followers, who responded with more cheers. For the first time Henrietta found herself caught up in the general mood. Perhaps it was the indomitable will of this middle-aged woman with the gentle face leading them seated in a trap because she could hardly walk after the recent attack on her, or the contrast between her frailty and the massed masculine ranks confronting them that moved her, but she felt an almost spiritual lift and excitement, and pressed forward herself in the general surge with scarcely more than a glance back for Popsy; she could not see her.

The procession had only moved a few yards before the police across the road ahead had forced a halt. There were angry shouts, but Mrs Pankhurst raised her hands to still them, then she climbed down from her seat and Henrietta lost sight of her. Presently they began to move again, very slowly as they were forced into single file. She felt her temper rise; what right had the police to treat them in this way; they were doing nothing unlawful. She had never seen so many police. The pace slowed even more; hemmed in, she began to loathe their smiles and condescending cheeriness.

They came to a halt again; voices rose to ask what was happening; she could feel the frustration building up, then shrieks and cries erupted some way ahead; a policeman was shouting orders and she heard other voices, men and women among the onlookers at the side calling 'Shame!' Gradually the sounds of the disturbance seemed to move away.

'They've started!' someone said close behind her.

She turned.

'They're taking them away!' The woman was in her twenties or early thirties; she had a soft voice and gentle eyes – about as far as one could imagine from a militant feminist, Henrietta thought, liking her immediately.

'Why?' she asked.

'They do *not* intend us to come anywhere *near* Parliament!'

'That's – *dreadful*!'

The woman smiled at her tone. 'Is this your first time?' Raising her reticule, she opened it and taking out a card, handed it to her. 'I'm Alice Davies. Do call if you would like to talk about things – any time.' She smiled again.

'I'm afraid I'm still at school.'

'A most progressive school I should think! Never mind. You do have holidays, I hope. Of course, you may not wish to –'

'Oh, no –' Henrietta started, when she felt a push from her other side; they were moving again. 'Thank you!' She waved the card.

They had only gone a few yards when a police officer, looking more important than the others, barred their path.

'You'll have to split up, ladies,' he shouted and waited impassively for the dissenting cries to die down. 'You cannot proceed in a column –'

'Why not?' Henrietta called furiously.

He looked down, and seeing her expression smiled.

'The law, Miss.'

'What law?'

A woman nearby repeated, 'What law?' and the cry was taken up by scores of others.

'Men's law!' someone yelled.

The noise rose. Henrietta felt herself being pressed from the right towards the officer when there was a flurry of movement and screams from just beyond him. She saw three bobbing helmets among the women's hats, their owners evidently engaged in a furious struggle; the screams rose in pitch to genuine fright. Others joined in hysterically. The press of people swayed, the woman immediately in front of her butted backwards in her anxiety to get away from the scrimmage; feeling Henrietta in the way, she lunged to the side, and in the space left Henrietta caught a momentary glimpse of a girl pinioned between two police; one had her arms behind her back, the other clasped her jerking legs. He had lost his helmet. She had an image of his red, curly hair and the uniform straining across his shoulders and the girl's frightened face as she felt another surge from behind. She took a step forward, but trod on someone's ankle and unable

251

to extricate her leg felt her balance going. She cried out in alarm.

A hand grasped her upper arm, steadying her, and looking up she saw the police officer, his expression grimmer now. Without a word he drew her towards him, turning and backing so that he moved her out from the knot of women. She felt so shaken she did not resist. Another pair of hands took her by the shoulders guiding her on towards the pavement.

'Come on, duckie!' A large woman wrapped in furs was stretching out her arms. There was a waft of cheap scent. 'It's *shameful* the way they're treatin' all of you.' She was gazing at her anxiously. 'All right, are you –?'

Henrietta nodded, bewildered by the sudden transition to the sidelines.

'You're best out of it, duckie – I've seen some things I never would've believed – mind you, they asked for it, some of 'em –'

There was a murmur of assent from others nearby.

She adjusted her hat, feeling her heart quieting. Turning back towards the road, all she could see were the backs of massed blue uniforms and helmets.

'They've taken 'em,' the woman said. 'Pals of yourn, were they?'

Anger and frustration welled up; she had allowed herself to be eased aside as if she were of no account while others were resisting and being taken away to face charges. She had failed them. Looking round, nodding, she felt tears pricking her eyes.

The woman put a hand on her shoulder. 'Best wait here with us for a bit.'

'I must get back.' She turned and began to move through the onlookers towards the Hall with an idea of finding Popsy and setting out again, and this time she would not submit tamely. She thought of Alice Davies, wondering whether she had become involved. She realized her card was still gripped between her fingers; it was bent almost double. She straightened it, committing the address to memory in case she lost it – 155 Palace Gardens, Kensington. Certainly she would visit her when the term ended. She felt as she had while

252

watching Mrs Pankhurst climbing up on to the trap to lead the deputation, a strong tie of sympathy and fellow-feeling. Now she had been a part of the fight, however briefly and ingloriously, she was committed in a way she could not have imagined before.

14

Everyone was in tears on the last day of term. Even Popsy's ultra manner slipped; she hugged Henrietta quite emotionally and there was a catch in her drawl as she said they must never lose touch. She would let her know directly she returned to London – she was staying with her father over the next few weeks – in any case they were bound to see one another often during the season.

Henrietta nodded, not trusting herself to say much as she walked with her to the car. Johnson was standing by the opened door like a statue. A wave of nostalgia for past times he had driven the two of them overcame her and she heard herself sobbing openly as she tried to say 'good bye –'

'*Dear* Etty –!' Popsy's eyes glistened.

Impossible to say why they cried; it was like an epidemic spreading from eye to eye. Outside the Baroness's rooms with several others waiting to make their final farewells, the sniffing and choking became pitiful. The butler, on his way in with the mid-morning tray of coffee – laced, it was said, with brandy – allowed his brows to twitch upwards as he passed, something which had never happened in her experience. When it was her turn to go in and make her last deep curtsey, thinking of the King, she managed to compose her face by repeating under her breath, 'I hate you von Witless –' But to her surprise the tough-jawed old face cracked into a smile when she entered, and she felt her own lips quivering in response.

'You have a *most* exciting and enjoyable time ahead of you, Henrietta. Do not forget us, will you. Do come back and tell us about it –'

She wiped her eyes. It was so *silly*. She learned afterwards that prisoners often cried on their last night before release.

The first days at home were bliss. She was eighteen, a *person*. When she looked in the mirror as she did for long periods while putting her hair up, or caught sight of herself in the reflecting surfaces of windows she was amazed to see it was so; she was no longer a girl, but a person, almost a woman.

The boys recognized it immediately they returned from school. So did Babs, who appraised her with some awe for a day or so. The change was most marked, although most subtly so in her mother; it was as if she regarded her now as an ally, or would like her to be one. Henrietta was unsure in her response; the habit of leading the opposition was too ingrained for her to shed it like an old skin.

Stretching ahead was 'the Season', and among the glittering dancers or sitting out, half-hidden by the palms in the conservatory or by the river perhaps on a June evening in striped blazer and flannels, a most unusual young man waited to claim her as his love. He was like no one she had known, not really *known*; on rare occasions she had glimpsed men whom she might have liked him to be, but always at a distance or in passing or in plays; the only time she had met anyone she thought probably resembled him was that day in the *Enchantress*. Of course it could still be Alastair, the new, immensely glamorous Alastair she had seen stroking fours along the Lords' grass; that would be revealed. In the meantime he waited as unaware of her as she was of his identity. How very strange to think of him somewhere out there leading his life oblivious for the moment to her existence.

But there were worms in her thoughts as well; as the days after her release passed, they grew larger. Chief was guilt. Images of Father Geoffrey among the ragged and starving of Plaistow, and of Mrs Pankhurst and Christabel, Annie Kenney, Alice Davies prepared to go smiling to prison for a cause she herself believed in but did nothing to assist, disturbed her.

She talked about it to Mary, but she had changed, or perhaps she wondered, might it be she herself who had

255

changed during the time they had been away at different schools. They no longer understood one another's thoughts instinctively. And whereas she looked at the world for which the Baroness had been attempting to prepare her, with scepticism – taking it for granted that the young man she would meet in that world would share her amusement at its pretences – Mary's Parisian education had aroused no such doubts. She accepted it all, its assumptions, its manners and its necessities. She was so impervious to Henrietta's stirrings of conscience it seemed at times as if she regarded *them* as affectations. Reminded that it was her mother who had first aroused their interest in the women's movement she gazed at her with those steady grey eyes, wondering what that had to do with it.

'But I still believe in it – very much. So does Mama. That doesn't mean to say we have to – I have to take the veil, honestly, Henry! We're bound to win soon. Look at all the support we have now.'

'How can you say *we*!'

'But I'm always talking about it. We have meetings still –'

On another occasion she accused Henrietta of being so conceited about her looks as to think she could dispense with the formalities.

'I can't though. I know that. And nor can you actually, Henry. You must be practical –'

Henrietta began to think there was no difference between Mary's concern for practicality and Popsy's belief in herself and her own enjoyment, except that Popsy's view was more honest – and more pathetic. She would be hurt because, at bottom, she had as wild an imagination as Henrietta; Mary had no illusions to be burst.

As the time for the first ball neared, Henrietta felt her inner tensions driving towards a resolution that she foresaw with awful clarity as she lay turning in the early hours of the morning, but banished from her daytime thoughts. Her mother, working with her on the details of clothes and lists of guests, dates and trains, carriages and chaperons, noticed her irritability; she put it down to quite understandable nerves, humoured her and took her side in increasingly bitter quarrels she had with Babs who had recovered from her awe and now took every opportunity to puncture Henrietta's still fragile adult persona.

Another cause of tension was her father. She had not been told why he had been away for so long; now he was back, she began to suspect he might have been to a 'Home' for those who had lost their reason. He could be as amusing as ever but his periods of talking utter nonsense had become more frequent and blatant, and his behaviour was often startling; he might start singing in the middle of someone else's conversation, or pushing back his chair in the middle of dinner, start hunting around under the table or tickling ankles. Sometimes he appeared not to recognize her; once in the drawing-room he asked why she had not fetched his hot water and yelled at her threateningly when she asked what he meant.

The morning after this deeply hurtful episode, she saw him in the orchard with Babs. They were playing 'he' around the trees, she evading easily, he panting after her, laughing each time he lunged and missed, as he always did. She felt herself torn with jealousy and pity for him – he was so slow and unsteady on his feet – and remembered his former grace and stature when he had played with *her* – and loved her. She turned away, as she did so catching sight of him fall; he rolled over on to his back, kicking his legs in the air and roaring. Babs, after a moment of surprise, pounced on him and they rolled about in the grass like infants.

Sick with inexpressible hurt and shame she wandered back into the house.

She was mounting the stairs when she heard her mother calling from the hall.

'You have not forgotten the blue tarlatan, Henry?'

She had forgotten. 'No,' she replied, and after a few more steps upwards, 'I'm having a fitting this morning.'

'When is she coming?'

'I'm going to her house, Mama. It will save time.'

Mrs Waring, who was making several of her less formal outfits, lived a short way down the hill in the end house of a terraced row. She was surprised to see Henrietta, and anxious; the blue dress was not quite ready.

'It doesn't matter,' Henrietta said, realizing she had been thoughtless to call without an appointment. 'I felt like a walk, it's a lovely morning –'

'Would you like to wait? It's nearly ready – you could almost try it on now. I won't be more than a few moments –'

'Thank you, Mrs Waring,' Henrietta smiled. 'Really, there's no hurry.'

'It is quite convenient.' She beckoned, and gesturing towards the door to the front room, 'Would you like to wait in – or – I work upstairs – the light is so much better –'

'Oh –' She felt thoroughly embarrassed. 'Can I come up? I should love to see your work room.'

'You must please excuse the disorder –'

There was very little disorder, considering. Most of the snippets of cut-off material and thread on the floor were concentrated to one side of the work table which stood under a window in the far, garden wall; sun streamed in, glinting off the silver knobs of a sewing machine which stood on the table, brightening the sinuous designs chased on its flat end, glancing off the shining hand wheel. The dress lay beside it; Henrietta experienced a moment of pure delight: the lace trimming was exquisite against the sunlit and shadowed folds of pale blue.

'It looks *lovely*!'

Mrs Waring turned and smiled at her pleasure. 'Yes, I'm sure it will look most fetching on you.'

There were two comfortable chairs against the near wall, and she motioned Henrietta to one, a moment afterwards swooping on it to remove a newspaper from the seat. Henrietta caught a glimpse of the title as she turned quickly away with it.

'*Votes for Women!*' she exclaimed. 'Do you support the suffragettes, Mrs Waring?'

'Oh, no.' She bent and thrust the offending paper beneath a gorgeous brocade lying across the seat of the other easy chair. 'I happened to be in the village yesterday when –' she fiddled with her glasses, 'I thought I'd see what all the fuss was about.'

'Do you mind if I have a look?'

258

'Do you think you should? What would your mother say if she knew you read such things here –'

'Don't worry, I won't tell her.'

Mrs Waring looked at her for a moment. 'Very well.' She bent again and taking the paper out from under the brocade, handed it to her. 'But pay no attention –' She went over to her table by the window and smoothed out the blue material, 'Really, I've never read such stuff!'

Henrietta sat down. The main article on the front page was about the by-election in North West Manchester contested for the Liberals by Mr Winston Churchill. He was, he said, being vigorously 'hen-pecked', but he promised, when returned, to try his best to help women obtain the franchise: 'I do think sincerely that the women have always had a logical case and they have now got behind them a great popular demand amongst women. It is no longer a movement of a few extravagant and excitable people, but one which is gradually spreading to all classes . . .'

'Trying his best', the article went on, was not good enough, particularly since their confirmed opponent, Asquith, was Prime Minister. Christabel Pankhurst had made it plain that the Women's Social and Political Union would not withdraw their opposition to Mr Churchill unless they had a definite understanding from the Prime Minister and the government as a whole that the Women's Enfranchisement Bill would be carried into law without delay.

Henrietta had an image of Miss Snape-Hervey. '*Pourquoi veulent-elles rendre visite à Monsieur Asquith, Henriette?*'

'*Parcequ'il est le grand ennemi des femmes . . .*'

They seemed no further forward than they had been two years ago; probably they were in a worse position since the Prime Minister then, the gentle Campbell-Bannerman, had supported their cause. Was it really two years ago? She heard Popsy's '*Au diable le Monsieur Lloyd George!*' and smiled to herself.

Turning the page, she caught sight of an invitation in bold, black type to join the women's demonstration in Hyde Park on 21 June. She froze, staring at the date; it was the weekend of her dance. Surely it must be a message. It was to be a record meeting. The greatest meeting ever held previously

259

in the Park had numbered 72,000; they were determined to gather at least a quarter of a million –

She seemed to hear Mrs Waring saying something.

'Henrietta!' Her voice was nearer, insistent. She looked up. Mrs Waring was standing, holding the blue dress. 'Are you all right, Henrietta?'

She gazed back for a moment. 'I'm awfully sorry, Mrs Waring, I have to go.' She rose. 'I have just remembered –'

'But it's ready for you –' The old eyes, enlarged by the glasses and pink from strain, were wide, 'that is to say – it is ready to try on –'

'Thank you very, *very* much, Mrs Waring, I'm dreadfully sorry if I've put you to – I forgot, completely.' She folded the paper and placed it on the chair behind her. 'I shall be in touch – or Mama will. I'm *so* sorry. I can let myself out – please don't trouble.'

She ran down the stairs with an image in her mind of Alice Davies's card: '155 Palace Gardens, Kensington'.

Messages of the kind she had received can only be interpreted by the prepared mind; she realized this years later. At the time she had no doubt that the impulse which had sent her to Mrs Waring, and the impulse – if it had been – which had led Mrs Waring to take a copy of *Votes for Women* were in the nature of Divine intervention, saving her from herself. The idea was reinforced by her visit to Alice Davies. But again, looking back from a distance she realized that it was, of course, the excitement she sensed there, the purpose and the cause which fired her. For the Davieses, Alice and her husband Charles, were between them in every kind of progressive cause from universal disarmament to co-operative handcrafts, not excluding she discovered some time after her first visit, eugenics and free love.

While Alice turned her drawing-room into a virtual meeting house for the ladies of the Kensington Suffragettes, and Charles's study with its telephone into an organizing post, he was out for much of the time at a press he owned in Chelsea, printing socialist tracts and the works of poets he had 'discovered', in the evenings attending Fabian meetings or trying to raise money for worthy plays; in brief interludes at home he quoted what Shaw or Wells or Granville Barker or Max Beerbohm had said to him the day before, or what Mrs Patrick Campbell planned, or the latest doings of the fascinating Olivier girls or their 'find' a brilliant young man at Cambridge called Rupert Brooke. It was a new world, as far from the Baroness's and the nineteenth century certitudes of home as it was possible to be; she was swept off her feet.

In retrospect, she was haunted by the images she could not shut out – her father stumbling round the trees in the orchard, her mother's tension whenever he was present, waiting, fearing his crassness, waiting for the next 'episode', his eyes gazing at *her* without recognition. She hated Babs, whom he loved; despite his grossness he could still love Babs; she wanted to kill her, but ran away instead – all this she saw in nightmares and woke to guilt. If she had recognized her mother's suffering, if she had stayed to help her, if at least she had not spurned all she had lovingly planned, contemptuous of her attitudes, consigning them to the past with the dreadful certainties of her new intellectual discoveries.

Here too her memory played her false. She did recognize her mother's agony, pitying her as much as she pitied what Papa had become, and she wrestled with herself for days after first visiting the Davieses before a hasty remark from her mother brought the inevitable outburst.

Her mother said nothing. She stiffened, her face hardening, then turned without a word. Afterwards when she spoke to her it was with icy correctness which made it impossible to apologize or reconsider.

This time it was she who asked Andy to go for an early morning walk up to the Heath. It was not as early as on the previous occasion, nor such a sparkling morning; the wind was bitterly cold, chopping the surface of Whitestone Pond into lines of miniature waves which made her think of George out at sea in his grey ship. She wished he were here; she needed his reassuring strength. Andy was cleverer, much cleverer she had realized recently, but he lacked George's solidity.

She had asked Andy rather than Willy because she wanted to know what he thought about God – whether He existed and if so why He should send such pain and confusion into His world. To her surprise she found that he did believe, but not in the Christian God, not in Church at all. His God, he told her, was in quiet places; he had found Him while resting below the branches of a beech tree in Savernake Forest, and in a hollow in the Downs, and innumerable other places away from people. He had written a poem about it, in fact, he confessed, several.

She was surprised; he had given no intimation in his letters. 'Why didn't you tell me! Tell me some now.'

'I can't – well, I can't remember exactly –'

'What are they *like*?'

'Well –' He hesitated.

His face seemed more *formed* than she had noticed before, or perhaps it was the peculiar, low early light; his spectacles no longer drew attention from his rather fine, lean nose and cheeks. There was something altogether firmer and more assured about his expression. His voice still quavered uncertainly, but he had grown up in the last term. Why had she not noticed before?

'Here the dappled thicket grows,' he started, studying her response.

She looked down as she walked to encourage him.

> 'Here the dogweed and the rose
> Are with the briar intertwined,
> Like tangled thoughts inside my mind.
> They seek the sun; so do I:
> My sun is in a wider sky.'

He paused, looking at her.

She turned in amazement. 'You wrote that?'

'Why not?' He looked pleased.

'It doesn't – sound like you.'

'Sometimes I feel it's not me. Lines just come into my head. I have to work hard at the others though. It's jolly hard work –'

'*My* sun is in a wider sky –' she repeated slowly.

'I was just lying by the roadside,' he said, 'with my bike, and there was a tangle of little wild roses and brambles and

262

the sun was shining. I was looking up at them and I realized they were all stretching out – the stems were stretching towards the sun, and it came to me – I didn't *think* about it – I sort of saw the boys at school all jumbled up against one another – without being able to get away from one another – no – no privacy anywhere – some good at cricket, some squash, some running, some – I wasn't much good at anything, I went on frightful "sweats" over the Downs with the other "wrecks". But I knew I was good at playing the piano and –'

'You're very good at Latin – and maths –'

'We were all different at any rate. But we were all *trying* – even the boys who don't try because they think they're no good, try at something. They suck up to the boys who are good at games or –' he gestured with his hands, 'even Reeves, who's only good at getting beatings – we were all trying – not for the school – all the fellows who play in teams say it's for the school, but it isn't, it's really for themselves. I like maths. That's not for the school, it's because – I just like maths.' He looked at her, knowing he was not explaining it at all well. 'We're just like the briars trying to get clear and into the sun – except it's something else – you don't see, do you?'

'Of course I do –'

'I don't see it now, not really, but it was absolutely clear then – when I was lying there on the grass –'

'Are all your poems like that?'

'No, they're about school mostly – about the things that happen.'

'Can I see them?'

'You wouldn't understand them. They're about people at school –'

Nevertheless, he showed them to her when they got back from the walk; they were written out in his small, neat hand in the blank pages at the back of a diary. There was nothing too difficult about them, and a few bits she thought amazingly good, but it was the one he had quoted from that remained with her, for the more she thought about it, the more she realized how it applied to herself. 'Coming out' – for what? To attract the young man she would meet, and marry and

263

do as all the others did? It was far more than that. She desired 'Life' – unguessed experiences and love, more even than that, something she could only sense drawing her on – where? She had no idea where or why, but she felt it. How amazing that Andy had expressed it more exactly than she could ever have done herself. She wondered if he would become a poet.

The 'sun in a wider sky' was God. Had Papa, perhaps, been smothered in his reaching out, and so – withered? That would mean the opposite of the compassionate God she wanted to believe in. It might explain suffering and evil better.

She wrote to Father Geoffrey. She had another reason for writing: she felt guilty after all her promises that instead of offering herself for his mission, she was going to work for the Kensington branch of the W.S.P.U. Yet after all, as she reminded him, he had told her how important the women's movement was.

My dear Henrietta,

Your letters are such a joy to me. Let me say first that I believe you are right to have made the choice you have, I hope it will not mean you become too busy to write to me! Letters are almost as good as talking, in some ways better for we often put on paper things we might not wish to express face to face, and we omit all those things we say lightly which have no meaning.

I agree with you about the lines you quoted from Andrew's poem, but I don't think you expect me to agree with your interpretation! It reminds me of the theories of the 'life force' of which one reads so much. I prefer to believe that life was given us by God and that we all have an innate sense of this in moments when our other senses are not overwhelmed by the concerns of the material world. It is possible to read that too into Andrew's poem. He was lying, probably tired, by the roadside and his spiritual senses were free to roam.

But of course you are right, pain and suffering and grief are perplexing problems. Surrounded by them as I am here, I cannot pretend to understand them. But life itself is a very perplexing and difficult business, and whether one believes in God or not one has to meet with the same disappointments, bereavements and a hundred other things that man is prey to. Yet if these things went out of life, would we not lose with them courage, compassion, fortitude, faith even? These are great mysteries, there is either no reason to it all; it is simply a stupendous accident with no beginning and no end, or there is a reason which it is not given to our mortal minds to understand. I think it unreasonable to suppose that we, reasoning beings, are the result of blind, unreasoning forces; on the other hand I, like so many others, have seen gleams of light, and I know I am right to follow them. I hope this may help you a little. Remember, our Lord knew suffering. He made all the suffering of the world His suffering and all who know and love Him, make His suffering theirs.

Do write again sometime. Good luck in your endeavours and may God bless and keep you always – Geoffrey.

I shall be praying for your success before some of your more extreme sisters go too far!

For Willy, the news that Henrietta was leaving home to live with another family in Kensington came as something incomprehensible, as numbing as Jack's death had been. In a way it struck him as even more final. Home without Henrietta could not be home; she had always been there, fierce, frightening at times, yet even in her maddest moments he had known he could rely on her more than anyone else in the world, for she could understand how he felt. George, he had always looked up to tremendously, but in rather a removed, no nonsense way. With Henrietta, he could confide his innermost feelings without thinking about it, knowing she would either tell him not to be so silly very sharply and immediately forget it, or give him her whole sympathy. She was as generous with love as she was quick with argument, as concerned for all of them and for fairness in their quarrels amongst themselves as she was prickly about her own position; she was Henry; he loved her in a way quite different from that in which he loved other members of the family, even his mother.

He had been aware of the tension at home almost since the beginning of the holidays; at first he put it down to the strain of the preparations for Henry's 'coming out' – preparations which had excited him almost as much as Henry although he pretended to Andy and the young Harry that it was just girls' stuff, worth only cynical amusement. He had loved it when Henry showed off her ball dresses, swirling round first one way, then the other. The rustle and lights in the satin captivated him, and the way the front of the dresses swept daringly low, leaving her shoulders and the upper part of her chest quite bare.

'Won't you be awfully cold, Henry?'

'*Silly* boy! I shall be *dancing*.' She had caught his hand and placed it round her slim waist and waltzed him round and round until he was giddy, and stepped on her foot.

'Don't they teach you *anything* at Dartmouth!'

He could not imagine home without Henry.

'But what will you do, Henry?'

'Work. I shall help to organize things, meetings, donations – there's any amount of work – getting out leaflets –'

'I mean how will you "come out"?'

She had laughed. 'It doesn't mean I can't go to balls, I'm going to Popsy's. That'll be about the best dance of the season I should think. She's having the *Entente Cordiale* as the theme,' and she had started taking off Popsy until he was doubled up with laughter, '– it will be too – my dear, patriotic is *not* the word, it will be positively *provocative*. I shouldn't be in the *least* surprised if we didn't start the teeniest war, I mean *think* when the Germans hear of it. We must be decidedly on the *qui vive*, you know how many spies they have here. Bobo, the poor thing, *begged* me to think of something less *à haute voix*. *Et pourquoi?* It is distinctly possible that when they blow the whistle, Bobo will be sent to France – even *he* knows that. The poor dear does *not* want to go, not during the polo season, that is distinctly not what he joined the colours for. Bobo, my darling, I said, the poilus may be rather – but can't you raise just a teeny bit of jingo spirit –' She stopped, and with a sudden change of mood,

'So you see, *everyone* will be there. And I'm going to Mary's and Flighty's and – well, practically everyone I know –'

'But they won't be going to yours.'

'Of course not! I'm not having one.'

'I know. It won't be fair.'

'Yes it will. *They're* not working for the vote, are they!'

Exasperated, he had said, 'Why do you want the vote so much, Henry?'

'Oh, dear! How would *you* like it – just think, Willy Steel, if we had the vote and you didn't. How would you like that? You wouldn't think *that* fair!'

She was determined to go, and nothing he could say would alter her mind.

Sensing his despair, she had said in a gentler tone, 'We'll still see each other – often – I'll come back to see you and you can come to Kensington and see me. It's not far. We can go out and have lunch together – at a Lyon's Corner House – it'll be such fun!'

It would not be the same.

Babs was the cause of it. She and Henry had been at each other's throats for most of the holiday. On the last occasion Babs had come to him sobbing desperately, saying she hated Henry. He had tried to calm her, and ask her what it was about.

'She said – she said – I – I told – Mama –'

'What?'

'She said – I was a sneaky – underhand – mean –'

'What did you tell Mama?'

'I had to – I had to tell her –'

'*What?*'

'She's seeing him, I know she is – she's going to the East End –'

'Seeing who?'

'Father Geoffrey. I know – I saw his letter. He writes to her –'

'*Babs!*' He had been really cross. 'Have you been reading Henry's private letters?'

'I didn't read it, I just saw it.'

'How did you know who it was from?'

'I saw the postmark.'

He could tell she was lying; she wouldn't look at him, but started crying again.

'You can't – read – other people's – letters –' he said severely, and as she started crying more desperately, 'I agree with Henry, that was a foul thing to do – you're a beastly little girl –' He had risen abruptly and left her wailing, disturbed to think that Henry was still going to the East End. Girls were the absolute limit; they picked away at each other until one or other was in tears, then came running for sympathy. He felt shaken and unhappy. The thought of Henry sneaking away to the East End was terrible – even if he was a priest.

He went straight into her room and tackled her about it.

'I suppose Babs told you!' Her eyes flashed danger signals. 'And what does it matter if I did?'

He stood up to her, angry now. 'You *did*!'

'Of course I didn't.'

She stormed to her chest of drawers and pulling open a top drawer, started taking out filmy pieces of underclothing and throwing them about the room. He wondered if she had lost her senses. Then she picked out an envelope and hurled it at him, and another.

'Look at those! D'you think he'd write all the time if I was *sneaking* out as you put it to see him. Look at the date. Read it – see what it says –'

'Why don't you tell Mama then, tell her he just writes to you.'

'Why should I? If she wants to believe everything Babs tells her –'

'Of course she doesn't. I'm sure she wouldn't if you explained.'

'You don't understand, Willy, it's no use.'

Unable to sleep that night after talking over the whole awful business with Andy as they lay in their beds, he thought of George; he was the only one who had ever had real influence with Henry. He must write and tell him; he wondered where he was now – the Channel Fleet – he couldn't be far away –

There was an air of expectancy on the bridge; only the 'Old

Man', pacing slowly with his right hand in the pocket of his reefer jacket, affected nonchalance. The dawn sky beyond him was a dusty red filigreed with orange, the land sleeping below was grey merging in the distance with the glistening, corrugating grey of the sea. The breeze blowing across the sea from the east was sweet and clean. George felt it sweeping away the miasmas of the shore and harbour routine, the tawdriness of the previous evening with its unrealized promises, half-desires, half regrets. Soon they would be clear away.

The Old man stopped at the extreme end of the bridge wing and raised his binoculars, gazing astern for a moment towards the flagship before dropping the glasses to his chest again and starting slowly back, passing across the *Commonwealth*'s silhouetted grey masts and funnels, smoke from one erupting suddenly and mushrooming against the luminous sky.

From the Old Man's expression he might have been taking a morning promenade. His dark beard, just tinged with a hint of grey, was immaculate as always, the white silk scarf around his neck turned elegantly between the lapels of his jacket which hung with faultless cut despite the strain caused by his hand in the pocket; was the full weight of his arm borne by that pocket or was the hand merely poised there as deliberately controlled as his character? George had been with him for two months but he still wondered; he couldn't even guess at his feelings; the plane of his authority was too far removed; probably he did not permit himself feelings – not the kind he himself was experiencing. Looking at his face as he passed, the creased brow beneath the oak leaves around the peak of his cap, deep-shadowed clear eyes and the taut skin of his cheeks testifying to the physical condition he maintained by daily exercises and gymnastics on the quarter-deck, George felt more keenly his own dissatisfaction with the complexities and disillusions of 'the beach'; the only true satisfactions and rewards were in duty done –

'Shorten in to two cables, sir!'

The Yeoman's call broke into the Old Man's measured pace; he glanced briefly astern again at the hoist dropping from the flagship's yard as he turned to the Commander, watching him.

'Shorten in!'

The Commander leaned over the forward rail and shouted the order to the fo'c's'le, not bothering to use the megaphone by his feet, so quiet was the morning. Number One had already seen, and before the words were out, he was nodding to Stinger by the ladder, who stooped, waving his arm to the Chief Stoker at the capstan below. The clattering, squealing sound of steel against steel began, the hiss of the hose directed at the anchor cable occasionally audible through the racket as the great links shuddered up; George imagined them jerking, turning under the strain as they came on deck.

The hammering of all the other capstans and cables carried clearly across the water; indiscernibly the fleet inched forward together.

After a while the young signalman leaning out over the bow straightened, this time holding aloft the '2' flag, and there was a pause, a quiet in which the roar from their funnels just abaft the bridge sounded louder than before. Another hoist rose to the flagship's yard; the Old Man nodded, the Commander wheeled on the little group behind him, and moments afterwards the pipes were shrilling from below and hoarse shouts echoing up the steel ladders and from the casemates, the thud of running bare feet on the decks as the hands went to stations.

Shortly after the ship had quietened again, the flagship's hoist dropped and the final stage began, the renewed clank and squeal of the cable coming in punctuated by laconic reports from the fo'c's'le and the Yeoman's voice as he read out new hoists burgeoning from the flagship's halyards. They were inverting the lines. The Commander sent his 'doggie', Brewster, to warn the guard, exchanging an ironic quick gleam with the pilot as 'Brewup' slid down the ladder like an eel. Moments later they heard a barked order from below followed by the thud of marine boots as the detachment doubled aft to the quarterdeck, and the thump of rifle butts and clinking of bayonets being fixed.

The fo'c's'le was quiet. The anchor hung out from the cat davit, a bare-footed bluejacket crouching on the flukes as he passed the chain around; he measured the distance and leaped back aboard; in seconds the davit was swinging after

270

him; the tackle parties hauled, then walked back and the anchor settled ponderously in its seating, mud spraying as the hose jet played over it.

They waited; the ship was free, prey for the moment to tide and wind; the rest of the still fleet stretched in its three divisions all about them, deep grey hulls lined with angled booms and rolled torpedo netting, great turrets at either end with lesser guns massed between and high above them the thin funnels drifting smoke down the lines; the roar of their own funnels and ventilators was a reminder of all the latent power.

George had an image of longer lines but with black hulls and gleaming white upperworks and yellow masts strung with flags overall sparkling in the sun of a long time ago when he was very young, and of his father releasing the *Peacock*'s tiller to spread his arms wide, 'Come all the world in arms, George!' He would always remember that moment – although not much else about the day. Pain bit deep; his father had looked so old and queer recently, and he remembered the letter from Willy – Henrietta was playing the giddy goat again – she must know the anguish that was causing Mama. Girls only thought of themselves – when they thought at all – and she wanted the vote! What she really wanted was to upset things and draw attention to herself as always. But it hurt deeply. Poor Henry, he could do nothing for her, badly as he wanted to. He had been there once upon a time to steady her; now there was nothing he could do; he felt strangely removed as if it had been another life –

Number One was coming briskly up the ladder; he saluted the Old Man. 'Anchor secured, sir!'

The Yeoman uttered and a halyard whirred above.

George looked at the other ships; a few had their signals up already, others were hoisting theirs as he gazed around, and presently he thought he caught the tinkle of engine room telegraphs from way astern. He stared at the flagship – surely the space between her masts was growing? Turning to the Old Man, he saw he had his binoculars on her.

She was turning slowly out of the line, bringing into view her after ports which glowed palely with electric light. Now she was swinging back, presenting her bow again, a feather of white playing over the thrust of her ram. A bugle sounded from *Hibernia*, her next ahead, and moments later her band started playing.

He heard the Commander shouting from the end of the bridge; as he looked, he straightened, moving the megaphone from his mouth to round on Brewster.

'A *head*! The wardroom pantry I fancy. My compliments to the messman, if I see it again I shall personally separate it from his shoulders –'

Brewster was already leaping away.

'– even if it does mean delaying breakfast! Sink the Dutch!' The Commander looked over the forward rail, scanning the hands on the fo'c's'le and down along the foredeck.

The flicker of a smile seemed to lift the Old Man's bearded lips.

The flagship had gathered speed; foam danced at her bow and played along her freshly-painted sides. The *Hibernia* was turning out of the line to follow her now, and a bugle sounded from her next ahead, the *Irresistible*. Over in the second division it was the same exactly, the *Venerable*, flying 'Snuffy' Custance's flag, steaming up the line.

Was it really possible that Snuffy and Charlie B were plotting to unseat Jackie Fisher? He thought of the gunroom guest night Hedgepig had invited him to aboard Percy Scott's cruiser, *Good Hope*. The rumours about Charlie B had been amazing. Even more amazing, perhaps, had been the gunnery devices he had been shown there. It was not surprising the *Good Hope* had licked every ship in the gunlayers' test last year. They were planning bigger surprises this time! He had suggested some of Scott's training gadgets to 'Guns' and he had seemed interested enough; so far nothing had happened though. 'Paintwork appears more in demand than gunnery' had indeed been the watchword in the short time he had known the Channel Fleet; now they were all brightened up to salute the French President – he still found it difficult to think of the French as allies –

The flagship was closing fast, the red cross of St George straining at her fore, high above three hoists of signal bunting, a fourth rising. The arms of two of the semaphores above her bridge flashed round and up and down. Black smoke

272

streamed from her funnels, almost obscuring the white ensign at the main; followed by the *Hibernia* and the *Irresistible* turning into their wake, she made a brave sight, the round of her bow, the sloping front plate of her great fore turret, the tompions in the long guns picking up hints of pink from the sunrise, which flashed from sudden curves in the waves swelling out from her side. The hiss and rumble of the water as it foamed at the stem and passed down the armoured belt and the noise of the draught for her boilers preceded her. And somewhere high over the fore turret and the still men lining her decks, among the officers clustered on the bridge was the Admiral, Charlie B; he could never forget his kindness to him in the Med. –

'Still!' the Commander said quietly.

The bugler on the ladder faced aft and sounded the 'Alert',

An order rang out from the quarterdeck and they heard the muffled crash of rifles coming to the present. A moment afterwards the band started playing 'Rule Britannia'.

On she came, not fifty yards of clear water between their sides as her bow passed their quarterdeck and the first wave struck them right aft. On her bridge George saw a bulky figure moving from the knot of officers a pace or two to stand alone at the very end of the wing, and recognized Lord Charles Beresford – the bulldog jowls, the mouth that could twist so genially, the heavy-lidded eyes set now in a firm expression as he gazed across the short space between them.

The band reached a climax as the flagship's bridge drew abreast of theirs – '*Rule Britannia* – Britannia rules the waves –' As one man they brought their heels together and saluted, the Old Man, the Commander, Number One, the pilot, the snotties, messenger boys, cone boys and the yeoman and his minions and the coxswain and helmsman, standing stiffly as the deck moved beneath their feet from the swell pressed out by the flagship, their eyes fixed on the great man, heads turning as he swept by in the roar and hum of majesty.

A few moments only and he had passed, and the boats above the battery were sliding by, the picket boat's brass funnel gleaming, then the after bridge with another knot of officers and men, and as that too drew ahead they gazed

273

down on the after twelve inch turret and the sanded sweep of the quarterdeck with its shining companion rails and the admiral's guard drawn up stiffly.

A bugle sounded 'Carry on'; the bugler on the ladder repeated the call and the spell was broken. George turned to look at the *Hibernia* steering up the pale whirls of the other's wake. The Old Man paced back from the bridge and slowly towards the telegraphs. George wondered whether he was moved. The Commander, obviously pleased that it had passed off without a hitch, stepped up to Number One, leaning towards him confidentially.

'Heard a good one last night. Miss Mabel de Vere of Mayfair – said I really have nothing to wear. I need a new dress, and must buy one unless – Percy paints me. Lord! Charlie will swear!'

Number One chuckled quietly.

'It's come to something! Sink the Dutch!' The Commander moved away to the front rail and peered down at the foredeck.

The *Hibernia* steamed past; they saluted her, and after a similar interval the *Irresistible*. The *New Zealand* was coming up astern of her.

'Slow ahead both!' the Old Man called.

The order was repeated by both telegraph midshipmen as they pushed the handles right down and immediately up again to 'Slow'. Answering bells jangled.

'Turn of starboard!'

The helmsman, his bare toes twitching on the raised grating as he was called into action, pressed the wheel round.

'Half speed starboard!'

They gathered way, turning into the path of the oncoming *New Zealand*; they were swinging fast as she reached them; it was a nice problem in relative motion; as she swept by, a stone's throw from their fo'c's'le they were pointing at her moving side, closing.

'Full speed both!' the Old Man called, as if to ram, and moments afterwards, 'Ease the helm!'

As always it seemed a minor miracle as the other's stern drew clear, and with an opposite turn of the wheel, they slewed neatly into the boil of her wake.

'Take her out, Pilot!' The Old Man started across to the other side of the bridge to inspect the last ship in the line, the *Britannia*, as they approached. George followed him.

After coming down from the bridge and having breakfast, he and Stinger wedged themselves in their usual spot in the shelter of the launch for a clandestine smoke before divisions. He didn't enjoy the smoking part of it much, but liked the texture and smell of the tobacco as he pulled it from his pouch and the feeling of the pipe's stem between his teeth; above all, he liked the sense of masculine dignity and calm, philosophical reflection which his pipe induced.

'I thought –' he puffed '–Old Charlie B looked pretty sick. Didn't you?'

Stinger was having difficulty getting his going properly, and grunted.

'I think,' George went on, gazing skywards as he blew out smoke, 'the Old Man is an anti-Fisherite.'

Stinger took the pipe from his mouth and knocked it against the strakes of the launch in disgust. 'Dare say he is. We didn't cover ourselves with glory last prize firing.'

George looked at him; there was no doubt he was sharp, whatever he lacked in exam ability. That was an aspect he had never considered. Pique at the new accent on gunnery and jealousy of the success in this respect of Fisherites like Percy Scott were not emotions he could imagine in the Old Man though; it was difficult to imagine him permitting himself emotions, certainly not such feline ones. He was one of the old school and a first class seaman.

'Besides –' Stinger went on between sibilant attempts at relighting, 'he's that sort.'

'What sort?'

'Old family. You know, what is he, ninth Baron? Look at your sister's chum, Popsy – her family hobnob with old C-C and he and Snuffy and Charlie B are thick as fleas – it's all a *social* row, you know,' he finished with an air of authority. 'The service doesn't get a look in.'

George was amused at the way he had managed to mention Henrietta; he usually did somehow or other at their morning sessions; he was quite stupid about her.

'Well –' Stinger said hotly, misconstruing his expression,

'look what they say about Jackie Fisher's parentage – and you can't say Percy Scott exactly has a family either!' He got his pipe pulling at last. 'What makes you think the Old Man's in Charlie B's camp?'

'He said to me just before he left the bridge,' and he imitated the Old Man's precise tones, ' "And men in England now abed, will think themselves accursed they were not here. Know where that's from Steel?" "Henry the fifth" I said. "You will have no difficulty in accounting for your activities, Steel. I served with Lord Charles Beresford! The Channel Fleet!" "Yes, sir," I said. "And in the Med." "Yes, sir." "The finest admiral since Nelson," he said, then he asked me whether I had enjoyed my evening in the *Good Hope* – how he knew we went over there I've no idea. "Very well, sir," I replied. He looked straight at me. "There are queer things happening in the Service these days, Steel." Then he went below. It was the look he gave me – I think he was warning me.'

Stinger nodded. 'No question.'

He raised his brows.

Stinger went on, 'Some officers have an idea it's detrimental to their careers to be associated with Charlie B. But if he comes out on top – it'll be the other way round.'

'No chance of that.'

'Let's hope not.'

They were silent, George thinking of the Hedgepig's enthusiasm when showing him the gunnery training devices aboard his ship and the director firing gear they were experimenting with – like all the other gadgets, designed by his extraordinary Admiral, Percy Scott. He envied him. He was at the forefront of the new Navy Jackie Fisher was forging. Besides which a good flimsy from Scott's flagship must carry a great deal of weight when it came to selection for the gunnery long course.

'You're wrong,' he said, 'it's not social. It's the old against the new,' and with a flash of inspiration, 'Charlie B would have been fine when we were going to fight the French. With the Germans, it'll be different.'

'Better not tell that to the Old Man.' Stinger squinted into the bowl of his pipe, sucking noisily. 'Wars!' He took it from his mouth and started pressing the tobacco down with his thumb. 'Bloody baccy must be green!'

George offered him his pouch.

Stinger declined it, looking at his watch; it was after nine. He started scraping out the bowl into his cupped palm. 'And you'd better not tell your people either.'

'My people?'

'Henry would hear probably – if she told Popsy!' Stinger left the sentence unfinished, looking up innocently from his scraping.

George felt sorry for him; he was pathetically naïve about girls, even the ones they met in Pompey. The poor devil had no sisters, that was the trouble.

'The least said to Henry, the better,' he replied briskly, taking out his own pipe and beginning to stub out the glow.

'On the other hand,' Stinger went on, 'she did warn us – when your mater was quizzing you about the paintwork business, so she'd have the sense not to let on –'

'So far as the other half goes,' George said with the authority of experience, 'it's never safe to assume anything.' He wished he would shut up about Henry. He had not told him about her leaving home, nor would he; it was like a stab when he thought of it, reminding him of the other difficulties at home and of what his mother was having to cope with, and of his own impotence. He couldn't afford to think about it all; he needed to keep his wits about him if he was to get a good flimsy and start preparing for the vital exams next year. If the Old Man was in the anti-Fisher camp, he was going to have to watch what he said in future, especially about gunnery.

'Come on,' he said roughly, 'we'd better go.'

15

It was good to see Flighty again. Henrietta had seen no one from the Baroness's since leaving. It was pleasant after the seriousness of her work at the Davies's to slip back into the old relationship – how distant Sunningdale seemed now although it was only a matter of weeks – and laugh together and speculate about everyone's doings, and who would be at Popsy's 'rout' that evening, who would not. It was quite surprising that Flighty was going, but her mother was in the social set; she was going to everything.

After a while her chatter about 'everything' palled; Henrietta, who had been invited to hardly anything that counted – apart from Popsy's – thought how boringly *comme il faut* Flighty was trying to be; it was amazing how friends changed so in different surroundings. Flighty had always been inclined to take the Baroness's nonsense rather too seriously, but now, in her own home, she sounded like something out of *The Ladies' Pictorial*. Henrietta had a suspicion it was because of her father, a small, stout man she had met as she came in – completely without tone. Popsy had told her once he had started life as plain Herbert Davison, and had amassed his huge fortune after succeeding to the family building firm, by knocking down beautiful town centres, erecting in their place '*the* most vulgar' modern department stores – 'he could certainly have bought out Croesus several times!' He had bought a knighthood instead, then the least attractive of the fflyte sisters – or the other way around – 'it scarcely matters, the man is absolutely too – I do mean it, Etty, he *is* a cad, and probably a Jew. David's-*sohn* I shouldn't be surprised. Look at the Balloon – all the daughters of Israel are round and comely –'

'Do shut up, Popsy, I'll bet he's perfectly charming – what's wrong if he did make heaps of tin.' She experienced a twinge of guilt about her own grandfather; she had never told anyone about the sewing machine accessories.

'Building shops! Oh, Etty!'

Certainly the fflyte-Davisons lived in the greatest style off Park Lane. It was strange she had not been before; that probably had to do with Flighty's father as well; she had never spoken of him at school, and Henrietta had sensed an air of tension when she was introduced, as if Flighty had hoped he would not be there that afternoon. He was not there at tea when she met her mother; she liked her at once; she was lively and natural, surprisingly natural for someone so much in society, also rather tired-looking, which was not surprising.

Afterwards she sent a maid up to help her dress, the most delicious time, marred only a little when the sight of the satin gown took her straight home and she thought of her mother's efforts and enthusiasm before that stupid quarrel. The maid was ecstatic about the gown; so were Flighty and her mother, who said she looked quite lovely.

She saw herself full-length in the great mirrors at the head of the stairs as they were starting down together, and shivered a little; the sparkle of her silver hairband and the settings of the pendant pearls in her necklace set off the cool cream of her skin. Her eyes were dark – how young she looked and, beside Flighty, sylph-like in the white satin. She experienced a sudden, peculiar sensation that it had happened before – here at the head of the stairs, turning from her reflection to look down into the hall with the two footmen and the ferns on either side of the double doors; she had known exactly what she would see as she turned. It was oddly disturbing.

She saw admiration in the footman's eyes as she passed through the opened doors. There was the carriage; she was glad they were not going by motor car. Ushered in first, she turned to sit with her back to the horses. lady fflyte-Davison rested her hand for a moment on her knee as she entered and sat opposite.

'I remember my first ball!' Her eyes were warm and encouraging.

She must have sensed the palpitating excitement she had begun to feel. She was wishing alternately she was there already or far away, anywhere else. The carriage jerked into motion; it was hardly any distance to Grosvenor Square. She hoped she would recognize lots of people – yet meet that singular young man she had not seen before. What would she say as they sat out? She had so little experience. She felt a bit sick, and heard herself exchanging absurdly clipped phrases with Flighty – about Popsy – about Bobo – and laughing too much.

'We are not going very fast –'

'I don't believe we are going at all!'

They giggled again.

Lady fflyte-Davison looked out briefly forward. 'I fear it will be a little time. There must be at least twenty ahead of us.'

Henrietta felt a quiver of alarm. 'We're there!'

The older lady leaned forward to touch her knee with her gloved hand as the carriage jerked forward a few paces and came to a halt again. 'I flatter myself I shall know most people tonight. Should you see someone you would *particularly* like to dance with – be sure to point him out.'

'Mother!' Flighty exclaimed.

'You have no idea how dreadfully shy young men can be,' she retorted. 'Particularly –' she gave Henrietta an appraising glance and left the sentence unfinished. 'Goodness knows I frightened away a good many during my first season –!'

They laughed delightedly.

'I mean it. I was so shy myself, if I saw a young man cast his eye in my direction, I *plunged* into the most animated conversation with my chaperon or one of my sisters. It was open to the very worst interpretation!'

'Did you enjoy it?' Henrietta asked, feeling the carriage moving again. 'Your first ball?'

'Oh, *yes* – then again,' she shook her head, 'no –'

They shrieked with laughter.

'It was *so* exciting and at the same time so *frightening*. If only I had known then what I know now. How I would have enjoyed it! But things are different today. You have no idea how formal we were. Society is so much more lenient. Now if we had been seen sitting out on the stairs – or in some corner or other it would have been quite all up with us!' She nodded, 'Bad style!'

The carriage jerked forward another few paces.

Henrietta felt the tensions mounting inside her. 'Lady fflyte-Davison, have you any other advice –?'

'Let me think.' She paused. 'I think, if there is one – *general* piece of advice, it would be – do not undervalue yourself. Remember, it is *we – women –* who regulate society. I do not say you should give yourself affected airs, like some, but so many young gels in their first season tend to –' she searched for the right word, 'act as if they are flattered when a man pays them court. That is quite altogether wrong. Every woman is a queen – I must say, my dear, you should have no difficulty convincing anyone of that! And she must learn to accept homage as her due – neither apologetically, nor on the other hand haughtily. You must strike a very careful balance.' She smiled. 'If you simply remember that you cannot go very far wrong.'

The carriage rumbled forward again.

'For example,' she said as it came to a halt, 'I heard one gel – I must admit she was up from the country but you would think *someone* should have told her – it was at Letty Beaumont's last year – "Yes," she said to Letty, "I have been introduced to Lord Rebe." Well! The poor dear realized she had said *something*, but had absolutely no idea what. I so wanted to take her quietly aside. But you see, had she just been thinking in the right *mode* – I am a queen – men are introduced *to me* – she could never have come out with such a *gaucherie*. Do you see?'

Henrietta nodded, smiling.

'So – simply hold to that thought and you can never go very far wrong. For instance, a queen would not allow herself to dance with anyone who showed her to disadvantage. Nor must you! If you find you are partnered by a buffoon simply stand still, say you are tired or you would like to watch the others for a while and lead him off. Never permit yourself to be made a sight of. It is entirely up to you whether you wish to dance or not.' She smiled suddenly. 'But I hardly think I need to tell you these things. From what Cynthia has

281

said,' looking fondly at her daughter, 'you will be quite able to cope.'

They moved forward another few yards, and she looked out ahead again. 'I declare! This is worse than Ascot! But there are only a few before us now.'

People had gathered on the pavement to stare at the vehicles and their occupants, and as their own carriage drew nearer the entrance to Lynne House, the sound of their chatter became more apparent. Henrietta felt herself the subject of curious stares, and heard snatches of talk which she suspected were about herself; it seemed they had recognized Lady fflyte-Davison and were arguing whether she or Flighty were her daughter. She felt herself colouring and was glad she was sitting on the side away from them; she turned to look out of her window, and saw another little knot of staring spectators beyond the traffic on the other pavement.

'You would think they had better things to do,' she said.

Lady fflyte-Davison raised her brows. 'But this is one of the events of the season. You can be sure their patience will be rewarded. In any case, this is nothing. Wait until we leave tonight! Then you will see a crowd, I assure you!'

'Do you think the Prime Minister will be there?' Flighty asked.

'I should not imagine he will venture into such a hornet's nest of Tories! I may be wrong. I have heard he is a brave man.'

Henrietta felt her heart pounding as the thought came to her that if Asquith *were* here, she might do something dramatic for the cause. She had a momentary image of confronting him, demanding to know why he thought so little of women – but it would be a terrible abuse of Popsy's hospitality and of her chaperon's kindness – she had grown very fond of Flighty's mama. She couldn't do it –

The carriage had come to a stop again, but this time a footman was opening the door; he was resplendent in the Lynne livery crossed with a diagonal blue, white, red sash – for the *Entente* of course! Miraculously it seemed not to clash with the predominantly green coat. His eyes were black against the pallor of his face and powdered hair – one of the

282

banditti she thought, tensing as she prepared to leave the safety and comfort of the carriage.

She placed her hand on his raised arm and stepped down to the red baize runner that led across the pavement along under the canopy to the front door. Strains of music heard as they approached were louder here and she sensed the stares of the crowd who were passing comments on either side, and from the corner of her eye glimpsed a policeman; then she was being ushered behind Flighty and her mother under the canopy towards the front steps by another of the banditti who had come forward from nowhere; it was beautifully organized.

Inside, they were directed to a small room with a marble floor and fluted columns to sign their names in a book – 'for *The Morning Post*, my dear!' Lady fflyte-Davison said in a low voice. Ushered out again, they were handed dance programmes tied with blue, white, red ribbons as they entered the hall; Henrietta scarcely recognized it. Large French tricolours and Union Jacks hung in tandem from the high ceiling on either side of a softly rippling stretched banner with *L'ENTENTE C'EST LA PAIX* emblazoned in gold. Garlands of flowers and green ferns were everywhere around the marble pillars, up the sides of the stairs, over every doorway; the band, in uniform with tricolour sashes was half-hidden behind a thicket of palms and hanging greenery in the stair well.

More captivating than the decor, however, was the glitter of the guests on the staircase, a queue on the right moving very slowly upwards, groups on the left coming down in leisurely style. The light from the chandeliers above flashed from tiaras and diamond necklaces; the colours of the older women's gowns made a shimmering tapestry to set off the white of the girls' and the glistening black of the men. All the wealth and beauty of London seemed to be here. It was a fairy-tale in modern dress. And above the noise of a hundred conversations the strings moved into the Merry Widow waltz.

The people at the end of the ascending queue turned, smiling as they approached, and Flighty's mother made general introductions. Close to, the scene was not quite so entrancing: many of the faces were etched with lines of

283

tiredness despite the early hour and heavy overlay of powder used by the older women; the smiles were often limp and artificial, the conversations heard during the long, slow climb up the stairs equally artificial. Recognizing all this with a part of her mind, Henrietta was still elated by the novelty and glamour and the sight of famous faces descending past them on the other side, the sense of being a part of something very splendid.

The Countess of Lynne was receiving the guests at the head of the stairs under great portraits of the King and M. Fallières, President of the French Republic, both surmounted by their national flags. She too had lines of strain but in her case they seemed to add to her beauty. Gazing at her as they neared, Henrietta wished that her own face was not so smooth and young, and wondered how long she would need to stay up late every night to achieve such mysterious shadows beneath her own eyes.

'Of *course*! *Etty* Steel!' she said as Henrietta was introduced. 'Popsy *will* be glad to see you.' Her smile did not seem to extend to her eyes.

Popsy was some distance away surrounded by a laughing group. On her low bodice she wore three fresh blooms, a blue cornflower, a white rose and a red carnation; her hair was caught in a tricolour band with a bow at the side. She looked radiant.

They waited for what seemed several minutes while the group about her chattered, and Henrietta was beginning to feel annoyed when at last they moved away.

'*Etty*! And *Cynthia*!' Popsy bowed to Flighty's mother, then pecked them both on the cheek without embracing. 'One must try not to crush the *Entente*!' and glancing down at the flowers at her breast, 'Actually I've dozens. In case! But apropos – *have* you seen the dreadful Bobo? I mean, he has come as the Kaiser! In full fig and *pickelhaube* – *pickelhaube*! Eggy swears he knew nothing at all about it but I have my darkest. It is absolutely a disaster. Do you know I feel so genuinely *loving* towards the French, I actually do, don't you? And I was most careful to insist, *no* frogs' legs at supper. You must tell him when you see him there was distinctly no mention of fancy dress, absolutely not. Be sure to talk to me again, *dear* Etty, *dear* Cynthy –' She turned away towards the group waiting behind.

'Poor gel!' Lady fflyte-Davison said, 'It is such a strain.'

'Popsy's always like that,' Flighty said.

She looked at her for a moment. 'Who is this Bobo? Do I know him?'

There was a burst of laughter from the hall below, spreading gradually up the throng on the stairs as heads turned, and as they looked they saw the cause resplendent in scarlet uniform with sword and decorations glittering at his chest, carrying beneath his arm an elaborately decorated Prussian helmet with a point sticking from the top; he was marching with stiff strides towards the foot of the staircase, where he waited, greeting someone, twisting the fiercely upward-pointing ends of his moustaches with his free hand.

'That is he, I presume,' Lady fflyte-Davison said, and turning to Henrietta, 'A case in point – you remember what we were discussing! Come!' She led them back from the head of the stairs. 'We do not need to go down yet.'

Henrietta felt disappointed. Bobo was the first person, apart from Popsy and her mother, she actually knew. She glimpsed an interested look in the eye of a young man with a pleasant fresh face who was waiting to be presented to the Countess; there were so many who appeared nice; how could one choose? And once one had chosen, what if another better one came along? It was not possible, surely, to make a *permanent* choice – to stick to one person for the rest of one's life when there were so many? How would one ever know one had made the best possible choice? One would be tormented with doubts –

Lady fflyte-Davison was talking to the people who had been behind them in the queue coming up the stairs, Sir Drax Phillipps and his wife and daughter, Prudence, recounting in a determined voice how she had always been a Francophile ever since her schooldays in Paris, and had never been able to understand why the French were so often regarded disparagingly. It was, perhaps, because they were felt to be a shade clever.

'But you know, I have not found them to be so, have you? Not remarkably.'

If Sir Drax was puzzled at being accosted on his way to the stairs, he did not show it, but responded gallantly. 'I agree. They do have a devilish high opinion of themselves though. Don't you think that is about the root of it? Of course –' he glanced round at the portrait of M. Fallières, 'one should not say so!'

Lady fflyte-Davison was equal to the new turn, wondering if that were not, after all, the accusation generally levelled against Englishmen abroad. She kept the exchanges going until, apparently judging the coast clear, she turned and led them with equal determination back towards the head of the stairs. The stage Kaiser was nowhere to be seen. They went down.

Refreshments were laid out in the supper room where Henrietta had eaten with Popsy on her first visit to Lynne House before Lords. It was packed, the noise so intense that everyone seemed to be shouting to make themselves heard above it. A footman weaved into view bearing glasses of champagne on a silver tray, and they helped themselves, Henrietta realizing suddenly how dry her mouth was from the excitement and heat.

Her chaperon was fanning herself as she looked around. Flighty appeared rather anxious as she too glanced about her at the massed groups, people leaning in towards one another to catch what was being said. It was not at all as she had imagined it.

She felt a touch on her arm; Lady fflyte-Davison was motioning to her. She followed dutifully, as she turned catching sight of two young men, one exceptionally tall with very blue eyes, looking straight at her. She looked away quickly before realizing she had seen that long face and figure before, and turned back. Of course it was Popsy's brother, Eggy. He looked different – extraordinarily distinguished in his long tails, his sandy hair smoothed down, brows straight and serious. She bowed to him; returning the greeting, he came towards her, a grave smile on his lips.

'Etty! Popsy said you were coming.' He stood for a moment looking pleased before remembering his companion beside him. 'May I present Mr Harry Graves –' he turned, 'Miss Steel – Etty – a great friend of Popsy's –'

Harry Graves had a merry eye in a wide, full face which was very brown as if he had just returned from the Riviera; she liked his smile. She turned to introduce them both to her chaperon, but she and Flighty had disappeared somewhere; there was a loud, laughing group in the direction they had been heading.

'So glad you could make it,' Eggy said and smiled again.

She tried to think of something interesting to reply.

Harry Graves came in, 'Have you any free spaces on your card?'

'Yes, by Jove!' Eggy reached into his pocket.

'It's a complete blank,' she replied.

'What a stroke of luck!' Harry looked down his programme. 'How many are we allowed?'

She laughed.

They started booking numbers, Eggy asking in a diffident way whether he might have the supper dance, looking pleased when she said that would be nice.

'You dog!' Harry laughed.

Several others came up to speak to the men; after being introduced they too asked her for dances so that her programme filled with remarkable speed.

She was wondering how to refuse the next one, for she had not yet seen the man she was looking for – she liked Eggy very much but in a sisterly way she thought – when they heard a raised voice by the entrance, and turned to look.

'*Moi* –!' It was Bobo in his fantastic uniform and moustaches waving his gleaming helmet above his head. '*Moi – c'est la guerre!*' He kicked a stiff leg high in the goose step. '*Mais oui – c'est la guerre, mes amis! Moi –!*'

'*Lord!*' Eggy muttered. 'He's bin drinkin', the ass –' and with a bow to her, he beckoned Harry and they left, making swiftly towards him.

The others clapped and laughed.

Bobo's voice rose in pitch as the two reached him and took him by the arms, swinging him around to face the other direction and his language changed with his tone. '*Mein Gott!*' Struggling as they propelled him towards the entrance, he shouted '*Danke!*' and '*Mein Gott!*' at random, then as he

287

disappeared his voice took on a more desperate tone and he changed his tongue once again. 'I will give no quarter! NO prisoners will be taken! As the Huns under – as the Huns –' the shout broke into a choking, gurgling noise as if he were being muzzled, and the buzz of talk in the room which had ceased, broke out again, shutting out even those sounds.

'Attila, wasn't it –?'

'Attila, the Hun!'

'His English isn't half bad, I'll say that for the fellow!'

'*There* you are, Henry!' It was her chaperon, Flighty looking flushed behind her.

For some reason she felt guilty as she turned and started trying to make introductions; the men helped, laughingly, afterwards asking Flighty for dances. Henrietta was amused by her efforts to take the homage as her due, hoping she had not looked so obviously as if she had won first prize in a sweep herself.

'Henry, you must meet the Inglethorpes,' Lady fflyte-Davison said when all the cards had been marked; nodding to the men they left; she felt very much like a duckling.

Passing out into the hall, where there was no sign of Bobo or his captors, they went through a wide entrance to their right into a room with pale blue walls and tall windows rising to classic mouldings; above, the ceiling was painted with scenes of gods and goddesses, naked save for filmy draperies, against a clear sky blue harmonizing with the walls, lit by glittering crystal chandeliers. She had not been in here on her former, brief visits. It was magnificent.

It had been cleared of all furniture save for tubs of palms and ferns against the walls, and the floor, bare of carpets, presented a clear sweep of parquet, or would have done had it not been for the groups of guests moving and mingling. The noise was much less, seemingly dissipated in spaciousness.

The Inglethorpes had disappeared; instead Lady fflyte-Davison swept them into a large, mainly female group in which the single elderly male confined his contributions to explosive agreement with whatever was said. Henrietta found herself next to a nervous young girl who spoke equally abruptly. Yes, it was her first season; she listed dances she had been to, a few to come. Henrietta was unable to claim any of these and they fell silent, pretending interest in a convoluted story told by the girl's mother. Henrietta could make no sense of it; also the champagne was acting, and she felt herself removed slightly from the group, her eyes straying, not too obviously she hoped.

She became aware of more movement than there had been, the reason for it soon apparent as the band began playing – it had been silent for a while she realized. It was the first waltz and she raised her programme to glance at it, remembering perfectly well she had promised it to Harry Graves. As, like the others, they began moving towards the side, she glanced back and saw the Countess of Lynne entering on the arm of a man with fierce black moustaches and brows; of no more than medium height, but absolutely upright, he moved with a sort of latent energy or power like an athlete and conveyed an impression of almost arrogant assurance; he and the Countess might have been the only people in the room.

'That is Lord Nunne.' Her chaperon was at her side, following the direction of her gaze.

She felt a shiver of excitement; perhaps it was Lady fflyte-Davison's expression and the hint of disapproval in her voice, or the dangerous look of the man. He and the Countess were lovers, she felt certain. It was like a play; they were actually living it.

Harry Graves claimed her, and they took the floor. He was a good dancer, quick and sure with his feet, with an instinctive feel for time and tremendous enthusiasm as he swung into the turns; he obviously enjoyed it, and so did she.

It ended all too soon; she told him so as they walked off, and he nodded, smiling even more broadly.

'We have two more!'

She was about to say she looked forward to them when she wondered if that might convey more than she meant, so she said it in a formal way – immediately feeling mean. He didn't seem to notice, responding with an enthusiastic, 'Rather!' She liked him a lot.

Then she caught sight of the Countess and Lord Nunne

289

again; they had stopped to talk to another couple just ahead, and as she and Harry approached, Nunne turned as if sensing her gaze and looked directly at her; she felt the shiver of excitement and sudden emptiness in her middle she had experienced before. His eyes were hard; there was a gleam though and a slight lift to his brow as if he had penetrated her thoughts. She looked away quickly.

She wondered if he would contrive an introduction. He would find no difficulty if he wanted to; she doubted if there were anything he couldn't or wouldn't do. He had looked right into her.

He did not approach, but she continued to wonder, half-hoping as she danced with successive partners, spun and galloped and romped in the barn dance and Roger de Coverley, polkaed with Eggy, then waltzed again with Harry Graves – aware of him all the time, glimpsing him on odd occasions but never looking directly for long lest he glance round and catch her eye again.

In no time it was the supper dance; Eggy was claiming her once more with the grave, pleased look he had worn earlier.

'We could get something to eat now,' he suggested, 'before the crush?'

Evidently he was not such an enthusiastic dancer as Harry. He was certainly not so good; he had seemed to find it difficult in the polka to get his long legs to follow the music; they were always a fraction late. She looked up into his eyes, crinkled at the corners with smile lines; his expression was serious now, even anxious; he was anxious to please her. She found it strange and touching that he should be so concerned about what she wished to do, but obviously he was. He was so extraordinarily different from Popsy and his mother.

'Yes,' she nodded, smiling. It would be pleasant to rest. 'Why not!'

'Capital!' He made a gesture towards the door. 'It's rather a splendid night. We might go outside.'

'I'd love to.'

He looked round, pleased at her response.

They went into the supper room, much less crowded than it had been although several people, mostly older, had also decided to beat the rush. Maids with starched white aprons and caps waited behind long tables spread with damask, laden with delicacies. The girls smiled, bobbing as he came to examine their wares, or teased them gently about the exceedingly thin slices of ptarmigan; he hoped he would be excused if he did not patronize their stall this time! They giggled and cast inquisitive glances at her.

'What would you like – Etty?' he asked.

It was difficult to choose; there was such a selection. 'Frogs' legs!' she said on impulse.

His sandy brows shot up and his moustache seemed to quiver for a moment as he looked down at her. 'Have you seen any?' He looked along the tables again.

'No – I didn't mean it. You choose for me –'

He turned back to her, then laughed. 'Frogs' legs!'

He seemed more at ease with the maids than with her. And he was so serious about not making a wrong choice, and took so long, continually asking her, that she wished she had said something, almost anything.

At last, armed with glasses of champagne and plates, they made their way out through open French doors into the garden. As he had said, it was a splendid night, cool after the heat of the ballroom, but not chilly and there was a fragrance in the air which was pleasant after the artificial scents inside. He led her down a gravel path bordered by shrubs until they reached a rose trellis, the flowers showing palely against the darkness of the leaves; turning under an arch, they came to a semi-circular marble seat; the trellis curved round behind and on the other side, almost enclosing it with rose blooms.

'Ah!' he exclaimed. 'No one here! What a stroke of luck!' He put his plate and glass down and immediately taking off his tail coat, spread it out on the seat, then straightening, took her plate and invited her to sit where he had arranged the coat.

She turned, as she did so aware of the bulk of the house against the night sky; several of the upstairs windows were lighted and the tall windows of the ground and first floors were all ablaze, illuminating nearby trees and bushes; the music and hum of talk carried clearly out to them across the

291

dark, intervening lawns and shrubs, and there were shrills of laughter from a girl somewhere in the garden, followed by a man's low voice and more laughter.

Looking up at him as she sat, she knew quite suddenly that the house and all the other houses and estates and titles he would come into were hers if she wished. It was a feeling of such certainty and intensity she wondered for a moment if it was a temptation of the devil. Then it passed; he was bending, setting her plate on the seat beside her, his shirt sleeves very long and white, a fresh, laundered waft of air passed her nose as he moved.

He sat and toyed with his glass, looking at her. 'What a grand night!'

'Isn't it! It is beautiful.'

They drank. He put his glass down and picked up his plate. 'How many have you been to so far – dances?'

'This is my first.'

'The first one!' He sounded surprised.

'And the best! By a long way!'

He laughed.

'What did you do to poor Bobo?' she asked to break the silence as they started to eat.

'Oh –' He chuckled. 'Popsy's not pleased. We removed his trousers. Thought that better than lockin' him up – the ass. He passed out.'

She laughed, thinking of the Kaiser with his splendid helmet and no trousers. 'Popsy thinks you put him up to it.'

'*Me!* Lord, no! It's bad enough wonderin' what *she's* up to! It was a lark wasn't it – till the ass started drinkin'.'

'I liked his goose step.'

He chuckled again.

She wondered what he was thinking. This was not at all as she had imagined sitting out. He hadn't attempted to come very close, let alone touch her. She didn't want him to touch her; she would have no idea how to respond. She didn't think of him in that way in any case. He was pleasant, gentle, with a diffident charm and she felt at ease with him; it was rather like talking to her brother, Andy – the same reticence, the same sense of feelings not allowed to surface, and most odd the same sense of unspoken affection although she had hardly met him except on brief occasions when Popsy or Bobo had stolen the scene. She felt she could like him, already liked him very much, but he was not the one in her imagination. Nor had she seen *him* tonight. Lord Nunne excited her, but that was a different feeling, an awareness of what he would be and do if she were ever to find herself alone with him, an awareness of the senses only; on her mind he exerted fascination and revulsion, eagerness and aversion in equal, fluctuating measure.

'I expect they'll all come out now,' Eggy said.

She realized the music had stopped. 'What a *shame!*'

He was gazing at her, swirling the drink in his glass. 'Yes, it is. I wish –' He twirled the glass so vigorously it seemed as if the drink must spill out. 'You must come down to Stokey – one weekend – would you care to?'

Stokington Park, seat of the Earls of Lynne! That sharp earlier intuition had been correct; she felt her heart beat as she replied she would love to, hoping he had not caught the slight tremor in her voice. 'Popsy's often talked about it.'

'Popsy doesn't like it much down there.'

She laughed.

'I love it.' He waved his glass in a sweep encompassing the garden and the house. 'I don't care for this so much –'

'It's *beautiful!*'

'Do you think so?'

'You know it is,' she replied, teasingly.

'Perhaps. I suppose – it's the life up here – you know –' He left the sentence unfinished, smiling as he gazed at her, 'my mother –'

'She is very lovely.'

He nodded, looking down into his glass. 'Yes, she is.'

For a moment her heart went out to him as it had not before; he sounded so sad. Popsy was not the only victim of their parents' giddy orbits. He was so large and looked so vulnerable, like an enormous schoolboy as he gazed down with bent head; she wanted to put an arm around his shoulders and comfort him.

How absurd –

Henrietta Steel, your fancies are ridiculous. This man, this very large man beside you is Lord Eggledon, heir to the Earl

293

of Lynne. There is no reason to suppose he has anything more than a passing interest in you as a friend, he supposes, of his sister, and because he is bored with the other girls here tonight. Undoubtedly his future wife will have been picked out for him. It is the height of folly and wickedness to suppose that glimpse you had of what it might be like – not to be his flesh and blood wife, that never entered your head – but as his consort, mistress of this great house, was anything but a dream –

There had been a sound of voices approaching, and now they were quite close on the path by which they had come, although the people, whoever they were, were hidden behind bushes at the end of the trellis. Eggy was looking in that direction.

A man appeared through the arch. He saw them and immediately stopped.

'So sorry!' He turned back.

'Not at all,' Eggy said rather late and without conviction.

Then she heard Popsy's voice, feeling an immediate involuntary twinge as she thought of the horrid inferences and inventions she would weave around them if she found her sitting out here alone with her brother. Popsy was asking the man who it was; he had not actually seen, he said.

'It's my brother!' she shrilled. 'The brute!' There were sounds of movement on the gravel. 'I bet it is! I bet it is!' She came through the arch, glass in hand, and gave a whoop of triumph.

Eggy was standing up.

'Lord Eggledon, I presume!' she stared at him for a moment, then became aware of Henrietta on the seat. '*Et tu – Brute!*'

'For heaven's sake!' Eggy said, annoyed.

'For heaven's sake!' she mimicked, 'but isn't it absolutely too cowardly, debagging my poor Bobo and *sneaking* out here – with Etty of all people –'

'Popsy –' There was a threatening note in his voice.

Popsy flashed her a quick smile. 'Of course I didn't mean it like *that*.' She turned to him again. 'But can you imagine – I'm utterly *shamed*. Probably not –' she addressed Henrietta, 'He never had much imagination –'

294

'Bobo brought it on himself,' Eggy said in a very controlled voice.

'There was no reason to humiliate the lamb –' Popsy looked as though she were enjoying herself; a man and another girl from her party had appeared through the arch and were standing awkwardly behind her. 'He has just created quite the most frightful scandal, and it is because of what you and Harry did to him –'

'Scandal?'

Popsy looked at Henrietta. 'He appeared in the supper room – the poor lamb was ravenous, he told me so,' and transferring her attention back to Eggy, 'in green – satin – breeches –'

'A footman,' he said quickly.

'A dago it was. But that is not the worst of it. He forced the breeches from the poor man at the point of the sword.' She swivelled large eyes on Henrietta. 'Can you imagine what the dago thought, I mean distinctly worse than death! He ran, screaming, from the room. Bobo, the innocent, has no idea still why his character is besmirched for ever. But it is sure to be all around London by breakfast and do you think anyone will believe Bobo's side for a minute –'

'Where did it happen?' Eggy interrupted the flow.

'That is the awful part of it – in a bedroom. He simply *rang* for the maid and *ordered* a dago.'

Eggy rubbed his long jaw.

'All the poor lamb wanted was a beef sandwich, he told me so.' She spread her arms. '*Who* will believe that? Mama is furious, and the Veil is backing her up –'

'He would.' Eggy muttered.

Popsy turned to Henrietta. 'You see, he is thinking of himself, never a thought for what will become of *us*. *How* can I marry a man who – when he enters a room people will say, "Here is Bobo, the famous bugger!" I mean even my upright bro. –'

'I'll go and see him,' Eggy said coldly. He turned to Henrietta. 'I'm terribly sorry,' and with a little gesture of his hands, 'I'd better go –'

'I'll come with you,' she said, rising quickly.

Popsy gazed at her as she passed. 'It's too bad – I *had* to

295

say it!' and as Eggy came up, shrugging on his coat, 'I did so want the *Entente* to be a great success.'

He passed her without a word.

'Did you have a pleasant supper with Lord Eggledon?' her chaperon asked much later as they waited in the hall, hearing the cries of the assistant linkman from the street, 'Lady fflyte-Davison's ker-ridge – Lady fflyte's ker-ridge –'

'Very!' Henrietta nodded. She had sensed a coolness in the older woman's attitude since supper, and Flighty herself had been offhand; she wondered how she might repair the damage – presumably jealousy, she could think of no other explanation.

'I did not see you –'

'No, we were in the garden,' she replied. 'Several others came out – Popsy and some friends of hers –'

'Everyone flirts nowadays – outrageously. But you do *not* want to get yourself talked about. It is exceedingly bad to be talked about in one's very first season.'

The injustice hurt. 'Really, I was not flirting, Lady fflyte-Davison.'

Her chaperon's brows rose, then she turned as her page came up to announce the carriage.

The linkman in his tall, shining hat and frock coat raised his lantern in a token gesture, smiling ingratiatingly as Lady fflyte-Davison came down the steps; she passed him a coin and he muttered a throaty, 'Thank you, my Lady!' From the crowd on either side and across the street came a murmur of conversation; the crowd before had been nothing to this.

'– Lady fflyte an' 'er li'tle angels!' someone said, and there was a gust of laughter.

It was shameful –

'– 'oo d'yer fink *she* is?'

'She do look lovely –'

'– see them pearls –'

'Much more quiet pearls is, than dimins –'

She was glad when they were inside the coach and had started to move. But it was an uncomfortably silent journey, Flighty pretending exhaustion – but really piqued, she thought, that *she* had stolen the prize of the evening, not that she regarded Eggy like that at all – her mother brooding, no doubt about her *flirting*, but that was quite unfair.

The evening had been a disaster from every point of view. Popsy probably thought she had designs on her brother; she would not invite her anywhere again; probably she would never even see her, and although she detested Popsy more than ever after what had happened, she also in an odd way liked her more; she had stuck up for Bobo. She would terribly miss seeing her.

The Countess had thought she had designs on the title too. Her reception when they came to say goodbye would have frozen an eskimo. And there was Eggy himself, so big and good-natured and friendly, yet he was almost the worst part of it; she could never feel anything more for him than affection; even if she were to think she felt more there would be the doubts that she was really convincing herself for his position and wealth – the temptation in the rose garden she remembered so clearly. She would be selling herself like a chattel, the very thing she was campaigning against in her work. She could never do that – not even if she came to love him – which she never could, she felt sure; he was too pleasant, too assured, too un-challenging, too thoroughly *nice* –

She thought of Lord Nunne – 'the Veil' – and smiled to herself.

'Did you enjoy it, Henry?'

Apparently Lady fflyte-Davison had relented.

She smiled. 'Yes – and then, *no!*'

Her chaperon laughed, leaning towards her and patting her knee. 'I could see that, my dear, but I do think there was rather more "Yes"!'

16

George was not really aware of what he was doing; he knew he had to reach the top and was determined he would, but his head was throbbing with queer sensations and noises and wasn't altogether of much use to him. His arms and hands were in tremendous form, his fingers extraordinarily prehensile. His bloody feet were slipping again, but he just had to hang on to this fellow's waistband and get his – other – hand – up – to his shoulder. He knew he was high and the ceiling was not far above. The idiot seemed to be trying to shake him off, shouting at the same time. From down below at the bottom of the human pyramid someone else was shouting at someone to get their bloody fingers out of his eyes. There was a background din of encouragement from some of the senior officers not taking part. The fellow he was hanging on to was swearing like a porter. He drew his right leg up, feeling around for a lodging place, but the whole quivering, grunting edifice had begun to move as if it had taken on independent life and might shift itself across the room, or flail against the wall or simply teeter from side to side, swearing. Lord! It was alive, and the long windows and curtains had begun to move towards him. He was going! Blood pounded in his chest; he felt part of the fellow's shirt rip away in his prehensile clutch. There was nothing to hold on to now; he was floating helplessly in an uproar of noise.

Lying on his back looking up into Fitz's face, he saw two green eyes come together, part into four with two rather flushed noses beneath. Concentrating, he brought them together again. There was a worried frown across Fitz's wide forehead which was beaded with sweat, queer little globules of sweat. Lord! He looked a mess; his hair was wild and half his hairy chest bare, he noticed; his shirt hung like a bent white board from the side of a still immaculate wing collar.

'Wass wrong with y'collar?' George asked, shaking with laughter at the witticism. Lord! He couldn't laugh: his ribs felt as if he'd been kicked by twenty mules. He groaned.

Fitz bent closer, going out of focus. Other faces he recognized were gazing down at him too. He remembered, he'd got a *first*! He had *six firsts* – he was a six-oner! He yelled and to hell with his ribs.

Fitz straightened, his face breaking into a relieved smile.

Someone said, 'Fetch a fire bucket!'

Fitz helped him to his feet. Fitz was an extraordinarily good fellow, but he thought he would rather have stayed where he was on the floor; everything throbbed in and out of focus, and without Fitz's steadying hand he would undoubtedly fall. He felt horribly sick and sweaty. Truth was – he was beastly drunk.

From what Fitz told him the next morning, it was as well he had been drunk or from the height he came down he must have broken a few limbs if nothing more serious. As it was his head ached – how much as a result of the fall, how much from the 'fizz' before and the brandy and assorted drinks after dinner he wasn't sure. His ribs on the right and his left elbow and knee were extraordinarily tender; again, whether this was the result of the fall or whether he had picked up a few of the bruises in the course of the obstacle race beforehand, he had no idea. He remembered a collision with a settee, but not a great deal else. He couldn't remember turning in; he wondered who had helped him up to his room; Fitz probably. Fitz had an awesome capacity; looking at him this morning you wouldn't know it had been anything other than a normal evening, indeed he looked a good deal healthier than he had since the end of the exams – relief at knowing the worst at last! And it had been pretty bad for poor old Fitz although he had worked like a horse all hours.

The knowledge of his own first was like an ember smouldering at the back of his mind, ready to burst into fresh flame whenever he thought about it. He'd wired home; he wondered if Henry had heard yet. He wanted her to know. He could telephone her at that women's command post she manned! Womanned! On the other hand he would like to see her. He thought of the drawing-room at Palace Gardens when he had called to see her two weeks before, and Mrs Davies had insisted he should sit and have a sherry and tell her what he was doing because she had heard so much about him. If she hadn't been older than he was he would have thought she was trying to flirt. She had smiled at him a great deal and her eyes had been very warm and interested although the details of the subs' course at Greenwich and the cricket he had been playing for the College could not have meant much to her. Obviously she and Henry got along very well; they were on 'Alice' and 'Henry' terms. He wondered how efficient Henry was. He couldn't imagine orderly work as her strong suit.

'Stop grinning at yourself,' Fitz said. 'Address yourself to the question, for the love of God!'

'What question is that?'

'What question is that! Holy Mother, preserve us from x-chasers! The question as to whether you've found yourself a suitable partner for this evening – or better still an unsuitable one. Have you found yourself a *partner – Steel –*!'

'Please keep your voice down, old man.'

Fitz had been talking about seeing his cousin, Kate, for days; he hadn't realized he intended him to come along as well. Fitz was never very coherent on the subject of 'Cousin Kate'; she was a combination of Zena Dare and a National Hunt champion and was quite as 'fast' out of the saddle as in it. He had no desire to meet her; the thought of her and Fitz talking horseflesh through the night was distinctly unappetizing – particularly in his own present condition.

'As a matter of fact –'

'As a matter of fact,' Fitz repeated, advancing menacingly on the bed and seizing the blanket as he hugged it to his chest, 'all you think about –' he heaved '–is – bloody – cricket –' He heaved again more violently and the mattress and everything started sliding.

'For God's sake – Fitz!'

'And "x" bloody chasing –' Fitz gave a final heave.

He landed on the floor on his elbow and let out a yelp of genuine pain.

Fitz stood over him. 'It's time you started thinking about *women*!'

'I don't want to think about bloody *horses*!' he shouted up angrily.

'Ah! That's it! Why did you not tell me! For the love of God, we'll neither of us mention a word about the noble beasts. There you are! It's a bargain! I'll not speak of them and I'll answer for Kate not doing the same.'

He wondered if Fitz answered exam questions in the same way. 'It may prove a quiet evening in that case. Why don't you and Kate –'

'Listen Steel! You said you'd come, and I've arranged for the transport for both of us directly we've finished lunch, so get to the telephone and call that sister of yours and tell her you need a woman. Tonight –'

'Henry!'

Fitz clapped a hand dramatically to his head. 'Who was it said six-oners were all bloody fools. And he'd not met you. You'd have proved his case for even if you weren't one then you were still a bloody fool –'

'*Please!* Fitz –' He had struggled up to sit on the edge of his bed; he was feeling ill again.

'She must know hundreds of girls,' Fitz went on remorselessly. 'She's in the woman's movement for God's sake! Tell her to pick one for you – a decent looker so she won't feel too bad when she sees Cousin Kate –'

'*Pax!*' George held up his hand. He couldn't listen to Fitz on Cousin Kate, not this morning. 'I'll have a bath. Then I'll call Henry. I'll let you know.'

Fitz was silent, staring at him as if weighing up the honesty of his intentions.

'Now be a good fellow,' George pleaded. 'Go away. And send someone for my man.'

A steaming bath in the splendid College bathroom was about the limit of his thoughts, but an idea had formed that perhaps Fitz had something: Henry's friend, Popsy, was, if not a looker in the conventional sense, a girl it was difficult to take one's eyes off. He'd back her to hold her own with Cousin Kate or anyone else Fitz cared to put up.

Fitz turned back with his hand on the open door, a suspicious look coming into his eyes as he saw George's expression. 'You are going to call her?'

'I've thought of someone. I'll guarantee she'll give Kate a run for her money.'

Fitz slapped a fist into his palm and uttered a view-halloo, slamming the door behind him as he left. George heard him making trumpeting noises all the way down the corridor.

The transport Fitz had arranged turned out to be Temple-Vane-West's car, a legendary vehicle at the Naval College, where bicycles were the usual mode. West was an equally legendary figure. A gunnery lieutenant on the extra long course, therefore a good deal older than the subs who formed the majority at Greenwich, he was also a good deal wealthier and, it was believed, irresistible to the fair sex. That he was formidable in this direction George knew: like himself West played cricket for the College and usually turned up for home matches on the Rectory Field with stunning beauties sitting beside him in 'the old girl', as he called his motor car. George sometimes wondered whether the fact that these beauties seldom lasted more than a couple of weeks was a sign that West was good at his game or whether he was simply good at attracting them and fell down when it came to performance. He had given it little thought; his practical knowledge of what counted for 'performance' was limited, while cricket – and tennis when he could fit it in – and swotting for a first, had left him no time even to think about the other half. West himself, when not actually batting or fielding, was so given over to poodle-faking he spent little time with the rest of the team; George hardly knew him except as a marvellously fluent and enterprising stroke-player.

He wondered whether West would have one of the lovelies beside him today, in which case he and Fitz would serve as ballast, general fitters, wheel-changers and dragmen in the back. It was well known 'the old girl' was lucky to travel five miles without attention of some sort. 'My dear old thing' went one of West's *mots* about his amatory exploits which had gone the college rounds, 'the point is to get far enough into the leafy lanes to allow "the old girl" a decent breakdown without too many bloody nosey onlookers.' He could not imagine why Fitz had chosen to go up to town in this most difficult way possible. Fitz, however, seemed extraordinarily pleased with himself – flattered no doubt by inclusion in the aura of West's sophistication.

The car was standing by the guard house pointing towards the gates when they came out after lunch, its red bodywork and black mudguards and polished brass tail and side lamps glinting in the sun. West, wearing an elegantly dented homburg and a light burberry over his suit, had one foot on the running board and was swinging a pair of goggles idly as he talked to a college servant on the other side of the machine. There appeared to be no one else about.

'There you are, old things!' He studied George from under dark brows. 'I must say I didn't expect to see you today. That really was a thrilling fall.'

'I've told him he should sign up with Barnums!' Fitz said.

West smiled politely as though the jest was a shade below the level to which he was accustomed, and taking his foot from the running board, asked which of them would like to sit in the front. 'There are certain tasks.' He raised his brows quizzically.

Fitz decided he was probably in better shape than George, and throwing his portmanteau into the back, climbed in. West slid into the driver's seat beside him.

'The change-gear stick's a beast,' he began in his decided, rather theatrically clipped voice. 'On occasions I have to use both hands to wangle it in –' He simulated a two-handed struggle with the lever. 'It is then necessary for you to take the helm. I'll sing out "Stand by!" as preparative when I anticipate trouble. But you must keep alert at all times – especially when I'm changing.'

'Changing,' Fitz repeated, nodding sagely.

'Don't be frightened to give her too much wheel if you have to. It's well geared down. She needs a couple of turns before she begins to answer.'

Fitz nodded.

'Now – here –' He pointed to a knob sticking from the

dashboard, 'is the throttle, and here –' pointing to a lever on the steering column, 'is the ignition –'

'Throttle – ignition –'

'That's it. If I need more juice, I'll sing out "Throttle out!" ' He suited action to the words. 'Less juice – "Throttle in!" If I need the ignition advanced, I shall say "Ignition forward!" ' He pushed the lever away from him. 'Or retarded – "Ignition back!" ' He pulled it to its former position. 'Think you've got that?'

Fitz took the lever and jerked it back and forth a couple of times. 'I have the ship, Captain!'

West studied him for a moment. 'My girls can do it with their eyes shut. Now. There's one more thing. So far as I know, we shan't be going up any mountains, but –' he bent to indicate something on the floor between them. 'Here's the sprag tackle. If the old girl cuts out while we're steaming uphill, I'll sing out "Let go!" Release the sprag, she'll come up all standing. In case the brakes can't hold her,' he added.

'Same thing if we're going downhill?' Fitz asked.

'I doubt if she'll cut out going down.'

'Ah!'

West took off his homburg, tossed it into the back seat beside George, and put on his goggles and a tweed cap with side flaps like a deerstalker, then he nodded to the servant by the bonnet.

'Stand by engines, Jenkins!'

Jenkins bent to take hold of the starting handle.

'Full ahead both!'

The car shook as the man pumped the handle round, the seat jumped and subsided rhythmically, the body swayed, the engine fired briefly once and died, fired again and died. Gradually the intervals between the turns grew longer; finally all movement ceased; Jenkins's red and glistening face appeared above the bonnet, his mouth hanging open, his breath coming in anguished gasps.

West pushed his goggles up and turned to Fitz.

'I'll have a try,' Fitz said, sliding from his seat.

After several minutes vain effort he, too, stopped and straightened, resting his hands on the radiator and shaking drops of perspiration from his forehead; his eyes were bulging, his mouth open, gulping air.

West turned round to George. 'We live in stirring times.'

George couldn't help smiling, despite rising doubts about their chances of ever reaching London. The idea of spending the evening with Popsy had grown in his imagination since morning; he was now very anxious to see her, and his anxiety was the more since Henry had been out when he had telephoned. Unless they got up to Kensington in reasonable time it would be too late to arrange anything with her or anyone else. He wondered if he should try calling her again.

Fitz came back looking worried, hat in hand, wiping his brow with his handkerchief. He slid into the seat and looked at West. 'What now?'

'I dare say the mixture's wrong.' West was fiddling with a knob on the dashboard. 'We'll allow her a couple of minutes to recover. I feel Jenkins went at it rather, don't you?' He looked up. 'Jenkins!'

'Sir.' The man came round slowly.

'More finesse next time, Jenkins. Handsomely to start with and work up to the big push – you understand?'

'Sir!'

West patted the side of the car affectionately. 'You can't rush the old girl. We'll try again in a couple of minutes.'

'Very good, sir!'

West looked at Fitz. '*Nil desperandum*. What are you two fellows up to in the wicked city?'

Fitz told him they were taking a couple of girls out to a theatre probably and dinner, and asked if he had any suggestions.

'That rather depends,' West replied, 'on the sort of girls.'

Fitz struggled for words to describe them. 'I can't answer for Steel's, but my Cousin Kate – well, I doubt if you'd believe – not unless you could see her for yourself –'

'Perhaps I could?'

Fitz was surprised into momentary silence, then went on, 'She has the best hands in County Wexford – or had –'

'Had?'

'Her people have moved over here.' Fitz grinned. 'You can be sure, she has the best hands in Suffolk now!'

305

West turned round. 'How about yours, Steel? Good pair of hands?'

Sensing some amusement in the dark eyes beneath the goggles, George felt an impulse to brag. 'She's known as Popsy. She came out last year. You may remember it – it was in all the rags. The *Entente Cordiale.*'

'I don't think I recall.' Interest had replaced the hint of amusement in West's expression. 'Who are her people?'

George tried to keep his tone very flat. 'The Earl of Lynne.'

'Gad!' West shifted right round in his seat. 'The Lady Lavinia! Didn't I hear something –' he frowned. 'Quite recently –'

Warnings flashed in George's brain; he had met Popsy only once and for scarcely more than a family luncheon; moreover it was not at all certain he *would* be seeing her this evening –

He was saved from comment by the approach of two long course officers.

'Aground again!' one of them called.

'He's just waiting for the tide,' the other said.

West turned. 'O, ye of little faith,' and looking across to where Jenkins was waiting in the shade thrown by the buildings, called out to him to stand by main engines.

He came across, twitching his right shoulder as if testing for soundness after his previous effort. The two long course men stopped to watch, smiling indulgently. One called out he knew where they could hire a couple of hacks.

West indicated the bonnet. 'I have *eight* under there.'

'Live ones old man!'

Jenkins reached the front of the bonnet and bent down. West pulled his goggles over his eyes and, making a final adjustment to the mixture knob, called out, 'Full ahead, both!'

The long course men doubled in helpless laughter, but at the first turn the engine came to life, the noise rising to a roaring, rattling crescendo. West tried to damp it with the throttle, then turned to the watching couple. 'Care for a spin. We're going up to the wicked city.'

They shook their heads.

306

West raised his hand at Jenkins, and pulled the change-gear lever, wobbling it about until he was satisfied it was in before starting to release the clutch. They jerked forward and continued, bouncing slowly towards the gates.

'I forgot to warn you,' he said, 'the clutch can be rather fierce.'

The uniformed gate-keeper looked on with interest as they bumped by. West touched his cap in response to the salute, then swung the wheel energetically to make an eight-point turn into Park Row. He had to stop at the end for a pantechnicon drawn by a single grey straining up from Maze Hill, and used the time to juggle with the change-gear lever to engage it more thoroughly.

A group of passers-by gathered to stare. He smiled and raised the peak of his cap to a girl amongst them, who looked down shyly. When the van was clear, he let out the clutch, revolving the wheel at speed again for the turn right, and they moved out smoothly.

'She's in!' he cried, and pulling out to overtake the pantechnicon, 'Hurrah for the open road!'

George, feeling the breeze on his face as they accelerated felt suddenly that he was going to enjoy the trip.

They passed the tall masts and yards of the training ship in the grounds of the Royal Hospital School to their left at fair speed and were rattling along approaching the King William Street crossroads, West squeezing the horn and peering from side to side to see if anything was coming.

'Stand by!' he called, seeing all clear.

Fitz held his right hand up tentatively towards the wheel as a grinding noise signalled failure to find the gear; West disengaged the clutch.

'Take the ship, Coxswain!'

Fitz leaned across and gripped the wheel as West started his double-handed fight with the lever.

'Steady on that! Take her up Nelson Street!'

'Steady!' Fitz replied cheerfully.

'A little less juice – throttle in!'

'Throttle in!' Fitz took his left hand from the wheel to make the adjustment.

A woman coming round the corner from King William

Street on a bicycle looked back at them apprehensively; not liking what she saw, she put both feet on the ground and stopped.

'Starboard ten!' West called, eyeing her.

'Starboard ten!' Fitz repeated, and with his eyes still on the dashboard reacted to the order by habit as if steering a picket boat, turning the wheel to port.

The woman froze, eyes widening as the car, free-wheeling at some speed, veered towards her; her mouth opened in a soundless scream.

West jammed on the brake. The back wheels locked and they slid out of control, turning through 180 degrees, the bonnet and mudguards swinging gracefully within inches of the woman's bicycle before the car started to travel backwards, mounted the kerb, swayed and came to rest with a dull metallic thud against the stone pillar of a shop.

They sat, shocked. A crowd had begun to gather already, and they heard hysterical screaming from where the woman had been; George couldn't see her, but two people were bending over something by the kerb ahead, and he guessed she had collapsed. The bicycle was lying on its side nearby.

'Begod!' Fitz muttered in a cracked voice.

West looked at him, then pushed his goggles up, jumped out and strode towards the gathering knot of people. Fitz slid out from the other side, turning a white face to George.

'He said starboard.'

By the time they reached the ring of spectators the woman had stopped screaming. Hostile eyes turned towards them and George heard remarks about 'speeding –' 'might've killed 'er –'

Disregarding them, West pushed through; the woman was being supported to her feet between two well-dressed young men.

'I'm frightfully sorry,' West began, but she had caught sight of Fitz behind him.

'That's 'im!' she shrieked, and started screaming again.

The crowd pushed closer. West gestured to one of the young men, relieving him of her arm. 'Now then –' He interposed between her and Fitz, 'what we all need is a cup of tea.' His assurance and extravantly clipped accent, or perhaps the contrast between his mode of speech and the ordinariness of the remark seemed to surprise her into silence. He looked round at Fitz. 'Pick up the bike. We'll go to the Meridian.'

Fitz bent to carry out the instruction while he turned the woman to lead her away.

' 'Ere!' A man in a bowler stepped in front of him. 'You can't get away with that!' Assenting noises came from others in the crowd. 'You was exceedin' the limit –'

'Stand aside!' West cut him short. 'This good lady is in a state of shock.' He looked at George. 'Clear a path Number Three!'

George came across, gesturing and holding out his arm to make a passage through the throng, now silent and regarding West with some awe. West supported the woman through, and George took over from the young man at her other side.

'Do your people have a motor car, Number Three?'

Why he had become 'Number Three', George was not clear. 'A Lanchester,' he replied.

'You had better change places with our Irish member for the next leg,' West looked down at the woman on his arm. 'A remarkably warm afternoon is it not.'

Henrietta wondered when they would arrive. George had said afternoon; there wasn't much of the afternoon left. Alice Davies had sent out for muffins and extra cakes, but soon they would have to have tea without them.

She had the restless feeling she had so often these days. It was stronger today. She wondered what Fitz would be like. She remembered George talking about him a long time ago, but couldn't recall exactly what. 'Fitz' had a certain ring to it; she could imagine a rather dashing young man with curling dark hair and an air of dissipation – undoubtedly an old family.

Oh, he probably had a spotty face and talked about picket boats and 'pussers' and evolutions – and heavens, she could scream sometimes at George. But even that would be preferable to the jargon she heard every day. She really could not stay here any longer. Where could she go? To do what? The sunlight slanting in through the curtains, lighting the floating dust, mocked her. She was wasting her life shut up in a single room in Kensington.

The Davieses were frauds. Alice Davies was pleasant enough but used her, just as she used the womens' movement itself – her husband being the rabbit he was, and with no children to give focus to her life. Most of the other Kensington committee ladies were doing the same thing, she was sure, scheming and manipulating each other because their husbands were bored with them or immersed in their business or drunk or dallying; she couldn't stand their silly parrot squawks.

The Fabians *he* brought home were as bad, ineffectual dreamers for the most part, like the women with their silly ideas about equality. It took some self-restraint to stop herself telling them a few obvious truths: if God had wanted men to be equal he would have created them so, not made some in the image of rabbits and others so pompous they couldn't see the nonsense they were talking for what it was. As for some of the ladies who declaimed loudest about equality with men, they should start in their own households with their servants – or even here with the Davieses' poor little overworked maid, Sadie – poor sad little Sadie who knew her position so well she would not even respond to her smile, but flattened herself against the wall.

The injustice and *cant* of it all stirred her to such anger at times, she had to leave the house and go for long walks in the open until she was too tired to think – or write to Father Geoffrey. That avenue was closed now he had gone into retreat; when he came out she would ask if she could join him. But in the meantime –

If it weren't for the occasional house parties when Eggy invited her to Stokington Park or one of his friends asked her for the weekend – and Eggy too of course – she would surely have gone insane – those breaks and her increasingly frequent returns to Felpham House were all that had preserved her, particularly the visits home. Babs was such a sweet; they got on so well together now they were living apart, and her mother was more gentle and understanding than she had ever known her. The only black spot was Papa, but he was seldom there when she went. Harry was growing into such a fine boy; Andy and Willy would be back for the holidays soon; she was reminded of George and Fitz.

Where on earth could they have got to? She rose and went to the window and looked out on the rectangle of lawn and bushes bounded by all the other trim green rectangles basking in the sun – the same sun that shone on the Downs and woodlands outside the purlieu. She wondered where Fitz came from. An old house – sun brightening the wistaria on the walls? A castle in the family since the Conqueror's time – dreadfully run down and mortgaged to pay his father's gambling debts. Fitz had inherited the same wild streak; he and George were friends because their differences complimented each other.

She thought she heard the doorbell and waited, listening – light steps running down the stairs – a man's voice from the hall and Sadie's – it must be George and Fitz. She went to the mirror. Could anyone guess at the despair behind her eyes? They returned the scrutiny, very clear and even slightly amused at the suggestion; there was a faint shadow beneath but nothing terrible, indeed it added a certain maturity – a suggestion of late parties – crossed love affairs. She tidied a wisp of hair falling over her ears, then pulled it out again, and some more after it and tousled it; she wouldn't look as though she'd been sitting, *waiting* –

Sadie was coming up the stairs as she started down the lower flight.

'Miss Henrietta – it's your brother and another young gentleman. I've shown them into the drawing-room.' Sadie, knowing it was unlucky to cross on the stairs, went down sideways before her.

There was another ring at the door as the maid reached the bottom; she scampered across the hall and pulled it open.

A tall man wearing a burberry and a peculiar tweed cap with ear flaps and goggles pushed up over his forehead stood there.

'You must be the gentleman –'

'West,' he said crisply, and seeing Henrietta as she reached the foot of the stairs, looked past Sadie directly at her.

Henrietta was reminded of Lord Nunne; this man looked nothing like him, but he had the same presence, the same steady eyes that looked right into you and could tell what you were thinking. Holding his gaze a fraction longer than politeness dictated, she felt the quiver of excitement she had experienced at first sight of Lord Nunne.

Sadie was standing aside for him to enter. 'Mr Steel said you would be coming, sir.'

He came in and handed her his cap and goggles – he had thick dark hair with a natural curl, very much as she had imagined Fitz.

'Thank you!' he said as Sadie helped him off with his burberry. He came towards Henrietta in an attractive, loose-limbed way. 'You must be Steel's sister – Henry.'

She smiled. 'Yes.'

'His chauffeur!' He bowed.

She laughed.

'I'm sorry if we're late – uncharted navigational hazards.'

She laughed again, leading him towards the drawing-room door. Looking back before she went through, she saw him gazing at her.

'I am exceedingly glad we eventually made it.'

She felt blood coming to her cheeks, and turned quickly into the room.

George had finished introducing Fitz to Mrs Davies and was about to take him up to the bathroom to sponge off the dust of the journey, when Henrietta came in looking rather flushed, he thought, and remarkably bright-eyed, with West just astern of her. He should have thought of that! He couldn't have guessed they would be so late, West would insist on driving them to the door, though, nor that the 'old girl's' radiator would boil over. The immediate thing was to get Henry on her own and tell her to organize Popsy for the evening. There was not much time.

West strode to where Alice Davies was sitting in a chair by the window, and bowed over her hand. 'I'm delighted to meet you, Mrs Davies.'

George saw from her eyes that West was exerting the same effect as it appeared he had on Henry. He felt a stab of jealousy; his own greeting from Alice Davies had been so warm he had read all sorts of things into it; it was absurd. The main thing was to detach Henry somehow.

As he moved towards her, she came bouncing up and hugged him. 'You *clever old thing*!'

'You know!'

'Mama told me. She is so pleased. You have no idea how thrilled she is.'

He grinned despite himself. 'It was quite a surprise –'

She pulled him close again and pecked him on the cheek. '*Rot!*'

He disengaged, smiling happily. Fitz was hovering, so he turned and introduced him.

'At last!' Fitz said with a grin. 'But I believe I know you already –' he indicated George, 'from all *he's* told me of you!'

'I didn't know he talked about such silly creatures as us!'

Fitz bellowed with laughter.

'Look here,' George said in a hollow voice, 'can you call Popsy for me?'

'Popsy!'

'We're trying to arrange a foursome for this evening.'

'Popsy's engaged!' She stared at him. 'Didn't you know! In any case – my name with Popsy!' She made a face. 'I hardly ever see her, and then only if she can't avoid me!'

George was devastated by his idiocy and scarcely noticed what she was saying. If West heard that Popsy was engaged, he would never be able to look him in the eye again; it was bad enough Fitz knowing – but with Fitz he could bluff his way out of it somehow.

'Her *sister* –' he said desperately.

Her brows curved up. 'Rather young for you.'

He turned to Fitz who was looking on in a puzzled way. 'Come on, let's wash!' He took him by the arm, leading him towards the door, then stopped and went back to Henrietta, saying softly in her ear, 'Don't tell West – about Popsy.' He looked round. West was standing by Alice Davies, glancing in his direction. 'I'll show you the bathroom,' he called.

'Yes,' Alice Davies agreed, smiling up, and placing a hand on West's arm. 'You go with George. I'll have tea sent in. Henry, dear, ring for Sadie would you!'

313

'We're doing rather well for tea this afternoon,' West said in the bathroom. He looked at George. 'Why so pensive, Number Three?'

'It's Popsy. She can't come.'

'Oh, dear! Oh, dear! Oh, *dear* –!'

Fitz started running water into the basin. 'It proves my point, all six-oners are bloody fools. I don't believe you could find yourself a whore under a red lamp, Steel. *What* am I to do with cousin Kate?'

'Take her for a gallop,' George said hotly.

West interposed. 'I was about to suggest I might ask your lovely sister to make up a sixsome.'

'Begod!' Fitz exclaimed. 'That's it!' In deference to West's superior rank, he stood aside from the basin which he had filled.

George felt suddenly protective. 'Henry's practically engaged.'

'Practically!'

'She goes down to Stokington Park most weekends – the Lynne's place.'

'Of course, if you object to my asking her –'

'Of course I don't object.'

West looked at him, then stepped to the basin.

'I thought you should know,' George said to his back.

'Of *course* we have no objection,' Fitz said, 'not at all, at all! What we have to do now is find one for Steel since he can't find one for himself.'

'How about the fair Mrs Davies?' West said, lathering his face vigorously. 'I think I can vouch for her enjoying extra-curricular diversions. You may find her stimulating, Number Three.'

George had begun to regret the whole thing. His ribs were aching again and his insides were in an uncertain condition; the last thing he felt like was a slap-up dinner with stimulation from Henry's landlady.

'I think it would be best if you two went.'

West looked round sharply.

'And take Henry,' he went on. 'She'll enjoy it. But West –'

West gazed at him.

314

He felt foolish, but had to go through with it. 'You will look after her.'

'Don't *worry*, old thing.' He reached for a hand towel and vacated the basin. 'She'll come to no harm, I promise you. But you must come.'

'Begod, you will!' Fitz agreed.

When they returned to the drawing-room in a body, they found Alice Davies's husband had come home. He was standing by the fireplace wearing a Norfolk tweed jacket and knickerbockers tucked into thick brown socks as though he had been out for an afternoon's golf or shooting. His face belied the impression; the forehead and cheeks were pale and smooth. George had not met him before. He was smaller than he had imagined; Alice Davies was quite a tall woman. His first impression was of quickness and intelligence – inquisitive eyes behind spectacles, a neat moustache, a vivacious manner as he straightened to greet them.

Alice Davies, sitting by the window with the trolley before her, started pouring tea after introductions had been effected; Henrietta handed round plates and cake forks while West and Fitz sat on the settee and George went over to the trolley for the cups as they were poured.

Charles Davies – as he had introduced himself – remained standing in front of the mantelpiece. He appeared amused by West's description of the accident and other tribulations on the way up.

'And what are your plans for this evening?' he asked.

'There's a thing,' West said, looking at George and Fitz. 'The exercise has not been planned with customary precision.' He looked back at Charles Davies. 'But it's an ill wind,' and turning to Alice Davies and Henrietta, 'it would be very jolly if you could all come with us. We plan to have a dinner to celebrate the end of the course.'

Alice Davies looked at Henrietta. 'It sounds a perfectly lovely idea!'

'Yes, it does.' Henrietta tried not to sound too enthusiastic although her heart was leaping.

'I'm afraid you'll have to count me out,' Charles Davies said. 'I have a meeting. But that need not stop you.' He looked at his wife.

315

'No, indeed,' she replied brightly, and turning her large eyes on West, 'It will be better for the numbers.'

'I'm so sorry, sir,' West said. 'It would be good to have you with us.'

Charles Davies's eyes flickered behind his spectacles. He looked round at his wife. 'Isn't it Sadie's evening off?'

'I'll speak to her when she comes in.' She looked at West. 'Have you decided on anywhere?'

17

George was not really surprised that 'Cousin Kate' bore no resemblance to Zena Dare. In repose she might even look ugly he guessed, although repose would not come easily. She had a formidable brow, making her eyes look deeper than most, and a wide, strong jaw, lending credence to Fitz's tales of her prowess in the hunting field. These somewhat heavy features were softened by lustrous piles of dark hair and a wide, remarkably feminine mouth seemingly formed for smiling. It was her eyes which made the deepest impression; changing greenish colours ringed by dark lashes, they were, George thought, the most direct and fearless girl's eyes he had ever seen, and when she turned to him at the table he could not help being aware of her interest in him. It provoked queer, palpitating feelings he was quite unused to; he was unsure how to respond.

Fitz was transparently, stupidly enamoured of her, egging her on constantly, roaring with laughter at the denouements of her anecdotes, it was positively embarrassing to watch, while her tongue made his attempts at repartee pedestrian. But stealing glances at the two of them when in conversation, George detected on occasions a dreamy look glaze her eyes which became at once distant and sad. These moments were fleeting. Had he not been drawn to study her with such interest, he would have been aware only of her bounce, her readiness to laugh, her engagingly funny way with an Irish story, her unconcealed interest when she looked at him. She really was the most direct girl he thought he had ever met.

He could hardly respond: Fitz was his friend. Dear Fitz! Watching his clumsy attempts to sweep her off her feet, he thought he liked him more than he had realized, hated the thought of parting now the Greenwich course was over and they would be taking such different paths. At the same time unworthy thoughts would surface; once he and Fitz had gone their separate ways there would be nothing to inhibit him with Kate. He had never felt quite like this before, excited, yet fearing those same intensely feminine things about her which thrilled him, impatient, shivery with apprehension lest through loyalty he lose her, perceiving somewhere in the recesses of his mind that she was a challenge he would meet – must meet.

She was sitting on his left; on his right, around the corner of the table, Alice Davies sat between him and West, opposite him on the other side; Henry was on West's right, Fitz at the other end of the table between her and Kate. He had a growing sense of unreality as he listened to them all. Whether it was the vintage champagne insisted on by West topping up last night's excess in his blood, or the splendid surroundings of the Ritz, the disturbing feelings provoked by Kate, or sheer tiredness, he seemed to be floating, disembodied, observing reality behind all the lively words and glances like a spectator at a dream play. He saw Alice Davies's eyes glow as she talked to West, but knew that West's real attention was reserved for Henry, fully reciprocated by her. Fitz of course was obsessed with 'Cousin Kate', but she –? When Alice Davies turned towards him and he heard himself fulfilling his conversational obligations, he felt Kate's vibrant force on the other side.

A waiter came to top up their glasses from the magnum in the beaded silver bucket; another cleared their dishes.

In the sudden pause in conversation he sensed Kate turning towards him, and looked round.

'Fitz tells me you're *living* in England now,' he said, the banality of the phrase causing it to return like an unwanted echo in his mind as soon as it was out.

Her face saddened dramatically. 'It broke my heart, it really did, leaving –' she checked herself quickly, 'But we're getting used to it now –'

'It must have been difficult leaving your friends,' West cut in from the other side. He and Henry had been having some fun at Fitz's expense over his promise that neither he nor Kate would mention horses or anything to do with horses during the evening. They had not baited Kate yet. George guessed she would give as good as she got.

'Why,' her eyes widened innocently, 'I brought my best pals with me!'

They laughed, and leaning towards George, she whispered, 'They have four legs. Don't tell your friend!'

'I dare say he guesses,' he smiled back; catching Fitz looking at him, he felt absurdly guilty.

A waiter appeared with the next course.

'Escalopes!' West said, eyeing Alice Davies's plate, and raising his shoulders rhythmically up and down, 'Es-calloped – Dirk galloped – we galloped all three –' He turned back to Kate. 'But it's not such good country, surely?' His expression was serious, interested.

'Oh, I like the country,' she flashed back. 'It's the town I don't care for, and clever people doing their best to fox a poor girl!'

Fitz bellowed with laughter. '*Fox* a poor girl!'

'Sure, Oi'll go to earth,' West said in a passable brogue; instead, looking round at the waiter, he ordered another magnum.

George wondered how much the evening was going to cost. He was in debt after three months at Greenwich on top of the previous courses at Pompey; last night's damages were going to increase that and here was West, who had never known what it was like to be short, running the bill up with special fizz – adding insult by chasing Henry. He was leaning closely towards her now, retailing some beastly anecdote with animation.

'You are a very close family, aren't you!' Alice Davies was addressing him. She must have noticed the direction of his gaze; he was probably looking grim.

He smiled. 'I suppose we are.'

'That is so good. I should so like children, but –' She seemed to sigh silently, shaking her head.

This was outside his experience; he had no idea how to respond. He busied himself with knife and fork.

'It is a pity you could not have come up to see Henry more

319

often while you were at Greenwich,' she went on. She had remarkably nice eyes, as he had noticed before, large and soft with sharply defined, upward curving brows.

'I cycled up to one or two matinees. I spent most of my spare time cricketing I'm afraid.' He cursed himself for being a bore; she knew that.

'Henry says you have no time for anything but the service and cricket.'

'I don't believe everything Henry says.' He looked across, catching Henry's eye as she laughed with West. He would warn her about him afterwards. Why the devil hadn't she clinched matters with Eggy? He was as decent a fellow as you could find anywhere, and as rich as Croesus.

'Will your first make a great deal of difference?' Alice Davies persisted.

'It'll push me up a bit. It should help me to get on the gunnery long course. I hope to specialize in gunnery, you see.'

'Oh, dear!' She shook her head again and looked at him intently. 'What do you think of all this battleship building? I suppose you have to agree with it, it will give you even *more* guns. But really, don't you think it too *wicked* when there are so many other uses the money should be put to? There are people *starving* – here – in London –'

He smiled at her intent expression. 'Yes of course. But it would be equally wicked to let the Germans catch us up!'

'You can't honestly believe that!' There was a hint of real annoyance in her eyes, quickly displaced. 'It's all a put-on. The armaments manufacturers are tied up with the Admiralty and they have produced this latest scare to get more orders, that's all.' George remembered Henry telling him something about the Davieses' pacifist inclinations. She leaned earnestly towards him. 'If they go on like this it will lead to war. It must. We are already so mistrustful of each other people actually believe what they read about the Germans – that they want war and are accelerating their building programme or whatever it is they're supposed to be doing. It is the most *wicked* nonsense put about by people like Mulliner and the *dreadful* Fisher.' She shook her head as if Fisher's depravity

320

were beyond belief, then noticed his expression. 'You think it's true, don't you?'

He wondered how to defuse her. 'I don't see how they can possibly take us on if we keep ahead of them – as far ahead as we are now –'

'Quite right!' West came in decisively from the other side, and turning to her, 'I'm afraid Jacky Fisher is doing much too good a job. They'll never dare to take us on as things stand at present.'

'*Afraid!*' She looked astonished. 'You want war!'

He smiled easily. 'Some of us think it high time we were given a chance. After all, we haven't fought for more than half a century – not a first rate enemy at sea –'

She leaned right back in her chair, staring with large eyes. 'I really can't believe you're serious.'

West's expression changed. 'How are we to prove we are equal to our forefathers?' He leaned towards her. 'More important, how are we to drive this cursed spirit of money-grubbing materialism from the land?'

She turned to George. 'And you feel like this too?'

He nodded, surprised nonetheless by West's unusual vehemence.

She threw her hands up. 'I see no hope.'

'Don't worry,' West said. 'There won't be a war. They simply haven't the ships. Their fleet would be on the bottom within the first week – then what would happen to their trade? They couldn't risk it. And Willy knows it.' He grinned suddenly. 'Unfortunately for us!'

She gave way gracefully. 'I see I'm in the minority. But I think perhaps, if we took a vote of the whole table we should have a rather more equal result.' She added, '*That* is why we must have votes for women!'

'Ah!' West laughed. 'Well – as I recall – let's see – didn't good Queen Bess support a number of rather – warlike adventures! And Isobella of Castille – she was hardly a milkmaid. To name but two –' He looked at George for confirmation.

George felt out of his depth. West was evidently something of an intellect. 'Absolutely!' he said with conviction.

'You would not get our modern women voting for war.'

Alice Davies looked up the table. 'Don't you agree, Henry?'

Henry looked at West, a teasing light in her eyes. 'I don't think they are going to give us the vote!'

'*Politics!*' Fitz bellowed. 'If you're talking politics down there, Kate and I are dashed well going to talk –' He stopped.

West leaned towards him, a hand up to his ear.

'Fences,' Kate said, 'and ditches –'

'And *drains* –' Fitz roared excitedly.

'*Drains!*' West raised a brow. 'My dear old thing!'

It was excruciatingly funny. Amid the laughter, West looked round and snapped his fingers at a waiter and pointed to the champagne.

Alice Davies was not laughing. She leaned towards George. 'The *dreadful* thing is, he means it. To think – in the *twentieth century* – and we can talk seriously of – oh, dear, oh, *dear* –!'

Something exerted gentle pressure on his ankle. He looked up at West, but he was engaged with Henry and Fitz. He moved his leg away.

'What are you doing now you have finished at Greenwich?' Alice Davies asked; she appeared to have reverted to normal although her cheeks looked slightly flushed still; perhaps it was the fizz.

'I have two days at home – then I join a destroyer for the manoeuvres before I –' What? He had no idea where he would be sent; he knew where he would like to go –

'Only two days! Have you any plans?'

'I shall be going to Lords. It's the Marlborough-Rugby match. My brother – Andy – is coming up – he's at Marl-borough –'

'Why don't you come and have some lunch beforehand? I shall ask the *charming* Mr West,' and with a meaning glance in Henry's direction, 'I've no doubt at all he'll accept! We can make it an early lunch. It'll give you plenty of time.'

He felt the strange pressure on his ankle again. Her eyes seemed very large and warm and rather bright. He wondered what to do with his leg. 'Thank you.'

'I don't think there is any need to include your friend, Fitz, do you!' and lowering her voice, 'I dare say he will want to see as much of his "cousin" as he can!'

George looked round. Lord! Whyever did she want to ask him to *lunch*! And this intermittent pressure on his ankle. He thought of West's remark about extra-curricular activities and his insides turned over. Kate was listening to some involved story of Fitz's; she looked round at him and smiled, then he heard Alice Davies again.

'After you have been to Lords, I should like to take you to the Anglo-German Society. I don't suppose you would find it *frightfully* amusing. I do believe you might find it interesting though. Some of them are quite civilized – the Germans, I mean.' She smiled.

There was no doubt about it; she had given up West and transferred her full attention to him. He thought of Charles Davies standing by the fireplace in his knickerbockers and golfing socks, an engagingly intelligent, but ineffectual little man. Lord! What on earth did she want of him?

George stood with Alice Davies by the window, watching as West led Henry out to the dog cart he had procured from somewhere and handed her up. She wore a blue dust cloak over a white dress caught at the throat with a deep blue velvet tie; her eyes reflected its colour. Her extraordinarily wide hat was trimmed with cornflowers and she carried a parasol with alternating pale blue and lemon yellow bands; she looked as lovely as he had ever seen her.

West waved to them cheerfully as he strode up to pass something to the boy holding the horse. George turned away. He hated to see them driving off; he felt absurdly, unaccountably possessive. He hardly saw Henry on more than a couple of occasions from one year to the next and he wanted her with him now; he wanted her to come to Lords with him on this splendid afternoon. She had made no sense at all at lunch! West had turned her head completely, and he might not have been there for all the notice she had taken of him.

'They've gone!'

He heard Alice Davies moving from the window, and looked towards her.

'I'm so glad for Henry,' she said, smiling. 'This is *exactly* what she needs.' She gazed at him, sensing his disapproval. 'It doesn't matter, it really doesn't matter, George.' She came up and put her hand on his arm. 'There is far too much made of – you mustn't *worry* about Henry. She's a perfect sweet and your *charming* Mr West knows it.' She smiled suddenly. 'Why don't you have a brandy before you go –'

'Thank you – no –'

'But I insist. You must not go thinking these *dark* things.'

She was very close, her fingers on his arm, looking up at him with a gleam of humour in her warm eyes and he could smell the fragrance she used. He smiled, wondering how he could get away without seeming to rush.

'I am going to fetch you one,' she said, releasing his arm and moving towards the door. 'Five minutes will not make the slightest difference.' She disappeared.

He moved to the window and looked out at the road where the dog cart had been. How empty it seemed now. Henry had looked absolutely radiant. He didn't really want to go to Lords; he was doing it from loyalty to Andy; he wanted to be with her and West driving past Green Park, looking at the lambs in the sun. It was not only Henry causing him dissatisfaction, West had lost interest in him since seeing Henry. Yesterday, driving in the 'old girl', West had been more companionable than he had thought possible, given his sophistication and seniority; the drive had been enormous fun and he had felt West liked him. Now West could only think of Henry, and here he was on almost his last afternoon going to Lords on his own –

He heard Alice Davies returning.

'I forgot to ask if you would like soda.' She was holding an enormous brandy balloon, generously charged.

He shook his head, smiling at the measure as he stepped across towards her.

'I have given Sadie the afternoon off,' she said. 'She had to stay in for Charles's meeting last night.'

He took the glass, her words ringing in his head, the queer sensation he had had last night taking hold of him again – 'I have given Sadie the afternoon off' – perhaps it was an innocent explanation of the reason she was bringing him the brandy glass herself; yes, surely that was it.

'Thank you,' he said, taking the glass.

'Come and sit down.' Her voice was very matter-of-fact.

He followed her to the settee, and sat at the opposite end to the one she took, relaxing back and crossing one leg over the other; he felt anything but relaxed. He raised the glass towards her, then circled it under his nose in the approved way, breathing in the heady vapours. He had more than a suspicion West had been right about her enjoying diversions, but had no idea what he might do to test the theory. She was married; he might be absolutely wrong. What would she think of him? And there was Henry to consider. He took a gulp of the brandy; it was excellent. The idea was preposterous. He thought of Charles Davies standing in front of the fireplace, arms spread either side on the mantelpiece.

'Aren't you pleased that Henry is in love?' she asked.

He considered the question. Certainly, that was the impression she had given.

'She hasn't been at all happy,' she went on. 'She's been meeting too many – she hasn't really seen enough people of her own sort – young people. In a way she's been *too* conscientious. I have a feeling sometimes she doesn't really believe in all we're doing now. She worked far too hard at the beginning, I think.'

He nodded. 'You can't stop Henry when she's keen on something.'

'Exactly so. I really think she's drained herself. And her weekends, when she goes down to Sussex – they are a strain too. I can tell when she gets back. That's why I say, this is the best thing that could possibly have happened – I'm really so pleased for her. So ought you to be.'

He looked down into the brandy, swirling it around the glass. 'West'll be off in a few days.'

She laughed. 'Not for good, I trust!'

He looked up again into her eyes. 'I don't know.'

'You don't trust the *charming* – Mr West!'

He smiled at her constant emphasis. 'I've seen him. In action.' Why was he telling her? He had meant to warn Henry, but had not been able to get her on her own, and in the mood she was in, she would not have listened anyway. 'I think you ought to warn her.'

She seemed amused. 'You don't know very much about us. I should have thought you would with a sister like Henry.'

He held her eyes, annoyed by the criticism and her playful manner.

'It would only add to his glamour,' she went on. 'There is nothing we like more than a degree of – wickedness! The idea that he has – *is* a little *dangerous*, oh, yes, danger, so long as we know it is not likely to get out of hand, is most attractive.' She smiled at his expression, and threw an arm wide, 'You men go off exploring – finding new lands to govern – that's how you find purpose – excitement. With us, it happens inside, in here,' she indicated her breast and laughed. 'I've embarrassed you, I'm sorry. Really. But there is a difference. Despite what you might expect a militant feminist to say!'

'That's all very well. Henry may get hurt.'

'I expect she will. We all do.' She leaned towards him with a suddenly serious expression, one arm along the back of the settee towards him. '*You* may get hurt. A fever in Africa or a bullet even – a shipwreck. You don't want to stay at home though and be a *clerk*. Do you?'

'That's rather different.'

'I don't think so. Love is as dangerous for us.'

A tremor ran through him at the deep look in her eyes, and his hand seemed to quiver slightly as he brought the brandy to his lips. He wanted to move the short space between them and take her in his arms; he had not realized quite how attractive she was, and the thought that she was married and knew all about that side of things added to the urgent feeling he had. His knee started shaking of its own accord and he uncrossed his leg, thankful to break the tension with movement. He crossed the other leg over it. His heart was pumping hard.

'Young girls can be too protected,' she said. 'It can be a mistake to go into marriage without knowing anything. Their husband has probably picked up a good deal one way or another –'

He couldn't meet her eyes. He looked down into his brandy as he felt the blood rushing to his face; he hoped his tan masked it.

326

'On the other hand, many haven't. Unfortunately!'

He seemed actually to hear his heart pounding in the silence as she stopped talking, and hoped desperately it didn't carry across the short space between them.

'I was lucky.' Her voice had taken a different timbre. 'I spent a great deal of my time in the country. My uncle had a farm on the borders. I used to spend most of my summer holidays there. You can't live on a farm for as long as that and grow up as ignorant as a town girl. Besides, I was friendly with the farm girls – I'd grown up with them. I remember one summer – I was about fifteen I think – several of them were talking about where they were going that evening. I gathered it was rather daring. They wouldn't tell me what it was. They bracketed me with my uncle and his family, which I was of course.

'Well – I determined to follow them. They walked quite a long way. I dodged about behind hedges praying they wouldn't turn and see me. They came to a wood. I couldn't tell which way they'd gone then – I'd had to leave a longish space in case they heard me. I couldn't hear anything. They seemed just to have vanished. I knew the wood went down to a rather pleasant little stream that bordered the farm, so after looking around to see if I could find any clues as to which direction they might have gone, I started along a path leading down towards it I hoped. I'd almost arrived and could see a flash of water through the trees when I heard men's voices. A little to my right. I went on more cautiously, I didn't want them to see me, I thought they might be swimming. I heard their splashing then, and was just about to turn back when I suddenly heard my friends laughing and calling out to the men. Of course they swam without anything on. The girls had been hiding, watching. The calls and laughs turned into shrieks – not real shrieks – play-acting, and I realized that one or two of the men must have come out of the water and were chasing them. I could hear them crashing about through the undergrowth. Then I heard someone coming towards *me*! I got right down and wriggled into a bush. Then I saw who it was, her name was Amy – I'll never forget her, never. She was giggling and crying out as she ran, and I saw a man coming after her. He was naked, still wet

327

from the river. He caught her not fifteen feet from where I was hiding and they fell into the undergrowth, laughing – Amy pretending to fight him off – not utterly convincingly I must say! I was terrified. I dared not move. I didn't even look in case even that somehow gave me away. I hardly dared breathe.

'Well – after a while I heard him get up and go back the way he had come, and a few minutes later Amy got up and walked away. I must have stayed there for an hour before I dared leave. I saw Amy the next morning and I think I probably stared rather! She seemed an entirely different person from the Amy I had known – I saw her with new eyes, d'you understand what I mean?'

He nodded, hardly daring to trust himself to speak. Waves of tension and desire were searing through him as she spoke leaving him shaking. His chest was pounding, his breathing seemed irregular; he doubted if he could lift the brandy glass without giving himself away by the tremble in his hand, or look at her without showing how much her story affected him. She had made it plain, surely she could not have made it plainer --?

He turned and leaned towards her, meaning to take her hand which he could sense was still resting on the top of the settee half way between them, but he was holding the brandy glass; it was not even empty. Awkwardly, still half-turned, he lifted it and gulped.

'I have bored you with my tale of nymphs and shepherds!'

'No, no, certainly not.' He looked at her at last. Was there a gleam of amusement still in her eyes?

'It was a corrective for some of the idylls we were taught. Do you like Alma Tadema?'

'I haven't seen many –'

'We have one in the guest room.' She stood in one composed motion. 'We were given it. I *refused* to have it anywhere else!'

She walked towards the door. He swallowed the last drop of brandy and rose too, his legs quite weak as he got up. She didn't look back, but turned outside the door and went up the stairs in the straight-backed way she had. At the top she turned towards the back of the house, opening a door beside a fern in a pot standing on a small white table. He followed her in. There was a large print on the wall of a classic landscape, two girls with milk-white skins bathing in a pool. Beneath the picture was a bed with a golden, quilted counterpane and shining brass rails at the head and foot.

She turned to look at him and moved closer to take the brandy balloon he was still clutching; stretching out, she placed it on a chest of drawers by the door. Then she pushed the door to gently, and taking his hand, placed it on her collar. She wasn't looking at him now; her movements were silent, rounded. He put his arm on her waist and pulled her towards him, surprised at how lightly she came. His boats were burnt! He quivered all over, feeling his heart thump as if about to leave his chest as she came against him and he felt her firm breasts and her supple waist and felt himself pressing into her thighs. She raised her head and he bent to kiss her mouth. How soft she was, and yielding.

He felt her pushing him gently away, and this time she placed his other hand on her collar as well. Again, he glimpsed that faintly amused light in her eyes.

'I should not like my dress to get crushed.'

He fumbled with the clasps, but his fingers were clumsy and she put her own hands up to do it; she released the catches, undid the buttons at the front and, turning, removed the sash from around her waist.

'Close the door properly,' she said softly, 'And count to twenty.'

He turned and did so, trying not to think about her or the pressure at his groin. It was agony. Why was she doing it to him? It was broad daylight. Marlborough must have passed Rugby's first innings' total by now – with this sun the pitch might be turning nasty. The sun was streaming in at the window and she was undressing; he could hear her. The pressure was terrible. He couldn't move, dare not lest he disgrace himself. Andy would be waiting by the entrance, expecting him; he had *promised*. He was letting him down badly. Marlborough had done so well yesterday. They had the game in their pocket if they just played steadily –

He could hear her moving. It was surely twenty. He turned carefully. She was in shimmering silk, taking clips from her

329

hair and shaking it free. It was cascading down over her shoulders in a shower of soft, light brown swirls. She saw him and smiled and came towards him, taking the lapel of his jacket and easing it from his shoulders. He let her take it off, his heart going again like a steam pump.

'What very large shoulders you have, George –'

She turned away to put his jacket over a chair back and he bent to untie his shoes. He took them off – anywhere – he didn't know what he was doing as he kicked them away, and started unbuttoning his trousers – but he still had his shirt on. Lord! The sudden release of pressure was almost his undoing. He dropped on one knee so that she wouldn't see, and started folding his trousers on the carpet.

She had come round in front of him and was pulling off the golden counterpane; she pulled the blankets back and sat down on the sheet; he could sense her gazing at him.

'I suppose that must be your Dartmouth training,' she said.

He looked up wildly.

She was looking down at the neat parcel he had made of his trousers.

He smiled with relief, then seeing one of his shoes almost under the bed, crawled over and took it, swinging round and placing it by his trousers in line with them. Turning again, he put a hand on her lap and raised himself to his knees in front of her.

She leaned forward and put her arms around his shoulders and smothered him. Her hair fell all around him, tickling. 'Don't *worry*, George! You mustn't worry so much –'

She pulled him up and sank back beside him on the bed.

He pushed down at his drawers, aching for release, feeling her hands guiding him when it happened.

'I'm sorry – I wasn't –'

'*George!*' She sounded irritated, 'It'll be all right – it'll be quite all right next time –'

Henrietta followed Mary down the aisle towards the altar rail where the groom and best man waited. She wondered why she didn't feel more – she wasn't sure exactly what she

330

should be feeling, but she and Mary had been so close once, and she was 'best girl' as Mary quaintly called it after the American fashion. Somehow she had felt much more involved at the four previous weddings of her friends; familiarity had staled her perhaps.

Popsy, whose invitation had come as a great surprise – a reward for no longer seeing Eggy she had supposed – had made a stunning bride. She had radiated excitement – not the usual sort. It had little to do with young love or her illustrious relations, certainly nothing to do with poor Bobo, splendid as he had contrived to look in his dress uniform! It had been more in the nature of a triumph; veiled as she was, her vital personality had dominated the proceedings; her clear voice had rung out through the church. She had taken Bobo for her lawful spouse to do with as she pleased; there could have been few in the grand congregation who had not sensed this.

Eggy, as best man, had seemed very straight and stern. He had not looked about him once. She had wondered what he was thinking. She had seen him afterwards at the reception, but he had avoided coming up to her. It would be his turn next; she had seen the announcement in the paper. She would not receive an invitation for that sparkling occasion!

Her feelings for Eggy were so mixed. He represented safety and kindness, tenderness and absolute honour and inconceivable wealth; the thought of his grave eyes was still enough to send shudders of regret through her and bring back memories of those early weekends at Stokey when it had been fresh and exciting and he had seemed so boyishly devoted to her. Perhaps he still was. He had taken her rejection as he must have learned to take a beating at Eton, without a sign, without display of any kind, just a little bow of his head and a smile that hadn't touched his eyes.

Why could men not be *friends*? Why did it have to be all or nothing? It was so unfair. She liked Eggy, even loved him in a way, but not *that* way –

They reached the chancel step. The groom seemed nervous as he turned – a good-looking young man with an eager face and keen eyes. He had a brilliant future at the bar, Mary

331

said. With the dowry she came with he would be able to afford to pick his cases!

Mary turned and handed her her bouquet, then her gloves; she smiled reassuringly back. It was doubtful though if Mary needed reassurance; she seemed the most composed person in the church, the Mary she had always been, matter-of-fact Mary following the path laid out for her. So she would continue while this young man climbed the ladder and became middle-aged and famous and she gave him children – alternately prudent and brilliant! She thought of all their talks on 'love' and marriage – and here they were and it was Mary, not her, who was first in the water, but she doubted if love was involved any more than it had been with Popsy –

'Dearly beloved, we are gathered here in the sight of God, and in the face of this congregation, to join together this man and this woman –'

She imagined standing at the altar beside Robin West. Some time he would ask her; he had more or less implied as much when he told her naval officers were not expected to marry young. And what did he consider young! He had laughed. He was devoted to the Navy, she knew; she could only ever be his mistress, the lover to whom he would run for solace from the stern demands of his grey wife. And she would always be on hand, if he was in the Mediterranean or on the China Station or in the West Indies or the Pacific, she would sail there to be with him between cruises, and when she had his children she would take them so that he could be with them. She would love him, sharing him with no one except his great wandering wife.

It was hard waiting. Looking up at the stained glass above the altar, she prayed, 'Dear God, if it be Thy wish, please show him how much I love him, and if I must *wait*, may it not be long –'

Willing her prayer fervently, she heard the priest's voice, 'Wilt thou have this woman to thy wedded wife, to live together in God's ordinance in the holy estate of matrimony –?'

Again she imagined Robin beside her, gazing at her with that humorous speculation in his eyes as if thinking of some

332

more amusing response than a plain 'I will!' He disliked conventional forms. She wondered what he really thought of marriage; probably he had never considered it. She didn't think he had considered many things at all – except his profession. He had said as much in his first letter to her; she could remember it almost word for word, she had read it so often.

– You have much to answer for, in a single week you opened my eyes to so many things not taught at Greenwich or Whaley, splendid things which seemed so natural to you you could not imagine anyone not having made these discoveries for themselves, and I had not the courage to say 'It has never occurred to me!' Did you think I was too proud on those occasions? In St James's Park we were looking at the ducks and you said you remembered you used to come here with your old nurse, Scopey, you wished she could see you now, and meet me. I looked at you, thinking what an enchanting little girl you must have been then. I said I so wished I had known you, and you said – it is graven on my heart – 'In three days you will have gone. It will be as if we had never been here.' 'Impossible,' I replied. You looked at me. You thought you had *always* known me, you said, not in the physical world, but in some spiritual world we carry along with us through all the physical changes. Otherwise, how could you have recognized me when I stood at the door that first day!

My heart, you have the courage to say things which take a fellow's breath away! It was not said for effect, you truly meant it. And now we are a thousand miles apart I have the courage to answer – how could I have recognized you? For I did – over little Sadie's head I saw your eyes and something I knew I had been looking for, and I can see them still in the smoking circle after dinner when the port has passed a few times and the other fellows are chattering away and when I look down into the wake as the ship carries me further from you and as I write these poor lines I can see you on that first day and ponder your *marvellous* theories! Even if they cannot be proved – you must remember I am a d——d scientific fellow and thoroughly despised here for it! – they make one think about all the things one has taken for granted.

I look at the photograph we had taken together, it is before me on my desk, and think it is not *you*, it is a representation, a mere sketch which means nothing unless one fills in the little quick laughs and thoughts and feelings and a thousand things that make the real *you*. Perhaps the world is like this, a photographish kind of place which we unthinking fellows take to be all there is but which you have a truer idea of with the spiritual world you carry around to give life and feeling to the print? Now you see you have turned a poor gunnery Jack into an amateur philosopher which is not altogether a good thing. I might be pondering such a knotty problem at our next target practice and coming to the conclusion that since the target was not there when you were feeding the ducks with Scopey it has no proper existence, making spotting corrections in the spiritual plane from perceptions of where the shells must surely land before I see the splashes! I fear I should be on the next P & O home with extreme rapidity. Sweet heart, my *rara avis*, my Keats-lover, my true love, your brother who is such an excellent fellow tried to warn me off by telling me you were *practically* engaged. I do pray you listen to your spiritual voices and wait at least until I come home again and show you we are truly linked in that other world to which you have introduced me –

How different he was in writing from the detached, sardonic character he assumed –

The words of the priest calling them to prayer interrupted her reverie. She had missed the ceremony. Mary had been married. It was awful, the most terrible, selfish thing she had done – the most important moment in Mary's life and she could think only of herself –

'Dear God, *forgive* me – and please bless Mary's marriage, send her joy and happiness always –'

She was still feeling guilty when she followed Mary and her new husband into the vestry and signed the register after them. Mary's grey eyes were as steady as ever when she handed her back the gloves and bouquet, but in some quiet

334

way she was transformed with happiness. It really did mean something. It meant something to her as well; her guilt heightened the love she felt as she embraced her.

'Dear Mary,' she breathed after they kissed. 'Please be very, *very* happy.'

'Dearest Henry,' Mary smiled.

18

Willy worked mechanically. He had gone beyond tiredness and wondering when they would finish, beyond thought itself. His mind was a machine, registering if a bag were unbalanced as he took its weight on his barrow, sending the necessary messages to his arms to shake it to a more central position as he backed and turned before setting off up the deck at a lope. Swerving automatically as he came to the spot where the canvas deck cloth was rucked up around the ventilating pipe, he was aware of the private formula repeating inside his head, 'One – two –' strides 'and *hup*!' as he jerked the handles towards the tippers standing over the circular opening to the bunker below. And swinging the lightened trolley to the left as the coal clattered down the chute, he would start back, aware of Barlow loping towards him with another trolley, but not looking at him as he jogged past, streaked grey with rain and dust.

Wind pressed the wet clothes against his skin, chilling him as he stood, waiting for the next hoist; his mouth was dry with the taste of coal, his eyes smarted; a thin trickle of mucus from his nose mixed with the rain on his upper lip and he tasted salt as he curled his tongue to lick it away. There was a dull ache in the muscles of his arms and wrists from shovelling earlier in the collier's hold, but he could go on for ever at barrowing if need be – if only the wind were not so cold.

Steam clattered in the winch; the wire guy beside him tautened as the hoist swung across and down, thumping on the deck. A cloud of black burst upwards, dissolving in the rain as the waiting hands leapt for the bags. Automatically

336

he moved closer to his loaders, tensing in anticipation as he saw them swing towards him. The bag hit the barrow, knocking it sideways for a moment before he righted it; they swore without force. He pushed the handles down, tipping the barrow on one wheel to shift the weight to the right as he backed and turned, then loped away, following the lines scored by his own and other wheels across the wet grime on the canvas – a quick swerve around the rucking, 'One – two – and *hup*!'

This time as he swung the barrow lightly away from the tippers, he became aware of a still figure in a waterproof standing by the casing door. The squat shape and belligerent thrust of head and jaw were unmistakable even without a glimpse of gold around the peak of the cap thrust down over the eyes – the 'Bull'! Willy came out of the machine-like dream, his pace quickening instinctively, and in his haste he almost slipped as he turned; he recovered quickly and ran the barrow aft as if they were going for a record. They had been at the start; all hope of that was long past though: the last hour's return had been something like 160 tons, he couldn't remember exactly, but well down on what they could do, well down on what the Bull expected. Whether it was the rain or the new coaling organization or the fact that the collier had come on to them from the flagship and her after holds were practically empty, whether it was because of the sullenness which had been settling on the ship's company since the Bull had relieved old Lightfoot as Commander, damping the extra effort needed for good results, Willy had no idea. One thing was certain, the Commander was angry. The thought of him watching their gang made him stiff with apprehension and all purely physical discomforts faded as he waited his turn for another bag.

Receiving it, he turned and raced up the deck, almost losing it from the barrow as he swerved for the rucked deck cloth, managing to hold it, just, completing two giant strides. '– and *hup*!' The low angle of the bag and the unexpected momentum of its arrival proved too much for the tipper on the right; he lost his hold with one hand, the mouth of the bag opened before it was properly positioned over the opening and coal spewed on to the deck. As in a nightmare,

Willy saw a knob about the size of a cricket ball bounce away over the grey canvas towards the Bull; so strong was the impression that he was aware of it bouncing right up and past the motionless figure although by that time he had swung round for the return journey and his back was turned.

'That man!'

The call froze him. He turned.

'You! Come here! Who the devil are you?' The Bull's eyes were narrowed as he tried to penetrate Willy's mask of rivuleted grime.

'Steel, sir.' He halted his barrow before him. He was actually taller by several inches than the Commander.

'Fourteen days leave stopped!'

'Sir!'

'Now get on with it!'

'Sir!' He swung his barrow and doubled off, almost colliding with an ordinary seaman charging up the deck with a load; they jinked their barrows around each other, Willy tensing for the inevitable yell. It never came. When he dared cast a glance back he saw the Commander had disappeared as suddenly as he had come.

Fourteen days leave stopped caused him no concern; with the Bull's arrival he had become used to staying aboard, and had not worked off his last stoppage yet. 'The beach' was not something he thought about in any case – except in his darkest moments as a final escape. Since joining the battleship some five months before, all his mental and physical resources had been needed for sheer survival; whether or not he went ashore was of no consequence beside the humours of the sub of the gunroom, 'Ginger' Ross, and the senior snotties who aided him in making the lives of the recently joined young 'warts' like himself as miserable as they could. Nothing in his previous training, hard and arbitrary as it had been, had prepared him for it, not Osborne, nor Dartmouth, certainly not the training cruiser which had taken him on what appeared now, looking back, a Caribbean idyll of blue seas and hot sands and picnics and dancing through balmy tropic nights with dusky partners. And of course Jollion Peters had been in his watch.

Now, for almost the first time since entering the Service,

he could not talk or laugh with Jolly, who was in a cruiser in the Med – enjoying gunroom life no end according to his letter. It was the knowledge that there *were* other sorts of gunroom which he might find himself transferred to at some time if he managed to weather this one that helped to prevent him throwing in the sponge in the first months. Uncle Richard's words in the garden helped as well; he remembered them so clearly – the apple fizzing back and forth between his hands.

'You don't know a man till you've bin through a scrape with him, Willy – it's whether he can stick it out that counts –'

The thought of this made him determined he would stick it out, and he prayed each night over his sea chest for the strength to do so.

Recently, a new threat had appeared; it was more dangerous than the physical torments and indignities, the frequent canings and constant sport made of the defenceless youngsters by the seniors; it was a mental torture, doubly insidious because he dared not allow them to see that it was a torture; once they found out they would have another weapon with which to hound him.

It had started on the spring cruise down to Vigo and Arosa Bay; the warm weather they met had encouraged cockroaches which bred behind partitions and in crannies between steam pipes in the old pre-dreadnought to come out in scores in the living spaces and pantries. To stem the invasion, Ginger had decreed that all warts hunt them and bring him a dozen corpses every night before turning in. It was not simply the futile waste of time involved – for with the colder weather on their return to home waters, the cockroaches had disappeared back into the woodwork – it was his distaste for killing anything that caused Willy agony. The first night he had made the excuse he was on watch, knowing the inevitable result – 'Why didn't you find 'em before you went up?' and the inevitable consequence: after dinner he had knelt on the timber form running along the inboard side of the gunroom table, bent to touch the stained cloth with his nose and forehead and taken six with the cane without a sound.

That night in his hammock had been his worst ever. He

could not take six every night, nor could he tell anyone the real reason for not producing corpses. The problem was insoluble. It led to the more profound, if less immediate problem of what he was doing in a fighting service. It was not as simple though, and Uncle Richard's words again helped him.

'We're very fortunate in England, you must never forget that, Willy, for I believe we shall have to fight for it – you and I and George and Andy and Harry –'

Fighting for his home and family, for Henry and Babs and Mama and everyone, he could understand that. He was quite prepared to kill Germans, he thought. Stamping on harmless cockroaches who had as much right to life as the bully he loathed with every fibre was a different thing –

Next day, with no idea what he was going to do, help had taken the unexpected form of the engineer sub, Wilkins, an older and normally rather silent member of the gunroom with the extraordinarily pallid face engineers had and dark brown eyes which seemed to Willy to have angry red rings around the pupils, although when he looked for them they weren't there. Wilkins had come up without a word, thrust a ketchup bottle in his hand and gone on his way. Surprised, he unscrewed the top; inside were scores of dead cock-roaches.

That night, as Ginger held out an open hand for the 'corps', as he called the cockroaches, counting aloud as Willy popped them one by one into his palm, Wilkins watched with his smouldering eyes.

A few days later Willy found him alone and thanked him.

'I'd like to see the bastard in hell!' was all the engineer said.

By the time the ketchup bottle stock ran out, Willy had found a new source of supply: the gunroom messman, Old Harper, who had access to places almost as warm as the engine room and stokeholes, had taken to selling corps at threepence a dozen to those warts who had failed to reach their quota. Willy had a regular order for a dozen, which the messman chalked up to his account in a little book he kept. Willy had no idea how much he had run up; undoubtedly with his normal mess and servants and dhobying bills and now Old Harper's account, he was exceeding his paltry pay and allowance from home, but he didn't waste time worrying about this; it was in his nature to take things as they came. What did worry him greatly was that getting someone else to kill the poor creatures was a cowardly way out of his dilemma. He tried to convince himself that he was powerless to affect Ginger's edict and since he could not take six or more over the table every evening, it was a question of either acceding to the system or throwing his hand in, which he was sure would mean having to leave the service; that would cause his parents terrible distress. He was simply choosing the lesser of two evils. But wasn't that only an excuse?

The whole problem set him thinking about Uncle Richard's belief that all the queer things that happened to a fellow were 'meant'. Wilkins's intervention must have been meant or sent by God in answer to his prayers. It was an intriguing thought for if queer, moody fellows like Wilkins were used by God, he too might be and in ways he could scarcely guess at, for he was sure Wilkins was not aware of his partnership with the Almighty; every other word, when he did speak, was a blasphemy.

The thought that he himself might be used on occasions as an agent of the Lord strengthened Willy's naturally helpful attitude towards others in distress. The member most frequently in distress was James Halliday, assistant clerk, lower in the scale of gunroom values than even the most junior wart, and gradually Willy had come to regard himself as the chosen one for preventing Halliday from doing away with himself; assuredly the lad had come close to it on occasions. In trying to help him, he found he helped himself, for it took his mind from his own misery.

So he stuck it out. But his stock of courage was now desperately low. He didn't realize this; it was not until years later when he chanced on Lord Moran's observations of men in the trenches, published as *The Anatomy of Courage*, that he realized what must have been happening to him in that first gunroom mess. Like the men in the trenches, he had been drawing continually on the balance of courage in his account.

Until coming across *The Anatomy of Courage* he had, consciously or unconsciously, submerged all memories of that
dreadful period of his life, never thinking, never talking of
it, not in his most intimate moments. Reading Moran, he
began for the first time to try and analyse what it had meant
to him, and like a dam bursting the images returned – the
large white-enamelled steel room on the lower deck, the
deckhead beams you just couldn't touch, riveted frames
projecting from the side between three polished, brass-bound
scuttles only three or so feet above sea level, great brass
screws to hold them closed. He saw the long mahogany table
at which they had eaten, worked, been made sport of – he
saw Halliday propelled along the table head first on his
stomach with a lucifer clamped between his teeth – again
and again until he contrived to strike fire from the match
rather than break it; he suffered the torments of having to
watch, and experienced the sinking helplessness he had felt
himself when used as a human torpedo and 'run' along the
same scratched surface with his hands as a matter of honour
by his sides. He smelt the slightly fishy odour of the cloth as
he put his nose to it after dinner to receive six for being last
out of the mess when Ginger brandished a fork towards the
deckhead beams, or not getting his hands up quickly enough
to his ears when the sub shouted 'Breadcrumbs' before telling
an obscene story. He heard the click of the locker where the
cane was kept, the sharp sounds all their boots made on the
brown corticene deck covering, smelled the close, cokey,
smoky fug when the stove in the corner was stoked up to a
red heat and the scuttles clamped tight shut. He listened for
the blank notes on the battered old upright piano lashed to
the stanchion by the for'd bulkhead as they gathered for a
sing-song; his stomach turned over with the old loathing and
fear, for Ginger Ross was there with his colourless brows and
almost white lashes, sensuous lips turned down arrogantly at

342

the corners. Ross had paid for his sins with his life in almost the first week of the war, but he was there still in the most secret recesses of his mind, challenging his self-respect.

. . . In the trenches a man's will power was his capital and he was always spending, so that a wise and thrifty company officer watched the expenditure of every penny lest their men went bankrupt. When their capital was done they were finished . . .

At the time Willy had little notion he was almost bankrupt. He knew he always felt tired; he knew he found studying during the instructional periods unnaturally difficult, and he couldn't summon enthusiasm for anything, not sailing his cutter or writing to Jolly or Henry, although he did so as a duty. He knew he loathed the very sight of the gunroom and braced himself every time he entered, but he accepted these things as the present facts of his existence; no thought that his capital might be almost exhausted entered his head; he was simply determined to stick it out for as long as he had to.

That was his mood when eventually, just before five in the afternoon, the bugle sounded the cease fire for the end of coaling. It was little relief; it merely exchanged the endurance of trundling his barrow for the endurance of the gunroom, and it was only when he reached his chest way down in the steering engine flat that he realized how physically tired he was; he flopped on the deck, resting his head on the lid.

The Bull was shaking him roughly by the shoulder; he panicked, trying to imagine how he could have fallen asleep in the middle of coaling and on such an extraordinarily large chunk of the stuff. Another fourteen days leave stopped –

The large chunk turned into the lid of his sea chest. McQueen, his face pink and clean, was looking down at him; his chest was bare and he had a towel around his middle.

'There's a panic on.' He seemed excited. 'The bandsmen have gone on strike!'

Willy sat up, wondering how long he'd been asleep.

Besides himself, McQueen was the only person in the flat; grubby coaling gear lay by the other chests, some of them with their lids up.

'On strike!'

McQueen had started towelling his hair. 'They're insisting on tea. You have to fetch your own water. Ginger's doing a war dance –'

The Bull's new routine Willy thought: no meal, not even a spell allowed until the ship had been hosed down, cleared up between decks, and all coaling gear scrubbed and inspected at divisions. There had been rumblings when it was announced. Wondering how long he had to get cleaned up, he opened the lid of his chest. The mirror in its mahogany surround gave him a quick glimpse of his matted hair and sooty features; beside it was the photograph of Henry and his father, curling up at the bottom right hand corner; below was Felpham House, solid, well-proportioned, framed in branches in strong sunlight. He lifted the tray containing his wash hand stand, hand towel, soap and flannel and looked beneath for his bath towel. He remembered; he'd given it to his servant for washing. Placing the tray on the deck, he rubbed the worst of the grime from his fingers on the hand towel, leaving smears of grey, then started lifting his uniform, his pyjamas, shirts, underclothes to peer beneath. Lord! A mess! He knew he had another somewhere.

By the time he had found it, raced up for a water can, forward to the galley for hot water and back to the gunroom flat, the bathroom was almost empty. The cramped enclosure seemed even dimmer than usual after his trip through the mess decks; it smelt of wet towels and bodies. Seizing the nearest bath, he upended it, sloshing the soapy contents over the deck tiles, and placed his hot water can inside it before going to the hydrant on the bulkhead and turning the wheel. Salt water hissed out. Splashing it up his limbs and body, ducking his head under and rubbing his hands through his hair, he got rid of most of the grime, he thought, then turned the hydrant off and returned to the tin tub.

The only other occupants of the bathroom were a snotty of middling seniority called Forbes-Jones and the assistant paymaster, Pritchett. They were discussing the strike and the

Bull's likely reactions as they towelled themselves down. Leaning forward in his tub, pouring the deliciously warm water slowly over his head, Willy allowed his mind to wander over the consequences if the entire band were locked up in the cells! Not that they would all fit in, he supposed. He thought of the gunroom piano secured in the centre of the quarterdeck for leaving harbour, 'Hearts of Oak' banging out with the blank B natural clicking down silently.

> Come cheer up me lads, 'tis 'click' glory we steer,
> To add something more 'click' this glorious year –

The bandsmen's strike proved only the beginning. Willy had scarcely tumbled down to the flat after divisions for inspecting scrubbed coaling gear than he heard that the stokers had boycotted the assembly – as indeed he had noticed himself, but he hadn't realized it was a boycott. Wilkins's absence from the gunroom when they gathered for dinner confirmed that something was up in the engine room department, and presently the Bull's doggie, Hesketh, appeared with the full story. He had been sent down to find out why there were no stokers on deck, and had been told by the senior engineer they were still trimming the bunkers and cleaning up the engine rooms and stokeholes. On hearing this, the Bull had stopped Hesketh's leave for fourteen days. He had then interviewed the Chief himself; as a result the stokers were to be fallen in on the quarterdeck at seven bells in clean night clothing. The Master at Arms and his minions had been ordered to attend; the Marine detachment had been alerted.

Hesketh hurriedly swallowed his soup and the first course and left again to attend his master on the quarterdeck, leaving the table alight from end to end with excited chatter. Pritchett, the acknowledged authority on King's Regulations and Admiralty Instructions, held forth on the possibilities if the stokers remained solid, turning their action into mutiny. He gave lurid examples from the outbreak of the mutiny at the Nore in 1897, stirring Ginger to bang on the table for silence and warn them all of their duty to defend the half deck if the stokers tried to rush the arms racks. In the thoughtful hush that followed, Forbes-Jones said that so far as he was concerned, he was with the stokers; he hoped they'd teach the Bull a lesson.

There was dead silence.

'Are you querying an order?' Ginger asked, dangerously quietly.

Forbes-Jones took a moment to choose his words. 'I'm saying that since the Bull joined, the atmosphere in this ship has become poisonous. It's not as though efficiency has gone up either. Look at the coaling!'

'Hundred and sixty-five point three,' Pritchett came in promptly.

'We're not going to win any cups for that!'

Ginger's curiously pale eyes were fixed on Forbes-Jones. 'Remarks intended to subvert discipline and morale,' he said quietly and looked round the table. 'You heard it. What is the punishment, gentlemen?'

He was expecting the usual chorus of 'Six with the cane!' Instead there was silence; they cast uneasy glances at one another.

Ginger turned to Pritchett. 'A.P.?'

The assistant purser looked up innocently.

'Punishment?'

'I'd say Forbes was calling attention to something we all know –'

He came to a faltering halt as Ross jerked forward, almost lifting his thick-set body from the seat and, eyes bulging, loosed a string of obscenities at him. Stopping suddenly, he banged his fist down on the table, shouting *Breadcrumbs!*

Willy clapped his hands over his ears, so missing the rest of the barrage which seemed to be divided equally between Pritchett and Forbes-Jones, both of whom paled as they stood the onslaught.

As it ended, he saw Ross turn his gaze on him, and cautiously removed his hands from his ears.

'Steel, you were last! Get up on deck and see what's happening. Report *pronto* on the first sign of indiscipline or breaking ranks,' and turning to the table at large, 'Gentlemen, hold yourselves in readiness – *Mac-bloody-Queen* take your fingers out of your ear'oles –'

346

Willy left the table as Ross called on them to be prepared to arm themselves, and went out and up the ladder to the half deck, which seemed remarkably normal and quiet after the row below. The Marine orderly was impassive against the sparkling white panelling of the Old Man's bulkhead; no one else appeared to be about. He wondered if the band was still 'on strike'; he'd heard the word used ashore, but had never thought to come across it in the Service. Climbing the ladder to the upper deck, he shivered. It had stopped raining, but the wind was keen; the sky was almost black with a faint lightening over the mass of Portland; nearer, the water rippled with a sheen of lights reflected from the other ships of the fleet.

He stepped across to the rail by the 9.2 inch turret and looked aft past the great bulk of the after twelve inch turret to the expanse of the quarterdeck glaring under electric light. The Marines with fixed bayonets were drawn up aft of the turret, shielding any sight of the Bull, who he imagined must be sitting at the defaulters' table surrounded by his acolytes; he could just make out the great figure of the Master at Arms, and he heard him barking at someone for not standing straight. The stokers themselves seemed to be divided into two groups, one on each side of the deck. He couldn't see much of the group on the far side because of the turret and the ranks of Marines, but as he watched, he realized that the starboard rank men were being called out one by one to the Bull's table, charged with not obeying the order 'Hands to divisions with coaling suits for inspection', then sent across to fall in again on the other side. He couldn't see any bandsmen; perhaps the earlier strike had not been brought to the Bull's attention.

Now and again a man raised his voice or swore after he was charged, and was promptly seized and marched forward by the corporals along the other side of the deck on the way to the cells. Most seemed too cold and dispirited to raise objections. He began to get bored.

He wondered what would happen to Forbes-Jones and Pritchett. It had been plucky of Forbes to speak out like that; what he had said was absolutely true. There was no cheer anywhere in the ship. The hands worked carelessly with

347

morose expressions unless directly under the eye of an officer, when their faces closed up as sharply as they snapped into more attentive attitudes. And the atmosphere in the gun-room, which had never been pleasant, had deteriorated; the line marking out the seniors from the others had sharpened, and since the Bull's arrival the warts as the lowest form of life, were being ground under the weight of resentment building throughout the ship. Now it had exploded. He wondered what would happen. Everything seemed calm at present – no sign of the massed rush Ginger seemed to be hoping for. He didn't think he'd ever met anyone as stupid as Ross; it accounted, probably, for his behaviour; it was the only way he could prove who was master. He had never heard him say anything clever or even knowledgeable outside Service matters.

He heard voices, and looking round, saw some of the others arriving on deck; they came across and asked him what was happening, and as it was the recognized smoking area a few lighted up pipes. Some wardroom officers came up shortly afterwards and strolled across; none stayed long; the wind was too sharp. He was soon alone again except for McQueen who came up with the great coat he'd asked him to fetch. He did not stay long either.

He wedged himself down on his haunches between the 9.2 inch turret and the rail, folding his arms tightly across his chest, and watched the slow process as one man at a time walked from the ranks towards the defaulters' table. Soon his eyelids began to droop. He forced them open, but they kept on closing again, and he found himself falling to the side asleep. He rose and walked about, shaking his head and slapping himself, then ran on the spot for a few minutes before he went back to his former position out of the wind.

The next thing he knew someone was pulling on his arm. He jerked free, wondering what he was doing sitting on deck at night. He must be on watch. The quarterdeck before him was bright with light, and the detachment was drawn up. He remembered the stokers –

'Mr Steel, sir –' It was his servant's voice. 'Mr 'Arper's done finished, sir. 'E sent up this for you.'

348

Willy stood shakily and took the twist of paper the man was holding out – of course – his quota of corps.

'Thank you, Brown – thank you very much.'

'Goo' night, sir.'

'Good night, Brown. What's the time?'

'Baht ten minutes afore pipe down, sir.'

At the thought of reporting, Willy realized suddenly he could not give the cockroaches to Ginger; it was so obvious he couldn't have collected them up here on deck – and there had been no time during coaling. Even Ross would be suspicious – more than suspicious. He felt his insides turn over and his knees go weak as he was forced to the conclusion that, to protect his secret, he must sacrifice himself tonight.

'Brown –'

The man looked back.

'Go down to my chest, Brown – it's not locked. My hand towel's in the tray – I think it's there. Bring it up would you.'

The man gazed at him for a moment before acknowledging and continuing towards the ladder down.

Willy looked back at the quarterdeck, hardly registering what he saw; he was aware only of Ginger's broad, stupid face and his colourless eyes gazing into his with that horrible expression of anticipation.

'No corps tonight, Steel! *No* corps tonight! You haven't done your duty, have you!'

The thinking about it beforehand was always the worst. When it was over and you hadn't given the brute the satisfaction of a squeak there was, through the agonizing pain, a sense of achievement. It was the waiting and the thinking that was the real torture. He tried to concentrate on what was happening on the lighted deck before him, but couldn't shake the gunroom images from his mind. His legs felt so weak he had to hold the rail to support himself. He must not let Ginger see he was scared. His lower lip hurt; he had bitten it. He tried to steady his cheek muscles. He could see the scratched initials in the surface of the table, and hear the sub's voice, 'Slave of the stick!'

And the footsteps moving towards the cane locker in the silence that always descended on the room.

In ten minutes it would be over; he would be in his

hammock; tomorrow night at this time he would have forgotten it; in a year's time he would be in another ship, in a hundred years he would be dead. No one would know or care –

By the time his servant returned with the hand towel he had composed himself.

'Thank you, Brown.'

The man looked at him. 'It needs a good wash an' all, sir.'

'I'll let you have it tomorrow.'

'Goo' night, sir.'

'Good night, Brown.'

He unbuttoned his coat, then his trousers, and pulling his shirt out, started pushing the hand towel down his trousers at the back, smoothing it and bringing the ends forward around his thighs, pulling and patting out the creases. It took a long time before he was satisfied. Then he tucked his shirt over his drawers and pulled it right down over his seat and smoothed that out too before drawing the fly of his trousers together and buttoning it up. He felt down the sides to check, pressing them in, and passed a hand over his seat.

How it came back to him from nearly half a century, that lonely descent through the brightly lit decks to the flat. He could hear the sounds from inside the gunroom as he pushed through the curtain. The only face he could distinguish properly through the waste of years was Ginger's – Ginger balked of his Mutiny. Ginger had known he would not have his quota of corps.

In the unending struggle between fear and the idea greater than fear he could find no rest – no moment's peace. He saw danger multiplied as a child sees its face in some distorting mirror, but he saw too through the same mirror the idea greater than fear till it came to be his religion.

'Sticking it out' had been all there was, all that he could remember at all events – that and his concern for Halliday. He wondered if he could have carried on without the assistant clerk to support. Strange, he could scarcely recall his features. He remembered the scrap, he could never forget that. Halliday had been on scuttle duty, closing the scuttle over

350

the port and putting on a clamp each time the ship rolled that side down, opening it for ventilation as she rolled back. He had become tired or an unexpected sea had caught him out; the water had sluiced in green over the settee and the table spread with books and journals, wetting several of those sitting there working, as well as Halliday himself. He would never forget the look in the lad's eyes as, oblivious to the howls of protest rising about him and even of the possibility of the next sea coming in the still open port, he stared at Ross, stiff with terror.

The sound of them all baying at the petrified boy and the exultant light in Ross's eye had been too much. Something had given way inside him; he had almost felt it break. He had shouted at them to leave Halliday alone. It had not been courage, he was sure, but sheer desperation; he was certain he had not known what he was doing. There had been complete silence, then Forbes-Jones had backed him up, and at the same time one of the seniors, incensed at being yelled at by a wart, had grabbed him around the neck. Without thinking, he had lashed out.

He remembered rolling about under the table exchanging blows with someone while sea water surged down intermittently from the open port; afterwards he remembered the fresh smell of the sheets in his cot in the sick bay, but not much else! What a scrap! The gunroom had never been the same afterwards. It had lanced the boil, and Ross, stupid as he was, had recognized it. Soon afterwards he had gone.

Ross had not left him alone; he had returned in nightmares; he still did so on occasions, and the footsteps of the 'slave of the stick' pacing to the cane locker, and the dents and initials carved in the mahogany top of the gunroom table so close to his eyes. He could see them still. He would always see them.

He was reminded of Andy back from France on the one or was it two days their leaves had coincided? Shouting in the night. Andy had told them little of what it was really like in the trenches; that had to be inferred from his manner and one or two of his war poems and that unnerving yelling from his room in the silence of the night. A man screaming on his own was the most fearful of sounds. What hells human beings

351

contrived to create, and other men were swallowed up in them – all other men, becoming a part of them themselves until the devils were exorcized. Then, if they were lucky, they changed back again to ordinary men.

He had never served again with any member of that first gunroom mess, but he was certain that if he had, with the exception of Ginger Ross, he would have found them eminently decent, harmless good fellows; they would greet one another when they met like long-lost brothers. How frighteningly paper-thin the defences of civilization were. Each man was born a savage.

19

Henrietta started thinking about Willy as she was coming downstairs; it was odd; there was no apparent reason for it. Going to bed the night before, her mind had been filled with Robin's return, and she had known immediately she woke, or perhaps before she was fully awake in the languorous half-world between dream and bright morning, that Robin was back and going to call. Then, starting downstairs, she began to think of Willy.

As she entered the dining-room, Alice looked up from a letter she was reading and smiled.

'Today's the big day!'

She couldn't prevent what must have seemed at that time of morning an indecently wide smile in response.

There was a single envelope by her place; she knew before really studying the handwriting that it was from Willy.

'Berehaven,' Alice said.

She went across and picked it up; it was the same size as the envelopes Willy always used, but so thick it was almost bursting.

'Willy!' she said. 'He's *always* at Bantry Bay.'

Something disagreeable seemed to communicate itself to her as she felt the weight of the envelope; perhaps it was because she knew how he hated the monotonous cruising in home waters, Bantry Bay especially, where they spent so much time firing the guns.

'He seems to have plenty to say.' Alice looked down at her own letter again.

She replaced the envelope on the cloth and went to help herself to a single rasher of bacon and an egg, and it was not until she had finished eating that she turned to the envelope again and opened it; it was extraordinary the feeling of reluctance she had.

There were two large sheets inside, folded several times; one was in thick cartridge paper – accounting for the bulkiness – the other was from an official book of some kind as it had H.M.S. in thick black letters followed by dots along which Willy had filled in the name of his ship. On the right was the word 'At' in equally bold letters, and he had filled in 'Bantry Bay'. It seemed to be a log book of some sort, for he had entered dates inside a column down the left hand side, following them with comments on the main page which was ruled with faint blue lines.

> Tuesday, April 4th At 0600 we weighed and steamed to the calibrating buoys, and the picket boat landed the navigator and his party on Observation Island. At 09.30 we commenced firing on the range buoys with 12″ and afterwards with the 9.2″ port turrets, and then with the port battery 6″. After lunch, we turned the ship between the buoys . . .

She scanned down the page, trying to find some clue as to why on earth he had sent it to her; probably he meant her to keep it, but there did not seem to be anything to say so. She put it down and started unfolding the cartridge paper, wondering if there was a letter inside. There wasn't – only a picture, rather a lovely one in ink and wash on the paper itself. It showed a rocky stretch of shore with cormorants – or were they shags? – ranged in different attitudes along the rocks, some holding their wings open in the heraldic way they had, some sideways on showing their angular necks and sharp beaks and a curious quiff rising from the back of the head – the 'shag' of course, they must be shags. Some were in the sea in front of the rocks, one had just caught a huge, flailing fish. It was an extraordinarily vivid picture; the birds looked so natural and at the same time so different in subtle ways they might have had individual personalities. Below the wash colour of the sea he had signed his name, 'W.L.S.Steel'.

She passed it across to Alice.

'Why –!' Alice's brows rose in admiration. 'It's lovely! What a shame he had to fold it. He seems to have a talent.'

'He's always been good at drawing animals and birds. But I can't think why he's sent it. There's no letter – simply nothing – just *this*!' She picked up the log book sheet, 'I can't make head or tail of it!' She started reading at random. 'We put a hole in the galley due to the topping lift of the screen derrick not being backed up sufficiently. The derrick therefore lowered the galley on to an awning stanchion – etcetera – etcetera –' She scanned down the page, 'We fired cannon tubes from both batteries at towed targets. The Commander, not being satisfied with the practice, exercised "Out Torpedo Nets" at evening quarters and ordered the picket boat and launch away to sweep with searchlights –!'

Alice held her hand out and she passed the sheet across.

She read in silence, then turned the page; after a moment she said, 'This sounds more interesting. Have you read this? "At 08.30 two great skuas appeared in the direction of Hungry Hill –' She looked up.

Henrietta shook her head. She continued to read.

'– harrying the gulls there. I wonder if they are breeding; they are probably on passage. Soon afterwards over 150 auks flew across the Bay in a north-westerly direction in straggly lines. It was a magnificent sight. Soon afterwards it rained. When the rain finished I saw the two terns I had observed yesterday fishing quite close off our starboard quarter; I think they were arctic terns. The skuas had gone. I was sorry as they were wonderful to watch through the glasses. They go at such a terrific speed, and their swoops are thrilling to watch. I never saw them fail once when they were after a gull. Eventually the poor gull had to drop whatever he had and the skua swooped down and claimed it –' She stopped reading to look quickly down the page '– and – so – on –' and looking up again, 'A distinct improvement on the first side!'

'But why? Why ever d'you suppose he sent them?' She felt

355

the unease she had experienced when handling the envelope first; it was stronger now.

'There's no letter at all?'

'Absolutely nothing.'

Alice Davies handed her back the picture and log book sheet. 'You had better show them to young Lochinvar! Perhaps he will be able to suggest something!'

Henrietta laughed, but out of politeness. She felt sure something was wrong. Willy's letters had been strange lately. There was nothing definite she had been able to pick out; it was the feeling he was holding back, not telling her things he wanted to tell her. They were not *Willy*, but dry husks of not very interesting information, and they came so frequently. She *would* show Robin this latest example. The more she thought about it, the more bizarre it seemed.

'Your tea'll get cold.'

She smiled and picked up her cup, shaking her head. 'It's queer –' She took some gulps of the tea which was rather disgustingly lukewarm, 'I knew – well, I was thinking of Willy as I came down this morning. And then –' She nodded at the open pages.

'It is funny when things like that happen.'

'Do they happen to you?'

'Not exactly that. But with the telephone – it's happened with the telephone. I've known who it's going to be as soon as I've heard the bell. Sure enough – it is.'

'It's so strange. It's as if we have senses we don't use – don't even know we have them until something like this happens. When it happens to you with the telephone, is it something bad? Usually?'

Alice Davies laughed. 'No – not so far as I remember. No, I simply know who it is that's calling.' She seemed to ponder, and a smile appeared fleetingly on her lips, 'And I think it only happens with *certain* people.'

Henrietta looked at her, wondering what the little smile signified, then she gathered up the envelope and two sheets of paper and rose, nodding towards her cup. 'I'm afraid it is cold.'

'I shall be extremely cross if you don't let me see Mr

356

Temple-Vane-West when he calls – for a moment at least. I shall not detain you!'

'He'll want to see you in any case.'

'Fiddlesticks! There's only one person Mr West is at all anxious to see, and as my great uncle Jack used to say, she is not a thousand miles from where you are standing now! What time are you expecting him?'

'He said as early as he could possibly get here!'

'Well – I have the feeling he generally means what he says. I think I had better do something with my face!' She rose and walked with Henrietta to the door. 'I read an interesting article about complexion yesterday. Apparently we should all walk in the rain as often as we can. It doesn't at all look as if we shall have rain today.'

It was the most perfect morning. The birds outside her window were cheeping busily as they went about their important parental duties, the fresh green in the gardens was bright with sunlight, laced with shadow, the branches of the trees, garlanded with tips of early blossom, swayed to the breeze, and above, small, puffy white clouds moved across a clear blue sky. She should have been in heaven; it was the day she had been waiting for so long. She couldn't shake off her anxiety about Willy. She had wondered if something like this – whatever it was – might happen. He could be so hurt; he was as sensitive as he had always been, but he had learned to hide it now under a guise of tolerant cynicism; he had become an amusing yarn-spinner too – like Papa had been. She had wondered if, perhaps, his extreme sensitivity came from Papa as well, if Papa too had learned to cover up with all those stories, but she had decided that Papa had never been really sensitive; certainly his behaviour nowadays was absolutely the reverse.

She put on her new grey wool coat with its lovely deep velvet cuffs and collar, then the beehive hat with a plume of ostrich feathers she had bought to go with the coat, and turned before the mirror to raise her spirits, but she only felt she was being selfish – thinking of herself while Willy was in despair in Bantry Bay – for what other reason could there be for this latest extraordinary letter after all the others?

She so wanted to see Robin again; she was so worried

about Willy. The concerns fused together; directly he came, she would ask him to look at the letter. She took off her hat and, sitting down at her dressing table, picked up the log book page again to read it more carefully; there might be something they had both missed.

She heard the front door bell; her heart seemed to miss a beat. Ages later, she heard his voice; she was sure it was his voice. She folded the log book page, then the picture that had come with it and pushed them both back into the envelope as she heard Sadie's footsteps on the stairs. There was a knock on her door, and she turned, calling to her to come in.

'It's Mr West, Miss,' Sadie's cheeks were flushed, and her eyes bright. Robin had worked his usual spell, really she ought to be more worried. 'I've shown him into the drawing-room, Miss –'

'Thank you, Sadie. Would you let Mrs Davies know please. And tell him I shall be down directly.'

'Yes, Miss.' It was evident Sadie looked forward to seeing him again.

She would allow Alice to get down first, then go. She had an image of the Countess of Lynne on that first occasion she had met her, the momentary pause she had made in the doorway, the gracious smile as she swept in. There was no reason why she should go down as soon as he arrived; he had kept her waiting for almost a year. She pulled the log book page out of the envelope again and tried to read.

The words made even less sense than they had when she had first looked at them. She heard Alice's door, and her footsteps across the landing and down the stairs. She would give her about five minutes. She reached out for the hat and put it on again and studied the effect from different angles. Probably it didn't suit her quite as well as the wide saucers she had been wearing the last time she saw him, but it was high fashion – and extremely spring-like. The thin purple tie at her throat matched the dyed ostrich feathers beautifully.

She wondered what he would say; he had the knack of saying the right thing. She thought of George's earnest attempts to tell her that he had taken other girls out in his motor car, and smiled. Dear George! What an innocent he was still; he would remain one too. He was so bound up with the Navy, he would never open his eyes to anything much outside.

It was obvious that Robin was no bashful novice, yet he could not have been more profoundly gentlemanly with her; she had only to say she didn't like motor cars because they always reminded her of the loss of poor Bacchante and Endymion, and he had hired a dog cart for the next day. And he had never made the slightest attempts at 'poodlefaking' as George called it. When he kissed her before he went away on the last occasion, it had been almost reverential. Very strange from such a sardonic character.

He was entirely different from the literary and intellectual men in the Davies's circle, who were all talk and no morals. He had confessed that his reading consisted of the *Gunnery Manual* and the *Sporting and Dramatic* for light relief, yet he had such a store of sound common sense most of *them* seemed to lack entirely, and a strict code of honour. H.G.Wells, the old ram, had promised to show her the gates of paradise. She couldn't imagine Robin proposing such a thing, or if he did it would arise naturally and honestly and seem right. Mary had said it wasn't much fun in any case; she supposed men enjoyed it, but she had been glad when she found that she was going to have a baby and had been able to keep herself to herself at nights. Extraordinary to think of Mary as a mother – *herself* as a godmother! Little Katherine was very sweet –

It must be at least five minutes by now, probably more, she had no idea. Picking up Willy's envelope and the sheet from the log book she rose and went out.

He was sitting on the settee pretending he was talking to Alice with great animation when she opened the drawing-room door, but he must have heard her coming; he looked round quickly and eagerly, and stood in a fluent movement as she paused for a second, then swept in, smiling.

He was very tanned, much browner than he had been; his eyes showed he was impressed by her outfit.

'Henry!' He seemed unusually lost for words for a moment. 'You look absolutely stunning!'

'Thank you,' she smiled.

'Not *quite* battleship grey!' Alice said in a teasing way.

He turned. 'It's rather like the colour we use in the Med though!'

She moved across to sit at the other end of the settee. 'I am positively not on the Admiralty List!'

'I'm so glad.' He sat down gazing at her. 'I should like a break for a few days!' and he laughed the pleasant, unforced laugh which brought back their last time together.

There was so much she wanted to say and ask him about, but she couldn't think where to start. She said how well he was looking.

'*And* you have brought the sun with you!' Alice said.

'Oh to be in England!' he replied, 'You've simply no idea how beautiful the country is looking to the exile. All the way up in the train I couldn't take my eyes off it. I felt like pushing open the door and just stepping out –' he waved his hand, 'rolling down the embankment and lying, looking up at the catkins and blossom.' He looked at Henrietta. 'D'you ever feel like that?'

'I've felt like running through woods as we go past – they look so much more exciting when you're travelling past, looking out at them –' When younger, going down to stay with Grandpapa, she had imagined playing hide and seek with a young man through the trees and grassy banks seen through the train window.

'Righto!' Robin slapped his thigh. 'We'll take a train. The first wood you'd like to run around in you must tell me. I shall pull the cord and we'll *jump*. Before the guard arrives!'

They laughed.

'I hope you can come and stay with my people,' he went on more seriously. 'I've wired them. They're expecting you.'

She turned to Alice.

'Of course you must go,' she said, 'Yes, you must,' and smiling at Robin, 'I dare say we shall manage somehow!'

'Done!' he said. 'Capital!'

'You'd better ring for Sadie to help you pack.'

Rising and going to the bell pull, Henrietta remembered she was still clutching Willy's envelope. She wondered suddenly whether she ought to show it to him. Probably it was meant for her alone. The Navy was so strange. But who else was there she could possibly ask? She must know. She held it out to him.

'I got this this morning. It's from my brother – Willy. It seems to be a page from a log book.'

He took it, a questioning look in his eyes.

'There was no letter with it, you see.'

They watched as he took the two sheets out and studied them.

He held the log book page up. 'Is this his writing?'

She nodded.

'In that case it's from his midshipman's journal. Snotties have to keep a journal.' He passed his finger down the edge. 'It's been cut out. Very neatly.'

'Why should he send it to me?'

'Why should he cut it out?' He leaned towards her, holding the sheet out and pointing to scrawled initials halfway down the page. 'That's the snotties' nurse –' He smiled at her expression, 'the officer responsible for their education and general well-being.'

'Do they often write about birds?' Alice asked.

He turned to her.

'In their journals?'

'Not generally.' He smiled. 'Why?'

'Look at the other side.'

He turned the page over and started reading. Henrietta watched his expression sharpen.

Sadie came in, and she told her she needed to pack some things for a few days; she would be up shortly.

Robin read to the end of the page, turned back and read through the first side again, his forehead creased in concentration. Finally, he looked up.

'I don't like it.' His voice was very quiet and even.

Her heart sank.

He indicated the cartridge paper. 'There was *nothing* else?'

She shook her head.

He sat back, staring towards the ceiling, waving the two sheets idly in his hands. 'What sort of a young feller is your brother?'

She thought for a moment. 'He's not at all like George.

361

He's much more – he *feels* things more. He thinks about things. He's not so – he doesn't care so much about doing well. I suppose really he likes going his own way –' It was difficult to explain what she felt about Willy, the essential unchanged Willy beneath the uniform and recently acquired pose of cynic.

'May I use your telephone?' He had turned to Alice.

She looked slightly surprised. 'Why, yes. Of course!'

Henrietta wondered who on earth he was thinking of calling. 'I'll show you,' she said, and led him out to the study she used as an office.

He gave her a reassuring smile. 'We'll soon have this sorted out.'

She left him, and went up to her room to find the things she needed to take away. She should have been so happy; she couldn't keep her mind from Willy, though, and the frown on Robin's face as he studied the page from his journal.

He jumped up when she returned to the drawing-room.

'The Atlantic Fleet's coming in to Portland to coal before the spring manoeuvres. If you travel down to Weymouth this afternoon you'll be on the spot to see young William on the morrow!'

She stopped in surprise.

He came towards her, both hands out to take hers. 'I think you should go. I'll gladly come with you if you'd like me to.'

She looked round at Alice, who nodded.

'Have you –?' she asked, 'Is there something you've found out?'

He shook his head, squeezing her fingers in his. 'Absolutely nothing. There may be nothing to find out. He may simply have slipped the wrong sheets into the envelope.'

'You don't think so, do you?'

'No.' Letting go of her right hand, he led her to the settee. 'We've been talking it over. The ornithological observations – they could have been a momentary impulse –' he smiled, 'made mad with too much gunnery! It's the fact that he cut the page out and *sent it to you*. With no explanation. That's the extraordinary thing.'

362

'He must want you to know something,' Alice said.

'Without actually telling you,' he added.

She looked from one to the other, wondering what they had said while she was out.

He handed her a scrap of paper with figures scribbled on it. 'Those are the trains to Weymouth. As I said –' he left the sentence unfinished.

'I think it would be best if Robin went with you,' Alice said. 'In case you run up against any difficulties. Robin will know the ropes.'

'Robin'! Henrietta thought.

'The snotties' nurse is an old ship,' he said. 'I checked up on the initials. John Medhurst. I can vouch for him. The trouble isn't there – if there is any trouble, of course.' He shrugged, 'We may be making a mountain out of some silly little molehill.'

The word 'molehill' took Henrietta back to that night Willy had insisted on springing the mole-catcher's traps. She wondered if he had done something like that again. She could imagine he might. He wouldn't get away with that kind of thing in the Navy.

'You want to go home,' she said.

He smiled at her. 'I'd far rather be where you're going!'

She looked down, embarrassed by his directness.

'I'd very much like you to come.' Her heart gave a sort of flutter as she realized the implications of what she had said, and she felt the blood rising to her cheeks.

He evidently realized what she was thinking, for he said at once, 'I'll go and book two rooms at the Royal Palm Court.' He turned to Alice Davies, 'If I may use the bush telegraph?'

'Of course!'

'I won't be a moment.'

'Don't worry,' Alice Davies said, smiling at Henrietta's expression after he had left the room. 'He's quite indecently good-looking, but I'm sure I don't need to chaperon you. You will be quite safe with Robin. I have some experience of these things.'

'What does he really think?'

'I don't know. Are you all packed? What train shall you

be catching? You'll need some money –' She rose. 'I'll see what we have.'

There was a knock on the door. She wondered if it was Robin.

A page boy entered with a small silver tray.

'A telegram for you, Miss.' He brought it across and waited while she opened it.

SHORE LEAVE STOPPED STOP THANKS COMING STOP LOVE WILLY

'No reply,' she said dully, not even thinking of finding a tip until some time after the door had closed behind the boy.

Then she stood, trying to remember the number of Robin's room. But she couldn't just go in. She crossed to the writing table and taking a sheet of hotel paper, wrote, 'What can we do now?', folded it and popped it with the telegram form into an envelope. After addressing it, she took it to the reception desk, this time remembering a tip. She went and sat in a wicker chair and waited, thinking of Willy.

'They've really got it in for him,' Robin said as he came up. His face was sterner than she had seen it. But he smiled at her anxious expression. 'Of *course* there's something we can do. I intend to do it! Right away, Miss Steel!' He thought for a moment. 'It's probably best if you stay here.'

'I'd much rather come.'

He grinned, taking her hand. '*I'd* much rather you came!'

It seemed amusing, and they laughed.

She hurried up to her room for her coat and boots and scarf. An elderly lady in the corridor smiled at her sweetly, looking as if she might have said something if she had not been moving so quickly. Returning the smile, Henrietta wondered if, perhaps, she thought Robin and she were married; she remembered seeing her glancing across at them from her little table the previous night at dinner. She had thought then she looked rather nice, and lonely.

'Normally I'd walk,' Robin said when she came back.

'I *always* walk!'

He laughed, looking at her hat. 'Secured for sea? There's half a gale blowing out there.'

'I've taken every seamanlike precaution,' she replied in one of his stock phrases.

He laughed heartily, pulling her arm into his and leading towards the entrance. The commissionaire stepped forward to see if they needed a cab.

'She likes to walk,' Robin said with a humorous lift to his brows.

The man grinned, tipping his fingers to the peak of his cap. How extraordinarily nice everyone was being! If only they would allow Willy ashore, how perfect everything would be. There couldn't be anything much more perfect – except being actually married as most of these people surely thought they were. She wondered what Mama would say if she could see her! She found it difficult enough to believe herself.

Outside, the wind struck and Robin clutched at his hat. She was glad of her gloves and scarf; there was a distinct chill despite the sun. It didn't look as if the sun would last much longer either; banking white clouds towered over the grim rock of Portland. In the harbour below she could see the masts and funnels of many more warships than had been there yesterday.

'The fleet's in!' He waved his arm out cheerily. 'They must have come in while we were dining last night.'

She thought of Willy on the bridge of one of those ships in the darkness while they were sitting with a bottle of the most perfect claret and the musicians playing Strauss and Offenbach. The sense of unreality came over her again as she remembered how she would gladly have had Robin lead her through those gates of Paradise afterwards. He had not even hinted at anything of the kind. Alice Davies had been absolutely right. He had led her around a palm at the foot of the grand staircase, making sure no one would see and kissed her gently, 'Night, my heart. And *don't* worry. We shall assuredly sort it out tomorrow!' then watched her up the stairs. Afterwards she looked down and saw him turn towards the lounge, she supposed for a brandy. How she had wished he was still with her, wished and trembled at her feelings. How strange it seemed now in the chill wind of morning –

'Penny –?' he asked.

She smiled. 'Actually, I was thinking of H.G.Wells.'

'The literary fellow – airships and all that –?'

'That's right.' She wanted to tell him about Wells asking her out to dinner and more than hinting at the delights to come if she accepted. Instead, she said, 'He used to come to the Davieses' quite often. I don't know why I thought of him just then.'

'I shall have to mug up on the literature if I'm to keep up!'

'Don't! I hate them!'

He laughed.

'They talk so much. Afterwards you realize it's simply hot air, they haven't said anything that anyone couldn't think for themselves quite easily –'

'Anyone! You may be selling them short. Not *anyone* has your marvellous imagination!'

She cast him a sideways look. '*Where* are you taking me?'

He laughed, putting his arm around her waist, 'At larrst I 'ave thee in my pow-wer!'

'Sir Jasper! My father does not know you –'

'Ah-ha-ha-harrh!' He squeezed her to his side, then changing character in mid-dastardly gloat, 'Unhand her, you brute!' and swinging his arm and releasing her, 'Take that! And that!' His hat blew off, and he ran back, chasing it across the grass for a long way before he caught it.

She laughed as she hadn't for ages, feeling a pain below her ribs as he came up again, breathing heavily with the hat jammed firmly down over his brow.

He took her arm again. 'Us'm goin' down to that therr shore therr –' he nodded to their left, 'to git out of this yearr infernal wind. Then us'll walk along a Bincleaves – that be wherr boats do fetch in from ships, ma'am – an' by my worrd as a gen'leman us'll find one as'll take a message to Mr Medhurst, if it please y'r ladyship.'

'It pleases me.'

'Capital!' He reverted to his correct self and held a hand out to help her down over rocky projections towards the beach.

It was certainly less blowy when they got down. The sea was smooth close in to the lee of the land, lifted by sizeable rollers sweeping in and breaking; further out, the colour of the water darkened amid moving whitecaps. A fishing boat was taking spray overall; beyond her, almost on the horizon, the square sails of a large five-master shone in the sun.

He put his hand in hers, looking at her without a word; she sensed they were truly close, and knew it was a moment she would never forget. Almost immediately her cursed sense of time passing took over, and as she looked again towards the breakwater of Portland Harbour and the massed yards and signal flags and grey funnels and bridges, she had a premonition there would not be many such moments. The Navy would claim him. She squeezed his hand. He responded, smiling at her.

'I'm the luckiest man alive.'

'I'm so happy.'

His expression changed as if he had had the same feeling that had gripped her a moment before, and he almost groaned, 'If only –'

'If only?' she prompted.

'If only – I were a *normal* man.'

He said it with such intensity she couldn't smile.

'If only –' he was looking down, digging his heels into the sand as he walked as if releasing violent impulses. 'I must not condemn you to be a sailor's wife.'

She tried to lighten his mood. 'There are worse sentences, I imagine!'

'None longer.' He shook his head. 'None longer.'

She walked beside him silently.

After a moment he looked at her and smiled, and swung her hand in his. 'My life was so infernally easy before you arrived. I should never have driven your brother up to town!'

'*Was* it!' she teased.

'I suppose he told you about the – my motoring companions!' He grinned. 'They meant nothing.'

'Is that what they thought?'

'Good Lord!' He swung her arm more violently. 'It was *different* –'

'I'm sorry.'

367

He looked down at her again. 'I shall have to be careful what I do when your brother's around!'

'He's just – rather protective.'

'I know. Good for him! So would I be. And you're rather protective towards Willy.'

She thought for a moment. 'I suppose so. I've never thought –' She stopped herself; she had been going to say she had never thought he was exactly cut out for the Navy, but she knew she must never say that to another officer, not even Robin.

'Yes –?'

'No – I never thought I'd be dragging you down here like this.'

'Not what you were going to say! You're loyal you Steels, I'm hanged if you're not!'

She smiled, thinking of them all, George and Willy and Andy, Harry and Babs. 'I suppose we are.'

'Good for you!'

They were nearing the breakwater, and he led up from the beach to the path again. All the battleships were clear in view now, moored in a double line inside the enclosing moles, slimmer cruisers further in and a knot of destroyers of low and menacing aspect, pouring smoke from their multiple funnels as if they were about to go out or had just come in. Small boats were everywhere alongside the big ships, under sail between the ships and the breakwater, picket boats with shiny brass funnels amongst them, one speeding under an admiral's flag with statuesque crew.

'Let's hope she's not coaling,' Robin said, screwing his eyes to try and make out which ships had colliers or coaling lighters alongside.

Most of the further battleships looked exactly alike to her except for differently placed white bands around their funnels. She wondered which was Willy's.

He took her by the arm and pointed to the nearest of the large ships. '*Invincible.*' She could sense his mood had changed. His voice was charged with a different kind of interest. 'Isn't she wonderful. But you must know about them all from George?'

'No, not much. I know she's a battle-cruiser, isn't she? We

368

heard a great deal about dreadnoughts and battle-cruisers last autumn – during the Naval Inquiry. The Davieses talked of scarcely anything else.'

'I can imagine whose side she was on!'

'Actually – I couldn't believe it – when it was announced Fisher was retiring, they celebrated – in champagne.'

'Poor old Jacky!'

'I said I had a headache. And went up to my room!'

'Good for you! I've felt much the same. I've been thoroughly ashamed of the goats my elders and betters made of themselves!' He laughed in a slightly embarrassed way as if even with her he felt uncomfortable about criticizing senior officers. 'Still – he's made the peerage – which is a feather in the Navy's cap! Perhaps one day the country will learn what they owe him. Look at her –' he waved a hand towards the *Invincible* again. 'I'd give my right arm to be gunnery Jack there,' and looking round at her again, 'One of his hard-boiled eggs!'

She raised her brows.

'Can't be beaten!' He laughed lightly with her. 'One of Jacky's *mots* I might say.'

'D'you think we'll stop building so fast now he's gone?' she asked. 'That's what they think – the Davieses – as though it was all his fault.'

'It makes me very angry, these wretched pacifists and Little Englanders. They've swallowed the Hun propaganda whole. The Germans *started* the competition – now they're whining because we've taken up the challenge, and accusing *us* of provoking *them*! No, we must go on, whoever's in charge, to make it absolutely clear we have no intention of sharing the trident with anyone. Hang it, we haven't challenged their *army*!' Realizing he was growing heated, he took her hand again. 'But what's a girl like you doing in a nest of pacifists?'

'I've begun to wonder myself,' she said. 'I've been thinking of training for a job – a *real* job I mean –'

'I see –' He looked down appraisingly. 'You *are* a feminist, then!'

'I agree with that part of it.'

'So, what's it to be?'

369

She felt herself bridling at his teasing tone, and released her hand. 'I don't know yet.'

He looked round quickly. 'I'm sorry. That was inexcusable. Of course – why shouldn't you – train for a real job.' Nevertheless, he evidently found it difficult to say it.

'*Exactly*! Why *not*!' She decided to relent. 'Actually – I thought of photography –' She looked up to see his response.

He checked a start of surprise. 'You'd make a splendid photographer.'

'You don't think so, do you.'

'Yes, certainly I do.'

She felt pleased at the way she had handled him. 'I should like to do portraits.'

He nodded. 'You'd be good at that.'

'Not simply the "great" – poor people as well. Have you noticed how much more interesting their faces are?'

'I can't say I have.'

'Your sailors for instance.'

'Yes, of course I have, yes, you're absolutely right! Good heavens, I could send you some marvellous sitters.'

They reached the breakwater and turned along it. A group of liberty men, talking and laughing as they swung towards them, grew quiet as they neared. She turned to Robin, making conversation to ease her slight self-consciousness at their eyes all over her.

It was a short distance to the steps down to where all the boats were coming in; several were rocking alongside one another, others waiting just off, others beating away under sail. There was an air of activity and controlled ebullience.

'Stay up here, old thing,' he said, leaving her. 'I won't be a moment.' He ran lightly down the steps.

She walked further along the breakwater so that it would not look as if she was actually *receiving* the men as they came up from the boats, and gazed out over the greeny-blue expanse of water and the scores of ships beneath the hard grey rocks and forts of Portland Bill, and thought of Willy as a tiny, unimportant part of this vast, masculine array geared for war. They said it was to preserve the peace – the *Pax Britannica* which the Germans were challenging. In their hearts they wanted war. Robin wanted war; he said so. He

370

longed to add more laurels to the legend of this mightiest service in the world. Probably he wanted to show what he was made of – prove it to himself. Looking out at all the ships and the ant-like activity aboard, she was more than ever possessed by the feeling that Willy did not belong here. She thought of him as a young boy dancing about on the path down to the beach at Thorpeness to avoid treading on *insects*. And here he was in one of those great grey conglomerations of armour and guns, learning how to sink other similar floating fortresses and kill men. He was such an *individual* among all those worker ants. Then, so was Robin –

'Henry –!'

She turned to see him striding towards her from the top of the steps.

'A stroke of luck. I've found their doc – he's going off now. Says he'll be happy to take us as his guests. He doesn't think they'll start coaling till tomorrow.' He took her hand and led her to the steps. 'Our boat's on the outside. I'm afraid we'll have to jump across a couple.' He looked a little anxious.

She cursed the tightness of her wretched skirt; if it wasn't for that she would show him a jump. She looked across at the picket boat he had indicated, the sailors holding on with boathooks and the young midshipman in charge gazing at her with some interest. It was curious how everything seemed to quieten when she approached as if they had never seen a girl before.

She pulled up her coat and skirt with one hand as they reached the sternsheets of the nearest boat and put out her other hand to an officer waiting there to help her – a little leap and she was aboard.

'Bravo!' Robin said, jumping on beside her.

She completed the transit across the next boat without difficulty and was greeted by a fresh-faced young man in tweeds with an Irish accent, who introduced himself as her host. He had been taking a man to hospital; he expanded on the medical details as he led her down to the cabin; there would be no difficulty with conversation while he was about.

Presently the engine-room bell tinkled twice and she heard

the midshipman call to the sailors to bear off; the deck and seat quivered beneath her as the propeller turned, and through the windows she saw the boat they were alongside appear to glide forward. A moment afterwards there was more tinkling, the vibration ceased momentarily, then started again and she felt the boat surging forward, heeling and bouncing into the waves which were not small even inside the harbour.

'Young Steel!' The doctor exclaimed when Robin told him she was his sister, and banged the side of his head with his hand. 'Steel! Aren't I the bright specimen! You told me so! A fine young fellow he is to be sure. Many's the chat I've had with him. We're both of us observers of the natural world d'you see, and by – Gad! He's a whale on sea birds, he can tell what they are after half a glance at five miles just by the flap of their wings. Mind you, I don't say he doesn't spread it a shade thick at times – but why not!'

'So, he's well,' Robin said, glancing at her.

'Fighting fit!' The doctor lowered his voice dramatically and leaned towards them. 'As much as any of us is. We've a new "Bloke" d'you see – a taut hand –' he glanced at Henrietta, 'taut as a Salvation Army drum. I've no doubt you'll hear about our little mutiny when you get aboard –'

'Mutiny!' Robin exclaimed.

'We're not supposed to mention it. Reporters –' He looked anxiously at Henrietta again, then back to Robin. 'But why not!' It seemed to be his stock expression. 'It's all round the fleet, and as we all know, between the fleet and Fleet Street is but a step today!'

'What was the cause?'

'The cause was – our new Commander. By the name of Turkey.'

'The Bull!'

'You're acquainted! 'Twas the engine room department only. The stokers refused duty, d'you see.'

'Refused duty! How did it end?'

'The owner was summoned aboard the flagship! What happened there no one is precisely certain. He didn't stay too long though, I can tell you that, and it was shortly after he came off the stokers' punishments were quashed – those confined in cells were released. It's on the *tapis* we'll have a new Bloke after the manoeuvres. Who knows –' He shrugged. 'If he knows, he's not giving it away!'

'Not the happiest of ships?'

The engine bell tinkled and they felt the urgent movements of the boat subsiding.

'I dare say you might say that!' The doctor grinned.

Henrietta saw through the windows a rope ladder and other ropes hanging from a boom standing out from a ship's grey steel side, and heard the wash of their own boat surging along the sides of other boats and the clink of hooks and blocks. The engine raced astern, then stopped altogether, and shortly afterwards she felt the faintest of bumps as they came alongside the platform at the foot of the gangway.

The doctor stood, steadying himself with a hand to the cabin top, and offered her his arm.

Emerging on deck and looking up she was surprised by the size of the ship, much larger than the one George had been in when she visited him at Portsmouth – perhaps it only appeared so because that one had been alongside. A boy was standing on the grating at the foot of the gangway; he handed her from the boat and watched as she started climbing the steps, sliding her gloved hand up the beautifully whitened rope rail.

A reception party of a smartly dressed lieutenant with a brass telescope beneath his arm, a young midshipman and a rather mature sailor with emblems on his sleeve saluted her at the top. The midshipman continued to gaze at her with ingenuous interest, the older sailor with less obvious but equally rapt attention, and other younger sailors standing stiffly nearby were casting glances. Beyond them the deck stretched wide and curving round the stern, shadowed by a white awning stretched overhead. The brass rails of a companionway in the centre gleamed, as did the ship's crests on the ends of two long guns extending from a huge grey turret; two rather smaller guns protruded from another turret rather further forward near the side.

This was Willy's home. How immaculate it was, complex and immaculate with little canvas hoods over the ends of pipes coming up through the deck near the side, round,

373

polished brass plates inset here and there into the scrubbed white planking delineated with sharp black seams, ropes from the davits coiled in perfect spirals – a sense of space and perfect order and, yes, artistry, and clean paint and polishy lived-in smells wafting occasionally on the sea wind which clutched at her skirt and the chiffon and ostrich plumes in her hat.

'I'll show you the way,' the doctor said.

She followed him forward a short distance to a companion and down steel-bound steps to an equally immaculate deck where the polishy, warm, lived-in smell was strong. Doorways with chintz curtains across, several blowing out gently, were spaced along white-painted panelling on both sides; at the end towards the stern the panelling stretched across the deck unbroken except for one door, beside which a marine with white belt and gleaming rifle stood silently. A polished brass bell shone above his head.

'Here we are,' the doctor smiled. 'If you'd like to come into my den – I hope it's presentable! I'll see if I can muster young Steel – and the Trader,' he looked at Robin.

An officer of Marines clattered down the ladder, glancing at them briefly with interest before striding towards the other side. Sounds of altercation came up the ladderway from the deck below.

The doctor grinned. 'May be our man!'

'The gunroom flat,' Robin explained, nodding downwards.

The doctor's den, labelled 'Surgeon', was a compact cabin with a bunk along the side beneath an open, brass-bound port with the same chintz curtains as across the doorway. There were drawers beneath the bunk and a wardrobe cupboard at its foot, all deep French-polished work. Against the bulkhead at the top was a desk with an array of photographs in ornamental frames and a table lamp with tasselled shade. There were two shelves of heavy looking books above, and beneath tucked between two columns of drawers, an upright chair. At the other end of the small space was a wash hand stand, French-polished, with a similar fitment on the bulkhead above holding a carafe of water and two plain glasses. The only other furniture was a heavy armchair covered in the ubiquitous chintz.

374

Waving her into this, the doctor left them.

She looked up at Robin. 'What did he mean by "Trader"?'

'Apparently what they call Medhurst. He's a submariner – it's known as "the Trade", the submarine branch. I dare say that's how it started. He's fearfully keen on his subs.'

'What's he doing *here*?'

'They have to do a couple of years' big ship time.' He smiled. 'They'd forget they were part of the outfit otherwise! They're an independent lot.' He pulled the desk chair round and sat, facing her. 'A bunch of pirates. I suppose they have to have something to compensate for spending their time cooped up in those beastly little sardine tins.'

'Have you been in one?'

'Yes. And I did not enjoy it. I like to know the ropes when I'm aboard. They tried to describe it all to us as they turned the wheels and opened the valves and goodness knows what, and we descended to the depths. But I was not entirely convinced. I wondered whether something might not go wrong and leave us stuck on the bottom turning quietly blue as we sucked in each other's carbon dioxide –'

'Oh, don't!'

'I prefer being on top, I must say. I admire them tremendously.'

The doctor pushed in through the curtain and looked at Henrietta. 'You're in luck. I've just seen the junior snotties breaking up from a class. I've no doubt he'll be along shortly.'

Robin looked at her. 'You'd prefer it if we left you for a few minutes. There's nowhere else you can be by yourselves.'

He looked up at the doctor.

'That's right,' he nodded. 'We'll leave you. We'll be in the wardroom.'

Robin rose, looking at his watch. 'I'll be back in about a quarter of an hour – twenty minutes,' turning to the doctor, 'if that's all right?'

'Of course! If a man can't do such a small service for a lovely lady!' He turned to Henrietta. 'We're put here to assist our fellow creatures, I say. Don't worry about a thing. You may stay here all the day if you wish. Why not!'

Robin smiled, raising his hand briefly as they left.

A minute or so later she heard footsteps approaching the door and a knock on the surround.

'Come in!' she called.

Willy poked his head around the curtain, a look of utter disbelief as he saw her. He stepped right in and stood, gazing at her, his expression changing through a sort of happy uncertainty to delight, and he shut his eyes for a moment as if wondering if she was real. There was a recently-healed gash on his brow, and she noticed there were faint shadows beneath his eyes and his cheeks were much thinner than she remembered; he seemed to have grown up suddenly; he was almost a young man, and a remarkably good-looking one with his tousled hair, well-defined eyebrows and fine, firm jawline. She felt immensely proud of him in his uniform, somewhat rumpled and in need of cleaning as it was. She rose from the chair and at the same time he stepped forward so that they collided with their arms around each other. He laughed as he clasped her, and hung on so tightly she felt as much as heard it. The laughs sawed up from his chest until, with a dreadful, sick feeling, she realized he was actually sobbing.

'Willy –!' she tried to pat his back, 'Willy – Willy – Willy –'

He couldn't stop. It was an uncontrollable torrent of emotion, shaking him as if he were a young tree.

Thinking that anyone in the next door cabin or outside must hear, she turned him and tried to ease him into the chair she had been sitting in. He collapsed into it suddenly, and leaned forward holding his head in his hands, the sobs still choking up. Gradually their intensity ebbed. Seeing the carafe of water above the wash hand-stand, she reached up for it and filled one of the glasses.

'Willy – *Willy* –'

He looked up, his eyes red, his cheeks streaked, then down again, ashamed as he tried to wipe his face with his sleeve.

'Here –' She looked round for a towel and finding one hanging by the side of the washstand, pulled it out and gave it to him.

He wiped his face and eyes, then handed it back, taking

376

the glass of water in exchange and looking at it for several seconds before drinking in deep gulps.

'I'm sorry, Henry.' He handed back the glass half-empty, and started laughing, really laughing this time. 'I just didn't expect –'

'It's all right.'

'No one told me –' he spread his arms, still laughing.

She looked at him, still shaken by the sobs, wondering whether she should ask him what had been happening and why he had sent her the page from his journal, or whether that would simply start him off again.

'Henry.' His features were more composed now, his expression serious. 'I've got something for you.' He rose. 'I'm going down to fetch it now. It's in my chest. I won't be half a minute – you will be here –?'

She nodded.

'Do I look all right?'

'Well!'

He turned to gaze in the mirror over the washstand. 'It doesn't matter.' He darted out, leaving the curtain shaking for a moment.

She drew a deep breath, realizing for the first time how her heart was going. She felt quite drained. It was even worse than she had imagined. Poor Willy. Whatever could have been happening to him? And yet the doctor had said he was fine. Had he been saying that simply to comfort her? Yet he didn't seem to be that sort of man; he had been genuinely helpful and kind; he would have told her if he had suspected. Obviously Willy was keeping whatever it was closely to himself –

He was back again quite quickly; she heard his heels as he stepped smartly to the door and pushed straight through the curtain. He had a Marmite jar in each hand, and when he was inside, he held them both out to her.

'I want you to take them off the ship. You must take them, Henry.' His expression was fierce.

'Of course – but whatever are they?' Taking them, she could see they did not contain Marmite. They were very light – as if empty.

'Cockroaches. There's one in each jar.'

377

'*Cockroaches!*'

'*Listen*, Henry. It's important. There's one in each. One is called Edward, the other's Edwina – at least I think she is, it's difficult to tell. I want you to take them home – Felpham House I mean – go up to my room and let them out –'

'*Willy*! Have you gone –' She stopped herself. There was a wild look in his eye.

'You must do it for me, Henry.'

'Why?'

'You mustn't ask why,' he was shaking his head distractedly. 'I haven't time to tell you. Will you?'

He had a pleading look now. She wanted to hug him and ask him what on earth it was all about, what had been happening. He looked like a little boy again. 'Well – if I must –'

'Yes, it's very important. And you must keep them warm until you get home, you must keep them *warm* –'

'All right, Willy, all right, I'll do it.' She was worried by his look. 'I'll wrap them in my scarf.'

He smiled, suddenly relaxed. 'Thank you, Henry. Gosh, I'm so glad you came. How did you know?'

20

The moment had arrived as she had known it would almost from the beginning of Robin's leave. Whenever you looked forward so much to something there was always this moment as it ended and you realized you had known it would come to it all along. This time it was far worse than anything she had ever experienced.

'Two years,' he had said, 'possibly a shade longer.'

It was the 'shade longer' that had really shocked her. 'Three at least,' she thought – '1911, 1912, 1913 – spring 1913 perhaps before he returns.' It was unimaginable, a yawning, unfillable gap. She had never before contemplated such a huge chunk of time as a whole. For two weeks they had been so close, ever since that first dash down to Weymouth together to see Willy; in half an hour it would simply be memory and they would be leading their separate lives, Robin heading eastward in this indecently sumptuous P & O for more weeks than she cared to think about with all these eager, unattached girls she had seen already casting predatory glances, looking at her as if she were an enemy. The voyage out would be longer than all the time they had spent together so far; his vows of constancy must crack under such temptation. He was very human.

He had been right when he said he couldn't condemn her to be a sailor's wife. She hadn't believed it then; it had not really meant much although he had been so serious about it. Now she knew exactly what he had meant – a life composed of partings and homecomings which only reminded one of the next inevitable, searing parting. How could anyone ever become used to it?

'There are worse sentences I imagine!' Her words sounded uncomprehendingly *silly* now. She saw him shaking his head in exasperation, not at her, at fate, digging his heels into the sand with every step like an angry boy.

That walk along the shore to Portland seemed so long ago, and yet so close, so full of sun and sea and excitement and portent all at once. She hadn't known then that he had been ordered to the China Station; he had known, of course, which accounted for his anguish and his moods. He hadn't told her until almost the end. And here they were aboard the *India*, and for all practical purposes it was the end; it merely remained to consummate it with a tear.

She looked for him past a group, obviously a family, entering the music room chattering, their eyes moving inquisitively around the people sitting and the lush decor. He had said he wouldn't be long. Time was going so rapidly. Soon it would have stopped for three unimaginable years.

Images of the early days of his leave tormented her, the time at Weymouth and Portland particularly because of their promise and because she had known then for certain that her feelings for him were truly reciprocated. He had been so worried about Willy, more worried than she had been herself, and she had realized almost with surprise how much he must care for her. She thought of the walk back to the hotel after they had left Willy's ship; he had been concerned to tell her all he had managed to find out from Medhurst, yet weighed his words carefully; she had had to press him.

'What d'you mean "giving him a bad time"? How?'

'A thousand ways, I'm afraid. A sub rules the gunroom much as a Captain rules the ship, only –'

'Yes?'

'There are unhappy gunrooms – just as there are unhappy ships. If you have a brute of a sub for instance, or if he takes a down on someone –'

'Why should anyone take a down on Willy?'

He had smiled briefly. 'Your brother is an independent kind of person, according to Medy – like another Steel I know! And apparently he has twice as many brains as the sub.'

'You mean the sub is jealous?'

'Your brother may have made the mistake of displaying his brains, on the other hand the sub may simply not realize what he's doing. He may think he's doing nothing other than carry on the sacred traditions of the gunroom – the Service is absolutely ruled by tradition –'

'Not to make people's lives a misery, surely! Anyway, if your friend is supposed to be their "nurse", why doesn't he do something?'

'That's not easy. In the first place – as I told you – the sub's word is law in the gunroom. Even the Captain can't go in without an invitation; in the second place it's difficult to find out exactly what is happening. No one is going to tell. Medy had his suspicions. It wasn't until he saw your brother's journal that he knew something was seriously adrift. He called him in and had a long talk. He's a rebel himself – can't stand big ships as he told young William to encourage him. He thought even more of him when he'd talked to him. At all events, he told him he must cut the offending page out of his journal – if you do it neatly enough it looks just like one of the inserts provided to stick diagrams on to – and generally encouraged him to hold on for a few more months – the commission wouldn't last for ever, and told him he could always come up to talk things over if he felt things were getting on top of him. He's a good man.'

'He sounds it.'

'There was nothing much else he could do except give the sub a general warning about over-use of the cane – although even that was risky and might easily have made things worse. As it happens, your brother seems to have taken things into his own hands. Medy doesn't know exactly what happened, but he believes it was something to do with the young assistant clerk – the sub was hazing him, he imagines, and your brother appears to have instigated a general revolt of the younger snotties against Ross and the seniors. Leading to the most fearful scrap. The youngsters came off worst of course. Three of them, including Willy, had to have some fairly serious attention in the sick bay – something our Irish host did not allude to! It taught Ross – the sub – a mighty lesson, so Medy believes. He thinks things are very much better now. Is that the impression you got?'

She hadn't really got an impression from Willy; she had been too worried she might bring on the awful sobbing again really to question him, and he had not volunteered anything, merely asked about things at home. He had looked fit enough though. If it hadn't been for his breakdown and the business of the cockroaches she would have thought he was perfectly well.

She and Robin had laughed so much about the cockroaches on that walk. She had asked him whatever she could do with them, how could she possibly introduce them secretly to Felpham House as Willy had asked!

Things were simple for Robin. 'You said you would?'

'Yes.'

'Then you have no choice.' He had looked at her for a moment. 'You Steels!' and nodding towards the Marmite jars wrapped in her scarf. 'They won't survive! If they do, it'll give the maids something to talk about!'

He had so much sound, common sense.

All the same, she had felt a traitor, letting them loose in Willy's room.

'Be fruitful and multiply,' Robin had said portentously as they knelt together on the floor, each opening one Marmite jar and shaking a reluctant creature out. 'Populate the wainscoting – aye up to the very beams and rafters of the roof!'

'I shall not say Amen to that!'

But he had gazed at her in such a deep way as they knelt together with their empty jars after Edward and Edwina had scuttled into the safety of the dark under Harry's bed, she had thought for a moment he was going to ask her, and held her breath. How strange it was, she had received so many proposals, some from men she scarcely knew, yet the only one she had ever wanted was denied. Denied for the most honourable reason she knew now. Would she still want it after three years? Could she ever be a sailor's wife? Would he still want her?

'Very pensive, old thing!' He was standing, smiling by the table before her.

She tried to match the show he was putting on, and said brightly, 'Actually I was thinking of Edward and Edwina.'

He frowned for a moment, then burst out laughing, more heartily than the memory warranted, she thought.

'I wonder how they're liking it in Hampstead. We must pay them a call when I get back.' She could tell he wished he hadn't said it almost before the words were out; an empty look like the emptiness of the years ahead seemed to dull his eyes, gone almost as quickly as she glimpsed it, and he smiled again, 'Would you care to inspect the ship, Miss Steel?'

She bowed her head in exaggerated politeness, and rose on his arm. Anything would be better than sitting, exchanging meaningless pleasantries, glimpsing that hopeless look in his eyes at unguarded moments as time slipped away.

They paused at the rail around the well in the centre of the room and looked down into the dining saloon below; light from the stained glass dome two decks above made blurred patterns of colours along several of the white cloths on the tables on the further side. Dark-skinned stewards in white coats moved between the chairs, swivelling them, polishing the cutlery by habit as they laid the places.

'They do you well in P & O!' Robin said.

She smiled. A sense of unreality had taken her over; the hum of talk all about her, the activity on deck glimpsed between the velvet hangings to the windows, the silent-footed Goanese stewards below were part of a world which had no possible meaning for her, a world he would know but she would only guess at between the lines of his letters.

They moved on, past two richly-jewelled Indian ladies talking in rather loud voices of purchases made at the Army & Navy, and went out between the library cabinets on either side of the doors at the end. The companionway was crowded, both flights of the grand staircase dense with people moving slowly because of the crush. An officer was trying to explain to an elderly man with a veined nose and bushy white brows how to get to the smoking room. The man had very blue eyes, and it seemed to her he paid more attention to her as she came out than to the instructions he was receiving. His eyes reminded her of her father and she smiled at him, feeling a wave of nostalgia overlaying her emptiness.

Robin eased a way through the press to the doors on the

side away from the quay, and they went out on deck. The wind caught them and she shivered, clutching his arm.

He looked round. 'I'm told there are some very fine paintings in the smoking room.'

'Do you think I should go in?'

'As a sightseer and art critic? I'm sure you should!'

The seams of white, /sanded planking stretched wide between the side rails and the inboard bulkhead all in shadow save for an area further aft bright with sun where the hurricane deck above them ended. The paintwork in P & O buff was spotless; two Lascar sailors in very blue tunics with red sashes and brimless red caps were even now swabbing down a part of the rail in the sunlit portion; their exotic look only added to her sense of unreality.

'Here we are!' They had arrived at a protruding section of accommodation with large windows through which a colourful interior could be glimpsed. 'I don't think too many people have found it yet.'

They heard footsteps on the deck behind them and turning she saw the elderly man with the bushy brows and blue eyes. He raised his hat to her, indicating with a courtly gesture they should precede him.

'The glass is falling, I hear,' he said, still gazing at her intently.

'Oh, dear!' Robin said.

Inside, the immediate impression was of sunlight and air. A glass cupola stretched overhead, the beautifully moulded framing and surround white-painted, gold-embossed. Below, between velvet-curtained windows, were the paintings done directly on the panelling. One that particularly caught her eye was called 'Evening' – all seemed to represent different times of the day – and she stepped across for a closer look. It suggested downland with trees and an ornamental lake or pond in the foreground, the surface of the water lit with pink from the sky. She knew why it had caught her attention, and turned to Robin.

'Does it remind you of anything?'

He studied it gravely.

She had been introduced to his parents and two younger sisters that first evening after coming up from Weymouth;

384

after changing quickly for dinner, they had gone out together on to the lawn at the back and strolled around the gravel path to the pond. A thrush had been singing in an old elm to their left and the sky over the trees ahead had been suffused with just such a glow as the picture held.

'I don't think so,' he said. 'Should it?'

'Not really – not if it doesn't.'

He laughed, studying it again with concentration. 'Now you have worried me!'

'You've passed inspection,' he had said as they stood looking down at the shape of a goldfish darting beneath weed. 'The old man actually advised me to stick this time – not twist!'

She had smiled, pleased.

'The Mater said I ought to have told her what a peach you were,' he had continued. ' "I did," I said. "Yes," she replied, "but you say that about them all." '

They had laughed.

'I liked them,' she said, 'very much,' and he had taken her hand and they stood in silence as if they had known each other perfectly for a hundred years.

'I confess myself beaten!' He looked round at her. 'Was I ginned at the time? Are you going to help me?'

She took his hand and moved him away around one of the heavy-looking, marble tables to the next picture. 'It doesn't matter.'

She had liked them very much, and they had been perfectly sweet to her, making her feel a part of the family. And now they were allowing her to see Robin off by herself, although she knew they would have liked to come down to Tilbury. She had told them they should; they had shaken their heads, smiling at her in a sweet way. She had got on particularly well with the elder of the sisters, Violet, who had all Robin's charm and sense of fun, and also the rather ambiguous, disillusioned feeling for the women's movement she herself had acquired. She had questioned her with great interest about her life in London on her own; she had the feeling she would like to share rooms if she left the Davieses. She *would* leave them; she couldn't possibly go back there to *wait* for the next three years to pass.

385

'*I know*,' Robin said, 'when we went out riding. We saw that old fellow –'

'No, really, it doesn't matter.'

He frowned slightly, looking at her, then with another obvious effort at cheerfulness, 'My man has been talking of nothing but the plumbing! Shall we inspect below decks!'

They went out and down a companionway near the doors to the spar deck, then forward again, along a shiny corridor smelling of polish lined with louvred mahogany doors, past the surgery and dispensary, the barber's shop, drying rooms, baggage room, the hum of the ventilation very evident. An ayah in a white sari with two children in tow flattened herself against the hand rail as they approached, pulling the children in behind her. Robin patted the elder on the head as he passed. From an open cabin door to their left a decided female voice was making it clear that she always put her hat boxes beneath the bed. Chattering from around an angle ahead heralded the approach of girls; there were two, the leading one very pretty in a vivacious way, and her eyes held Henrietta's for rather longer than simple interest dictated. Henrietta returned a hard stare, sure that this one was travelling and would make a determined cast for Robin. She wondered if he had noticed her; he didn't seem to have paid particular attention.

They arrived at a door marked bathroom, and he opened it for her. She stepped over the coaming and across to the nearest cubicle door, pushing it open, and gave a little exclamation. The bath was long, reminding her of the baths at Stokey for it was carved from solid marble. At the end was an array of huge taps and pipes and controls for the douche and spray which even Stokey could not boast.

'Rather splendid, isn't it!' Robin said behind her. 'I fancy I shall be wasting a good deal of time in the tub!'

'It might be better than some other occupations,' she replied, thinking of the girl they had passed.

He gazed at her for a moment. 'How I *wish* you were coming out.' Again he seemed to regret the words almost before he uttered them, and frowned.

There seemed nothing she could say that would not make it worse.

'Would you like to see my cabin?' he asked. 'We're not far away. They dignify it by the term "stateroom".' He wiggled his brows.

She smiled, and they went out into the corridor again, past more louvred doors, some open with people inside.

He stopped and turned to her. 'We've passed it. My stable-mate was inside. I didn't think – we'd have to introduce ourselves and so on –'

'I'd rather go on deck.'

A warning bell sounded as they reached the grand staircase.

'It's all right,' he said at her ear. 'It's only the first bell.'

But already she could hear a voice calling for visitors to leave, and her heart went cold.

The crush on the stairs and outside the music room was worse than it had been before, and it seemed ages before they managed to push their way up the next flight and through the heavy doors out on to the hurricane deck by a cluster of tall radiators between the bridge and the first of the two raking, black funnels. She saw several officers at the end of the bridge nearest the quay and heard the call again from somewhere below, 'All visitors ashore please – visitors ashore!'

She looked round wildly at Robin.

'We've a few minutes yet,' he said, but his eyes were dark with emotion, and she felt his fingers gripping with unusual force as he took her hand and led her towards the rail between two lifeboats.

'What would happen if I stayed aboard?' she asked, thinking again of the girl with vivacious eyes.

He seemed to be considering it. 'I fear they'd bundle you off in the pilot boat.'

She looked down at the warehouse sheds and the grey quay; already people who had left the ship in response to the bell were gathering in little knots, looking up towards friends or relatives on board, ready to wave farewell. What a dreadful thing – she had never realized what a dreadful thing a ship's departure was. It happened all the time; every week throughout the year and down the years from this quay P & Os were leaving, tearing loved ones apart, perhaps for ever. An image rose of her cruise in the *Peacock* so long ago, and a glimpse of the P & O liner steaming up-river in sunlight and her father telling them there'd be tears aboard. She hadn't understood at all. Tears at homecoming – tears at parting. One only learned from experience; no one could really tell you what a thing was like.

Robin was looking down at the quay as well. She wondered what he was thinking. It wasn't so bad for him; there was the excitement of the voyage ahead, the excitement of the East and new sights and people – then his duty. In between, he would think of her and loyally write and look forward to receiving her letters, but his real life would be with his ship; she would be an ideal of the past, a promise for the future, not a real, living, feeling person. He would love her in the abstract – a 'sweetheart' to toast and think of fondly after dinner on Saturdays – while her heart was breaking –

He seemed to be staring rather fixedly down, his fingers very tight around her hand. Could it be that he didn't trust himself to meet her eyes? She felt her lip beginning to quiver, and tossed her head in an attempt to stop tears coming into her eyes, and looked wildly around for something to comment on to break this dreadful silence between them. All she could see was a thin line of people descending the gangway.

The bell went again; as if stung, Robin turned to her, this time unable to conceal the anguish behind his eyes. He drew her towards him and kissed her fiercely, pulling her into him, crushing her.

He had never kissed her like this before. She felt all the control she had built up snapping, and knew there was nothing she could do about it; tears started down her cheeks.

He drew slightly away, looking aghast. 'It won't be long, I promise. It'll seem like no time –'

She let herself go, clutching him and sobbing quietly on his shoulder while he patted her desperately. Then, feeling ashamed, she stopped. It was over; there was no time left. She stepped back and smiled, blinking away the remains of her tears.

'I'm sorry. That wasn't fair!'

He offered her his handkerchief and she dabbed her eyes and cheeks.

'I had better go. Please don't come down.'

He stretched out both hands for hers with a look of such hopelessness she felt sorry for him, and bobbed up to kiss him lightly on the mouth.

'Goodbye Robin! Good luck!'

She turned quickly away so that he had to let go and made towards the companion doors, not really aware of what she was doing, hearing his steps behind, following her. There weren't so many people on the stairs now. An English steward was coming up the other side calling, 'Who's for the shore!' in a mechanical way; it meant nothing to him. It was his job. At the bottom, she felt Robin's hand on her arm, guiding her towards the doors out to the deck. They threaded through groups making their final goodbyes and she didn't look round until they reached the top of the gangway. She wished he had not come with her; she had already said goodbye. She stopped and turned, smiling up at him to say it again.

He bowed his head, standing very stiffly, gazing at her.

'Take care of yourself, Henry.'

'I shall. So must you!'

He smiled, a strained, drawn smile, but seemed lost for words. She bobbed up again and kissed him on the cheek, then turned, almost cannoning into the elderly sailor standing with his hands behind his back at the head of the gangway as she made for the steps. She side-stepped and started down, looking round once and waving.

There was a throng several deep on the quay by now, but a woman with a kind face smiled and made way for her to stand beside her. Robin was where she had left him near the head of the gangway, gazing down. She waved and he responded, stern-faced. How very distinctive he was even amongst the other equally lean and well-dressed young men, looking as if they were probably soldiers going out to join their regiments. She had a vision of the Indian Empire and the East sucking all the vital young blood from the homeland and felt the futility of so much caring and loving, generation after generation leading to this inevitable heartbreak and emptiness, and for what?

Because it has to be, Robin would say in the sententious manner he adopted when talking of serious matters of that sort. The game is more than the player of the game, the ship is more than the crew. She had never really understood that either before. Looking up at the crowded promenade deck at the young men who would not come home for many years and the elderly men, district officers and judges and cavalry colonels, their faces tanned like parchment by a lifetime in the sun – probably several were in commerce but affected the bearing of imperial administrators – and their ample memsahibs, and the young girls, 'the fishing fleet' Robin called them, travelling out to find a husband, and here and there a brown face – standing here, gazing up at the liner, she comprehended it fully.

The warning bell for visitors rang again; renewed calls sounded through the decks, 'Last bell! Now, then, quick please – who's for the shore –?' The ship's siren emitted a shuddering blast. She saw movements at the end of the bridge; the Captain was leaning out, looking down towards the gangway, the sun glinting on the gilt around the peak of his cap and the broad gold band on his shoulder. His beard was trimmed to a point. A clean-shaven officer beside him was looking down in the same direction. Some sort of commotion on deck by the head of the gangway diverted her attention and she saw two women almost jump on to the steps in their hurry, looking back shouting with silly laughter at whoever it was they had just left. On the hurricane deck above, a Lascar in brilliant blue and red was looking down impassively from the rail between the lifeboats. Above the black funnels glistened; their smoke drifted across the third of four elegantly tapering buff masts. More black smoke was coming up from tugs out of sight on the other side.

Further aft she saw the second class gangway was already being raised. People had begun calling to each other there, back and forth between the ship and the quay. It was more fun in second class, Robin said; she wondered if he would think so this time with that girl she had seen in the alleyway below. She looked along the faces to see if she could see her now, and found her – just forward of where Robin was standing, separated from him only by an elderly man and woman. She was sure she hadn't been there before; the girl who had been with her was beside her, on her other side naturally. She looked back to Robin, seeing the pattern of his voyage in her mind. He was looking down at her and he smiled and waved as he saw her eyes move to him. Four weeks, five weeks of laziness under the tropic skies, watching the sea and the sunsets, dancing on deck, she wondered how long he would really miss her. She smiled and waved back, then looked at the girl again.

The primitive possessiveness gripping her subsided as she tried to rationalize her feelings. For after all, what did it matter? Robin had known any number of girls before her, he would meet lots more in the East. As for herself, she had found out today she could never be his wife – not while he remained in the service. Yet leaving the service would mean deserting his first love, and he would not be Robin then. She wouldn't want that either.

She felt empty and alone, more alone than she would have thought possible before she had met him. She thought of Father Geoffrey, and for an instant decided to visit Plaistow on the way back to try and find out when he was coming out of retreat. She dismissed the idea. She could not keep running to him with her troubles. This was her own affair; she had to face it. She had to face the fact that she was alone, completely and utterly alone. She had only herself to rely on, her own life to lead; she would lead it by her own effort without relying on anyone. She remembered on that walk to Portland teasing him with the idea that she might become a photographer; had it simply been teasing? Had she known even then that this was going to happen and she would have to make her own way without him?

She looked up again and waved and smiled, fighting back tears as he returned the waves, for he looked as grave and splendid as when she had first glimpsed him in the Davieses' hall, and she still wanted him more than she thought she had ever wanted anything.

It seemed an age before the ship cast off finally. Shouts from relatives and friends rang about her and the siren blasted. The liner drew away, revealing the yacht-like black

391

hull beneath the shadowed decks, lined with people. Gradually Robin's face and waving handkerchief and the faces of the girls nearby receded into patterns of light and shade above the rail. It was over; she was alone. She couldn't even imagine the space of time between now and 1913.

BOOK TWO

1914 – 1918

1

Willy had good reason for looking back to June and July 1914 as halcyon days. He was twenty-one, wore the two gold stripes of a full lieutenant, and was serving in an old cruiser suffering chronic boiler trouble which kept her almost permanently in one or other of the home ports, usually Chatham. As a result, and thanks to an agreeable Commander, he enjoyed more shore leave than in all his previous years at sea together. More than this he had been accepted provisionally for the submarine branch of the service and during the summer his name reached sufficiently high on the list of applicants for their Lordships to send him a posting to the submarine depot, H.M.S. *Dolphin*, for training in September. The thought of exchanging the 'big ship' Navy for the reputedly freer, pioneering spirit of 'the Trade', not least the prospect of command at an early age, gave him fresh life. At times he found himself lightheaded with relief; indeed it was not until he received the posting that he realized how much he abominated the formality and monotony, not only of the life in the Home Fleet with the cruising and endless exercising between Portland and Bantry Bay, but the crushing uniformity of thought itself – or so it appeared to him.

Another cause of his intense feelings that summer was Isobel, one of Jollion Peters's twin sisters. He had spent his Christmas leave with Jolly and his family at their father's vicarage near Guildford, and to his surprise found in place of the somewhat plump, feminine versions of Jolly he remembered from visits to Peters in the holidays from Dartmouth, two slim things of nineteen with dark, expressive eyes and mouths that smiled a great deal, especially when he told

395

stories. They had rather round faces like Jolly still, and they still giggled together for no reason that he could understand; otherwise the transformation seemed as magical and complete as the emergence of two butterflies from very ordinary chrysalises.

He had difficulty in deciding which one he liked most – not that he tried, he was just happy to be in unfeigned feminine company after some of the walking compendiums of the Navy List met at dances in the restricted round of ports they visited.

'You should show more interest in social occasions,' the Commander had warned him one night when they found themselves coming off in the same boat, 'otherwise you might be taken in by the wrong sort of girl.' In an expansive mood, he had gone on to give him more fatherly advice. 'Youth and beauty will undoubtedly fade, but a well-filled purse, looked after properly, will never lose its sparkle.'

The Commander was single, still looking for a well-filled purse. In his eyes Dora and Isobel would have been undoubtedly the wrong sort. The Reverend Mr Peters found it difficult enough to provide for his growing family on his living and the interest from a small sum of inherited capital; neither of the girls, nor their younger sisters would bring much to marriage beyond themselves. To Willy this was of no importance. He had no ambitions of the worldly or social sort, consequently had never felt the need for money, indeed he seldom thought about it, sure from experience that whenever really short he only needed to wire home and a 'loan' would arrive within the week. He had no idea how much his loans amounted to; they were only small sums and he was never asked for them. So his view of Jolly's metamorphosed twin sisters was the straightforward view of a young man released from the masculine, at times monastic disciplines of the wardroom, and surprised and flattered by attentions he was quite unused to.

Since he could not make up his mind for himself which of them attracted him most, they made up his mind for him; he realized this afterwards, a long time afterwards. At the time it just seemed that Dora often had other things to do when it came to a family walk up Box Hill or archery in the meadow

396

on the other side of the road, and usually chose to partner her brother, Jolly, in charades and other evening entertainments they got up, leaving Isobel demurely silent for him to ask. Also he found Isobel shared all his own enthusiasm for butterflies and birds – again it was not till many years afterwards he learned she stayed awake for hours at night surreptitiously reading rather out-of-date books on these subjects from her father's library shelves.

By the end of that Christmas leave, he had become distinctly attached, and had ventured to write to her after returning to the ship. She had responded with a long letter, the first of many; they were rather prosaic, diary-like accounts of everyday happenings, but he enjoyed reading them for they took him away from the cruiser into a world he had enjoyed so much, if briefly. Also it gave him kudos in the wardroom, where the regularity and extraordinary length of the epistles was taken as a sign the girl was dotty about him. He had never had a regular, corresponding girl before except for Henry, who not only didn't count, but was far from regular. He had been in love several times and on two occasions, once with the Creole in the West Indies, once with a girl of Scottish descent in Halifax, Nova Scotia, had expressed his feelings in letters. The Creole had not replied; the one in Halifax had written once without any hint of the passion he had expressed, after which the correspondence lapsed; he had never been back to either port again.

The Creole had been his first love; she had woken in him the ecstacy and heartache of adoration. It was a dance at Government House, St Lucia; she was in a shimmering silver-white, low-backed creation. With much trepidation after dancing, he had asked if she would care to sit out in the garden. Her bare shoulders had shone in the fairy lights, the warmth of the night, stars as sharp as arrows, the fragrance of the vegetation, throbbing with cicadas, and his physical closeness to her were things he would never forget. She had seemed perfection; her figure and everything about her, slim forearms, beautiful hands, the ease and grace of her walk, the delightful way she spoke ungrammatical English spiced with French captivated him; he had not realized such extraordinarily, exquisitely feminine creatures existed.

Jacquelene – 'Jacq'len' she pronounced it – and the aromatic, blue-black West Indian night were entwined in his heart. He had not been quite seventeen, his dress trousers somewhat crumpled from lying squashed in the bottom of his sea chest, his starched white shirt, one sleeve ripped off in a guest night free-for-all, attached by two safety pins, dress studs borrowed from Jolly, white gloves from Harrison – duty boat that night – and uniform dress buttons sewn on his white waistcoat at the last moment in a panic; how the shirt had clung after dancing, how heady the night outside, how cool the lime juice squeezed from fruit fresh picked! He had not touched her save for taking her waist very lightly in the waltz, but if she had replied to his letter he would have thrown up the Service and everything to be with her in that paradise.

Isobel was very different. He was attracted by her warmth and liveliness and interest in the things that interested him, and probably because she was Jolly's sister, so that he felt he knew her from all that Jolly had said of his family, but had he tried to analyse his feelings he might have concluded they were more brotherly than love-struck. And when, at the beginning of June, the cruiser was in dockyard hands in Sheerness and Andy had suggested he might like to come up for the May races in Cambridge – for he was rowing in the Pembroke first boat – he thought at first he would invite both twins and felt guilt when deciding eventually on Isobel alone.

His stronger feelings really dated from the days they spent in Cambridge. Isobel and Henry had travelled up with him from Liverpool Street, and they stayed with a big party gathered by the parents of one of Andy's friends in Selwyn Gardens. The talk and jokes had been of Cambridge people, or in serious moments poets and poetry, and he had been surprised to find Andy regarded as someone of note in this field. He had known that he had written verses at Marlborough; Andy had shown them to him one Christmas leave and he had thought them extraordinarily good, but to hear him talk with authority about established names like Masefield – whom even he had heard of – familiarly about others whom he did not know – Rupert Brooke was one that cropped up a great deal – was to discover a new Andy altogether, one who he realized in a short time, had left him way behind in intellectual matters; he felt very much out of things.

Henry had been all right; well able to cope with the names that were dropped on all lips, she added several larger ones of her own that had them hanging on her words. Inside stories of rows among the Fabians she had heard during her time at the Davieses', and embellished – particularly one about George Bernard Shaw besting H. G. Wells, whom she seemed to dislike – established her intellectual credentials. She created even more of an impression when she announced casually that she was a professional photographer, and went on in answer to questions to list some of the famous journals to which she contributed portraits. He thought she had really overdone it then, but was amused to see how even older guests afterwards sought her opinions on socialism and the Labour movement or the militant tactics of the suffragettes; she did not seem to like them much either.

Isobel was as lost as he was though; helping to look after the younger Peters in the country vicarage had not fitted her for the intellectual badinage and name-dropping, and as he felt responsible and very protective towards her, they were thrown closer together than they might otherwise have been. They excused themselves from a picnic on their second day to look around the colleges; neither of them had been to Cambridge before. Andy felt obliged to act as guide, and Henry came with her camera. Isobel was thrilled with everything, the garden at Sidney Sussex, the windows of King's College Chapel, wherever Andy took them she exclaimed with the ingenuous delight of a schoolgirl.

In the afternoon they had strolled along the river path with the throng of visitors and undergraduates for the 'Bumps', flannelled young men in gaudy blazers talking in the jargon about the prospects of their college boat, past punts hauled in along the bank and summery girls casting quick, inquisitive glances up from cushions at the passing parade. Other punts glided up, 'youth at the pole and beauty at the prow' as one correspondent had it next day; the eights slid by on their way to the starting queue, oars dipping and emerging powerfully, leaving patterns of whirls enlarging in the smooth water. He remembered watching drakes ahead of a boat swimming towards the side with unhurried judgement of the relative motion problem, the moving blades missing their tails by inches. Swallows swung low; linnets flashed from the willows. A foal, excited by the noise and crowds, galloped round and round its mother who collapsed on her back and kicked her legs in the air for joy. They must have missed Andy's eight while they stood watching them.

They did not miss him when the race was in progress. Shouts from further along the bank heralded the boats' approach, first Jesus, then Third Trinity with Pembroke close on their tail. Noise and excitement spread towards them along the towpath as the crews neared, bending and pulling with everything they had. As Trinity sped by a goodish distance astern of Jesus, they saw there was barely six feet of clear water between her rudder and the sharp prow of the Pembroke boat. And there was Andy straining mightily at number five. Yesterday Pembroke had bumped First Trinity; today it looked as if they must make another on Third Trinity and move themselves into line for taking on Jesus for the headship of the river.

Hearing later that the Trinity boat had just managed to hold them off, he felt an almost personal sense of let-down.

Andy mimed total exhaustion when they met him.

'What wretched luck,' he sympathized.

'I thought we had them. I really thought we'd got them!'

'It was jolly close when you passed us.'

'We'll have them tomorrow.'

Unfortunately tomorrow was the last day of the races and there would be no chance of challenging Jesus until next year.

That evening they drank champagne and danced at the Athenaeum Club ball at the Corn Exchange, honoured, so they learned, by the presence of 'Q', Sir Arthur Quiller Couch, and some time early in the morning a rather drunken Andy rounded them up for an expedition in three punts to breakfast at Granchester. On the way they had alternated songs with a 'bad limerick' competition, soon degenerating into arguments over which was 'absolutely and positively the most execrable' – and from there to a struggle between Andy and a fellow in the bow of the punt following. Both went into the water. Willy, balancing aft to retrieve the pole, was upset when the other punt collided with them, and trying to avoid falling on the girls, found himself toppling into the river. Choking with laughing as he went under, he was struck by the thought that Cambridge balls and wardroom guest nights had much in common. The jargon here was strange, but he enjoyed the presence of the girls and their colourful, rustling gowns; it was decidedly better than dancing with officers with a handkerchief stuck in their waistbands to denote gender.

They never reached Granchester, nor the following afternoon when they all walked across the meadows, for he and Isobel detached themselves and lay on the bank of the river in the sunshine side by side. It was a perfect day. From the distance the soft hum of voices, nearer the splash and swirl of water as a punt floated by, two girls lying out, arms trailing over the side, straw hats covering their faces; he felt peace soaking in and envied Andy his three years here. It would almost have been worth having short sight and spectacles –

And yet, despite the miserable times in the Service – despair – the tedium of the same circle of faces and knowing exactly what each would say before he said it, and how he would react in most situations, there had been the splendid times and splendid friends and he would not willingly have done anything else. He had held responsibilities Andy had never known, had proved himself in charge of cutters and picket boats in the vilest weather while Andy was still at school. He had learned to handle men coming off the worse for drink, shouting abuse, had been responsible as watch-keeper for a million pounds worth of ship and her complement; he could navigate, fight a turret, take charge of a landing party; it was quite surprising all the things he could do when he thought about it, and when he set them against what Andy and these other Varsity fellows could do – actually *do* – they could certainly talk –

'Is Henry really a photographer?' Isobel asked. 'I mean a *professional* –'

He laughed, rolling over and pulling out a stem of grass to chew. 'Better not ask her that!'

'But why? I mean – she's so, well, I should think hundreds of men must have wanted to marry her.'

He smiled, thinking of some of the more amusing conquests Henry had regaled him with. 'The trouble with Henry, she's rather critical!'

'I thought she probably was.'

He raised himself on one elbow to look at her, wondering what Henry might have said to call forth that tone of voice. Henry could be beastly; Isobel was so inexperienced by comparison. He hadn't realized it before; it was probably what he liked about her; she was a total unsophisticate, absolutely direct, almost childlike – like Jolly – no poses, no artifice, no lies. Henry was such a liar –

'Isn't there anyone?' Her dark eyes were wide with a kind of surprised interest.

He nodded. 'One of the whitest fellows you could find.' His mind had skipped back to the time Henry and West had come aboard to see him at Portland – those ridiculous entries in his journal – it was another world and so long ago. He shut the memory out. 'The trouble is, she's decided she can't marry him I think. He's in the Service you see. She has an idea she's not cut out for a sailor's wife.'

'He's asked her?'

'I'm not certain.' Henry had never told him much about West; he had had to deduce most of what he knew from her mood and odd remarks when he had seen her for a brief spell of leave after the Bull left the ship. That had been soon after West had sailed for the China Station. She had been more argumentative and disagreeable than he had ever known her. West had been back from China for over a year now; she had seen him, he knew from her letters, but what the position was between them, he had no idea.

'Do *you* think it's hard to be a sailor's wife?'

She was gazing at him so anxiously, and was so patently applying the question to herself – as girls seemed to apply everything to themselves – although they had never spoken of anything like that, he felt suddenly he loved her, and without thinking, shifted position to take her hand. 'It's not a question I've considered.'

402

She looked down and he thought he saw a flush. Lord! It must have sounded the most fearful snub.

'Not before last night,' he added quickly.

She looked up again with a questioning expression and the protective feeling flooded over him again; she could be hurt so easily. *He* must never hurt her – for Jolly's sake as well. He loved Jolly – he loved *her*. He squeezed her hand. 'At the dance last night, I felt –' He didn't know how to put it. 'I mean a fellow can't get married on a lieutenant's pay, so – Oh, Lord, Isobel –!'

Her eyes had cleared. 'I know. That's what Jolly says.' She lay back, staring up at the sky. 'Oh dear, money is *such* a bore!'

He laughed, rolling closer. He wanted to clasp her to him, she was so slim and slight and her breasts were so delightfully rounded.

'I hope –' she started, and looked round into his eyes, so close now. 'Do you think there *will* be a war – some time?'

He looked away, adjusting his thoughts.

'Jolly says there is certain to be,' she went on, 'when the Germans are ready.'

'He's right, I'm sure,' he nodded smiling at her expression as he looked back at her. 'But they're not ready! They'd be mad if they tried to take us on at present.'

'D'you think so?'

'Of course.'

Lying so close to her in the early summer sun, war was remote, unimaginable, a total anachronism. The Kaiser huffed and puffed to curry favour with his own people, but when it came to it, that was all he ever did, all he would ever do.

'What do you mean, "this *wretched* Irish business"?' Kate asked in a low, carrying voice.

Lord! George had been aware of the tension building up inside her for some time. Watching anxiously as the group exchanged pleasantries that meant little to her, he had noticed her eyes wandering and that distant, sad look he had seen the first time he met her. She reminded him dangerously of Fitz. Beneath her elaborate coiffeur and the jewellery which had shocked the older women too obviously and brought startled looks from her contemporaries, beneath the equally stunning ball gown in shades of green, she was half wild. Uncle Richard had warned him the first time he had brought her to Felpham House, 'That one's a bolter, make no mistake!' He could see now what he had meant. And Leroy, the ass, had sparked her off.

'What do you know of Ireland!' she went on, challenging Leroy with her eyes and formidable jaw. 'Have you the slightest notion of what it means to be Irish?'

Leroy's mouth opened as the others turned to him, but no sound came out.

'Have you ever *been* to Ireland?' Kate pressed her advantage.

The faces turned back to her in the awkward silence, then one of the officers, Daniels he thought, gave an involuntary laugh, followed by the others.

'Shure,' Daniels adopted a stage brogue, 'Is not Bantry Bay joined on to th' emerald oisle, Oi'm thinkin'!'

There was another shout of laughter. George, not joining in, felt desperate for Kate. Even the girls were laughing now, although they probably had little idea why.

Kate obviously had no idea. She turned the full force of her attention on Daniels and a little shiver passed through her body as if with the effort of holding herself in. Daniels stopped smiling. In the silence, the Marine band which had been reassembling inside the wardroom mess, converted now into the ballroom, blared suddenly.

Kate, still holding Daniels's eye, said, 'I've been pleased to see your relations here tonight.'

He looked surprised but relieved at the mildness of her tone. 'I rather hope not!'

A chuckle went round the circle.

'Oh, yes!' Kate turned her head on her long, slender neck to look through the open doors into the messroom. 'Have you not seen them?'

There was a shout of laughter from the others following the direction of her gaze to the stuffed heads of game poking from the walls.

Daniels, hands clasped behind him, rocked back and forth on his heels and toes, a broad smile on his face. When the noise had subsided, he asked, 'Which ones in particular?'

Kate took a step towards the doorway and looked all around the room before nodding, 'I think that fellow, don't you?'

'The Canadian moose!' Leroy exclaimed delightedly; there was a sort of similarity.

'I was rather afraid it was going to be old rhino!' Daniels said, gazing in at the lugubrious features of the moose.

'Is that because he has two horns sticking up from his head!' Kate flashed out.

George was glad to see the Commander coming up, smiling at the hilarity, white shirt and waistcoat rounded out over the great chest that had earned him his soubriquet, 'the gorilla'.

'I hope I don't break up the party!' he boomed, and bowing to Kate, 'My number, I believe, Miss Gallwey!'

'Gallwey!' Leroy said quietly, nodding to himself as Daniels and Eagle-Howlett also claimed their partners and left. 'Well – I must say – I believe I do have *some* notion of what it means to be Irish. Now.'

George smiled.

'I suppose it adds a certain –' There was a look of genuine interest in Leroy's eyes. 'I mean – does she often go off like that?'

'Not unless someone drops a lighted match.'

'I say, I'm frightfully sorry, I –'

'Don't think about it. She doesn't mean it –' Catching sight of an attendant with a tray of champagne glasses, he nodded to him.

Through the doorway he could see the dancers coruscating under the line of lanterns, the filmy swirl and colour of the ladies' gowns set off by the dark blue and white and glittering gold of the officers' ball dress; he couldn't see Kate or the gorilla. Taking a glass from the tray, he raised it briefly. He hadn't realized how dry his mouth was. The evening was not turning out as planned. He had pinned so many hopes on it in the weeks of anticipation. It was to be the high occasion during which he set the seal on his relationship with Kate, not putting the question direct, he was hardly in a position to afford marriage yet, but using the atmosphere of the summer ball to establish a permanent claim on her affections. Instead, she had been growing more distant. The polite exchanges in the intervals, rather too frequent reliance on Whaley jokes or naval terminology to produce a laugh, had bored her, and his attempts at liveliness had gone flat; she had been brewing up for some time; Leroy had not been to blame really.

'I'm going out for a breather,' he said.

Leroy frowned. 'I hope I didn't shove my big hoof in it –'

'Good Lord!' He shook his head.

There was a distinct chill outside, and a suggestion of dampness in the breeze and he thought he caught a faint trace of the mud and salt-weed tang of the foreshore one smelled crossing the swing-bridge at low water. The coloured lights strung in the trees had lost their earlier magic for there were few people now to be seen and beyond the lit area and the striped marquee, the lawn stretched away flat into outer darkness. The lights of Portsmouth glimmering beyond the trees at the far side, seemed unusually distant; there were no stars.

A pipe would be a consolation, but of course he hadn't one with him. He lifted his glass and took several gulps. How could he retrieve the position? He had the next dance with her; perhaps he should suggest they sit it out? He could take her across to see Backhouse's rock garden and ornamental fish ponds, and the aviary and wallaby pounds; he imagined what she might have to say about those conceits in her present mood! It was simply not the kind of evening to sit out. It was distinctly muggy. In need of cheer, he found himself moving towards the lighted entrance to the marquee.

Entering on his own, he felt rather conspicuous.

'Bin deserted, Steel!'

Lord! It was the Old Man himself, sitting with his party finishing bowls of strawberries or ices.

'Outranked, I'd say, sir!'

The Old Man and his guests obliged with a shout of laughter. He saw the C-in-C at the table too, smiling broadly, and felt a thrill of pleasure.

'One of the Wexford Gallweys, is she?' the Old Man asked.

George was surprised he had remembered Kate's name. 'Yes, sir. Actually, she's translated recently to Suffolk.'

There was a gratifying chuckle.

'A nailer wherever she's from! By George!' The Old Man turned back to his guests. 'You see, it's not true what they say about my staff officers. They do have other interests!'

Amid the laughter, George thought he heard the C-in-C muttering into the ear of the lady next to him, 'Gas – and – gaiters –'

He extricated himself as soon as he could and left the marquee, quickening his pace back to the wardroom block as he realized the music had stopped. It started again as he strode through the doorway; inside officers milled in search of their next partners or escorted them towards the messroom doors. He looked for Kate.

Not seeing her anywhere, he went through the doorway amongst the couples dancing. It was odd, she was not there either, nor could he see the gorilla. It was not as though either of them was small. He came out searching the groups in the hall again, then went through into the billiard room.

Both Kate and her recent partner seemed to have vanished.

'Looking for someone?' It was Daniels with his fiancée, Veronica. She had an attractive smile.

'Kate – have you seen her?'

Daniels raised both hands in front of his face and stepped backwards so smartly that a waiter crossing behind him with a tray of empty glasses had to jink sideways, nearly losing them all.

Daniels turned and set two of the fallen glasses upright. 'Practising the new drill! I should have warned you.'

'They left,' Veronica said, 'both of them before the end –'

'Not long after it started,' Daniels agreed. 'We thought they were probably going out for a spot of refreshment. The gorilla was a shade flushed! My Aunt, Steel! How am I to look that moose in the eye again! Have you tried the marquee?'

'That's an idea!' Probably they had come in while he had

407

been embroiled with the Old Man's party, and they had not realized he hadn't seen them. 'Thanks!' He raised a hand and hurried out and back across the lawn to the marquee.

She was not inside. He saw some of the Old Man's guests look up curiously as he searched the tent with his eyes, and turned quickly and left. Where else was there to look? He couldn't search the island. They would not have gone to the rock garden or the marsupials or sit out anywhere come to that – the gorilla was married – his wife was here. The exasperation that had been growing turned into the anger of mortification.

Walking slowly back towards the wardroom block, preparing himself for the necessity of somehow masking his seething feelings, he heard the thud of hooves on grass and had a sudden presentiment of Kate. How he could have imagined it might have been her he had no idea, for when he turned to look the thrill of recognition was mixed with incredulity. How could she possibly be riding – in her gown – in the middle of the ball? And where had she found a horse? He stopped and strained his eyes through the darkness over the grass towards the road from the guardhouse.

Beast and rider formed a moving shape against the night, but there was a lighter tone to the rider's clothes. He had a moment of doubt, dispelled as they cantered into long swathes of light from the windows of the wardroom block thrown between the young trees lining the lawn in front. It was her!

The shimmering greens of her gown were strangely muted out here, but the lustre of her piled hair and diamond band, and the way she held her head and the slim curve of her neck were unmistakable. And he recognized her mount; it was 'Beastie', the staid old mare from whose bowed back the gorilla took the parade each morning. Both horse and rider seemed transformed. Perhaps it was the absence of the gold-bordered blue saddle cloth he associated with Beastie's daily appearances, or the unusual speed of her progress that gave her an anarchic air as if she were enjoying the night and forbidden jaunting, perhaps it was the champagne inside him, perhaps Kate's white face, her eyes in darkness beneath her wide brow, her mouth and thrusting chin set in triumph

– or disdain? It was pagan – this mare and the nubile girl balancing with her left leg down to the stirrup and her right bent before her over the high pummel of the gorilla's saddle hidden by rippling folds of her gown, her slender body, silhouetted, swaying in harmony with the horse's motion. The back of his neck prickled and a sensation he had never experienced surfaced from locked primeval memory of blood and rite –

A moment only, and passing from the shadowy paths of light on to the road before the wardroom block and the illumination of the windows, she was Kate again. He shivered with the strength of feeling that had possessed him. But what in heaven's name did she think she was about!

He called to her.

She seemed not to hear. Perhaps she had not: Beastie's hooves were pounding on the metalled surface and the music was loud through the doorway and half-open windows. Certainly she would not be able to see him. He ran forward through the line of trees, beneath the coloured bulbs on to the road and called her name again. By this time she had reined in before the entrance and brought Beastie's head round away from him towards the door.

Lord! He couldn't believe it: she was going in! She was leaning forward over the mare's neck cajoling her to mount the low steps of the doorway.

'Kate!' he called desperately, 'KATE!'

This time he was sure she heard. But she was committed, and Beastie was rising, one leg hesitantly, then the other. She could talk to horses; he remembered her introducing him to Golden Lad at Verney Park before their ride along the river; he remembered her gentle hands with the animal and the quiet look in her eyes, her usual restlessness quite gone – to return afterwards at dinner –

He saw the startled face of Petty Officer Fellowes in the doorway, and ran forward again. It was far too late. All he could do was watch the rump of the animal as, surprisingly delicately for so heavy a beast, it manoeuvred its hinder legs up a step, and Kate bending low passed under the white stone lintel and inside.

Word had passed. The hall was crowded with couples who

had been dancing and more were pressing through, almost silent, staring, grinning up at Kate. Only Fellowes was taking an active part, talking to her with remarkable restraint while Beastie, moving her head from side to side, forced him backwards.

'– I'm sorry, Miss – no hanimals permitted in the building. You'll 'ave to remove 'im, Miss –'

'All right, Fellowes,' George called, coming round on the left side and resting his hand on the animal's neck. He looked up at Kate. 'You'll have to take her out –'

'*George!*' she cried as if in utmost surprise, 'I've been looking for you *everywhere*!'

He never lived it down. For the rest of his time at Whaley, which was not long as things turned out, and whenever afterwards he met those who had been with him there in 1914, the greeting was usually the same, '*George!* I've been looking for you *everywhere*!'

The episode assured him of laughs at strange dinner tables for the rest of his life. The only people not amused when he told them were his mother and Henrietta.

'Absolutely typical!' Henrietta said.

'I think it took a lot of pluck, I mean, getting up like that on the gorilla's saddle – in her ball gown –'

'The gorilla must be as stupid as you are. And *how* did she get him to give it to her!' There was a nasty innuendo in her voice.

'As I understand it –'

'The trouble is you *don't* understand. You don't understand her. If you did you'd realize she's *simply* a show-off. That's all there is to her. She thinks because she's Irish she can behave – like the Irish behave. They don't though. I know *heaps* of Irish girls. They don't do that sort of thing and they know that if they did they wouldn't get away with it. *She* thinks she can get away with anything –'

'Henry –'

'No, don't "Henry" me –'

He lunged towards her and seized her by the arm.

'Don't be so childish!'

'Why do you dislike her so much, Henry?'

'Dislike her! My *dear* – *boy*! I'm thinking of *you*. You

410

seem to be – for heaven's sake, she's no good for you, can't you see *that* even!'

His mother was almost as disappointing although not in such a direct way. 'Too highly strung' was her complaint; she was, however, always interested to hear about her family.

His chief memory of that summer ball, overshadowing even Kate's episode with Beastie, was later in the evening when he walked her determinedly but with trepidation to the rose garden and they 'sat out' on the grass between the bushes, and she laid her head against his shoulder and sang, lightly at first, but with increasing strength. He had known she had a lovely voice; he had heard it after dinner at Verney Park, but hearing the pure tones in the garden rising high in the silence of the night with the pale blooms of roses all about them, and from the distance the strains of the band, was like nothing he had ever experienced before, nothing he was ever to feel again.

> 'Once a young maiden climb'd an old man's knee,
> Begged for a story, "Do Uncle, please –
> Why are you single? Why live alone?
> Have you no babies? Have you no home?" '

How many times had he sung it in the old *Peacock*; it was his father's favourite. He joined in gently.

> "I had a sweetheart years, years ago
> Where is she now, pet, you will soon know.
> List to my story, I'll tell it all
> I believed her faithless – af-ter the Ball."
> After the ball is over – after the break of morn,
> After the dancers leaving, after the stars are gone –'

Others heard her voice and quite soon a sizeable group had gathered around them, hushed for the most part, sometimes joining softly in the choruses.

Her last song, he never forgot, and over the following years as he thought of her on lonely nights, he wondered if it had been coincidence or the second-sight of the Irish that caused her to save it to the end and then, apparently drained

411

of emotion, refuse all requests for more. It was 'The last rose of summer'.

> '– Thus kindly I-I scatter
> Thy leaves o'er the bed
> Where thy mates of the garden
> Lie scent-less and dead.'

2

The two men stood close as they read the evening paper together. It was a scene Henrietta never forgot, Robin and Uncle Richard, the westering sun on their flannels, a thrush singing in the high branches of the elm as one always had she realized. Their rackets lay on the grass where they had dropped them. Andy was approaching from the net, studying Uncle Richard with keen eyes behind his spectacles.

She could not believe it. Men had talked of a European war for years – 'the coming war' – dinner table speculation. They had not expected it for heaven's sake? George, the devil had hoped for it, so had Robin. She had never taken them quite seriously. She had never felt even a twinge of alarm because it had seemed a chimera, utterly remote, unthinkable, beyond the bounds of imagination for civilized nations to fight a war. It was too fantastic to have contemplated.

'Anything new?' Andy asked as he came up to the two men.

Robin stopped reading and looked across at her, his expression serious.

'Austria's declared war,' Uncle Richard said, and lifting his head with a sort of numb shake, he held the paper out towards Andy.

'Are you *playing*?' Harry called from the other end of the court.

'Shush, Harry!' her mother said, appearing from the direction of the house. 'You must not talk to Uncle Richard like that!'

Uncle Richard smiled.

413

'What do you think of the news?' she asked him.

He put a hand up to the end of his moustache. 'Doesn't look too good.'

Henrietta saw Robin walking towards her in the loose, swinging way he had, smiling with his mouth, but his eyes were examining hers. She heard Uncle Richard say, 'I don't believe they're bluffing.'

'What does it mean?' she asked when he reached her chair and stood looking down.

'Looks rather like war, old thing.' He was trying to keep his voice steady, but she detected the tremor of excitement. He *did* want it, he really wanted it.

'*Why?*'

'Russia's bound to come in – if that report is true,' he gave a nod back towards the paper in Andy's hands now.

'It has nothing to do with *us*.'

'Germany is bound to support Austria in that case –'

'It still has nothing to do with us.'

He smiled. 'Let's hope so.'

She could tell he didn't mean it, but it was so appalling she couldn't reduce it to an argument. She saw him looking towards the house, and turning saw Willy coming out dressed now in his suit, Babs jumping beside him. Her mother and Uncle Richard turned too, her mother starting quickly towards Willy, her hands flying out for a moment before she collected herself. Babs caught sight of Robin and came bounding across like a nine year old. It was difficult to think of her as *fourteen*.

'Robin West – Robin Temple-Vane-West – are *you* going to be recalled?'

Henrietta felt again the awful sinking inside she had experienced when the telegram had arrived for Willy – little over an hour ago now she supposed. Probably Robin's was on the way, but he had telephoned his home when Willy's had come, and there had been nothing then.

Robin was smiling. 'Their Lordships move in a mysterious way.'

'I know where that comes from!' Babs said brightly, 'Their wonders to perform.'

He laughed.

'You don't know?'

'I do not know.'

'D'you think there's going to be an absolutely *tremendous* battle in the North Sea?'

'Babs!' Henrietta said.

'Willy does,' she retorted, 'And the Huns probably won't declare war before they attack us.'

Robin laughed. 'We'll be ready for 'em.'

'But *you* won't be there – they haven't sent you a telegram.'

'In that case, I shouldn't think they'll start the battle!'

Babs squealed, pretending to punch his arm. She was simply so spoilt she was uncontrollable.

Willy strode across to them, holding his hand out towards Robin. 'Goodbye. Sorry I couldn't stay to finish the set!'

'Goodbye, old man!' Robin clapped him on the arm. 'Give 'em toko!'

Willy grinned. How good-looking he was, Henrietta thought. Why he bothered with that Peters girl, she could not imagine. She was nice enough and quite pretty, but he had depth and *quality*; things really mattered to him; he would need someone with more intellect than Isobel – had needed someone – if there was a war now –

He was looking down at her, smiling, 'So long, Henry!'

She jumped up and threw her arms around him. 'You take care of yourself William Steel.' She heard the catch in her voice.

'Don't worry,' he replied. 'We're too slow. To get to the scrap in time,' he added quickly, pretending to Robin it was a great joke.

She clung to him. 'Write to me.'

'It's *your* turn!'

She released him, trying to pretend annoyance. 'If you don't I shall never write to you again.' She wondered if she had caught Babs's childishness.

He bent quickly to kiss her. 'Of course I'll write, Henry.' There was a slight hardness to his voice and he held her eyes very seriously with his after he straightened.

'Aren't you going to kiss *me*?' Babs said.

He looked round. 'You can carry my case.'

Her mother called out that he would miss the train if he

415

wasn't quick, and Harry came over, still holding his racket as if he expected to carry on with the game directly they had said goodbye. Then they all turned and walked with Willy to where he had left his case, and down the path towards the stables.

Mackinnon was standing by the Lanchester. Henrietta thought of the boys going off to prep school and Bliss waiting by one of the harnessed horses. It reminded her of George; she had been so looking forward to seeing him when he started his manoeuvre leave next week. That would be cancelled now. It was extraordinary that he had been sent to the cruiser *Bacchante*. No doubt there had been ships of that name before her, which Papa had named one of the horses after; it was still odd. Bliss had been killed in the Boer war. She looked at Willy desperately, thinking of him as a young boy and those summers that would never return. It might be the last time she ever saw him. It was impossible. The whole thing was like a nightmare –

Willy turned to his mother and they embraced.

'Do take care of yourself, Willy.' They were practically the words she had used.

'I'm sure it's all a false alarm,' Willy said. 'I just hope they'll allow me the rest of my leave afterwards!'

Her mother smiled bravely, and they called out goodbyes and good luck as he stepped in behind Mackinnon, who had already started the engine; he turned and waved as the car started forward.

'It seems we were fated,' Robin said as they walked outside by themselves after dinner. 'It was that confounded spell in China that started it.'

'Started what?'

He looked at her and took her arm. 'Your *confounded* independence!' He laughed lightly.

'I think I was quite independent before that.'

'You were different, very different.'

She looked down. She wished she knew what she felt towards him now.

'This wretched photography –'

She halted, shaking her arm free and looking up at him furiously. 'What *do* you mean!'

416

'Good Lord, I don't mean *that* – I don't mean you ought not to do it –'

'I should think you don't.'

'I simply meant – since you took it up, you've changed so –'

'It's quite hard work,' she said acidly.

They stood staring at each other for a moment until he smiled suddenly and took her arm again.

'Come on, old thing –'

She couldn't get Willy out of her mind. He would be on the train down to Portsmouth now – and all the talk at dinner had been of war. Uncle Richard was certain there would be war.

'The Germans have been working up to it for years. It's an absolute fact. They mean to squeeze a colossal indemnity from France, it'll make the thirty milliards Bismarck collected from them in 1871 look like nuts –'

'Uncle Richard, what has that to do with Austria and Servia!'

'Servia's a pretext, Henry. I'm sorry to say it, but the Kaiser wants a European war. There's no other explanation of the way this thing's been got up. I mean – the note to Servia. No nation on earth could have swallowed it – and when the Servs did – bar the odd phrase which stuck in their gullet – what do the Austrians do? March on Belgrade! The Ruskies can't stand back and watch them giving the Servs toko. And the Kaiser can't stand back and watch Austria bein' rolled up by the Ruskies – and that pulls in France y' see – she's allied to Russia. No, this whole business has all the marks of the Prussian I'm afraid –'

'It still doesn't mean *we* have to come in.'

'Ah! *There's* the question!'

'If we don't,' Robin had said, 'we'll never be able to hold up our heads again –'

'*Albion Perfide* indeed!' Uncle Richard nodded. 'And, Henry – in case you're about to say somethin' about honour bein' a funny pretext for war – if we let the Prussians overrun France, it'll be *our* turn next!'

'They'll have all the Channel and Biscay ports,' Robin said quietly.

'You simply want a war, both of you.'

'Not at all. No. You're quite wrong, Henry.' Uncle Richard shook his head. 'No one can want a war with modern weapons – the South African business should have taught everyone that.'

'If no one wants a war, why do we have to have one?'

He laughed. 'I ought to have said no one in their right mind. The clique around the Kaiser have wanted war for years. They've worked up such an agitation in the country, I fancy they believe it now themselves! If you was to read the German press, Henry – as I've had to for me sins – you'd know what I mean. They say England has contrived their encirclement to check their rightful power and influence in Europe – and France and Russia are preparin' a descent. The facts are just the reverse. *They have* been preparin' to descend on France and Russia to force their power and influence on Europe by the only means the Prussian understands – blood and iron! The encirclement they speak of is simply an alliance of the prospective victims! No, Henry, they've planned it all down to the last wagon and railway siding.' He leaned forward. 'You mustn't breathe a word of what I'm about to say. They're comin' through Belgium. We've known it for some time. But don't worry. All arrangements have been made for their reception!'

'The real worry,' Robin had said, 'is the pacifists in the cabinet.'

'It'll be a close run thing I grant you, but I can't believe, no I can't think we'll not.'

'D'you mean we may stay out of it?' Her mother had asked very earnestly.

Uncle Richard shrugged. 'It's a possibility.'

'How can we!' Robin said. 'We've more or less come to a working arrangement with the French over joint military and naval action – so I understand.'

'Quite right. It's difficult to see how we can possibly stand aside. I fancy once the Huns start pouring through Belgium even the pacifists may have second thoughts.'

'Let's hope Grey manages to get the Ambassadors to London before that happens,' her mother had said.

418

'Let's hope so.'

He had no real hope of it, she could tell.

Willy was on his way back to join his ship, and George was already at Portland or Portsmouth perhaps by now –

Robin had stopped and turned to face her, his starched shirt front shining in the glow of light from the house, his eyes very clear against the night.

'You know what I meant about being fated?'

She had a sudden feeling he was about to propose to her. If he did, she would have to ask for time to decide. She shook her head.

He gave a little, exasperated laugh and swinging her arm, turned and started walking again slowly.

'I'd worked out in my queer scientific way the reason for the change –' he looked round '– the change in you. I'd been taking you for granted – taking it for granted that – some time – we've *talked* about it, but we've never come to a firm arrangement. I'd left it up in the air so to speak. That's what you must be thinking, I thought. But if I'd asked you directly I got back I expect you'd have wondered how on earth you could engage yourself to a fellow who was never in the country – liable to be sent off to the other side of the world for another three years. In any case I couldn't come back from not seeing you for so long and simply – it would have been a bit of cheek. I was hoping to take the opportunity today. If by any chance – well, I'd hoped to see your father. That's what I mean by fate! This war business! On top of that your father's not even here!'

She smiled as they turned and started walking slowly back towards the house again. She felt he hadn't given all his reasons. Her 'independence' was how he had started – her 'wretched photography'. It was difficult for a man to think of his future wife living outside his reach and control – especially a man like Robin who, for all his understanding underneath, had a fixed code of behaviour and such pride. He had made no secret of his distaste for some of the people she had introduced him to from her world. He would expect her to give them up and treat her photography as a mere hobby. At the same time, he had the understanding to know she couldn't. It would have been different if he was going to

419

be at home. He wasn't and never would be for long until he retired from the Service.

'Things are so – uncertain now,' he went on. 'When they get back to normal, would you – *could* you –?' He gazed at her. 'There's never been anyone else, Henry, not like you, I promise. There never will be.'

She squeezed his arm into her side, torn by his sincerity and her own doubts. 'There's never been anyone like you.'

He stopped and pulled her into him and bent to kiss her as he had on the hurricane deck of the *India* as if there was hardly any time.

'You might?' he said at last, raising his head.

She should have been ecstatic; it was what she had wanted so much once. Now she couldn't be certain. But then, at any moment he might be recalled to his ship and sail out to meet the German fleet; how could she simply reject him and let him go away – like Willy she might never see him again. She gazed up desperately.

He drew away a little and felt in the pocket of his jacket and pulled out a small jewellery box, handing it to her. 'Whatever happens – whatever you say – or don't say – I'd like you to have this.'

She opened it, knowing there would be a ring inside. There was. She pulled it out of the satin mounting and held it up towards the light from the windows; diamonds shone.

'You don't have to wear it,' he said, 'if you don't wish to. I'd like you to keep it.'

She turned and threw her arms around him. 'Thank you!'

'I bought it quite a time ago. Oh-nine wasn't it?'

'Who for?'

'Who for! *Oh-nine*, don't you *remember*! When I drove your brother up to town in the old girl –' He glanced towards the house, 'Oh, dear!'

She looked round and saw Uncle Richard and Andy coming out with lighted cigars. Seeing the two of them they stopped and seemed to be about to walk around the other way when Robin hailed them and said what a splendid night it was. They came on to join them on the lawn.

She held up the ring. 'Look!'

Uncle Richard's brows rose, and he looked quickly from

420

her to Robin, back to her. 'You don't mean to say –?'

'Robin has asked me to marry him.'

'You don't say so!' He turned to Robin. 'My dear fellow!' and thrust out his hand and pumped Robin's up and down while Andy made congratulatory noises. 'My dear fellow! Does –?'

'I was rather hoping to be able to ask for per this evening – if –' He looked at her.

'Of course!' Uncle Richard's eyes darkened. 'Yes, of course. Poor Robby. But I know he will be absolutely delighted.' He stepped towards Henrietta, holding his cigar well behind him. 'May I –?'

His moustache tickled as always as he kissed her.

He turned to Robin again, holding her arm with one hand and squeezing. 'I've known this since it was an infant. You've taken on something I dare say you know that!'

Robin smiled. 'It has come to my attention!'

'It's always the best are the most difficult – so they tell me at all events.' He squeezed her arm again. 'You'll not find a more difficult one than this –' he leaned close to her ear, 'nor a better!'

'I know.' Robin gazed at her.

'Well,' he released her arm, 'I vote we give your mother the glorious news. It'll take her mind off things I dare say.'

Andy came up beside her to give her a hug as they walked towards the house.

He had been unusually silent at dinner. She wondered if the possibility of war had upset his plans – whatever they were. She had hardly seen him since that time at Cambridge and he had been quite undecided then about what he would do when he came down – apart from writing poetry. She slipped her arm into his. At least he would not have to fight. She wondered where Willy had got to now, and then why she had suddenly announced her engagement like that – she supposed it was an engagement –

Her mother smiled as widely as she had ever seen her when they told her, then her eyes started to glisten, and she came up rather hurriedly to embrace her.

'I'm so glad, Henry. I had been hoping, you know –' Her voice seemed to give way.

Henry felt her own eyes starting and fought to keep her lips from quivering. She had never been so happy, nor so apprehensive; it was too stupid. She felt shocked with joy and dread at the same time. It was simply unbelievable. Yet she felt the presence of war like the heavy, oppressive air before a summer storm.

3

George gripped the bridge rail as he scanned the faces of
the men coming up the for'd gangway; thus far he'd not
recognized one.

The Commander, beside him, turned his head, fiddling
with his eyeglass in the way he had when upset. 'Great Percy
Scott, Guns! They've sent us a brand new outfit!'

George nodded. The reserves they had worked up for the
test mobilization and manoeuvres had left the ship barely
five days before. They would have to work this lot up from
scratch – in earnest this time –

'D'you think this is someone's idea of humour?' The
Commander's tone was one of disbelief.

George smiled. There was little use in replying with the
racket Chippie was making demolishing the wooden doors
to the charthouse; the Commander heard little at the best of
times on this side. Why they hadn't cancelled demobilization
after the manoeuvres was a mystery; it had been fairly clear
from all accounts what the Hun had been up to –

'Gad! You're right!' the Commander said suddenly, and
as George turned in some surprise, 'The orders only came
through this morning. I should wring someone's neck, but
whose? We'll have to do the best we can with this lot. I'll go
down and make a bonfire of the watch bills for Jimmy
starters. Come and see me when you've had your tea. I'll
have their tallies by then.'

'Aye-aye, sir!'

His head ached and he had a griping pain in his belly; he
didn't know whether from the kromeskies he'd been rash
enough to finish at lunch despite their foul smell, or his

anxieties in trying to extemporize half modern communi-cations for the guns in a rush, or whether it was a symptom of the raging despair he felt at the trick fate was playing on him. The sight of the reserves jauntily mounting the gangway as if they thought they'd be in action with the Kaiser's fleet tomorrow only increased his tension; it confirmed it was real, they would be at war at any moment – the war he had dreamed of and longed for and now it was nearly upon them had to pinch himself to believe.

It could not have come at a worse moment. Even two weeks later and Norris's application for him to join the other sportsmen he had assembled in the *Princess Royal* might have been accepted. And here he was; here he would stay. He felt like shouting down to the fools mounting the gangway they could wipe the idiotic grins from their faces; they would not see action; if they did it would be their last. The *Bacchante* was too old and slow either to fight or run away; she had barely the speed of a battleship in the best conditions; her Belleville boilers were suspect; the Commander was an amus-ing old boy but deaf on the starboard side and as out of date as the ship herself. Most of the other officers were RNR, or long-retired lieutenants; the gunroom was formed of cadets under fifteen years old filched from Dartmouth after one term. He still found it difficult to believe it was happening to him. Top of the gunnery long course and retained since then either at Greenwich or in the experimental department at Whale Island to perfect the new director firing gear and associated instruments, working up new ships fitted with them, to be relegated at this supreme moment to an old cruiser that should have been dispatched to the knackers years ago was as undeserved as it was bitter. That they were flying the flag of a rear admiral and leading four other armoured cruisers of the same vintage served only to deepen his despair; it was a dangerous charade.

He saw a telegraph boy cycling past the crowd on the dock as if making towards the after gangway, and was reminded of Kate. That was the other thing! One more week and he would have been on leave – staying with her at Verney Park. He would have asked her, by God! He had decided on that since the Whaley Ball, and hang the tin! They need not marry

424

at once. But he must stake his claim. He thought he knew what the answer would be; she had made her feelings for him very clear in the rose garden at the end – his stomach still turned over when he thought of it. He could not eternally worry about how Fitz would take it. It would be a kindness, in fact to put Fitz out of his misery. Kate would hardly be content with anyone with so little prospects as Fitz – nor would her father, 'the long 'un'. He smiled to himself: Colonel Gallwey would want something more than a good hunting man for a son-in-law, and old Fitz, daredevil good fellow that he was had neither financial expectations nor the hope of rapid advancement he himself had already achieved. But, of course, Fitz was Number One of a destroyer in the First Fleet up at Scapa now, or poised perhaps to waylay the Huns off the Norwegian coast. Fitz might easily have the chance of action he would never get; once the enemy had been soundly trounced they would never dare show their face again; it would be all over in three months at the outside while he was rotting in this bug-trap.

In that case, would Kate and her father look more favour-ably on a war hero than on a former 'coming man' tipped for the highest posts whose career had been blighted by the hellish bad luck of not bearing a part in the twentieth century Trafalgar in the North Sea? It was all too dreadful to contem-plate.

He turned from the rail, fists clenched. He would not go down to the wardroom among the elderly lieutenants, he would see how the armourer was progressing; at least they talked the same language. The pain in his middle gripped, and he thought perhaps tea might ease it and changed his mind again.

The only sound in the wardroom was the rustle of news-print. Poring over the latest editions for pointers to the European situation, they scarcely looked up at his arrival.

'Another border outrage!' the doctor exclaimed. 'The Huns have torn up the line at Moncel-sur-Salle – seized the Froggy rolling stock –' He was as excited as he might have been at the report of a close test match.

'Good luck to 'em,' the old paymaster said, leaning towards him and raising his voice, for the doctor was as deaf as the

425

Commander. 'Have you ever travelled on a Froggy train!'

The doctor nodded shrewdly, pretending he had heard.

'Waiter!' George called as he saw the man disappearing towards the hatch, 'Tea and toast!'

He had scarcely sunk into the one vacant easy chair when a messenger appeared carrying an orange telegram envelope, and to his surprise made his way across to him.

'For you, sir. Boy said as 'ow 'e'd wait –'

'Thank you.'

His heart lifted for an instant as he thought it might be Norris telling him his berth in the *Princess Royal* was secure, but he realized almost as the thought struck him the battle cruiser was in Scapa Flow or at sea, and even if it were possible to wire, they would not change gunnery officers on the eve of battle. He tore the envelope open.

IN POMPEY QUEENS HOTEL STOP MUST SEE YOU STOP HENRY

Henry! What in heaven's name could she want at this time! He couldn't possibly get away.

He realized the silence in the room had deepened. They were gazing at him. He rose, waving the form.

'It's off! The Kaiser's called it off!'

'*Sir!*' The Marine waiter, approaching with tea and toast, stopped, a look of utter astonishment on his face. 'War's *off*, sir!'

Amidst the laughter and barracking, George strode towards the door, telling the messenger to follow.

He made straight for the Commander's cabin, knocked and pushed through the curtain into a haze of tobacco smoke. The Commander was sitting at his desk shuffling through sheaves of watch and quarter bills, the reeking pipe sticking from the side of his mouth. George manoeuvred towards his good side and shouted. He jumped round, his hand flying up to his eyeglass.

'Guns!' He looked relieved. 'The very man! Had y'r tea?'

George waved the telegram form. 'It's my sister, sir.'

The Commander frowned.

'She seems to want to see me – I can't think why. Would it be in order – since I can't get away –!'

426

'Can't get away?'

'No, sir.'

He looked surprised. 'You can't get away?'

The trouble was, the Commander's sudden turn had cancelled out his earlier manoeuvre to get around to the good side, but he seemed to realize it for he now tilted his head towards the door, cupping a hand over his left ear. 'What's keeping you?' His tone was sharp.

George offered the telegram. 'Permission to have my sister aboard for half an hour this evening, sir?'

The Commander adjusted his eyeglass as he stared at the message. He seemed puzzled as he looked up again.

'Who's Henry!' He turned his face abruptly for the answer.

'Henrietta, sir, my sister.'

'Sister!' He turned back. 'Gad! Perhaps she can assist – write a fair hand, does she?'

George smiled. 'Thank you, sir.' He took the form back and waved it. 'I'll let her know.'

'They can't Jimmy spell. Never understood why. Ever met a woman who could spell, Guns?'

'Henry can't spell, sir.'

'Good! Good!' The Commander had omitted to turn his head. 'Send someone for Pay as you go. I've a mind to wring his neck.'

George left, feeling the first genuine smile on his face for more days than he could remember. The 'Bloke' was an endearing old stick.

He scribbled a few words instructing Henry to be at the dockyard main gate at six, handed it to the messenger with a small coin for the boy, and returned to the wardroom. Telling the paymaster he was required, he warned him to be prepared. The old man raised his hands to his neck and wiggled his head. He nodded.

Someone had filched his toast!

'Waiter! Where's my toast!'

'I put it down there, sir –'

'I thought you'd gone,' a round-faced RNR lieutenant called Stewart was looking up from the next chair.

George sank wearily into the leather. 'Bring me some more!'

427

'Sir!' The waiter made off.

'Sorry, old chap!'

George picked up his cup and saucer. Stewart was learning. He was quick and competent, he'd noticed before; he wondered again about bringing him into the control top in place of old Prior-Matcham whose brain must have become addled during his years on the beach. What could he suggest for Matcham that would not make his dissatisfaction too apparent? Lord! He couldn't worry about personal feelings; the cruiser had enough disadvantages if it came to a scrap without adding to them gratuitiously. He would suggest Stewart for the job.

In the choking fug of the Commander's cabin afterwards, scribbling lists of guns' crews made up from strange names with nothing to go on but age and rating, it was the Commander who reminded him about Henry, asking when she was due.

Lord! It was past six, and he'd clean forgotten to tell anyone off to meet her. He rose quickly.

The Commander frowned, but seeing his expression, gave a little shrug and threw his pencil down on the papers.

'Cut along then! I need a spell. But what an infernal Jimmy nuisance! I mean to say! If you or I were to interrupt the preparations for one of their infernal dinner parties great jumping Jehosephat! Give her half an hour, Guns. Don't stand any Jimmy nonsense!'

'No, sir.'

He went out, dashed across to the wardroom to collect his cap, and up the ladder at the run. He would have to go himself at this stage. What a curse Henry was with her inspirations. She probably wanted to take his bloody photograph – something equally demented –

'Thank you for coming,' she said icily, when he arrived to find her in conversation with the policemen on the gate. 'You should not have bothered to run!'

He looked at the men, who had eased away respectfully, then back at her.

'Sorry I'm late. We actually have a few things to see to!' He turned, gesturing to her to follow.

'If I'm in the way –'

'Lord!' he hissed. '*Come* on! I've only got half an hour!' Amazingly, he saw her eyes begin to fill with tears. He stepped up to her. 'I'm sorry, Henry,' and leaned to kiss her, very conscious of the impression they must be making on the policemen.

'I just wanted to see you,' she said, looking down.

He stared.

She looked up, her chin thrust out. 'Is that so strange?'

He realized suddenly how glad he was to see her. He smiled, taking her arm and leading her round gently.

'I'm sorry, Henry. It was just – you've no idea what a panic there is. We've just had a brand new draft of reserves and –' he looked round. 'It's marvellous to see you.'

'What is it, George – really?'

He shrugged. 'I don't know.' He did know. The sight of her and the sound of her voice had made him realize how much he had allowed things to get on top of him. There was no one on board he had been able to unburden himself to. He tried to laugh. 'Everything, I suppose!'

'I thought you *wanted* war.'

'That's just it!' He flung his arm out desperately. '*Not* in the seventh cruiser squadron. You've simply no idea, Henry. We're an absolute – another week and I'd have left for good – I'd more or less been promised the *Princess Royal* after the manoeuvres. Her gunnery Jack got his step in the June promotions and old Norris wanted me. It's the most damnable thing.'

She was gazing at him. 'You mean you're annoyed simply because you're not in the ship you want to be in!'

'If you put it like that –'

'And the war – doesn't mean *anything*?'

'Of course it does. But don't you see, Henry, I've been working with – well, actually I can't tell you, it's absolutely secret – I've been working on the thing for years ever since I finished the long course at Whaley. I could be some *use* in the First Fleet, that's the point –'

'Are you of no use here!'

'Good Lord, if we ever get near a Hun, it'll be a miracle.'

'I'll tell Mama. She'll be pleased at any rate.'

He looked round at her tone, feeling dreadful. She was

429

right. Whatever had come over him? 'How are things?' he asked. 'How's the old man? Is he any better?'

'Sure you're interested?'

'Look here, I'm *sorry* if I've been grousing – you did ask.'

'I know I did.' She pulled his arm into her. 'You sounded so strange, not like I imagined. I thought you'd be so *keen*.'

'Well –' he smiled, 'It's ripping to see you, it really is. How *is* the old Pater? How's Andy? What's he going to do now?'

'Andy's as bad-tempered as you are. He thinks he'll have to apply for a commission.'

'A commission! Andy! Whatever for? Good Lord, it'll be all over by the time he's learned to get fell in! He wasn't even in the corps was he, at Marlborough?'

'We've all tried to tell him that. He says it's his duty. I don't think he really wants to, but he seems to think he must do something – I *think* it's to prove he's not an intellectual or a pacifist or something –'

'Good for Andy!'

He laughed, but an image of the brass bedstead and the Alma Tadema girls with marble skins in Alice Davies's guest room brought a sudden rush of shame he had not experienced for some time. He saw the half-amused, yet far-away look in her eyes as, shivering with anticipation, he drew her towards him on those tempestuously exciting afternoons – for *him*. She had simply wanted to pump him for ammunition that she and Charles and the pro-German people could throw at Fisher. He shuddered, closing his eyes momentarily in self-disgust –

'Even Harry's thinking of leaving Marlborough and joining the army.'

'Harry!' He tried to think how old Harry was now; he must be seventeen – a good deal older than the *Bacchante* cadets.

'George, I do think – it's so utterly – *dreadful*.' She gave a little, hopeless shudder. 'I simply can't believe it.'

'I know,' he said. 'I feel like that –'

In the half world, poised between peace and war, whenever he stopped for a moment, his mind filled with the blast of guns and images of the German battlefleet lined along the horizon, fountains rising about the ships as they did about the lattice targets at battle practice, and the glow of fire and

430

black smoke from hits he remembered from the old *Empress of India* firing trials. The hammering of the riveters from the dockyard and the noise of winches and rumbling barrows loaded with stores and ammunition, the ceaseless activity day and night added to this phantasm of events driving to a thundering, fore-ordained conclusion. And each time the vision came he cursed the old *Bacchante* –

'Uncle Richard's at Felpham House a lot now – Oh, and Kate called.'

He looked round sharply.

Henrietta saw his expression change. She had had a feeling about Kate and Uncle Richard. It was not so much what they had said to one another when they found themselves together at Felpham House, rather the *care* they had taken not to. Uncle Richard flirted with any attractive girl; Kate was outrageous with men she thought worthwhile, as Uncle Richard most certainly was, with that slightly worn air of experience combined with still good looks and huge animation that was so captivating. Yet neither had drawn fire from the other. They had seemed to avoid each other; it had been odd. She had wondered –

'She was in town,' she said. 'She asked if there was any news of you.'

He smiled at her expression, but he wished she didn't detest Kate so.

'And –?'

She returned his questioning expression.

'Did she *say* anything?'

'Gracious! Have you ever known her *not* say anything!'

'Did she send a message?'

'How could she? She didn't know I was coming down.'

They rounded a building to open a view of the cruiser at the end of the basin. He pointed her out.

'She's *big*!' she exclaimed.

'*Big* enough –'

'*George!* Please!'

'Why didn't you tell Kate you were coming down to see me?'

'I didn't know. I only decided this morning.' She looked

431

at him. 'I'd seen everyone else off before they went – Willy
– Robin –'

He shut his eyes. 'You've seen West!' He should have
asked her. 'How is he?'

'Cheerful!'

'I should think so! I should be in the *Invinc*! Mind you,
she's in for a refit – completely new hydraulic machinery for
the turrets. It'll take time. She may miss the show too!' He
realized she was very silent, and looking round, saw her
expression had closed; he'd said the wrong thing again. He
joggled her arm. 'Did you go down to Devonport!'

'No. He came to London.'

'Lucky dog!'

'I just can't make my mind up, George. He came up to
see Papa you see – only Papa's still in hospital –'

'You mean –' He stopped dead, turning to face her, 'He's
asked you!'

'Is that odd?'

'No, but – West –' He pulled her arm and they continued
walking towards the ship. 'And what did you say?'

' "Yes", I think I said "Yes". But I don't *know*, George
– thinking about it –' she turned her head towards him
suddenly, 'You must never tell him.'

'Of course I won't! What d'you take me for!'

'I don't know if I could bear it – seeing him for two weeks
and then –'

'It's not as bad as that. Look at me – I've hardly had two
weeks *away* for years – you know that –'

She gazed at him as if he were protesting too much. They
walked on in silence. Nearing the cruiser's gangway, he
stopped and turned to face her.

'If you want my opinion old girl, I'd say congrats were in
order all round. You'll never find a better fellow than West.
And he's very highly thought of – he's certain to go to the
top – he's not exactly short of tin either – and he's a thumping
good bat. If he hadn't been away so much he'd have been
certain to make the United Services' side –'

'Of *course*! I hadn't thought of that!'

'You know what I mean, Henry. Look – you don't really
want to come aboard this old bug-trap do you? My cabin's

in the most fearful mess at present. I'm trying to concoct telegraphs for the batteries – if I go up and make my number with the OOW – tell him where we are – we can have a stroll. I need to get away from the ship anyway.'

She nodded, and he strode away to the ladder and took the treads up two at a time.

Poor George, she thought, watching his uniformed figure bounding up with that extraordinary, thick-set agility of his – so oblivious most of the time of anything outside the intense beam of his ambition, so loyal and understanding when it penetrated that she was worried, so competent, so *schoolboyishly* transparent; he had never changed and wouldn't now – although it was funny how he had been so antagonistic towards Robin at first!

She uttered a silent thanks to God for sending him to this old Third Fleet cruiser instead of to the battle fleet, where he wanted so intensely to be, and thanked Him that the *Invincible* was undergoing a refit at this time. She had had no idea. Robin hadn't breathed a word.

'Dear God, please keep the *Invincible* in dock until after the battle, and please preserve dear George and this ship he is in –'

The evening was so perfect; if it were not for all the activity about the ships and the noises and hammering and the air of barely suppressed excitement she could see in the moving figures and hear in their voices it would have been difficult to believe the unimaginable things that were happening. Had she been so dull and thoughtless all her life as to think they were poised for ever in a haven of security where the history she had been taught at school, for the most part the dates of wars and battles, had been suspended for the onset of science and material civilization and the greatness of the great British Empire! The warnings had been sounded often enough. Why had she not taken them in? Uncle Richard had told her; Alice and Charles Davies and all their circle had worried constantly; she had read countless articles about German militarism. Why did she find it so difficult to believe now? Why was it such a terrible shock?

She heard the clear note of a bugle; a stillness seemed to descend on the ship and she saw the gently waving white

433

ensign at the stern jerk at the beginning of its slow descent and the ensigns at the sterns of all the other ships were beginning to drop quite slowly. The *Bacchante*'s flag disappeared from view as the last, long note hung in the air. Moments afterwards she saw George at the top of the gangway, waving his hand to someone on deck, hidden from her sight. Then he started down; the gangway bounced under his weight. He would hardly be able to answer her doubts about Robin, but she was so glad she had come to see him.

The moment of the outbreak of hostilities caught George by surprise. The warning telegram had stated midnight GMT as the expiry time for the ultimatum, and he had been too busy since to concern himself with the newspapers or he would have known it was a mistake; midnight, Berlin was the time – eleven p.m. GMT. They had steamed to Harwich the day before, and were coaling. He was in the foretop with a cadet named Henderson testing the new voicepipes and extemporized dials the armourer's gang had completed for the batteries when he was startled by shouting from the direction of the ship ahead; an instant afterwards it spread to the decks below and at the same time the whole harbour seemed to come alive with cheers and calls carrying clearly across the water, followed by siren blasts and whistles from the direction of the flotillas. Glancing at his watch, his first thought was that the German High Seas Fleet must have made its anticipated pre-emptive blow on the First Fleet, now under Jellicoe and been chased home with a bloody nose. He leaned to the voicepipe and blew. The response was not long coming – a roar which caused him to lift his head. A moment and he realized what the armourer was yelling.

He looked round at Henderson. 'It seems we're at war with Germany!'

The cadet had heard. '*Yippee!*' he yodelled in his cracked voice. 'Sir!'

George smiled. 'A moment you'll not forget!'

'You can bet I won't, sir!'

It was not a moment George ever forgot. The winches had

434

stopped while the cheering was at its wildest; as it died orders sounded and they started again. Looking out from the top it seemed to him the wires were running faster through the blocks, thumping the sacks more decidedly in the glare on deck, the figures there inspired with a new urgency as they seized and swung them silently to the barrows.

Caught up in the mood, he turned to the cadet. 'The Kaiser will be sorry he started this, Henderson!'

'Yes, sir. You can bet he will, sir.'

Early next morning they slipped and steamed out past the concrete forts and observation posts at the entrance into a luminous dawn, followed by the *Aboukir* and *Euryalus* of their own squadron, and the *Amethyst* and *Arethusa* leading the first and third destroyer flotillas, and with two submarines and their leader set course northeasterly for the German coast.

With the prospect of action, George's mood of self-mortification had dropped away. His doubts about his raw guns' crews, the rawness of the whole squadron and its lack of speed remained, but pushed into the background by the sense of high events. Every perception on this first bright morning of the war seemed extraordinarily sharp, routine occurrences charged with significance. He could tell that everyone else was affected in the same way. Behind shadowed eyes from missed sleep there was a light of anticipation; underlying more than usually clipped remarks at breakfast in the wardroom, now stripped of all easy chairs and extraneous woodwork and combustibles, excitement was guarded beneath unspoken questions about the mettle of the enemy and the nature of real battle.

When, after noon, they altered course easterly along the Dutch coast towards Heligoland, George felt his own tension mount; his mood alternated between a longing to see the German ships and direct his fire into them, and speculation about how it would feel to be under fire oneself, how he would react. It was like waiting to bat next wicket down; there was the same slight dryness to the throat and moistness in the palms he experienced wondering if the bowling was as fast as it appeared from the pavilion. He told himself that once out in the middle and concentrating on the bowler's arm all doubts disappeared. It didn't work. The seesaw of mixed anticipation and apprehension persisted, and he could not rid his mind of the thought that if the German battle cruisers were out, the squadron would never see Harwich again. Yet surely the Admiralty would have sent stronger support for the flotillas if there were any chance of that. For all he knew, of course, Beatty might be steaming down towards them even now with the battle cruisers.

He thought of West in the *Invincible*, then of Henry. From what he had told her, she would scarcely imagine him heading straight for enemy waters on this first day! What an impulsive creature she was! It had been marvellous of her suddenly to decide to come down like that – a tremendous relief for him to be able to talk at last.

She had tried to warn him off Kate again of course. It was queer; he had tried to warn *her* off West at the beginning, but now, since he'd come to know him more, he couldn't think of a better fellow. Probably she would come round to Kate. It was simply sisterly jealousy. Harwich was a perfect base so far as seeing Kate was concerned; he could almost steam up to Verney Park in the picket boat! Not that leave would be granted until the German fleet was settled on the bottom. He felt the throb of anticipation and that odd, instant apprehension that kept catching him at unexpected moments. It looked as if he might see action before Fitz! He imagined Kate's green, black-lashed eyes wide in smiling adoration as he came to her, the conquering hero!

For all his fantasies and perceptions the afternoon passed off uneventfully. If the enemy were out, they were not in the waters off Heligoland, and the squadron returned for home without sight of a hostile warship. Only the *Amphion* and her flotilla, swinging off in chase of a suspicious vessel reported off the Outer Gabbard, found and sank a minelayer to draw first blood in the naval war. Returning early next morning, the *Amphion* struck one of the mines laid by her prey and while abandoning ship drifted on to another which caused her to go down at once with heavy loss of life. The squadron was diverted to the Downs until the field could be swept.

Laying mines in international waters where unsuspecting

neutrals or passenger vessels with women and children aboard might run into them came as almost as much of a shock as the outbreak of war itself. It was contrary to all former principles of warfare and fair play, a sign of scarcely credible frightfulness in the enemy.

'I don't believe they mean to give us a fair fight,' the Commander said at lunch. 'They mean to stay in their bolt-holes and sow these infernal devices everywhere. When we've no ships left to fight they'll come out and claim a victory. It's Jimmy not good enough. Great heavens, I'd like to have the Kaiser here! I'd wring his neck.'

The doctor, next to him, remarked that he preferred the Kent to the Essex coast.

The Commander nodded. 'We'll have to force 'em out,' and turning to George, 'What d'you say, Guns! You're infernally up to the minute, how would you say we might ferret 'em out?' He turned his head with interest for the answer.

George thought rapidly. 'Aeroplanes.'

'*Aeroplanes!* Did you say aeroplanes?'

He articulated clearly. 'Aeroplanes carrying torpedoes.' Considering it, he thought it not at all a bad idea.

The Commander looked down at his plate and, forking up a portion of sole, turned to the doctor, 'I'll say this, there's capital fishing off the Dutch coast.' He looked across at George again, a speculative gleam in his eye as he chewed. 'That's the sort of beastly dodge they'd cook up. They'd be certain to follow suit anyhow,' and brandishing his fork triumphantly, 'How many torpedoes d'you suppose they could carry in one of their infernal Zeppelins! No, we must play a clean game, Guns. We always have.' He looked down the table for approval. 'Leave the Hunnishness to Jimmy Hun!'

The doctor leaned towards him. 'I remember the time Margate was a very decent little spa town before the day trippers found it, y' see.'

437

4

Henrietta was surprised to see Andy as she opened the door; a glance told her he was depressed.

'Andy!' She went up to him and pecked him on the cheek. 'I'm so glad it's you!'

'Are you expecting someone else?' His eyes behind his spectacles looked so hurt. She guessed where he had come from.

'Of course not.' She turned and led him into her sitting-room. 'I'll put the kettle on.'

He threw a copy of *Punch* he was carrying to the table and remained standing, staring at her morosely as she went out. She heard him following.

'You look as if you've just got in.'

'I have,' she replied. 'You'll never guess where from!'

'The war cabinet.'

She laughed. 'Warm!'

'The Admiralty – *Winston* –'

'No, you're getting colder.' She picked up the kettle and took it across to the tap and started filling it. 'I don't suppose you've met Popsy have you – a "chum" of mine at the Baroness's –' She looked round with a dubious expression, 'Off and on! And do you know, they've interned her! As a spy!' She finished filling the kettle and brought it to the stove.

'Popsy?'

'Silly! The *Baroness*. But when you think about it, it was the most perfect position really – for spying. Goodness knows how many ministers she must have met among her fathers. She expected us to be able to hold our end up with a cabinet minister for ten minutes. Can you imagine!'

438

'She made a bit of a mess of it then.'

'What d'you *mean*!' She looked round sharply.

'She must have confined her spying to the pacifists.'

She adjusted her thoughts. 'They really didn't expect us to fight?'

'Of course not. It's been the most frightful shock.'

'Oh – I thought – from what Uncle Richard and everyone said they'd planned it for years.'

'Exactly. They expected us to let them get away with it. With a few *douceurs* of course. I dare say if they hadn't been so unutterably foolish as to go through Belgium they'd have got away with it. But then, what can you expect from a Prussian war lord.'

'Andy! You look so *cross*! Go into the sitting-room and I'll show you George's letter.' She pointed to the door.

'You've had a letter from George!'

'Poor George!' She followed him out. 'He seems to think the Germans chose the moment to spite him personally – to keep him in the *Bacchante* for the duration!'

Andy stopped in the sitting-room, wheeling on her with his hands clenching. 'At least he's *in it*.'

'Not far enough apparently.' She went across to her desk and pulled out the drawer in which she kept her personal letters; one of Robin's was on top of George's; she wouldn't show him that. 'They won't come out, you see. Well, I expect you know that.' She handed him the letter. 'I think it's a very good thing, don't you? It's surely very much easier if they simply shut themselves in than trying to sink them all.' She started back towards the kitchen. 'There's quite enough killing in Belgium.'

'*Don't!*'

She turned. 'There must be any number of other things you could do –'

He stalked to the window angrily. 'There may be,' and rounding on her again, 'I must go to France, Henry. This is our *chance*, don't you see that!' He started pacing, 'It's the chance we've actually been waiting for. Of course we didn't *know* it. To match our sentiment with *deeds*. If English ideals mean anything, if justice and freedom and – civilization mean anything we have to prove it by going out there and suffering

439

for them.' He came and stood over her, visibly agitated. 'Can't you see that, Henry! How can I –' He threw his hands up, 'How can I write another line if all I write is words – words – words – words –'

'*Andy!* You must *stop*. It's no good.' She heard the kettle begin to hiss from the kitchen. 'Do sit down for heaven's sake, and see what George says.'

'I'm sorry.' He collapsed into an arm chair. 'I got through the top line on the card today, but I've found out, you have to read the first *four* lines. It's absolutely hopeless.'

She gazed at him.

'It's always the same. "What school?" "Marlborough." "Ah! The very fellow we're looking for! Step along to the medic would you –" You see, if it weren't for my cursed eyes, I'd probably be out there already. They're absolutely jumping at fellows from the public schools.'

She was wondering why on earth, if he wanted it so much, he didn't ask one of the others due to go in before him to memorize the top four lines and tell him when they came out. Or he could put on his spectacles and memorize them himself for the next time he tried; most of the cards were sure to have the same letters on. He wouldn't think of anything as simple as that! She certainly wasn't going to tell him. Uncle Richard's latest estimate was that the war would last much longer than anyone thought; if that were true she was not going to help him get in now. She turned and left, calling back, 'You'll manage it one day –'

'It'll be too late,' he shouted.

He seemed in a better mood when she came in with the tea tray; there was actually a slight smile on his lips although he was trying not to show it as he jumped up to take the tray.

'You should have called me.'

'Fiddlesticks!' She moved a small table across.

'George writes a better letter than you'd expect.' He placed the tray down on the table.

'Can't you just hear the "Bloke" and the "Doc" when they sit next to each other!'

'I like the Bloke's idea for smoking them out – to give 'em

our word we'll meet them with the same number of ships they care to send out!'

'Isn't he perfectly priceless! I wish I'd gone aboard and met him.' She sat and started pouring the tea.

'Have you heard from West?'

She handed him a cup and pointed to the plate of muffins. 'You can turn the fire on and toast them if you like. *Two* letters actually. I expect there's another on the way. They hold them up until after the ship has left wherever she is.'

He nodded at George's letter as he took the muffins and a toasting fork and went across to the little fire. 'Robin was in the Heligoland fight.'

'Isn't George green! Actually, he said it was very small beer. He felt sorry for the Huns – which is something from Robin! They put up an amazingly plucky fight despite the odds. One of them was burning from end to end and her funnels and masts all falling in and they couldn't see her flag so they stopped firing at her. Then they saw she had hoisted another flag somewhere and fired a torpedo so the *Lion* just blasted her out of the water. They had just blown another cruiser clean out of the water on the other side – so Robin said. He had very little to do as the *Invincible* was at the tail of the line. By the time they got up to these poor little cruisers they were either blown up or turning over on their sides. It sounded funny, but I'm sure it wasn't.'

'It won't encourage them to come out.'

'That's what Robin says. He thinks it demonstrated amazing nerve, charging right in to the enemy's ground like that. "Nelson has come again," he said. They were less than fifteen miles from Nordeney and all those islands, and the German fleet must have been in the Jade all the time.'

'Nordeney,' he repeated, staring into the fire. 'I remember at Birchfield House, one of the masters used to read us *The Riddle of the Sands* before lights out. Lor'! We used to look forward to that – a chapter at a time. I could never wait for bedtime.' He looked round at her. 'I've read a lot of books since then, I can't remember one that made quite the same impression. I could just imagine being there myself in the old *Peacock* – Nordeney – I can see the mist and those seas *sluicing* across the sandbanks now.'

441

'There were so many books like that. I was thinking the other day –'

'Not like that!'

'What I meant is – we *knew*, didn't we. All the time. We knew it was coming – and then when it came we simply couldn't believe it. So strange.'

'In a way, I suppose.' He turned the muffins. 'I expect we'll say that when we die though!'

She ignored it, raising her cup thoughtfully. 'I still find it difficult to believe it's actually happening – all those men killing each other – in *Europe*. It seems so perfectly senseless – and the frightful casualty lists – every day –'

'Frightful?' He looked round with the intense expression he had worn earlier, 'Fighting for what they *believe*! How can you call that frightful! What could be – it's what anyone would want, isn't it?' His expression changed and he went on in a seemingly calmer tone, 'But there you are, I have no right, absolutely no right – words again! Words can only have meaning through action, surely you must see that, Henry.' He turned back to the fire. 'I have to get out there.'

Her heart went out to him. Of course he was right. If one felt as deeply as that one had to do it. She could see the predicament so clearly and was so sorry for him in his despair. Everyone seemed to be getting a commission these days. Yet she couldn't bear to think of him at the front, and felt the same tremor of apprehension she had when Uncle Richard had predicted a long war – 'several years, I'm afraid.' He had been right before. So many of the men she knew were fighting already – besides Robin and George and Willy at sea, Eggy and Bobo were in Belgium, Popsy had told her –

'I wonder if Popsy can do anything,' she said, regretting it immediately as he turned with such a hopeful look. 'She knows absolutely everyone. She's Eggy's sister. You must remember Eggy – I used to go down to Stokey –'

'Of course I do! Will you ask her?'

She saw smoke rising from the muffins and called out.

He turned, snatching them from the fire and tossing one gingerly from hand to hand, brought it across to drop it on her plate. 'You must ask her, Henry!'

She started scraping black rime off the edge of the muffin.

'If you really want me to. I shall be seeing her tomorrow. I'm helping her with a soldiers' and sailors' wives' club in Lambeth. It's amazing fun actually. I do like them, the wives. They're so *honest* – in their feelings I mean and the way they come out with simply everything instead of – you know – they're so different, like children in a way – very, *very* grown-up children. They know so much more than we do. And they have such marvellous faces –'

She rattled on about meaning to take her camera there, and about how Popsy was so good at organizing knitting and sewing comforts for the men at the front as well as organizing games and sing-songs in the evenings, but the thought never left her that if she did actually ask Popsy, and she decided to help, Andy would almost certainly obtain the commission he wanted in very short time indeed, short-sight or no short-sight, and she couldn't think whether it was her own pure selfishness that urged her not to do it or whether she was thinking of Andy as well for she was sure he was not cut out for a soldier.

'You'll be certain to ask, won't you,' he said at the door as he was leaving.

'Of course!'

'You know how much it means to me.' He grinned suddenly and hugged her, lifting her off her feet. 'Eggy's sister! If that doesn't do the trick! Thanks for tea. I enjoyed talking.'

He looked as if he really meant it. She had enjoyed it too. She felt lonely quite often now that Catherine had left the flat.

Almost the first thing Popsy said to her when she arrived at the Lambeth club next day with her camera was to ask whether she knew Alastair Vauncey. She tried to think where she'd heard the name.

'It's too utterly –' Popsy said with an unhappy look, and leaning closer, 'He was absolutely too – if poor Bobo and I had not been destined for each other – surely you must have met him, Etty. He was at Stokey quite often –'

Henrietta had an image of the Eton-Harrow match, and Alastair hitting the most perfect fours all along the ground as she and Popsy went round indulging pleasantries. She

443

heard herself saying, 'He had a castle.' It came unbidden. She wondered if she had actually said it.

'Lor' lummy!' Popsy turned suddenly and hissed in her ear, 'It's that there Mrs 'Ope! You must look after her, Etty. I shall say something very rude otherwise. She is too – *mal à propos*!'

Afterwards Henrietta bought a paper and, sitting in the bus on the way back to her flat, opened it with a sick feeling and turned to the 'Roll of Honour'. Her eyes seemed to find their own way to his name.

Captain Alastair Luke St. Adair Campbell, elder son of Lord Vauncey, was gazetted in August, 1908, after passing out from Sandhurst with the Sovereign's Sword of Honour . . .

Her eyes misted as she read. The brief details of his life were unknown to her; she couldn't even remember exactly what he had looked like – only his grey, frank eyes gazing at her so long ago. She felt as if a part of her childhood had been excised, and when she got back to her flat and closed the door to the world, she began to cry.

The next day there was a picture of him in the paper. He had grown into a remarkably good-looking young man. She cut it out and slipped it between the end pages of the diary she had begun to keep since leaving the Davieses' and starting to train as a photographer; it was not so much a diary as a record of her inmost thoughts.

Last night I cried for Alastair although I didn't know him. It was strange. I wonder if it was because I have been thinking so much of Robin and George and Willy and what it would feel like to see their names in the paper. Sometimes I imagine it and feel I know exactly what it would be like. But how can I? Am I preparing myself for something I know will happen some time if this war goes on? I wonder if crying for Alastair was like that, a sort of rehearsal. Or was it because he was the first boy I fell in love with? I think it was partly that because I really felt as though I had lost something. I wonder if he had time to

444

feel he was dying for his country and freedom and justice that Andy talks of. I suppose he is right. I hate the Germans so much for what they are doing, but how can it be right to hate like this? I shall write to Father Geoffrey.

As so often, when she had put her thoughts on paper, she felt soothed, and clearer in her mind. She would get in touch with Father Geoffrey; perhaps she could help start a soldiers' and sailors' wives' club in Plaistow?

'Good Lord! Steel!'

George could not remember having seen West look really surprised before! He grinned, advancing into the cabin and thrusting out his hand. It seemed he had caught him just in time, for he was dressed in tweeds, the trousers tucked into matching, flecked socks; as ever he looked immaculate. Behind him on the bulkhead above his bed near the red curtain to the port, he caught sight of Henry's face smiling wistfully from a large picture frame. He had not seen the photograph before. He wondered if it was one of the famous self-portraits.

'Where on earth have you sprung from!' West grasped his hand, a genuinely pleased look in his keen eyes. 'The last I heard, you were in the –' he snapped his fingers, 'You don't mean to say they've sent the rest of you up here! Because of the unfortunate –'

He shook his head. 'No. They sent *me* to the *Inflexible*.'

'Our new chummy ship!' West's expression changed. 'Something happened to V-W? I hadn't heard –'

'No, I'm additional to requirements. She's to be fitted with director firing. I was sent along to assist when she arrived back from the Med.'

West looked dubious. 'And how is V-W taking that!'

'I can't say it's all plain sailing –' That was an understatement: Verrier-Walker had appeared to take his appointment as a reflection on his own abilities as gunnery officer of the battle cruiser. Relations had been icy. 'Especially as said gear did not turn up before we were ordered up here!'

'The proverbial spare prick!'

445

He laughed, looking round at the amazingly colourful fabrics with which the cabin was furnished and decorated. West evidently spent a great deal on his aesthetic comforts! There were, besides, rows of books and academic-looking journals on shelves above the desk to his right – a side of him he had not guessed at before. Everyone else he knew had pared their personal possessions to the minimum in expectation of the coming battle. He wondered if West had guessed the Germans would not come out. Below the bookshelves and standing on the surface of the desk – although they would surely not remain there at sea – were dozens of elaborately framed photographs and pictures; one whose startling colours caught his eye was a Drury Lane programme, *La Legende de Joseph* by the Russian ballet – Michel Fokine and Mme Karsavina; he remembered Henry enthusing about it to him –

West had a hand on his shoulder. 'You are having a bad time. Henry's been rather worried about you. Look here, I'm for the beach – as you might possibly have guessed – can you come?' and as George looked down at his uniform greatcoat, 'Don't worry about that. I'd lend you some togs but the boat'll be going any minute. We'll stick to the paths – if there are any in this *Gord*forsaken 'ole!'

'Righto! I'm game!'

'Good man! We've been given four hours. I intend getting as far away from coal and lyddite – and several of my brother *orfi*cers – as I decently can!' He turned to pick up a raglan laid over the brilliantly-embroidered counterpane of his bunk and shrugged it on, then a deerstalker and gloves from nearby, and opening the wardrobe door, 'My fellow invariably forgets –' he produced a walking stick and made a lunge like a fencer at the curtain across the door and lifted it aside. 'Lead on, Macduff!'

They went out, turning aft past the rifle racks in front of the smooth white enamel of the funnel hatch casing, ducking through the open watertight door into the flat between the curving armour of P and Q turret hoists, West's boots echoing like dulled hammer blows on the corticene. It was so similar to the *Inflexible* with the feeling of wrongness he had still not quite overcome, officers' cabins and wardroom where the mess decks should have been, yet it was entirely different. It was odd how even sister ships acquired such individual characters.

A small group of officers for the most part in uniform caps and greatcoats was waiting near the side party at the head of the companion ladder as they stepped on to the quarterdeck; they turned as they heard West's boots; one pretended to back away in alarm.

'You didn't tell us you'd joined the Force!' someone called out.

Another rejoined, 'We wouldn't have 'im!' Obviously the captain of Marines.

West raised one sardonic brow to indicate that the remark was unworthy of a reply, and introduced George.

The one who had mimed alarm, Bingham, pretended shock. '*Two* gunnery officers in one ship!' and looked anxiously at West, 'You're not thinking of applying for an assistant?'

West turned to George. 'Forgive them, they know not what they say. Without our guns, they know they'd all be on the beach looking for jobs –'

Shouts of ribald laughter drowned the rest of his words, then they heard someone calling that the boat was here.

Turning for the ladder, West pointed out large paintings of submarines submerged, their periscopes just breaking the surface, which George had noticed decorating the after screen as he came aboard.

'How d'you like our murals? We were having sub scares every night – never got any sleep. Someone had the bright idea of showing the Jacks what a periscope actually looks like!'

' 'Twas me,' the officer ahead of them said. 'A small thing but mine own!' and peering round at George. 'But I admire your side artist old man!'

George grinned. The *Inflexible* was an amazing sight as he'd seen for himself for the first time properly when coming across, a Mediterranean grey light cruiser going the wrong way overpainted on the dark grey of her sides, and her funnels and masts striped like barbers' poles.

'We took the idea from the *New Zealand*,' he replied.

They started down.

'The trouble is,' the other called back over his shoulder, 'Who is she supposed to be?'

'That's the idea, surely,' West said. 'Can't you see the poor devil of a Hun captain thumbing through his Janes!'

'*Donnerwetter!* Two beeg funnels, two leetle funnels, and alvays she steams stern-first –!'

They climbed in to the picket boat convulsed with laughter at the image.

'The trouble is,' West said as they found seats in the cabin, 'the Hun mines are not known to discriminate.'

'If you ask my opinion,' the navigator came in, 'the officers in these bloody minelayers – if we ever *catch* one – should be summarily shot, and the bodies sent to Berlin for instruction –'

'I think we know your opinion, Pilot –'

'One has to say a thing several times in this ship –'

The chaff subsided as the picket boat throbbed into life and headed away from the side, gathering speed and bouncing into the grey waves of the Flow; spray whipped overall, slapping against the cabin top and running down the windows through which they tried to gaze out at each great ship as they passed. The fleet was in – truly the Grand Fleet now; it was an awesome sight, more powerful and businesslike than the same array drawn up in review order in the Solent a few weeks before the start of the war. Perhaps it was the background of windswept water, bleak grey hills and rolling mist, the absence of colour save the white and red of the ensigns blowing out that induced this feeling; perhaps it was the knowledge of war that lent the scene the shades of war. Looking at them, line after line of dreadnoughts, and cruisers and colliers and the myriad destroyers like packs of tethered hounds, George had the feeling the High Seas Fleet would never come out to meet them. He'd had the same feeling a few weeks ago soon after joining the *Inflexible* when, with the other battle cruisers, they had met the Grand Fleet at sea for a sweep towards Heligoland. The horizon had been filled with ships, the sky overlaid with the gloom of their smoke. He had wondered why the Germans should come out to meet all this; what on earth could they hope to

448

achieve against such odds? Villeneuve at least had numerical superiority when he sailed before Trafalgar. He saw Jellicoe's flag above the *Iron Duke* in the distance before a sheet of spray momentarily blotted out the view.

After landing, West made it clear to two others evidently expecting they would walk together that he and George had particular things to discuss. He soon found out what these were. Almost the first thing West said as they strode out on their own along a shepherd's or crofter's track through the grass was to ask what news of Henry. George told him how she had suddenly appeared at Pompey on almost the last day before the war.

West turned eagerly. 'I can imagine it! That's just her. It's what makes her so – *Henry*!' They laughed. 'I really think that when she thinks of something she either *does* it or *says* it! Pronto! Have you noticed?'

George smiled. 'She can be a fearful embarrassment! Is that what you mean?'

West laughed again. 'But it's always the *right* thing, that's what's so extraordinary.'

George had not realized quite how badly West had got it. He had always regarded him as a super-sophisticated real colonel of the nuts with a knowledge of women far wider than his own, the very last man to be taken in by the see-through wiles Henry deployed; his confidences came as a surprise.

'I can tell you a few times it was definitely the wrong thing,' he replied.

West waved the remark aside as if he hardly heard it. 'D'you know much about Nelson – the *man* I mean? There's something Collingwood said about him, I've always remembered it – something like this –' he thought for a moment. ' "An enemy that makes a false move in his sight is ruined and –" this is the bit "– it comes on him with an impetuosity that allows him no time to recover." Isn't that a marvellous way of putting it! It's Henry to a T. Things come on her with an impetuosity that allows her no time to recover!' He looked round, evidently expecting enthusiastic support for the view.

George couldn't help being infected by his look. 'I'd agree with that!'

'Lor'! She's taught me so much, Steel. I mean, when I look back at what I thought about before when was it – that trip up to town, that damn-fool what's his name – knocked that dreadful woman off her bike –'

'Fitzdunnon.'

'Fitz, that was the fellow's name. I don't think he'd seen a motor car before.'

'He's in the second flotilla now.'

'Up here! Lor' help us!'

'He's a good fellow,' George laughed.

'Anyway, as I was saying – had it not been for your sister I don't like to think of how I might have finished up in China. It was only the thought of her and her letters kept me on the rails, you know how it is out there – before the revolution at all events. It's still all too easy for a fellow to drink more than's good for him – and the other things of course.'

He strode on, digging his walking stick into the peaty soil or taking swipes at upstanding tufts of the mist-sodden grass, then as if making up his mind, turned his head suddenly.

'I expect you know I asked her to marry me. We came to an informal arrangement– that's how I see it at all events, I don't know what she makes of it. I've been doing a good deal of thinking since then – when I've been able to think with these infernal sweeps. I know she doesn't like the idea of becoming a sailor's wife – who would! I've more or less made up my mind to throw my hand in – you mustn't breathe a word of this to her –'

George gazed at him in astonishment. 'The Service?'

'Not until we've tidied up this little affair of course.'

'You can't throw it up –'

West turned his head, his eyes very steady under the dark brows lifting fractionally.

George looked down, numb with surprise. West was the pattern of the dedicated career officer; he was undoubtedly marked out to go high, given a fair wind First Sea Lord was entirely within his grasp. The idea of him throwing it all away for Henry was too much for him to take in.

'There is a problem,' West went on. 'She must not know I've done it for her – that would damn it from the start –'

George's restraint broke. 'Of course she'll know. Why on earth should you otherwise?'

'I know. Don't think I haven't given that a fair amount of thought.' He swiped out with his stick. 'So far as I can see it's heads I lose her, tails I lose her.'

George wondered if the strain of constantly keeping at sea without a break except for hurried excursions like this between coaling and preparing for the next sweep had affected his judgement. 'Wouldn't it be better to give it time. You said yourself – it's impossible to think properly.'

'I intend giving it as much time as it takes to break these swine –' a biting edge had come into his voice, 'break them completely and utterly so they can never again infect Europe with their God-forsaken "culture".' His tone lightened. 'Then, my dear, I believe our task will be accomplished! We can retire on our laurels!' And putting his hand on George's shoulder, 'Gentlemen in England now abed shall think themselves *accursed* they were not here! But – I fear it might not come to that. It'll be the long, slow haul – like Nelson's storm-tossed ships girdling the French coast. Year after year.'

'You don't think it'll come to Trafalgar?'

'They'd be mad to allow it. The only chance might be if they become desperate about our blockade – or about their position on land. It *would* be a desperate throw, wouldn't it? Do you read the *Naval Review*?'

George shook his head.

'You should. It gives one another dimension. History,' he added. 'What actually happened. *Not* what they taught us in the old *Britannia*!'

They laughed.

Striding into the moist wind, they talked as if for both a dam had burst – of the fall of Antwerp and the conduct of the war, the escape of the *Goeben* and *Breslau* to Constantinople – about which strong feelings still wrankled in the *Inflexible*, fresh from the chase when George joined her – of the recent loss of the cruiser, *Hawke* – 'almost certainly torpedoed by a sub,' West thought – which led on inevitably to the loss of three old cruisers of George's former squadron to subs while patrolling at ten knots off the Dutch coast. They had discussed which members of the Board of

451

Admiralty should be shot, then the chances of breaking up the German nation so completely it could never again disturb the peace of Europe, then of Henry again, then Kate – 'that nailing, half-wild Suffolk colleen of yours,' West called her – and the proper age for an officer to marry – whether an officer should *ever* marry! And how many children one should have, then back to Henry again, and somehow they got on to director firing; the *Invincible's* system was still incomplete although installation had begun before the war. They wondered how it was that such an obviously vital innovation had been obstructed for so long while so much money was being poured into even larger guns. George had been able to open West's eyes to the extraordinary attitudes struck by senior officers at firing trials, and his conviction that the Fisher-Beresford feud had left its mark here as elsewhere.

By the time they arrived back at the landing stage, pleasantly weary and flushed and cleansed in lung and blood and mind by the keen, wet wind, George felt that he knew and liked West better than anyone he had met except for old faithfuls like Fitz and Selby, but West was different. And he was more than ever certain that Henry could not do better. West had the intelligence and strength and individuality to control her – when he had shed his present fantastic image of her as Helen of Troy, saint and genius – comparing her with Nelson! It would have been laughable if he had not been so utterly serious – and of course when he had thought better of giving up his career for her. The isolated life they led up here did strange things to one's mind, as he knew himself.

The Flow had emptied while they walked; besides the battle-cruisers, they could only see the *Iron Duke* now and three other battleships. They heard a heavy gun like the crack of distant thunder, muffled by the cloud, and ten seconds later another; George imagined the giant water columns standing up by the battle practice target.

On the way back, the *Invincible's* boat dropped him off at his own ship.

'Good hunting!' he waved.

West raised his gloved hand courteously. '*Der Tag!* My best chin-chins to V-W!'

He had scarcely shed his greatcoat and sunk back on to his bunk for a moment to ease his legs when the bugle sounded action stations, and the decks began to throb with the sound of running. He leapt up and dashed out and up the ladders to the bridge.

The Old Man was there already.

'There's a sub inside the Flow. Alert the four inch guns' crews, then hop up to the main top and keep your party up there on their toes!'

George darted back down the ladder, passing V-W on the way up, and swung forward by the searchlight. While informing the party there, he saw Acheson standing on top of A turret by the quick-firers, looking up as he listened to the Old Man just above. George turned and raced down the next ladder to the guns on the flying deck.

Climbing the rungs up the angled strut to the main top after doing the rounds of the light gun positions, he wondered if there really was a sub out there somewhere in the gloom or if this was another of the pieces of driftwood or seals that had disturbed previous nights. Having escaped the seventh cruiser squadron's debacle off the Dutch coast to join the battle-cruiser élite it would be ironic if he found himself torpedoed inside the Grand Fleet base.

He found his snotty, Adams, and the three men in the main top gazing out studiously as he climbed in through the lubber's hole and went to his stool in the starboard forward corner.

'*Vincy*'s got the best plan, sir,' the rangetaker, Tomkins, said after a moment, 'She's securin' colliers alongside! Both sides, sir!'

'Never mind her. Keep your eyes on the water.' He added, 'I'd say that was a defeatist view anyhow.'

They chuckled politely.

A few minutes more of straining their eyes out among the flecked waves and Tomkins said, 'Reckon this one's a *proper* sub, sir?'

'If it is, I trust we'll give her a proper surprise.'

They seemed to find this mildly amusing too.

'One a them phantoms, I dessay, sir.'

453

'Take care she doesn't put a mouldy into us before you see her Tomkins – or you'll be the phantom!'

An unrestrained burst of laughter greeted this – no doubt at the image of Tomkins's solid flesh metamorphosed into spectral form. He called for quiet. 'Put a stopper round that tongue, Tomkins! Keep your eyes skinned!'

'Sir!'

They never discovered if it was a real submarine or not. It became evident from volumes of smoke from the funnels that they were raising steam, and as the murky twilight gave way to dark, the Old Man's voice came through the voicepipe, 'Steel – we're clearin' out! Come down!'

5

There was a crackling fire in the Old Man's fireplace. George was reminded of other fifths of November at his prep school – old Phipps becoming so excited as the chestnuts exploded, talking to his wife as if she were another prefect gathered in his study, 'Now then, Mater, where's that bag. By Jove! There goes another! Quickly now, we must keep it going –' He wondered how old Phipps was and what he made of the war – whether he'd been telling the boys it would all be over by teatime. That was roughly what everyone had thought in August – himself included. West seemed to think it would drag on for years.

He wondered where they were off to. The Old Man would not tell them of course. Every kind of rumour had been flying around; it was said the Admiral was striking his flag and the two of them, *Invincible* and themselves had orders for Berehaven. Steam had been ordered for twenty knots by 12.30, that was a certainty. He'd seen quite enough of Bantry Bay before the war; it was difficult to think what useful purpose could be served there. Pray God it wasn't something to do with the wretched Irish business. He had an image of Kate at the Whaley Ball, the expression in her deep-set eyes –

There was a knock on the door surround and Wigram came in, tucking his cap under his arm rather hastily. 'I'm sorry I'm late, sir. One of the young seamen got himself caught up in a reel –'

'All right,' the Old Man waved him to a chair, and after glancing round to check that everyone was present, looked towards the open doorway to his sleeping cabin. 'Dixon!'

His servant appeared in the opening, cloth in hand. 'Sir!'

'Clear out for ten minutes, Dixon. And tell Campbell, belay early lunch. Meals at the usual times.'

'Aye-aye, sir.' Dixon steered around the officers seated by the dining table as he made for the door. 'Usual time, sir.'

The Old Man took a pace nearer the fire. 'Tell him to make my soup thick and hot.'

'Thick an' 'ot, sir! At the usual time!'

George imagined the adjectives he would apply to these instructions as he passed them on to Campbell.

Perhaps the Old Man was thinking the same, for a ghost of a smile hovered on his lips as he watched Dixon push out through the curtain; it faded as he turned and looked along their faces again.

'I've called you together, gentlemen, because – as you probably know by now – we're off on detached service – the *Invincible* and ourselves.' He pulled his shoulders back in the characteristic way he had, his hands clasped behind him. 'I can't tell you where we're goin' – but be sure y'r hot weather kit's in good order.' The silence in the brief pause he made was rapt. 'Admiral Moore is leavin' us to hoist his flag in the *New Zealand*. Admiral Doveton-Sturdee will take his place.' This time there was an audible sound of surprise. Sturdee was chief of staff at the Admiralty. 'We are both proceedin' to Devonport to take on the necessary additional stores. However – enemy submarines have been reported in the area and we shall not now be sailin' until after dark. That is all I have to say, gentlemen. I'm sure you have some questions – I'm sure you know I am not permitted to answer them!' He smiled, trying to hide the keen anticipation he evidently felt, and looked at Wigram. 'We shall be sailin' at six, Commander!'

'Six o'clock,' Wigram replied, 'Aye-aye, sir!'

'Thank you, gentlemen!'

George stood, hopeful and puzzled at the same time as he took a place in the file moving towards the door. The detached service was undoubtedly of some moment, that had been clear in every syllable of the Old Man's deliberately understated homily. He wondered if it was the Mediterranean; perhaps the *Goeben* had come out through the Straits and the French had asked for assistance in bringing her to book. The Med at this time of year was hardly 'hot weather' though. And Sturdee! It was common knowledge that Fisher, now back as First Sea Lord in place of poor old Prince Louis, hounded out by the gutter press because of his German blood – and setbacks in the naval war perhaps – detested Sturdee. He had been Beresford's chief of staff at the height of the great feud, now thank heavens almost forgotten. However much he might wish to boot Sturdee from the Admiralty, he would hardly do so at the expense of the Grand Fleet battle-cruiser squadrons; that would be ridiculous. In any case, the Old Man's eagerness made it quite certain this was a significant mission.

Outside, still in single file as they passed the Old Man's spiral ladder up to the bridge, they began quiet speculation; once through the watertight doors into the wardroom flat all restraint broke; Wigram had to remind them they should not discuss what they had heard where the wardroom attendants might hear.

The solution to the riddle was not long in coming. George had started to dash off a brief note home to warn them not to expect letters for some time as they were being detached on foreign service, when V-W pushed his head in around the curtain. There was a light in his wide brown eyes and an eager lift to his brows that made George think for a moment he was going to make one of his ritual sallies about going into or out of director control; instead, he said, 'Heard the news?'

'No.'

'Report of an action in the Pacific. *Monmouth* sunk with all hands. *Good Hope* ashore in a burning condition; *Glasgow* severely damaged off Valparaiso. Strictly unofficial. It's from German sources. But –!'

George nodded towards the Old Man's flat.

'Exactly!' V-W responded. 'I'd hazard we're off on a Pacific cruise!'

George leaned back. 'Poor old Cradock! I wonder how much is true.'

'They're obviously taking it seriously in Whitehall. I smell

457

our old friend, John Arbuthnot Fisher!' His large head disappeared. A moment later it was back again around the curtain. 'What price your director gear awaiting us in Devonport!' The curtain fell into place again.

George smiled. V-W's present attitude was a welcome improvement. Those first weeks after he joined had been a nightmare – the most difficult in his whole life. Never before had he known he was actively unwanted. And since V-W had refused to delegate any responsibilities, he'd had most of the day and night to brood. Apparently his own attitude had not helped. From prep school and even before he had been used to starring in whatever he undertook; he had not known how to deal with this sudden, unexpected blow to his self-esteem. He had lapsed into stubborn hostility according to Wigram, who had taken him aside and told him he must buck up – pull together with V-W who was a first rate officer; the *Inflexible*'s gunnery was second to none. The spirit of the ship was second to none, and he intended to keep it that way –

He wondered if Wigram had given V-W a similar talking to; he had been making real attempts to be friendly over the past two or three weeks – cloaked always by some sarcasm. The latest visit was an example. It crossed his mind that perhaps West might have said something. He wasn't aware of any opportunity the two of them might have had to speak to one another recently, but he might have sent a note across. He had quizzed him about V-W on that walk at Scapa. Ostensibly they had been discussing the *Invincible*'s incomplete director firing system.

It was unlikely he would find out. He threw his pen down and went out towards the wardroom anteroom to find out if there was any further news. Horniman, the paymaster was expounding to a small group. Horniman had the Old Man's ear; he usually had a good idea of what was going on.

What he learned was confirmed in the press by the time they reached Devonport. A German squadron under Count von Spee, consisting of the *Scharnhorst, Gneisenau, Leipzig, Nuremberg* and *Dresden*, had sunk Cradock's flagship, *Good Hope*, and the *Monmouth* off Coronel on the west coast of

South America, and seriously damaged the only other war-ship in the squadron, the light cruiser, *Glasgow*, while she and the armed merchantman, *Otranto*, made good their escape. The Germans had suffered little or no damage apparently. Why such a hopelessly inferior British squadron had been chasing von Spee was not clear; there was talk of the ancient battleship, *Canopus* not far away – probably left behind by Cradock, they decided, as her lack of speed would have made it impossible to catch the enemy cruisers.

Whatever the causes, the damage to the prestige of the Royal Navy was obvious and brutal. There was no doubt in anyone's mind when they cleared Devonport in haste on the eleventh, every alley and mess deck piled with crates of stores and dockyard workmen still busy in the *Invincible*, that their new admiral with the splendid title of Commander-in-Chief of the South Atlantic and Pacific, was under the most urgent injunction from the great Jacky Fisher to wipe out the debt. They only hoped that Admiral Stoddart, who was already out there – or worse still the Japanese – would not find von Spee before them.

'My dearest Kate,' George began, thinking immediately how inadequate it was to express the mixture of fierce desire and tenderness and possessiveness he felt, and anxiety lest one of the bloody fox-hunting Jimmies was paying her court in his absence – yet what rights had he! None as yet. The hot weather had been playing havoc with his emotions.

> You can have no idea how much I've been thinking of you recently. We are in the tropics and with the sun and heat I haven't felt for so long – *real* heat *sinking* right into one as one lies out on deck, I *long* for you –

He paused, wondering if that wasn't a shade too much. It was exactly how he felt, but Lord! He crumpled the sheet and threw it in the bin. Thinking of Hopkins coming in to empty it, he bent to retrieve it and tore it carefully into shreds.

My dearest Kate,

You have no idea how much I've been thinking of you and wondering what you're doing and *cursing* every man who speaks to you while I'm away! I'm starting this now as we reach our next place the day after tomorrow and there *may* be a steamer for the mails.

We are enjoying A 1 weather, it's rather difficult at times to remember what we're coming down here for –

He stopped again, wondering if 'down here' was giving it away. Hell! By the time she received it, they might be anywhere. It was a depressing thought. He put a full stop after 'for', and thought for a moment.

On Saturday, His Oceanic – and needless to say Britannic! Majesty, King Neptune came aboard attended by Court, concubines, bears, musicians and the whole shoot! You would have been amazed to see how lovely some of our young bluejackets are when got up in rope-yarn skirts and paper *fleurs-de-mer*!

Amazed too at their oversize, heavily paint-ringed nipples like archery targets – but perhaps she would not have been!

His Majesty's Herald made a gracious speech to the Old Man standing on the bridge – as much of it as we haven't chucked overboard – with numerous allusions to the purpose of our cruise of course, all of which received with the most rousing hurrahs by our Jacks. There really is a tremendous spirit in this ship. Now that I've more or less got over a personal difficulty with someone which I can see on reflection was quite natural but which made me very miserable when I first came here I really don't think I've ever been in a happier ship and everyone loves the Old Man – 'Fidgety Phil'. After the speeches, the real fun began. I was rather glad I had crossed the line before. If they treat the Huns the way the bears treated some of the poor young fellows who had to go through the bath look out! No one was actually killed!

He had heard someone pounding down the ladderway to the flat; now the footsteps crossed towards the door, there was a quick beat on the surround and the round, flushed face of Wigram's doggie appeared.

'Commander's compliments, sir – and where are you? They're all ready to start, sir –'

He looked at his watch, guessing what Wigram might actually have said. 'Tell him I've lost my shin pads. I'll be up in a trice.'

'Sir!'

He looked down at the letter.

I must finish now, Kate. I have to go up and play deck hockey for the two-ringers against the S.O.B.s – silly old bumblers or words to that effect! I'm centre forward and we're well ahead in the tournament –

He put the pen down, annoyed with himself for the last sentence. Rising quickly, he turned towards the wardrobe for his plimsolls and stick.

Heat shimmered over the rocks around the anchorage. Sun glared off the water and the burnished fittings; the timbers of the deck radiated heat. One of the gang waiting by the crates piled beside the torpedo hatch swore as he touched metal with his bare forearm. It was a good thing they were not coaling; that would be intolerable. It would come later – in the evening he hoped, thinking of the thousands of tons they had sweated across and poured down the chutes since the hunt began.

Hearing a heavy step, he turned to see V W approaching in the large, lumbering way he had by the guns of P turret.

'Care to go calling!' he asked as he came up.

George tried to raise a smile. 'It rather depends! We're still trying to find the six inch for the *Glasgow*.'

'The *very* place, old dear! I feel we should glean what we

461

can of the enemy practice. I've had a word with Wigram. He agrees.'

George looked round to where the *Glasgow* lay off their starboard bow, looking very normal and clean for a cruiser that had been in such deadly action recently. 'We should,' he agreed. 'You want *me* to go?'

'Can't think of anyone much more suitable!'

It was quite remarkable how the atmosphere had changed with the sun and the relaxed, almost holiday feeling it had brought over the past week or so. 'Right away!'

V-W waved towards the crates. 'Don't worry about this. I'll send young Jerrycan up to sort it out.'

They moved forward.

'Backhouse is Guns over there,' V-W went on. 'A thorough fellow as I recall. If he hasn't made out a report in triplicate with "Schemes" and "Observations" and Lord knows what else, I'll eat my hat. I've ordered up the picket boat by the way. I think you'll find it waiting for you.'

It was. They shoved off as soon as he jumped aboard and, making a sweep around the stern to avoid a cluster of boats laden with stores for the *Kent*, headed for the *Glasgow*. Beyond her, he saw smoke pouring from the funnels of the *Defence*; evidently she was leaving them – which explained why Stoddart's flag was flying in the *Carnarvon*. There was still more than enough force gathered here to deal with von Spee, wherever he was now. One report had it that he had rounded Cape Horn and was heading towards Africa, another that he was still on the west coast of South America. He imagined what it must be like for the Germans and what he might try and do in their place. It would be tricky. They would have even less idea of the moves of their world-wide enemy; it was unlikely they were even aware the two battle cruisers had been sent after them. No time had been wasted. Decision had been swift, execution sudden – the Fisher of old. Evidently he had lost nothing in retirement. And now this concentration with Stoddart's cruisers off the coast of Brazil amid parched rocks and sandbanks tossing up and smoothing the long, deep blue rollers of the Atlantic, put the cap on it. It merely remained to gather firm news of the Germans' whereabouts. Then *look out*!

Backhouse greeted him warmly when he went aboard, only too happy it seemed to discuss the action.

George remarked how little damage the cruiser appeared to have sustained.

'We were fearfully lucky. I estimate that between them they chucked about six hundred bricks in our direction – of which only about half a dozen landed – mostly on the water-line in the bunkers. The coal saved us. Don't draw any conclusions from that. Shooting conditions were atrocious – seas coming over swamping the guns' crews, whiting out the layers' telescopes and by the time we came within effective range it was dark. After the first quarter hour or so I never saw them! We were just firing on their gun flashes. Their big ships though, I take my hat off to them. You know the *Gneisenau* won the Kaiser's Cup for shooting last year?'

George nodded.

'Doesn't surprise me in the least. They started with salvoes – three guns I think. The *Scharnhorst* hit *Good Hope* with her third salvo! 12,000 yards! The *Gneisenau* must have done the same with the *Monmouth* – I saw a huge fire on her fo'c's'le within minutes. It was a bloody massacre – no other way to describe it. Cradock kept on altering towards them, trying to close quickly to take advantage of the light. We had the *Otranto* with us though and she couldn't keep up. We were steaming bang into the most almighty seas and a force six. Well – perhaps he should have detached the *Otranto*. It was a nightmare whichever way you look at it.'

'You forced the action?'

'They were not shy! We had no idea they were in the area actually. We were poodling up the coast spread in line of search. We'd picked up a lot of Hunnish chatter on the wireless, but thought it was only the *Leipzig* talking to some colliers. Then at four-thirty we sighted smoke on the starboard bow, altered towards it, and there they were! Large as life! *Scharnhorst*, *Gneisenau* and some light cruisers. It fairly woke us up I can assure you! We didn't spot the others till they'd formed their line. Well, we reported them and legged it back to mother! That must have put Cradock in a spot. As you know he was the last fellow on earth to run away from anything. On the other hand *Good Hope* and

463

Monmouth were raw ships – no chance to work up their gunnery since commissioning and here we were faced with the Kaiser's crack-shooting armoured cruisers –'

'Where was the *Canopus*?'

'About three hundred miles astern. Escorting the colliers up to our next rendezvous. I can't vouch for this, but there's a story that when we picked up the telegrams after the action there was one from the new Board instructing us on no account to act against von Spee without *Canopus*. The *Defence* was on the way to join us. Of course poor Cradock never saw that. If it's true.'

George was reminded of all the talk in the *Inflexible* when he had joined about the decision Troubridge had taken not to engage the *Goeben* in the Mediterranean. The *Goeben* was in a different class from von Spee's protected cruisers, but everyone had thought Troubridge should have gone for a torpedo attack after dark when the German's gun superiority would have been less use to her.

'He didn't hesitate a moment,' Backhouse was continuing. 'The *Good Hope* altered towards us – we were about 25 miles east of her at the time – nearest the enemy – and the other two were ordered to concentrate on us as well. Von Spee altered towards us immediately. There was no hesitation.'

'Not surprising!' George said.

'Quite!' Backhouse made a rueful expression. 'Given we were hopelessly outranged by their 8.3s, Cradock had to close the range as soon as possible. The light was crucial. The sun was very low as we closed – sixish. They were to the east of us so as long as the sun was above the horizon we had the advantage; they were beautifully lit up. Directly it went down of course the positions were reversed. We were thrown into the most beautiful silhouette against the afterglow. I have to hand it to von Spee. He played his hand absolutely to perfection. He had the speed advantage. The *Otranto* couldn't seem to keep up and we had to ease down for her. As von Spee was obviously trying to get to the south of us, taking the weather berth and crossing our T, we had to alter south with him. So between about six and seven we were both steering south, converging slightly. Von Spee judged it beautifully. He kept away just outside extreme range while the sun was up. Immediately it disappeared he allowed us to close and a minute later he opened fire – three gun salvoes. We must have made lovely targets.' Backhouse shrugged. 'With the seas and general murk we could hardly see anything of him at all.

'Well – *Good Hope* and *Monmouth* were hit repeatedly. Within ten minutes *Monmouth* was yawing out of the line heavily on fire. Cradock altered towards the enemy – a magnificent sight – it took one's mind off one's own peril somehow to see her advancing like that firing with her six inch guns, funnels lit by flames and the enemy making uninterrupted target practice. I hope I never see anything like it again. But it was a glorious sight.'

He stopped, then went on quickly. 'The end came about seven-fifty. There was an almighty explosion – a sheet of flame from amidships right over her masts and her forward half disappeared, you could just see flames from a sort of shadowy afterpart. After that they concentrated on the *Monmouth*. The range must have come down to under 5,000 yards but the light had gone completely. The *Monmouth* managed to haul round stern to sea and put her fires out – she was badly down by the bows – then the moon came out from behind the clouds and we saw the enemy closing. It was not a pleasant moment. We tried to signal her. No reply.' He paused. 'There was nothing to do but leg it. It wasn't the proudest moment of my life. The *Otranto* had left the line earlier. Of course she had no fighting value, I dare say Cradock only kept her there to draw their fire.'

'You didn't see the *Monmouth* go down?'

'We heard her. I think she went up like the *Good Hope*.'

'Magazines?'

Backhouse nodded. 'I've been thinking about it a good deal since. At the range they blew up the shells would have had a more or less horizontal trajectory. It seems unlikely they would have penetrated a magazine directly. There's no doubt in my mind fire must have spread along the ammunition passages.'

George nodded; there had been a good deal of talk about the likelihood of that.

'I've beaten it into my ammunition numbers,' Backhouse went on, 'they uncover the igniters at peril of their lives. The trouble is in the excitement of action, they tend to forget.'

'So far as we're concerned,' George said, 'it looks as if we should keep outside 12,000 yards.'

'No question, absolutely no question. I told West that this morning –'

'He's been here!'

'He was aboard almost before you secured. I loaned him a copy of my report. He promised to bring it back this evening, you can have a look at it then if you like. The Old Man's got the only other copy.'

'Let's hope Sturdee reads it.'

'He's be a fool not to. Their rangefinders must be superb and their salvoes are wonderfully closely bunched – even at that range. If they're allowed a couple of lucky hits early on –' He raised his brows in a dubious expression.

6

'Etty! What do you suppose this means!'

Henrietta thought she recognized Andy's writing on the envelope Popsy was waving at her and guessed what it might mean. 'I've no idea –'

'It's quite the most outrageous letter I've ever had.' She pulled it out and opening it, started to read, 'My dear Lady Beauchamp – rather formal!'

'He's never met you.'

'Ah!' Popsy's eyes widened a little. 'You know that!'

'Well! Has he?' She was annoyed. Popsy might run the Lambeth club and generally boss people about, but she should not think she could quiz her like a headmistress.

'No. He has not,' Popsy replied decidedly.

'I didn't think he had. I'm sure he would have told me, he always does when he meets unusual people.'

Popsy looked at her for a moment, then down at the letter. ' "Dear Lady Beauchamp, I am writing to express my thanks for your extraordinary kindness." ' She looked up again, her brows and shoulders lifting to suggest hopeless incomprehension. 'My *extraordinary* kindness!' and looking down once more, ' "You will be pleased to know that it did the trick. I am to travel to Colchester tomorrow to join the Suffolks –" ' She looked up. 'The *Suffolks*, my dear!'

Henrietta couldn't help smiling. 'Popsy, you are hopeless!'

'If I had wanted to be so extraordinarily kind, Etty, would I have chosen the *Suffolks*! I take it that's what I'm supposed to have done for the lamb.' She started reading again. ' "I can't resist telling you how they worked it –" ' She raised

467

her eyes dramatically towards the ceiling, 'I ask you!' 'and looking down again, 'Where are we – "I came into the medic's office, specs on. He looked at me for a moment, then without a word rose from his desk and went over to a cabinet at the back of the room and started pulling out drawers – I'm not certain what he was doing exactly because I had seen the eyesight card stuck up on the wall. Of course I started memorizing the lines as if my life depended on it. By the time he came back from whatever it was he was doing I knew the top four which are the vital ones. He asked me a few questions. I don't know what he made of the answers because I couldn't think of anything much but the order of the lines and letters! He must have realized this because he then told me to take my spectacles off and read the card. I fairly rattled off the first four lines – still worried in case I might muddle them – then came to an absolute full stop. It was a complete blur. He looked at me for a moment as if to say 'I know your game young fellow, but I trust this will go no further than these four walls,' and said 'Good! You'll do!' and started writing out a chit for the orderly. That's how it was done – all strictly above board! Please don't tell a soul –" '

Popsy looked up. 'I hope I'm allowed to tell you, Etty!' And reading again, ' "And I can't thank you enough. I had to write and let you know. Believe me, you have saved my life. I don't know how I could have carried on much longer knowing that I was one of so few of my sort who have not answered the call. I am," etcetera – etcetera – a perfect fool, I'd say, Etty!'

Henrietta flared. 'He is a poet you know.'

Popsy's eyes widened again. 'He should be allowed his fantasies, you mean? But why – whatever made him hit on your poor Popsy as his unsuspecting correspondent? I mean this could go on for simply ages. I *always* answer letters, it is a point of honour as dear Bobo says, and I simply haven't the time – my war work. And I am not at all good at nonsense. Is he a nonsense poet, Etty?'

'Do shut up, Popsy. He's been desperate. He might have mistaken something I said –'

'Ah –!'

468

'I might have said something. He misunderstood me, that's all –'

Popsy folded the letter deliberately and putting it back in the envelope placed her hand on Henrietta's arm. 'Why did you *not* ask me, Etty? You know Bobo is so well placed with General Frog and truly loves doing things for his friends, and you are a real friend Etty – I mean I don't suppose we could have quite got him into the cavalry – not with specs – although even that is not impossible –'

'You disgust me Popsy. I can't go on working here –'

'Etty!' She looked stunned.

'No! What you've been saying, I don't know how you can. It's the limit. If Andy wants to go out and die for his country –' She felt herself shaking with emotion, whether genuine or manufactured because of her disgust with Popsy, she didn't care, but rushed on, words tumbling over themselves, 'What difference does it make if he's in the Suffolks or the Household Brigade, it's simply –' She couldn't find words to express her revulsion. 'And as for your *poor* Bobo, if I have to listen once more to that silly *hocus* about all the polo he can't get I'll, I don't know what I shall do –'

Popsy had taken a step away, and was staring, wide-eyed, and she became aware of two others, 'occasional ladies' as Popsy called them ambiguously, also gazing at her from the doorway and behind them in the dark, frosted panes of the angled glass she caught sight of herself, dark-eyed as a veritable avenging angel. It was too much. She felt her lips trembling, her fingers digging into her palms, and turned, shaking towards the occasionals, who seemed to melt aside.

'Etty!' Popsy sounded distraught.

She went blindly out, hearing Popsy's running steps behind.

'Etty – you can't leave me –'

She hurried on.

'*Etty!* For heaven's sake Etty! It was a joke. For heaven's *sake*. I adore getting letters –'

Henrietta turned on her, about to give her some home truths about her attitude and the fat, spoiled puppy of a husband she had, but saw that she too was desperate. She was reaching out both hands to clutch hers and there was a pathetic look she had never thought to see in her rather prominent, hazel-green eyes.

'*Etty*, I do so rely on you for so much. They all *love* you here, all the wives. I know they put up with me because I amuse them, but they love you, Etty –'

Henrietta felt her lips trembling again. 'Flighty asked me,' she made a deliberate effort at control. 'She's running a canteen – on Victoria Station – actually her mother, but Flighty asked –' she couldn't go on.

'Etty.' Popsy's eyes were moist. 'I promise I'll not say a word about my poor –' she seemed to crumple, leaning forward and turning her head, sobbing, 'I'm so desperately worried about Bobo, Etty – you have no idea how much I worry –'

'I know,' Henrietta said, feeling her own control slip, 'I know you do –'

'So-so I w-wouldn't have – I really wouldn't –' her words rose between choking sobs.

Henrietta put her arms around her.

'– Not the – ca-cavalry – Etty – *really*.'

7

After dinner George went straight to his cabin. They would be getting the collier early in the morning; he intended to catch as much sleep as he could beforehand, but first, he must finish the letter to Kate. There were several colliers in; one would surely be taking the mails.

Dec 7th We have arrived Kate, a queer sort of place reminding one very much of Scotland. We got in this morning, a guard of penguins in full fig turned out to do us the honours as we rounded in to the anchorage, rather nice after our last place, also sea lions and yesterday we passed quite close to a school of whales a-blowing, a magnificent sight. It is ripping weather, the air sharp and bracing, a pleasant change after the heat and we have been in blues several days. We carried out a practice shoot on the way at 14,000 yards – nearly eight land miles! Some of us have been urging this for years, it's sad to think one has to have a war to change people's ways of thinking. I still find it hard to think of all those splendid fellows of my former cruiser squadron *sacrificed* to d——d *thoughtlessness* –

He thought of Sturdee, wondering as he had before, just how much he was to blame for that disaster – and for the Coronel business. He had been C.O.S. at the time.

Coronel was another needless *sacrifice* to incompetence – although Kit Cradock has added a glorious page to our roll, which should never be forgotten. I hope the papers

471

in England have done him justice. They are rather too fond of trumpeting the winner – if he's ours! – and brushing everything else under the carpet. What was it Kipling wrote about those two imposters, triumph and disaster? Make no mistake, Kate, we shall triumph, however long it takes us. At present it looks as though it could be some months yet. There is still no firm news of our quarry although one wireless from Montevideo said they were in the Straits of Magellan on the 2nd – last Wednesday – if that is true they can't be far away, but there are so many reports all saying different things it is almost impossible to judge which is likely to be correct.

I managed a run ashore with Acheson this afternoon. A dead and alive place the town here – it puts one in mind of one of those out of the way Scots villages on a Sunday – three churches! Unmade, stony roads and for such a wee place a considerable graveyard. Many sailors I'm afraid including an admiral! Most of the people, those we saw anyhow seem to be Scots or Irish – but more sheep than people! No fear of our succumbing to the flesh pots here! Some of us are rather hoping the Germans lead us to more exotic pastures! I must close now and turn in since we shall be coaling at an early hour and probably leaving afterwards, goodness knows where for. I hope one of the colliers will be going back with the mails. Goodnight, Kate, and God bless you, I think of you always and can't wait until we have completed our task out here when I am sure we'll be allowed leave – in the spring perhaps! Some people seem to think the Huns will not be able to last out much longer than the spring – not West who thinks it might go on for years. We all hope it won't end before we've evened the score for Cradock's gallant fellows. I'll leave this open in case we hear something tomorrow. Good night, *dear* Kate.

He addressed the envelope, gathered the fresh pages together with those he had written earlier and folded them into a bulky package which he just managed to ease into the envelope. Propping it carefully against the back of the desk so that he would not forget it in the morning, he rose and went out and

472

across to the heads. The flat was strangely quiet for such an early hour, not even any noises from the direction of the gunroom aft; they knew they would be hard at it in the morning.

On the way back, he crossed V-W going forward. They nodded greetings and goodnight; he had evidently been in the armaments office, doing what? There was no question of his efficiency, nor of the outstanding gunnery achieved under his direction in the two years of the battle-cruiser's commission. Once they found the enemy there was no question as to the result. He was disturbed nevertheless as he returned to his cabin and, flinging his jacket over the chair, went to the basin. He liked V-W and was as fiercely proud of their shooting prowess as anyone in the ship's company, but there was always this irritation in the big man's presence. It was irrational, he knew; he loathed himself for it, knowing it resulted simply from his own status as junior. At least in the old *Bacchante* he had the whole gunnery organization of the ship under his control and direction; here he was neither fish nor fowl. He wondered as he had many times whether he should apply for a transfer on the grounds that the director gear had not arrived and showed no signs of doing so and he could be more usefully employed as sole gunnery officer somewhere else. The somewhere else was unlikely to be a battle-cruiser – he had missed his opportunity with the *Princess Royal* – nor a battleship in the Grand Fleet. At least he would have a real task.

He was wrestling with the idea as he undressed. After the heady spirit of the battle-cruisers, the cavalry of the Grand Fleet, it would be difficult to adjust to a more humdrum level. Turning in and switching the light off, he tried to think of more cheerful things – perhaps tomorrow they might receive firm news of the enemy.

He was asleep almost immediately.

Someone was moving inside the cabin.

'Mr Steel, sir, collier's coming alongside, sir – Mr Steel – sir –'

'All right!' He hung on desperately to an image of Kate riding a magnificent black horse away from him. If only she would turn and see him. He was running after her trying to attract her attention by shouting, but it was no good –

He was in his bunk and they were anchored in Port William Sound in the Falkland Islands – about to start another perishing coaling –

'What's the time?' he called.

There was no reply. His man had gone. He tried to brace himself. There was nothing he could think of to sweeten the pill, no landing afterwards for games, no sights to see – they had seen everything there was yesterday – no shows, no one to take in any case, no Kate – if only she had turned when he called so that he could have seen her face for a moment. The only thing it was possible to look forward to was a bath after they finished, and long draughts of beer to wash down the suffocating taste of the coal dust.

He reached up and pulled the curtain from across the port; it was dark and bitterly cold as he felt directly his arm left the blankets. He brought it back and hugged the warmth of the bunk. Footsteps were sounding across the flat outside and from the mess decks below he heard the ship waking to life. The bedclothes were infinitely desirable in the last moments before turning out. Summoning all his will, he pushed the sheet back and rolled out on to the deck, and across the short space to the basin.

After dowsing his face in the hot water his man had left he was crossing to where his coaling gear had been laid out on the second, unoccupied bunk when he felt the deck move beneath him. The collier had arrived. He heard the squeal of wire through fairleads, brief, shouted orders, the hammering of steam winches, and presently from below the shrill of the pipe, followed by the call for the hands to fall in. Buttoning his trousers he thought he could already sense the acrid smell of coal in his nostrils. He opened his wardrobe and pulled out the ancient monkey jacket that served on these occasions with threadbare sleeves and two rings of braid grimed and dull; throwing it on, he buttoned it around his muffler and made for the door.

'Had a queer dream last night,' Acheson said to him as they strolled to their stations when the hands had been reported correct. 'I was saying goodbye to a crowd of people. Went back to my room and found two strange maids clearing up. They were talking in German! I asked them what they were doing here – they said they'd taken the place! It'd be funny if we met 'em today wouldn't it!'

George thought of Kate on the splendid black horse; there was little chance of that coming to pass today! He was glad; it had been too vivid and deeply frustrating on several counts: his own prowess on a horse left much to be desired.

The hands, spurred by the chill, were tumbling across to the collier and down the hatches, shovels and bundles of sacks thrown after them over the coamings. On the battle-cruiser's deck parties unfolding the canvas deck cloths bobbed ferociously like participants in an obstacle race at a children's party; others ran away with the wire whips, reeving them through blocks to weave the familiar patterns between the derricks.

The bugle sounded. Like a machine at the touch of the starter, the apparatus came to life: shovels crunched in the collier's holds, winches rattled, hooks descended, swinging and hung for moments out of sight before rising triumphantly with a clutch of bags, swaying and spewing little knobs of coal and dust; the blocks jumped and quivered as the whips tautened, rumbling round the sheaves and the bags flew across, landing with a crash on the deck cloths, black spores rising as the waiting men converged like rugby forwards and the marines ran their barrows up behind. Time ceased, superseded by the rhythmic swing and crash of the hoists, the squeal of the barrows' wheels and the competitive tally, hold against hold, every man against the ship's previous record. In the first hour they clocked up 205 tons and were well on the way to exceeding this when the bugle called them to breakfast.

'One thousand, two hundred and eighty-eight tons to go,' Wigram said, pushing his empty plate aside. 'In round figures.'

As the others finished eating and sat back with their coffee the usual queries about the latest messages and speculation about their next destination surfaced. Then all talk was silenced by two electrifying summonses, one for Wigram, one for the Engineer Commander. Strange ships had been sighted to the southward; the Admiral had ordered steam for full speed. There was a scramble for the door and a dash up the ladders. George turned aft for his cabin instead and pulled his binoculars from the 'battle bag' he kept ready for sudden calls before following up on deck. Judging that the fore top and bridge might be crowded, he swung aft and climbed the mainmast strut to the after control top.

The strangers were immediately visible over the land rising beyond Port Stanley Harbour to the south; two were steaming in a north-easterly direction as if making for Cape Pembroke at the mouth of their own anchorage, another group could be seen further off on the rim of the horizon. It was a perfect morning now, the air so clear and bright the division between sea and sky was as if incised by a knife. Focusing his glasses on the nearer ships George could make out every detail. It was scarcely credible, yet there was no question, the larger of the two was an armoured cruiser of the Scharnhorst class. Wondering if perhaps he had willed himself to see her, he lowered the glasses and counted under his breath to ten before raising them again. It was a vision: the sea was blue and calm, the intermittent flash of the wakes so white, and there steaming towards them, the very ships they were chasing! He moved his glasses to the group just over the horizon and was confirmed. He couldn't see the hulls, but the four tall, evenly spaced funnels between symmetrically disposed masts with round fighting tops, and the peculiar chimney-like appearance of the narrower tops of the funnels identified the larger as another Scharnhorst class protected cruiser.

Two maids speaking in German in Acheson's room! What an extraordinary coincidence – if that was what it was. Henry occasionally had these odd dreams that foretold aspects of the future, so did Willy.

The next hour matched that first morning of the war he remembered so vividly in the old *Bacchante* – intense excitement about everyday tasks alternated by sudden catches at the heart. They resumed coaling while the engineers fired up, then shoved off the collier and went to stations for leaving harbour.

By this time the two nearer Germans, obviously recon-
noitring, possibly also intending to bombard the wireless
station near Hooker Point, had approached within about
eight miles of the old battleship, *Canopus*, moored at the
eastern extremity of Port Stanley Harbour with her guns
pointing seaward. She fired ranging shots, then a salvo; all
fell short, but the Germans altered away. Once out of range
again they continued their northerly course to look into the
Sound. The briefest glance was all they required: two pairs
of tripod masts under the thunderous rolls of smoke were
unmistakably the sign of dreadnoughts or battle-cruisers.
They turned away again, this time keeping a southerly course
to join their further division, then made off together under
a spreading black pall.

The guard ship, *Kent*, had already weighed, and she
steered after them, then the *Glasgow* went out after her. Half
an hour later the engineers reported all boilers connected and
they weighed and threaded their way past the observation
mines laid across the entrance; the *Invincible* came out just
astern of them, then the *Carnarvon* and *Cornwall*, leaving
only the *Bristol* still inside. Action stations sounded before
they passed Cape Pembroke. George dashed down to his
cabin to grab his battle bag, then up again to his position in
the after control top, where the rest of his little party, with
dust-blackened clothes and faces smeared black where they
had wiped them with hands or sleeves, had already
assembled. Dumping his bag, he pulled out his glasses and
trained them on the German squadron, now hull down on
their starboard bow; only their topmasts and the tops of their
funnels beneath thick smoke were visible and these were
blotted out from time to time by drifts of smoke from their
own funnels just below.

'Reckon we'll ketch 'em, sir?' Tomkins asked in a breathless voice.

'Sure to,' he replied. The morning remained perfect, not
a cloud in the sky, only a light breeze behind them ruffling
the gently heaving surface of the ocean and the air so clear
and crisp one could have seen to the ends of the earth if the
horizon had not been in the way. He made a rapid calculation:
assuming the enemy made a shade under their designed

477

speed of twenty-two and a half knots – for they could not have been in dock recently – while they themselves managed a shade more than their twenty-five knots on paper – which they had made on previous occasions – a four knot difference – about two hours to get within range. 'We'll catch 'em by dinner,' he said.

Tomkins clicked his teeth. There was a strange light in his eyes, accentuated by the mask of grime like a Christy minstrel. He was too young to have seen action; he would be wondering – as he was himself – he hoped his expression did not betray it.

There was a whistle from the speaking tube. He took off the cap.

'T.S. – after control – testing communications –'

By the time they cleared the Cape all routine tests had been carried out. George looked round at the flagship astern; she was coming out under a heavier than usual cloud of impenetrable smoke, against which Sturdee's flag and two ensigns decorating the halyards above her bridge blew out whitely; others he saw occasionally through the murk surrounding her main. Astern of her the heavy cruiser, *Carnarvon* and the slightly smaller *Cornwall* wore equally brave displays. They themselves had five ensigns, he thought, although it was difficult to see through the fog above the funnels.

The *Invincible* overhauled them gradually to port, and he saw Sturdee's flag lieutenant climbing the foremast strut to enter the director tower just below the foretop. With his glasses he made out West and his party in the top looking as grimed as his own men; scanning down to the bridge he saw the Captain, Beamish, standing at the starboard rail looking towards their own bridge. He saw him take off his cap and wave it, evidently at their Old Man. Signalmen were busy below, and a hoist climbed to the yardarm.

Moments later there was a call up the voicepipe, 'Signal from Flag – General Chase!'

The words thrilled him, conjuring images of victories under sail and the great names he had learned of first in the *Britannia*'s classroom, Hawke and Rodney and Boscawen –

478

He turned and repeated the signal to his party. They cheered rather wildly he thought.

Looking forward again and raising his glasses, he trained them on the Germans; already they seemed closer; certainly the *Kent* and *Glasgow* were much nearer; they were being overhauled fast. With the calm day and the following breeze some of the sensations of speed were lacking, but there was the usual juddering and roar from the ventilation below, the jagged lacework of foam passing rapidly down the side and the angled rollers pressed out, stretching away on the quarter throwing light reflections. He felt an elation of a different kind from anything he had experienced, his mind over-whelmed by the thought that it was real.

They quickly overhauled the *Kent* and left her astern; the *Carnarvon* and *Cornwall* had dropped far behind; only the *Glasgow* was able to keep up; she hung some three miles ahead on the port bow. He sensed an appreciable easing of their own speed though, and soon afterwards heard the pipe 'Hands to clean and dinner!' He looked at his watch – 11.40 – the morning had flown. Leaving his seat to turn for the hatch, he saw their cruisers well astern; no doubt Sturdee hoped they would catch up before he closed the range.

In the wardroom between mouthfuls, he thought he de-tected an unnatural curtness to his words and tried to make his voice more relaxed. Images of the coming action pressed to the forefront of his mind. What would it be like watching those closely-spaced German salvoes arriving? What would it be like when they were hit? What were the chances of damage to the fore control sufficient to allow him a chance to take over? The thought was beastly disloyal. Yet a single shot might sever the navyphone cables and voicepipes through the mast strut –

He glanced across at V-W, hoping he could not read his mind. The big man looked up and caught his eye. Perhaps he could; *he* would not relish a mere spectator's role.

After eating he went to his cabin and took off every stitch of clothing and rinsed himself down all over from the basin before putting on clean underclothes and socks in case of wounds.

Action stations was sounded again at 12.25. Climbing to the top, straining sounds and spasms of shaking and the sight of foam sliding faster down the sides made it evident they were working up to full speed again. They tested communications quickly. The German squadron was within eight miles now and making a splendid sight against the bright horizon; they seemed to be in line abreast with the *Gneisenau* on the left, then the *Nuremberg*, the *Scharnhorst*, flying von Spee's flag, the *Dresden* and the *Leipzig* at the extreme right and a little way astern of the others. They were steaming away to the south-east directly before the wind, which blew the smoke back over their masts.

He glanced back; Sturdee's attempt to let the *Carnarvon* catch up had failed; both she and the *Cornwall* were trailing some five miles astern with the *Kent* about half way between them. As their own speed increased the two were left further astern; even the *Glasgow*, now broad on the *Invincible*'s port bow, could not keep her former position ahead. The distance to the fleeing Germans was closing as fast.

Through the voicepipe from the transmitting station he heard the fore control rangetaker's call repeated, 'Range oner – height – four – double ho – Range oner – height – three – double ho –' then he heard the Old Man in the conning tower tell V-W to open fire on the left hand ship, *Gneisenau*, when he was ready. He looked at his watch – 12.53 – and cautioned Ashwell at the time of flight clock.

Looking forward he saw out of the corner of his eye the outspread shape of an albatross. There was an incongruity about the scene – the limitless sea shimmering in the sun, the white bird gliding against the brightness of the sky making nonsense of the game they were about to begin.

A crash sounded from the left hand gun of A turret – Acheson's. He made out brownish-orange traces of the cordite thinning under the funnel smoke, but couldn't see the shell itself as it rose on its way. He lifted his glasses, ready to put them to his eyes. Clouds of the funnel smoke from below crossed the range continually, obscuring his view.

'Twenty-four –' Ashwell said, 'twenty-six – twenty-eight – thirty – thirty-two –'

480

Through a fringe of smoke, he saw a water column illuminated by the sun stand up short of the target, and heard V-W's immediate correction repeated in the transmitting station, 'Up 400!' They had begun! It was exactly like battle practice, but at a greater range than anything he had witnessed before. His pulse was quite steady.

The right gun of A turret fired. He waited, but at the crucial moment a cloud of funnel smoke blotted out the target. The shot was evidently still short, and out for line, for he heard 'Left two! Up 400!' Then the *Invincible*, which had pulled rather ahead of them on the port bow, also opened fire, he guessed at the *Gneisenau* for after one more shot from A turret, he heard the Old Man telling V-W to shift target to the right hand light cruiser, *Leipzig*, now well astern of the others.

As alternate guns from A turret crashed out at deliberate intervals, interspersed by ranging shots from the *Invincible*, he realized both were aiming at the *Leipzig* – no doubt to try and force von Spee to drop back to cover her with his heavy ships. The *Leipzig*'s captain handled his cruiser consummately, altering every time he saw the flash of the guns by the look of it, so that even when they found her range, the rising white columns were always just off for line.

He heard the Old Man order an alteration to starboard. As they came round, bringing the enemy squadron finer on the bow and the light wind almost right astern funnel smoke began to wreathe the top, shutting him from all sight of the action. It was like entering a tunnel in a train without being able to pull up the windows; smuts and cinders drifted in until his party were looking as if they had not been to wash. He told Tomkins to let him know directly he saw anything more, and squatted down, coughing, his ear by the voicepipe, trying to interpret the course of events from the terse comments passing between the Old Man, V-W and the transmitting station, interspersed by the crash and slight shaking as one or other of Acheson's guns fired.

All he could make out for certain was the ever-decreasing range – down to 15,000 yards – 14,000 – they must start hitting soon.

'Sir –' Tomkins was pointing.

He leaped up to his seat and took his glasses. It was the *Leipzig*, but broader on the starboard bow and appreciably larger in his field of vision. A fountain erupted ahead of her as he watched, so close as to be scarcely visible between the low side and the smoke cloud hanging over her, but he was certain he saw the flash of water in the sun and thought she must have steamed right through it. She appeared undamaged still.

A moment later he saw her alter sharply away until she was showing her starboard quarter; soon afterwards the *Nuremberg* emerged into view from behind the smoke, also showing her quarter, making off in the same direction. He leaned to the voicepipe, expecting to hear they were turning to starboard after them. Instead he heard the Old Man say 'Light cruisers are scattering!' and a moment afterwards the voice of the chief yeoman, with him in the conning tower, reading out a signal for a turn to port.

Looking towards the *Invincible*, he saw her begin to turn; they followed her round until she was ahead again, leading them north-easterly at right angles to their previous course. The funnel smoke hung horribly to starboard, obscuring everything, but it was evident from the way all turrets swung to point their guns a little abaft the starboard beam that the enemy heavy cruisers were out in that direction. Von Spee must have altered round to accept action in an attempt to allow his light cruisers to escape – a noble decision. He could just make them out, all three of them steaming away, and right aft where the air was clear of smoke, he saw the *Glasgow* crossing their own curving wake to go in chase, and beyond her the *Kent* and *Cornwall* also turning to follow the enemy light cruisers. Beyond them, a good ten miles off over the edge of the horizon was the old *Carnarvon*.

Through the voicepipe he heard the Old Man give *Scharnhorst* as the new target; the communications number in the transmitting station intoned, 'Range – oner – fife – six – double ho –'

Trying to penetrate the passing banks of smoke, he caught occasional glimpses of one or other of the enemy heavy cruisers. He saw the *Scharnhorst* as she fired at them, bright

482

flashes twinkling along her side, then she was blotted out again and he could just make out the *Gneisenau* ahead of her. It was a distinctly odd sensation, waiting for the salvo to arrive; he thought of the Hun spotting officer over in the other ship staring at them, counting under his breath, a man of flesh and blood like himself, concentrating all his powers on their destruction. It was a disturbing image. Somewhere high up beyond the smoke the shells were on their way, their trajectories now ordained. Lord! He had too much time to think; if only there was something he could *do*. For a start if he could *see* properly through this wretched fog rolling out of the funnels below –

Three water columns rose magically from the sea, considerably smaller than those made by their own shells and some thousand yards short he was glad to see. They had a poisonous yellow-green tinge at the base, and after they collapsed they left rings of noxious mist hanging on the surface. He imagined the German control officer ordering an 'up' correction.

The next three shells arrived soon afterwards, considerably nearer, tightly bunched; it was marvellous to see how close together they were at this range. This rapid opening fire seemed to sting V-W to reply in kind; through the voicepipe he heard the order for 'Salvoes' repeated, and shortly afterwards, in place of the thud of the single ranging gun from Acheson's forward turret, there was a louder crash below and the top was shaken as if by giant hands as Q and X turrets went off.

Tomkins gave a sort of low growl. From Q turret immediately below he heard or thought he heard the hiss of compressed air through the barrel, followed by a subterranean rumbling as the chain rammer thrust the next round home. He knew exactly how Tomkins felt; he felt his own fists clench as he counted the seconds and strained his eyes into the smoke. There they were! He could see both enemy cruisers now; the *Scharnhorst* seemed to have closed the gap to her consort; it seemed she was intent on overhauling her to take her rightful place at the head of the line. He saw the *Gneisenau* fire, evidently at the *Invincible* for it was not the twinkling effect he had observed when they were the target,

483

but distinct flashes. Seconds afterwards a salvo from the *Scharnhorst* crashed into the sea shockingly close off their starboard quarter. Startled exclamations sounded in the top. The nearest of three water columns rose not thirty yards from the ship's side and he heard the whizzing sound of splinters through the air. As the white pillar collapsed a section of rainbow gleamed briefly through the spray. The unexpectedness of it had caused him to lose his count of the seconds, but it made no difference; when he looked back the enemy was hidden behind smoke. Their salvo evidently landed over for he heard a 'down' correction, and shortly afterwards the top shook again as the right hand guns crashed from all turrets.

His ears were still ringing with the concussion when he heard the close screaming of the *Scharnhorst*'s next salvo through the air above, followed by explosions to port as the nearest of the shells landed some hundred yards away.

'Jesus!' Tomkins exclaimed.

The German shooting was superb. Backhouse had not exaggerated. He thought of the enemy control officer ordering 'Down 200!' The next bunch must surely straddle, and closely spaced as the shells were, one or two must hit. He tensed involuntarily as he waited. What was V-W doing? Why wasn't he firing? Through the voicepipe, he heard 'Up 200!' That sounded more like it!

The top was shaken again as a salvo crashed out. Through a momentary thinning of the smoke he saw the shells rising away into blue sky, and below them the strangely symmetrical shapes of the enemy ships with their four upright, evenly-spaced funnels with chimney-like extensions, and upright masts at a similar distance either end. The *Scharnhorst* had almost caught the *Gneisenau* and was about to overtake. Picking up his glasses, he studied her; she looked in splendid shape, not a mark on her, and as he held her in view he saw along her side the winking red lights of her guns magnified in the lenses. For the first time he felt anxiety about the result.

The feeling was reinforced by the tearing, rushing sound as her previous salvo arrived. The nearest shell dropped almost alongside; a ring of foam surged outwards and he

484

heard the hum and metallic clang of splinters. He watched the water column in fascination as they sped past it leaving it collapsing in the rolling froth of their progress.

'*Jesus!*' Tomkins said again, in hollower tones this time.

Through the voicepipe he heard the closing ranges intoned. It was distinctly nerve-wracking to have to watch this kind of shooting without being able to affect the result one way or another, or even *see* the enemy for periods. It was lack of occupation causing these jitters. He wished V-W would find the range and give the Hun control something to think about.

The top shook to another four-gun salvo, and another shortly after it. He was waiting to hear what corrections would be ordered when an exultant cry came up the voice-pipe, '*Hit!*' He felt a physical thrill and his mood reversed itself; his anxiety dropped away. He turned to tell his party, grinning as they cheered. Then they scored again. Shortly afterwards he heard the Old Man ordering a shift of target; evidently the flagship had taken the lead.

Moments later he was able to see the ships again; they looked magnificent steaming in close line ahead, *Scharnhorst* leading, two white columns from V-W's last salvo standing high before the *Gneisenau*'s funnels, blotting out all sight of the after two. They were straddling her! He strained to make out any signs of a hit, but only saw the red lights from her own guns winking along the side as she fired, and the bursts of smoke. The shells rose high, dark specks quickly growing in size as they began their descent until he lost them in the smoke. Three fountains rose five hundred yards or more short.

Her next salvo was closer, and within five minutes shells were again dropping alongside, alternately just short and whirring like giant bluebottles overhead. He heard the Old Man's voice echoing inside the conning tower, cursing the *Invincible*'s smoke. In desperation it seemed V W went into rapid salvoes. The top shook to repeated, thunderous discharges, George's head rang; he willed each clutch of shells on its way, wondering with some disconnected part of his mind when they themselves were going to be hit by one of these beautifully-controlled enemy salvoes. It was a miracle they had not been struck already. They had surely used up all their luck by now. It was only the very high trajectory of the shells at this extreme stage, the consequently small danger space as they fell almost vertically that had saved them so far.

He realized he could see them again. A single water column stood up, hiding the *Gneisenau*'s mainmast and simultaneously the reddish-black glow of a hit appeared on deck between her after funnels. He repressed an urge to yell as he snatched his glasses. He was studying her still when another hit went home, this time in the side below her forward funnel, knocking out one of her casemates he imagined. Magnified in the glasses it was as if dark chaff erupted from the interior of the ship, followed at once by bright flames, then thick, black smoke obscuring everything, hanging at the base of the funnels.

The distance to the enemy had been falling, but as their own funnel smoke rose to obscure the view again he heard opening ranges repeated. Looking back along the course marked in pale whirls across the deep, sunlit blue of the sea, he saw they had altered to port. It was Sturdee, not Spee, hauling away! Evidently West had succeeded in impressing him with the importance of staying outside 12,000 yards! No doubt the *Scharnhorst*'s shooting had driven the point home. He wondered if the *Invincible* had been hit.

The enemy salvoes dropped short as they drew away, finally ceasing altogether, while their own fire grew more deliberate, but he saw the bright glow of another hit between the enemy's funnels before they checked fire altogether. Relaxing from the tension, looking at his watch, he was astonished to see it was almost two o'clock. It struck him that it was taking rather a long time to finish them off; at this distance and with the flagship's smoke fouling the range hits were obviously difficult to obtain. Unless they could start shooting more effectively the enemy might succeed in drawing out the fight for long enough to escape in the dark.

Von Spee evidently had that idea for when he was next able to make them out both enemy ships were turning away sharply. They continued round until they were showing their

486

formerly disengaged starboard quarters, heading about due south, he estimated.

Peering forward, he saw the *Invincible* beginning to come round after them; there was a large hole in her side at about mid-length just above her armour – a few people would miss their cabins tonight, he thought, or the wardroom perhaps. The top began to heel as they followed the flagship round.

He was seized with a strange deflation of spirits, perhaps the concussions he could still feel echoing in his head and the suffocating smell of smoke. He was possessed by an urgent need to do something.

'After control –' It was the Old Man himself.

'This is after control, sir.'

'What did you see?'

'Very little, sir.'

There was a pause, then, 'Come down to the conning tower. Bring your glasses. You've another officer up there?'

'Adams, sir, Midshipman –'

'Good!'

His spirits lifted. Slinging his glasses around his neck, he told Adams he was in charge of the top, squeezed around Tomkins to the hatch and lowered himself on to the rungs of the starboard mast strut.

P and Q turrets were still training to port as he stepped on to the flying deck. The muzzles of the guns had changed colour; he could smell the fumes from the blistered paint. The next thing that struck him was the second cutter; it looked as if it had been opened out by a giant blow. The strakes bulged or hung in strips like kindling – the effects of the blast from Q turret. Something similar seemed to have happened to the starboard boats forward of the two turrets, although nothing quite so drastic. Otherwise he could see no damage. On impulse he crossed behind the funnel to the port side ladders and called down to the four inch guns' crews sheltering on the quarterdeck behind X turret. They appeared most cheerful.

'We're hittin' 'em ain't we, sir?' a reserve man called Livingstone shouted up.

'Hard! Two on the Flag, three for certain on *Gneisenau*!'

487

They cheered.

By the time he arrived at the conning tower and clambered inside through the massive armoured hatch, fire had still not been re-opened. The enemy were ahead on the starboard bow but scarcely visible through the dense black cloud trailed by the *Invincible*. The Old Man was in a fever of impatience, attempting to pace a few steps in the cramped space, shooting interrogations up to V-W every few minutes, but he could see no better from the top, and his rangefinder was useless.

'We're certainly closing them, sir,' Carrington said.

'What damn use is that, Pilot, if we can't see to shoot!' The Old Man rounded suddenly on George. 'What do you say, sir!'

'No use at all, sir.'

'No thundering use at all! Odds teeth!' It was evident he felt like saying more; instead his tone calmed, 'Guns suggested you might be of more use to him down here. He thought you might make out somethin' under this infernal smoke.'

'I see, sir.'

'Hanged if I do! There's no harm in tryin', I suppose. It can't make it any worse!'

'No, sir!'

George, exchanging a glance with Carrington, stepped around him to the forward observation slit to starboard of the wheel, and gazed ahead at the smoke pall hanging down the range. He wondered why Sturdee had not ordered at least a quarter line with a greater interval than their present close line ahead – or simply allowed them to choose their own course to clear the range as his original general chase signal had suggested.

They heard the flagship's guns; orange-brown smoke mixed with the dark grey haze ahead. The Old Man called into the voicepipe to V-W to open fire if he could see anything.

The concussion of the resulting shot from A turret immediately in front had scarcely ceased ringing inside the chamber when George felt as much as saw the blinding flash of an explosion from the top of the turret. Splinters dinned on the armour plating before him and he felt something hum by his scalp, parting his hair just above his left ear, clanging against metal somewhere behind. It had happened before he could move. Choking fumes blew in through the observation slit.

'Love a fugin' duck!' the quartermaster said softly without thought of where he was.

George, coughing, looked round. The Old Man was stepping to Carrington, who had his hand up to his forehead; his fingers were bloody when he took them away, and blood flowed from a gash above his eye in a little stream down his cheek.

The Old Man pulled a handkerchief from his pocket and pressed it to Carrington's brow. 'This is clean.' And turning to the messenger, 'Fetch a dressing – quick man!'

The damage report came through presently: 'A' turret rangefinder and both four inch quickfirers knocked out; otherwise everything was in full working order.

'Two rangefinders blinded by smoke,' the Old Man growled, 'the other one shot out! How d'you suppose the devils saw us when we can't see them!'

Carrington took the bloody handkerchief away from his brow as the messenger handed him a dressing. 'Lucky shot,' he hazarded.

The Old Man stepped to the voicepipe and again asked V-W what he could see.

'Precious little, sir!'

'Keep firing! Don't let the devils have it all their own way!'

Acheson's right gun crashed out and they felt the ship quiver; gun-smoke drifted to port óver the two four inch mounted on the turret roof. They looked a sorry sight; one barrel was skewed and pointing skywards.

'Signal flying from flagship!' the Chief Yeoman sang out. 'Turn twenty degrees to port together!'

Acknowledging, the Old Man raised his glasses towards the enemy. 'What d'you think, Pilot?'

'I believe they've come round, sir –'

'I believe you're right. I'll say this – they're not short of pluck. The devil's tryin' to close the range again!'

'Execute, sir!' the yeoman called.

489

George heard Carrington order, 'Starboard ten!'

'Starboard ten, sir! Ten of starboard on, sir!'

As they came round, he saw a full-rigged sailing ship on the port bow. She must have been visible for some time, but all his attention had been concentrated in the other direction. Her white sails gleamed in the sun; what an extraordinary apparition! She might have drifted in from another world.

With the enemy on the beam again at the completion of the turn, V-W resumed four-gun salvoes. It was a comforting sound. The splashes seemed to prevent the *Gneisenau*'s gunners making their former good practice, but George could not see any hits going home. The *Invincible*'s smoke still fouled the range horribly. Something must happen soon; the range was closing rapidly –

Sturdee evidently thought it was coming down too fast; he ordered another turn to port together and almost immediately after it a large turn which brought them round on to their former southerly heading; this time they were leading ship.

'See how he likes *our* smoke!' the Old Man said grimly.

The enemy was clear in view now, showing up brilliantly at 15,000 yards. It was evident the *Invincible* had been hitting the flagship; one of her funnels was leaning, she had a fire forward, and a large hole in her side. V-W quickly found her range and began to straddle; immediately von Spee turned away; the *Gneisenau* followed in beautiful formation and the Old Man turned to conform, keeping the enemy flagship sufficiently broad on the bow to allow three turrets to bear.

They began hitting almost at once. At first George kept the score, puffballs of white smoke from lyddite or dense black from common shell, but the hits became too numerous and many were obscured by smoke from the fires started. The flagship continued to fight bravely but with an ever-decreasing number of guns, and no longer in controlled salvoes; only occasional shells came close. He found his first elation at hitting change to something like sorrow for the poor devils receiving such fearful punishment. In his glasses, the glow of numerous fires was plainly visible through gaping holes in her side, areas of formerly grey paint were hideously

490

blackened, her upperworks a shambles of twisted, black steel, her funnels holed like colanders, two shot away completely.

In less than half an hour the battle had been decided. By then the *Scharnhorst* was little more than a smoking hulk, listing and obviously sinking, but her colours were still flying, and she turned towards them in a last, vain effort to sell her life dearly – just as the *Good Hope* had done at Coronel. Cradock was avenged, but it was a sad sight.

The *Gneisenau* passed her, and the Old Man told V-W to shift target. Astern, the *Invincible* took over the task of sinking the wreck, now practically stopped in the water. West would not be enjoying it. George shivered involuntarily as he turned to watch for splashes about their new target.

The navyphone bell rang.

'The Commander, sir,' the Old Man's doggie said after a moment, 'We've been hit on the main derrick. No serious damage. Three casualties from the quarterdeck being taken below.'

The Old Man nodded.

George glanced back towards the *Scharnhorst*. She had turned over on her beam ends. He thought he could make out dark, ant-like figures on her horizontal side. He looked away.

The *Gneisenau* was already suffering as the *Invincible* turned her guns on her, and it was plain the end could not be long. There was a brief hiatus when Sturdee instructed them to take station astern of him, and they completed a 360° turn to come round into the flagship's wake. Immediately the range was obscured.

'Holy catfish!' the Old Man exploded, and after interrogating V-W about what he could see, 'I've a mind to leave the line, Pilot. What d'you think?'

'We're not doing much good here, sir.'

'I've a damn good mind to leave the line!' He glowered at George. 'Nelson would've!'

'He did, sir!'

'By God, he did!' He looked at Carrington a moment, then at the quartermaster, 'Starboard fifteen!'

'Starboard fifteen, sir!'

'What did old Jervis say when Nelson turned out of the line?'

George wondered who he was addressing; he was staring out, head turning to watch the *Invincible* as they hauled out.

'Bravo, sir!' Carrington hazarded.

He glared at him, then turned to the swinging compass card. 'Steady on one two oh!'

'Steady on one two oh, sir! Midships!'

'Midships, sir!' the quartermaster repeated.

They headed away from the *Invincible* on almost opposite courses, leaving the curtain of smoke surrounding her well on their quarter.

The Old Man leaned to the voicepipe. 'Guns, see what you can do now!'

The salvoes had already commenced.

Once again they watched as a splendid ship was reduced to a hulk, the *Invincible*'s and their own guns concentrating from different directions with devastating visible effects. Within a short space the enemy guns had been reduced to silence; they checked fire and started to close at full speed. The day had clouded and a slight drizzle begun, and with the smoke from her fires it was difficult to see whether her flag was still flying. She answered the question a moment later: a single shot directed at the *Invincible*, closing her from the other direction. They altered and opened fire again. In six minutes, as she had not fired, they checked and headed towards her once more. Again she fired a single gun, this time at them, and they had to turn and open fire once more.

'I don't like this,' the Old Man said. 'She can do no more than she has, for heaven's sake! Good Lord –!'

Carrington had drawn his attention to something on the port quarter, 'the *Carnarvon*!'

The cruiser was straining up under dense clouds of smoke.

'Too late!' the Old Man grinned. 'Too late, old chum!'

Within ten minutes it was evident that the *Gneisenau* was going. She had turned and was lying bows towards them inside 10,000 yards, listing heavily to starboard, smoke drifting from fires on deck.

'Cease firing!' the Old Man called into the voicepipe, then, hearing a salvo from the direction of the *Carnarvon*, he wheeled on the yeoman, 'Make to *Carnarvon*, "I think the enemy have hauled down their colours",' and to Carrington, 'Take her alongside, Pilot! Full speed!'

'Port ten!' Carrington said, and rang the engine room telegraph handle round twice.

The Old Man swung on the messenger, 'Pass the word to all hands. "The enemy is sinking. You may come on deck," ' and to his doggie, 'Tell the Commander to get all boats over to pick up survivors!' He turned to George, 'You can take the first one in the water, Steel! Tell him I told you so.'

She went down before we could reach her. Her starboard list increased gradually until at the end it was very fast and she turned right over. The hands were fearfully excited, rushed up to the fo'c's'le – those who weren't manning the few boats that could still swim, and started cheering as if it was 'No time' at a footer match. The Old Man very properly ordered the 'Alert', and they stopped and came to attention to watch her sink. It was very moving in a horrible way, Kate. It is so different from looking at a picture, or trying to imagine it, it is sad and terrible and awe-inspiring all at the same time to see a great ship go down even if she is an enemy.

It was even more awful when we reached them in the boats, the ones who had managed to grab a lifejacket or a hammock or a piece of wood all crying out for help. It sounded exactly like the bleating of lambs. It was difficult to have anything but sympathy for them – queer considering the intense hatred we have always felt for the Hun.

The water was absolutely clear and we could see several of the poor devils sinking way down below us as we came up. The water was 39° – it was cold enough in the boats with a beastly icy drizzle. It was surprising we managed to save as many as we did, but between us we collected up nearly 200, we have a number aboard now, including their Commander – an officious piece of work – and their gunnery Jack who has been spilling the beans famously. Why they didn't hit us more often no one can understand. They were after *me* all right! Three splinters went through the main top, and my rangetaker told me afterwards in some glee one of them passed clean through the place I normally occupy! 'You would've bin a goner, sir, an' that's the truth!' Then, no sooner had I got into the conning tower than a shell burst on top of Acheson's turret, the splinters buzzing in like hornets, one removing a piece of skin from above Carrington's eye, one I felt *through my hair*! An inch or so to the right and I'd have been a goner and that's the truth!

We only had four casualties – one man killed by a splinter when the main derrick was hit, and three slightly wounded. The *Invincible* only had one slightly wounded – her Commander! – although she suffered many more hits than we did, they have counted twenty-one and there are probably more, we only had three. That was through no fault of the enemy gunnery as I told their 'Guns', a pleasant enough fellow by the name of Busch – Boosh! He gave us a graphic description of the state of affairs on board towards the end. Our shells had progressively broken down through the decks right down to the armoured deck, systematically wrecking the batteries, blowing out whole sections of the ship's side plating, in one case an entire casemate complete with eight inch gun and crew simply tumbled overside. The light guns' crews were kept below as reserves for the six inch and 8.3s. All were required! Finally there was, practically speaking no one left alive at the guns. Communications were completely destroyed.

At the end Busch was asked by the Captain, 'Why don't you fire?' 'I cannot speak to the guns' he replied. The Captain then ordered the second artillery officer to go and have a look. He reported that he could not get around the ship – there were no decks left – but he could *see* all the guns, and they were all disabled except for the fore turret that had a single round left – nothing could be got up from below. 'Order them to fire!' the Captain said. That was the one they fired off at us as we were closing to get the men off – the last shot in the locker! There is no question they put up a gallant fight. At the end they opened the valves to scuttle her. There were about 850 in the ship's company and they reckon there were about 300 alive and mustered on the quarterdeck and fo'c's'le as the ship went down. Their after hospital, where they had collected some fifty wounded was completely destroyed by a shell in the last phase of the action. One wonders how men can live through such an experience without being *changed* somehow, yet they all seem cheerful now, talking away in their guttural jargon to all hours. It makes one think a bit.

V-W is very buffed, as you can imagine, says that provided he is allowed a clear range – without the flagship fouling it! – and a steady course he is now confident about engaging targets at considerably greater distances than we have ever practised. As for myself – I don't think I'm cut out to be a spectator, Kate, I'm terribly pleased about our victory naturally, but feel rather as if I'd been out for a duck in both innings and hadn't done much work in the field either! A curious, disappointed sort of elation!

Anyhow, as you probably know by now the *Leipzig* and *Nuremberg* were brought to book by our cruisers, leaving only the *Dresden* at large, and we heard yesterday she has been interned at Sandy Pt in the Magellan Straits, so it looks as if our task is complete – if the reports prove true – and we can return and perhaps be granted forty-eight hours to enjoy what the King has been pleased to call our *opportune* success! It *was*, believe me! Had we been twenty-four hours later they would in all probability have taken the place, that was their game, they told us. They got the *fright of their lives* when they saw our tripod masts!!! Had no idea we'd been sent out! That was Fisher's doing – let those who will decry him. Wasn't it queer about Acheson's dream though? I had a dream that night too. It was about you and you would *not* look at me! I hope that will not be borne out by events!

Must close now, Kate – I'll need another envelope in any case to fit in this latest edition! We are due in at the place from whence we started tomorrow afternoon, there's sure to be a mail going. So long, *dearest* Kate, God bless you, I do so long to see you and hope now it will be sooner rather than later –

He put his name at the foot, and sat back, feeling guilty at

495

having spent so much time writing to her. He would have to repeat much of it now for the family. Henry would be furious if she knew his priorities!

He wondered again how he might bring about a rapprochement between her and Kate. Once she really came to know her – yet she was so *wilfully* contrary. They were both such strong characters in their own right, that was the difficulty. Now they had started off on the wrong foot it was going to be the devil's own job to bring them together; neither would bow the knee, that was certain.

8

As a child Henrietta had always been pleased her birthday came in January; it had extended the Christmas season marvellously, and there had been snow for parties – at least in recollection – and snow fights during which she had been able legitimately to make a thorough mess of the party dresses of anyone she didn't care for. Nowadays she thought of January as a dull month, and her birthdays depressed her. She was particularly depressed in January 1915; twenty-five had a rounded, horribly final feeling; it was not only divisible by five, therefore altogether lacking in subtlety, but halfway towards fifty which was positively the end of life. Twenty-five was the end of youth. It was deceptive of course; like every other age she could remember she could feel no difference, and when she examined herself from all angles in the mirror she could see no difference – if anything her skin was smoother, her jawline finer, her eyes more devastatingly clear than they had been at twenty-three or twenty or eighteen even.

And of course she *was* no different; she felt the hollow, thrilling tug inside – the mysterious ritual she had put off, not altogether put off, she would not have minded at all if Robin – it was the middle-aged men she had put off and the young hopefuls who looked on it as sport and drank too much in order to give themselves courage. The few young men she had really cared for had been honourable; if, as with Robin, she might have thought she was signalling once or twice that she would not have minded going some of the way, they had misunderstood, whether deliberately or because they had not expected it and so failed to interpret

497

the signals – if indeed she had made them clearly – she had no means of knowing. The fact remained, she had not passed through those mysterious portals – she was still a girl – of twenty-five – and five years could be swallowed in a season. Heavens, she had thought at twenty she was rather mature! If this war lasted five years, and Uncle Richard seemed to think it might, she would be thirty, absolutely the end of any possible pretence of being young –

There were times when she felt she would marry Robin tomorrow if he would only appear. That would be a mistake. She had chosen her course; her friends might look down on her for not acquiring status by acquiring a husband – she looked down on them for being unable to stand on their feet without one. They simply proved everything men said about the 'weaker half' –

She wondered where Robin could be – probably Gibraltar since the *Invincible* had need of repairs and Uncle Richard had said Gib was the most likely place outside the British Isles. It might be Malta. It didn't really matter where he was if he wasn't here. It was annoying all the same. After a victory like the Falklands one would have expected them to have allowed the ships home and the men the leave they deserved.

Her mind turned to the verses someone had made up after the battle to be sung at the *Invincible*'s concert party. She had copied the choruses on to large boards from the sheet he had sent, and sung it to the wives at the Lambeth club. She smiled, remembering the encores. She had been so proud of him, she had been quite unable to keep her voice steady as they joined in the choruses, bawling them out at the tops of their lungs –

> 'It's a long way to far-off Chile,
> It's a cup full of woe.
> It's a long way to where our squadron
> Lay a-shattered by the foe.
> Stand clear little Willy!
> Kaiser Bill beware!
> It's a long way – to far-off Chile,
> *But brave hearts – died there –*'

'Miss –' the Cabbie was looking at her. 'You did say Felpham 'Ouse, Miss –?'

'Thank you,' she smiled, and glanced out at the taximeter. Good heavens! Thank goodness it was not every day one was twenty-five!

The wrought iron gates were as they had always been, the mysterious scarlet and gilt armorial device worked into the centre which no one had been able to explain satisfactorily shone bright. The latch clinked with just the same sound as she pressed it up. At the end of the gravel drive the house stood tall and welcoming; it was something to do with the proportions of the windows or the warm red of the old bricks. The stone balustrade around the cornice above brought back those forbidden, breathtaking circuits of the roof which George had led – the dizziness when one looked down over the edge, leaning back, careful not to rest one's weight on the rough, pitted stone lest the mortar gave way –

She wondered if Harry and Babs did the same now. They had passed that stage though. Harry was a prefect at Marlborough – a fug! – disgusting name – with dreadful powers over the poor little boys in the house. Babs was almost fifteen. Would the war be over by the time she came out? How long ago her own coming out seemed! How silly her ideas then – and running away to the Davieses, what a waste! Not that she would have enjoyed the grind of parties, but at least she had been able to choose. Babs might not be able to if this terrible war went on. Would there be any young men left in any case? The senselessness of it struck her as it did on odd occasions, breaking through the ordinariness the war had acquired over the months to shock her again into horrified realization. For some reason she thought of Eggy – a fond, nostalgic tug of regret for those absurdly innocent days, his grave devotion which she had taken for granted. It astonished her now when she thought of it, and her acceptance. Popsy had been uncontainable the morning the news of his M.C. had come through. It had appeared in the papers later; she had cut out the paragraph and preserved it in the pages of her diary like the cutting about Alastair's death, afterwards thinking superstitiously that perhaps she ought not to have done so, perhaps it would mean he would join Alastair. It had been too late by then; she had done it; it would have been worse to take the cutting out and throw it away because once you had done something it was done for ever and all time and there was no use trying to expunge it. God knew that she had done it – if He was up there, and like Andy, she sometimes wondered, and more often lately. In any case she had written about it in her diary and she could not tear the pages out. She had felt vague unease, and she felt it now as she ran up the steps to the front door and pulled the great polished knob of the bell.

She heard it ringing inside, and immediately afterwards thought she heard someone moving across the hall. It was strange, they seemed to be going quickly towards the dining-room. She saw her mother's face for an instant, staring at her from around the curtain in the nearest dining-room window, her eyes dark with anxiety. Something was wrong: George? Willy? She felt all strength drain from her legs and her heart pound in her breast. The steps were coming towards the door now, and she heard her mother call to one of the maids that she would see to it. She didn't want the door to open; she was sure it was Willy – how he could go down in those submarine boats she had never been able to understand –

'Henry!' Her mother sounded relieved, but her expression changed quickly. 'Is something wrong?'

Henrietta gazed back, waiting for the blow to fall – yet it seemed her mother's anxiety was for *her* –

'No,' she replied faintly.

'Are you sure, Henry?' She took a step forward to take her arms in her hands. 'You're so *pale!*' then leaning, kissed her. *'Many – happy – returns!'*

'Oh – don't!' she smiled. 'I'm feeling quite ancient enough already –'

'Fie!'

As she started in, she saw her father in a dark suit lying in a rolled-up position at the foot of the stairs, one leg rising up the lower steps, the other bent beneath him, his head on the floor, thin, white hair straggling; he looked like a very large old doll that had been thrown down stairs; if she had not seen his chest moving she would have thought he was

500

dead. The unexpectedness of it made her want to scream; she checked it and it came out as a kind of squeak.

Her mother had tried to interpose between her and the sight. 'I'm sorry, Henry – it happened just before you came, I was – go on into the sitting-room, I'll –'

'*No*, Mama,' she turned on her. 'I shall help you.'

An infinite sadness passed for a moment behind her mother's dark eyes, so like George's in their power and assertiveness, even in distress – and she seemed to wilt a little as she nodded without a word, and turned. Henrietta followed towards the recumbent form, seized by agonies of guilt.

She relived the scene over and over again that night as, unable to sleep, she walked, not knowing or caring where or what happened to her, wrapped in the dark mantle of her thoughts, beyond which the blank houses, people she passed, groups of men shouting out sad, drunken ditties, rattling hooves and wheels, the stark coldness of the air, the raw places she rubbed on her toes with every step, the aching in her muscles, occasional lascivious greetings called out, leering faces remained unfocused blurs from another world.

All she could see was the sadness behind her mother's eyes and the hopeless, defiant small movement of her shoulders as she turned towards the bundle that was her Papa – and the change that came over her as together they started to lift him, her tender absorption in *him*, her poor, broken father, dragging breath through gravelly lungs, veined cheeks shrunk behind his whiskers, the blue eyes which had been his glory, so sunk and dull.

'John –?' he had asked, staring up with a horrified expression, as they eased him away from the steps.

'It's all right, Robby –'

'Iss John there – my man – John –?'

'Yes, yes, John is all right –'

He seemed not to have hurt himself by the fall, and it was comparatively easy to help him to his feet, and with his arms around both their shoulders walk him slowly up the stairs. She had expected to smell drink on his breath, but there was only a stale odour. He had recognized her, and half-way up

501

started struggling, telling her to go back below and fetch John –

'John is on deck,' her mother said. 'It's quite safe for her, Robby.'

'Yes, it's eased off –' He had started up again with firmer tread, but his forehead creased in puzzlement. 'When did he get back?'

'He's not back yet, but he will be soon –'

He had started sobbing, gently at first, then in spasms, and they had difficulty in getting him up the last steps.

At the top he turned to her, his eyes still swimming. 'You heard, Henry? You heard of his glorious victory?'

She nodded, glad that he had remembered her name – so often he couldn't – and smiled. 'It was a splendid victory.'

'You had better go down now, Henry,' her mother said when they had got him to his bedroom, 'the others may arrive. I can see to him now –'

The *others*! What an effort they had made for her. Uncle Richard had come, and Andy looking lean and very fit had managed to get the afternoon off from his training camp, and Mary had come over as if she still lived around the corner, and there was a wire from Willy and even George had managed to send a cable from wherever he was, and Babs had tried to restrain herself, although without a great deal of success; they really had made an effort. She had tried to respond, but had found herself casting glances at her mother, seeing her expression as she looked at Andy, imagining her life now with the boys fighting or about to go out, Harry impatient to complete his time at Marlborough, Mackinnon already at the front and the other servants leaving one by one to work in the munitions factories where they could get more money – and upstairs her poor Papa –

She had made a tremendous effort to be cheerful, but she had wanted them all to leave so that she could talk to her mother alone and tell her how sorry she was not to have helped more – had thought only of herself –

But of course when at last they had gone it had not seemed the right time to say things like that; her mother had been determinedly cheerful, shrugging off her father's fall as something one expected with his present condition. What *was* his condition? She had thought before that it was brought on by drink –

'He was so looking forward to your birthday, Henry, it was such a shame –'

What *was* his condition? If it was not drink, was he insane? If so was it hereditary –?

'Thank you, Mama – *so* much –'

'I was so glad George remembered too. What do you suppose your Uncle Richard meant!'

Uncle Richard had hinted that the war might not, after all, last as long as he had feared; there was something in the wind. He was not at liberty to divulge –

They hung on his words, her mother and Andy for quite different reasons, Andy desperate lest the war be over before his battalion was sent across to France. Uncle Richard had refused to say more.

'It may not come off. I mustn't raise your hopes –' and realizing of course from her mother's face that that was just what he had done, he had tried to change the topic quickly. 'At all events George has had his show and that's more than many other naval officers will be able to say. So far as fighting *ships* is concerned.'

He had laid so much emphasis on 'ships' with such a meaning look they had asked what he meant.

'I doubt they'll send their fleet out. After such a drubbing they'll not risk another. There are other targets for ships' guns,' and pausing again significantly, he had gone on to say something to her mother which had puzzled her slightly at the time, even more when reflecting on it since, 'George may yet get his chance.'

It had surprised her because she wondered how he knew of George's disappointment at his part in the battle. George's letter had only arrived recently; so far as she knew she had been the only one to read it that afternoon while waiting for the others to come.

'Shore targets?' Andy had come in quickly. 'In support of landings –?'

'Warm!' Uncle Richard had nodded approvingly.

'Is that what you meant? For shortening the war?'

He had nodded again. 'But not another word! And you must keep that under your hat!'

'Why are we *always* talking about the war?' her mother had come in, 'Do you really think it will be finished soon?'

They laughed.

'Isn't there a slight contradiction there?' Uncle Richard said, 'But yes, if I were a betting man, I'd give it evens. Of course it depends – if we want to smash Germany. As a nation. *Delenda est Germania* –' shaking his head, 'In that case I dare say it could drag on.' He had caught her mother's quick look across at Andy, and reached across to put his hand on hers. 'Don't worry. Saner counsels will prevail – on both sides.'

'I wonder,' her mother had said, 'When you think of that German captain – *deliberately* prolonging the fight after all hope had gone – those poor wretches in the water –'

'I know.' He patted her wrist.

How had he known? George had described those last two futile shots from the *Gneisenau* in his letter, as he had described his own feelings of disappointment at being little more than a spectator, and Uncle Richard had seemed to know about both.

The nigglings of doubt fed the feeling she had had about him and Kate since she had seen them together at Felpham House in the last fateful July days before the war. For George would have written to Kate – probably even before he wrote home. If Uncle Richard was seeing Kate – if he was her lover, incredible thought, yet not so fanciful with someone like Kate and an adventurer like Uncle Richard – if so he might easily have been shown the letter. That was another thing, her mother had mentioned George's letter and his description of the battle at tea. Uncle Richard had expressed interest then, but had made no attempt to follow it up afterwards. Of course he might have forgotten –

Her unworthy suspicions might have more to do with her dislike for Kate and possessive feelings for him; she had always thought him extraordinarily attractive, and he had always been so fond of her –

The chimes of a clock close by beat into her thoughts; there was a church to her left. She turned as if recognizing this was where her steps had been leading, and climbed the steps to the great, studded doors.

Inside the darkness was intense; she could just make out the windows as arches of paler dark either side. The door clanked behind, shutting out the world and its sounds. She stood while her eyes accustomed themselves, then picked her way cautiously towards the central aisle between the pews and started walking towards the altar, which she still couldn't see, although the pale shape of the window above showed her the direction. Her heels sounded like hammers in the silence. There was a nice, faint smell reminding her of the church at home, of woodwork and polish and care, old prayer books and consecrated space.

Coming to the altar steps, she moved sideways until she found the rail, then knelt, feeling suddenly enormously tired. Looking towards the cross, whose shape she could just make out now, she wondered if He were there. She willed Him to be, feeling perhaps He was, for He had known despair, and she remembered suddenly that Father Geoffrey had done just this as a boy. Perhaps she had been guided here. Perhaps eventually everyone was guided here, only for some the despair came later than for others. She was much older than Father Geoffrey had been; she had less excuse; she *ought* to have realized –

She bent her head desperately in her hands, asking aloud for forgiveness for her total selfishness, her deliberate lack of thought for her mother – for she realized it had been deliberate. She had known, she must have known, but had chosen not to, excusing herself with the pretence that she was breaking away from the subservient role allotted women by society, showing the way for others – not like Alice Davies by demonstrating and going to prison and refusing food – but mastering her own profession, mastering her own life instead of fulfilling her duty as an unmarried daughter –

She saw the little movement of her mother's shoulders as she turned away towards where her father lay at the foot of the stairs, and could feel the weight of her sadness in her own head; it had been going on for so long and she had not been *there* to ease the burden. And now the boys were an additional worry. Darkness shrouded the way ahead, lit only by gunfire; she saw a line of battleships stretched against yellowish mist, the thinning pall of smoke from their funnels cutting off the tops of their masts, and felt the heavy breath of the coming storm and heard Papa's voice, 'The Fleet's at sea! We shall sleep soundly in our bunks tonight!' How alert and very blue his eyes were; how confident he looked, but she could see the squall about to overtake them and began to pray for them all, especially for Papa, that he might bring them through –

When she woke, the church was filled with the grey light of morning; there was an excruciating pain in her right knee, bent beneath her; her shoulder and arm ached, and she felt cold, her mind numb but clear, thank heavens, of all the disturbing images of the night before. Slowly, crying out once with the pain, she straightened her leg, then sat up and gripped the rail. She felt quite different; the church was entirely different in the light: the cross with the figure of Christ crucified had lost its mystery. He had gone now – if He had been there – but she thought perhaps He had for she knew what she had to do. Closing her eyes, she thanked Him briefly for sheltering her in His house, and showing her the way, then rose and started walking unsteadily back down the aisle between the pews.

Her mother looked startled when she told her, but she could tell how pleased she was underneath.

'You don't have to, Henry, really – there is no need –'

'But I *want* to, Mama.'

She smiled. 'Very well then, I'll let Mrs Harding know. I know how pleased she'll be. Would you like to have the green room?'

'*Yes!*' She laughed. 'Please!'

'And you'll need somewhere for your dark room won't you? What about one of the boys' rooms?'

She smiled. 'I don't need anything as large as that. Actually it's easier if there's running water –'

'I'll ask Mrs Harding. Perhaps we can shut off a part of the scullery – there are so few servants –'

That night after Babs had gone up to bed and they were alone in the sitting-room, her mother's reserve cracked a little. 'I'm so glad you've come back, Henry – even if it's

506

only for a short time. I had thought you might –' she smiled, '*hoped* you might. It seems to make it all complete again somehow. Now when you go – well, it was so unsatisfactory before.' They both knew well enough how unsatisfactory the parting had been.

Again she wanted to say how sorry she was, but did not think her mother would want her to – coming home should be a *positive* thing. Nor could she say what was really in her mind: she would be on hand to share the blow – or blows – if they came.

'It's *lovely* to be back,' she said. 'I really feel I'm *home*.'

They laughed.

The next morning at breakfast the telephone rang. Millie answered.

'Miss Henrietta – it's the Countess of Lynne,' her eyes were bright, 'she'd like to speak to you –'

Henrietta had a horrible flash of intuition.

'Henrietta –?' How long since she had heard that imperious tone?

'Lady Lynne –'

'Henrietta – Popsy asked me to call you, she is rather too distressed –' she sounded as if she was about to invite her to a ball. 'It's her brother, you see. We have just heard. He has been killed, you see. Popsy does not feel quite up to going in to the club and she wondered if you could kindly see to things –'

'Of course – I'm so –' Numb.

'Thank you *so* much. I shall tell Popsy – poor gel. She was fond of him you see. As we all were. He will be a great lorss. Thank you *so* much, Henrietta. Goodbye!'

'Please tell Popsy –' The phone had gone dead.

She stood, thinking of Eggy –

Popsy returned to the club two days later, her eyes shadowed, but she was otherwise as exquisitely turned out and looking as bright as ever. 'Etty, please don't say anything, I couldn't bear it. I have to work or I sit around *thinking*. I never was much good at that as you know. Do you think I was too horrid to poor Eggy? I do. I can't bear it, Etty, I really can't. Do you think he will forgive me – where he is now –?'

507

'Don't be silly –'

'He left this for you,' she pointed to a small package which she saw was addressed to her in Eggy's once-familiar hand. 'Please don't open it here, I don't think I could bear it –'

'Of course not.'

'I suppose you think he did his duty, Etty, and all that tosh – I suppose you do, don't you?'

'Of course –'

'I thought you would. He was murdered by the bloody Boche.' Her expression was fierce.

Henrietta put a hand around her shoulder; she turned her head away defiantly.

'Do you believe –' she nodded upwards, 'Do you pray still, Etty?'

'Yes.'

'I wish I could, oh, God, I so wish – I'd ask Him – why the *hell* did you take him –' A shriller note had come into her voice. Henrietta gripped her shoulder. 'I know what he'd say,' she made an effort at control, 'He never held back – he wasn't a bloody little runt like some of the – Oh, *Christ* Etty, I knew they'd get him – sooner or later I knew. He wasn't afraid of a thing. He never made a fuss, even as a boy. You wouldn't catch him going round the wall. I was too *beastly* to him. I couldn't *bear* him being made such a fuss of –'

'Popsy!' Henrietta dug her fingers in. 'You must stop. Of course he loved you, I'm certain he still does –'

'Do you think so, Etty –' she gazed at her, then seeing something further off, 'Oh, *God!* It's the *bloody* occasionals! Etty, do go and tell them they must not say a word – I simply couldn't bear it –'

Henrietta went out briskly to take the occasional ladies aside.

She did not get home until late that night after a party of amateur entertainers had finished a dreadful performance. She looked in quickly to the sitting-room, where her mother was alone with a book at the end of the settee – how many nights had she sat up alone? Calling a cheerful 'Good night' she went straight up to her room and, sitting on the bed, took out the package Popsy had given her and held it on her lap, staring at Eggy's writing.

508

'It's rather a splendid night. We might go outside –?'

The house loomed against the night sky, tall windows ablaze with light which shone out on the foliage; voices came from somewhere around one of the hedged paths, a man and a girl; the girl had laughed. It was unbearably poignant. She remembered Eggy's long white shirt sleeves as he swept his coat on to the bench and invited her to sit, and thought of his eyes so clear and direct, like the man himself – and now –

Her fingers trembled as she undid the knot in the string. She didn't want to cut it; if he had taken the trouble to do it up, the least she could do was untie it decently. She thought of his living fingers on the string where hers were now.

Inside was a small jewel case; she had guessed it might be. She opened the single, folded sheet with it. It was headed Stokington Park with the crest, and dated 'Aug. 3, 1914'. He had written it before he went to France!

My dear Henry,

I shall have gone when you read this. I should like you to have the ring. It came down on my father's side. There is a story that one of my ancestors at the time of the Mutiny in India had it set for his love. He was coming home to marry her, but he was killed. It was saved from his body by his faithful bearer who knew where he kept it close to his heart, so the story goes. Please keep it.

Goodbye, Henry. May you find your happiness, Eggy.

Do what you can for my poor sister, she has little to hang on to.

She opened the box. A large ruby blurred in the mist over her eyes.

Acheson, in the role of Priest of the Parish, struck the deck with the stonachey made of a rolled *Sporting and Dramatic*. 'The Court is open!' and pointing at V-W on the left of the semicircle of officers seated facing him, wearing monkey jackets with bow ties. 'Tell off by caps!'

V-W saluted. 'White Cap, sir!'

Acheson looked at West.

West saluted. 'Percussion Cap, sir!'

George, when it was his turn, called himself 'Cricket Cap': it may have had something to do with Henry's letter, which had arrived that day; she had a lot to say about Uncle Richard at her birthday party, and his mental image of him always included those lavender flannels and the striped cap with the glorious I Z band.

Acheson looked at him a shade longer before passing on; George thought he was probably for it early, and tried to bring some clarity to his mind, pleasantly loose after the port.

After Blaker as 'Man John' had reported himself in splendidly crawling manner, they told off again from the other end, George trying to devise methods of fixing each Cap in his mind as they snapped them out; with the Inflexibles he managed it, but it was difficult with a couple of the Invincibles, whose names he had forgotten; one rather drunken two-and-a-half-striper helped by calling himself 'Dud Cap' – Drunk – Dud – D – D –

'The Priest of the Parish has lost his considering Cap,' Acheson began in a brisk voice. From the group around the piano beyond the curtains someone was 'Gilbert the Filbert, the Nut with a K', and Acheson raised his voice, 'Who claims this very fine piece of money? Some say this and some say that, but I say Mr Cricket Cap.'

George was not surprised; he saluted. 'What me, sir!'

'Yes, you, sir!'

He saluted again. 'You lie, sir!'

'Who then, sir?'

'Mr White Cap –'

The drunk two-and-a-halfer yelled, '*Watch* Mr Cricket Cap!'

There was some laughter at the ferocity of the challenge. Acheson struck the deck with the rolled paper stonachey.

'Mr Cricket Cap watched by Mr Dud Cap! Who claims this very fine piece of money?' He waved the stonachey.

The two-and-a-halfer saluted, 'I, Dud Clap claim that very fine piece of money –'

Several challenges rang out, V-W's fractionally first, and

the two-and-a-halfer broke off, giggling quietly to himself.

Acheson brought his stonachey down hard on the deck. 'Mr Dud Cap watched by Mr White Cap! Who claims this very fine piece of money?'

V-W saluted. 'I, White Cap, claim that very fine piece of money, likewise Mr Dud Cap, who, bringing a very fine flipper to the front, did during the course of this most divine ceremony make a complete and utter cock-up of his dialogue in that he did refer to that noxious affliction, "the clap", thereby bringing the Court into disrepute. I therefore beg leave to award him with one good flip over the tautest of taut bundoons.'

Appreciative chuckles greeted his near perfect perform- ance as Acheson, granting the award, passed the stonachey to him and the two-and-a-half-striper rose clumsily, swayed and bent to receive the whack. V-W, smiling at the cheers, laid it on, then saluting, passed the stonachey back to Acheson.

'All just debts and dues duly paid, most noble Lord!'

West challenged whilst he was still speaking.

'Mr White Cap watched by Mr Percussion Cap!' Acheson called, bringing the stonachey down. 'Who claims this very fine piece of money?'

West saluted. 'I, Percussion Cap, claim that very fine piece of money, likewise Mr White Cap, bringing a very fine flipper to the front did during the course of this most divine ceremony smirk whilst in possession of that very fine piece of money, thereby bringing the Court into disrepute. I therefore beg leave to award him with one good flip over the tautest of taut bundoons.'

Amid the guffaws, Acheson handed over the rolled maga- zine and V-W rose and bent to present a very taut backside.

The opening challenges set the pattern in their suggestion of rivalry between the Invincibles and the Inflexibles, the single officer from the *Caesar* and the Governor's ADC, who had not played before and was treated with leniency in his bewilderment, were seldom heard; the challenges between the rival ships grew faster and more inconsequential, taxing Acheson's judgement as he and 'Man John' Blaker strove valiantly to preserve the dignity of the Court. George, for his part, thought he probably gave as good as he got, but was almost helpless with laughter by the time the proceedings veered right out of control and Acheson, shouting, declared the Court closed.

They rose, flushed with noise and laughter, straightening their jackets, and drifted across to join the glee party around the piano, leaving the drunk two-and-a-halfer claiming 'this very fine guillotine – Off with his head –!'

'Bloodthirsty bugger!'

Much later, George accompanied West out to the quarter-deck to bid him farewell. Pools of rainwater between the railway lines along the jetty reflected light from the shaded lamp over the accommodation ladder.

'Bye, old thing,' West said, gripping his hand. 'If you're back before us – see what that sister of yours is up to for me!'

George smiled. '*You'll* be home first!'

'I wonder. Good hunting!' West held up his palm briefly as he started down the gangway, 'Wherever they send you.'

George watched for a moment as he went down, dark hair shining under the light, the flaps of his long, beautifully cut greatcoat blowing up in the wind, then he turned and walked back, sad at the parting and envious. If they were not going home, he would rather stay here a while like the *Invincible* than hare off on another chase across the seas. They had been constantly at sea since he joined the battle-cruiser. He felt an urge for a longish spell with firm ground beneath his feet. The Rock, looming darkly to starboard, the top edge sharp against the stars, looked inviting. He no longer felt light-headed, nor even tired.

If only their orders were, after all, for home. They would not be; there was too much secrecy about, too many rumours. A fleet was gathering in the eastern Med. They were too well-placed here for their Lordships to resist the temptation to send them to augment it. Uncle Richard had hinted to Henry of a stroke that would shorten the war, now bogged down in the trenches stretching across France and Belgium. Perhaps this concentration of ships on the southern flank was what he meant. So far as he himself was concerned, the war could go hang for a bit. He longed for home, chiefly he

512

realized, he longed to see Kate. He wondered what she was doing; he wished she would write more often and rather more fully when she did. She was not a good correspondent – but then her genius lay in her quick tongue and it would be unfair to expect her to wield a flashing pen as well. He could expect no news of her from Henry of course –

Strange to think of Henry living in the old house again. It would be marvellous once he did get some leave. He felt a pleasant glow to think that she and Mama had made it up so completely.

They cast off from the South Mole the following evening and anchored outside in the bay, still with no certainty of their destination. A lighter was towed out to them with spares for the new picket boat and charts under escort in a sealed package which Carrington took under his personal charge. It was certain then, they were not going home; they hardly needed charts of the North Sea or Scapa Flow!

They weighed at nine, speculation high as they waited to see what course would be set; it turned out to be south for Africa! The Straits were dark and eerily deserted; the usual torpedo boat patrols appeared to have been called in – to ensure that no one saw which way they went? After the Rock merged into the night astern they altered to port, into the Mediterranean.

For George the attempt to force the Dardanelles with the fleet stood out all his life distinct from other engagements he took part in. It was more thrilling to every nerve than the deliberate target practice at the Falklands, a sharper spectacle than the confused affair that was to come in the mists off Jutland. All ships and the forts were clear in view in sunlight, the battleground and its simple goal delineated starkly by the closing trend of the shoreline on either hand towards the Narrows. It resulted in his first, shocking experience of the mutilation of men close to him whom he learned to value fully only afterwards. It was the contrast between splendid beginning and sad end that impressed itself; when over the years details faded, it was the clarity and inspiration of the beginning, the distressing sight of V-W at the end which remained as vivid almost as when the events took place.

He had not liked the plan to start with, nor, he guessed, had V-W. The bombardment from outside the Straits in February had demonstrated the difficulties of ships taking on forts – despite the success of their own contribution. This time they were to steam right in past the silenced fortresses at the entrance to engage the works on either side of the Narrows at long range. They would be unable to anchor because of the tide sweeping them into such an alignment that only the forward guns would bear and because they would be exposed to close range fire from the batteries set up on either shore to protect the minefields; above all they would have no spotters ashore to direct the fire. Spotting was to be by aeroplane, but with the number of ships taking part and the lack of serious practice between ships and 'planes he was sceptical.

Even if they were to succeed in mastering the main forts, there remained the problem of the minefields and the mobile batteries covering them. It was difficult to see how these self-supporting defences could be overcome without landing troops to occupy at least one shore – which would at the same time eliminate the chief objection to the attempt by allowing spotters for the ships' guns to be stationed on the heights. He wondered whether the Admiral had taken any advice from gunnery officers. The organization and staff work that had come to his notice during their recent period as flagship had been amateurish. He had been scarcely surprised when Carden's health broke. De Robeck was a stronger figure. It would take more than strength to accomplish the plan.

'The general idea is to silence the defences of the Narrows and of the minefield simultaneously so as to enable sweepers to clear a passage through the Kephez minefield; if this is successful that attack to be at once continued on the remaining defences until the fleet has passed through the Dardanelles . . .'

To George, this read rather like the proliferating articles in the newspapers heralding the imminent arrival of the fleet off Constantinople, to be followed by the collapse of Turkey and other large consequences which would lead to a speedy conclusion to the war. He had no opinion on the consequences; as a gunnery officer he simply doubted if it were possible for the fleet alone to force the Narrows.

Once they had weighed, though, and closed up for action stations and were steaming towards the undulating hills of the peninsula, draped prettily in morning mist, his doubts vanished; the sun lifted them as it lifted the haze and lit the white beach below Cape Helles and the extraordinarily blue water stretching inside. Their own group of four – line A – the new *Queen Elizabeth*, the very image of compact power with her fifteen inch turrets rising in perfect balance to the bridge and director control top, de Robeck's flag blowing out above, the less pleasing but businesslike *Agamemnon* and *Lord Nelson*, and their own battle-cruiser led the rest of the fleet, whose line stretched back to the horizon, dropping the peaks of the islands astern like sharp, dark clouds.

The armada looked splendid, the morning so clear for target practice, the headlands and the pale old walls of the forts so plain to see and hushed, George felt they would do it; the end of the day would see them in the Sea of Marmora at least; it looked but a step to the heights above the Narrows. Constantinople tomorrow! *Look out* Enver Pasha!

The destroyers ahead of them swept in between the silent, devastated walls of Sedd el Bahr to port, Kum Kale to starboard. The *Agamemnon* with the honour of leading the line entered close astern of the flotilla with the ancient battleships, *Prince George* and *Triumph* on either beam to take on the mobile shore batteries. Funnel smoke drifted away slowly to port and from the after control top, George trained his glasses on Kum Kale: the damage from the bombardment and the demolition parties that had landed afterwards was visible above cratered earthworks and through gaping holes in the masonry. Sun flashed off what appeared to be the remains of a searchlight projector. He saw no sign of life.

They were well inside the Straits and inclining to starboard to take position at the extreme right of the bombarding line

515

when they heard the first report. George saw greyish smoke drifting up from behind a scrub-covered mound to the left of Kum Kale and immediately trained his glasses there. The Old Man had told him to look out for the shore batteries and report what he saw as he intended to get the four inch guns on to them if there was half a chance of annoying them. He could see no sign of the gun – a six or eight inch howitzer he guessed from the report; it was evidently behind the mound with a forward spotting officer – no doubt a German – directing it.

'See him?' the Old Man came through on the voicepipe.

'Only his smoke, sir.'

Two more guns cracked out from the same direction. He wondered who they were aimed at; he had not noticed the first round coming in their direction. Lowering his glasses he looked forward. Two water columns rose a cable's length to port of the *Triumph*. Part of his mind registered their grace in the sunlight as he turned back towards Kum Kale, searching the scrub again through his glasses.

He heard the thud of heavy calibre guns from the direction of the *Triumph*, and soon afterwards the crack of a four inch from the flying deck below, followed by an irregular volley from the other quick-firers up the starboard side and on the turrets. The Old Man had decided to start annoying them! Lowering his glasses to see the fall of shot, he saw the flash of an explosion on the broken masonry of the fort way to the right and a cloud of dust rising with the smoke, then three bursts below the mound, two near its crest; from their timing and the size of the bursts he thought all but one had come from the *Triumph*. Their own shots winged over; he saw two flashes close together at the side of a gully beyond, and smoke from several other hidden bursts some distance away from where he judged the battery to be.

Two more rising puffs of smoke confirmed this. Shortly afterwards he glimpsed from the corner of his eye a water column rising astern; the devils had shifted to them! Another appeared about a hundred yards to starboard. He felt the strange quiver and elation of danger.

Splashes continued to rise nearby, and he was aware of the drone of overs as, listening for the reports of their quick-firers below, he tried vainly to gauge which bursts each might be responsible for. Gradually they overhauled the *Triumph*, whose smoke began to blow down between them and the shore, and as suddenly as they had begun, the fountains near them ceased; he saw them glistening about the *Triumph* as their own four inches fell silent and felt encouraged and rather surprised they had not been hit.

'After control!' It was the Old Man.

'This is after control.'

'Did we worry them?'

He considered it for a moment. 'It was hard to see, sir.'

There was a pause, then in defiant tones, 'They didn't hit us.'

'No, sir.'

'See if you can do better with the next lot.'

'Aye-aye, sir!'

Annoyed, he turned to Adams and told him to keep his eyes peeled for gun smoke. They had been told there would be at least one battery, probably several in Erenkoi bay, which they were fast approaching. He looked astern. Numbers of picket boats were following, sun glancing off their paintwork and the quartering pattern of waves in their wakes, white ensigns flying splendidly in the breeze of their progress. About a mile astern of them the four French battleships of line B had entered the Straits and were spreading in line abreast; he saw a water column glint short of the *Suffren*, like themselves on the right of the line. Beyond them the third line of old pre-Dreadnoughts were approaching the Cape under dense clouds of smoke. The sea and air sparkled before them, the forts were shadowed in silence. He had a feeling the fleet was irresistible. *Here we come!*

He turned to look forward towards the shallow curve of the bay they were approaching; several balls of smoke appeared from separated points inland.

'Sir!' Adams called excitedly, 'They're firing!'

The reports reached them almost simultaneously. He raised his glasses to examine the scrub beneath the nearest, hearing the shells landing in the water some way ahead. Once again, there was no sign of the guns themselves. He lowered the glasses below his eyes to await the next rounds, fixing the spots when they came and subjecting the area to another close scrutiny. This time the Old Man didn't ask what he could see, but as succeeding salvoes crept nearer, he heard the four inches below come into action. Trying to spot their bursts ashore, he didn't look at the splashes of the enemy shells, but it was impossible not to be aware of their explosions close on either hand, and the sounds of falling water, occasional spray on the deck and the whir of splinters. As at the Falklands, he wondered when they were going to be hit. It seemed only a matter of time.

'After control – T.S. – message from fore control. Am about to pay the enemy some attention.'

He smiled. 'This is after control. Shall observe with interest.'

A shell burst against the side about the waterline; he glimpsed a white surge of foam as he heard the tearing sound of another shell through the air above. From the sudden heel of the top, he realized they were turning sharply to port. The turn continued until they were heading away from the bay towards their consorts in line A; furthest off under the far shore, he saw the *Queen Elizabeth* broad in the water as she showed them her stern. A shadowed gully ran down between the hills of the Gallipoli peninsula behind her masts. In the clear air she seemed close although she was almost two miles away; her side and the backs of her great fifteen inch turrets pointing to starboard were bright with sun.

Their own turrets were already on a starboard bearing for the four inch, whose crews had now taken shelter below; they swung a few degrees to point the great pieces towards the centre of three low-lying forts on the Cape closing the Narrows on the Gallipoli shore seven miles away. He could see several ships moving in the blue straits beyond; one was a small warship. On the opposite headland was the square castellated bulk of Hamidieh 1 fort, and beyond it, just visible the white houses of Chanak; he wondered if the people there had been evacuated. Above, two aeroplanes shone, specks of silver against the blue.

He turned to Tomkins and Adams and made sure they knew which of the distant, sunlit walls was their target, Fort 16. Their small rangefinder was not much more use than a toy at this distance, but working a range and deflection would give an illusion of taking part – keep them on their toes.

From a distance, he heard the boom of a salvo and a rumble of heavy shells through the air – the *Queen Bess* – and shortly afterwards the close concussion and shaking as their own turrets fired. Orange cordite smoke thinned away on the beam. He watched the shells rise into the clear sky, growing smaller, waiting with interest to see if he would be able to make out where they fell on land; at the same time he became aware that the Erenkoi batteries, thrown out by their sudden turn, were beginning to drop their salvoes uncomfortably close again.

The splash buzzer went, but he saw nothing. Putting his ear closer to the voicepipe, he heard a 'down' correction repeated in the transmitting station, and from the conning tower, the Old Man's order to open fire with the after flying deck four inch on the batteries at Erenkoi.

'After control!' It was the Old Man.

'This is after control, sir.'

'See if you can spot for the four inch.'

'Aye-aye, sir.'

He rose and squeezed aft, exchanging seats with 'Knocker' White at the navyphone cabinet, and began to search the bay, glasses at the ready. There was a tearing sound and a thudding explosion close astern; jagged white water rose in their wake. He wondered about the propellers, but the whirls they were throwing to the surface appeared unchanged as they moved away, leaving the splash collapsing into rings of waves surging outward.

Gun smoke stood out again from the shadowed green ashore. He raised his glasses to the nearest trace when the top was shaken by the discharge of a salvo and he lost it for a moment. He heard the crack of one of the four inch guns below and lowered his glasses, keeping his eyes on a pale shape made by an exposed area of rock or earth just above the point he had been studying. The darker burst of the four inch appeared way to the left. Without knowing which of the several smoke traces the gunlayers were aiming at, it was going to be difficult!

A close whirring noise and the burst of a shell sounded

simultaneously from below and just behind him, followed by the drumming of splinters on steel and the high whine of others in the air.

'Where was that?'

'Between P and Q,' Adams answered.

He hoped the four inch crews were well out of the way.

Their wake started to bend; the Old Man was evidently trying to throw out the fire control ashore. He heard two bursts in the water close to port; he had succeeded this time! V-W would not be pleased at the alterations, though. The wake began to twist in the other direction and he realized they were turning right round to steam back along the line towards Erenkoi. He saw X turret training towards the port beam.

Relaxing, he permitted himself an inspection of the Narrows' forts. They were shrouded by smoke and dust, augmented continually by eruptions. The ships in the Straits beyond seem to have vanished, and so far as he could judge the forts themselves were not returning the fire; most of the guns were outranged, but they were supposed to have several fourteen inch pieces. He had an exultant feeling they were on the way to success.

He felt suddenly very hungry and his mouth was dry. Since the funnel smoke on this course made it impossible to do anything very useful about the Erenkoi batteries – now engaged by the forward four inch – he sent Adams down to see what he could find in the way of sandwiches and cocoa. An ice would be more appropriate! He hoped the lad wouldn't run into a shell burst on the way. He was just as likely to catch one up here. Able now to study the bursts on the water, he thought they were probably using shrapnel.

The smoke obscuring his view ahead was beginning to blow quite sharply to port, hanging down the range towards the Narrows and interfering with V-W's spotting he guessed. The Old Man's occasional alterations to throw out the shore batteries' aim would not be appreciated either! He was keeping up a good rate of salvoes nonetheless; perhaps the aerial spotting was proving useful. From here it was quite impossible to make out much through the spreading haze from the funnels.

Looking to starboard, he thought the *Suffren* seemed closer than she had been. He trained his glasses on her, then on the other French battleships of line B, feeling another catch of triumph as he saw they had begun to steam up to pass them, the *Suffren* and *Bouvet* on their own side of the Straits, the other two steering towards the *Queen Elizabeth*. De Robeck must feel they had achieved sufficient mastery of the forts to allow the second line in for a close range bombardment. He pointed them out. Tomkins waved his arm and cheered.

By the time Adams appeared with a heaped plate of corned beef sandwiches, the *Suffren* was almost up with them, heading to pass between them and the shore so as not to foul their range. He was contemplating leading a cheer for her and the *Bouvet* close astern of her, when he felt a tremendous concussion from somewhere forward, followed by the whizzing, drumming sounds of splinters or shrapnel. Jumping round in his seat, he saw the fore topmast with its aerial array toppling down through the fog above the funnels; he thought at once of V-W, but couldn't see the fore top itself through the murk.

Adams was standing by him, a shocked look on his face. George indicated the shelf and the lad placed the plate of sandwiches down.

Brief exchanges through the voicepipe confirmed the awful feeling he had about the fore top; a moment later the Old Man came through.

'After control! Fore control's bin hit. Take over main armament! I'm altering to starboard.'

He felt sick for V-W and Blaker and the others.

As they came round, he saw the glow of a fire about the bridge and glimpsed flames licking up the foremast. He tried to concentrate on Fort 16, but the thick smoke from the fire and the funnels combined to obscure the Cape so frequently as to render it impossible. He reported it.

Some minutes later, the Old Man came through. 'What can you see now?'

'Nothing, sir.'

'Put the turrets into "local", and hop up to the fore top. See if it's possible to re-establish control there.'

'Aye-aye, sir!' He had the queer sensation in his stomach as he thought of V-W and the others silenced, and tried to shut out thoughts of what it would be like to see them all. Arriving below the bridge, he found Wigram with the fire brigade directing hoses at the charthouse, which was burning with a fierce, roaring noise. The heat was intense. The paint on the mast and mast struts above the charthouse was also on fire, flames darting towards the base of the top, which was already blackened. He wondered how many were alive up there; the doctor was gazing up, a party behind him waiting with bamboo stretchers; evidently they had not all been killed.

'We'll never get it under control in time,' Wigram said.

He was not expecting an answer, but staring at the flames and the volumes of thick, oily smoke wreathing the top. Turning suddenly on his doggie, Rawlings, he told him to let the Captain know that if they remained on this course the survivors in the top would be burned alive. 'He'll have to come round,' he muttered, pulling at the sides of his mouth in agitation.

George asked if he should fetch another fire party.

'I've sent for one.'

Rawlings dashed back in quick time. 'The Captain says he's coming round to sou-west, sir. Will that answer?'

'Tell him I think that will do very well.'

They steered out of the action, increasing speed so that the wind blew the flames aft away from the top. In time the fire was forced under; the hoses were turned on the port strut to cool it sufficiently to allow the doctor and his party up. George looked at Wigram, and receiving a nod, followed up, choking in the fumes from the blistered, yellowed and blackened paint. The rungs were still warm.

He had never seen anything like the sight that met him. The entire control party was either dead or wounded. The range-taker, Taylor, was slumped forward, quite still, against his instrument, gripping it with stiff fingers, his head twisted to reveal the lower half of his face and neck torn away by splinters or shrapnel. V-W was propped near him below the corner spotting shelf, one side of his head, neck and all the visible part of his shirt dyed with blood, his jacket torn open to reveal dark, gleaming areas. One eye seemed to have gone although it was difficult to tell; a raw gouge stretched horribly across his left cheek to the bridge of his nose. He was drawing breath through open lips that twitched when he saw him as if he was trying to say something, then the doctor's figure intervened.

On the other side, Blaker lay in an equally torn state next to the stiff, hunched form of a signalman, head resting on one side; part of his skin looked as if tattooed in black; his eyebrows were charred, his fixed, white eyes staring, hands clawed in a last attempt to remove shrapnel from his chest. A dead bandsman lay next to him, lapped in blood. At the rear another bandsman crouched, groaning; an A.B. named Smedley who seemed relatively undamaged, knelt as if to comfort him with a lost look on his face. Petty Officer Munson was propped, ashen-faced against the side of the navyphone cabinet; an A.B., Riseborough, lay slumped on the other side of the cabinet. The thin, sweet odour of blood seemed to blow through the chamber on the breeze.

'Goin' to finish the job, sir!' Munson got out, his eyes moving towards where he thought the enemy forts were.

George nodded with an attempt to match his cheeriness. 'We'll pay them out for this!'

He picked his way over the dead bandsman towards V-W. The doctor had given him morphia, and was bending over Blaker.

'Shish – kabob –' V-W's lips were dark with congealing blood. 'Thought – we were going to be – done – to a turn!'

'No danger of that now.' George attempted a smile. 'The fire's out.'

The doctor turned to him, nodding towards the open emergency aid case. 'Tourniquet! Round his upper arm!'

'Director – control –' V-W went on, giving up the task of trying to fix him with his good eye. 'Next time –'

George eased his arm up to get the tourniquet around. 'I'll make certain it's lined up for you.'

V-W gasped involuntarily as he was moved, drawing in hoarse breaths. 'Not *me* – you – old dear –'

His fortitude and amazing cheer was equalled by Blaker and the other wounded as they were patched with emergency dressings, eased on to bamboo stretchers and lowered down vertically through the hatch to waiting hands on the ladder; it was what George principally remembered alongside the horror of the scene.

He found that the rangefinder, Dumaresq and Argo clock had been put out of action by the explosion or the splinters which had scoured the men, but all communications were untouched, and as the Old Man turned and headed the ship back towards the firing line, he called Adams up with him with his Dumaresq and with Tomkins and Knocker White established a scratch control party.

During this time he noticed little outside, and was astonished when Adams told him the *Bouvet* had struck a mine or been torpedoed and had disappeared in next to no time; another French battleship had been so knocked about by the forts she had limped away down by the bows and with a heavy list, and the remaining two had also retired more or less damaged. The 'Aggie', next but one to them, had taken a round turn out of the line after being centre of a storm of shot, and now the old British pre-Dreadnoughts of the third line had gone in to take the place of the French at close range. He saw them manoeuvring gamely two or three miles ahead as they neared Erenkoi bay again. He looked through their drifting smoke at the new target the Old Man had given him, the large fort Hamidieh 1 before Chanak. It had been silent earlier; now it was firing steadily at the closer third line ships – as were several batteries along the shore; *Irresistible* was steaming through a thicket of glistening fountains.

They were greeted again by the Erenkoi batteries as they resumed station in the long range bombarding line next to the *Lord Nelson*, but he was scarcely aware of them as he concentrated all his attention on the fort. He knew the flagship had been firing at it all day in director control, and at least one of the pre-Dreadnoughts was dropping salvoes in the vicinity, yet judging by the number of gun-flashes and the controlled salvoes hurling up splashes around the *Irresistible*, little if any serious damage had been done. He soon realized they had small chance of remedying it. With the smoke of the close-range ships and their own funnel and gun smoke blowing up towards the Narrows, out of contact

524

with the spotter aeroplane since losing the wireless aerials, having to make constant adjustments whenever he thought he had succeeded in ranging on as Carrington manoeuvred to keep the ship in position with all turrets bearing, it was little better than firing into the brown, hoping for a lucky chance. He slowed the rate of fire.

'Somethin' wrong!' the Old Man came through brusquely.

'The target is obscured, sir.'

Silence for a moment. 'D'you want to go into local control?'

'I doubt if they can see any better from the turrets, sir.'

'Keep it going! Keep 'em busy!'

The enthusiasm of the morning had gone; he felt low. Thoughts of the poor mangled forms of V-W and Blaker and the other men obtruded even as he concentrated on the constant corrections needed for the guns. Their inability to affect the enemy fire, the difficulty of judging where his own shot was falling, the strain of staring through the smoke haze, the concussions ringing and echoing in his head played a part in his darkening mood.

They turned to starboard at the inshore end of their line and he closed his eyes to rest them briefly, opening them with a start as the top shuddered from a tremendous explosion forward. His first thought was that they had been hit by a fourteen inch salvo from Hamidieh; he realized it must have been a mine; the picket boats had been firing at them; one mine had already accounted for the *Bouvet*; evidently the devils were floating them down on the current.

A report came up that all power was lost in A turret, and he heard the Old Man tell Carrington to take her out. He thought he felt the ship settling down to starboard as they steered away. The thud of a distant explosion carried across the water from somewhere astern and looking back, he saw the *Irresistible* stopped dead, pouring smoke from amidships; he wondered if she, too, had struck a mine or if perhaps they were firing torpedoes from the shore. As he watched, another group of white fountains climbed around her, blotting her from sight.

The Old Man came through. 'We're clearin' out. Send

your party down for their lifejackets, Steel, and report to the Commander!'

'Lifejackets!' Adams's eyes were large.

The Old Man called him in late that evening after they had crawled like a plough into mercifully calm, greening water close off the north shore of Tenedos, almost dazed at having made it still afloat, and dropped anchor and rigged mats over the great hole torn in the starboard plates.

'I shall recommend your appointment to succeed Lieutenant Commander Verrier-Walker as gunnery officer, Steel.'

'Thank you, sir.' All he felt was deep despondency and weariness.

'Verrier-Walker has represented – on several occasions – how much he valued your enthusiasm and support. He thinks very highly of you.' He seemed about to take a pace up the slope of the deck, but thought better of it. 'It was a sad day.'

'Very sad, sir.' The thought of it was like a nightmare recalled through waves of tiredness. This was not how he had wanted it – not at V-W's expense –

'I've bin to see them,' the Old Man went on. 'I'm afraid the doctor doesn't expect Verrier-Walker or Blaker to last the night.'

He stared, shocked.

'Poor fellows,' the Old Man went on. 'They showed great pluck.'

'It was a chance in a million,' he heard himself say. 'Hubbard was in the lower top. He thinks it must have struck the yard. Three inches either way and it would have gone clean past.' The scene of carnage was vivid in his mind.

'Yes – fearfully bad luck.' The Old Man gazed at him for a moment. 'I don't imagine we'll make another attempt.'

'I shouldn't think so, sir.'

'Not without the troops. When you've had some sleep, see what you can do about getting the fore control into shape again. Smoke is a problem aft?'

'It makes it extremely difficult, sir.'

The Old Man was silent for a moment, then he nodded. 'Good night, Steel!' He looked grey with tiredness.

He found 'Pay' sitting with V-W and Blaker when he went

526

forward to the temporary sick berths in the Admiral's flat. Nearly all V-W's face was covered by bandages, but one eye flickered open when he heard or sensed him come in and greet Horniman in a low voice, and there was a small movement of the brow in recognition. He placed a hand on his good shoulder very gently, feeling inexpressible remorse.

'Verrier-Walker has represented – on several occasions – how much he valued your enthusiasm and support –'

He sat down beside him with what he hoped was an encouraging expression, and thought of the first dreadful weeks in the battle-cruiser, and how he wished he could have them again and do something else with them. He wanted to tell V-W that, but he must not disturb him; the single eye in the swathe of bandages had closed.

Starting awake, he saw the doctor gazing at him in the dim light. 'I should turn in, old man.'

He looked round at V-W. The sheet had been drawn up over the helmet of bandages.

9

There was a look in Robin's eyes Henrietta had never seen before this evening. She could tell he had not heard what she said although he was nodding, pretending he had as he brought his napkin up to wipe his lips. Then he glanced round at the next table with that frightful ferocity; she had noticed him doing it several times since they sat down.

The tension just below his joy in seeing her had become evident soon after she had met him at King's Cross those few short days ago. It was understandable; he had so little time; the sudden release into freedom and normality – if wartime London could be termed normality – accentuated probably all the bottled up emotions of the months of strain he had endured. And here they were, and already it was nearly over; it was not surprising his thoughts were elsewhere. It was absurd they allowed him so short a time.

'So, he's not gone yet!' he said in a fierce voice.

She tried to keep her tone even. 'No – but –'

'I dare say he's getting impatient – any man would who called himself a man –'

'Robin!' The people at the next table were looking round. His voice was so loud. She leaned towards him. 'I *said* he was. I have just this minute said so –' She was annoyed now. Did he not allow her any feelings? Could he imagine what it was like to wait at home, wait for news, praying there was none – ?

He scarcely seemed to hear her; he was snapping his fingers for a waiter.

'I am sorry, sir,' the waiter bent to take her plate.

'Leave that, man! Find us another table!'

528

'Another table, sir!'
'Another table.'
The waiter looked round for his chief.
'The air is unpleasant here.'
'*Robin!*'
He glared, turning again to the occupants of the next table, who were obviously listening.
'Would you like to go, Robin?' she said.
He reached out to place his hand over hers on the cloth.
'We are going, old thing – far enough.'
'You wish another table, sir?' the head waiter murmured discreetly. 'Something is wrong?'
'Everything is perfect, thank you, except,' indicating with his hand, 'these tables are too close.'
The man's eyes flicked briefly towards the next table, down again, 'If you would care to come with me, sir –' He leaned towards her to ease her chair out. 'Miss –'
Robin rose, offering his hand. She turned instead silently after the head waiter, trying to remind herself what a strain Robin must have been under. Of course it was understandable. It was so unlike him though; it was intolerable. If he felt able to treat her in this manner – listening to strangers while she spoke to him, demanding to be moved without a word to her – what would it be like if she were ever to marry him? How very differently the leave was turning out –
'I'm so sorry,' he said when they were seated again in the far corner, near the musicians playing Lehar. 'I'm afraid I saw red. It's no excuse I know.' His fingers gripped hers tightly across the table.
He had such a contrite look she felt like crying. The tension was catching. 'What on earth was it all about? They seemed perfectly harmless to me –'
'Harmless! Not how I should describe them. You didn't hear what they were saying?'
'Of course not. I imagined I was talking to you.'
He looked down briefly. 'I couldn't help overhearing – the most awful stuff –' his tone was angry again. 'International capitalism is at the root of the war – did you know that! We are quite as much to blame for it as the Huns, if not *more*! If we had made it clear to the poor things we would fight,

they would not have marched into Belgium – which seems to me to spoil the argument a bit, don't you think! The rape of Belgium was simply a trumped-up excuse on our part. The capitalist press is whipping up anti-German feeling with a campaign of lies – which we, you and I and everyone,' waving his arm to encompass the room, 'except *them* – are too sheep-like to see through. D'you wonder I saw red! Hang it! If I hadn't been with you –' He leaned back as the waiter came with their dishes, whipping the covers off with a flourish as he put them down.

After serving them vegetables he asked if everything was all right here.

Robin had the grace to smile. 'Perfectly, thank you!' He turned back to her. 'What annoys me about these fellows – all their jargon –' he nodded as the wine waiter proffered the bottle and poured a sample into his glass. 'It boils down to one thing. Funk!' He tossed the wine back with uncharacteristic disregard, nodding again at the wine waiter.

'You *can't* say that, Robin,' she retorted as soon as the man had gone. 'If that *is* what they think – I mean if everyone *has* to think it absolutely right to fight, we are no better than the Germans, so why are we fighting them?'

He smiled at the roundabout logic. 'I'm not sure I follow. But I know what I'd do with fellows of that sort. I'd have them shot, their heads paraded on Tower Hill.'

She cut into a roast potato, spreading some of the delicious sauce onto it. 'You're not serious!' She thought he might be, although it was more probable he had said it to shock.

He gazed at her steadily. 'When I think of V-W and a score of other splendid fellows who've gone – and the thousands in France – and Gallipoli now – no – I'm perfectly serious.' He looked down at his plate, moving his knife and fork in an agitated way. 'Good Lord, to think we're up there – watching, hoping they'll come out and give us a chance at 'em – and down here these carrion live off the fat of the land.'

'Not many of them.'

'Enough.' He looked round at the other diners. 'Not much sacrifice here, would you say!'

'You can't expect everyone to – anyway most of them are

on leave I expect. Look over there –' she nodded towards a group of two young men with two girls who probably were not ladies a few tables away to his right.

'I know.' He looked dejected suddenly and shook his head. 'I've been an ill-tempered brute. I don't know why you put up with me.'

She put her hand out towards his.

'You've no idea how much I'd been looking forward to seeing you,' he went on in an anguished way. 'It's queer, but I'm still up there, a part of me at least. I can't leave it behind –'

'Of course you are. You're bound to be –'

'And then to hear that sort of talk.'

She shrugged. 'Socialists. You'd find them whether there was a war or not.'

'The *class* war!'

Her mind was only partially on what he was saying. The other part was mixed up with impressions of the two girls and the young men who looked so hard and fit in an open-air way, like Robin, as if on leave from the trenches.

'Traitors on two fronts,' Robin was saying. 'That's the worst of it, the sheer, nauseating *arrogance* of these fellows. They have the key to the universe. Here we are – poor boobies – on both sides – stumbling around in the dark fighting one another when with a grain of common sense – Shaw's brand of common sense – turning on the officers and shooting them! – that's an Irish way of bringing about the millennium if you like! – brotherly love and harmony would prevail throughout the world!' He was leaning towards her, dark eyes alight. '*They* think *we* are the deluded fools!'

She smiled. She loved him.

He nodded towards their previous table. 'I'd like to introduce those skunks to Petty Officer, first class, Makins. He'd make 'em sit up – mind you,' he smiled, 'they'd probably understand about as much of his unprintable jargon as he understood of theirs!'

'All the same, you can't believe it's right – so *many* dying – every day –' she spread her arms, thinking chiefly of Andy, so impatient it seemed to join them.

'They're dying for what they believe – for their country –

their loved ones. Gloriously. What better way for a man to go?'

Looking into his eyes she felt a little shiver as if for an instant she could imagine the fires dulled, the keen intelligence finally – awfully still.

'Are you certain they are not simply words too?' Why was she carrying on the discussion? Whatever they said the war would go on –

He was leaning back with a little smile as if regretting having allowed his feelings such forceful expression. 'They may be! They're words I believe in though. I rather fancy I always shall.'

'I'm sure the Germans say exactly the same.'

His expression changed and his voice became hard again. 'Declaring war on civilians – women and children! Glorious!'

She had asked for that with the *Lusitania* so fresh in everyone's memory. She was only conducting the argument with half her mind; the two girls were laughing uninhibitedly with the young men she was sure were from the trenches. She must wean Robin from the war and the gloom of the northern Flow; she had an awful premonition that like these young men, he might not have very much longer; like the girls with the young men she wanted to demonstrate tonight – for all time – she loved him.

He filled her glass, seeming to read her thoughts in part for he smiled. 'Curse the socialists for setting us off on that tack,' and raising his glass, 'Curse all socialists!'

She drank to it, thinking of the Davieses and Shaw and Wells and the others with a stirring of guilt. Poseurs all with such a childish view of the world, yet who could deny they had *something*? No one could be happy with the way things were ordered at present –

He raised his glass again. 'To the rest of us – *sinners*!' and leaned towards her. 'It's a funny thing, you know. I dare say most socialists are sinners too – not all of *course*! But they never allow for it in their philosophy!'

'Sinners!' she smiled, lifting her glass to his, and holding his eyes with hers as they drank. She saw his expression alter; she could scarcely have made it plainer.

He put his glass down quietly and picked up his knife and fork again. 'The war's changed so much. D'you think things can ever get back to normal?'

'I hope not!'

He laughed delightedly.

'Robin –' she started.

He looked up.

She couldn't say it. What would he think of her? It was up to him.

Again, it seemed to her, he sensed what was in her mind; his hand trembled slightly as he touched the base of his glass. 'I know, old thing –' and smiling rather grimly, 'If it weren't for the fact you have chosen to live at home!'

'If I hadn't?'

'If you hadn't? Then – I should feel sorely tempted to ask if you might care to see the night away with a confirmed sinner! No!' He shook his head suddenly violently as if reaching a decision, and she felt all his sincerity as he gazed at her. 'It would be wrong. I promise you when –' He stopped, looking down briefly. 'One of my cousins has a shooting box on the Dee not far from Ballater. Have you been up there?' He was looking at her again, and he smiled. 'I'd rather planned it all. It's the most perfect place in the world – especially in the autumn. The air on the hills – the heather – so *sumptuous* you feel a brute to tread all over it! You can hear the burns tinkling down before you see them. I can't describe it – it's simply –' he spread his hands, shrugging happily.

She smiled at his enthusiasm.

'I thought that's where we'd go.' He added rather quickly, 'If you'd care to –'

She laughed. 'I'd love to!'

'I've thought about it so much, I almost feel – and you –' his eyes were serious. 'When we're married.'

She caught her breath at his look. But 'when' – always '*when*' –

He reached his hand out for hers and squeezed it urgently. 'So you see, old thing –'

She did see; she was moved by his passion, but strangely disquieted, why she didn't know. He had thought about it

533

so much. But why was everything always in the future? It had been like that ever since she had known him. Waiting for the perfect moment. He expected too much of her. Perfect moments caught one unawares. It was now, she was certain it was now. She shivered a little. He wouldn't see it; he wouldn't see her as she was, only as he wanted her to be –

He was gazing at her steadily. Had he sensed her feelings? She thought she saw a hint of perplexity in his eyes. Perhaps the question was not entirely closed.

She raised her glass and drank. He refilled it gravely without a word.

Henrietta looked out of the sitting-room window at the sunset framed between the trees beyond the lawn and shrubs. The evenings were drawing in. It was the time of year they returned from Thorpeness as children; the Christmas term would be almost upon them; the weather, warm and sunny, reminding them of the holiday behind, mocking their coming incarceration inside the classroom. She felt the tug of nostalgia, deliciously poignant; if they had known then what was to come – if one ever knew the future, how could one bear it?

The clouds were spectacularly disordered, edged with fire low down, the sky glimpsed through jagged gaps suffused deep red. She thought of Andy in France and wondered if he was watching it too. Perhaps, if a cloud were high enough they might both be looking at the same one. She twisted her head to see as far to the south as she could. She would ask George; he was certain to know the mathematics of it.

Andy was not so happy as he tried to suggest in his letters, their frequency testified to that, she was sure. Four had arrived already. She had always been able to tell when he was unhappy at Marlborough by the number of letters she received. She wondered where he was. Eternal secrecy was one of the curses of the war. If one only knew where they all were, it would make them more tangible; one could place them on a map or just think to oneself comfortingly of the name of a town; towns could not simply be wiped out. Travelling insubstantially from one 'place' to another 'place' they might almost be ghosts already.

'Rolling chalk hills,' he had written, 'rather like the Downs but less grand, much more open. All the wild flowers and copses here remind me so much of England, especially Hampshire. I almost expected to see the spires of Winchester as we breasted a ridge, but no, it was the same fields of golden wheat and the pointed, square tower of a church with red and grey slate roofs clustered around it practically hidden by apple trees – the local cider knocks one's head off! I long for the Bull and a pint of "the best" in the tap room with the old bike leaning outside. This mixture of the familiar and unfamiliar is strange and unsettling –'

'What are you thinking of, Henry?'

She turned. Her mother was looking up at her from her book.

'I was thinking of Andy.'

A shadow passed momentarily across her mother's eyes. 'Yes. I wonder how he is.'

There was no more to be said – not aloud. She walked across to the writing table and sat at the chair.

'I think I'll write to him.'

She had become the centre of a web of communication among them all – relaying news as it was received from separated outposts here at headquarters in Felpham House; that was how she viewed it. It had become her chief preoccupation now that the Lambeth club had been wound up as the wives had taken on the jobs of their menfolk away at the war. She often felt she ought to be doing something more useful. Popsy had become a V.A.D.; yet she was working out her penance for past thoughtlessness, and knew her mother liked having her, not for physical attention to Papa – a living-in nurse looked after that side of things – but for companionship and moral support in seeing out the awful uncertainties hanging over her sons – even Harry now he was training in Sussex. If the war lasted, by the inexorable law of averages their names must surely begin to appear one day in the 'Roll of Honour'. She had imagined it so often, sometimes she felt it had already happened and there could be no more terrible pangs to bear when it did, only the dulling ache of memory.

The feelings were strongest when she found herself in one of their rooms, fingering a cricket bat or a cup, gazing at a group photograph of their prep school when the three of them had been together; how large boys' heads were in comparison to their bodies; she had not remembered noticing it at the time. They were almost like strangers in the picture, yet they hadn't really changed: George looked purposeful, utterly confident, his wide head inclined slightly as if challenging the world; it was not in the least surprising he had won the D.S.O. at the Dardanelles; if anyone in that picture was going to win a medal, one could tell it would be George. She was glad his ship was back at home, far from Gallipoli – something had gone dreadfully wrong there –

Andy was smiling out broadly, his eyes without spectacles keen but trusting; it was before he discovered solitude at Marlborough. Willy was most changed, and most unchanged; he had the naval veneer of smiling, matter-of-fact briskness, but off guard she had caught that dreamy look, and when she was being annoying that humorously philosophical lift to the corners of his mouth that always inspired her to worse.

Willy was the one she would miss most; it was dreadful even to think of it, but she knew it was so; his possessions caused her the most distress, his drawings of animals especially; even as a schoolboy he had been able to catch more than simple appearances; he had stalked his subjects so long and sympathetically he had managed to show their characters, although sometimes she thought it was more a projection of his own character: she was sure moles were not such innocent victims as he represented. She had not realized before quite how obsessed with them he had been. She remembered old Abe, the mole-catcher, telling them what vicious predators and fighters they were.

Willy's moles with their brilliant black coats and large human hands scrabbling at the earth or raised as if to ward off blows provoked her tears for they seemed like portents, leading her imagination in horrible directions; she thought of herself looking at them after news of the loss of his submarine, thinking of all the love and care that had gone into the pictures extinguished for ever, the speculative imagination which had delighted her first on walks along the beach at Thorpeness no more than traces in her memory, his ideas for the future cut off as cruelly as the animals whose lot he hoped he might improve somehow. Already he had become a vegetarian. That he should undergo all the difficulties this must cause him while prepared to kill and be killed by *man* was so hopelessly quixotic it pulled at her heart. Besides such true sacrifice, the arguments of the pacifists and C.O.s seemed, as Robin said, simply 'funk'.

'We should be hearing from Willy soon,' her mother said.

She turned, wondering if it was coincidence or some form of telepathy; she was sure it was the latter; similar things happened too often to be always coincidences – it was even possible Willy was thinking of both of *them* at this moment.

'I think I should order some more of that jam and cake he liked so much from Fortnums,' her mother went on. 'He hasn't said much about Isobel recently, has he. Do you think it's cooling off perhaps?'

She smiled at the strange juxtaposition of ideas. 'He's a very loyal person.'

'That's what I'm rather afraid of.'

'Mama!' Who was she to talk though! She had just as little enthusiasm for the match.

Her mother disregarded it. 'I used to worry about Willy more than the others. He used to be such a dreamer.'

'He still is, I'm sure. Underneath.'

'I know. But you know, I think old Mr Phipps was right. I think the Navy was the right thing, don't you?'

She thought of his sufferings in that dreadful gunroom in the battleship; all boys seemed to have to go through this sort of initiation – except George of course, but if he had he would never have admitted it – and she thought of the strongly individualistic Willy that had emerged, hating groups and group conventions, a non-smoker because everyone smoked, a vegetarian because everyone shot or hunted animals for sport, a submariner because he couldn't stand the conformity of big ship life, now of all things a bagpipe player, to make more noise than the others, he insisted; she was sure it was because most people played the piano; he had played the piano rather well himself when small. 'I think he would have been much the same anyway,' she replied.

'I'm sure he would, but he is *practical* now. I was so afraid he would never do anything practical. And he's ambitious. I never thought he had any ambition in him. You remember that argument he had with George –'

'I don't think that was ambition. I think he enjoyed teasing him; he would have command before George was even a first lieutenant. George rose, I'm sure that was all it was.'

'I think that shows ambition. No –' she looked out thoughtfully towards the sunset. 'Andy's the one I worry about now. He did so well at school – and Cambridge – now he seems to have lost his way.'

Henrietta didn't reply. She thought it was probably true, but not in the way her mother meant it.

'I mean no one makes a living from writing – not from poetry –'

'Mama! Why does everyone always have to be *practical*!'

'Because that is the way the world is.'

'No it isn't –' She must not start another argument. 'Well, I don't think it is. I think it depends on how you look at it.'

'Poets look at it from the window of a garret, I have always understood!'

She smiled. 'Perhaps other people should live in garrets! Anyway –' she turned, 'I must get on,' and she picked up Andy's last letter.

'Ask him if he'd like another hamper – no, ask him what he liked best in the last one. Perhaps we can just send those things. Ask him if there's anything he particularly needs.'

She nodded, 'All right,' and started to read.

Dearest Mama, Henry, Babs,

Greetings from the front! You will doubtless be disappointed to learn that I have still not seen 'Fritzy' as Frost, my servant, terms what I used to know as the Hun, but which the Jocks of the 51st Highland Div, our mentors in 'static warfare' – e.g. digging! – have taught us to call 'Jerry' or 'the Boche'. I have however seen his manifestations. They are rather unpleasant. He does passing good imitations of express trains rushing about above our heads – and so do we – they always end in a 'crump' and there's another 'ole to stumble in on the way back to the support lines, or another wall knocked out of an inoffensive cottage or the grand chateau or the church. The Boche is democratic in his treatment of our ally. But so are we. There is a little village immediately before our present position whose buildings – those that stand – are mere skeletons, the church tower a single tooth sticking up from bleeding gums, the orchards scrumped not simply of apples, but of leaves, branches, even the *trees* themselves! We have done all this because that village and another close by stands or stood amid the lowest of the meanderings of white chalk which mark out the Boche's mole runs on the slopes. Oh, the chalk after rain. Oh, the rain at the bottom of the craters in the chalk!

What else is there to tell? There are woods on the slopes, poisonous woods where tree-loads of leaves turn brown before their season. I swear no flowers grow there although I have not seen! The Boche is there. And there are sunken roads which echo at night to ghostly carts and horses rattling, rattling. And there are fireworks at night. Every night is a firework party for the Boche. We like to join in but we haven't so many beautiful coloured flares as he has. Oh, we know he's there! There is one road which has escaped his grasp. It has run out of the village that was a village, *very carefully* over no man's land through the thistles and poppies and hogweed, past the craters with pools of still water at the bottom and cautiously through our wire. Oh, the wire! Someone is getting very rich in this war, there is so much wire and it is always being crumped and cringled and more wire is unrolled and that is prounded and thrumped in its turn and so it goes on – for ever I believe! Eventually, passing safely under our wire, the road has escaped. It is ours and we make good use of it in the communications to our mole runs, you may be sure. I can report we have won the heart of a brave little French road.

And that is how the war looks from a mole's point of view. Do you remember when Willy's moles ran their communication trench across the tennis lawn? I swear they had as little idea of the great games about to be played above, the funny scoring, the proper height of the net – the rules are so important – as we have of the great game being played above us here. I have seen the Brigadier. He has a red band around his hat and red tabs on his collar and a very red face – after scrambling along our communication trench – and it is said he breathes fire. He came to look at the Boche through one of our periscopes. Rather tall, he had to bend. 'Hrmmph – d——d awkward! Are the men short?' 'Er – um – er – we have our full muster sir.' '*Short* man, *short*! Good G-d! Hrmmph!' We can't tell what he is thinking but we think he *is*, and he knows all about the game you may be sure. I hope he has mastered the Yankee service. But what is that to us! Our existence is bounded by our diggings and moley companions. We are very close, we mole subalterns, not just physically but in every way. We may have started out with the usual pretences of society around ourselves, but they come down, piece by piece until one is nothing but one's bare mole self. We know the length of one another's foot. And over there is the Boche, and his life is much the same. But that is what happens to moles, it is strange and a little sad when you remember how eager we were to come out here and 'give the Hun toko!' But we shall, you can be certain of that, only it will not be quite how we imagined it.

I have yearnings to write verse again but cannot seem to find new forms, my old ones won't do any more. How do moles write? There is someone I should dearly love to talk to here, an old Marlburian named Sorley. I met him at Shorncliffe last September, in the Suffolks too, but the 7th Batt., so in another place. He wrote splendid poetry then. I long to hear how he writes now, whether he has undergone a mole-change, and a hundred things not dreamed of in the philosophy of my mole companions – of Masefield – also out here somewhere – and Rupert, dear Rupert whom the gods loved too much. Sorley has not Rupert's looks so perhaps he will be spared, then I am certain the world will hear of him. I shall write to him –

'How do you think he is?' Her mother's voice broke into her absorption.

She looked up, wondering herself. The consciously 'literary' style was to disguise the horrible realities; how much did it hide of his own real feelings? 'He sounds cheerful enough.'

'I know. But *moles*, I mean to say!'

'*Mama!*'

'I always did detest them.'

Henrietta had an image of George and Andy knotting sheets together, Willy dancing from one foot to the other as he watched, and she remembered her palpitating heart.

10

The last red had gone from the clouds visible above the trench. The evening cacophany was under way. With the automatic part of his mind, Andy registered from somewhere between the staccato outpourings of machine guns and the screaming five nines a thud as a 'canister' was sent up, and automatically looked up over the sandbag parapet; with another part of his mind he found himself at Marlborough. He seemed to think of Marlborough rather often now; it was as if Cambridge had been an interlude, a waking dream permitted him between the real demands of being a boy and a man. From the window of his dormitory in Preshut he had seen just such a restricted area of torn cloud in the September dusk.

The clumsy-looking oil drum rose into view with a wobbling noise, trailing sparks from the lighted fuse, and he moved towards the traverse to his left; it was going to be short, otherwise close. The explosion seemed to make even the solid sandbags tremble.

'Oi'll be dalled!' he heard young Hawkins mutter.

'Oi doubt Fritz'll be sindin' a good toidy few a-they,' Sawyer said. 'Us shoon't a-blowen that moine. He din't loike it, Fritz din't –'

They accepted 'Fritz' as they accepted their 'guvnors' in Suffolk, an unfortunate but inevitable part of the struggle for existence which was all they knew. The worst thing for them, he had discovered talking occasionally in a night watch, was homesickness. Most had never been away from their families or their villages; eager at the start to escape the cycle of long, grinding work for a pittance, jubilant to be going to fight the enemy of that abstract 'England' of which they had suddenly heard so much, nothing had prepared them for the loneliness they felt, herded together under army discipline. In that respect Marlborough had given him and his sort decided advantages.

He walked round into the next bay. They turned their heads as they heard his step on the duckboards, stolid faces, roughed red by exposure, smeared with mud and dust, jaws like fields of thick corn stubble for the most part, their eyes clear, their fixed bayonets glinting in the last of the light as instinctively they drew themselves up.

What were they all doing here? It came on him at times, this nightmare unreality. Here they were, and less than 200 yards away on the other side of the dip and the new mine crater, the Boche was standing to as stolidly in his lines, hurling projectiles from *Minenwerfers* and occasional larger oil drums filled with high explosive surrounded by scraps of rusty metal to perforate *this flesh*.

It was a madness no one could stop; all of them were tied into it, the Brigadier and the generals above him as much as these raw farmhands and saddlers, grooms and bricklayers who knew nothing of the earth-moving forces that had drawn them from their towns and villages. It was a natural cataclysm: Ipswich and Halesworth and Needham Market, Eye and Eyke and their counterparts in Bavaria and Brandenburg had been sucked into this deadly chalk angle between the Somme and the Ancre, there to stick it out. And in sticking it out they had *become* the force, this group and all the other sections and platoons building up into the grand opposing armies. They were both fuel and fire, and would continue to be until one side or the other burnt out and collapsed; only then could the thing end.

These were the faces of war, the ordinary faces of the men he knew; his own face was among them. With his rational side he knew why they were here: for Belgium, for their ally, France, chiefly for England and the Empire. The Boche could also explain; he had been encircled, he had to break out before he was crushed by the hostile alliance and in any case he had his mission to spread *Kultur* to a philistine world dominated by Anglo-Saxonism. As Sorley had put it to him

543

at Shorncliffe, 'It seems to me we are not fighting a bully, but a bigot.' Looking along the red faces and clear, trusting eyes of these men he saw, beneath rationality the simple reality, the primordial instinct of the first man born of woman to loyalty. They and the Boche opposite were sticking it out for the lads beside them in the trench and for their officer fellow who knew more than they what it was all about, and who spoke to them of 'England' – or *der Vaterland* – and who seemed mysteriously immune to the terrible fear of death and mutilation – Lord, if they *knew*!

And beneath this reality was the harder truth that, perceiving the folly as they all could in their hearts, he must continue to pursue it; it was his duty and his care to ensure it was not *his* group that collapsed; he would do so for all the rational reasons on the surface of his mind and the irrational ones below; as much as his men, or Sir John French, or the Kaiser himself, *he* was fuel and fire, atom and charge in the grand conflagration, and there was no way out for him or anyone.

In a strange way Marlborough had prepared him for this knowledge.

'*Wartch owt!*'

He caught a glimpse of the thing himself an instant after the yell, rolling across the clouds, and this time they all flattened themselves for it was going to be close.

The explosion sounded as if at his feet; the noise and echoes of the noise ringing in his head blotted out every other thought, leaving him with the idea that he was dead and it didn't hurt. Lumps of chalk and earth and hard things started falling on and around him and, as he felt them on his shoulders and heard them clatter to the duckboards, and an unnerving screaming from somewhere in the next bay to the right where he had been minutes before, he realized he was alive. He scrambled to his feet – everything seemed to work – and forced himself around the traverse, shocked and dreading what he would see.

The canister had landed feet behind the trench, blowing in a portion of the rear wall and the hollowed out sleeping holes beneath; corrugated iron revetments were splayed to reveal the crater from which black smoke was thinning. The sweet, pungent odour of the high explosive overlaid the usual trench smells of earth and chloride of lime. The screaming had stopped. Beneath earth and chalk debris piled over the duckboards a pair of legs with muddy puttees and smeared boots protruded. Young Hawkins and Sawyer and others beyond the pile, still in much the positions they must have thrown themselves when they saw the thing coming, were staring with shocked eyes. Blood was running down the side of Sawyer's neck from somewhere in his cap, but he seemed unaware of it.

'On your feet, you men!' Andy moved quickly towards the mound of earth, and started shovelling away with his hands about where the head should be.

The others, jolted from their numb state, joined him. Soon they uncovered the face. It was Patterson, his mouth wide in what might have been a grin, blue eyes fixed, glazed already behind clotted dust.

He straightened. His Sergeant, Webb, had come up.

'There's nothing to be done, Sarn't.'

Webb looked from Patterson towards the crater. 'Best put him in thar, sir, f'r now.'

He nodded. 'Carry on, Sarn't!'

Turning, he saw Sawyer on the ground, resting on one elbow. Seeing his glance, the man tried to get up, but toppled over with an exclamation and rolled away, his eyes still looking up, puzzled.

'Sarn't!' Andy called. 'Stretcher!' and heard the cry repeated.

'Oi be in a fare owd flummox –' Sawyer started, his eyelids flickering, pupils not focusing.

Andy motioned to Hawkins, and together they eased him to a more comfortable position on the duckboards, feeling him lose consciousness as they did so. The hair beneath his cap and the band of the cap itself was stiff with blood, but it had stopped streaming now; he decided to leave the cap as it was probably playing its part in staunching the flow.

'Thet thing give Oi a fare judderin',' Hawkins said in a shaky voice. His youthful cheeks looked very pale in the half light; saliva spotted the fine hairs at the corner of his lips. He reeked.

545

'Look after him until the stretcher party gets here,' Andy said, adding, 'Lightning never strikes in the same place twice,' whether for the lad's spirits or his own, he was not sure. His knees felt shaky.

Webb had detailed two men to remove what had been Patterson, and make a temporary passage through the rubble that had covered him. Webb was a steady man; he was fortunate to have such a born soldier as his sergeant. Strange to think of him before the war serving behind the counter of an ironmonger's.

He was glad when the batteries behind them opened and he heard the enemy trenches in front of their sector being strafed. He walked two bays along and, tapping the sentry's shoulder, took over his periscope. The western sky was still light enough to make it dangerous to show anything above the parapet. Their own wire filled the picture, grey thorn rolls with the thicker outlines of the supports leaning at all angles. Through the tangle, the familiar low bushes in the dip crouched darkly, and the split tree with its one remaining, twisted branch leaned as always like half a man about to cartwheel. Beyond, on the rising ground shell bursts glowed briefly, their smoke merging into the darkness above the enemy lines; between them, as if unaffected, the lights of rifle fire winked on and off. The noise was deafening; still the canisters and the 'minnies' kept coming, their closer bursts punctuating the steady concussion of the batteries. It was a devil's medley. Their own machine gunners joined in again; three whizzbangs whined overhead; a rifle bullet chinked on wire; he heard it turn over and over and over as it sang away behind.

He stepped back from the 'scope, and the sentry, Hayes, moved up again.

Brenton, the company commander, appeared around the angle of the traverse, leaning and peering. 'Is that you, Master?' He was known in their little circle as the Master of Pembroke. 'See anything?'

'Nothing out of the ordinary.'

'I don't think they're coming, do you?'

'There's no sign of them.'

'You lost Patterson.'

He nodded, thinking of the man's bared teeth.

'I got our guns down on to 'em.'

'They're strafing well.'

'Everything all right?'

'We sent one fellow back on a stretcher.'

Brenton's eyes flicked round momentarily as machine gun bullets zipped into the ground somewhere in front and small fragments of earth spattered against the sandbagged parapet. 'I dare say they'll quieten down. I don't think they're coming over.'

'Probably annoyed about the mine.'

'That's it!' Brenton raised his torch like a swagger stick and walked on with his slight limp, a tall, slim figure, scarcely older than Andy but already a veteran: he had landed with the original expeditionary force and been through Le Cateau and the Marne, where he had received a shell splinter in his left hip and been recommended for the Military Cross. He was known in the mess as 'Limpopo' or 'the great Limpopo', or 'the great grey-green', but no one called him these things to his face.

The fury of the fire subsided after he had gone, and by the time he returned, things were back to normal for the time of evening; he told Andy to stand the men down in ten minutes if nothing else blew up.

Webb had sent back for empty sandbags and was standing by a small pile of them, waiting with obvious impatience to begin the task of rebuilding the blown-out portion of the wall when Andy came to tell him to stand the men down. Immediately he detailed a working party to fill the bags, and sent others back for the rations. Andy stood with him, not anxious to go to the dug-out with the others, nor yet to stay, but there was nowhere else.

A section of sky towards the enemy slopes had cleared and several stars were out. He felt an impulse to climb the parapet to prove there was no danger – it was an illusion – and down the dip – somehow over the wire – and up the forbidden slopes on the further side, through the rubble of the village and up, taking care to avoid the woods inhabited by darkness, over the rolling fields to the top of the ridge you could only glimpse from certain positions, to stand

and breathe in the night air and look down over all the labyrinthine workings on both sides. But he would not be alone even there. He could hear the cart wheels and the horses and the boots already. As at Marlborough, it was hard to be alone.

'Good night, Sarn't!'

'Goo' night, sir!'

'Don't work them for too long. I shouldn't think Jerry'll drop another one plumb into that 'ole. Not before to-morrow!'

'Oi hopes not, sir! Come tomorrer Oi doubt Jerry'll think a some place else to frazzle.'

He turned, wondering if that had been a pleasantry or a rebuke, and made his way back along the windings of the trench, past the sentries like statues with their eyes above the parapet, past details coming up with ration bags, and turned into the Norwich Road, squeezing round the outside of a recent crater that had bitten out the walls of the alley, following the twists, registering the broken-down parts by habit until he came to the entrance to the dug-out. The fusty smell of earth and concrete and damp, and Barnabee lighting up for the evening meal met him as he started down the steps.

The mail had come up with the rations, he saw; an envelope and what looked like a roll of magazines was lying on the corner of one of the sheets of old newspaper spread over the table. Carfax and Limpopo were sitting at the table, smoking, mugs beside them and the two Johnny Walker bottles between. Carfax, who was looking at an illustrated magazine with shiny pages, glanced round as he heard him coming down the steps, the great Limpopo remained absorbed in a letter spread out before him. The light from three candles stuck in beer bottles on the table accentuated the hollow skin beneath his eyes and his long, fine nose, twisted slightly to the side, and the firm contours either side of his mouth leading on to the hollows of his cheeks. Andy admired him more almost than anyone he had met. He was like a quieter version of Uncle Richard. He put on no 'side', treated them all as friends he might have known all his life, yet when he looked at you with his steady light grey eyes you wanted to

548

be worthy of him, have him think well of you, follow him to hell if need be.

From the corner of his eye, he saw the shape of a rat move out from the entrance to the sleeping chamber in the dark, darting way the creatures had; immediately behind it he saw and heard 'Nails' Nailor brandishing the knobkerry-like stick which he had spent hours fashioning with a knife. He was swinging round the doorway on one arm, yelling, and he launched himself after the rat, a big fellow, between two of the rough wooden posts supporting the roof. The rodent evaded him easily, shot under the table between Limpopo and Carfax, and out beside Andy's legs.

'*Christ* almighty! *Master*! You could've had him!'

Limpopo turned his head and looked up at Nailor without a word.

Nails pursed his lower lip like a sixth-former caught out in some peccadillo; he was scarcely more than a sixth-former. The thick moustache he sported and his dark jowls and dark, button eyes and general pushiness made him seem older, but his remarks and behaviour in the mess suggested a rather undeveloped schoolboy. His talk consisted of undigested scraps picked up from the press, the more bellicose pieces, and lascivious comments on his prowess with the village girls - 'mawthers' he called them in the patois of his platoon. Andy found nothing in common with him except the unhappy accident of close confinement in D company mess.

'I'll bring you one tomorrow,' he replied curtly. 'That do?'

'There's a letter for you,' Carfax said as if interposing between them.

He had already recognized Henry's writing on the envelope. He picked it up and stood, ripping at it fiercely. He could feel Nails's gaze on him, then Barnabee came in with a rattle of cutlery to lay up for the meal, and the tension eased. Nails, swinging his stick, disappeared into the gloom of the sleeping chamber. Andy sank wearily to a biscuit box by the table.

'You'd think there was enough of a row outside!' Carfax said.

He smiled. He liked Carfax; he hadn't much more in his head than Nails but he was personally thoughtful beyond his years and there was nothing evil in him. He eyed the Johnny Walker bottles, and looked up at Barnabee. 'A mug, Barrabus!'

'Sir!'

'You lost a man,' Carfax went on.

He nodded, drawing Henry's letter out of the envelope. He didn't want to talk about it. It was his first experience of death in action; he hadn't comprehended it yet. His mind was still bumping with noises and the air down here was so stale and thumping he didn't want to think. He needed to put something on paper about his revelation of the paradox of war, and about Patterson's face when they scraped the chalk debris away; was that fearful scream he had heard the man's only epitaph, or had he laughed as he went over the edge? The suddenness and arbitrariness was shattering. A line from Horace ran in his mind – heroes and cowards die the same death. Horace had known about war; he would be able to appreciate Horace better now. He felt the urge to write himself though –

He realized he was looking at Henry's letter without actually reading it, and pulled his mind back to the page.

Dear Andy,

Isn't this too like the letters we used to write each other when you were at Marlborough? Mama has just asked 1) Do moles like Fortnum's hampers? 2) Which morsels do moles like most? 3) Is there anything moley needs partikler? We are all well and *much* looking forward to seeing you when you come home on leave – *when will that be?* – although of course, poor Moley will not be able to see us we do so look forward to seeing him.

Willy has just this moment telephoned; he sounded marvellously cheerful although another dud patrol he said. He told us a funny story about winning a motorbike from his skipper at poker – I never know whether to believe him but Mama improved it by crying out 'Oh, Willy, do be careful!' Even she laughed afterwards, poor dear.

Nothing from George, but we don't worry about him now he is up at that place in the north. Uncle Richard is positive the German fleet will not come out, and if they do will get so dreadfully knocked about they'll run home with their tails between their legs like their battle-cruisers did when Beatty went after them. He is very depressed about Gallipoli tho', says it's been bungled and we shall be lucky now to get out of it without worse than the August casualty lists. 'Does that mean you think the war could go on for a lot longer then?' I asked. He simply looked at me. I could tell he thought it would. I'm so glad you're not there.

Isobel Peters came to dinner last week, she looked so tired. They work them like absolute slaves at the hospital but it is worthwhile she said; it made me feel such an idler – I was rather beastly to her, Mama told me that afterwards which of course made me feel even worse! She is such a *true* little *brick* and so utterly devoted to Willy I really feel so sorry for her especially as I have a feeling Willy has *other* fish to fry now. You must *not* tell him I said so, he would never forgive me, he hasn't said anything himself. Oh dear, retailing gossip as usual! I am only idling here for Mama's sake, and Papa. Next year I have decided to do my duty as a slave like Isobel and Popsy. Popsy has been sent out to France. Morale will rise out there! I hope it lifts *yours* to know Popsy might greet you if you get a *little* wounded –

Barnabee placed a mug by his hand, returning him abruptly to the present. He sensed Brenton gazing at him and looked up to see an amused light in his eye. He realized he was smiling.

'My sister,' he explained.

'Ah! *Henry!*' Brenton pushed the Johnny Walker bottles towards him. 'On form?'

'She's decided she ought to become a V.A.D.!'

'Something to look forward to if we get a Blighty one!'

He shook his head, thinking of Henry in a uniform pretending to be demure. 'Difficult to imagine though.' He poured from the half-golden bottle and topped it up with chlorinated water from the clear one, nodding towards Brenton's letter. 'Does she still love you?'

'She says so!' Limpopo smiled rather shyly.

He raised the mug. 'Here's to them all!' He thought of Cynthia cycling along the towpath by the Cam yelling encouragement as indecorously as any young man, and wondered what she was doing now, whether she'd married Bertie, where Bertie was now – probably out here somewhere –

'To them all!' Limpopo said with a strange, ardent expression as he raised his mug, and Carfax joined them in the toast.

Nails emerged from the other room, his hair tousled on the left as if he'd been lying down. 'Where's the Mac-bloody-conachie! I'm out at – *Chrrrist!*' He stared towards the far wall, then very quietly, 'Don't move anyone!' and turned and tiptoed back towards the opening from which he had emerged.

They looked round. A rat was peering at them from a gap in the boards between the torn poster of Kitchener pointing his gloved finger at them and a road sign 'Albert-Villers-le-Vert'.

They laughed. The creature tilted its head, pin-points of candle light in its eyes as it studied Carfax, who was nearest, tiny nostrils at the end of the sharp snout dilating.

Limpopo banged his hand on the table, and Andy and Carfax joined in heartily. The rat jerked its forepaws as if about to sit up, then swivelled suddenly and disappeared along the crack behind the road sign, its tail following nakedly, a spatter of chalk falling to the floor.

They looked back as Nails entered with his stick.

'You *bastards*! You –' He looked at Brenton, realizing he was leading the drumming and stopped himself.

They shouted with laughter.

He came up and placed the stick very deliberately by his place on the table.

'That was awfully – bad – luck!' Limpopo gasped, tears on his cheeks.

Nails, unused to being a butt, sat and muttered about 'bloody Barrabas'.

It was Barnabee's appearance with a dixy of soup that calmed them. Limpopo wiped his eyes and with a very obvious steadying of his voice, said, 'We'll need plenty of wire tonight. I've sent word back to Brierley.'

Nails gazed at him, then at his watch. 'My job again!'

'Well – let's hope it's come up by the time you go on.'

'There's a bloody great 'ole in the Norwich Road,' Carfax said.

'I know. Stalky knows about it.'

Nails looked up at Barnabee. 'What the hell *is* this?'

The man's pale brows lifed, 'Toidy bi'a moost things, sir. But thet oon't dew yew no harm.'

'Slugs and snails,' Andy hazarded. 'Trench rat's tails?'

'Ooh, noo rats, sir – owd rat, he woon't a-let yew fang him, sir. He's hully tew sharp.' His eyes widened. 'Doon't he jis' goo, sir!'

Nails studied him suspiciously.

'Mr Nailor thinks you exaggerate,' Limpopo said.

'*Oi*, sir! Ooh, no-oo, sir, there been't no rats in thar.' He looked at the dixy. 'Howsumdiver –'

Limpopo raised his hand. 'We don't want to know.'

'Noo, sir. Well – it oon't dew yew noo harm, Oi prarmiss.'

'That's good enough for us!'

'Thankee, sir.'

Smiling, Andy turned to the last page of Henry's letter to glance at it quickly before folding it away.

– otherwise there is nothing to tell. I do think of you so much, so do we all, Mama sends fondest love, we are so proud of you.

Till the seas gang dry, yr everloving Henry.

P.S. Uncle Richard asked me to send his best salaams and be sure to let him know as *soon* as you come home, he will stand you a slap-up evening anywhere you wish with *the girl of your choice*!!! Ah – hum! I wish I could do more, he said. So you see – I can't wait to see our moley again.

He folded it and tucked it back in the envelope. He wished he hadn't reminded himself; it was all a million miles away.

He had forgotten what it was like to lie in the sun – simply lie with the warmth sinking in. Old longings stirred, and memories that had been buried under winter. Moving patterns of light played inside his closed eyelids like the patterns on the water rippling just beyond his stretched arms and the shadows of the spring leaves rustling in the branches overhead. A warbler chrr-chrr-chrrd as it flew in and out of reeds; the marvellously varied liquid notes of another bird rose from quite close above.

With his eyes closed like this he could imagine himself lying by the Cam.

He had never been able to fathom why he had not guessed Cynthia found Bertie so attractive – if she did and it was not simply Bertie's social position. That would not be Cynthia though. She was honest. It hurt to think of her honesty. It hurt to think of her in the May sun, shining hair against the cushion, slightly freckled, pale forehead, dark lashes of her eyes cast down as she read aloud while he toiled at the punt pole not really listening to her, happy to let the cadences flow past, happy to declaim with her if she came to lines he remembered, happier, much happier than he had ever been. So far as he knew Bertie had never read a line of poetry –

He felt the rising urge to write again. He had not written anything since Sorley had been killed.

'The Seventh Batt.'s got stick –'

Jumping up, he had crossed to look over Carfax's shoulder at the paper spread on the table.

BATTLE FOR LOOS
Attack on the Hairpin Trench . . .

His eye skimmed down the column until he came to the name he knew he would find: Captain C. H. Sorley, taking over after the loss of his company commander, had been killed whilst leading the charge.

He had begun a correspondence with Sorley a few weeks before – a lifeline he had hoped. The line was cut. The shock had faded now, but his sense of loss was even greater.

The same night he had led a patrol out from their line on the outskirts of La Boiselle; it had been an extraordinary experience. Followed by Webb, he had crawled up to the head of an occupied sap extending in front of the enemy wire, surprised three Germans in it, killing two he thought, taking the third back as a prisoner for intelligence. Limpopo had ensured his mention in the dispatch; Carfax had been enthusiastic about the credit brought on the battalion. Nails's manner towards him had shown a marked change. He had felt extraordinarily good about it, a warrior, even a hero. Yet he knew how very differently it might have turned out if he had not been feeling so strange about Sorley's death; he had not gone out to get himself killed, but the possibility had not worried him; he had felt no fear of any kind; neither life nor death had meant much.

Going to see Sorley's people during his six days' leave in November, he had been moved by that last, prophetic poem found in his kit.

> When you see millions of the mouthless dead
> Across your dreams in pale battalions go –

How did it go on? He had the book they had sent him afterwards in his pocket. That and the other war poems made him despair of his own efforts.

Walking on the Heath with Henry, he had rather let his feelings pour out; the new forms he was searching for to match the shock of new experience, they came at night; he confessed he thought that perhaps the search for expression was cathartic and alone kept him sane in the awful nights, but when he wrote the lines remembered in the morning they seemed worthless; he hadn't the heart to work at them, nor the energy. His energies, his whole mind were sapped by the banal and temporary nature of his existence and the need to adapt at all times to its petty routines and to his fellows, who never really touched his intellect. The truth was, he was not cut out to be a soldier. His mental exhaustion built up intolerable frustration for he wanted to write more than he ever had, to explore the effect on himself of this constantly changing camp existence where every small event was charged with the imminence of arbitrary mutilation, and death had become as ordinary as lice, and companionship was closer than he had ever known; he would move out from himself to his fellows, merging individuals and individuality into the larger outlines of the war which had taken them over and so write an epic, not from an observer's point of view, but as it was experienced by everyone from inside, totally subjective, totally real –

'Perhaps you are being too ambitious, Andy. Perhaps you should *start* on a smaller canvas –'

'Yes, I know I *ought* to, but honestly – then, you see – the language – obviously when I try to describe the way the men are affected I should use *their* language –' he laughed, 'I hardly understand them myself at times! And dialect is so dangerous – I'd be accused of aping Kipling or Masefield –'

'You must be yourself, Andy.'

'Of course I know that, Henry! Who *am* I? Sometimes I have the feeling I'm thousands of my forbears who went to war. What have I to say that's new? Horace knew all about war – why does everyone have to find everything out for *themselves* – no it's not true. I do want to say something. About the *impetus* inside the – the anthill – the company, the way that war, *imposed* on all these men, changes them and makes them a part of itself and gives them the power – the way the power moves up as well as down – the way we adapt to it and it adapts to us – the continuity of it all. Through the ages too. You know you used to ask me whether I believed in God and I said my god was not the Christian God? I think I'm coming back to Him – not so much in a Christian sense, in a Roman sense, because our forbears worshipped Him so He has permanency, d'you see? If I am what went before who am I to say I cannot worship at that shrine? It is the only shrine that has truth – the truth of those who *believed* –'

'Some of us still do!' she had come in as he paused in the reckless rush of words, wondering how much she understood of what he was trying to say.

'I'm glad, very glad.'

'Surely you must have written something?'

'Nothing. Not since I heard about Sorley.'

'Well – before?'

When they returned, she had persuaded him to show her his pitiful efforts.

'You lost a man today?'
I heard him scream;
My flesh was like a nerve
In agony.

'You lost a man today?'
His lips were parted;
From behind his eyes
The soul had fled.

'You lost a man today?'
Why he? His eyes,
Lips, teeth, grimace threw back
The mystery.

'You lost a man today?'
I don't know where he went.
I heard him scream;
His lips were frozen in
That farewell cry.

He thought that had shocked her a little; she had looked at him in a strange, quiet way. He had pared the language down too much; he had lost the nuance – who would want to read it in any case?

Poor Henry. He doubted if it would shock her now. She must have been three months at Guy's. She had probably seen more wounded than he and have attended them rather more intimately. She said as little about it all in her letters as he told her about the front in his. She wrote of her up and down relations with Sister and some of the regular nurses, of the other V.A.D.s, not of the wards themselves; her letters were less frequent now and much shorter. It was obviously a struggle to keep up the network of communications between them all, but she managed it.

It was strange, that dream she had had the night before Papa died. He could remember Papa's eyes when they had been clear blue, his hair full and dark just as she had described it. He had come to her bedside at the nurses' hostel as he used to to hear their prayers when they were small. On his rounds. He had smiled and patted her hair as he used to.

557

He thought of Henry and Mama and Babs and Uncle Richard in black behind the coffin, and the black figures of relatives with complacent faces half-remembered from childhood. Poor Mama –

The warmth faded as a cloud passed in front of the sun, and he shivered a little. The April air had a decided nip. He rolled over on his side, then sat up and with his hands behind him, gazed at the reeds and the water beyond covered with lily leaves. The clouds were banking high over the trees beyond, which marked the line of the Somme. He had seen the best of the sun today; the wind flicked over the water in the spaces clear of leaves; it looked suddenly dark and unfriendly.

He thought of the 'big push'. The scale of preparation visible on every road and in every village behind the lines stretching back even behind their present divisional rest, and building every day; it was going to be a big push indeed. He wondered when it would start. There was no question the Bosche knew all about it. Henry knew in London!

Carfax had died as he had lived, without fuss, decently as a gentleman should; he could imagine he might have been smiling in his warm, sympathetic way for others when the sniper's bullet struck – a chance in a million. There had been no reason for it. His men had been fearfully cut up; they had idolized him. His own worst time had been next morning when they lowered him into the grave. He had been unable to compose his face. Oh, Lord, Carfax had talked of his sisters so often.

The wings of an aeroplane caught the sun above the reaching clouds. The clouds had outlines like trees – changing shape as they drove before the wind – 'Fear not, till Birnam Wood do come to Dunsinane.' The top of the right hand tree widened and spread like a wing, reaching out; some way along another shape was rising like a closed fist – a head – a narrow head. For a moment he saw the German eagle, hooked beak turned to the left, then the beak widened and the head leaned and the wing to the right turned into a dog's or wolf's head with a large eye of blue; the eye widened diagonally almost cutting the back of the head from the snout which had changed into a puffy, elongated cloud again, thinning grey-blue at the edges.

He thought of the permanence of the scene. The sky and the grand clouds over the trees or other trees would be here for other eyes long after he had ceased. The lilies would open on the *étang*; the Somme would flow. Life was priceless.

Rolling on to his left elbow, aware of the miraculous wholeness of his body and hard muscles as he moved, he tugged the book from his pocket and opened it against the rich grass, flicking over the pages that he knew until he came to XXVII:

> When you see millions of the mouthless dead
> Across your dreams in pale battalions go,
> Say not soft things as other men have said,
> That you'll remember. For you need not so.
> Give them not praise. For deaf, how should they know
> It is not curses heaped on each gashed head?
> Nor tears. Their blind eyes see not your tears flow.
> Nor honour. It is easy to be dead.
> Say only this, 'They are dead.' Then add thereto,
> 'Yet many a better one has died before.'
> Then, scanning all the o'ercrowded mass, should you
> Perceive one face that you loved heretofore,
> It is a spook. None wears the face you knew.
> Great death has made all his for evermore.

11

George looked along the row of young faces behind the Captain's table and settled for Carew-Porter.

'Porter, suppose we are detailed target-towing ship –'

There was a knock on the door surround and he turned. It was Dixon.

'Beggin' your pardon, sir. Capting wants 'is pictures took down, sir, for firin' sir.'

George looked back at the midshipmen; their faces had become rather interested.

'I shall expect you to be able to describe in detail how you would prepare the target – hoist it out – the towing wire you would use – the whole shoot –' he paused for some laughter at his unintentional pun. 'All right – hop it!' and turning to Dixon, 'Carry on!'

'Thank you, sir.'

He went straight up to the bridge. 'Pat' Acheson was in the charthouse, his eyes looking as though he had been roused from his post-prandial nap; Carrington was pencilling on the chart, the Old Man watching. He looked round as he entered.

'Ah, Guns!'

'Sir! Dixon is preparing your quarters for firing.'

The Old Man nodded towards some signal forms on the table, and he picked them up. They were intercepts from the *Galatea*, leading Beatty's light cruisers, to his flagship, *Lion*: the earliest, timed 2.21, read 'URGENT. TWO CRUISERS PROBABLY HOSTILE IN SIGHT BEARING ESE COURSE UNKNOWN.' The latest at 2.35, reported a large amount of smoke as from a fleet bearing ENE.

'I dare say it's Hipper's battle-cruisers again,' the Old Man said. 'How far off d'you put them, Pilot?'

'Eighty miles, sir.'

George saw that Carrington had marked the approximate position for Beatty's battle cruiser force sou-sou-east of the 2.30 cross marking their own D.R. position off the Skaggerak. If it was indeed the enemy battle cruiser squadron that had been sighted, it seemed an odd position for them to be, hugging the Jutland coast.

The Old Man had the same thought. 'What d'you suppose they're up to over there?'

'Having a go at the Danish holiday resorts this time, sir?' Acheson suggested.

The Old Man gave a short grunt of a laugh. 'Safer for 'em! I expect it'll turn out to be someone burnin' rotten coal!'

Another washout, George thought, not entirely sorry about it. If it was Hipper, he would turn tail as soon as he became aware of Beatty as he had on every previous occasion, and there would be no chance of their own squadron catching up from eighty miles astern. If they were going to meet him, he would far rather it happened when their squadron was back in its rightful place in Beatty's line.

'Sir John's taking it seriously, sir,' Carrington said with a hopeful expression.

'He has to! Find out how they're gettin' on down below, Pilot!'

Carrington moved out to the voicepipe to the engine room. George followed, gathering from what he heard that they were working up to full speed. He walked along the bridge wing, looking out beyond the *Indomitable*, following in the pale green smooth of their wake, to the cruisers in line abreast, and beyond them the smoke from the Grand Fleet battleships hull down over the horizon; from the density of the clouds, it seemed Jellicoe was raising steam for full speed too.

He became aware of Acheson beside him.

'Do you think they are out?' he asked him.

Acheson shrugged. 'They'll show us a clean pair of heels in any case.'

They turned and paced back. The sun was very pleasantly

warm. The familiar, wide shape of the *Invincible* hung just ahead over the piling froth of her stern wave, and just visible through the smoke pouring from her funnels, Hood's flag blew out. George thought of West on her bridge, speculating sceptically no doubt on the chances of a scrap. West had not been altogether too pleased about Henry joining the V.A.D.s; he seemed to take it as a personal reproach that they had not managed to finish off the Hun before such extreme steps became necessary! Perhaps he was also concerned about her proximity to young doctors and officers back from France who might steal her affections. He had seemed in an oddly excited, nervy sort of mood when he had last talked to him two days before, more than ever determined to give up the Service for her when they had completed the job. It was surely the monotony of the waiting and fruitless sweeps across the North Sea preying on his mind, as it preyed on his own when he thought of Kate. Her people were talking of turning a wing of Verney Park into a convalescent home for officers.

The Old Man came out of the charthouse and gazed round, squinting at the horizon towards the sun. 'Good visibility, Guns!'

'Couldn't be better, sir.' Yet there was a suspicion of haze beyond the bright edge of the sea.

'Just our luck if it is Hipper!'

With the fifth battle squadron, the latest 'Queen Elizabeths', occupying their place in Beatty's line while they were up with Jellicoe, it would undoubtedly be a massacre: the fifteen inch guns of the Queen Elizabeths would hit the Germans far outside the range at which they could reply. George had an image of von Spee's cruisers listing, burning at the end of the Falklands Battle. 'I shouldn't think there'll be much left by the time we arrive, sir.'

The Old Man grunted.

They had worked up to full speed now, over twenty-five knots; the ventilator fans roared; the deck vibrated underfoot; the wind of their progress was strong on his face. Ahead the *Invincible* had her stern tucked deeper into the boil from her screws; the sun brightened her starboard plates and shone from the moving swell spreading from her side across the lightly ruffled blue of the sea. George was again reminded of the Falklands; yet there was a heaviness in the air, that suggestion of haze around the sun and a thickening of the sky; there was not that extraordinary sharpness they had experienced in the south Atlantic, nor the sense of great distances. Ahead of the flagship, the four destroyers of their anti-submarine screen clouded the sky with smoke.

A signal rating pounded up the ladder with another wireless message clutched in his hand; he speculated on its content from the Old Man's expression as he read it. At the same time the chief yeoman began reading out a course alteration easterly; looking ahead, he saw a flag hoist below the *Invincible*'s yard.

The Old Man handed Acheson the message form. George looked at it over his arm; another from the *Galatea* to the *Lion*.

SMOKE SEEMS TO BE SEVEN VESSELS BESIDES DESTROYERS AND CRUISERS. THEY HAVE TURNED NORTH.

'Hipper, sir!' Acheson said.
'Looks uncommonly like it.'
'Execute, sir!' the yeoman called.
'Take her round, Pilot!'

Hood was evidently going to try and interpose the squadron between Hipper on his northerly course and the German bases; if he succeeded, *look out!*

The *Invincible*'s flag hoist dropped; moments later they saw her port side ribbed diagonally with the torpedo-net booms open gradually to view; what a splendid sight she made at speed, the wash spreading from her long hull, high white stern wave creaming behind – a greyhound mounting the great turrets and long guns of a battleship. It was what they looked like themselves, he thought; as always it gave him a thrill of pride. The destroyers were coming round ahead of her, and away on the port bow the cruiser, *Canterbury*, showed her slim stern.

They had scarcely followed the flagship on to the new course than another message came up. The Old Man looked at it for a moment, then turned to Acheson with one of his grunting, short laughs. *'Galatea*'s tryin' to draw the Huns nor-westerly – towards Beatty I assume,' and reading from the form, ' "They all appear to be following"!'

They laughed.

'I wonder for how long.' He looked out towards the flagship then back to Acheson. 'You'd better send the hands to tea. We'll close up afterwards.'

Going down the ladder, George saw they had already drawn well away from the cruiser screen, while the Grand Fleet was no more than a suggestion of murk over that part of the northern horizon not obscured by the *Indomitable*, close astern. The sight of the wave mounting the forward thrust of her stem, spray glistening in the sun and all the sounds and straining movements of their own speed gave him a momentary feeling that perhaps there was a chance, then he reminded himself of the previous false alarms. Directly Hipper saw Beatty, he would turn and leg it for home.

After tea on the way up to his station in the control top he looked in at the charthouse, finding the Old Man and Carrington staring at a new signal form on the table as if trying to decode it.

'It's Hipper all right,' the Old Man said as he saw him. 'They're engaging.'

'Have they turned back, sir?'

The Old Man's lips twitched wryly. 'I think we can assume it!'

George glanced at the chart.

'Not a hope,' Carrington said pointing, 'unless they manage to slow 'em.'

The Old Man stepped to the door. 'I shouldn't place too much reliance on that. Hipper left the *Blücher* to her own devices at the Dogger if you recall.' He looked at George. 'We'll let you know if they turn north again!'

George grinned. 'I look forward to hearing that, sir.'

He followed the Old Man out and turned straight down the ladder to the mast strut, stepping over a stream of water from a hose, whose handler, humming in a low monotone to the rhythm of 'Tipperary', lowered the jet for him.

'Fritz out, sir?' the man asked mechanically; he knew the answer well enough.

564

'He is indeed!'

'We'll 'ave 'im this time, sir!'

The other members of the hose party grunted assent.

'I hope you're right, Lambert. Unfortunately we'll have to go like hell to catch him first!'

They chuckled.

He hitched his bag over his shoulder and started up the rungs as the jet of the hose swung up across the deck again. Climbing through the hatch into the control top, he looked round quickly; everyone was in place; they had already started the routine tests.

'Hipper's out!' he said.

They cheered.

He moved to his stool forward, and taking his glasses out swung his bag into the corner below. Listening with half his mind to the familiar reports, he looked round the horizon. To starboard the day was bright and clear with the path of the sun sparkling on the blue sea. The little *Chester* was some four miles on the quarter; well astern of her were the distant columns of smoke above Jellicoe's cruisers. Was it smoke, or were there also patches of mist? He turned to port; conditions looked ideal; the *Canterbury* on the bow was lit up beautifully, the horizon beyond as sharp as a cut-out.

'As we suspected,' the Old Man said when he reported all turrets prepared for firing in director control, 'they're headin' south!'

He relayed the news and an audible groan sounded round the top. He found 'Tipperary' going through his head again.

> Twas a long bill those hard men owed us,
> Twas a sad bill to pay.
> With a strong will behind to goad us
> As we hit them hard that day.
> Stand clear little Willie!
> Kaiser Bill beware!
> 'Twas a big, big price you paid to England
> For your work – out there.

West had been in cracking form at the Falklands first anniversary dinner in the *Invincible*, most amusing on the punishments he would hand down to C.O.s if appointed to an examining board. He hadn't shared the general view that the new army troops and the colonials and Indians being poured into France would settle the issue some time in the spring or early summer; he had been nervous nonetheless lest the politicians sign a peace before they were allowed a crack at the High Seas Fleet – not that he really expected Scheer to come out. The Kaiser would preserve his battleships as bargaining counters at the peace negotiations, he thought.

'Funny sort of counters that daren't be allowed outside the Jade! I dare say the politicians will fall for it though. It will all have been for nothing then – we'll have to go through it again – when the Crown Prince comes to the throne!'

West was a fire-eater on the subject of Huns!

It was rumoured the big push would start any day now. He wondered what part Andy had been allotted. There was a fellow in Andy's platoon who had been a groom at Verney Park and knew all about Kate, spoke of her with great awe! Lord! If only they could settle the business; he had felt on his last leave something was missing; it had been difficult to place: Kate had been as lively as ever but he had not felt the *force* of her interest as he used to. She was absolutely direct; if she felt something, she showed it, and this last time he had sensed she did not feel so strongly for him. Their unofficial understanding remained, he had assured himself of that: directly peace returned they would become engaged formally. It was intensely frustrating, this eternal waiting and cruising, knowing every time one went out that one was not going to catch even a glimpse of the enemy.

'It's funny we can't hear the guns,' Bousfield said. 'You'd think we'd be able to hear something.'

'They're half way back to the Jade by now,' he replied; if there were any prospect of catching them, surely they would have heard by this time.

As the afternoon wore on with no further news from Beatty's force, the feeling of haring off on yet another abortive chase took firm hold. It was reinforced as the visibility started to close in in patches: at times the *Chester*, five miles away at the most, disappeared completely in mist. In the north where they had left Jellicoe's cruisers and the smoke haze of the Grand Fleet far astern, featureless sea merged into humid sky. For all that could be seen or heard, they might be racing through waters empty of everything save their two cruisers and the destroyers, the *Invincible* ahead and the *Indomitable* like their own shadow in their wake.

He was wondering when they would call it off and come down to economical speed when the Old Man came through on the voicepipe, his normally calm voice sharp-edged. 'Guns! Signal from *Southampton* – "Have sighted enemy battle-fleet bearing approximately southeast, course of enemy north"!'

'*North*, sir!'

'*North!*'

It was incredible. There was stunned silence for a moment in the top, then a frenzy of speculation, increasing as they saw the *Invincible* altering to the southward.

'Wars!' Bousfield exclaimed, grinning immediately at his reversion to gunroom idiom. He looked hardly older than a snotty. He was a sound man, a very quick brain.

A minute or so later the Old Man came through again. 'Message, Commander-in-Chief to Admiralty, Guns – "Fleet action is imminent"!'

There was a wild cheer in the top, and they heard it echoing from other positions as the news was relayed through the transmitting station below.

Asking permission to load, George had an image of V-W, almost as if he were beside him for a moment in the top. How he would have revelled in this moment! His training would not be wasted though; he would see that if he were looking on!

They heard it then, a low concussion like distant thunder as if the haze had been split. He felt a thrill, half apprehension, half anticipation, running through him. Glancing at his watch he saw it was nearly 5.30; the afternoon had flown by. The sounds appeared to be coming from somewhere off the starboard bow, the familiar thudding of heavy guns firing salvoes, this time in earnest. He tried to picture the situation: Beatty, chasing south after Hipper must presumably have come upon the High Seas Fleet steering north, and immediately wheeled to draw them towards Jellicoe. Even with

567

the Queen Elizabeths he would have the legs of Scheer's battleships; it was probable, therefore, that the firing they could hear was between Beatty and Hipper, who must have wheeled northwards at the same time as Beatty and was now chasing him. It seemed as if Hood had indeed managed to bring the squadron into a position from which they might interpose between the Germans and their bases for the firing was certainly to the westward. A hollow feeling gripped him inside, deeper than the earlier thrill as he thought of their three battle-cruisers barring the way home for the entire German fleet! They were playing a far more serious game than they had in the south Atlantic.

He thought of West in the *Invincible*'s control top, imagining the exultation he must be feeling at this unexpected fulfilment of his most heartfelt desire; it was a calming image. They would give them toko, no question. He couldn't see the control top where West was sitting because of the screen of impenetrable black smoke thrown up from the flagship's funnels as always at high speed; he caught occasional glimpses of Hood's flag; it was an inspiring sight. Everyone had faith in their extraordinarily youthful Admiral; West considered he had more brains than anyone on the flag list except for his beloved Jellicoe.

His momentary attack of nerves had gone, leaving him buoyed up by a sense of impending high events – Trafalgar in the twentieth century. He had an image of his mother at home and completely unaware that he was poised on the edge of history, and of Henry at Guy's; he wished he could let her know somehow; he remembered games they had played on rainy days at home trying to project thoughts from the nursery to someone in a bedroom above! It reminded him of his father, and he felt the anguish again; he had died four months too soon. How certain he had been in the old days that they would have to fight the Hun sooner or later. Lord! How had he imagined a sea battle then? He couldn't remember.

The sound of the guns piercing the haze on the bow was like the thunder they had heard before the storm on that last cruise in the *Peacock*; he had an image of the line of battleships the colour of the squall behind them, and the tense expressions on Henry's and Andy's and Willy's faces as they gazed out from the cockpit, and his father with deep-shadowed eyes before the stroke that finished his sailing life – and with it most of his interest apart from themselves, his children. A wave of regret passed over him that he hadn't realized more or been more at home then – had not even been able to make his last farewell – and with it an absurd compulsion to take it out on the Huns when they appeared –

The haze, rather similar to the opaque haze before that storm, was extraordinarily patchy. He wondered if West was giving Hood advice on the best bearing for gunnery; at present he thought ships to the west would have the advantage, but that could change quickly as the sun got lower; much would depend on the banks of mist. The *Chester* was moving in and out of sight as if passing through thick white drapes; it was North Sea weather at its most perverse.

The sounds of gunfire grew perceptibly louder, drawing ever broader on their starboard bow; it was difficult to tell how far away; the mist played tricks with sound as with sight; he guessed it was over twenty miles distant. Still they held their sou-sou-easterly course, the little *Canterbury* on the port bow, the destroyers ahead, the *Chester* invisible again somewhere abaft the starboard beam. The sun hung, a yellow orb with a clear, bright outline. The horizon below was indistinct. Time was suspended, only the sounds of battle moved towards them, towards the beam, ceasing for periods as if mist had intervened, breaking out again in violent spasms.

As the firing passed the beam it grew suddenly louder and continuous, rolling through the mist like long-drawn peals of thunder almost deafening in intensity. A climax of some sort had been reached; perhaps the fleets had met – but that was impossible: Jellicoe was well astern; the battle was only just abaft the beam.

Still Hood held on the straight course to the southward as if bent on over-running the fight so that when Hipper and Scheer turned, as they must when they became aware of the trap into which Beatty was leading them, the third battle-cruiser squadron would be there to greet them! Surely it was impossible. They would be massacred.

The silence in the control top was intense; all stared out to starboard, trying to penetrate the haze that shut out any view of the shattering events passing by. He cautioned Bowles in the director tower just below to get his sights on to the first object he saw; for all he knew though the first ship to appear might be one of Beatty's; he might have worked his way around to the east of Hipper somehow in the run northwards. Rapid identification was going to be critical. He passed down to the transmitting station an initial range of 10,000 yards, which he thought was about the limit of visibility westwards.

A burst of fire from lighter guns sounded from close on the starboard quarter, rising quickly to a crescendo. He guessed they were approximately six inch pieces – a cruiser action. Not even shapes were visible through the mist curtains. He realized they were turning. Looking forward, he saw the flagship's starboard side open, and the eager destroyers now on her port bow racing round, waves swelling up their sides, sterns low in white water. Their leader was the *Shark*, where Willy's great chum, Jollion Peters, was Number One.

The *Invincible* continued right round to starboard until she was leading them north-westerly, bringing the gunfire from the cruiser action on to the port bow. Below the turrets swung as Bowles trained his director sight towards the sounds and the trainers in the turrets followed the pointers round. Looking forward, he saw the *Invincible*'s guns pointing in the same direction.

He looked back towards the firing, straining to penetrate the haze, and thought he saw a momentary brightening, then another. Bousfield was staring in the same direction over his Dumaresq. More flashes showed; the question was, from whose guns?

The Old Man came through. 'Guns! Look out bearing red two seven! Gun flashes!'

An area of the mist seemed to become denser and he saw a continuous glow low down; seconds later a cruiser broke through at speed, trailing smoke from her funnels and fires which could be glimpsed through holes along her side. It was the *Chester*. She was close, scarcely four miles he judged, heading from west to east across their course. Three water columns stood up around her bow as he brought his glasses on to her; she drove through them and he saw them collapsing on her fo'c's'le and bridge; immediately another three rose beyond her, and four others on the near side, obscuring her after part, where he thought he had glimpsed a puff of cordite smoke from the discharge of one of her guns.

He trained his glasses left towards where the enemy must be, again making out a slight thickening and darkening in the haze through which the glow of gunfire flickered palely.

'Got it?' he asked Bousfield.

'Red – four six!'

The bearing was passed to Bowles; George turned quickly to make sure Clarke on the rangefinder was lined up in the same direction.

A moment after he turned back he saw them, spectral shapes scarcely denser than the mist from which they emerged, solidifying into two – three – light cruisers heading north-easterly at speed, flashes from their guns rippling along their sides. *Yorck* class! They looked in magnificent shape. A single water column stood up short of the leader; a fourth ship of the same class began to emerge some way astern.

The Old Man came through, 'Open fire on the second in the line!'

'Stand by to open fire on the second cruiser from the right! Bearing red four four.'

The target began to shorten, turning towards them.

'Turning to starboard together,' Bousfield called.

'Range – oner – ho – niner – double-ho –'

It flashed through George's mind that the enemy cruisers were in an ideal position for firing torpedoes as he slipped into the routine monosyllabic quick question and answer to establish an opening range and rate with Hemmings on the plot in the transmitting station. Settling on 10,200 yards, closing at 400, he gave the order to shoot. The target was well round on her turn. He heard the fire gongs in the turrets.

The mast shook as Bowles pressed his button and all left guns fired. He watched the four shells climb away against the bright western sky, counting the seconds under his breath. A split second after the buzzer sounded, the splashes stood high beyond the target and towards her stern.

'Right two! Down 400!' She was coming round towards them all the time.

'Down 400 on the plot!'

'Right guns ready!'

'Shoot!'

Again the judder as if the control top had been shaken by giant hands; orange-brown cordite smoke blew back from the guns; the shells grew into specks against the sunlight.

This time one splash rose short and he saw the glow of a hit under the cruiser's bridge. There was an exultant yell up the voicepipe from Bowles, echoed from behind him in the top. He went into rapid fire. The cruiser ceased altering to starboard; her hull began to lengthen in his glasses as she turned to port. Two more splashes rose just short which were not from his guns and he saw another hit; he wondered why West should be firing at his target. Two more hits glowed from his next salvo, and seconds afterwards she erupted in an explosion whose dense smoke hid all but her stern from view. She was slowing; the water was no longer white at her bow and her stern wave had dropped away. He saw through the gloom amidships the light from a raging fire and watched another salvo from the *Invincible* plunge in. He took his eyes off her momentarily to see what had happened to the other cruisers; one was a long way astern completely shrouded in smoke and steam; the others had disappeared. There was a tremendous noise of light gunfire from the direction in which they must have gone. Looking right again he watched another salvo straddle the burning, scarcely moving target as they raced from her and she became a blur of smoke merging with the mist.

'Check fire!'

Now that he was no longer concentrating on the fire control corrections, he realized the thunder from the main battle was closer than before off their port bow; looking ahead he saw the *Invincible* turning to port as though making directly for it when Bousfield shouted a warning of torpedoes. He jerked in the direction he was pointing and saw two parallel tracks some 800 yards off the bow. He reported them to the Old Man and heard him order a starboard turn. They watched the tracks pass clear astern as they came round; at the same time a third torpedo, evidently at the end of its run, bobbed slowly down the side some twenty feet away, its red nose showing clearly through the water. Looking towards the flagship as they passed it, he was surprised to find her way out on the starboard side and still turning as if her helm had jammed. Whatever she was doing, she started to come back soon afterwards, and they manoeuvred into her wake again.

She led round westerly towards the sound of the heavy guns; the *Indomitable* followed in perfect station astern, but of the damaged *Chester* and the *Canterbury* and the destroyers there was no sign; they had all disappeared as completely as the enemy. There was no doubt from the tremendous noise that Hood was leading them towards the main action, but whether it was still Beatty and Hipper, or if Jellicoe had arrived on the scene he couldn't think. Glancing at his watch, he saw it was just after ten past six; since he had not noted the time they turned back from the original southerly course, he couldn't begin to calculate where Jellicoe might be.

The shape of a large cruiser appeared off the bow, heading southerly across their course from starboard to port; snapping his glasses on her, he recognized the *Defence* from Jellicoe's cruiser screen, flying Arbuthnot's flag; another cruiser of the same class followed her, and moments afterwards he saw a squadron of light cruisers heading towards them – then destroyers. They had arrived immediately ahead of the Grand Fleet! The sky was dark with hanging smoke, and to port in the direction the *Defence* was heading, it was ripped like lightning with gun flashes; columns of water stood up against the gloom. The uproar was deafening. It was anyone's guess where the enemy was.

He began to see among the water spouts and flashes to port long grey shapes of ships; they were steaming east on the opposite course to their own, trailing widening layers of dense black smoke from their funnels, white water at their sterns; as they closed they rapidly became distinguishable as

Beatty's battle-cruisers in perfect line ahead, *Lion* leading, guns cocked up, firing to starboard; he had never seen anything so magnificent. The *Lion* had a large hole in her side and Q turret appeared to have been knocked out; her guns were still and pointing away from the enemy to the southward, but salvoes from her other three turrets crashed out with beautiful precision. Glancing quickly back along the line, he wondered where the second battle-cruiser squadron and the fifth battle squadron had got to; Beatty only had three ships following the *Lion*, then the *Defence* and her consort shut out his view, seemingly on a collision course with Beatty's flagship; they too had begun firing at the enemy in the south.

He heard a shout of torpedoes and saw tracks crossing ahead as the ship began to heel into another hard starboard turn. They came right round after the *Invincible* through rather more than 180 degrees until they were heading back east-south-easterly in the same direction and some one and a half miles ahead of the *Lion*, which he saw had somehow avoided collision with Arbuthnot's cruisers! They were lost to view beyond the battle-cruisers' smoke.

The glow and heavy smoke of a vessel on fire could be seen on the starboard beam, fountains from shell bursts erupting around it, and from just beyond, enemy gun flashes lit the murk. He was cautioning Bowles to train his sight on them when the Old Man came through and told him to fire directly he could make anything out. The range was going to be short. He doubted if he could see five miles.

Moments later the leading enemy became visible on the beam, a battle-cruiser of the *Derfflinger* class heading almost directly for them, huge in his glasses. He experienced a heart-stopping moment of exultation as he realized they were across the German T; he heard himself calling urgently for a range.

The leading enemy began turning to starboard as he watched; astern of her he saw a ripple of gunfire from what looked remarkably like a *König* class battleship, also beginning to turn, and astern of her the shapes of two other battle-cruisers. Why had no one given him a range? What was a battleship doing with Hipper's battle-cruisers?

The Old Man came through, 'Open fire on the second in line!'

'Range – eight – seven – double-ho –'

He couldn't wait for the plot below, but asked Bousfield for a snap rate and deflection; passing it down, he gave the order to shoot. In a fever of impatience for the turrets to come to the ready, he watched the *König*'s shape lengthen as she turned. What on earth were they doing down below –?

The top shook as the first salvo crashed out. He thought he saw the enemy battleship's turrets training towards them and put his glasses on her for a moment. They were! An involuntary shiver seized him. Taking on a battleship, and at this range! She filled his field of vision. He had an image of the massive thickness of plate the shells would have to penetrate to reach her vitals.

He lowered his glasses to watch for the fall of shot.

'Stand by splash!'

The buzzer went. He saw nothing save an angry red glare from the enemy's guns like tiny furnace doors opened briefly.

'See that?'

'No.'

'Down 400!'

'Down 400 on the plot!'

'Shoot!'

Moments later the right guns roared. He watched tensely, wondering where the enemy's shells would land. He had seen the brief glare of three salvoes in quick succession. She had almost paralleled them now. The rangetaker intoned behind him – down to eight thousand three hundred. Obviously the instrument was reading high. Where on earth were the enemy salvoes? Could it be they were not the target?

'Stand by splash!'

The buzzer went. He thought he saw water columns standing beyond the gap between her funnels.

'Down 400!'

'Down 400 on the plot!'

'Put it on and open the rate 200!'

'Rate 200 closing!'

'Shoot!'

575

On his third salvo he saw two splashes abreast her forward turret; they were straddling! He went into rapid fire, hearing Bowles blaspheme as a hit went home, a warm, red glow beneath the forward funnel. The next three salvoes all straddled as both they and the enemy held a steady course, and he saw the burst of another hit forward, followed by a brighter glow of flame obscured at once by thick black smoke rolling out and up over her bridge and funnels. Salvoes from other ships were beginning to stand up around her, at times almost hiding her from view. Why was West always interfering with his target? It was not only West this time; it seemed as if half the fleet were concentrating on her; the salvoes stood up thickly all around her. Her forward turret had been put out of action. She was firing from her other turrets, but no longer in controlled salvoes; still none of her shells appeared to come anywhere near. He was able to concentrate undisturbed as at target practice. He saw all four of his own shells splash up short as the buzzer went again, and called an 'up' correction by instinct. Perhaps she was zig-zagging, perhaps turning away. Surely she couldn't take this punishment for long?

For a moment he had an uninterrupted view between the water spouts and saw she was indeed turning away. Bousfield had seen it too, and called out an increase in the rate. He passed it down to the transmitting station as the buzzer went; one of the shells splashed short, and he saw another hit aft. He willed Hood to close; she was beaten and turning from them; he felt a savage intoxication; now was the moment to press the advantage. Instead he felt the top tilt slightly as they turned away to port, and for a few moments he was completely unsighted by a cloud of smoke from a wreck they were passing close to starboard. Glancing down quickly as they raced by, he saw two ends of a ship sticking perpendicularly out of the water, red with heat and between them a handful of men on something in the water; elation gripped him; they had accounted for one of them at least!

By the time they had passed through the cloud, his target and the others of the enemy squadron had melted away into the haze. He checked fire, wondering why on earth Hood had not altered after the fleeing enemy.

576

Looking ahead, he found the *Invincible* no longer there. For some extraordinary reason they were now leading ship. Two of Jellicoe's light cruisers were haring across their course from the starboard bow, otherwise the sea ahead was empty. He looked aft. The *Indomitable* was in position astern, and about a mile beyond her, the *Lion* was leading her squadron in their wake; beyond them was a confusion of light cruisers and destroyers, then the van of the battle fleet in line stretching back into the smoke overcast, tongues of flame leaping from their guns. It was an amazing sight. The flashes extended in a thunderous arc around the north-western horizon far beyond the point at which the great ships themselves merged into the fog. Jellicoe had achieved what seemed a perfect deployment!

Where was the *Invincible*?

He turned to ask Bousfield.

The young sub's face looked pale, and he seemed surprised by the question. 'She's gone,' he said after a momentary pause.

'Gone!'

'She went up. You didn't hear?' He stared at him. 'She seemed to come apart – she just opened up – amidships –'

'Opened up!' he heard himself repeating. He thought of the two ends of a ship they had passed so closely, and felt a chill across his heart. It was impossible. He couldn't visualize the flagship he had seen minutes before turning so grandly to lead the line, reduced to a cloud of smoke and two glowing ends pointing up out of the sea. Impossible to think of West and all the rest of them – where? There had been a few men in the water –

His mouth was quite dry with a foul taste; the rims of his eyes pricked with strain. He thought of Henry, and prayed that West was one of those in the water. There had been so few.

12

Willy followed the skipper up the depot ship's gangway, looking forward to a bath. There would be a letter from Isobel – what was he going to do about her –?

'Any luck?' the torpedo lieutenant, Jenkinson, greeted them cheerily.

The skipper shook his head. 'Sighted one of their subs going home. Managed to get in one shot, but he turned away and dived. Must have seen it. We never saw him again. There's a rumour you have some waterholes here, is it true?'

Jenkinson looked after him as he turned away forward. 'You haven't heard?'

The skipper glanced back.

'The fleet action,' Jenkinson went on.

The skipper stopped, his expression suddenly sharp.

'Off the Jutland Bank. They must have passed you in the night. They legged it back to the Horns Reef,' he added.

'What night?'

'May 31st – June 1st.'

'We were lying on the bottom. As per instructions.'

'You didn't hear them!'

'We heard a good deal of thumping.' He turned to Willy, and looking back at Jenkinson, 'Thought it was some poor devil being bombed. How many did we bag?'

Jenkinson's expression became dubious. 'That's the thing. You'll see the accounts. The papers are all in.'

'Do I detect some reluctance, my old Torps?' His brows had risen. 'Don't tell us they got away?'

Jenkinson started forward with them. 'It's worse than that

actually. They put rather a lot of ours on the bottom,' and as they stopped dead, 'Three battle-cruisers, two armoured cruisers –'

'*Three battle-cruisers!*'

'Unfortunately. That was the tally –'

'Which ones?' Willy asked, his mind numb with shock. Jenkinson turned his eyes on him. '*Queen Mary, Indefatigable, Invincible.* Magazine explosions. They simply blew apart. There's a fearful panic on.'

'How many survivors?'

'Practically none –'

'The *Invincible*,' Willy interrupted. 'Was anyone saved from her?'

'Six, I believe.'

'*Six!*' He tried to imagine a thousand men blown apart in the instant; it was impossible to take in. 'D'you happen to know if West –' He stopped, appalled at what the answer might be.

'West was with a small party from the control top who found a raft somehow.' Jenkinson paused. 'He left it to go after some poor fellow in the water.'

Willy stared. What did he mean? 'Did he reach him?'

'I'm afraid he wasn't seen again.'

He closed his eyes; he had known as soon as he heard the name, *Invincible*. West and the *Invincible* were inseparable; impossible to imagine him surviving his ship; he was an all-or-nothing fellow.

Lying in the bath, he could think only of the effect of West's death on Henry. He knew he had to go to her. He was the only one: George would be up in Rosyth or Scapa Flow, Andy in France. Yet he knew he couldn't go. The skipper was off on leave as soon as he had made his number with the S.S.O. He couldn't ask him; he had been talking of nothing for the past week but London with his lovely bride of six months. Anyhow 'compassionate grounds' hardly extended to one's sister's unofficial fiancé; he wouldn't understand.

He wondered for a moment about asking Henry to come down to Harwich, but dismissed the thought; even if she could get away from the hospital, it would defeat the object.

He must go to *her*. As she and West had come to him, miraculously saving his life in Portland.

As he lay, allowing the sweat and oily grime of the patrol to lift from his pores in the steaming water it came to a stark choice between letting Henry down or letting down the skipper, the S.S.O., the submarine service – the Navy itself. Strangely, when he thought about it afterwards, the issue was never in doubt. He did not argue it out with himself, he scarcely agonized except about means, he simply knew: it was an imperative of the blood; he had to go to Henry.

He planned it with some care. He had lunch, allowing the skipper plenty of time to get away on his motor-bike to Dovercourt, where his wife was in rooms, then he changed into tweeds and slinging his binoculars around his neck, announced he was off to the links for a bird watch. His strange habits were well enough known to draw no comment.

Waiting on the platform at Parkeston was his worst time. He stood close by the entrance to the Gents, ready to dart inside at the first appearance of the skipper, although he thought it scarcely conceivable he would either want or be able to achieve such a rapid turn-round. When the train drew in he established himself at a window seat towards the front and kept watch on the barrier, his heart racing at the sight of a tall man whose head was turned away towards a young woman half-hidden behind the ticket collector. He thought he had never felt such relief when he saw the guard shaking out his green flag. A shrill whistle, the familiar juddering of the bumpers and steam wisped by the window as the supports for the platform roof and the dark red bricks behind with posters for Bovril and Pears' Soap began to move astern.

An old lady seated opposite was eyeing him curiously and with disapproval, he thought. His legs felt quite weak, his pulse pounded and his mouth was dry; he was utterly drained. It was worse than the time in the Bight he had seen two shining, pointed things beneath the water racing towards the conning tower; his heart had stopped, then they emerged, two porpoises leaping over a wave and turning swiftly on re-entry to dart and sport around the bow. Lord! He would rather go through that a thousand times than have this agonizing feeling he was letting down everyone and every-thing. When discovered, as he must be this evening it would look as though he had sneaked off directly the skipper's back was turned; it was an unbearable thought. His legs and insides went weak again and he twisted desperately in his seat, feeling an almost irresistible urge to rise and pull the communication chain, then jump out and run back along the line before it was too late.

It was the thought of Henry that calmed him. If there were any time in her life she needed him, it was now; was he too cowardly to break the rules? The chances of the boat being ordered out during the night in defence of the coast were too remote to contemplate and he would be back by the time the hands turned to in the morning.

'What are the binoculars for, young man?'

The old lady was staring at him with cold, blue eyes behind spectacles, her rather thin mouth puckered and pinched with lines and turned down at the corners; fine white hairs grew above her upper lip. Lord! Did she take him for a spy! He smiled.

'Looking out for birds.'

'I wasn't aware there were many birds to be looked out in London.' Her tone was accusing.

He attempted another smile. 'I like to have them with me, in case.'

He hoped the flat reply would shut her up. In his anxiety he had not bought a paper or magazine which he might have hidden behind. Some old ladies were the very devil. It was strange how delightful and modest and smily and altogether charming girls were, or at any rate tried to appear, yet elderly ladies often seemed to delight in being quite the reverse. He looked out at the sunlit countryside flashing past, neat fields of ripening wheat between hedgerows, and wondered if this one had been modest and smily when young, and he thought of Nora, experiencing the catch of guilt about Isobel he always felt in Nora's presence. He couldn't imagine Nora growing old like that – couldn't imagine her without her generous smile and gurgling little inclination of the head as she laughed at his sallies. Lord! She was sure to be at the Dovercourt Tennis Club this evening; she always knew when his boat was in – but by this evening probably he wouldn't have a boat. The weak feeling flooded him again.

'What do you think of the Military Service Bill, young man?'

She was staring at him still in that sharp intimidatory way, and he sensed the heavy-looking elderly man who was creating a fog of pipe smoke in the car corner had looked round to judge his response. So, it was an army-dodger they took him for, not a spy.

'I think it a great pity.'

Her eyes opened fractionally as if this were the very answer she had been expecting, but she made her voice incredulous, 'You think it a pity!'

'A great pity that men should have to be compelled to fight for their country.'

She was silent for a moment.

'I take it you will not require compulsion?'

'Quite right!'.

He shifted in his seat so that he could lean one shoulder against the window surround, crossed a leg over, rested his head back and closed his eyes, feeling the awful sinking sensation take him over again. There was still time to get out at Ipswich and take a train back, and no damage would have been done. He thought of Henry, and knew he couldn't. He had put his hand to the plough.

He felt himself being appraised by the cold eyes opposite and realized his whole body was tense, his leg shaking. He tried to relax his muscles and sink back into the seat. It was intolerable to return from enemy waters, sitting on the putty listening to that fearful thumping all around, to be accused of cowardice because he was travelling in civvies and looked white probably. Lord! He must pull himself together! What she thought was of absolutely no consequence.

There was nothing he could turn his mind to without depression or anxiety. Henry's distress was not something he wanted to dwell on, that would be difficult enough later. Nor West's death. It was how West would have wanted to go; there was no better way. He was to be envied. It still left a horrible gap for those who were left, one that could not be filled. He had been one of those rare characters who were

582

completely individual. It had been West who had persuaded Henry to visit him at Portland that time, and what would have happened if the two of them had not turned up then? He had everything to thank West for. And what would Henry do now?

He tried to shake his mind free of all thought. An image of Nora rose, Nora in her white tennis outfit, gloriously slim and graceful and absolutely dependable in defence, partnering him in the American doubles. There were not many girls who could be relied on on the backhand side. Would he ever be admitted to the Dovercourt club again? By tomorrow he would be an outcast. Nora and Isobel were twinned in his mind, though, and to think of one was to feel guilt about the other. One day he would have to make a choice –

At Ipswich he jumped out, strode to the platform kiosk and bought a copy of *Punch*, hoping it might lighten his mood. Even *Punch* was at war. There was a double cartoon showing on one side 'Vivian Vavasour, the melodrama actor' with stage boulders falling about him, lightning splitting the sky, and in the other half the same character, now in uniform, smoking a pipe and reading calmly while sitting on the fire step of a trench in France: 'the comparative peace of the trenches', the caption ran. He thought of Andy and wondered what it was really like. Their leaves had only coincided for two days since he had been in France, although he had seen a lot of him before; all he really knew of his life out there came from Henry; she seemed to think he was having a rotten time. He never said so; it was his nervy manner when he came home that gave it away.

Turning to the 'Charivaria', his eye was caught by 'Alleged Cannibalism in the German Navy'.

The prisoners got the same food as the submarine crew. Here is the bill of fare: Breakfast consisted of coffee, black bread, submarine commander and the pilot. *Provincial Paper.*

He chuckled.

The train started, and he turned back to a story he had

noticed about a V.A.D. hospital in France. Perhaps he could learn something more about Henry's life than she liked to disclose! The tale proved merely flippant; he found his eyelids drooping as he read, and lulled by the jogging motion of the seat was content to give way to sleep, almost waking as they drummed through stations, feeling sudden clutches around his heart as he remembered where he was going and what he was doing, dozing, dreaming of Isobel and Jollion Peters at their father's vicarage.

He had not realized they had so many tennis courts there; he could see them all below as the train jiggledy-jogged, jiggledy-jogged along the embankment. Henry and Isobel and the whole Peters family lined the side of the courts, looking up waving at him as he leaned out of the window, wondering how he was going to get down to them and realizing he would not be able to. He must get out somehow. Jolly was calling something to him, but he couldn't hear because of the noise the train was making. Isobel was sitting in the pew beside him, crying. He didn't want to look down as she was holding a telegram in her hand, and he knew it announced Jolly's death. He knew he had to leave the church and go back to the courts where he had seen him waving and calling. He couldn't stand, though, his legs wouldn't get him up and the pew was rocking from side to side and juddering –

He woke as they drew to a halt in Liverpool Street station, gripped with the nightmare certainty that Jolly was dead. Yet the official Admiralty communiqué he had studied in the wardroom before lunch had not mentioned the *Shark*. Could he have missed it somehow? Shocked by the fate of the battle-cruisers, all his thoughts had been for West and Henry. He passed a hand across his eyes, trying to exorcize the image of that telegram form.

Before alighting he studied the faces of the passengers coming up the platform lest the skipper had somehow managed to catch the train. He was not amongst them. He jumped out and hurried to the Great Eastern Hotel to find a telephone.

'*Willy!*' It was his mother, and he guessed she must have dashed to reach the telephone so quickly. 'Where are you –?'

584

'Liverpool Street.'
'*Liverpool Street!*'
'We got in this morning –'
'How marvellous! It's so good to hear you –'
'It's marvellous to hear you, Mama. I've – I've just heard about West. I wondered – Henry isn't with you –?'
There was a short pause. 'I'm so sad for her, Willy, so dreadfully sad. She's at Guy's. She simply refuses to take any time off. I'm so worried about her –'
'I thought she might take it like that.'
'She's tired, you see. They work them like galley slaves.'
'I thought I'd look her up.'
'Are we going to see you as well?'
'I don't know, Mama. I haven't long. I'll have to see how things turn out.'
'Do try, Willy –'
'I will. I promise. I must see Henry though –'
'Of course you must. I'm so glad you could get up. I know it'll be a great comfort to her.'
'I hope so.'
'I know it will.' Her voice sounded quite shaky.
'I'll try and get over afterwards. If there's time. I have to get back tonight. I can't promise –'
'I'm so glad you're back, Willy. Did you see anything?'
'Not a thing. We didn't know there'd been a battle until this morning, when we got in.'
'They made such a mess of the announcement, didn't they? Everyone quite thought we'd lost. We didn't, did we?'
He laughed. 'I should think not! When did the losers occupy the field and the winners bolt for home! No, they're back in their funk-hole again. I dare say we shan't see them for another couple of years now – well – actually I haven't seen them at all yet!'
'But those battleships blowing up –'
'*Battle-cruisers*, Mama –!'
'Whatever they were.'
'I know. It's hard to imagine it –'
'Do you think we shall be able to do something about it before next time?'
'I'm sure we will, but Mama –'

'I know. You have to go. Oh, it's so good to hear you, Willy –'

'I'll try and get over –'

'Do try.'

'Goodbye, Mama!'

'Goodbye, Willy! For now.' There was a catch in her voice. He felt almost guilty as he hung up.

He went out to the taxi rank.

'Guy's Hospital!'

He wondered if she was still working the same hours; he ought to have asked while he was telephoning. If she was on night duty he would probably be able to see her straight away, otherwise it would be a very long wait like the time he had visited her on his last leave.

To his surprise, his enquiry at the desk stirred a period of activity culminating in an invitation to see the sister in Astley Cooper Ward. The porter, wearing two rows of medal ribbons, pointed towards heavy doors to his left.

The hospital smell struck him as soon as he went through, disquieting in its implications of surgery and disinfectant dressings. The high walls of the corridor and the parquet floor gleamed with cleanliness. A nurse with starched white cap and apron over her pale lilac frock looked round from an open door, smiling briefly. She had nice eyes. He marvelled at the way nurses contrived to look so fresh and human in the midst of the horrors they dealt with every day. A rather older woman with a blue dress beneath her apron was standing talking to another nurse where the corridor opened into the ward. She turned as she heard his steps.

'You must be Mr Steel.' Her voice was starched, her eyes tired, but keen.

'Yes.'

'Come this way please!' She held her arm out towards an open door marked 'Sister', which led into a small cubicle of a room, preceding him and indicating a chair against the wall as she sat at the desk.

'It is a very good thing you've come.' Her expression hardly matched the words. 'How long have you?'

'Twelve hours at the most.'

She permitted herself a moment of surprise. 'A pity. It's

586

something at any rate. We are anxious about your sister. You know about her –?'

'That's why I came up.'

'I see. I had hoped you might be able to take her away for a day or so. I'll send for her now and tell her she can go off duty immediately as you have so little time. See if you can persuade her to go home for a while –'

'What is the trouble?'

'Grief. With your sister, it seems to be a refusal to grieve. That is how it appears to me. It was only by pure chance we learned about –?'

'Commander West –'

'Commander West. She told no one. The other V.A.D. with her had met him on his last leave – that's neither here nor there. She refuses to take off-time. She reported for duty on her half day. I sent her packing, but we learned afterwards she had reported to another ward where one of the V.A.D.s had gone down with flu. I've been told she stays up half the night writing letters – she sings in the choir – she never rests –'

'I see.'

'Had you not come I should have had to send her home anyway before she collapses. I hope you can persuade her to take a rest.'

'I'll do my best.' He couldn't remember ever having persuaded Henry of anything –

'Good.' She rose, motioning him down like a puppy as he stood with her. 'Wait here! I'll send her in to you. Then you can take her away. Make sure she changes from her uniform.'

He felt he should have saluted, and was distinctly uncomfortable to be seated as she left with firm tread. Henry might have been a blanket in need of repair for all the feeling displayed.

Hearing footsteps presently, sharp on the parquet, he rose out of his chair, turning towards the door and bracing himself for the sight of her. Amazingly, she looked more strikingly lovely than he thought he had ever seen her. The fine modelling of her face and brave chin was accentuated by an unusual tautness in her skin; her eyes, clear and blue and large with a serious look were lent depth by shadows and

587

little puckered lines beneath. The pallor of her forehead and cheeks, lit by points of high colour, gave her an almost ethereal quality, sealed by the neat blue V.A.D. dress and apron. She was a vision; she was also very tense, he realized as she gazed at him. She didn't seem in the least surprised to see him; Sister must have told her, but all the same –

'*Henry!*' He stepped towards her.

Her lips broke into a smile of recognition but her eyes remained questioning. 'How long have you got?'

'Long enough!' He leaned and kissed her on the cheek; she smelled of hospital. 'Come on! We're going out!'

She turned her head towards the ward, then looked back uncertainly. 'Yes, Sister said –'

'*You* have to get out of that uniform!'

It was intended as a light remark, but her brows drew in and her eyes lit angrily. A nurse carrying a waterproof sheet over her arm looked in curiously as she hurried by.

'Look here, Henry, I've only got about – I have to leave by midnight at the latest. I must see you –'

The words seemed to have a magical effect; her expression softened. 'I know.' She took his hand in hers for a moment, turning her head again as if looking for Sister or someone in the ward, then letting go, beckoned him out into the corridor.

She led him back and turned left down another corridor towards the rear of the block. Sun streamed in across the deep recesses of the windows; he caught a glimpse of lawn, the windows of the wing beyond wide open. They emerged on to a flagged path lined on one side by plane trees throwing patterns of bright sunlight and shade across newly-mown grass. The fresh smell was a delight. Some way off in the sunshine a group of men sat in bath chairs; two others limped slowly past with crutches.

'You can wait for me here.' She pointed to a bench under the trees. 'I shan't be long.'

Notwithstanding, he talked for half an hour or what seemed like that with a one-legged officer from the Royal Welch. Learning that Willy was in the Navy he quizzed him on the Horns Reef battle, but when told of the thumping noises about the boat that night – the only first-hand account

Willy could give him – started moving uncomfortably, his eyes darting from side to side. Willy changed the topic.

They discussed the prospects for the big push; the officer, Williams was his name, doubted the quality of the new army regiments. Willy told him of Andy's pride in his battalion. 'An exception to every rule, old man – understood! *Montis Insignia Calpe.* There's nothing wrong with the Suffolks. Their second b'ttalion was with us in the Salient. I'll never forget 'em on Minden Day – roses in their bonnets, every man jack – you should've seen 'em. Lord knows where they found 'em. "Expressed from Harrods!" the Adjutant told me! "Filched from the garden of the Chateau!" I told him! Filched from the garden of the Chateau –!'

By the time Henry came out, metamorphosed in a yellow dress, they had progressed somehow to women bus conductresses and ticket collectors, a subject Williams seemed to find particularly fascinating since he had heard and read of the phenomenon, but was still waiting to experience it.

'My sister, Henry,' Willy said, jumping up.

'Lord! We know each other, old man! *Sister!* Too bad! Thought at first you were the lucky fellow!' He laughed. 'Bad luck!'

'He's a dear,' Henry said when they were out of earshot. 'He's frightfully nervous, poor man. He jumps if you cough.'

'I got that impression.' He found her manner extraordinary. Was she acting, or had she managed somehow to thrust West's death from her mind? Yet behind the self-conscious normality he could sense her tension.

'Would you like to see the chapel?' she asked.

'Yes.'

'I sing in the choir.'

'I know.'

'Sister must have told you! Sometimes I go to Southwark Cathedral. Really I prefer the chapel here; it's more intimate, the atmosphere's more real.'

It was empty when they arrived. They walked to the altar in silence.

'Don't you think it's lovely?'

She was gazing at him with peculiar intensity; it tore his heart to look at her.

She laid a hand softly on his sleeve. 'I heard about Jolly.'
He stared, his dream in the train returning, numbing in the certainty of Jolly's death.

'I'm so sorry for Isobel,' she said.

And so guilty, she thought. She had prayed for Isobel and her own forgiveness. Willy was looking so queer. He and Jollion had been close from the beginning. She squeezed his arm with her fingers. 'You've seen her?'

He shook his head. 'No. I shall have to. I rang Mama.'

She wondered what he meant. He stood quite still, gazing through her, a million miles away. She took her hand away from his arm and walked back to the stall she usually occupied. She was glad he had come. Now, when she came in to sit by herself and think or pray she would be able to visualize him here with her, dear, dear Willy. He looked so pale and strained and he was very tense. He had always felt things so deeply.

Robin had liked him. She must not think of Robin. There were so many who needed her; if she allowed her emptiness to overcome her as it threatened to do, she would not be able to cope. Robin didn't need her any longer; the others did. It was fortunate or she didn't know what she might do with herself. Robin had gone in the way he wanted – for his country, for his Service, his beloved grey wife, for a fellow sailor – gloriously. Closing her eyes she could see the intensity in his dark eyes as he assured her of that. If it had not been for what George had said in his letter – if only George had not told her. She felt like crying every time she thought of it, but she couldn't; she had used up all her tears for Robin and the others before he went, knowing he *would* go.

She wondered who the third one was going to be. Bad things came in threes. It must not be Willy – that she knew she couldn't bear –

She would show George's letter to Willy afterwards, cautioning him to give it back to her without comment of any kind. That would be the end of it then. She would put it on top of the pile of Robin's letters, tie them all together and put them away. One day – when she had joined Robin – someone would find them perhaps. What would they make of them all? So much love frozen in his heart's blood transformed into ink. If only she and Robin had had a child, *he* would find them, sheets and sheets with that perky little penguin in the top left hand corner, nose pointed in the air, and 'MALVINAS' on the scroll beneath – frozen in time for all time. She had a sudden intuition that time was not real; the letters had always existed. The thought made her want to cry again.

She *must not think.*

She realized her eyes were closed as if she were praying, and opened them, hoping they did not look too red. Willy was coming back slowly towards her, looking down. She stood and tucked her arm into his as they walked out.

Railton blinked when he saw him at breakfast, and passed a hand across his forehead in exaggerated indication of a hangover.

'Where were you last night?'

'London,' Willy replied.

'I see!' Railton did not believe him. 'That accounts for my missing you! Oh *Gawd*! Some benjo!'

'Did A.K.W. ask where I was, d'you know?' He had a dreadful feeling he knew what the answer would be.

'A.K.W.? I've no idea, old bean. Tommers came to see me, wondering where you'd sugared off to. Wanted to report a couple of the hands adrift I think. I told him in your zeal to claim the greater shovel-headed auk you had no doubt missed the boat. It has been known for far less pressing engagements – *Gawd*!' He pressed his hand to his head.

'No panics?'

'You should ask someone else. I must say I don't know who!'

'You didn't see A.K.W.?'

'To tell the truth, I didn't see much. After about – ten-thirty I don't believe I saw anything!'

Willy heard other reports of a lively evening aboard the depot ship; nevertheless he spent the rest of the morning in acute apprehension of a summons to account for his absence. The coxswain, Tomkinson, keeping a splendidly solemn tongue in his cheek asked whether he had been fortunate in finding the auk. A deuced awkward customer to find, he replied.

By the time lunch was over and parties were being made up for golf and tennis, he felt it possible he had escaped; after dinner with A.K.W. present and in top form, he felt certain of it. It was a minor miracle. Until he caught A.K.W.'s eye and received a broad, frank smile he hadn't realized quite how much the fear of disgrace had been weighing him down.

With that hanging sword removed, the other matter became more pressing.

He was not certain when he had first come to the resolution; probably it had been maturing from the moment he had learned of Jolly's death. Henry had been unable to give details; Isobel had sent her a brief note simply repeating the words of the telegram, and she had not contacted her since except to write a letter of condolence. He had managed to find out a little more since returning to Harwich. The *Shark* had been leader of four destroyers detailed to screen Hood's battle-cruisers; they had led in to attack a cruiser squadron Hood had been engaging, and in the resultant *mêlée* with enemy destroyers the *Shark* had been brought to a standstill by a shell in the engine room or boilers, and later sunk, a sitting duck, her one remaining gun firing and her colours flying. Only six had been saved from her – the same number as from the *Invincible*. Was that a coincidence of some sort? Looking at the original Admiralty communiqué again, he had seen what he should have noticed the first time; the *Shark* was not named among the destroyers lost, but 'six others are not yet accounted for'.

He stared at the blank writing paper on his desk. He had made his decision, but how on earth did one put such things?

His mind wandered to Henry, and George's letter to her. He had come to know West very well over the two years in the battle-cruiser squadron, he had written, and was certain from numerous conversations – the last only two days before the battle – that he meant to throw up the Service directly their task was completed. He hoped it would be some comfort to her to know this since it demonstrated the strength of West's devotion to her.

'For myself,' he had gone on, 'I never hope to have a better friend. The dear man, it was not until he had gone I realized how much I loved him and how much I'll miss him. We are all sorrowing up here, but I am sure you know it was how he would have wanted to go in the very midst of battle. Several people have told us how magnificent the flagship looked, leading the line, firing with marvellous precision and rapidity up to the very end. One still cannot take in all that it means –'

He had returned the letter to her silently as she had made him promise.

'I wouldn't have wanted him to,' she said, 'I couldn't have borne it. I wonder if he knew that. I'm sure he did.'

They had walked on in silence. On London Bridge they had stopped and leaned on the balustrade looking down at the tugs and lighters and little river steamers coming up with the tide. He had turned to catch her gazing at him, and thought he had detected the first crack in her composure, but she had looked away quickly and they walked on.

It was she who had suggested going to St James's Park. He relived the helpless anguish he had experienced as they stood gazing at the paired drakes and ducks, and he realized she was crying silently. He had felt her shaking helplessly and pressing against him; it was worse now than it had been at the time. Then he had been with her, able to put his arm around her and hold her firmly –

Footsteps were approaching the door, and he looked up to see Railton's head appearing round the curtain. '*This* is where you're hiding! I thought perhaps you'd gone up to town for another show!'

He smiled.

'Come and make up a four. We've decided we should have a quiet evening!'

He looked down at the blank sheet on his desk. 'The trouble is, I have a letter to write.'

'Can't it wait?'

'It's waited rather too long already.'

Railton's expression had changed. He stepped inside the cabin. 'Something wrong?'

'Not really.'

'You don't look too hot.'

'I'm not sure how to start.'

'Oh, dear! One of those?'

'Not exactly, no.' Suddenly he wanted to tell him. 'It's a proposal actually. I've never written one before.'

Railton's rather protruberant eyes seemed to enlarge. 'Lor' lumme! You don't have to *write* old beansprout. Sugar round to the club tomorrow. She'll be there. We saw her in the Alex yesterday – teased her a bit as a matter of fact about your greater devotion to the shovel-headed auk! She rose rather prettily.' He laughed.

'Yes – well – that's the trouble.' He looked down, utterly miserable. 'It's not Nora.'

'Not Nora?' Railton stared. 'I say! You are in rather deep.'

He stared at the writing paper.

There was silence for a moment, then Railton said, 'Well – I'll go and dig someone else out –'

Willy looked up. 'Sorry.'

'Sorry *I* can't be of more assistance. To a brother officer in distressed circumstances. Lor' lumme!' He turned to go out, then looked back. 'Have you tried K.R. and A.I.? Something for every occasion!' The curtain fell into place behind him.

Willy thought of Jolly, and despised himself for his hesitation.

'It'll probably mean I shall have to become a parson!' For some strange reason he remembered that moment at the finish of the naval entrance exams although practically everything else about the day had vanished. The downcast look in Jolly's normally eager brown eyes, his own sudden realization on seeing the expression that he too would have to do something rather unpleasant if he failed, he saw it as if it had been yesterday.

They had sat at adjacent desks; their names had come out one above the other in the list of successful candidates; that was not surprising; the only surprising thing perhaps was that alphabetical proximity had turned into such close friendship.

He could see the fixed expression on Jolly's face as he

594

came aboard the Admiralty tug, close to tears after leaving his mother and sisters on the quay; he had not known Isobel then, nor for some time afterwards. They had stood together, he and Jolly, looking across the blue and greening water flecked with white to the Isle of Wight and Osborne. The sky had been clear blue above green fields and woods; it had been such a crisp, clear day, perfect weather for the start of a big adventure –

'*Mr* Peters! You 'aven't got your sweater on!'

'I'll go back with you, Jolly.' Running together up the path to the dormitory to fetch Jolly's sweater; what had happened when they returned to the pitch afterwards? It was queer the way some moments stuck in one's mind –

The boat closing the cruiser's side in Castries harbour, St Lucia, was a riot of noise and colour, shining black arms and faces and white teeth as the 'washerladies' vied for attention. 'I mother Flora, I wash for darling midshipboys –' The vegetation swept down to the shining water on every hand. He saw his first enormous Blue Morphos with Jolly in the Botanical Gardens, delighted by the iridescence of their wings, changing shade and colour as they flew, and his first humming birds darting from sunlight into deep shadow; he could almost smell the heavy tropical scents of the flowers.

He had not been quite straight with Jolly about Jacq'len, why he could not think, but he remembered his guilty feeling at concealing the fact he had written to her. It was one of the few things he had concealed from Jolly. He would have thought his idea of running away to live with her in the island paradise absurdly romantic. It had been. He wondered what had become of Jacq'len.

He had a duty to Jolly, now more than when he had been alive. Now it was no longer possible to withhold or to explain. He picked up his pen and wrote determinedly, 'Dearest Isobel'.

How on earth did one start? There *were* no words. He scribbled the date. It couldn't be done. There would have to be two letters, the first with his sorrow and sympathy, the second asking her to marry him. He had hoped to combine them in order to ease her loss a little; he knew what Henry

595

would feel like if it had been one of them. But the letters would arrive sufficiently closely together to serve the same purpose. Dear Isobel, he did love her –

He was torn by the thought of Nora. He would not be able to face the Dovercourt club again.

13

The barrage before the big push took Andy by surprise. He had seen the proliferating field gun batteries under camouflage and the heavy 9.2s and fifteen inches pointing wickedly from behind barns and ruined farmhouses, over hedges and through copses, throwing straighter shadows than the trees; he had seen the ammunition dumps spreading under canvas along the roads behind the lines, and all the transport paraphernalia of animals and drivers, wagons and motor vans, field railways and engines; he was still not prepared for the pandemonium that broke loose in the last week of June. From one end of the line to the other the summer sky split apart; the clouds shook, the earth erupted; a shivering veil of white or earth-coloured haze and smoke vibrated in the passage and blast of projectiles; at night bursts played like fire, lighting the dust cloud above and the clouds themselves. It was terrifying to hear; what it was like for the enemy who had to endure it day after day, night after night, defied comprehension.

Their battalion was not detailed for the assault so they held the front line trenches during these seven days softening up. On 30 June they moved into reserve outside the little village of Carnoy. They had carried out two night raids during their week in the line and these had revealed men still alive in the German trenches, but demoralized; it was supposed the enemy in general must be so stunned as to be all but knocked out; it merely remained to cross over and dig him out of the ground, after which the 'war of movement' could begin. They had heard the whinnying of horses and seen the Indian cavalry massed in barns and beside the woods behind.

The morning of 1 July dawned fine. The sun rose in a clear sky. Andy waited with growing impatience for the assault to start. It was what the training and early hopes, the recent troglodyte existence had been for, the hard winter, boredom, the moments of stark fear and growing familiarity with horror – the looking at the firm flesh of one's own arm or leg and imagining it greening, returning to the earth like the parts of what had been men one stumbled across frightfully in no man's land – the sight of men swimming naked in the river, wondering which would be whole and unblemished next week, next month, which dismembered, decapitated, putrescing, it was a problem of mathematics, not humanity, like the attrition of companions in the mess. Nails had been the last to go; only Limpopo and Stalky and he remained now of their original number. All would be rendered worthwhile, all the futility and misery transformed into necessary suffering once they broke through and drove the Boche from this tormented land, anachronistic feudalism and militarism from Europe, letting the fresh winds of progress and enlightenment blow in the new century. Lord, grant victory! The price will not have been too high –

At 7.30 the barrage lifted from the enemy front line; rumblings of subterranean thunder were followed by earthquakes away to the left, and smoke rose, obscuring the tortured slopes beyond. Whistles sounded and brief orders; the first dun figures appeared from that small section of the front line he could see below him somewhat to the left. Sun darted from bayonets and the metal identification triangles on the men's backs, gleaming more dully on those queer, round steel helmets he had still not become fully accustomed to, and on accoutrements hanging from back pack and side, entrenching tools, wire cutters, water bottles, the long barrels of the Lee-Enfield rifles. From all along the trench he could see they were emerging, filing bulkily through gaps prepared in the wire, and spreading out over the pitted earth beyond with its brave little patches of green splashed with the red of poppies and occasional purples and mauves of vetch and clover flowers, thistles and scabious. Groups split around craters, coalesced beyond, separated into wedges, moved out of sight for long intervals while others re-emerged, identification triangles winking like heliographs. Andy was touched by the grandeur of the scene, and its profound mystery. Each of the small, sunlit and shadowed figures in the living pattern was a sentient being, carrying his past and present, fears and hopes for life in the world contained below his round helmet – so many worlds unknown to him or even to those immediately beside them, all linked for the present moment by common faith, common loyalty and will to victory which transcended their separateness. It was very strange.

Some of those worlds would cease quite soon; their passing would be marked tomorrow or the next day by small wooden crosses with a name and number.

He had had a talk a few nights back, one of those encounters with strangers which assumed significance from the circumstances of the line. It was in an angle of communication trench near the headquarters dug-out; the large man had introduced himself as 'Brew' – an American who had volunteered for the ambulance service. He was awaiting the probable results of a night raid. Andy had been unable to sleep in the close atmosphere below, and unable to control his whirling thoughts had come up for a smoke in the air. Amazingly, they found they had rowed against each other at Cambridge; Brew had been at Trinity after Harvard; he had been number seven in the first Trinity boat Pembroke had bumped in the May races of 1914.

Reminiscence had passed somehow to the topic of morality plays, probably because Andy had been reading a recent edition of *Everyman* Henry had sent out to him. The message of the imminence of death and judgement had acquired new reality in the trenches. 'All earthly things is but vanity' was as starkly manifest here as it had been to the medieval authors, and it was clear that at the end 'Everyman' lost beauty, wits, strength and discretion, 'foolish friends and kinsmen that fair spake'; his good deeds were all that were left him.

A definition of 'good deeds', the question of how Andy's 'good deeds', as he saw it at present, killing Germans, could be reconciled with German Christian ideas on the subject or with Brew's duty to save life, had occupied a lively half hour.

He had enjoyed it because of the contrast to what passed as discussion in the mess. Before parting they had exchanged addresses, agreeing to continue the debate 'when the guns stopped'.

Gazing now at the groups approaching the enemy wire which was supposed to have been flattened by the bombardment, hearing beneath the bursting thunder of the artillery, the rattle of German machine guns, seeing falling figures spinning or clutching at a limb or shoulder, others crawling, some lying still, Andy had an image of rough wooden crosses springing out of each motionless form, marking in this world the ultimate 'good deed' compensating for everything that had gone before, and making that life immortal.

Eternal life – it was a curious concept – natural for man with the knowledge he had but three score years and ten on this earth, rather less out here. In the rational world that was all it was, a hope for poor, thinking man that at the end he and those he loved would be united in eternity. Was that the only secret of the astonishing spread of Christ's message – simple fear of oblivion and hope of everlasting love? Or were there worlds beyond rationality to which the carpenter's Son from Nazareth and religious leaders of all faiths provided windows for believers to glimpse the truth? Had those forms he was looking at, spread in dark patterns up to the enemy wire like sea-wrack after a tide released their shining souls to heaven? Was it a mere animal matter of torn nerves and arteries, breaking the system of conscious, individual life so that the constituents returned to nature – blackening meat for rats?

He wished he could believe. Henry believed – or at least said she did. He wondered if that were perhaps another of her attempts to buck him up, like her letters in his dark time at Marlborough. There had been times recently he had needed all the bucking up she could provide. At last it was possible to see a hopeful end; the bad time at Marlborough had come to an end; looking back on it, he could recognize with Wordsworth that misery and hardship were bricks on which character was built; he could remember the lines Henry had written as if he had read her letter only a moment ago.

> . . . a needful part in making up
> The calm existence that is mine when I
> Am worthy of myself

He was not certain he had reached that state. There had been times, known only to himself, he hoped, and God – if He was there – when he had funked it. He could have pressed on further for longer when they had been out looking for Thompson and Miles that early morning they failed to return. The hint of first light he thought he glimpsed had been an illusion. There had been the bombardment when he lay on his cot in the dugout, shaking and had to stuff his knuckles into his mouth to prevent himself yelling out and disgracing himself. There had been other moments. The great Limpopo looked on him with favour still; his platoon was loyal. He had a sudden feeling that perhaps he would only find true worth in the moment his body was transforming into one of the wooden crosses he could see so clearly in his mind's eye.

The scene before him had become thoroughly confused; smoke drifting from enemy mortars and from bombs thrown by the attackers made it difficult to discern how far the assault had progressed. He glimpsed field grey through gaps torn in what had been a hedge along the side of the road up to Mametz, and raised his glasses. A file of Germans without weapons so far as he could make out from the upper parts of their bodies, which were all he could see, was heading towards the British lines with hands raised; some had steel helmets on their heads, some little grey caps with scarlet bands; one seemed to have a bare shoulder, his uniform hanging loosely. As he watched they seemed to fall or throw themselves down. Why? He could see no cause, but he couldn't see a great deal from back here in any case.

Further to the left, beyond the bank beside the Fricourt road, he glimpsed ant-like figures moving up a slope towards a copse of blasted trees; he raised his glasses, inwardly urging them on. Surely they must be beyond the enemy front line over there? He found it thrilling and terrible beyond compare, this first battle he had watched. Puffs of dark earth or smoke rose below the advancing figures and they flattened themselves or were flattened, it was impossible to tell. He

601

kept his glasses on them. Yes, most were moving off again; a few remained.

He heard cheering from his platoon, grouped on his right, and looking back towards the scene immediately below, saw another party of Germans without rifles moving towards them. Evidently the assault had reached its first objective. In front of the Germans, two runners were coming back, and nearer still stretcher parties had begun to move out, and he saw the heads and shoulders of a field telephone section disappear over the slope to his right, their wire jerking behind them over the raw earth rim of a crater.

He searched the line of the ridge beyond for the tip of Montauban church spire; it had been there earlier. There was no trace of it now. He turned his head with an almost superstitious feeling towards Albert. Yes! The golden Virgin was there still, a distant gleam of sunlight beyond the far ridge. It was odd how myths took hold of one despite oneself; when she fell, so the men believed, the war would end! He remembered his first sight of her when they arrived last year, leaning from the dome of the ruined basilica with the Infant in her outstretched arms as if, in exasperation at the evil of the world, she was about to dash him to the rubble-strewn street below. It was an extraordinary sight. And she was there still.

He turned back to what he could see of the battle. The barrage was moving into the trees before the village of Mametz. Nearer, where the air was more or less clear and the sun threw clean shadows, a lark rose before a lone runner breasting the slope towards them; he could just hear the bird's high notes above the rushing, tumultuous noises and awful crashing of the barrage, or thought he could. Probably it was imagination; there were larks everywhere, and crickets; he thought he could hear them too, but it may have been the ringing in his ears. The lark hovered against the blue sky singing its heart out; he was sure he could hear it. Beyond, observation balloons glinted like silver. He looked down again, resting his gaze on the pretty display of wild flowers, chiefly yellows and purples and shades of mauve in a corner that had not been trampled. A nearer clump of blue flowers looked as if they had been cultivated, they were so large and perfect, but they could not have been out here on the edge of the road. Perhaps seeds had blown from the village or been deposited by a bird. The petals each had delicate gradations of colour from blue to purpling blue to a lighter shade at the centre, from which long stamens stood out with blackish ends. Two – three – five bees were homing in, clinging, flying out and round to the next flower. He heard the summer drone of their wings, but this was surely imagination. Another bee darted in on a single petal that had fallen from somewhere and was resting on one of the intricate, long-pointed leaves. It clutched at the petal with its legs, dislodging it and, still holding on grimly, fell like a stone into the grass below. He smiled at its silliness. It rose and lighted on a real flower.

A fly was exploring the bowed head of a wild oat, and below his eye was caught by an ant moving across a broad leaf, switching direction, switching again, busily intent on some plan. And across there on the smoke-shrouded slopes below Mametz men murdered one another or were blown to pieces, or lay still under the sun.

He felt a need to move – anywhere – and swung his legs back over the sandbag parapet on which he was sitting to slide into the trench behind, and started walking towards the village and the old farmhouse basement that served as company headquarters.

His eyes had to adjust to the gloom when he went in. Limpopo was looking up from trench maps placed carefully alongside one another on the table.

'Master! The very man!'

Nails's replacement, Murray-Downs, spread palms on the table beside Brenton's, gazed up at him intently, his candid young eyes very clear and serious. He felt sympathy: to be pitchforked from training camp in England straight into the biggest show of the war could not be comfortable, although it was probably exciting enough! He wondered how he would make out; he didn't like to predict; he had been wrong on former occasions.

'We're required to carry up water and ammo,' Brenton went on. 'It seems we've got them on the run towards Montauban. Have you been able to make out much?'

'A fair number of Boche coming over.'

'That was my impression. Look here, I've told Barrabus to brew up. What d'you feel about giving the troops a tot before we start – I dare say it'll be fairly unpleasant.'

As always he felt flattered to be consulted. Probably, the great Limpopo had already made up his mind, but it gave him a good feeling.

'I think it would be a good idea.'

'Good! Well, that settles it.' He turned to Murray-Downs. 'Care to pass the word old man!'

The lad moved quickly towards the doorway.

'Is it your impression they're sending them out rather young?' Limpopo asked in a low voice as they heard him shouting outside.

He smiled. 'He looks all right.'

'Keep an eye on him.'

'I'll try.' Again the intense pride in his confidence.

'They expect to be in Montauban soon.'

'I could hear it being strafed well.'

Barnabee appeared, and Limpopo moved to the rough table that was serving as a sideboard and picked up the Johnny Walker bottle.

'Good man, Barrabus! Just what we need!' He unscrewed the bottle and poured a sizeable splash of whisky into both mugs of tea that Barnabee placed at the edge of the trench maps. He looked up at Andy. 'You've never been in a big show.'

Andy shook his head.

Limpopo handed him one of the mugs. 'It can be disagreeable.' He brought his own mug up to his lips. 'The sights.'

'I imagine so.'

'Yes – well. Here's hell!' He sipped the steaming brew. 'Ahhh –!'

Smiling, Andy returned his honest, grey gaze. Hell? He'd passed through that region once or twice in recent weeks. 'I'll settle for purgatory!'

'No philosophy, please, Master!'

Limpopo had not exaggerated. Clattering across the boards and old corrugated iron someone had laid across the enemy wire the heat and stench and sight of the dead on either hand brought on waves of nausea. He tried not to look, yet it was impossible to be unaware. In places bodies lay on top of one another as if second waves had been swathed down while scrambling over dying comrades; they were gripped in every kind of position. Moans or small wavings or writhings marked those still alive who had not yet succeeded in attracting the attention of the medical parties. Here it was not possible to philosophize. Surrounded by reality, abstractions lost their power, words their meaning. Sorley had expressed it. 'Say only this, "They are dead." ' Sorley must have been in a big show.

Despite his attempts not to see, he glimpsed the blue, sightless eyes of a youth on his side with his head propped up by an angle of ground as if on a pillow. Why that face caught his eye he couldn't tell, but he stared for a moment. The lad looked scarcely seventeen, his features seemed as if carved in wax, sensitive mouth half open, sparse silken stubble on his upper lip. There was a resignation in the attitude that caught at his heart.

> . . . should you
> Perceive one face that you loved heretofore,
> It is a spook. None wears the face you knew.
> Great death has made all his for evermore.

'Any questions?'

Brenton's eyes, looking strangely dark in the early grey of morning, rested a moment on Andy, and the signal passed unspoken: 'Looks like it this time, old Master! The chances are, by tomorrow one or both of us will be out of it, probably for rather a long time. We know each other as well as men can. You've taught me things I'd not dreamed of, I've shown you some honest soldiering, I trust. Chin-chin, old Master. Look up Edie for me if you get back. I'll do the same for you with Henry – like to meet her in any case –'

That was what Andy perceived, and rather more, and his unspoken signal was in the same vein. 'You've taught me more than simple soldiering, Great Limpopo. You've kept me on the rails. Heaven knows what might have happened if it hadn't been for your example and encouragement. Here's hell, Limpopo – or purgatory! What's philosophy beside mighty death?'

He had no questions. The orders were clear enough: they were to follow the 8th Norfolks, 6th Berkshires and 10th Essex Regiments up to retake Longueval, there to form up on the line of Prince's Street as jumping off point to assist the South Africans in clearing the enemy from Delville Wood – 'Devils' Wood' – which had been taken and part re-taken like every other devils' wood in this tortured corner of the system. Now the time had come, his legs felt like hollow canes and flutters of apprehension caught at his heart. His palms were moist, his mouth dry. Until he got himself under control, his voice would probably betray him.

They had been keyed up to it for days; prepared to attack Guillemont on the 18th – yesterday – the operation had been postponed the day before and they had marched back to bivouac in Talus Boise. His immediate, instinctive relief had been followed by the knowledge that it would come some time – if not here, somewhere else. There were reports of failures in other sectors, every other sector it seemed and everyone expected they would be transferred to make good the huge losses rumoured.

Instead they had been woken shortly before 1.30 this morning, and marched in the dark through the ruins of Montauban back to Bernafay Wood, their original jumping-off point. Making their way up the eastern edge of the wood, the sky above the slope ahead had been criss-crossed by coloured Very lights and German star shell; to the left front they heard the enemy strafing the Montauban-Longueval road; to their right Trones Wood, which they remembered stripped and blackened by fires from incendiary shells, had seemed to gather a deeper darkness to hide its shameful wounds. They had stumbled over recent craters and fallen timber, fought off branches, been surprised by shallow excavations that had served as trenches in the recent fighting; splashing through the rainwater which gleamed from the bottom of every hollow; they had avoided half-submerged bulky shapes that had been men or parts of men, still treading sometimes on soft things emitting nauseous stenches. The troops had kept up their courage with black humour and bravado. In the hollow hours of the morning it had taken bravado; there had been no other comfort.

Reaching the rendezvous position at four, Limpopo had left them, disappearing along the single railway track along the northern edge of the wood towards the quarry where the company commanders had been summoned.

Now they knew. He supposed he felt relief that the uncertainty was over, yet his body was not in tune with his will – or vice versa. His nerves, constantly strung tight and released, were reacting independently it seemed. He scarcely trusted himself to move his hand lest it tremble. He must control himself. He knew he would; he had become used to doing so; it was a matter of philosophy and will and a little time –

'That's all I can tell you, gentlemen.' Limpopo looked down at his map lit by a single candle resting on a Boche ammunition box. 'Once we're in the wood – we stick. Like glue!' He looked up as the sporadic thudding of bombs from the direction of their objective swelled up momentarily, then glanced down at his watch. 'We've a little time to explain it to the troops!'

The best part of three hours. It was this infernal waiting, allowing one to think –

Murray-Downs's face shocked him out of his panic. The boy – as he still looked despite the stubble on his jaw – had been introduced unceremoniously to unspeakable sights which most of them had been able to grow accustomed to slowly over the months in France. Even then they had not been prepared for the scale of the new carnage. Murray-Downs's lips were clenched tight, but his eyes gave him away; they moved, refusing to settle on his or anyone else's. His shoulder seemed to be jerking, and looking down, Andy saw that he was punching a tightly balled fist rhythmically into the flesh of his thigh, unaware of what he was doing.

He would be all right once they started off, he had proved that. It was imagination that pulled the mind off balance beforehand. It was nearly three weeks since they had carried ammunition up through the debris of the first assault on the slopes towards Montauban. The next day they had watched a more desperate contest for Mametz Wood. They had provided working parties to remove the dead and rebuild parts of trenches reduced by shells to little more than outlines winding through craters. Steeling themselves day after day to scenes that tortured their waking dreams, they had learned to banish feeling; it was of no possible consequence to the dead how smashed or disfigured the remains they left behind. Feelings would not be pushed under. Glimpsing a man's teeth as he laughed, one caught sight for a moment of the marbled green face and bloated torso of a corpse in Mametz Wood. Field grey and khaki intermingled, peopling the scored and splintered trees with tableaux of their end: green hands clutched distended bellies where the bayonet had been withdrawn; figures crouched behind sandbags in the act of loading a field gun, but there was no gun; they had no heads. When one moved a corpse after several days in the open, arms or legs might snap off like rotten branches; heads with jet black faces rolled away; foul liquids oozed from unexpected cavities. Like his own, Murray-Downs's imagination would be overflowing with such images. Two weeks in reserve, providing carrying parties and parties to identify remains and load them on to carts for transport to burial points was an ordeal that demanded as much as going 'over the top'.

Limpopo rose, signalling the end of the meeting. Andy stretched to put a hand on Murray-Downs's shoulder. He jumped as if stung, then laughed loudly at his reaction.

'Sar'nt Turncott,' Andy said softly; he was Murray-Downs's platoon sergeant. 'I happened to overhear him yesterday. He's near the end of his rope.'

The young man's eyes widened.

'He's been out too long,' Andy continued, rising. Murray-Downs rose with him. 'I've seen it before. These thick, stolid fellows you'd think hadn't a nerve in their body, they go quickly once it starts.'

'Are you sure? What d'you think I should do?'

'Watch him if I were you. Make up your mind who you want in his place. If it happens, you're prepared.'

'Turncott!' Murray-Downs's eyes were incredulous.

They started walking back towards their platoons. Andy put a hand on his shoulder again. 'He was telling all and sundry he was certain we were going to fetch up in one of these buggering "Bois" – all of us!'

'It looks as if he's right.'

'*End* up, old man. He meant end up –'

Images of green waxwork dummies acting out the last moments of the men who had gone into Mametz Wood were never far behind Andy's own thoughts. He was near the end of the rope himself. As for Turncott, it had been his manner and voice rather than the actual words that raised suspicions. He had seen it before. He had meant to speak to Webb about it; events had overtaken that. Looking at Murray-Downs, he thought he would be all right; his eyes seemed steadier with a thoughtful look. Since their platoons would be advancing adjacently, covering each other's rushes if it came to that, he had a personal interest in his soundness. He wondered how far the enemy had penetrated into the ruins of Longueval. From Limpopo's account of the pow-wow it was very much a last-minute 'wind-up' stunt without firm intelligence. The sound of fighting from the direction of Delville Wood was growing by the minute. The sky was getting lighter.

He saw Webb approaching as they neared the men seated or lying, trying to make up lost sleep on the rising slope beyond the line of the railway.

'We're bringing up the rear,' he said as the sergeant came up. He stopped, and holding his map out flat, turned himself until he had it aligned with the ground. 'Behind A Company. We shall be moving up the valley beside the sunken road. We'll shake out into artillery formation as we near the top.' He pointed.

The sun was well up by the time B Company started off. It was going to be a fine day. The birds remaining in the ruined wood recognized it. Ahead, in the direction they were going, was a small knoll under a blackthorn hedge which bordered the sunken road; it had been spared by shells, and men had marched around it, leaving it an oasis of colour amidst the churned clods of earth and chalk and flint. His eyes were drawn there continually for solace. There was a

609

patch of 'eggs and bacon' trefoil, recalling all his school summers back to the cricket outfield at Birchfield House, and a mass of camomile daisies with bright yellow eyes. A few poppies stood out amongst them, and purple vetch, and above, the white and delicately purpling heads of hogweed stretched to where the colours ended in the bare rim of a crater.

He heard a twig snap, and turned to see Limpopo coming towards him, limping rather more than usual he thought. His wound was evidently playing up after the showery weather of the previous nights. He was waving the walking stick he had picked up as a souvenir as if it were a rolled umbrella.

'All ready for the kick-off, Master!'

He felt the sudden clutch at his heart and glanced at his watch – twelve minutes to go! The rattle of machine gun fire augmented the sounds of the bombardment along the way the leading companies had taken. Limpopo stopped and leaned on his stick, gazing at the waiting men of the platoon.

'This is your chance now, you fellows. I know you've been waiting for it. Let's show 'em how the Suffolks can fight!'

There was a rumble of approval.

He nodded towards their objective. 'The Springboks are having a hard time of it in the wood. You can hear them I dare say. Our job's to go smack in there and clear the rest of the wood for them.' He looked round at Andy for a moment, then back at the men. 'Good luck, you men!' and waving his stick cheerily, he made off towards Murray-Downs's platoon. He might have been organizing a grouse shoot.

'Reckon Cap'n Brenton, sir, he's enjoyin' hissel',' Webb said.

'*We* shall be soon, I dare say!'

Webb looked at him, then up the rising ground over which A Company was moving. 'Oi moight,' he said at length as if he had been chewing it over, 'But me owd stomick keep tellin' Oi, Oi din't ought-a goo!'

Andy smiled. It was the first time he'd heard Webb say anything quite so candid. On the other hand it might have been intended as a wry joke. He looked at his watch.

'Ten minutes now, Sar'nt!'

'Oi'll warn the bors, sir.' Webb always referred to the platoon as his boys.

He strode off and shouted that if anyone wanted a piss they'd better have it now.

Several walked out of the groups as if it were an order, and there was a rattling and clinking of metal as others adjusted straps or accoutrements they had probably adjusted several times in the past minutes. Andy pulled out his map and studied the details he had committed to memory; the important one was missing of course: where precisely was the enemy? He folded the map carefully and replaced it in his pocket. He looked at his watch again. Time that calls us all away.

Now that it had come to it, he was impatient to go. The minute hand was moving extraordinarily slowly. The sounds of the bombardment on the road seemed to be increasing.

'One minute, Sar'nt!'

Webb cautioned the section leaders.

Well – this was it! It was rather like the moment after committing oneself to a dive before cold water embraced tingling flesh. Except that the sun was already warm, and the first part of the way was a not unpleasant stroll up the slope. It was only the din of the enemy shelling, and the evil connotations of the wood they were making for that engendered these fatalistic feelings.

His nerves were quite steady as he gazed down at his watch and put his whistle to his lips. He blew, hearing the other whistles along the line, and stepped out to take his place beside the leading section. Limpopo was across the railway track already, limping, swinging his stick, followed by his small retinue. They might have been setting out on any of the innumerable marches that had punctuated their time in France. For a number of them this would be their last. Lord! If it was his, he wanted it quick and clean. He had a feeling it might be his turn. Death was entirely arbitrary.

Two larks rose from the field to their left as larks had risen at every assault he had witnessed. Now it was their turn – as he had known it would be one day.

A runner came down from the top of the rise towards

Limpopo and spoke to him for a moment, after which he turned and held up the flat of his hand towards them.

They halted. He wondered why. It was intensely frustrating, unable to see anything, listening to the strafing the leading companies were taking. Waiting, not knowing what was happening was the pattern of war, even it seemed in an assault. He had hoped that once they started there would be no time to think.

They moved off again after some quarter of an hour, spreading into open order as they neared the top of the slope. Andy led his platoon into the dip to the left of the sunken road. Dark puffs of shell bursts showed ahead, and beyond them as they breasted the rise the top of Delville Wood appeared in the distance. A little further and he could make out, through bare, blasted trees and a haze of erupting smoke to the left of the wood, the ruins of the houses of Longueval village. The sun was warm on his right cheek. Along the top of the bank hiding the sunken road the isolated remains of a blackthorn stood in straggled silhouette against the bright morning sky.

It was another day. Everywhere normal morning things were happening. At Marlborough, along the path to Preshut boys with kishes and fresh penny buns bought hot outside the gates were hurrying back from early school and chapel, thinking of breakfast, butter and jam on the tables, and old Tim slopping tea from his huge can. At home the servants were moving in the downstairs rooms. The family was asleep; he lay there, hearing the quiet clink of an ash-bucket, thud of a broomhead against the skirting muffled by intervening floors, silent feet on the stairs, creaking, thinking of school with dread. There was dew on the tennis lawn and early thrushes playing a deadly game of tug of war with worms in the earth as he waited for Henry –

The ground flattened towards the outskirts of what had been Longueval. Some of the dispersed figures of their leading companies could be seen moving across a patchwork of cratered mud and golden wheat, splashed with the brilliant red of poppies, erupting with explosions. The whine and crump, or devastating crash as a 'coalbox' landed, the express train noises of their own shells through the air above, the

612

chatter of small arms impressed themselves more hellishly now the effects were visible.

He heard a familiar rushing sound and threw himself flat, smelling earth and crushed grass and clover still damp from the night as the shell exploded some fifty yards behind. He heard bits of stuff pattering to the ground. Rising and casting a quick glance towards the smoke drifting above the new crater to see if anyone were hit, he became aware of machine gun fire from closer than it had sounded before. He turned; it seemed to be coming from somewhere in the bank above the sunken road where it entered the village about half a mile ahead. Figures advancing in that direction seemed to be falling or throwing themselves down.

He hurled himself flat again; whether he had heard the noise fractionally before, or whether it was some sixth sense, he wasn't sure. This one exploded not twenty yards away, roughly where Noyce had been when he last looked. There was no one when he turned, only the rim of another crater and smoke blowing away.

He rose, thankful after a moment to see the rest of the section rising from the ground beyond the crater; he waited, waving them on with his pistol arm, watching as they came, keeping almost field day open order, long bayonets shining in the sun, faces harvest red under the shallow round helmets. How splendid they looked! He felt intense pride in them. Noyce had gone. The mathematical chances for the others had increased perhaps.

Behind, other sections bunched somewhat as they slowed; he shouted at them to spread out, gesticulating at the same time since they would hardly make out what he was saying above the din.

Turning to see what Murray-Downs was doing, he found his leading sections had gone to ground. Smoke was drifting across the sky; he had not been aware of the explosions, but there must have been more than one. He could see Limpopo again now, his head at least, looking over the bank from the sunken road, and lower down the heads of the leading section of Stalky's platoon. He jogged forward to catch up with his own front.

Another runner came back to Limpopo and they were

halted again. He sank into a patch of trampled wheat, annoyed at this second interruption; once committed one should be allowed to go on until the task was finished. The staff had miscalculated of course, sending them on a mile-long trek in broad daylight across open country which the enemy had under observation. Now they had probably found the whole village in Boche hands! The leading companies were obviously being held up by more than the bombardment.

The sun climbed as they waited. He loosened his tie and collar. His mouth was dry and he had a loose, empty feeling in his stomach. He unscrewed the top of his water bottle and gulped at the rather disgusting liquid, tepid already. He felt no better for it afterwards and there was a nasty taste in his mouth.

He became aware of his man, Frost, propped on his elbows some fifteen yards away, looking in his direction. Lord! Where had he sprung from! He shadowed him, turning up at the queerest times with a mug of tea or a scrap of information he thought he ought to hear – an extraordinary fellow! What was he thinking now? He appeared to have no personal life; he seemed to live entirely vicariously through the members of the platoon, especially himself. Was he speculating on his master's chances of catching one?

All had an equal chance out here. Noyce had gone. Death was simply the crump at the end of the screaming trajectory, mutilation several yards away, and beyond that if one were fortunate, a blighty one. Was that what he wished for? Had his fine talk to Henry of service to his country and freedom narrowed to preservation of his own skin?

He had an image of George, and felt ashamed. George fought to win. Compromise was not in him; cowardly thoughts never troubled him.

He looked around again in the direction of the village as he heard heightened machine gun and rifle fire and bombing. He could only see the trees from here and the broken stump of the church tower. Above, the sky was wide and blue like the Suffolk skies he remembered as a boy at Thorpeness with the same brightness and clearness. He was often reminded of Suffolk in this long, rolling country; so was Frosty; he was disparaging in his comparisons of Froggy farming methods.

When would they move?

It was extraordinary to think of Willy engaged. He thought of the girl he had seen coming from church with her family that Sunday at Etinehem. She had looked up at him briefly as they passed, dark eyes from a pale, perfect face, demurely down again. She had been so fine, so aware of her quality, and there had been interest in her look. Her family, all the womenfolk, were obviously respected there. He had wondered who they were, imagining a chateau surrounded by ornamental gardens, her father and all her brothers at the front. He had thought of her a lot but had never seen her again. As for the others, the sort Stalky and Nails found in Albert, he had been too fastidious. He had wished he were not so. He had been tempted to find out what it was like. When it came to it, he had been repelled by the calculation behind the girls' laughter.

What difference did it make? If he were caught today and scattered into parts by a coalbox what would it have mattered that once in this world he had paid for lust? Did anything matter on the edge of eternity – unless, of course, there *were* a God? This cursed waiting! Philosophy! Without God, it mattered *more*, not less. It mattered that he was worthy of himself; without that there really was nothing –

The sun was high by the time they moved off again, the day hot. The intensity of the strafing on and around the village had increased; the continuous shrieking of projectiles, the crash and shock of explosions from both the enemy and their own barrage close beyond numbed and overwhelmed his mind; it was as though they were advancing into the centre of a titanic storm. The air itself seemed to rush and quiver, the ground shook. Yet the sun was high and the sky blue beyond the smoking branches of the wood.

They were halted again. Another runner approached low from the right front where the bank above the hidden road disappeared behind the stumps of apple trees and the red brick ruins of what might have been a barn. Shortly, the order came to deploy for the assault. So this was it! They had watched others do it.

He passed the word to Webb and crouched along the line

615

as his sections came up into position. The staccato, revving noise of an enemy machine gun startled him, and he felt bullets through the air, zipping into the earth, spattering dirt and little bits of green in an arc horribly close in front of him. He bent lower, feeling something hard knock against his knee and unbalance him; a trampled patch of grass with furry seed heads rose towards his face; one of them seemed to flick his neck inside his collar. He rolled over on the ground and reached up to rub at the irritation, feeling an extraordinary wetness under his fingers. His knee throbbed. He wondered if he would be able to get up again; the cursed machine gun must have winged him. He had begun to feel rather faint. Surely the day was darkening? He stared up, seeing a bilious, yellow-green burst of shrapnel smoke against the midnight blue of the sky and the clouds like puffs from the hellish guns he could hear. The sun was hot on his face, but his hands were cold and he hadn't the strength to move them. He heard a voice, apparently calling his name, and thought someone was standing there, casting shade. All he could see properly were the clouds above, soft and feathery light as the ground bearing him like a wave beneath the old *Peacock*.

14

Henrietta's first thoughts when she awoke were of the christening. Little Jack was a darling boy. She still couldn't quite get used to the idea of Willy as a father. He had been determined to call the boy Jack. Isobel had been rather amusing about it; she had reeled out name after name; Willy had listened attentively as if weighing up each, then repeated, 'I think I prefer Jack.'

'John? Why don't you say John, then?'

'I mean John.'

He still went on saying Jack. Eventually Isobel had given up.

She was looking forward to the christening. It was the first thing she had looked forward to for so long she could hardly remember. Robin's leaves had been the last occasions – the torture of those leaves, knowing they would be over almost before they became accustomed to seeing each other again; could she ever forget? After Robin, what had there been to look forward to? The end of the war had seemed an impossible dream. When, out of the blue, the end had come she had only felt lost. Flares and maroons and the sirens of all the ships in Le Havre, church bells pealing crazily, strangers taking hold of one another and kissing, whooping and drinking everywhere except in the wards where the pale men tried to adjust to the miracle that they would never be sent back to the trenches; they were not going to die. But most of them had in the influenza epidemic.

She had been unable to go to the celebration dinner on Armistice night; she could only think of those who would not be going to any celebration, dear Eggy and Robin, Andy and Harry and others she had nursed and grown fond of. She had walked out by herself and thought of them, consciously thought of each one in turn so that, looking down, they would know their sacrifice had been worthwhile. Even if they were not looking down, if they had simply ceased as individuals as Andy had seemed to think likely, they remained individuals with her and very dear; this was *their* day. She had felt extraordinarily close to them that night.

Andy was the closest, no doubt because he was a part of her childhood; she had seen him change from one school holiday to the next from a carefree boy very much under George's influence to a rather solitary, thinking boy – 'They seek the sun; so do I. My sun is in a wider sky.' The thought of his aspirations glimpsed that early morning on the Heath saddened her more than almost anything. Robin had been glad to die in battle, she felt sure. Andy had had only a brief time of fulfilment at Cambridge, but his real fulfilment as a poet with things he really wanted to say had been stopped by the machine gun bullet at Longueval.

'Wawn't afeart a narthen, Mr Steel, he wawn't. Oi c'n see him as Oi stand yare, Miss – a-shuggin' his owd pist'l to git us in a fare loin. He were a heero, Oi rickon. Oi see him goo dowen. They divils git him yare – jes' yare, Miss. Oi rickon he were did afore he fare t' starp a-fallin'. That were a bootiful look in his oiyes, Miss, a roidin' up t' hiven, Oi rickon he were, on a gowden hoss. He look arter me, Miss. Happen Oi moight a blubbered suffen cause Oi din't hear him nix day – "Frarsty, whare's moi suffen shavin' warter, Frarsty?" Allus kip hisself hully clean an' shuv, he did. He were a prarper gin'leman.'

'He thought a lot of you, Mr Frost.'

'He were a heero. They din't give him no midal – he wawn't reg'lar, see – not reg'lar army. He ought-a had a midel, God's truth, Miss.'

After the christening, she would go back to France to visit his grave. She had been meaning to do it, but there had been no opportunity in the few days since she had taken off her uniform for the last time. Harry had no grave. She would visit Paschendaele where he had been.

Babs was already in the dining-room when she got down

for breakfast. Almost the first thing she said was that Willy had promised her she would be godmother next time. She had probably been working on poor Willy ever since he got home. She hadn't changed in the least.

'To think,' she replied, 'we're aunts!'

Babs thought about it silently. It was like her not to have registered this elementary fact before.

Mama was next down, looking happy and relaxed. Little Jack's arrival had done wonders for her. She smiled widely as she greeted them.

'It looks as though it will be a nice day for it.'

Henrietta felt disoriented suddenly – 'a nice day'. She saw men laid out in rows outside the tented ward of the casualty clearing station just as they had been carried from the wagons, and heard their croaking calls for 'Water – water, nurse –', saw their horribly stained dressings and mud-clotted uniforms, bloodless faces and dark, sunken eyes, and the way they had of twitching their shoulders out of habit for the lice infesting their under garments. She saw forms carried from the emergency operating theatre, hollow folds in the covering sheet where there had been a leg or legs, felt her nerves quiver as she prepared herself to remove dressings from a suppurating wound – would she ever be able to forget?

Her mother was looking at her with a rather questioning expression, and she smiled. She would have to try. Goodness knows, Mama had lost more than she had, and she was always so brave about it. She had caught her looking towards Papa's empty chair; she found it difficult enough herself to realize he would not be coming down and shuffling through the envelopes before opening the morning paper. He had been spared receipt of those two envelopes. Mama must have opened them –

They heard Willy's footsteps on the stairs.

Babs gave him a fanfare through puckered lips as he entered, the man of the hour! He returned his wide, lazy grin, the same old Willy. The Navy hadn't really changed him in the least. As he went to the sideboard Babs called out that he was a beast.

'Caroline!' her mother said, displeased.

'He *is*, Mama! He's made us *aunts*!'

619

Willy laughed. 'Ah – something I hadn't bargained for!'
He looked at her. 'I don't think you're quite ready for it.'
'Of course I'm not. I haven't even come out yet – not
properly. What will people *think*!'
'If they're anything like you – not much!'
'At the moment,' her mother cut in, 'we're *thinking* of
little Jack.'
Willy looked at Henrietta as he came to the table with his
plate, and lifted his brows fractionally.
'I *saw* that!' Babs cried.
Isobel came in, looking happy and Babs gave her a pen-
etrating stare, before looking at Willy again.
'How is he?' her mother asked.
'Sleeping like an angel.'
'A decided improvement on last night!' Willy said.
Isobel smiled, an admiring look in her brown eyes as she
turned to him. 'I expect that was the journey.'
'He'll have to get used to travelling!'
They laughed.
'Can I watch while you feed him?' Babs asked.
'*Caroline!*'
'*May* I!' Willy corrected her.
She pulled a face and mimicked genteely, '*May* I? After
all, I am his aunt.'
'I'm afraid there's nothing we can do about that,' Willy
said. He turned to Isobel. 'We should have thought about it
you know.'
She smiled; how just like Jollion she looked when she was
happy, Henrietta thought.
Her mother was looking at Babs. 'You should be very
pleased.' There was a sharp edge to her voice that even Babs
recognized, and she picked up her coffee cup, wiped her
mouth, rolled her napkin and rose.
'Excuse me!'
They exchanged glances, and her mother looked up at her
as she walked towards the door with a very straight back.
There was no doubt, when she did 'properly come out' she
would be centre of some storms; she would certainly break
a few hearts too.
Uncle Richard entered a moment after she had left; they

must have crossed in the hall. He gave her mother a quizzical look as he went to the sideboard.

'When are you expectin' George?' he asked after seating himself to the right of Papa's chair and starting to eat.

'George will be arriving after lunch. With Kate,' her mother replied.

Henrietta looked at Willy, wondering if he, too, had caught the timbre of her voice. He returned her glance with raised brows. He had not heard! Men were *so* unobservant. Uncle Richard was silent, concentrating on his plate. She had not been mistaken then; there had been something between him and Kate. She had rather wondered at her mother's obvious disapproval of a match which, on the face of it from George's point of view, looked quite brilliant. Poor George; he was mad about Kate. How she detested the scheming baggage, but there was absolutely nothing that could be done about it; she had George in thrall.

Her mother handed her the folded newspaper. 'Pass this along would you!'

'Thank you,' Uncle Richard said, taking it, and spreading it on the table beside his place. He looked up at her mother. 'What's the bettin' that ass Wilson's dreamed up a fifteenth point!'

His voice and manner reminded her so much of Papa, Henrietta suddenly wanted to cry. She must keep control. She excused herself quickly and rose, feeling her mother's eyes on her as she walked to the door. Really, she would have to do something about herself; she felt these stabs of emotion at the most ridiculous times – and breakfast now! Sometimes she couldn't stop laughing; more often tears welled uncontrollably.

Mounting the stairs, she found herself thinking of Scopey. She couldn't visualize her features now; she was a remembered presence in the nursery with a large, warm breast to lean one's head against, and the feel of a comb passing through one's hair, combing it out, combing, combing it – and nursery rhymes with soft vowel sounds – Rumpelstiltskin – she had wanted to call her little brother Rumpelstiltskin because his face had looked so red and rumpled.

Scopey was that letter she had kept, and a remembered

ache as she reached the head of the stairs and looked down towards the end of the corridor and the white-panelled door that had been hers. It had been her fault that Scopey had had to leave. She had made Andy wear a dress for Harry's christening. She could remember the drive to the church and the awful feeling of letting Scopey down, and inside the church praying that nothing would happen. She had an image of little Jack jumping up and down beside her as she tried to pray, but she couldn't for the life of her think what he had looked like. She wondered again why Willy was so keen on calling the boy Jack. Why not Harry? Or Andy if he wanted to perpetuate the names of his dead brothers?

She was lying on her bed, crying for Scopey and the letter she had written, which she still had, when she heard footsteps outside her door; she thought they sounded firm like Willy's and sat up quickly, wiping her eyes. There was a knock and the door opened. It was Willy.

He looked at her for a moment, then came in and shut the door, standing with his back against it.

'Like a walk?'

'Who with?'

'Just us.'

'You and me?'

He nodded, a strange look in his eyes. He obviously knew she had been crying; she must look ghastly.

She smiled, nodding. 'Five minutes.'

'All right.' He went out. A moment later, he put his head back around the door. 'I'll be in the orchard.'

How odd, she thought; it reminded her of something; she couldn't think what.

Willy walked back and down the stairs thinking of West and how useless it was to wish that he had not died. Henry would get over it – not completely, but she would have to come to terms with it. She obviously hadn't yet. He wondered how long it would take. How old was she – twenty-eight now? She looked more fetching than ever with those little puckers of maturity under her eyes and a sad, almost haunted look off guard when she didn't think she was being watched. If only he could *do* something for her, if only it could be as it used to be. He felt so powerless. And what must it be like for her to see him married and with a marvellous son. She had seemed very pleased when he had asked her to be godmother, genuinely pleased; it had seemed to mean a lot to her. Lord! he was glad he had asked. Who else though! Who else could he have asked? Isobel had wanted her sister of course, and now Babs was trying to stake her claim for the next one –!

'Going out, Willy?'

He saw his mother.

'I thought I'd take a stroll. With Henry,' he added.

She smiled. 'I'm glad.'

He saw from her expression, she was worried about Henry too. 'We'll be back in good time.'

'Don't worry. Everything's been seen to. Just so long as you don't miss the christening!'

He grinned; he had nearly missed the wedding; what a race that had been! 'No fear of that this time!'

She smiled again.

He went into the back hall and out through the colonnaded way, hoping he would not meet Babs or Uncle Richard. It would seem churlish to say that he and Henry wanted a walk together; he would never be able to say it, he knew, but it was what he wanted, what Henry wanted too.

He thought of her in her slim yellow dress in the Guy's chapel when he had realized Jolly had been killed. What had she said that told him that? Or was it the dream in the train on the way up? All he could remember was how she had looked against the altar – so contained, her shadowed eyes wide and very clear; he had marvelled at her composure, thinking how strange she had lost West and he had lost Jolly and here they were together in a chapel, and how much he admired and loved her –

He heard her steps in the grass and turned. She smiled; it was exactly the same smile as when they were young. Her eyes were clear again, and if he hadn't seen her a few minutes before he probably wouldn't have guessed she had been crying.

They walked through the trees on the old, dead leaves in the long grass, across the forlorn-looking unmarked tennis lawn, and out through the side gate.

623

They were half way up the hill towards Whitestone Pond before either spoke.

'It's queer isn't it,' Willy said, 'the family.'

She knew exactly what he meant. Half of them were here just like the old days, half of them weren't, and they were all trying to pretend to each other and to themselves probably that nothing had really changed.

'I feel so sorry for Mama,' she replied.

'What do you think you will do now?'

She smiled and took his hand in hers, swinging it. 'I'm not sure. I haven't had time to think really. I thought –'

'Yes?'

'D'you remember Father Geoffrey?'

He looked round sharply. 'I remember the time you practically forced Andy to sell his trains –' Once committed he had been unable to prevent himself finishing the sentence. He wished he hadn't said it though. He felt her fingers gripping his tightly for a moment. 'I never met him,' he went on, 'no –'

She thought of Jinny, wondering what had happened to her. It was only too probable she had 'fallen'. She would have to ask Father Geoffrey.

'It was just something I thought,' she said. 'He went out to France you know. I heard of him from some men who were brought in after Paschendaele. It was so strange. To hear his name out there I mean. They thought the world of him. I wondered if –'

'Harry?'

'Well – I wondered. And then – I've been wondering what I can do – I want to do something *useful* –'

'Henry!' He squeezed her hand. 'You've done *more* than enough for heaven's sake –!'

'I can't think, Willy, honestly I can't think, I simply don't know. Can we not talk about that –' She turned with an almost desperate look. 'What are *you* going to do?'

He grinned. 'I have certain responsibilities now! In any case I rather like it you know. Captain of all I survey! There's a lot to be said for it – even if it is rather small –'

'Was it too marvellous, seeing the High Seas Fleet coming in like that with their tails between their legs!'

'You should ask George when he arrives. He had a much better view of it all. I was expecting any moment to have to start loosing mouldies off. I simply couldn't believe it when they followed in meekly like a row of sheep. It was so different from everything we'd heard about them – *Der Tag* and all that. Then of course, if their officers had had their way, it would have been rather a different story!'

'*George* will only tell me what Beatty said to him and what he said to Beatty!'

Willy laughed. 'That's what matters to George.'

'Do you think he really is on such good terms with him?'

'Knowing George, it wouldn't surprise me. And once he springs Kate on him – well!'

'Irish, you mean?'

'Huntin'! Good Lord, Henry, huntin' an' all that!'

'Of course!'

'You have to hand it to George! He keeps his eye on the ball!'

'I think you're wrong. In this single, solitary instance I think, no, I *know* he's absolutely pots about her.'

'I don't suppose he's entirely unaware of her potential uses, though!'

She laughed. Poor George! He wouldn't understand why they were laughing at him; they ought not to. She was really so proud of him.

They were at Whitestone Pond. It was a blustery day, the tumbled clouds scooting across the sky in a way that would have excited her once, and the water was grey with lines of moving wavelets chasing across. In the old days she had imagined them scaled up to the size of rollers in the North Sea and had thought of George, and later Robin, in their grey ships. It looked the same now; it was the same, but not for her. It could never be the same again. Everything and everyone was simply how one saw them. She looked away, allowing Whitestone Pond to change back into what it had been once – in her mind. Robin would always be as she knew him. She dreaded to think of his features and mannerisms, his *presence* ever fading from her mind. Surely she would always remember.

Willy was looking at her with a strange expression. Probably he was quite right to! Mother thought she was a little crazy at times, she was sure. She grasped his hand and swung it. 'D'you think he'll make a frightful noise?'

He looked puzzled.

'*Jack!* I'm so looking forward to seeing him in his robes.' She clutched his arm to hers.

A slow smile at her enthusiasm spread across his face. 'To tell the truth, I'll be rather glad when it's all over!'

She joggled his arm in mock annoyance, feeling an urge to challenge him, 'Race you to the lamp post!' She managed to resist it. 'I suppose you're just thinking about the cake!'

Nurse untied the satin ribbons with one hand and removed the hood before passing the little bundle to Henrietta. He didn't make a sound, but looked up with serious blue eyes into hers. How like Willy he was! Would he, too, delight in butterflies and birds and all the world of colour and living things? If Willy had anything to do with it, he surely would. She rocked him slightly and his lips parted in a smile. What an adorable little creature he was! He was of Willy's flesh and blood. The mystery was too deep.

She thought of Andy's and Harry's christenings, feeling again that stab of remorse, and the first little Jack she could scarcely remember, and of the thing that Father Geoffrey had written to her which had stuck in her memory through the war and the losses and sights in the casualty clearing stations – 'there is either no reason to it, it is simply an enormous accident, or there is a reason which our mortal minds cannot understand –'

The Rector was addressing the godparents directly.

'Dost thou in the name of this child renounce the devil and all his works, the vain pomp and glory of the world, with all covetous desires of the same, and the carnal desires of the flesh, so that thou wilt not follow, nor be led by them?'

'I renounce them all.'

She looked down; what an awesome vow. She had not really listened to the words before; she had heard them as if for the first time. They expressed what she felt deeply, for what was there now she wanted from the world? What desire could she feel? She was barren. But to make the promise for a new little life, for Jack – well, he would make his own decisions. His wide eyes stared up into hers.

'O, merciful God,' the Rector intoned, 'grant that the old Adam in this child may be so buried that the new man may be raised in him.'

George's 'Amen' sounded firmly from close beside her, and she glanced round, catching him looking down at the baby. She wondered what he was thinking. It was difficult to tell these days. He was so completely the naval officer, a smiling quip for every occasion, an unequivocal opinion on every topic, brisk assurance concealing whatever feelings ran below the surface. Underneath, she was sure he was still the same George. He had greeted her with such warmth and sympathy when he arrived, but had been so anxious, as of old that she and everyone else should realize how well he was doing – and so anxious they should all like Kate of course! She had felt really sorry for him.

Kate, aware of their coolness, had been unnaturally re-strained. So far as she had seen, she had hardly passed a word with Uncle Richard either; the two of them had avoided each other, confirming once again everything she suspected. George seemed not to notice; why should he? His feelings for Kate obviously blinded him to everything. She wondered if he would ever find out. He would be so hurt if he did, but he would never let anyone see. He would hide his feelings perfectly under that charming, no-nonsense exterior.

George, catching Henrietta's look, felt a pang for West. Mother had warned him she had not got over it; she was still in a very low and confused state. He wondered if she ever would get over it. She had such loyalty; he couldn't imagine her feeling for anyone else what he knew she had felt for West. Lord! And West for her. He couldn't imagine her settling for second best either, and she would never find anyone quite like West again. Nor would he himself. He felt again the awful, hollow sensation, the disbelief when Bousfield told him the *Invincible* had gone.

'*Gone!*'

He remembered his glimpse of the few men in the water between the glowing ends of what he had taken for a Hun as they rushed past. West had been one of those men, and if he hadn't left the raft – pointless to dwell on 'ifs'. West would certainly not want it. He would only want Henry's happiness; that was what he had wanted all along. It had been his principal concern now he thought about it. Lord! When he remembered those walks in Scapa –

He smiled at Henry and caught her answering gleam. If only she were not so beastly cold towards Kate –

Looking at George, Henrietta thought how lucky she was that he and Willy had been spared. Many other families she knew had not been so fortunate. Some had no one. She had them. She thought of Kate and Isobel and was gripped by possessive, nostalgic yearnings, and felt tears about to come. She *must* pull herself together. She must not think of how it was before. She must break away –

She was alone – utterly alone. Standing on the quay, watching the *India* carrying Robin away had been a preparation. One was never sent things one could not bear. She had been tested once, and that made it easier.

Little Jack gurgled in her arms. She looked down into the blue, wide eyes and smiled. What dreadful, selfish thoughts she was indulging. She rocked him, thinking of Willy and how proud he was of his son, and how the tiny bundle would grow up probably with all Willy's sensitive, enquiring thoughts and fantasies and would have to go through the trials that boys like that went through. He was adorable.

She became aware of the Rector holding his arms out towards her. She passed the baby to him, and he moved a step to the font. She couldn't see the blue eyes now but guessed they were staring up into this alarming new face. She thought, 'If he cries when he's dipped it will mean they're here with us – all of them – Papa and Andy and Harry, Robin, Eggy, Jollion – that after all was what a christening meant, continuity of family and those one loved. She was sure they were here –

'Name this child!'

'John Jollion Thackeray.'

Mama had suggested Papa would have liked 'Thackeray'.

The Rector stepped closer to the font and inclined the bare head warily downwards. She held her breath. She remembered Scopey telling her that all babies ought to yell at christenings because it was the Devil being cast out.

'John – Jollion –'

The bundle shook a little and the Rector seemed to pause, brows raised in anticipation. The next instant the church filled with Jack's piercing screams.

'– Thackeray,' he raised his voice above the cries. 'I baptize thee in the name of the Father – and of the Son – and of the Holy Ghost –'

She felt her lips trembling on the 'Amen', and hardly trusted herself to look round at Willy. He was watching his shrieking son, a broad smile on his face; so were the others. Was she so odd she wanted to laugh and cry at the same time. She wiped her eyes and managed a smile. What an appalling noise little Jack was making. She had only asked for a token.